The
Daughters
OF THE
Mayflower
Groundbreakers

THE
Daughters
OF THE
Mayflower
Groundbreakers

MICHELLE GRIEP
KIMBERLEY WOODHOUSE
KATHLEEN Y'BARBO

BARBOUR
PUBLISHING

The Mayflower Bride © 2018 by Kimberley Woodhouse
The Pirate Bride © 2018 by Kathleen Y'Barbo
The Captured Bride © 2018 by Michelle Griep

Print ISBN 978-1-64352-773-4

eBook Editions:
Adobe Digital Edition (.epub) 978-1-64352-775-8
Kindle and MobiPocket Edition (.prc) 978-1-64352-774-1

Scripture quotations are taken from the King James Version of the Bible.

This book is a work of fiction. Names, characters, places, and incidents are either products of the author's imagination or used fictitiously. Any similarity to actual people, organizations, and/or events is purely coincidental.

Published by Barbour Publishing, Inc., 1810 Barbour Drive, Uhrichsville, Ohio 44683, www.barbourbooks.com

Our mission is to inspire the world with the life-changing message of the Bible.

ecpa Member of the
Evangelical Christian
Publishers Association

Printed in the United States of America.

The
Mayflower
Bride

KIMBERLEY WOODHOUSE

DEDICATION

This book is lovingly dedicated to my fellow "super-pants" wearer: Tracie Peterson.

For two decades you have taught, mentored, loved, and cheered me on. Now, umpteen published books later, I hope you know how much you are appreciated.

Without you, I wouldn't be where I am, and I know it's to God that the glory be given—not only for this gift of story and publication, but for the gift of you. You are my dearest friend other than my precious husband—and sometimes I wonder how or why you ever put up with me. But you do. Through thick and thin. And I'm so very grateful.

Precious lady—my prayer and Bible study partner, accountability partner, and listening ear. I love all the opportunities to learn from you, teach with you, write with you, and laugh with you. What a privilege it is to have you in my life.

Thank you for telling me I was a storyteller all those years ago and encouraging me to keep working at it. I also need to thank Jim. Without his encouragement, consistent help, and prayers—and let's not forget all the bunny stories—I would be lost. Give him a hug for me.

This dedication could never encompass my heart of gratitude for you, Tracie. So I will leave you with these simple words: Thank you. For everything.

DEAR READER

What an awesome joy and privilege to write the first book in the **Daughters of the *Mayflower*** series. Writing historical novels is a passion of mine, and I must admit I got caught up in the research. But this is a first for me—most of the time as an author I get to make up the majority of my characters and then sprinkle in real people from the time period. This time was different. With historical events surrounding the *Mayflower* and her passengers, I had to research each person on the ship and then bring aboard only a few fictional people.

But just so you are aware, the main characters—William, Mary Elizabeth (along with her father and brother), and Dorothy's family—weren't real people on the *Mayflower*. Nor was the character Peter. I did that for a reason. I didn't want to take anything away from the ones who lived the true story and live on in history. Rest assured the remaining characters were true *Mayflower* travelers. I pray I've done them justice in this story.

To keep this book enjoyable for today's reader, I have written *The Mayflower Bride* with both modern English and spellings (i.e., I didn't use *thee* and *thou* in the characters' speech. After I trudged through all the historical documents and journals, my eyes and brain were exhausted just from trying to figure out what they were saying, so this decision was for your benefit. You can thank me later). English of the day didn't have common spelling, so a lot of it was phonetic, with spelling changing from person to person. A sample of the way things were written in 1620 is the handwritten copy of the Mayflower Compact from William Bradford's book. Here is a small sample of it so you can experience the spelling and language:

Haueing vndertaken, for ye glorie of God, and aduancemente

*of ye christian faith and honour of our king & countrie, a voyage
to plant ye first colonie in ye Northerne parts of Virginia· doe by
these presents solemnly & mutualy in ye presence of God, and
one of another, couenant, & combine our selues togeather into a
ciuill body politick; for ye our better ordering, & preseruation &
furtherance of ye ends aforesaid; and by vertue hearof, to enacte,
constitute, and frame shuch just & equall lawes, ordinances, Acts,
constitutions, & offices, from time to time, as shall be thought
most meete & conuenient for ye generall good of ye colonie: vnto
which we promise all due submission and obedience.*

Notice the various uses of *u* and *v*. If you try to read an original
copy of the Geneva Bible, which the Separatists used, in addition to
the interesting spellings and language of the day, you'll see the *s* that
looks like an *f* without the cross bar.

I used scans of an original Geneva Bible (1560) for the Biblical
quotations throughout this novel, but again, because spelling wasn't
modernized yet, I modernized some of the spelling to make it easier to
read. It's a beautiful piece of work—the original Geneva Bible—and
there are two copies believed to have come over on the *Mayflower* in the
Pilgrim Hall Museum. And while the King James Version would have
come out by the time the Separatists journeyed to the New World, they
would *not* have had anything to do with it because it was authorized by
the Church of England and their persecution for many years had come
directly from the King whose name the new version held.

Many readers may equate this period with Puritans, but remember that these brave souls, the Separatists, were different. The Puritans
wanted to change the Church of England from within and thus fully
reform it, while the Separatists wanted to completely separate themselves from the Church of England.

Another important thing to note is the timeline. Back in 1620,
the Julian calendar was still used by the English and the colonists.
That meant that the new year didn't start until March 25. To try to
keep this novel as historically accurate as possible—and yet still understandable for you, the reader—I've time-stamped the dates from
January 1 until March 24 with the year notation 1620/1. To the passengers, these events happened in 1620, but we would now think of

them as taking place in 1621.

You'll notice throughout the book that there are variations on the spelling of "Plymouth." Modern spellings of both the US destination and England are "Plymouth." But to keep things as accurate as possible and yet clear to you, I used "Plymouth" for Plymouth, England, "Plimouth" to depict how Captain John Smith has this area labeled on his map of New England from 1614 which the travelers used on their journey, and then "Plimoth" for the original settlement. Plimoth Plantation is a fabulous place to visit at the original location.

While a lot of different conversations have taken place about the details of the *Mayflower* and its passengers, many particulars aren't known as fact. I did extensive research, but as always, this is a work of fiction. In trying to stay true to the historical story, I may have made a choice here or there that was based on opinion or supposition because the facts weren't clearly known. Please check the note at the end for more details. Any mistakes are purely my own.

Hopefully, this story will give you a glimpse into the lives of people who sacrificed everything for a better future almost four centuries ago—and were the beginnings of our great country. If you have a passion to read more about this historical time period, might I suggest the following nonfiction books: *Of Plymouth Plantation* by William Bradford (the true account/journal written by one of the passengers of the *Mayflower* and the eventual governor of the area—the edited version by *Mayflower* historian Caleb Johnson is phenomenal with footnotes and other journals included); *Here Shall I Die Ashore* by Caleb Johnson; *Plymouth Colony* by Eugene Aubrey Stratton; *Thanksgiving* by Glenn Alan Cheney; and *Mayflower* by Nathaniel Philbrick. My favorite website was MayflowerHistory.com by Caleb Johnson.

I pray you enjoy this series full of fascinating history from our incredible country.

It is a joy to give you *The Mayflower Bride*.

Enjoy the journey,
Kimberley Woodhouse

Glossary of Terms

Aback: wind from wrong side of sails

Alee: in the direction in which the wind is blowing

Aft: near or in stern of ship

At hull: to lay at drift with the wind

Battens: Narrow strips of wood used for several purposes on ships. One of the main uses was to fasten down the hatches—thus the phrase "batten down the hatches."

Bow: front of ship

Bulwark: The planks that made up the "sides" of the top deck to keep crew and passengers from being washed overboard (what today we might think of as the *railing*)

Caulk: The pushing or driving of fibrous materials into seams to make them water-tight. Not to be confused with modern caulk compounds.

Companionway: staircase/ladder between decks

Gangway: The long, narrow board used as a walkway onto ships. Most times it had smaller strips of wood across the width of it to aid in climbing onto the ship without slipping. The term changed to *gangplank* in the 1700s.

Gun deck: Where the passengers lived on the *Mayflower* and *Speedwell*. So named because in time of conflict, the guns—or cannons—would be brought out of the gun room to fire out of the gun ports. The gun ports were open only during a conflict or during nice weather to provide light and allow air to circulate.

Hold, the: cargo hold, bottom level of the ship

Larboard: left side of ship, changed to *port* officially in 1844

Masts and sails:
> **Fore mast** (front) held the fore-course sail and a bonnet sail
> **Main mast** (midship) held the main sail and a bonnet sail
> **Mizzen mast** (aft) held the lateen-rigged mizzen (a triangular sail on diagonal)
> **Spritsail** came up off the bowsprit (a long diagonal-looking mast that hung well over the sea past the bow of the ship)

Poop deck: deck above cabin of the ship master on the aft castle—highest level above the stern

Shallop: Also known as a *tender*, the shallop is a vessel used to ferry supplies and people between the shore and the ship.

Shoal: submerged natural ridge or bar that can be very dangerous to a ship

Steerboard: right side of ship, changed over time to *starboard*

Stern: rear of ship

Thatch: dried plant material such as straw, reeds, grass, and leaves

Ton or tonnage: Does not refer to the weight measurement we use today. Back then it was used to show the cargo capacity of a ship. A ton referred to a wine or beer barrel that was used for food stuffs, as well. So the *Mayflower* was listed as a 180-ton ship. That meant she could carry 180 barrels, each holding an equivalent to about 250 US gallons today.

Whipstaff: Device used to steer the ship. (The large wheel that we think of for steering large sailing vessels hadn't come into use yet.)

CAST OF CHARACTERS

Saints from the Leyden Congregation:
Fictional:
Mary Elizabeth Chapman
Robert Chapman, Mary Elizabeth's father
Elizabeth Chapman, Mary Elizabeth's mother, deceased
David Chapman, Mary Elizabeth's little brother
Dorothy Raynsford, Mary Elizabeth's best friend
Dorothy's mother and father, Mr. and Mr. Raynsford
Historical *Speedwell/Mayflower* passengers:
Isaac and Mary Allerton and their children: Bartholomew, Remember, Mary
William and Dorothy Bradford
William and Mary Brewster and their children: Love and Wrestling. William was head of the congregation because Pastor Robinson stayed in Holland.
John and Katherine Carver; their ward, Desire Minter; and their servant, Dorothy
James and Susanna Chilton and their daughter, Mary
Francis Cooke and his son, John
John Crackstone and his son, John Jr.
Moses Fletcher
Edward Fuller, his wife, Anna, and son Samuel, about twelve years old
Samuel Fuller (eventually the colony doctor) and his servant, William Butten. Fuller's wife, Bridget, stayed behind and arrived in 1623.
Degory Priest
Thomas Rogers and his son, Joseph

John and Joan Tilley and their daughter, Elizabeth

Thomas Tinker and his wife and son

John Turner and his two young sons

William and Susanna White and their son, Resolved (approx. five years old). She was pregnant when they left England.

Thomas Williams

Edward and Elizabeth Winslow

(Myles and Rose Standish also left with the Leyden congregation from Holland, but they were not part of the congregation. He was a military man hired to be the colonists' militia captain. But he appeared to have strong Separatist leanings.)

Strangers from England who joined the Saints on the venture:

John Alden, hired to be the ship's cooper and given the choice to stay at the colony or return with the ship to England

John Allerton

John and Elinor Billington and their children, John and Francis

Richard Britteridge

Peter Brown

Robert Carter

Richard Clarke

Edward Doty

Francis and Sarah Eaton and their son, Samuel

Mr. Ely

Richard Gardiner

John Goodman

William Holbeck

John Hooke

Stephen and Elizabeth Hopkins and their children, Constance, Giles, and Damaris. Elizabeth was pregnant when they left.

John Howland, manservant to John Carver

John Langmore

William Latham

Edward Lester

William Lytton (fictional)
Edmund Margesson
Christopher and Marie Martin and her son, Solomon Prower
Ellen, Jasper, Richard, and Mary More: four children aged four to eight, who were sent without parents
William and Alice Mullins and their children, Joseph and Priscilla
John and Alice Rigsdale
George Soule
Elias Story
Edward Thompson
Edward and Agnes Tilley with their nephew Henry Samson and niece Humility Cooper
William Trevor
Richard Warren
Roger Wilder
Gilbert Winslow

Crew of the *Mayflower* (about thirty men, but we know the names of only those listed):
John Alden, cooper (barrel maker)
John Clarke, ship's pilot and master's mate
Robert Coppin, master's mate
Giles Heale, ship's surgeon
Christopher Jones, master (captain)

Other crew members:
Boatswain: responsible for all the ship's rigging and sails, along with the anchors and longboat
Leadsman: kept track of the depth of the waters around them, could have had another crew title, as well
Master gunner: responsible for the ship's guns, cannon, etc.
Quartermasters (four): maintained the shifts and watch hours, in charge of the cargo hold, and responsible for fishing and maintaining lines

Ship's carpenter: responsible for fixing leaks and anything else ship related

Ship's cook: responsible for feeding the crew

Other sailors climbed masts, worked the sails, and performed other duties

Native Americans:

Massasoit: sachem (chief) of the Wampanoag in the area

Samoset: native from Mohegan

Tisquantum (the English nicknamed him "Squanto"): from Patuxet, which was the native village that had been where Plymouth is located

But here I cannot but stay, and make a pause, and stand half amazed at this poor people's present condition; and so I think will the reader, too, when he well considers the same. Being thus passed the vast ocean, and a sea of troubles before in their preparation (as may be remembered by that which went before) they had now no friends to welcome them, nor inns to entertain, or refresh their weather-beaten bodies, no houses, or much less towns to repair to, to seek for succor.
–William Bradford, *Of Plymouth Plantation*

A splinter of wood pierced Mary Elizabeth Chapman's thumb as she crept behind her lifelong friend Dorothy Raynsford. Resisting the urge to cry out, she stuck the offending appendage in her mouth and tasted blood. Adults weren't supposed to sneak around in the rafters. Why she ever agreed to follow her friend on this escapade, she'd never know.

Well, she did know. She was as curious as Dorothy, just not as brave. The thought of the elders below hearing and catching them? It was enough to make Mary Elizabeth want to faint. But she pressed on behind her bold friend and crawled like a small child up in the attic of the meeting room. The smell of hay filled her nose as fear crept up her throat. This meeting would decide her people's fate. And Mary Elizabeth wasn't sure she was prepared to hear the answers.

Dorothy stopped a few feet ahead of her and laid flat on her stomach, peeking over the edge of the rafters. Placing a finger over her lips, she waved to Mary Elizabeth.

As Mary Elizabeth reached the lookout spot, voices from the room below became clearer.

Pastor John Robinson spoke to a room full of their congregation's elders. "It's clear that the time has come. With the patent from the Virginia Company for a colony, and with the investments of the Merchants and Adventurers, I believe a small contingent can go on ahead and begin the settlement. Within a few years, we should have our whole congregation there and our debts to the investors for the trip paid in full."

Murmurs resounded throughout the room.

"Can these Strangers be trusted?" A voice from the back put words to Mary Elizabeth's own thoughts. She'd grown up with the stories of how their congregation had fled England and King James' religious persecution. The first attempt had been thwarted by a ship's captain who swindled all the passengers and turned them in to the King's sheriffs. When they tried again, a number of families were separated for a year as one ship deserted them, leaving many behind.

But that hadn't deterred them. Eventually, they'd all made it to Holland.

Labeled as Separatists because they wanted to separate themselves from the Church of England—which didn't exactly please the King since he was the "head" of the church—everyone outside of their small group became known as Strangers. Their longing not to abide by the church produced persecution they endured and that was almost as bad as when Bloody Mary reigned.

It was no wonder several folks voiced their concerns about trust this evening.

Twelve years had passed, and here they were again. Discussing a way to leave. This time, not so much to flee persecution, but to secure a better future. The memories of dishonest people, though, were still fresh to all who remembered. No one wanted to go through those atrocities again. They'd lost everything.

Pastor Robinson spoke in a soothing tone. "While no man is without sin, I do believe we can trust them. The investment is sound, and the contracts are binding. We all know the worries that have arisen. It's getting harder to make a living, and our children are being influenced too much by the culture around them. Sin and evil abound. If we stay, we risk losing the future generations to a dangerous course."

Nods accompanied many affirmations.

Mary Elizabeth tuned out the conversation. How would they even survive? Stories of tragedy abounded for those who had ventured across the ocean. And to start a whole new colony? There wouldn't be stores or supplies or. . .anything.

A shiver raced up her spine. Even though they were often looked down upon by the Dutch because they were outsiders and resolved to live out their faith in ways that went against the norm, she'd felt at home in Leyden. To be honest, it was the only home she remembered. But her people had worked menial jobs and longer hours to support their families, and times *were* getting tougher.

A poke to her shoulder made her look at Dorothy.

Her friend's face lit up in an exuberant smile. She raised her eyebrows. "Can you imagine the adventure?" The words floated toward Mary Elizabeth in a soft whisper.

"What?" Had she missed something important?

Their pastor's voice echoed through the room. "It's decided then. We have chosen the first group to go."

As they waited for the room to clear, Dorothy filled her in on the families who would venture to the New World. Dorothy's family—which made her even more animated than usual as she talked with her hands—and the Chapmans, Mary Elizabeth's family, were part of the group.

Mary Elizabeth went numb. She didn't register anything more that Dorothy said. Even as they walked home, her heart couldn't make any sense out of the jumble of words.

Dorothy must have recognized something was wrong and followed Mary Elizabeth home. "Mary Elizabeth. What is going on in that head of yours?"

Lifting the latch to the door of her home, Mary Elizabeth clamped her mouth shut.

"Don't shut me out. Aren't you excited about all this?"

She turned and stared at her friend's eyes. Eyes that sparkled with excitement and joy. Why couldn't *she* feel that way?

Dorothy's warm hand reached out and covered her own. "Come. Let's get some tea and discuss what you're thinking. My parents aren't expecting me home—I told them I was staying over with you—and as long as I am there to milk Polly in the morning and feed the chickens, I should be able to stay as long as you need me."

All Mary Elizabeth could manage was a nod. They entered the door to the small rooms she called home. Familiar smells greeted her. Running a hand over a chair her father had carved, she let the feel of it seep into her soul. How could they leave all of this behind?

Heavy footsteps sounded on the stairs, causing Mary Elizabeth to jump and put a hand to her chest. "Father." Releasing a sigh, she looked down at the floor. He didn't know where she had gone—did he?

"I need you to stay with David." His face was alight with anticipation. "I have much to discuss with the elders."

"Is there anything I need to know?"

"Not yet, my dear. But soon. Very soon." He kissed her cheek and strode out the door.

Dorothy pulled out a chair and pointed to it. "Sit. It's time to destroy this fear and doubt that I see etched all over your face."

Tears sprung to Mary Elizabeth's eyes. They burned as they overflowed and ran down her cheeks.

Dorothy stayed up with Mary Elizabeth in the kitchen, talking about the meeting until daylight crept in through the windows. While Dorothy's voice held excitement and wonder, Mary Elizabeth felt only worry and fear. Her friend quoted scripture and hugged her. Told her it would all be all right. God was in control. This was a good thing.

But what would become of them? Too many of their group were elderly and would have to stay behind, and the elders made it clear that only so many could make the journey. That meant only a small fraction of all the people she'd known the whole of her seventeen years would venture across the vast ocean to the unknown land of the New World.

"Mary Elizabeth?" Dorothy placed her hand over Mary Elizabeth's cold one. "Mary Elizabeth, have you heard anything I've said?"

All she could manage was a nod. "I just need some time."

"All right. I'd better get back home. The chores won't get done by themselves." Her cheery voice did nothing to soothe Mary Elizabeth's nerves.

She doubted anything could.

"Mary Elizabeth, may I go play with Jonathan?" Her little brother pleaded the same thing almost every day.

And she always said the same thing in response: "Have you finished your chores?"

He nodded and smiled.

She tousled his hair and handed him his cap. "Be home in an hour."

"I will."

Brushing her hands on her apron, she watched him run down the street. He wouldn't be a little boy much longer, but oh, how she adored him.

"Mary Elizabeth," Father called from the stairs, "I need you to sit down with me for a moment."

"Of course." The flutters of her heart couldn't be stopped, knowing all too well what he would say. She eased herself into a chair across the table from him.

"We've been chosen to go to the New World. Actually, I volunteered." The smile that lit his face was one she hadn't seen since before her mother died. "It will be good to have a fresh start and finally have land to call our own." His gaze went to the window as the smile disappeared. "And there are too many sad memories here."

He turned back to face her and shook his head. "Forgive me." The smile returned. "The journey is soon. It's all very exciting, but we have much to prepare and I need your help."

Odd how the body worked. She remembered forcing herself to nod, trying to look like she was interested in what he had to say, and tamping down all the fear and frustration inside. But she didn't really hear a word after that. So many emotions erupted inside her that she didn't know how to contain them. Before she knew it, Father stood, kissed her cheek, and walked out the door.

A sob choked its way to the surface. Without thinking, she stood and raced out the door.

Mary Elizabeth's heart pounded as her feet thudded against the ground. Running for all she was worth, she didn't care that it was unseemly for a young woman her age to run. How could Papa be so willing to volunteer?

She reached the edge of the cemetery and slowed down. Tears streamed down her cheeks as she opened the gate, walked through, and quietly shut it behind her. There always seemed to be a hushed reverence in this small plot of graves surrounded by trees.

Mary Elizabeth walked through a few rows and stopped in front of her mother's grave. The fresh flowers she'd left yesterday were already wilting.

Just like her heart.

She fell to her knees in the grass and sobbed harder. "Mother, I don't know what to do! Father has agreed for us to go to the New World. . . ." She couldn't even finish her thoughts.

This place—this hallowed ground—had been her sanctuary in the year since her mother had died. When she had no words to express her thoughts, she came here. And her heart spilled out.

How could she leave behind her mother?

Oh, she knew that her mother no longer resided in the body buried beneath the place where she knelt, but it still felt wrong.

It meant she'd have no refuge. No place to come and hash out her thoughts and questions.

Mother had been the only one to truly understand her. Dorothy was a dear friend, but she couldn't fill the hole left by the woman who'd given Mary Elizabeth life. The one who'd kissed her head good night every evening and sung her awake every morning. No matter how scared Mary Elizabeth had been about trying something new, her mother had always been there to encourage her and tell her she could do it.

Could she do *this*?

No. It wasn't possible.

But the elders had decided. Father had readily agreed.

The reality of the situation sank into her stomach like a rock.

Leaning back on her heels, she cried like she had when her mother had died. "Mother. . .I can't do this. I can't."

CHAPTER 1

Saturday, 22 July 1620
Delfthaven, Holland

Gentle waves rocked the *Speedwell* as the vessel left behind the only home Mary Elizabeth remembered. Salty air stung her nose, and the breeze tugged at wisps of her hair—threatening to loosen them from under her confining cornet.

Standing as close to the stern of the ship as she could without bothering the crew on the poop deck, Mary Elizabeth inhaled deeply. If only the crisp air could clear her mind like it cleared her lungs. Breathing out a prayer for courage, she clung to the bulwark. Courage had never been her strength. The past few weeks had confirmed that indeed it was all happening. And here she stood. On a ship.

Could she do this? Truly?

She'd armed herself with her prized possessions: her mother's red cape draped comfortingly around her shoulders; treasured receipts from generations prior sat safely tucked into the pockets tied around her waist; and the memory of the woman who loved her and modeled what it meant to be a godly wife and mother resided, always and forever, in her heart. Reaching her hand behind her apron, she slipped it through the slit in her skirt and found the string of pockets tied around her waist. The one with the receipts hung in the middle. She ran her fingers over the edges of the worn papers. Grandmother's savory egg-and-spinach pie receipt, a boiled pudding receipt from her mother, and her favorite—Mother's rye-and-barley bread—were among them.

If only mother were still alive. Maybe this journey wouldn't be so difficult.

Even though their time in Holland had been full of difficult stretches, God had been good to Mary Elizabeth there. She'd had her family, her dear friend Dorothy, and plenty of work to keep her busy. Besides that, it was familiar. Safe.

But no more. The land she knew had drifted out of her sight hours before. Never to be seen again.

The Saints, as they preferred to call themselves, had left England twelve years before while under persecution from the King and the Church of England. When they left for Holland, they wished only to separate themselves from England's church so they could study the scripture more and follow the state's rules and taxations less. They believed only what the Bible told them, so they considered all the man-made rules and traditions of the Church of England to be wrong.

She didn't remember England. But Holland would remain forged in her mind for the rest of her days.

Now it all seemed surreal. Listening in the rafters that night had been the beginning for her, but the group's preparation had been going on for years.

Correspondence to grant the Saints permission to start a colony in the New World had gone back and forth to England. And then John Carver and Robert Cushman were sent to London to negotiate an agreement.

Finally, permission from the King had been granted. In fact, he seemed to bless the endeavor with his words, "as long as they went peaceably."

Memories of their departure from Leyden washed over her. The rest of the congregation that stayed behind and many of their Dutch neighbors had come to see them off. There had been shedding of tears aplenty. But when Pastor Robinson dropped to his knees, tears streaming down his face, Mary Elizabeth had lost control of her emotions, as well. As he prayed for the Lord's blessing and commended the travelers on their journey, she wanted to gain strength from his words. But she'd only felt weaker and more inadequate.

A spray of salt water hit her face and brought her back to the reality of where she stood. The planning was done. The packing was over. Goodbyes had been said. And now Holland had vanished from sight. She and the others on the ship would reach England soon, and after they met up with the *Mayflower* and her passengers—the other brave souls who would journey to the New World with the Separatists to establish a colony—they would be on their way.

To what, she was unsure.

Squinting, she gazed toward the horizon in the west. What would this New World hold? Papa had regaled her with stories of lush, fertile land. Land unclaimed by anyone else. Land supplying an abundance of food. Land that held no persecution for their faith.

Her faith. It meant everything to her. And the thought of freedom to worship and learn and grow in God's Word thrilled her beyond imagining. It was the one thing that helped her through the past weeks when she'd had to swallow the reality that yes, she was going to the New World. Dorothy helped her to focus on the positive, and Mary Elizabeth clung to the thought of her faith.

Years ago, her father had spent almost a month of wages on a Bible so they could read it themselves. The first time she'd been allowed to hold the volume in her hands, she'd cried. She found it such a privilege to read the Bible, translated in its entirety to her own English language and printed in 1560, and understood why her people—the Saints—longed to separate themselves from England's Church. Why didn't *everyone* long to read the Word as she did? Why were they content to sit in church, pay homage to their country, and listen to passages read from the *Book of Common Prayer* and nothing else? Church was an obligation, a ceremony, a ritual to them. But followers of Christ were called to share the Gospel and be set apart. The difference in thinking didn't make sense to Mary Elizabeth. Especially since so many had been persecuted for it.

The New World held more than just release from persecution. Papa and the other men dreamed of working their own farms with land as far as the eye could see. In Holland, the hard labor they'd all put in for decades had given them nothing of their own.

To think the New World could hold the answer to all their hopes and dreams.

It sounded lovely.

So why did her heart hesitate so? She'd shed enough tears to create a river the past few weeks, and she'd finally told the Lord that enough was enough. The only way she could make it through was with His help. Her new recitation became *I can do this.*

Papa's excitement rubbed off on her younger brother, David, but most of the time she'd had to force a smile. No matter. It wasn't her place to go against Papa, and his mind was made up. They'd been chosen.

Her father had kept himself busy with the plans to go. So much so, she'd hardly seen him in a fortnight. His absence made their departure that much more difficult to bear.

It made her feel. . .alone.

And now she stood on a ship. Going.

She felt lonelier than ever.

She shook her head. She *could* do this. Her mind just needed to stay off these thoughts of loneliness and instead keep occupied.

Papa was engaged in excited conversations with the other men, which would probably be the daily activity for him the entirety of their voyage. So she must find something to keep her mind occupied and off these thoughts of loneliness.

She *could* do this.

But the recited phrase couldn't keep the questions from filling her thoughts: Would the New World be as beautiful as Holland? Would she make friends? Would she find a God-fearing husband?

Or would the savages kill them all in their sleep?

Another tiny shiver raced up her spine. Such thoughts were not appropriate. Papa would have a fit if he knew she'd listened to the sailors' stories. He'd scolded David for repeating the derogatory name *savages*. But what if that's what they were? Were they sailing into their own demise?

"Mary Elizabeth!"

Dorothy's voice drifted across the deck of the ship, and Mary Elizabeth waved and smiled at her friend. She must not allow her foolish doubts to dull Dorothy's enthusiasm for every aspect of this new life.

"I had a feeling I would find you here. Fresh air is always your first choice." Dorothy smiled and leaned on the bulwark as the ship listed to the right. "Your father is teaching David about Jamestown and the New World."

"David is thrilled, to be sure." Mary Elizabeth looked back to the water. She really must swallow this doubt and fear. Far better to grab hold of the thrill and joy she saw on her friend's features.

Dorothy laid a hand on Mary Elizabeth's shoulder. "I've been praying for you. I know this isn't easy, leaving your dear mother behind and all."

All Mary Elizabeth could manage was a nod as an image of the cemetery flitted through her mind.

The gravestone with her mother's name—Elizabeth Chapman—denoted the all-too-short span of the beloved woman's life. It would lay bare now. No flowers. No one to visit.

Even though Mother's memory resided in Mary Elizabeth's heart and mind, leaving behind the grave—the place she visited weekly to pour out her heart and soul—hurt more than the loss of any other physical object in Holland.

"Here." Her friend offered a brown-paper-wrapped package. "I wanted to give it to you on your birthday, but I couldn't wait."

Mary Elizabeth smiled and took her time unwrapping the gift. The brown paper could be saved and used again, and they wouldn't have access to such frivolities—or anything of the sort—for quite some time. As she turned it over in her hands, she found a deep brown leather book with a leather string tied around it. There weren't any words on the cover or spine. "What is it?"

"It's blank pages. For you to write down your thoughts. I thought it would help since you won't be able to visit your mother's grave anymore."

Tears sprang to Mary Elizabeth's eyes. Only Dorothy knew her heart and the lengthy visits to the cemetery and what she did there. She clutched the treasure to her chest. "This must have cost you a small fortune." Paper wasn't a commodity most could afford. Mary Elizabeth looked back down at the precious book. "Thank you so much." The words seemed all too inadequate.

"I know you have a quill and pots of ink with you since I helped pack them"—Dorothy laughed as she patted Mary Elizabeth's arm—"and once we have a settlement and regular shipments coming in, you might want to write even more. You've always had a talent for stringing beautiful phrases together."

Tears flowed down Mary Elizabeth's face. She didn't even want to wipe them away. What a treasure. Not just the book, but the friend.

Dorothy bounced on her toes. "I will be with you, dear Mary Elizabeth. Through every step of this new journey."

Mary Elizabeth smiled through her tears. "I know you will, and I'm very grateful, I am. The journey will just take some getting used to."

"Well, don't take too long. Adventure awaits!" Dorothy's arms stretched out, and she spun around. Her friend's eagerness for the unknown made Mary Elizabeth laugh and wipe the tears off her face.

Mary Elizabeth folded up the brown paper and tucked it into her cloak. God had truly blessed her. With a wonderful family and a delightful friend. She *could* do this.

Courage. Her prayer from before sprang back to her mind.

The pounding of boots behind them made Mary Elizabeth turn and wrap her cloak around her tighter. The sailors weren't the most gentlemanly of sorts.

The ship master emerged from the group and looked straight at them. The weathered man always appeared tense and stern, but today another expression hid behind his eyes. Was it fear? "Go get your men. We need all able-bodied hands on deck. Including the women and children."

Mary Elizabeth nodded and moved to do the ship master's bidding.

But Dorothy tugged on Mary Elizabeth's cloak and stopped. "What's happened, Mr. Reynolds?"

Seeing the other sailors' grim expressions, Mary Elizabeth felt a knot grow in her stomach. She faced the man in charge.

Mr. Reynolds's mouth pressed into a thin line, and he clasped his hands behind his back as he glanced out to the water and then back to Mary Elizabeth and Dorothy. The severe expression grew dim. "It's not the best etiquette to speak to women of such calamity, but since you will carry the message below and there's not a lot of time, I feel it's best to be honest." He took a deep breath. "The ship's been leaking for some time now, and we're taking on a good deal of water. It is far worse than I suspected. If we don't do something about it, we'll sink before we ever reach Southampton."

❦

Tuesday, 1 August 1620
Southampton, England

William Lytton lifted the last crate and his satchel of tools and readied to walk up the gangway of the *Mayflower* one more time. His leg muscles burned from the numerous trips up the steep, narrow walkway, but it was worth it.

The New World.

For years, he'd longed for change—a fresh start. The opportunity before him now presented all his dreams in one nice package. And the *Mayflower* would take him there.

If he could just make it through the weeks at sea, he'd be fine. They would all have to start with nothing. They would have to build or create everything with their own hands. They would be far away from everyone and everything they'd ever known. That was fine. Making a new life took hard work and sacrifice.

He was ready.

In a matter of weeks, he'd be standing on shores across the vast ocean—literally on the other side of the world. The thought made him smile. He might be an orphan, devoid of family or anyone who cared about him, and unworthy of English society's approval, but he was done with all of that. In this new land, in a new settlement, he could be someone else entirely.

A hand on his shoulder made him start and lose his grip on the crate, but he caught it with his knee. The man standing there didn't look like a thief.

"I'm sorry to disturb you, and I don't wish to startle you, but I have a proposition." The more closely William observed, the more he noted why the man's appearance exuded wealth. A shimmer of gold on the man's right hand didn't escape his notice. Only the wealthy donned such adornments.

William nodded. "Sir. Let me set my burden down, and we can discuss whatever is on your mind."

The man glanced around and moved to sit on another crate. As he reached into the pocket of his vest, the embroidery on the man's sleeves caught William's attention. The man must be rich indeed.

The mysterious stranger cleared his throat. "Are you William Lytton?"

Who was this man? The ring and clothing reminded William of royalty, but he'd had little experience with the upper classes, much less royals. "Yes, sir. I am."

The man smiled and motioned for William to move his crate closer. "I don't wish to take a lot of time, nor do I wish to be overheard, so I'll be brief. I'm with the Virginia Company and am also one of the Merchants and Adventurers. You may know that we have heavily invested in all who will be journeying with you to the New World."

It was no secret. The Merchants and Adventurers provided the monetary backing for the trip, and the Planters were the travelers to the New World. Every Planter over the age of sixteen received one share, while the Adventurers could invest and buy as many shares as they wanted. Once all the debts were paid in seven years, the profits would be divided by those shares. A rush of thankfulness hit William's chest. He had two shares when most Planters only had one.

"Yes, sir. I am aware."

The man leaned closer, his voice hushed. "We need to hire a man with integrity to keep records for us."

William felt his brows raise but attempted to keep a plain expression. "Records? What kind of records?"

The man coughed into his fist as another sailor ran up the gangway. When the young man was past, he continued. "A journal of sorts recording all the comings, goings, workings, business—all that takes place at the new settlement. The ten-point agreement we have with you all, the Planters, is to come to fruition in seven years. While seven years seems like it can go by quickly, it is a good length of time, and the New World is a great distance away. We don't have a man available who can pick up and leave his life and family here, so we thought it prudent to find someone who would be a part of the new colony to help us out. Your name was given to me as a recommendation. We wish to see this venture succeed with the utmost honesty and respect."

Respect. If he'd learned nothing else, William had learned the importance of respect in business matters. As for honesty and integrity? Well, as far as he was concerned, there was no other way to act. And it gave him a boost in his confidence to learn that someone had recommended him. He lifted his shoulders and nodded. "How may I help?"

"We would obviously compensate you for your time—as I said, we are seeking to *hire* someone." The man held a small velvet pouch and a leather book out to William. "This would be your first payment. We will send a messenger down on the *Fortune* next year with another hefty sum. After we have reviewed your report and see how the settlement is doing, there will be additional duties and payments. The book is for your record keeping. Details and exact quantities are important. While we will be receiving the wood, salted fish, and other goods made by the Planters to sell, we need to know that they are abiding by the agreement. Four days' work for us. Two for themselves. We believe them all to be honest people, but we also know many who are going are not a part of the Separatist's congregation and do not abide by the same strict moral laws.

"In essence, you will be our representative there, but we don't want to alarm anyone or create any chaos by making that fact known. Far better to keep this information. . .among those who need to know it. Just until the colony is well under way, you understand. Then we may have a higher position there for you since you will have gained everyone's trust."

William took the book and then the bag, a bit startled at the weight of it. The man's logic was sound. Everyone would have to work together if they were to build a lasting colony and survive. He could handle another job like this if it was just keeping records. It was honest. Even if it was a bit secretive. The extra money would definitely help.

Decision made, he nodded. "I would be honored to assist you, sir, the Virginia Company, and the Adventurers."

"Thank you, William." The man stood and turned on his heel. "I will be in touch."

William launched himself at the man and tugged at his cape. "How did you know my name, sir, as I do not know yours?"

The man's face softened with a slight smile. "Your master was a close friend. He spoke highly of you and often." He straightened and nodded at William. "As for me, you may call me Mr. Crawford."

As Crawford walked away, a tiny pang of grief hit William's chest. *His master.* The only kind person William had ever known. Twenty years ago, he'd been abandoned as a baby and left on a family member's doorstep. They'd barely clothed him and fed him occasionally. But he would have taken those conditions over what happened next. At the tender age of nine, he'd been kicked out and told to find his own way.

Many other orphans his age had been out on the streets, but William soon learned to work as many odd jobs as possible so he could put bread in his stomach.

Then one day—after years of misery, filth, and almost starvation—this man appeared. His master, Paul Brookshire. The man who'd taken him in at thirteen, taught him the valuable trade of carpentry, and given him hope for life. The man who'd loved him like a son for seven wonderful years when no one else wanted him. The man who bought an extra share for William—costing almost an entire year's worth of earnings—before he made his apprentice promise to make the most of his life, throw off the baggage of the past, and seek God.

William never had much of a use for God. The thought of a loving heavenly Father was foreign to a boy orphaned and shown contempt in the streets of London. But his master? He'd started to change William's mind.

Questions he'd longed to ask would go unanswered. Alas, his master died.

William had cared for the man until he took his last breath and had kept up with all the orders for their shop by working into the night. The day he buried Paul—his master and friend—was the hardest day of his life. Harder than living with a family that did nothing but show him contempt. Harder than living on the streets of London. Because he'd lost the only person who ever cared—the one who had. . .*loved* him.

If he were to be honest, no one else knew William—not even his customers—because he'd never given anyone else a chance.

A scuffle on deck of the ship made William look back toward the gangway. He shook his head. These thoughts were best left for a later time. He had work to do and a long journey ahead.

Tucking the bag inside his shirt, William breathed deeply. The grief that often hit in waves needed to be tucked down into his heart, away from probing eyes.

William Lytton was on a journey to a new life. The old had to be left behind.

CHAPTER 2

Peter watched Mr. Crawford walk away from that lousy carpenter. Anger bubbled up in his gut. That should have been *his* job—*his* money. As he'd followed Crawford to the dock this morning, his hopes were that all the pieces were falling into place. Apparently, he hadn't thought through the fact that they might hire someone else. All the times he'd gotten an invitation to meetings or gatherings, all the times he'd spoken to Crawford and offered to help the venture in any way that he could. His cousin had told him he'd made a good impression. Not that it did any good. Not now.

Venturing forth from his hiding place behind a large crate, he squinted toward William Lytton. Why had the Merchants and Adventurers chosen a carpenter, of all people? What did he know about business dealings?

All the work Peter had done to get a look at the contracts and plan for this were now for naught. His piddly savings were depleted. He'd counted on getting hired for the endeavor ever since his cousin had told him about the plan. Now he was stuck going to the New World with no foreseeable income.

His dreams of being established as a respectable and honored person in the new colony were dashed.

Unless. . .

He tilted his head and let the thoughts grow into fullness. It wasn't the craziest idea. Maybe it would work.

Maybe there was another way to earn trust—and to obtain the job he desired.

Saturday, 5 August 1620
Southampton, England

After more than a week of repairs dockside to reinforce the patching done at sea, the master of the *Speedwell* declared her seaworthy once again. While several of the crew had left the ship as their ship master released them during the repair work, all of Mary Elizabeth's congregation stayed on board. Not wishing to risk any mishap or reason for the King to change his mind, the elders had thought it best to stay out of sight.

But now as they left the port, Mary Elizabeth longed to stand on dry ground rather than on the deck of this ship. This very *small* ship—where the confining spaces threatened to trap her. Panic rose in her throat. She did her best to swallow it down, but it reached prickly fingers into her mind.

Would this be the last time she'd see land? What if they didn't make it to the New World? What if they got lost and ran out of supplies?

Shifting her gaze to the north, she forced her thoughts elsewhere. Across a small expanse of sea, the *Mayflower*'s crew worked her sails as the ship cut through the water beside them. The ship was much larger than the *Speedwell* and carried the rest of their supplies for the New World as well as many other colonists.

It was wondrous to behold and gave her a calming thought. They wouldn't be journeying alone. The panic subsided a bit.

But a sense of foreboding replaced it in full force.

"Good morning, Mary Elizabeth." Dorothy's voice pierced through the black fog threatening to overtake her.

Mary Elizabeth took a breath and then another. "Good morning." The smell of fish and salty sea air filled her senses.

Dorothy came alongside her and grabbed her arm. "What's

wrong? You're whiter than the sails."

Shaking her head, Mary Elizabeth closed her eyes. "It's nothing. I just had a wee bit of fear as we left."

"It doesn't look like it's 'nothing.'" Dorothy placed her hands on her hips and raised her eyebrows. "I've a good mind to go get your father."

"No. Please." Mary Elizabeth raised a hand in protest. "He doesn't need anything else to worry about. Besides, he's too busy with plans and meetings with the elders. I'm very well. I just need to breathe through it." Maybe her facade of bravery would appease her friend. But the niggle of fear that something bad would happen made her heart race. What had come over her?

"You may try and fool me, Mary Elizabeth Chapman, but I can see you are struggling." Dorothy grabbed her hand and squeezed. "Why don't we recite the Twenty-Third Psalm together?"

Mary Elizabeth nodded and kept trying to breathe, but the shallow breaths weren't giving her enough air. This couldn't be happening. Not now. After all she'd overcome. But the deep sense of foreboding wouldn't leave her. Why?

Courage, she just needed courage. Why was that her constant prayer now? And why was she so weak when everyone else around her appeared to be strong?

Dorothy started quoting from the scripture, "The Lord is my shepherd, I shall not want."

Mary Elizabeth let the words flow over her. She inhaled deeper and joined in the recitation. "He maketh me to rest in green pastures, & leadeth me by the still waters." Breathing came easier. In. Out. In. Out.

"He restoreth my soul, & leadeth me in the paths of righteousness for his Name's sake.

"Yea, though I should walk through the valley of the shadow of death, I will fear no evil: for thou art with me: thy rod and thy staff, they comfort me." Mary Elizabeth's voice grew stronger with every word.

"Thou doest prepare a table before me in the sight of mine adversaries. Thou doest anoint mine head with oil, & my cup runneth over." Her breaths calmed to a regular pace.

"Doubtless kindness & mercy shall follow me all the days of my life, & I shall remain a long season in the house of the Lord."

Dorothy smiled. "Now, don't you feel better? The color in your cheeks is back."

"Yes." The honest statement surprised her. It was true. The simple quoting of her favorite passage brought calm to her spirit. Mary Elizabeth hugged her friend. "I feel like our Lord has banished the fear from me."

"Wonderful." Dorothy bounced on her toes—a habit that she'd had since childhood.

Mary Elizabeth faced the west and grabbed onto the bulwark. Water as far as the eye could see.

"Isn't it wonderful?" Her friend's exuberant voice bubbled up and spilled out, making Mary Elizabeth feel foolish for her anxious thoughts. "Like I said, adventure awaits. New land. New home. New life. New. . .everything!"

A small laugh escaped her lips. She'd never tire of Dorothy's positive outlook. "Yes, God is so very good to us." And He was. She knew that. She would conquer this fear and doubt with His help. The fear was because of her doubt and worry—neither of which was honoring to God. She'd have to work on those areas of her life. If she was going to become a Godly woman like her mother, she had a long way to go.

"I'm proud of you."

Mary Elizabeth furrowed her brow. "Whatever for?"

"I can see the determination on your face. It's a brave thing you've done, Lizzy." She covered her mouth after the nickname from their childhood came out. "Sorry, it slipped. I know we're not children anymore."

Mary Elizabeth hooked arms with her lifelong friend and smiled. "It's all right. You're the only one I'd allow to call me that, and I think you have the privilege after all this time." She lowered her voice to a whisper. "Just don't use it in front of David. He'll start calling me that again, and Papa would have a fit. He said it's not becoming for a young lady and implies ill character." She took another deep breath as they took a few, slow steps to the other side of the ship. "Thank you for thinking that I'm brave, but I'm not near as strong as you are."

"That's rubbish." Dorothy put her other hand on her hip and turned toward her. "It's extremely brave. Everything you've done and had to endure. This was a huge step. . .walking into the unknown. It takes a lot more courage when you're not one prone to adventure."

"Like you."

Dorothy giggled. "My other friends in Leyden thought me daft. Always excited about something new. But you never ridiculed me for my unusual and impetuous spirit. I'm very grateful for that. You're the steady, compassionate, dependable one. I'm the—"

"Good morning, ladies."

Mary Elizabeth turned around and noticed Myles Standish, the adviser and guide they'd hired in Holland. "Good morning, Mr. Standish."

"Good morning," Dorothy echoed and grabbed Mary Elizabeth's arm again.

"It's a wonderful day to set sail, isn't it?" Standish stood at the bulwark with his feet spread wide and his hands clasped behind his back. He obviously was accustomed to the rolling seas and was confident in his stance.

Mary Elizabeth studied him and moved her boots apart under her heavy skirt and petticoats while Dorothy chattered. Surely she could hide the unladylike carriage underneath all the layers she wore. It was awkward, but if a wider posture helped her stay steady on the ship, she'd learn. Wouldn't Dorothy be proud and get a laugh out of this later? With a grin, Mary Elizabeth imagined how that conversation might go—and how she could prove she was at least trying to be courageous.

"Mr. Standish." Dorothy's tone brought Mary Elizabeth back to the talk around her. Her friend moved toward the man. "I hear you have copies of Captain Smith's writings and maps."

"Indeed I do, Miss Raynsford."

"Might we see the map of where we hope to land?" Dorothy had tried ever since they'd left Holland to speak to the man, but there'd never been an opportune time. Now her chance had come. And Dorothy was one who never passed up a fortuitous situation like this.

"Of course. Let's find a place below where we can be out of the wind. I don't want to risk anything blowing away." Mr. Standish stretched out his arm, indicating the girls should precede him.

Her friend clasped her hands together. "Thank you very much, Mr. Standish, I'm quite excited to see them."

As they navigated the narrow companionway to the deck below, Mary Elizabeth felt some of Dorothy's excitement. She'd always been a bit fascinated by Captain John Smith and his adventures in the New World, but his reputation as a swashbuckling braggart and his quoted prices to lead their expedition had made the elders search out another adviser.

Now to get a glimpse of the maps thrilled her. Maybe she had a bit more of an adventurous spirit than she thought. Maybe all those prayers for courage were being answered with an affirmation from above.

When Mr. Standish opened the book and pulled out several folded pieces of paper, he became very serious. "Please don't touch the maps—they are tedious to reproduce. I'm sure you understand."

"Of course." Dorothy's head bobbed up and down in a vigorous nod.

"Yes, sir." Mary Elizabeth knew the man was serious about his duties. And ruining a map they needed would be disastrous for their whole colony.

An English soldier who had also been living in Holland, Myles Standish's reputation was pristine. He seemed to be a good and knowledgeable man and agreed to the Saints' rules.

Carefully unfolding a large square, Mr. Standish cleared his throat and held it up so the light from the door above would shine on the paper. "Now this is the map of Virginia."

Dorothy scooted in closer. "And where will the new colony be?"

He pointed to the most northern section of the map and then went off the map farther. "Somewhere in here. Right at the mouth of the Hudson River."

"That's a good deal north of Jamestown." Dorothy pointed and tilted her head.

"Yes, it is. But that is where our patent lies. It will be beautiful and have plenty of water."

Mary Elizabeth studied the detailed map. It must have taken Captain Smith days upon days—possibly even months—to explore all that territory and coastline. The hours invested made her shake her head in wonder. The map itself was exquisite in its detail. "Is there anything else north of Virginia?" She hadn't paid a lot of attention to the discussions about the New World because they seemed to cause her a lot of stress, but now she was fascinated. All she remembered was that Florida was somewhere south of Virginia.

"Yes, there is an entire region Captain Smith named New England." Mr. Standish folded the Virginia map and pulled out another paper. He opened it up. "All of this is north of Virginia and a good deal north of where we are destined. But we won't be headed that far up the coastline. Maybe one day you'll get to explore that area. I hear it's quite beautiful."

"Look, Mary Elizabeth." Dorothy pointed. "There's a place here on the map called 'Plimouth.' Oh, and one named 'Oxford.' And there's even a 'London.'" She giggled and turned to Mr. Standish. "Are there actually settlements or cities there?"

"No. It's barely been explored, although the fishing waters in that area are quite good and many vessels are familiar with the bays and harbors. Captain Smith took the liberty—with Prince Charles's help—to name locations, harbors, points, and such after good strong English names. Thus the title: New England."

"This area is named Cape James?" Mary Elizabeth studied the hook-shaped piece of land at the bottom of the map.

"Indeed. Although another captain named it Cape Cod quite a while before Smith. I think most of the sailors still think of it as Cape Cod because of the abundance of the fish."

"What about the section in between? Do you have a map of that?" Mary Elizabeth's curiosity was piqued. Between the two maps, she could almost picture the coastline of the New World—and instead of inciting fear, it created a new excitement.

"Well, that part is uncharted so far. There are dangerous shoals and other areas that ships have had to avoid."

"I'm terribly glad we're not headed there." Dorothy's light laughter filled the close quarters. "Thank you so much for showing us, Mr. Standish."

"You are quite welcome." He bowed and closed his book. "And don't you worry. We know exactly where we are going."

❦

Wednesday, 9 August 1620

The slight breeze ruffled William's hair as he stood at the bow of the *Mayflower* and watched the *Speedwell* lazily cut through the water. They needed more wind if they were going to make any headway. Their ship master—Christopher Jones—had been ordering the crew to work the sails all morning.

"William!" John Alden's voice made him turn around.

"Afternoon, John." William greeted his new friend.

This was new ground for him. Actually having a friend his own age. Although John was a year past William's own twenty years, they continued to discover how much they had in common.

John had been hired as the cooper—or barrel maker—for the *Mayflower*. An important job, since all the provisions were stored in barrels. His responsibilities were to build, repair, and maintain the hefty number. And since William was a carpenter, they enjoyed working together and discussing shared ideas for building and for working with wood.

"We need some good gusts of wind, don't we?" John patted him on the back.

"That we do." William looked back toward the *Speedwell*. "I'm pretty sure everyone else is having the same thoughts. We're all anxious to get to Virginia."

"Aye. I've got so many things I want to try—my dreams for the future have made my imagination work around the clock." John pulled a small book out of his pocket and looked around them. "I haven't shown this to anyone else, but what do you think? Do you think it will work?"

William studied the drawing of what appeared to be a specialized wood-cutting machine. His friend was much like him. Young and unafraid of the future, William was ready to take on whatever the new settlement might need. He too had lots of ideas for how to improve the way things were done. But he had never shared his ideas with anyone. "I think it's a grand idea. Will you have all the parts to make it?"

"I tried to use only what I knew we would have with us." He turned the page. "But for some of my other ideas, I'll have to wait for the *Fortune* scheduled to arrive next year."

"What about Jamestown?" William eyed the next few drawings. "Do you know what kind of supplies they have?"

"It's such a long way from where we will be. It could take a few days by ship to get there, don't you agree? I don't know if it's worth traveling that distance. I've already requested certain items be sent on each of the next three ships. It was one of my requirements when I hired on."

William nodded. He didn't realize they'd be so far from Jamestown. But it didn't matter. Excited energy built in his heart. There would be a lot of firsts to come. He'd love to be the first one recognized for his craftsmanship in building. He dreamed of building cathedrals and churches as beautiful and elaborate as some of the prized ones in Europe. His mentor and master had shown him several drawings of them. Would his name one day be associated with something beautiful in history?

John's head jerked up from the book and jolted William out of the thought. "What do you think of that?"

William followed John's gaze and watched as the *Speedwell* appeared to be turning around. "I don't know, but it doesn't look like a good thing." He pointed. "Look, there's someone on the bow waving a flag."

Hurried footsteps sounded behind them. William turned.

Master Christopher Jones came toward the bulwark with his spyglass held out. He looked through it.

A small crowd gathered, but silence reigned as everyone watched their captain.

William realized he was holding his breath while he waited for news.

The ship master grimaced then let out a long breath. "Looks like we are headed back to England, chaps. The *Speedwell* has sprung a leak."

❧

Thursday, 10 August 1620

The bucket sloshed as Mary Elizabeth climbed up the companionway once again. Prayerfully, her hour of work was almost done because everything ached. Who knew a bucket of water could weigh so much after these many trips?

The shipmaster yelled down from the poop deck. "She's still sittin' too low, lads. We're takin' on too much water!"

Mary Elizabeth looked up to where the man stood. Leaning over the stern of the ship, he shook his head. "Everyone needs to move faster!"

Faster wasn't something she was sure her muscles could take. There weren't enough people to make a bucket line from the bottom to the top, so they all trekked back and forth. Going down with an empty bucket was easier than climbing up with a full one.

Their group of passengers had been divided up into four groups. Men, women, and children were all included. Each group took an hour shift. A brutal hour of going down to the deepest level of the ship, filling up a bucket with the sea water that continually seeped in, climbing up the two levels, and dumping the water back where it belonged. Afterward they'd rest for three hours while the other groups worked and then start right back at it.

The first shift, everyone was passionate about the job. No one wanted to sink. Fear drove them. But after little sleep and hefting and hauling, most had grown silent. They were soaked and weary.

As she threw the water over the bulwark, Mary Elizabeth saw her father bring his bucket up. For the first time in a long while, he looked tired instead of excited about the journey. "Papa, are you doing all right?"

A forced smile lit his features. "As well as I can." He nodded to her bucket. "We best get back down below."

"Yes, Father." She nodded and followed him down the companionway. Her younger brother made it to the steps as she reached the bottom.

He set his bucket down and wiped his brow. Only half full, it was still too much for a small boy to have to carry.

"Let me help you, David." Mary Elizabeth reached for the rope handle.

"No. I can do it. I just needed a breath."

The poor little chap. Trying so hard to be a grown-up. It didn't make sense that the ship master expected the children to assist. But then again, every able hand was helpful.

David headed up the steps, and she turned and went down the other companionway.

At the last step, her boots hit water. Much higher than before.

The master's mate continued to shout orders from the stern where the leak was worst. Mary Elizabeth sloshed her way to the others. Why was there so much more water? How would they ever get it all out?

What met her eyes caused her to gasp.

The crack in the bottom of the ship wasn't just a thin gap—it had grown.

And water poured in.

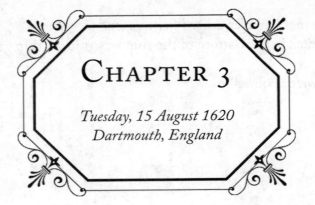

CHAPTER 3

Tuesday, 15 August 1620
Dartmouth, England

William bent over his journal with his quill. So far, there hadn't been a lot to report, but he wanted to be honorable and write down everything—to prove that he was a good steward for his new employers.

Now in port at Dartmouth for repairs on the *Speedwell*, he was anxious to get back to sea. Dry land was wonderful, but it couldn't match the thrill of the new life ahead of him. Going backward in his journey hadn't been part of the plan. And he did *not* enjoy deviations from his plans.

He and John took turns going ashore since neither one of them wanted to leave the whole of their worldly possessions to thieves who might try and get aboard while docked. So every time John went into town, William took the time to make notes of all he could remember having seen and heard.

The delay in getting to their destination would mean delay in getting the settlement set up. But it was a miracle the *Speedwell* had made it back to port without sinking. Thanks to the crew and the passengers, they'd kept her afloat.

But as the calendar days moved later into the year, the possibility to arrive early enough to plant anything this year vanished. While everyone tried to stay positive, the unspoken fear was palpable.

The delay also could affect their preparation of the ground to produce food next year. The risk to the Merchants and Adventurers' investment could be costly. But it wasn't his job to speculate. Only to report. Nevertheless, he couldn't help the little niggle of worry that started in the back of his mind. The delay would affect them all. But how much?

John came down the companionway of the *Mayflower* toward him. "What are you working on, my friend?"

"Just a journal." William shrugged and closed the book. "How was your trip to town?"

"It was good to stretch my legs and run, but it's quite boring to not be of use. Ended up offering to help on the *Speedwell* with repairs, and they said they needed another good carpenter—would you be interested?"

"Of course." William stood. "Anything to get us back out to sea faster." Tucking the journal into his trunk, he covered it with a few other items. Then he pulled out a satchel of tools and locked the chest. "Lead the way, my friend."

John nodded and took the steps two at a time. "I've hired a young lad to keep an eye on our belongings."

"Do you know him?"

"Yes. He's actually my cousin, so I know we can trust him."

A gangly young boy appeared at the top of the companionway. "I'll make sure everything is tip-top, John."

"Thank you, Matthew." John tousled the boy's hair. "This is my friend, William Lytton."

"Nice to meet you, Mr. Lytton." A scrawny hand went over his waist as the lad bowed.

William laughed. "How about we just shake hands"—he held out his hand—"like gentlemen."

"Yes, sir." The boy smiled and gave William's hand a hearty shake.

"It looks like everything will be in good hands." William looked to John. "Let's see if we can help get the *Speedwell* seaworthy again."

John took long strides ahead of William—his eagerness to be useful quite apparent. Such an interesting man this new friend. The simplicity of calling someone *friend* was still a bit unusual for William.

But he'd enjoyed the ease of their conversations and the camaraderie. No one on the ship knew that he was an orphan. No one knew his past—being kicked out to fend for himself as a child and being taken in by the man who'd taught him a trade. Instead of an outcast, he was part of a group—the Planters.

This was new territory.

Seemed like everything about the life ahead of him would be new. A completely fresh start.

John looked back to him. "Have you met Stephen Hopkins yet?"

William kept to himself a lot. "No, I can't say that I have."

"Oh, well now. . .there is someone that you simply must meet. He's been to Jamestown, was shipwrecked and stranded on Bermuda. He even attended the wedding of the famous Indian Pocahontas."

"So you know him?" He had to admit the man sounded intriguing.

"He's a passenger on the *Mayflower*, mate!" John chuckled. "He's been telling us these stories the past few nights."

But William had kept to himself and written in his journal while the men stayed top deck to swap stories.

"Maybe it's time you join us." John elbowed him.

"You've asked me every night—"

"And every night you answer the same." One of his friend's eyebrows raised.

"Well, perhaps this time will be different."

"Perhaps it will." John slapped William on the back.

They reached the *Speedwell* in swift time, thanks to John's fast feet. William raced up the gangway behind the cooper and held tight to his tools. Sounded like he needed to meet Mr. Hopkins. As he followed John toward the door to the lower levels, several people walking about the tiny main deck caught William's attention. He'd heard a lot about the Separatists and was curious to meet them and understand them. Anyone devout enough to stand up to the Church of England fascinated him. Not that he had much use for God or any church.

John stopped at the top of the steps. "Good morning, ladies." He tipped his hat, and a broad smile lit his face as he looked down into the mouth of the ship.

A white bonnet appeared at the top of the companionway. Then a knot of brown hair and a blue cloak. "Good morning." The lady nodded to John and turned to William. "Good morning." Her eyes danced as she smiled.

William was fascinated with the joy on her face. "Good morning to you, miss." He hadn't met many women in his line of work. Especially not any close to his age. And if he guessed correctly, this woman was younger than him.

She turned back to the opening. "Mary Elizabeth, hurry up. It appears we have some dashing men to greet us."

John carried on a conversation with the jovial girl, but William's attention was drawn down.

As he looked back to the square hole in the deck, he saw another white cap emerge. This time, blond hair—the color of his own—was tied in a neat knot at the lady's neck, and a red cape covered her form. Her head was lowered—obviously keeping an eye on her steps. William found himself anticipating another joyous expression.

But when she lifted her head, instead of a large smile, her face bore a timid expression. Unsure. And a bit embarrassed? With brisk steps, he strode to John's side and offered a hand down to assist. "Good day to you, miss."

"Good day." She took hold of his hand. "Thank you for your assistance." Shaking her head, she ascended the last few steps. "You would suppose I could be better at that climb by now."

"Not at all, miss." William found himself smiling. Brown eyes searched his. "Ships can be difficult to navigate. Especially for the fairer sex."

Half a smile. She tucked a strand of hair back under her cap.

He bowed slightly. "I'm William Lytton, aboard the *Mayflower*."

The smile that had started now blossomed into something radiant. "Nice to make your acquaintance, Mr. Lytton. I'm Mary Elizabeth Chapman."

It took a moment to gain his bearings. John's chatter went on beside him, but William was mesmerized by the woman in front of him. Was she one of the Separatists? She must be to be on the *Speedwell*.

"Again, thank you very much for your kindness." She turned to her friend. "Dorothy, we need to let these men get to their work."

Mary Elizabeth—in the red cape—tugged at her friend's arm. With a look over her shoulder, she sent William a slight smile.

As they walked toward the bow, he couldn't tear his gaze away.

"William."

A tap on his shoulder.

"William."

Another tap.

"Will–i–am." John slapped him on the shoulder.

He jerked toward the cooper. "I'm sorry. What were you saying?"

His friend's laughter washed over him. "Nothing. I just had to call your name three times. We need to get down to the hold, but I take it a certain lady has caught your attention?"

"What?" William furrowed his brow and shook his head. Couldn't exactly tell his friend that he'd never had much interaction with young ladies, now could he? "No. Of course not. I was just thinking about our journey."

More laughter from John brought a few stares to land in their direction. He slapped William again on the shoulder. "If you repeat that to yourself over and over, maybe you'll believe it."

Heat rushed to William's cheeks, but he couldn't admit to John that he was right. Best to just get to work and attempt to get a vision of Mary Elizabeth in her red cape out of his mind.

"Well. . ." Dorothy clasped her hands—a sure indication she was about to interrogate her subject—and walked backward up the deck in front of Mary Elizabeth.

"Well what?" No matter how hard her friend tried, Mary Elizabeth wasn't about to take the bait.

"You know exactly what I'm asking about, silly."

"Do I?"

Dorothy stopped and placed her hands on her hips. "Don't play games with me, Mary Elizabeth Chapman. I saw how you smiled at Mr. Lytton."

Even using all her energy, Mary Elizabeth couldn't stop a new smile from forming on her face.

"See? Just like that." Dorothy looked around and then grabbed Mary Elizabeth's arm and dragged her to the bulwark. "He's a handsome man, isn't he?"

"Dorothy Raynsford, you need to hush right now. You know he's not part of our congregation—he could be a heathen for all we know—"

"His friend John is a God-fearing man," her friend was quick to interject.

"And you discovered this fact *how*, exactly?"

"While Mr. Lytton assisted you up the companionway, John and I had quite a lively discussion. I found out that he is the cooper on the *Mayflower* and that his friend is a carpenter. And quite skilled, I'm told."

"Oh, I'm sure."

Dorothy huffed. "You are not playing fair. I've never seen you take interest in any young man. Ever. And you would deny me the pleasure of being a part of this—your best friend?"

For a moment, Mary Elizabeth *almost* felt guilty. But that was always Dorothy's way. Granted, Mr. Lytton was indeed a handsome man. But was she ready to admit that out loud? His hair was the same color as her own, but his eyes are what drew her. Blue and piercing. His gaze had been intense.

Dorothy giggled. "You don't even have to say anything. I can read your face. You're thinking of him again."

"Oh gracious, Dorothy, you could try the patience of the Good Lord above." She wrapped her cloak tighter around her and leaned on the bulwark. The scent of salt water was much better than that of unwashed bodies. And to think they still had weeks to go aboard this ship.

"So. . . ?"

Mary Elizabeth shook her head.

"I'm not saying you have to marry the man, but you are taking all the fun out of this. Can't you at least admit to thinking he's handsome?"

"What about Mr. Alden? You spoke with him longer than I did with Mr. Lytton. Am I to assume that you found him handsome?"

"Diverting the focus of our conversation is cruel, Mary Elizabeth. And yes, I found Mr. Alden quite handsome, as well. But please remember, I didn't get to take a man's hand as he assisted me. It's totally different."

Warmth rushed up Mary Elizabeth's arms as she remembered the simple touch of Mr. Lytton's hand. How could the gentlemanly gesture feel so different from him than from any other man? Once again, she couldn't keep from smiling.

"You haven't smiled this much in a long time." Dorothy's elbow poked Mary Elizabeth in the side.

"All right. You've beaten the subject to death. Yes, I found Mr. Lytton handsome. I've never felt anything like I did when we met. Happy?"

"Yes, quite." Her friend laughed and hooked Mary Elizabeth's arm. "Now, let's take a stroll around the deck and discuss what we hope to find in a husband."

For the love of all things good, Mary Elizabeth couldn't decide what was worse—embarrassment of the topic or admitting she found a Stranger handsome.

David sat on his mat and stared at the toy in his lap. The top was one of his favorites normally, but on a ship it wasn't as fun—extra space wasn't known on the small ship, and when they were out to sea, the rocking motion made the top fall over. It would be nice if he had a friend to play with. But all the other children his age were busy.

It was hard growing up. Ever since he'd breeched—at age six—he'd wanted to be like his father.

A man.

He'd gotten to wear the breeches and clothes like a man, but he'd been small. Too small for any real work. And then Mother got sick and died.

Everything changed with Father then.

At eight years old, David was still small, but before they were chosen to go to the New World, he thought he might like to learn the art of weaving. Many of their congregation were very good at the trade. But Father wanted him to study the Bible more instead of learning a trade like most boys his age. While he loved the Bible, he didn't understand. Why was Father treating him differently now that Mother was dead?

His future was uncertain. But he loved his family. He would obey Father and study as much as he could. Maybe when he was stronger and bigger, he could help the family more.

Maybe then, Father wouldn't be so sad. At least he'd shown excitement about the trip. But two nights ago, David found him crying.

They all missed Mother.

Sometimes at night, he wanted to cry too because he missed her so much. His heart often ached with the loss of her. Now they'd left her buried in Holland. And he could barely remember her face.

He shook his head and stood up, the top in his hand. His thoughts weren't honoring to either his father or mother. If he wanted to be a man, he'd just have to start acting like one.

Taking the toy over to the trunk, David opened the lid and dropped it in. He needed to prove that he was growing up. Father would see that his son could work alongside him in the new colony. Maybe then happiness would return on a permanent basis to the Chapman household.

CHAPTER 4

Monday, 21 August 1620
Dartmouth, England

William watched the *Speedwell* once again cut through the water, this time with a good wind in her sails. Too bad he couldn't see any snippets of a red cape. What could Miss Chapman be doing? How was she? The thoughts had recurred many times over the past week. Too many times.

Shaking his head, he gripped the top plank of the bulwark. It would be weeks before he'd get to see her again, and even then, he wasn't worthy of her attention. Especially since her whole reason for the trip revolved around her faith. Faith which William didn't understand.

Maybe it was time to learn more about it.

"Afternoon, Mr. Lytton."

William turned and saw Robert Coppin—the master's mate. "Afternoon, Mr. Coppin. What can I do for you?"

"Master Jones was hoping you could help him build an idea he has for his cabin."

"Of course, I would love to be of assistance."

"You would be compensated as well." The man's weathered face concealed his age. But he was an imposing presence.

"While it is much appreciated, sir, it isn't necessary."

"Master Jones insists." Mr. Coppin bowed and nodded. "He's heard of your skill as a carpenter and knows that an honest man is worthy of his wages."

"Thank you, sir." William gave a nod of affirmation. "Please lead the way."

Coppin headed toward the stern of the ship where the master's cabin sat on the main deck behind the steerage room. Above the cabin was the poop deck—the highest level of the ship on the aft castle.

William had studied the ship at great length over the last few weeks. The whipstaff inside the steerage room was how they steered the *Mayflower*. The precise movements of the sailors as they worked the sails fascinated William—climbing to and fro on the large masts. Harnessing the wind was indeed a science.

But this would be the first time he'd seen the ship master's quarters.

Coppin opened the door to the cabin, which wasn't much bigger than an eight-foot square—if that.

Master Jones stood by an old cabinet. "Mr. Lytton. Thank you for coming."

"Of course." With all three of them in the room, it felt quite cramped.

The ship master pointed to the cabinet. "I'm hoping you can remake this into more usable space."

Mr. Coppin bowed to the master. "I'll be on the poop deck if you need me, sir."

Jones nodded and turned back to William. "Do you think you can reuse the wood?"

"What do you have in mind, sir?"

"Something a bit more practical." As Jones described what he was hoping for, William measured the wood with the width of his hand.

"I think it can be done and will give it my best effort."

"Thank you, Lytton. I've heard you've earned quite a reputation as a carpenter in London."

"Thank you, sir." The praise made William's heart swell. If only Paul were still alive. His mentor would have loved the adventure of the New World.

"I'll leave you to it, then."

Christopher Jones walked out of the room, an air of authority surrounding him. No doubt years of commanding ships gave him the confidence to be comfortable with the man he'd become.

Maybe one day William would be able to embrace the man *he* was as well. Maybe one day he wouldn't think of himself as an orphan. Maybe one day he could earn the affection of a beautiful woman like Mary Elizabeth.

Monday, 28 August 1620

Mary Elizabeth leaned over the mat where her brother David struggled to breathe. What else could she do? Father had stayed up all night with the boy and now slept next to him. Dorothy tried to convince her to get some air while the seas were calm, but Mary Elizabeth couldn't leave little David. The ship's surgeon—Mr. Smith—was concerned it could be pneumonia.

The only other time she'd heard that term was when a neighbor in Leyden died from the dreaded disease.

Why had he been out in the rain? She put her face in her hands. Ever since they'd all had to walk around in wet boots and stockings to help stop the last leak, David had had a cough. Even with her warning to stay out of the rain, he'd gone out to help with chores on the ship's deck.

The past couple of weeks, David had acted differently—instead of sitting and playing, he'd tried to work with anyone who would let him—and Mary Elizabeth wasn't sure what had prompted the all-fire independence. He'd always been a busy child, but very cooperative and docile. To see him lying still and lifeless. . .

The thought of death sent her into another bout of uncontrollable tears. God understood the appeals from her heart. She knew that. But was she deserving of His grace in this matter?

Oh, Father God, please forgive me for my foolish ways and sinful nature. And please, Lord. . .please. . .spare David.

Her tears soaked into the blanket covering her brother. What would she do without him? What would her father do? Her brother was so small. . . .

Footsteps sounded behind her, and Mary Elizabeth swiped at

her cheeks. Most of the congregation had stayed away because of the fever David couldn't break, but maybe someone approached with help.

The makeshift curtain separating her family's small space swished to the side. "Miss Chapman"—the surgeon's clipped tone held a sense of relief—"Master Reynolds is turning us about. The ship is leaking again, and so we make for Plymouth for repairs."

"How bad is it?"

"Not as bad as the last, I'm told, but I'm thankful for David's sake. He needs more care than I can give on the ship."

The words sunk into her heart. That meant David was worse than she'd imagined. With a swallow, she choked back the tears. "How long will it take us to return to port?"

"A few days. But if we can keep the boy's fever down, we might be able to help him more once we reach land. I'll be back this evening to check on him." The man turned on his heel and left.

While his words were not encouraging, the surgeon did give her a slight reason to hope. God could heal David. Of that she was certain. And even though they would be delayed further, maybe it was Providence that brought them back to England. But what about the leak? Would they be able to keep it from growing like the last? For the third time, their ship would have to limp its way into harbor. Her heart sank as fear built in her mind. She shook her head. The time was needed to be faithful and positive. Not doubting or anxious. *Oh Lord, please help us. I need Your courage to fill me.*

For David.

For her father. He'd already lost so much. Losing David would crush him.

No. She wouldn't allow her thoughts to go there.

Thankfully, they had a surgeon aboard. Mr. Smith appeared very young, and she'd been told that he was betrothed to a young lady back in England—but this wasn't a time to doubt his abilities or to question his experience. From what she could tell, he was very knowledgeable.

Father shifted on his blanket. "Mary Elizabeth?"

"I'm here, Papa."

He swiped a hand down his face and sat up. "Was someone talking? Any news?"

"Mr. Smith came to give us some news—"

"Mary Elizabeth, how is our sweet boy doing?" Dorothy slipped in beside her.

The sound of her best friend's voice soothed her worry. "The surgeon just told me that we have to keep his fever down. We're headed back to England, and we will need to get him help there."

"I just heard Master Reynolds telling the people on deck. People are worried about the delay, but no one wants to be on a sinking ship. Especially after last time. I think we're all still drying out." She smiled and brushed some hair back from David's forehead. "And we can get help for David."

Father got up, his face grim. "I'm going to check on the details of the leak and ask the elders to pray."

Mary Elizabeth nodded and reached up for his hand. But he didn't look at her.

"I'm sure he's just tired." Dorothy took the outstretched hand.

"I wish it were only that. After Mother passed, he went to a very dark place—you know that. Ever since David has gotten sick, I've seen the same look in his eyes, and it scares me."

"Don't let your thoughts go there, Mary Elizabeth. God will get us back to England, and then we can get help for your brother."

Mary Elizabeth nodded. If they could keep him alive until then.

CHAPTER 5

Friday, 1 September 1620

A warm hand touched her own as she peered up into startling blue eyes. "Good day to you, miss."

Mary Elizabeth woke with a start. It wasn't the first time she'd dreamed of that day. The day she'd met William Lytton and his friend. The thought of seeing him again made her insides do a little flip. His eyes held such depth—unlike anyone else she'd ever met. Were there secrets hidden behind them? Would she have a chance to speak with him again? At the moment, she'd like nothing more.

David moaned next to her.

She shook her head at her foolish and selfish thoughts. How could she think of her own desires when David struggled with each breath? Good thing Father couldn't know her thoughts. He'd certainly scold her for such behavior.

Unsure of the time of day down on the dim and dreary gun deck where all the passengers resided, Mary Elizabeth wiped the sleep from her eyes. It must be the middle of the day because she'd stayed up all night with David. She'd torn strips from one of her petticoats and soaked them in cool sea water. All night she'd bathed David's forehead and chest, hoping to keep his fever down.

His breathing was quieter now, but what did that mean?

Sitting up, she pulled her knees to her chest. Mother would know what to do. But she wasn't here.

That made Mary Elizabeth long for Leyden and the cemetery. That wasn't a possibility, so she longed to pour all her thoughts into the journal from Dorothy. But now wasn't the time.

Only one thing remained certain—life wasn't easy. And probability ran high that it never would be again.

Every prayer she'd sent heavenward of late asked for courage. Yet here she sat next to her sick brother in the depths of a ship. The future unknown. Everything in tumult.

The *least* thing she felt was courage.

Lord, please help me. I'm weak and little of faith. But I know You are almighty God.

With a deep breath, Mary Elizabeth ran her fingers through her hair and tidied it as best she could. Replacing her cap, she sent another prayer heavenward for David's healing.

"How is he?" Father opened the curtain a slit and peered down at his son.

"He feels a bit cooler now." Hoping her words came across as confident, Mary Elizabeth swallowed her fears.

Father nodded. Dark bags under his eyes portrayed his worry and lack of sleep the past few days. His hunched form appeared weary. "We are almost to port in Plymouth. The surgeon will escort us into town. The ship master knows of another good surgeon there."

Mary Elizabeth stood as best she could, but the ceilings were several inches short for her stature. Wasn't it bad enough there were no windows? They had to walk around all bent and crouched.

"Mary Elizabeth, there's something else you should know. The decision has been made to leave the *Speedwell* behind. No one wants to risk a leaky ship, and Mr. Reynolds has done nothing but complain. The crew will stay behind, as well as some of the passengers. The rest of us will all have to move to the *Mayflower* for the remainder of the voyage."

While a change of scenery would be nice, Mary Elizabeth had gotten used to this particular ship. It also meant that everything needed to be packed. "I'll get our personal belongings put away right now."

Father nodded and knelt beside David. "I'll get the curtain down and help roll up the mats." He touched his son's head. "He does feel cooler. Let's pray the Good Lord sees fit to heal him before we need to depart."

That thought hadn't even crossed Mary Elizabeth's mind until Father put it into words. What would they do if David wasn't strong enough to make the voyage? They'd sold everything to get this far and only had meager possessions on the ship. Everything else was invested in the voyage and venture in Virginia. Besides that, they were Separatists. And without the support of their congregation, how would they deal with the persecution?

"Don't worry, Mary Elizabeth. I can see it on your face." Father's hand rested on her shoulder. "The Lord knows our plight. He will see us through." A thin smile stretched across his weary features. "I have no doubt we will be on the *Mayflower* when she sails."

As he pulled down their small dividing curtain, Mary Elizabeth packed the trunk they'd brought aboard for their necessities. Everything else was below them in the cargo hold. Making quick work of the few items, she felt the ship lurch.

"We must be in the harbor." Father tucked the blanket around David and lifted the small boy into his arms. "I'll meet you on deck with the surgeon."

Urgency filled Mary Elizabeth's heart. Looking around their tiny space that had been their home for all these weeks, she checked to make sure everything was ready.

"Mary Elizabeth. I just saw your father." Dorothy was at her side and hugged her. "I'll make sure it all gets transferred over, and I'll set up your curtains again."

"Thank you."

"Think nothing of it. I'll be waiting for word on my little King David." Dorothy sniffed and wiped at her cheek.

Mary Elizabeth's friend had called him that since he was born. And David loved her for it. As he grew from baby to gangly boy, he often said he wanted to be a man after God's own heart just like the real King David from the scriptures.

"Now go. I'll take care of everything here."

Mary Elizabeth hugged her friend one more time. She took her cloak and raced to the main deck.

Fresh air and bright sunlight greeted her for the first time in several days. Spotting her father, she made her way toward him just as the sailors lowered the gangway.

The walk was steep, but she followed her father's confident steps.

"Look. The *Mayflower* is a good deal larger than the *Speedwell*. The journey should be a good one." He nodded to the ship tying in next to them.

All at once, the reality of the situation hit her. They'd be joining everyone on the *Mayflower*. For the entire journey across the ocean. The *Speedwell* had been full of their congregation and the crew. But now they would join a new ship's crew and many Strangers.

She allowed a smile to ease onto her face as her insides fluttered. David *would* get better and maybe just maybe. . .she'd have that chance to speak with Mr. Lytton again after all.

Monday, 4 September 1620

William watched Miss Chapman's friend walk up the gangway. Obviously resolute in her objective, she took determined steps and placed her hands on her hips when she reached the main deck. Her brow furrowed.

"Looks like Miss Raynsford needs assistance." John patted William's shoulder and headed toward the young woman.

"How did you guess?" William stifled a laugh and followed his friend.

After crossing the deck, John bowed. "Miss Raynsford, how can we be of help?"

"Mr. Alden, Mr. Lytton." She curtseyed, then put a hand over her heart with a sigh. "I can't tell you how glad I am to see you. I need to make accommodations for the Chapman family."

William moved closer to her. Was Mary Elizabeth all right? "I know they've been transferring everything to the cargo hold, but I didn't think they were moving passengers until tomorrow."

"They're not." She clasped her hands under her chin. "That's why I need your help. You see, little David—Mary Elizabeth's brother—took ill, and they are in town at a surgeon's. I need to help move my own family tomorrow, but I promised I would take care of Mary Elizabeth's belongings. She's my dearest friend in the whole world, and I need to make sure they have a good space. Especially for David to recover." She finally took a breath. The pleading in her eyes couldn't be mistaken.

"Mary Elizabeth's not ill, is she?" William couldn't help but question.

A soft smile split Miss Raynsford's face. "No. She's not. But thank you for asking."

John offered the young lady his arm. "We'd be glad to assist. But let's do it quietly so we don't trouble anyone else."

"Do you know where we should set up their things?" Miss Raynsford looked hopeful.

"I'm not certain. . ." John shot William a questioning glance.

Several thoughts passed through William's mind. His spot was one of the choicest, at the stern in a corner. There was less movement of the ship at the stern and less water seepage. There was also a bit more privacy since it was up against the walls of the ship. "They can have my spot." The words were out before he knew it. "It seems we will have to make room for a lot of people, anyway. Let me give my area to the Chapman family."

Miss Chapman's friend covered her heart again. "Mr. Lytton, that is so very generous of you."

"It will be my privilege, Miss Raynsford." William eyed John and noticed his raised eyebrows. "There could be enough space for your family to be next to them as well."

"But where will you go?" Miss Raynsford appeared doubtful.

"I'll just have to find a space near John." He gripped his friend's shoulder.

"We will probably need to share the tiny area I already have." John nodded. "With as many passengers as we need to house, we will have to economize space."

Within minutes, the trio had collected all the Chapmans' belongings and were headed back to the *Mayflower*. When they reached the top of the gangway, William noticed the crew struggling with a large burden on deck.

As soon as he got a better look, he realized what it was. "Look, John. It's a house jack." How exciting that they were bringing this with them to Virginia. From a carpenter's perspective, it was amazing. They'd be able to get houses up a lot faster.

"I've actually never seen one." John stopped and studied the wood-and-iron contraption that resembled a giant screw.

"Gentlemen, I know it's fascinating, but my arms are getting sore." Miss Raynsford shifted her burden.

"Oh, of course. My apologies." William moved ahead. "Follow me."

When he'd first boarded the *Mayflower*, William had been proud of grabbing his accommodations. Never would he have thought that he would so readily give them up for someone else. Of course, he never thought that the passengers and belongings from two ships would be making the journey on one. But at this point, he didn't mind. They hadn't even gotten one hundred leagues past Land's End when the *Speedwell*'s master had turned her about again.

Master Jones wanted to get back under way as soon as they could replenish a few supplies and get loaded. This would make the third trip out from England. First from Southampton, then from Dartmouth, and now from Plymouth. William could only hope they'd make it all the way across the ocean this time.

Ducking into the short space of the gun deck, William steered Miss Raynsford and John to the back corner. "Let me just store all of my belongings and get them out of the way."

"I'll hang their privacy curtains." Dorothy laid her burden down and went to work.

John shuffled over to William. "Hand me whatever is ready to go, and I'll haul it to my quarters."

William made swift work of his packing and had everything out by the time Dorothy had the curtains hung. He moved the Chapmans' things into the tiny space while John carried items across the ship to his area. A sense of pride filled William as he realized he'd been able to help the beautiful Miss Chapman and her family.

Dorothy touched his arm. "Thank you."

"I was honored to do it, miss." Bent over, it was hard to acknowledge her in the proper way, but he sent her a smile.

"Not every man has as much honor as you, Mr. Lytton. You gave up a very agreeable space—for a long journey no less—to perfect strangers."

In his mind, Miss Chapman wasn't a stranger. He'd thought of her and their meeting often. But to the rest of the world, Dorothy made a valid point.

He didn't *know* the Chapman family.

Something he'd like very much to change.

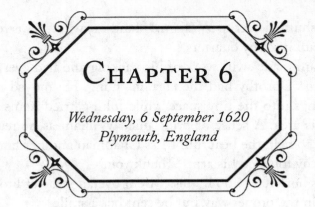

The good alee wind they'd enjoyed leaving Dartmouth seemed to follow them as the *Mayflower* once again left England's shores. William prayed it would be true and not just his fancy as the sails billowed above his head. At this rate, he wasn't sure when they would reach Virginia. As he'd studied all the writings he could find on ships crossing the Atlantic to the New World, everything pointed to a September departure as too late. Disastrous even.

Stephen Hopkins had been telling them of the storms that happened this late in the year, and then of the trouble the colonists at Jamestown had had with the Indians. While the stories were fascinating, William didn't need more doubt entering his mind.

No. He couldn't allow the negative thoughts to reign. He'd overheard enough conversations to know that the entire ship full of people were tired of the trip already. And now they were packed into every inch of space. With over 130 souls aboard, the 180-ton ship was full to brimming.

He thought that in such confined quarters the chance to see Mary Elizabeth Chapman again would be high. But ever since her father carried young David aboard, the pretty Miss Chapman had stayed within their curtained-off area.

Maybe once the boy was doing better, he'd have a chance to speak with her again. His hopes would just have to hang on that thought.

Why was it that for the first time in his life, he was fascinated with a female? Possibly because he'd been so concentrated on learning all he could from Paul in years prior. He tried to be logical about it. Perhaps a lady capable of capturing his attention never before crossed his path. And if he were honest, he knew it was because he found Mary Elizabeth enchanting.

Being an orphan had a profound effect on William. Even the family who took him in as a baby treated him as less than their own child. He was more of a slave. And then to be kicked out at such a young age—forced to live on the streets and beg for food? It was the worst possible scenario in William's mind. No child should have to suffer in such a way. To always be scorned by people. To have things thrown at him. To always be covered in dirt and grime but hoping that someone would see past that and cherish him for who he was.

But no. People had been cruel. He'd slaved for every penny he'd earned. Each twopence, each sixpence—and once he'd worked for weeks and weeks to earn a whole shilling. He thought it would be his lot in life for the rest of his days.

Until Paul Brookshire saw him on the street one day haggling with a merchant over a loaf of bread. By that time, William was hardened to the world. It didn't matter that it was common for families who took in orphans to put them out again at age nine. It didn't matter that once in a great while a stranger would come along and give him a sack of discarded clothing. What mattered? Four years, he'd fought to keep food in his belly. Thirteen years, he'd been treated as less than everyone else.

Paul changed all that. But it took years for William to trust the man.

The years passed. When his mentor tried to convince him to spend time with people his own age, William always refused. Why would anyone see him as anything other than a despised and rejected orphan?

The tangy scent of the sea made him take a deep breath and shake his head. No sense in digging up the anger and hurt of the past. Things were different now. No one knew what he'd been—or where he came from. Now he was a respected and well-trained carpenter. His master had seen to that. William Lytton's name had become known for quality workmanship. And this opportunity to start something brand new, in a setting around the world and away from everything and everyone he'd ever known was *exactly* what he wanted.

Would Mary Elizabeth be able to see him as someone special?

Shaking his head, William knew the thoughts were fruitless. She was a Separatist. And he'd learned in the past couple of days that those who called themselves Saints also thought of everyone else as Strangers.

John had brought up the subject yesterday. He didn't want to be known as a Stranger to the Leyden congregation—his beliefs lined up with the people. But since they'd faced such persecution for so many years, having lost everything on multiple occasions because of betrayers, the lack of trust was understandable.

Something William understood all too well. While he wasn't ready to discuss his background with John quite yet, he found himself respecting the man more each day. But the discussions on God and the Bible—two of John's favorite topics—made William more uncomfortable. For years, he'd hardened his heart, basing his thoughts of God on how the world around him had treated him. But for the first time ever, he was seeing a different side in people.

With the open ocean before him, William looked to the sky. If God existed the way Paul believed—the way Mary Elizabeth and John believed—then maybe it was worth asking questions and educating himself.

Peter watched William with a close eye. The man never seemed to do anything untoward or questionable.

Who was the carpenter, anyway? Maybe there was something in the man's past. Something that would plant a seed of doubt.

Once they were on board from Southampton, Peter had hoped he'd have a chance to go through Lytton's things, but William chose too good of a location for his quarters. Then when he'd given up his spot for that Chapman family, Peter thought maybe he had another chance. With all the people milling about, certainly, he could disappear and look...

But no. So far he hadn't had any luck.

Well, he had the whole voyage to put his plan into action. Maybe he just needed to sit back and be patient.

The time would come.

Saturday, 9 September 1620

"The sea is calm, Mary Elizabeth." Father looked down from his crouched position. "As long as you and I have a good hold of David, nothing can happen to him. I think the fresh air will do him some good."

"Please, Mary Elizabeth?" The illness had made her little brother's voice scratchy and weak.

Looking from him to Father made her realize how overprotective she'd become. Maybe this was another chance to show courage. "All right. Let's head up to the main deck together." She stood from her kneeling position and pointed a finger in David's direction. "But you must promise me that you will not let go under any circumstances."

"I promise." The twinkle in his eye lifted her spirit.

She hadn't seen it in a fortnight—or more. "I've been longing for a bit of fresh air myself."

"And sunshine." Father chuckled.

"Yes, and sunshine." Helping David with his shoes, Mary Elizabeth realized how thin he had become. "We need to fatten you up, young man."

"That won't be a problem. I'm starving and could eat a whole loaf of bread by myself." He rubbed his stomach.

"Well, we don't have any loaves of bread, but let's see what we can find." Mary Elizabeth shook her head. Her brother's active personality had often gotten on her nerves before, but now she would be thankful for it. After watching him be almost lifeless for so long, she wouldn't trade his energy for anything in the world.

"I'll meet you at the steps." Father tousled David's hair.

The way to the companionway was dim—another ship with no windows on the gun deck—but her eyes had grown accustomed to the lack of light. When she saw the sun shining down from above, she couldn't get there fast enough.

"Not so fast, Mary Elizabeth." Her little brother tugged at her hand.

Slowing her pace, she smiled. "I'm sorry. Is this better?"

"Yes, much."

"Before long, I won't be able to keep up with you."

"You couldn't keep up with me before I got sick, Mary Elizabeth. It must be because you're a girl."

"I beg your pardon?" Laughter bubbled up. And it felt good.

"You're a lot older too."

"Is that so?"

"Yup, you're more than twice my age. Old people don't move very fast."

"You little imp." She stopped and pulled on his hand so he would face her. "Then I think we need to make a deal."

"What kinda deal?"

Mary Elizabeth tapped her lip with her forefinger. "Hmmm. I think we should see just how 'old' I am when we get to our new home. We'll have a race and see who is faster. But that means you have to eat everything I tell you so you grow big and strong."

His giggles floated around her. "You'll never beat me. I'm too fast."

"We will just have to see about that, now won't we?" Tugging on his hand, she nodded toward the steps. "But no running today, all right? Master Jones said it isn't safe for the children to run up there."

"Yes, Mary Elizabeth."

"Good." The companionways on ships were not much more than a glorified ladder. What with all her petticoats and skirt, climbing up was always a cumbersome chore. If only there was a blue-eyed gentleman named William waiting for her at the top to offer a hand again. She shook her head. She probably needed to repent of all the thoughts she had of Mr. Lytton. Goodness, she'd only met him once.

At the top, she reached down for David. "Come on up, it's a beautiful day."

His ascent was slow but steady, and it thrilled Mary Elizabeth's heart to see him moving so well.

"Hold on to my hand now." She straightened to her full height and squinted in the bright light. Stretching her legs felt better than anything had in a long while. Looking down at David, she caught his smile.

"This is a big ship, isn't it, Mary Elizabeth?"

"It's bigger than the *Speedwell*, yes."

"How much?"

"About three times bigger."

Mary Elizabeth held a hand above her eyes to shield them from the sun. Days without bright light had made her eyes sensitive. Several groups of people stood around the small deck. Master Jones had made sure that everyone knew the rules. If the seas became at all rough, no one but the crew was allowed on the main deck. He didn't want to risk anyone getting washed overboard or getting in the way of the sailors as they did their jobs.

They were fortunate to have beautiful weather right now. It gave them the opportunity to walk around upright and be out in the fresh air.

Father nodded at her and reached for David's other hand. "Let's get some exercise, shall we?"

At eight years old, her brother was still a small boy, but he wouldn't stay that way for long. Mary Elizabeth relished the feel of his small hand in her own. She'd never take for granted the time she was given with him. Not after almost losing him.

And then there was Father.

The stoic man God had blessed her with was beginning to show age that would attest to him being a much older man. The past year since Mother died had taken its toll on him. Gray sprinkled his dark hair, and lines around his eyes gave evidence of his penchant for smiling and laughter.

But there hadn't been as much of either since her mother had died. Mary Elizabeth longed to see him return to his jovial self. A new thought struck her—would Father ever remarry?

He definitely wasn't an ancient man beyond marrying—not even forty years of age.

"What are your thoughts, Mary Elizabeth? Your brow is quite quizzical. . ." Father's voice intruded on her thoughts and made the heat rise in her cheeks. Could she tell him?

David laughed and pulled on her hand. "Her face is turning red, Father, look."

Best to tell the truth. She couldn't allow them to think she was thinking anything unworthy. "I was thinking of Mother. . .and if you'd ever marry again."

Father's face softened a bit.

Mary Elizabeth couldn't decipher the emotions that seemed to spread across his features. Her father had always been so strong—and so in love with their mother.

"Your mother was a wonderful woman. No one could ever compare." Facing forward, his shoulders stiffened.

"I'm sorry, Father."

No response.

Even David ducked his head and kept his eyes down. Would they ever be able to talk about it without being overtaken by pain and grief?

Silence surrounded their little family as they walked in a slow pace around the deck.

Father looked at her. "It seems David is doing quite well. I need to discuss some things with Elder Brewster."

His desire to depart was all her fault. She'd wounded the man she loved and adored above anyone else. "That is fine, Father." While Elder Brewster was the head of their congregation because Pastor Robinson had stayed in Holland to prepare the others to join them in Virginia, Mary Elizabeth wasn't so sure what could be so important.

Other than avoiding the topic she'd voiced.

"Don't let go of your sister, young man." Father gave his stern look to David.

"No, sir. I won't." The power in David's voice surprised Mary Elizabeth. After just a few short minutes, he already seemed stronger. Or maybe it was just for her benefit—since she knew she'd hurt them both with her words.

"Good, good." Father nodded and walked toward a group of men from their congregation.

Mary Elizabeth tightened her grip on David's hand. Things needed to turn around. "Where would you like to go next?"

"To the front."

"To the bow?"

"Yes." David wasn't overly talkative.

Mary Elizabeth understood, even though her heart ached to hear his happy chatter. Why did she have to bring up Mother?

Taking slow steps, Mary Elizabeth thought of ways to shift David's attention.

While there wasn't a lot of room to meander, Mary Elizabeth enjoyed being outside. The crates of animals were fun to see. Goats, chickens, pigs, and a couple of dogs resided on the main deck. Maybe she could engage David that way.

"Can you make the sound of a pig?" She stopped in front of one particular crate.

Her little brother looked up at her and then back to the animal. "I'm not sure. . .but I can make the sound of a rooster, I think."

"Why don't you give it a try. Let's go see the chickens."

"Maybe it would be better to cluck like the chickens."

"Whatever you want to try." Mary Elizabeth watched as David crouched by the crate.

He clucked at them and giggled at the random noises they made back at him.

She tugged at his hand to resume their walk. At least he'd laughed.

When they reached the bow, Mary Elizabeth spotted two familiar figures. She sucked in a breath.

"Mary Elizabeth, what's wrong?" David's pull at her hand made her look down.

"Not a thing. I'm sorry. I just wanted more fresh air."

But by the time she finished speaking, two pairs of boots entered her vision.

"Good morning, Miss Chapman. Such a pleasure to see you again." Mr. Alden greeted her. "This must be young David that we've heard so much about."

The comment puzzled her. "Good day to you, Mr. Alden. How have you heard about David?"

"Your charming friend—Dorothy—has kept us apprised of the situation."

No doubt she had. Dorothy could regale anyone with her stories. She never seemed to run out of words.

Mr. Lytton stepped closer and looked at her brother. "I'm so thankful to hear you are recovered."

"Thank you, sir." David gave a slight bow. "I'm David Chapman."

"Yes, I know." Mr. Lytton looked up at Mary Elizabeth and smiled before he looked back down at her brother. He put a hand to his chest and bowed. "And I am William Lytton. This is my friend, John Alden, the cooper of the ship."

"Nice to know you both. But what's a. . .cooper?" David's curiosity energized his voice.

As John answered, Mary Elizabeth enjoyed watching her little brother. He, of course, had more questions, and the men were patient in their answers. But the thrill at seeing William again caused the blood to pound in her ears. A feeling she hadn't had ever before. Everything in her cried out to stare at the man who'd offered his hand the first time they met. But she forced herself to keep her eyes focused on David. And snuck a peek here and there at the handsome man. The racing of her heart only caused her breaths to be short. Why was she so nervous? Maybe they would keep talking until she could calm down and trust herself to speak in a normal manner. Maybe then she could get to know the intriguing Mr. Lytton a little better.

CHAPTER 7

The look on young David's face as John explained his job as a cooper made William smile. But Mary Elizabeth appeared uncomfortable.

"What do *you* do, Mr. Lytton?" The young boy's enthusiasm was contagious.

"I'm a carpenter." William smiled at him and then peeked at Mary Elizabeth.

"So that's how you knew so much about Mr. Alden's job too. You both work with wood and build things." David scrunched up his brow. "I might like to do that when I'm older."

"I'm sure you'd be very good at it." John patted the child's head.

Memories washed over William. He was barely older than this boy when he'd been left on the streets to fend for himself. But seeing the lad hold tight to his sister's hand gave William a thankful heart. His desire would be that no child ever go through what he'd endured.

"William's done beautiful work." John's words cut into his thoughts.

"Mr. Lytton." Mary Elizabeth's soft voice drew his attention upward. "Could you tell us some of the items you've made?"

As he listed off some of his most recent pieces, he watched her face. Deep brown eyes stared into his own. Her skin was quite fair, and he saw a few blond locks of hair attempting to escape her starched linen cap. The red of her woolen cape set off the loveliness of her full, red mouth. If he wasn't careful, he'd be caught staring.

"Have you ever built a ship?" Little David's question made his attention turn back to the boy. The lad twisted and turned under Mary Elizabeth's arm.

"No. Not yet. But my master taught me some of the best techniques."

The younger Chapman swung the hand that held his sister's. Always movement, even though he'd just recovered from sickness. The energy of youth. "Do you think you could build one as big as the ark?"

Mary Elizabeth chuckled at the question and then covered her mouth.

John tapped William's elbow with his own. "We were just discussing the ark this morning, weren't we?"

"Well. . .could ya?" David persisted.

"It's plausible that yes, I could build a ship that size, but I'm not sure what I would use it for—do you have any ideas?" Maybe the way to get to know Mary Elizabeth would be through this boy. William shrugged. It was worth a try.

"It sure would hold a lot more than this ship. So we could bring lots of animals and people to the New World, and we could teach them about the Bible." He rubbed his chin. "But the ark didn't have any sails, so I wonder if it would work."

John knelt in front of David. "You're correct, it didn't have sails, at least from the description in Genesis. And if I understood the passage, they didn't direct where the boat was going—that was God's job. But those are very intelligent thoughts."

"Mr. Alden, would *you* like to build a boat as big as the ark?" The boy never seemed to run out of questions.

"I think that would be a fun project, but remember, it took Noah one hundred years to build the ark, and I would need Mr. Lytton's help. He's better at that kind of work."

William watched Mary Elizabeth as John and David continued to discuss the ark.

She turned to gaze back at him. "Thank you. You are very kind to indulge him." Her voice had lowered in volume.

He moved a step closer so he could hear her better. "He's a wonderful boy. I'm very glad to see he's doing so much better. You must have been pretty worried."

An expression he couldn't decipher flittered across her features as she looked down at her brother and then back into his eyes. "Yes. After we lost our mother last year, I couldn't bear the thought of losing him as well."

"I'm so sorry about your mother."

Tears appeared at the corners of her eyes. The sheen made her eyes all the more beautiful and rich. "Thank you. I fear my father has suffered the worst of it, although losing Mother was the worst thing I've ever been through. But thankfully we have our faith, and the Lord has taken care of us."

What would it be like to have such faith? "It must be very difficult for a husband to lose his wife."

"Yes. He loved her very much." She bit her bottom lip and paused for several moments. "Where are you from, Mr. Lytton?"

"Please, call me William. And I'm from London." Not wishing to give anything away, he kept his answer vague. Lots of people were from London.

"Well, I'm not sure it would be appropriate to be so familiar quite yet to use your Christian name. I haven't known you very long." An attractive blush swept up her cheeks.

"My apologies. I do not wish to offend." How did a man go about getting to know a woman? Paul never gave him any training in courting. He'd made sure his young charge knew the manners of society, but that was the extent of his advice. Besides, Dorothy had insisted that John and William use her Christian name.

"There's nothing to apologize for, Mr. Lytton." She looked down at her hand—still swinging with her brother's. But the boy was engrossed in conversation with John.

What a good friend. Taking the time to talk to a child so William would have the opportunity to talk to Mary Elizabeth. He'd have to thank his friend later. "I'd love to get to know you better, Miss Chapman." The words were out before he could stop them.

The pink in her cheeks deepened. "I'd like that." She cleared her throat. "Did I understand correctly that you and Mr. Alden have been discussing the scriptures?"

The question made his heart sink. How much did he tell her? As one of the Saints, she may look down upon him if he didn't share her beliefs. Choosing to be vague once again, he pasted on a smile. "Yes. It's been very enlightening discussion."

"Do you do that often?"

"Of late, yes. There's more time for it while we are on the ship. But John has been hired to do a job as we sail, so he gets called away often to take care of the barrels."

She nodded and tilted her head to the right. "I see. I know we are all thankful—especially since those barrels hold our food stores." Her bottom lip crept into her mouth again.

William found it very appealing—the way she did that seemed to indicate another question was on its way.

"What made you decide to go to the New World with us?" She smiled.

"It's exciting to me to start something new. To be a part of something bigger than myself." He couldn't risk telling her more, could he? "And I must admit that I admire the passion of your group. It's inspiring—to stand firm on your beliefs."

"I am glad that our little congregation can inspire you, Mr. . . . ." A deep voice accompanied a large man in dark breeches and coat. He took several steps and stood next to Mary Elizabeth.

Where had he come from?

"Father. . .I'm so glad you could join us. This is Mr. Lytton and Mr. Alden." Mary Elizabeth's cheeks had turned very red.

William bowed. "Mr. Chapman, it's an honor to meet you."

John bowed as well. "At your service."

The man's stern expression was undecipherable.

"Father, Father, you won't believe what we've been talking about."

David saved the day. "Mr. Alden is a cooper and Mr. Lytton is a carpenter, and they both want to build a boat as big as the ark!"

Mr. Chapman's expression softened as he looked down at the lad. "Is that so?"

"And Mr. Alden says that Mr. Lytton is a master carpenter. The captain even had him build something in his private quarters."

"Do you mean *Master* Jones? Remember, they are only captains when they sail military vessels."

"I forgot that part." David looked back to William and smiled. "Do you think we can see what you built for Mr. Jones?"

William opened his mouth—

"We don't need to take up any more of Mr. Lytton's time." The stern look was back on Mr. Chapman's face. "It was a pleasure to meet you, gentlemen." He bowed.

So much for William's conversation with Mary Elizabeth.

"Thank you, Mr. Alden"—she curtseyed to John—"and Mr. Lytton"—she curtseyed to William—"for helping David with his questions."

"But of course." William bowed, attempting to look as respectful and honorable as possible. He didn't need a reason for Mr. Chapman to keep Mary Elizabeth away from him. But it appeared as if that may have already happened.

As the family walked away, John poked William in the ribs. "Did you have a nice chat with Miss Chapman?"

He couldn't help the smile that sprang onto his face. "I did. But it wasn't long enough."

"Young David sure is inquisitive."

"Weren't we all at that age?"

"You're probably right."

William crossed his arms over his chest. "What did you think of her father?"

"I'll be honest. He didn't seem too fond of us, William. But remember, they are proud people. Steadfast in their beliefs. And they've been hurt multiple times by people outside of their faith." He clapped William on the back. "Give it time."

"What if he doesn't give us any chance to have more time together?" The thought made his stomach churn. How had a woman gotten into his heart and mind so swiftly?

"Then I suggest you pray." John beamed a smile at him. "A lot."

The big boat rocked back and forth under David's feet. Somehow the sickness had made him feel even smaller. How was he supposed to help out and show Father that he was capable of work if he couldn't even navigate the deck?

Mr. Lytton and Mr. Alden sure were nice. Maybe he could ask one of them to take him on as an apprentice. That's what men did when they wanted to learn a trade. The more he thought about it, the more he'd like to be a carpenter.

Jesus was a carpenter.

To him, there couldn't be a better job. But Mary Elizabeth would probably tell him it was dangerous, that he wasn't strong enough after being sick. And Father. . . Well, what if he said no?

Mr. Lytton was so tall and strong. David wanted to be like him.

Perhaps a week or two of gaining his strength back would help them all see that David was serious about learning carpentry.

He would be obedient and help out wherever he could.

Nodding his head, he knew he had a plan.

Father would be proud of him. And one day soon, he'd help build them a house in Virginia.

CHAPTER 8

Tuesday, 12 September 1620

Tightening the strings at the neck of her shift, Mary Elizabeth thought about the last few days. Short walks on deck, entertaining David, and Bible reading with her father. Not once had he brought up Mr. Lytton and Mr. Alden. Which was a great relief, even though he hadn't seemed too happy to meet them.

William.

He'd asked her to call him by his Christian name. And while she already thought of him that way in her mind, she knew it wasn't appropriate until they were better acquainted. Many other young men were aboard the ship, but most of them were sailors with questionable morals and profane mouths.

Not William. He'd been respectful and courteous. A perfect gentleman.

A shiver raced up her spine, and she pulled the blanket around her shoulders tighter. She needed to mend one of her sleeves on her dress—not think about Mr. Lytton. Again.

As she pulled out needle and thread, she focused her thoughts on the task at hand. The constant wear was taking its toll. That and no way to wash clothes. She had one other dress in the trunk that was for Sundays and worship since that was their sacred day. They spent the whole day studying scripture, singing worship to the Lord, and absolutely not working or playing.

Her other clothing was in the hold with the rest of their belongings. Not that she had multiple trunks full of skirts and shirtwaists, but they weren't poor by any means. Mother always insisted that they look their best—because they represented the Lord.

The thought made her smile. Her mother had been such a beautiful lady. Mary Elizabeth hoped she would one day be as fine. She'd inherited her mother's hair, eyes, and coloring. But Elizabeth Chapman had had something else that made her glow.

Might it have been the love she had for Mary Elizabeth's father?

Would Mary Elizabeth have that same glow one day?

The ship rolled and heaved on the waves and almost knocked her over. She'd learned to stand with her feet apart to give her a sturdier stance, and when she sat on the floor in their tiny quarters, she bent her knees and crossed her feet to give her a stabler foundation. But the wind had kicked up this morning. And not in the direction beneficial for their sails. The sailors called it *aback*, and Mary Elizabeth knew the term wasn't good.

Then the rolling began.

With more than one hundred people crammed into the gun deck's small area, families had put up blankets or thin wooden walls to give them privacy. But nothing could take away the sound of retching nor the smell that accompanied it.

She could only hope that the seas would calm and this turbulence would pass.

Even Dorothy had succumbed to the seasickness that troubled so many souls aboard today. But her mother hadn't been well for several days, so Dorothy hadn't gotten any fresh air for a while.

Mary Elizabeth needed to remember to check on her friend tomorrow. The Raynsfords might need her help.

The last stitch in, Mary Elizabeth held the sleeve out to examine it. Not too bad considering the circumstances.

David's deep breathing from the corner was music to her ears. Her precious brother slept better each night, for which she was thankful. She should be sleeping as well, but she hadn't been able to get her mind to obey.

A snore from her father reminded her that she *needed* her sleep.

Tomorrow would be another long day aboard ship. And the day after, and the day after that. Until they reached their destination.

Snuffing her candle inside the lantern, Mary Elizabeth shifted down onto her mat. Life on board the ships had been different. Sleep was harder to come by because she didn't labor as much during the day as she had at home. But a weariness also seemed to affect everyone as the days passed. Whether it was the travel, the constant weeks aboard ships, or the lack of fresh air and exercise—the problem was real.

Then she also dealt with the pesky problem of reining in her thoughts. Sometimes, it seemed to be more than she could bear.

Her dreams of marrying one day still held true. But she'd never imagined marrying someone outside their congregation.

Ever since meeting William Lytton, she couldn't get him out of her mind. Handsome in his green doublet and breeches, he invaded her thoughts and dreams with his blond hair and blue eyes.

He was strong and a hard worker, and he seemed to be very respectable.

But all of his wonderful traits did not change one fact: he was still a Stranger.

One she didn't know much about other than that he came from London and Mr. Alden seemed to think highly of him. Even the ship master must, if he'd hired William to build something for him in his personal quarters.

Father's stormy expression the day he met William was not encouraging. While she couldn't read his thoughts, she'd seen that look before, and it didn't communicate his pleasure.

So what could she do?

Her heart longed to see more of William. Was that wrong? Why did she yearn to spend time with him? These feelings were all so new and exciting. And she was normally the stable and calm one. Mary Elizabeth let out a sigh. Dorothy would be thrilled to know that thoughts of Mr. Lytton kept Mary Elizabeth awake at night. Her father on the other hand would be mortified.

Shoving her face beneath the blankets, she worked to rid her mind of all the spinning thoughts.

But one question continued to haunt her.

Did he believe as she did?

Saturday, 30 September 1620

The rolling seas they'd endured a few weeks ago were nothing compared to the tumultuous seas the last couple of days. Every time Mary Elizabeth didn't think it could get worse, the wind raged and churned up the seas around them.

Many people had battled seasickness from the beginning of their journey, but now almost every passenger aboard had succumbed.

Father was so sick he didn't have the strength to lift his head anymore and slept most of the time. David wasn't sick, but he complained of the awful stench they couldn't eliminate from the stuffy quarters.

"Mary Elizabeth?" Dorothy's voice penetrated the curtain.

"Come in, Dorothy." Mary Elizabeth stood as much as she could without hitting her head on the low ceiling and hugged her friend. "You are a wonderful sight to see."

"I'm much thinner than I was, but at least I'm not sick all the time. My parents aren't so fortunate."

"I'm sorry. We've been taking care of Father, and I should have checked on you."

"That's why I'm here, Mary Elizabeth. A great many people have been in misery for days, with no one to care for them since everyone else is sick. Mr. Jones won't let anyone up on deck for fear that someone will get washed overboard, and I think the lack of fresh air and inability to see the sky is making matters worse."

Mary Elizabeth looked down at Father. He slept. Not unlike the past few days. "I suppose David could look after Father when I'm not here."

"I can do it." David nodded and lifted his shoulders.

Turning back to Dorothy, Mary Elizabeth furrowed her brow. "Do you think you and I would be able to handle *all* of the passengers?"

"I've gone to each family's and person's quarters. Only three others aren't sick, but they have several to look after already. Then there's Elizabeth Hopkins—she looks like she may give birth any day now, and she isn't faring well. We must try to help. It's the Christian thing to do."

Mary Elizabeth nodded. Her friend was right. "Let's start now, shall we?" She tied her apron over her skirt and gave instructions to David. "I need you to be strong now and take care of Father."

"I told you I can do it, Mary Elizabeth. And when he's sleeping for long periods, I can help you." David stood and lifted his chin.

"Of course you can." Dorothy chimed in and gave David a hug. She turned back to Mary Elizabeth. "There's something else I need to tell you."

The tone of her friend's voice reminded her of when someone shared bad news. Breathing deeply, she took Dorothy's hand. "Please, tell me."

"William is very sick. John was taking care of him, but many barrels have been damaged by the rolling of the ship, and he was needed to repair them, so he asked me to check on Mr. Lytton. I'm afraid it's much worse than seasickness. He has a high fever."

The rats had eaten the last of his bread. Right through his sack too. Now he didn't have anything to eat, and he'd have to fashion a new bag as well.

Tears threatened to spill down his cheeks. Why was life so hard? Didn't anybody care?

"Hey, William. Why are you crying?" The taunting voice belonged to one of the older street boys.

"I'm not crying." He sniffed and wiped at his face.

"Look everyone, little William is crying. He can't make it on the streets like us. He's nothing but a baby. A crying little baby."

William grabbed his blanket—the only thing he had to call his own and to ward off the cold at night—and ran as fast as his feet would take him. He'd have to find another place to hide. Now that the big boys knew his spot. They always took his spot.

He had to get far away. He'd have to make it on his own. Could he do it? Yes. He was ten now. Those ruffians couldn't tell him what to do anymore or steal more of his food.

William ran until his legs ached. His stomach felt raw. Smells from a local chop house drew him. Maybe he could work for their scraps.

Looking down at his hands, he tried to wipe off some of the blood and dirt. Would they help him?

He was so tired of feeling alone and unwanted. So tired...

"Shhh..." Someone soothed William's brow. "You're all right. Just rest."

He shook his head back and forth. Why couldn't he open his eyes? Where was he? He wasn't on the streets of London anymore. Nor was he that lonely, starving boy.

He fought the arms that held him down. Why couldn't he get out of here? He had to get to Virginia. Start over.

Everything burned. Why was it so hot?

"Lie still." That voice. He knew that voice. A vision of a red cloak and soothing brown eyes—an angel?

But exhaustion pulled at him, dragging him back into the depths.

CHAPTER 9

Friday, 6 October 1620

I don't know what to do for him, Dorothy." Hot tears streamed down Mary Elizabeth's cheeks. William's fever had come down, but he still slept fitfully and mumbled in his sleep. "Every time I check on him, he's having a nightmare of some sort. He seems so miserable and alone, I can't bear it."

"Have you prayed for him?" Her friend grabbed her hands as they knelt on the floor next to Mr. and Mrs. Raynsford.

With a nod, she bit her lip. "But I don't know what to say. I've prayed over Father and every person on board that I've tried to help. No one seems to be improving."

"Well, the seas don't seem to be improving, so I doubt their sickness will pass until we have some calm days."

"Is God even listening?"

"You know He is, Mary Elizabeth. You're just tired. When was the last time you slept?"

The candle's glow made Dorothy's brown hair appear almost auburn. She was beautiful and smiling. How did she do it? "It's been awhile. I fall asleep, but then either the smell gets to me or I hear someone retching and know they probably need my help. Then I think of William and can't go back to sleep. I hate it that he's suffering so. Father isn't doing well, either. David has been such a big help taking care of him, but I can tell he's wearing out. And I don't want *him* to get sick again. He's too thin as it is."

"Why don't we pray together?" Dorothy squeezed her hands and bowed her head. "Our Father, we come to You now with heavy hearts. We are tired. Many are sick. And we don't know what to do other than come to You. In the prophet Isaiah's book we know that '…But they that wait upon the Lord, shall renew their strength: they shall lift up the wings, as the eagles: they shall run, & not be weary, & they shall walk and not faint.' Help us to wait upon You, Lord. Please renew our strength. In Jesus' name we pray, amen."

Mary Elizabeth felt stronger, but she couldn't think about herself right now. "Lord, my heart is heavy for William Lytton. Please comfort him in his sleep and bring him peace. And Father God, please help my father grow stronger—along with all the other people suffering from illness. In Jesus' name we pray, amen."

"Amen." Dorothy released her hands and sat back on her heels.

"Well, well, well, if it ain't the little saintly women praying again." The twisted voice boomed outside the Raynsfords' quarters.

Dorothy's expression clouded over. "That man!" Standing up as much as she could, she grabbed her candle and swept out of the area to confront him. "You should be ashamed of yourself. Coming down here to taunt the sick like you do," she yelled at her assailant.

Mary Elizabeth followed Dorothy. The filthy young sailor had taken it upon himself to torment the sick passengers as often as he could. As long as Master Jones wasn't around. And since so many were sick, the profane man came down way too often. "You aren't welcome down here. I've a mind to go speak to Master Jones about you and the filthy words you speak."

Dorothy turned to face her, eyebrows raised.

While speaking up in courage wasn't normally something Mary Elizabeth would do, she shrugged. Maybe she was made of sterner stuff than she thought.

"You're not allowed top deck, *miss*." The man sneered, showing off his dirty teeth.

"And I'm certain you're not allowed to harass the passengers of the ship on which you were hired!" Dorothy's voice edged on a shriek.

Mary Elizabeth moved forward and tucked Dorothy behind her.

"You need to leave now. Or I will speak to Mr. Coppin or Master Jones or whomever I need to speak to about your despicable and insidious behavior."

The man growled. "We shouldn't even be taking this trip. It's far too late in the season. Maybe we just need to throw all of ya overboard like Jonah since you seem to love your stories from the Bible so much." Another sneer and then he started laughing. "Let's just see if your God saves you then." He stepped closer.

Mary Elizabeth bristled. "I warned you." Stepping around the man, she held her lantern as high as the ceiling would allow.

The man grabbed her arm. "You'll do no such thing, missy." He flung her down to the floor, spit at her feet, and stomped toward the companionway.

"Foul man." Dorothy leaned over Mary Elizabeth as the man disappeared. "You all right? That was quite brave of you."

Mary Elizabeth shook her head and laughed. "I don't know where that came from. Truly. And I'm fine." She gave Dorothy a look. "I had to do *something*—you looked like you were about to murder him."

"Well. . .maybe not murder. . . But I wish I could clean up the man's mouth. I've never heard anything but profanity and insults exit it."

"There's not enough soap in the world to clean up that young man." Mary Elizabeth stood up and wiped off her skirt.

Dorothy laughed until tears streamed down her face. "I just envisioned you trying to wash the man's mouth out with soap."

Mary Elizabeth hugged her friend and joined in the laughter. "That would be a sight to see, I'm sure. But I think someone is going to have to talk to Master Jones about him."

"You're probably right. But only a few of us aren't sick, and I don't think the ship master or his mate would be too happy if we tried to go on deck while the seas are so tumultuous. Besides, I think he realized you were serious. Maybe he won't be as bad from now on?"

A nod was all she could muster. After their little confrontation, Mary Elizabeth thought she might wilt right there on the spot.

Dorothy took Mary Elizabeth's hands. "Why don't you go take a nap, Mary Elizabeth? I think you'll feel better."

A nap sounded heavenly. "All right. As soon as I check on William."

"William?" A sweet sound broke through the fog of sleep. "William? How are you feeling?" The voice was the most beautiful thing in the world to him.

The sound pulled him out of the dark recesses of his mind. "Hmm?" It came out more of a moan.

"It's me. . .Mary Elizabeth. Mary Elizabeth Chapman. I'm here to check on you and see how you are doing." The soft words washed over him and brought him awake.

As he blinked his eyes several times, the blurry image in front of him transformed. Mary Elizabeth. With a soft halo of light around her linen cap. She was a beautiful sight. "M–Mary Elizabeth." His throat was so dry.

"Here, let me get you something to drink." She left his side and after a few moments reappeared with a small cup. "The only thing we have is beer right now. The fresh water barrels are empty, but this will at least help ease the parch."

He lifted his head with her assistance and took a sip. "Thank you, Mary Elizabeth. It's so kind of you to check on me."

"I've been worried about you. You had a fever for a long while." It was dark, but not enough to cover the flush that crept into her cheeks.

"What day is it?"

"The sixth of October."

Another swell lifted the ship and dropped it again. He never wanted to take another trip like this. Leave the ocean-crossing to others. "I've been sick a long time, then?"

"You don't remember anything?"

"Here and there. . .a little. But not much."

She sighed. "It's probably for the best. You've had a tough time."

"How many others are sick?"

This time she ducked her head. When she lifted it, tears shimmered at the corners of her eyes. "Almost everyone—that is, of the passengers."

He nodded. Their situation was graver than he'd ever imagined. "And you haven't. . . I mean, that is. . . You are well?"

A tiny smile lifted the corners of her lips. "I am well. Thank you for asking."

"Are you taking care of everyone all by yourself?"

Her smile grew. "No. Dorothy and David are helping. A few others aren't ill, but they are weak from lack of sleep taking care of their families and friends."

He lifted his hand from his side and took hold of hers. "Thank you, Mary Elizabeth." A feeling—foreign to him—shot up his arm and into his chest and spread throughout his whole body.

Her cheeks were crimson now, but instead of ducking her head—this time—she stared into his eyes. "You are most welcome. . . William." She gave him another smile. "I best see to the others." Gathering her skirt, she stood up from her kneeling position.

"Will you come back?" What he wouldn't give for her to stay with him all day.

Her face became radiant with a broad smile. "Of course. . . I've been here every day."

He watched her go and felt his heart swell. She'd come to take care of him. Every day. The thought thrilled him.

CHAPTER 10

Tuesday, 10 October 1620

The rocking of the ship increased as another storm hit their ship. Mary Elizabeth looked up to the ceiling over her head. *Lord, we need help.*

Not only was she worried about all the sick, but she'd overheard the shouts from above. Could they survive this journey? It only seemed to be getting worse.

Stumbling through the gun deck, Mary Elizabeth worked to keep her balance. Buckets—used as chamber pots—littered the entire area of the ship. Along with prostrate bodies—they posed great obstacles when it was hard enough to walk in a straight line without falling down. She wiped the sweat from her brow and knelt beside tiny Mary More. The four-year-old hadn't kept anything down for more than a week, and it had begun to worry Mary Elizabeth. The connection she felt to the wee girl wasn't just that they shared a Christian name; it was the child's sweet face—her innocence—that grabbed Mary Elizabeth Chapman's heart. Even though there was gossip about the More children traveling without parents, Father had kept the truth to himself, and Mary Elizabeth couldn't help but feel sorry for the little things.

"How is she doing?" Dorothy knelt beside her.

"She's so small. I don't know if she's going to make it." The sting of tears pricked her eyes. Did anyone care about these precious children? "Dorothy, do you know the story? About the More siblings?"

Her friend ducked her head. "Sadly, yes."

"Father wouldn't tell me when we first set out." She stroked little Mary's head. "Would you?"

Dorothy sighed and sat on her heels. "Samuel More of Shropshire paid for their passage." She fiddled with a string at the cuff of her dress. "The gossip has produced some outlandish stories, but Mr. Brewster told us the truth when he took in Richard—Mary's older brother. Apparently, Katherine—the children's mother—was unfaithful to Samuel, citing their unhappy, arranged marriage. Over time, Mr. More discovered his children's likeness to another man. He divorced Katherine."

Mary Elizabeth gasped. "Divorced? Truly?" These things were simply not done. Didn't God hate divorce?

"Yes. He also retained custody of the four children—who didn't appear to be his."

"Goodness." She laid a hand over her heart. "Now I understand why Father wouldn't speak of it."

"Samuel sent them off with us—'honest and religious' folks—so they wouldn't have the stigma of their illegitimacy following them. But alas, the gossip has made it difficult."

"The poor children." Mary Elizabeth shook her head. "Can you imagine what they've been through?"

"Their family was prominent and quite wealthy. I imagine having nothing and being sent to a new home is quite difficult."

The tears let loose. "Dorothy, don't you understand? These children have no understanding of money yet. The oldest is barely eight years old. That's David's age!" She sucked in her breath. "They've been ripped from their mother's arms...and the only father they ever knew. And now they will never see them again. This ordeal will most likely scar them for the rest of their lives."

Dorothy leaned over and covered her hand that was still on top of the child's head. "I'm sorry, Mary Elizabeth. I didn't mean to sound so callous. The life of the wealthy is just beyond my comprehension." She turned her face away. "The gossip has portrayed them as hedonistic and unruly because of their...um...heritage."

"And the gossip has stained your view?" Mary Elizabeth huffed. "No wonder Father wouldn't allow talk of the children. I can't believe our own people have judged these poor souls so grievously!"

She stood to do—*what* she was uncertain. Never had she been someone to lose her temper over arguments—but the children! Would they be tainted because of their mother's infidelity for the rest of their lives? She loosened the strings to her shift at her neck. What she wouldn't give for some fresh air right now.

Dorothy stood as well and grabbed Mary Elizabeth's shoulders, and they both nearly fell over with the horrendous rocking of the ship. "Mary Elizabeth, I am so sorry. You're right. We've been wrong to look down upon the children. And we've been wrong to listen to the gossip. I know many of the elders are wanting to use it as an example to teach us to remain pure and faithful, but I don't have any right to think less of the Mores."

Mary Elizabeth nodded. Their faith was of utmost importance. The Bible spoke strongly of judging others. But the Separatists wished to remove themselves from worldly behavior—and the attitude of judgment seemed prevalent. This was the first time she'd ever realized it. Was there some way to find a balance? To protect the innocent in all this?

Dorothy knelt back down by the child. Her shoulders slumped. "The poor dear didn't ask for this. . ."

"No, she didn't. They all deserve our love and encouragement. Not our hesitation and scorn. If they are to come to understand almighty God, they need to see us shining His love to all. No matter their background."

Her friend nodded and bit her lip. "Please forgive me, Mary Elizabeth. I will see whatever I can do to help them. The Brewsters have taken in Richard and Mary, the Carvers—Jasper, and the Winslows have the eldest—Ellen. Maybe over time we can help them overcome the difficulty."

Mary Elizabeth felt spent. The realization that so many people looked down on the More children hurt her heart. To think that

Dorothy was one of them made it worse. "I think I will go check on William now. Will you stay with little Mary for a while longer?"

"Of course." Dorothy's words were hushed.

As she staggered her way through the maze, Mary Elizabeth thought through the past few weeks. She'd prayed for courage before this drastic change in her own life, and God had granted it. But not in the way she expected.

She *was* stronger now. Amazing how life had a way of bringing out hidden traits. She shook her head as she thought of her discussion with Dorothy. Never in her life had she stood up for anyone else. In fact, she used to be the quiet and meek one while Dorothy was the bubbly and outspoken one.

Maybe leaving Leyden had changed Mary Elizabeth.

Most extraordinary to her was that while most everyone else was sick and weak, she had been healthy and strong. Without thought, she'd jumped in to take care of first David and then Father. Now she was one of the caregivers of close to one hundred people.

Before Mother's death, she'd thought of herself as frail and insignificant.

Now, months after leaving her home, she realized she was a different person.

As she reached the front of the ship where William shared a small space with Mr. Alden, the boat lifted up on another giant wave. Sea water seeped in through the gun ports as the bow smashed back down. When she sat down beside him, she found William's blankets were wet.

"William?" Mary Elizabeth used her fingers to lift his hair from his forehead. "Can you hear me?"

"Aye." He licked his cracked lips as he blinked his eyes open. "It's good to see you."

His words made her happy—even in the midst of the stench and the storm. "Let me help you drink."

"Thank you." He lifted his head without too much assistance. "I'm feeling a bit better today."

"Thank the Lord! I've been very worried about you, and John has checked on you often, but he looks a bit green himself."

"Is John all right? I haven't seen him in what seems like weeks."

Mary Elizabeth wiped his brow and braced herself as the ship rolled again. "I think so. He looks a bit peaked, but he's had to constantly work on the barrels with all these storms."

William sighed and closed his eyes for a moment.

Mary Elizabeth thought he might be going to sleep.

Then he opened them, and the blue brilliance reached into her heart. "Why don't you tell me about your day so far? I need something to keep my mind off the misery around me."

"Of course. . ." She clasped her hands and laid them in her lap. "Well, the sailor that I told you about?"

"The one who taunts everyone and says he hopes to throw us all overboard?"

A moan erupted from her mouth. "Yes. That's the one." She rolled her eyes. "He came back down here this morning and started in on us all—that it's all our fault these storms are so horrendous—that God must be punishing us for our stupidity."

"He's an insolent fool, isn't he?"

"I heard Mr. Bradford praying for the sailor this morning, and he used those exact same words." She smiled.

"Mr. Bradford is an intelligent man—and a much better man than myself since he's praying for the ruffian." William smiled up at her. "How about the other passengers? Is everyone still sick?"

"For the most part, they have all gotten worse as the storms have tossed us about."

"I was afraid of that. But I'm thankful that I'm beginning to feel slightly better. I just can't move too fast—that brings the sickness back on." He scrunched up his face in displeasure. "How's your father? And David?"

It warmed Mary Elizabeth's heart that even though he'd been seriously ill himself, William asked about her family. "Father is still very ill, but David is doing fine. He's been a big help hauling buckets and anything else we need. He seems to grow stronger every day."

William's hand reached out to cover hers. "Just like you, Mary Elizabeth. You appear stronger in spirit and joy every time I see you." He smiled and paused. "And in beauty too."

She felt the heat rise to her face. Never had she been paid a compliment from a young man. It made her heart flutter. The feelings she felt for William were unlike anything she'd ever known.

She'd always assumed that Father would arrange a marriage for her to someone within their congregation and over time she'd grow to love whomever God had set before her. But now she wasn't sure she could settle for such an arrangement. Not when she'd had a glimpse at what attraction could make her feel. Was that wrong?

"Mary Elizabeth?" William searched her gaze. "I'm sorry. I didn't wish to offend."

She blinked. "You didn't offend me. I thank you for the compliment."

"You deserve it, Mary Elizabeth. And so much more. I. . .I—"

The ship lurched to the right and Mary Elizabeth fell onto her side, her shoulder slamming into the hard, wooden floor.

"Are you all right?"

"I'm fine." The cries of children filled the air. "But I better go check on David and the younger ones." She hated to leave William. Every time she did, she longed for more time with him. And she yearned to share with him about the God who gave her hope. "But I will be back later."

"I look forward to it."

CHAPTER 11

Thursday, 12 October 1620

"One more step." John helped steady William up the companionway to the main deck.

This was the second day of calmer seas, and William couldn't wait to breathe in the fresh air. Weakened by the fever and seasickness that had claimed him the past weeks, he hoped that the worst was past.

On the deck, John released him and walked toward the bulwark. "The wind seems to be at our backs again."

William looked up at the sails—full and taut in the wind. "And the air smells clean." He couldn't help but close his eyes as he inhaled.

His friend laughed and clapped him on the back. "Aye. Which is much better than below. That reminds me, I promised to help Miss Chapman and Miss Raynsford open all the gun ports and hatches. They wanted to air out the living quarters while the weather was nice." John turned and then shot over his shoulder, "You'll be all right for a bit?"

"Yes. I believe I'll be fine."

John's footsteps echoed behind as William looked out to the sea. The great gulf before him stretched as far as the eye could see. Beyond it—somewhere—a new land awaited. Behind them was all civilization as he knew it.

Had he made the right decision? Venturing into the great unknown? In London, he'd had regular work and customers who'd come to respect him.

But there was always the past—lingering around every corner.

And William wanted to forget the past. At least the part before meeting Paul.

Now he was ready for the future. As soon as he thought about building a new life in the new colony, Mary Elizabeth's face appeared in his mind. He didn't know her very well, but his heart hoped his future included her.

The sickness had kept him unaware most of the time, but he remembered hearing her voice, quoting scripture to him as he lay feverish and weak. Something about the Lord being a shepherd.

John had been discussing the Bible with him, but William's opinions had been so long shaped by his unwillingness to see God as a loving Father. Paul—his mentor and only friend—had shown him love and grace for several years. Never pushing for William to see things his way. Just quietly living out his faith. But time and again, William found any excuse he could to keep a wall up between him and God.

On days like today, William wished more than anything that he could sit down with Paul one last time and ask all his questions. But it was too late. By the time he'd been willing to soften his heart and listen, Paul was dead.

William had thought his life might be coming to an end many times in the last few weeks. Was he ready to meet his Maker?

He shook his head. No. He wasn't. But he didn't know how to move forward from here.

God, if You're truly a loving Father and up there listening to me, could You show me how to learn more about You?

Mary Elizabeth's voice floated over to him. He turned and saw her assisting an older gentleman to the bulwark where William stood.

"Good morning, Miss Chapman." He bowed slightly.

"Good morning, Mr. Lytton." She helped the man until his hands were safely on the boards. "Have you met Mr. Brewster? He's the head of our congregation for the new colony."

William smiled. "I believe we've met, yes."

Mr. Brewster looked him over. "Ah, yes. The carpenter. It's good to see someone else up and about."

"I agree, sir."

"Are you feeling strong enough to stand here by yourself while I go help someone else?" Mary Elizabeth laid a hand on the man's arm.

"Yes." Brewster smiled. "I've got Mr. Lytton here to help me if need be."

"Well then, I shall return in a few moments."

"Thank you, Mary Elizabeth." The older gentleman nodded.

William watched the man close his eyes and take in the fresh air just as he had.

How providential that after he'd prayed, this man had appeared. But where did he start?

"I fear many will be too sick to walk up here, but it's divine, is it not?" Brewster looked out at the sea.

"My thoughts are the same, sir." William glanced down at his feet. The time couldn't get better than this. Sucking in a deep breath, he ventured forth. "Mr. Brewster, I was wondering if I could impose on you. . ."

"Of course. Go on."

"I'd like to expand my knowledge of the Bible—and of your faith as well. Might I be able to persuade you to teach me?" There. He'd said it.

The older man's face transformed with his smile. "I'd be honored, young man. Before the seas sought to shake us out of this ship, I was teaching a younger group through the Gospels. Would that interest you?"

"More than I can say, sir. Thank you."

Peter barely had the strength to stand, but he'd made his way to the main deck with Miss Raynsford's help so he could spy on William Lytton.

What didn't make sense was that the man stood talking to one of those Saints. Their leader, too.

What game was he playing?

Was this how he would gain information? By infiltrating their ranks?

As far as Peter knew, the Saints were wary about accepting any of the Strangers. So what was Lytton up to?

The seasickness had been miserable and had slowed down his plan. So far, he hadn't found anything that could help him, but there was still time.

The ship rocked under a swell and it made his stomach lurch. Maybe all this fresh air wasn't so great of an idea.

David watched several sailors climb the masts and rig the sails. What it must be like to be so high in the air! They swung on the great masts and worked with the ropes and sails in a swift manner. Master Jones ordered commands, and the men complied.

The ship's space had begun to feel confining. There were so many people on board and not enough room. All the other children were sick, and it made David feel more grown-up. He'd been able to help take care of people. But what he wouldn't give right now to play a game or run around. Straightening his shoulders, he realized his thoughts were childish. Mary Elizabeth sent him top deck to take care of the animals. He'd best get to it.

As he collected the eggs from the hens, the ship's surgeon—Mr. Giles Heale—passed by him looking quite grim. David followed to the crate closest to the aft castle and listened in as the man reached the ship master.

"Dead?" Jones frowned. "That was quick."

"It was a grievous disease, sir." Mr. Heale said something else under his breath.

Jones looked to the westward sky. "The body will need to be disposed of immediately. More storms are on the horizon." With a nod, the master of the ship retreated up to the poop deck.

Someone died? David wondered who. And what had the surgeon said to Mr. Jones?

Mr. Heale walked toward the forecastle of the ship, where the crew took turns sleeping.

David once again followed. "Mr. Heale?"

The man turned and raised his brows. "Yes?"

"Who died, sir?"

"Ah, so you heard that, did you? It was a member of the crew."

Relief poured through him. Then he felt guilty. What if the man didn't know God? "Will there be a service for him, sir?"

"It's unlikely, son. Master Jones is worried about new storms coming in. But the crew will assemble on deck for the burial."

"Burial, sir?"

"As a seaman, it's only fitting that he be buried at sea." The surgeon turned.

"But sir, if others die, will they be buried at sea as well?"

The man slowly turned back and crouched down in front of him. "Yes, lad. It's the only thing we can do while we are in the middle of the ocean."

David nodded. He didn't like that idea at all.

The surgeon left, and David went back to gathering the eggs.

The thought of dying on the ship made him shiver.

Shuffling behind him caught his attention. Two sailors carried a blanket-wrapped, man-shaped bundle. The rest of the crew followed behind. When they reached the bulwark on the larboard side of the ship, someone said something David couldn't understand, Mr. Jones nodded, and then the two sailors heaved the body over the edge.

The water splashed.

The men dispersed.

David ran over to the side and peered down. Nothing but a large white circle of bubbles as the ship sailed past. He imagined what it must be like in the depths of the sea. Dark, and full of large fish and creatures. Another shiver raced up his spine.

"We all cursed, we be."

David turned at the words and watched two of the crew climb the main mast.

"Lefty shouldn't've cursed and tormented 'em. Their God has done cursed us now."

As the men climbed higher, their words floated in and out. Is that what people thought? That God cursed them if they upset Him in some way? The conversation made David want to speak to Father about it, but he'd been so sick. Maybe Mary Elizabeth could help him understand. But what would she say when she found out the sailor who'd thrown her to the ground had died?

Master Jones stomped down the deck and rushed to the forecastle. "Son, you need to get back down below. Tell them to shut all the gun ports and hatches."

"Yes, sir." David wrapped the eggs in his shirt and ran toward the companionway. The wind whipped at his hair. What had been a beautiful day was now turning dark and gray as they headed farther into the west.

"Storm's a'comin'!" Master Jones's deep voice carried a fearsome undertone.

David hopped down the steps as a drop of rain splattered on his forehead. The people hadn't had enough time to recover from the last bout of seasickness and another storm likely meant days of rolling and crashing on the waves. Would they be able to survive this again? He looked around the dark gun deck and spotted his sister. "Mary Elizabeth! Close the gun ports! Hurry, there's another storm."

CHAPTER 12

Monday, 16 October 1620

Mary Elizabeth knelt beside Elizabeth Hopkins. The squirming baby in her arms let out a squawk. As her heart cinched with longing to have a family of her own, she handed the brand-new baby boy to his mother. "Oceanus is a very fitting name."

The ship continued to roll and quake in the constant storms they seemed to face. The fact that this woman had bravely given birth in the midst of it dumbfounded Mary Elizabeth. Not that the poor woman had much choice in the matter.

"Thank you." Mrs. Hopkins laid back. "I believe I will rest a while longer. Thank you again for all you've done, Mary Elizabeth."

"I'll be back to check on you later." Mary Elizabeth inched her way to the next set of quarters. With so many people packed into such a tiny space, it was amazing they weren't all claustrophobic.

If only the calmer seas had lasted longer. The fresh air had been lovely—what little she'd had of it. But at least they'd had a bit of time to air out the deck and clean up a little.

But the poor passengers. The majority of them were still sick. Only a few of the young men seemed to be recovering. The stormy seas made the rest of them worse.

The *Mayflower* creaked in the torment of the wind, and water sprayed down upon the ill who were already miserable.

Mary Elizabeth had been praying for each person she attended, and the days had all run together. But at least she was busy. William appeared a bit stronger each day and helped the small band of caregivers. But since he wasn't sick anymore, Mary Elizabeth didn't have the opportunity to visit with him as much. She'd only seen him twice the past two days and had only been able to give him a smile.

Besides, although Father was still very ill, he probably wouldn't approve of William. Her new friend wasn't part of their congregation—he wasn't one of the Saints. He was a Stranger.

Thoughts of her father made her feel guilty. Had she neglected him to take care of everyone else? She shook her head. She couldn't allow those thoughts to take root. If she only sat by her father's side all this time, so many other people would have suffered—possibly even died.

As she made her way from person to person, Mary Elizabeth saw Elder Brewster speaking to William. They were huddled under the companionway with what appeared to be a Bible. While the sight encouraged and lifted her heart, she wondered what the outcome could be. Was there hope for her to follow her heart?

She'd never allowed herself to even think such a thing.

"Mary Elizabeth?"

Dorothy's voice jolted her. "Hmm?"

"You were staring at Mr. Lytton and Mr. Brewster. Everything all right?"

"Me? Staring?" Mary Elizabeth looked to the men and then back to Dorothy. "I'm sorry. Yes, I'm fine." She'd better change the subject and fast. "I saw the new baby a little while ago. He's so beautiful."

"You don't fool me for a minute, Mary Elizabeth Chapman." Dorothy grinned. "But yes, the baby is beautiful. Don't you just love his name? Oceanus. It sounds so strong and adventuresome."

"From what I've heard, his father has had quite the adventures already."

"Like father, like son, I suppose." Dorothy shrugged her shoulders. "Well, I need to get David to haul some more buckets for me. You know, when we finally reach dry land, I don't know if my legs will remember how to walk on steady ground."

"Mine either." Mary Elizabeth hugged her friend and headed toward the stern.

When she reached their meager quarters, Mary Elizabeth peeked at Father through the curtain. His complexion was still a pale gray, and he hadn't eaten anything in days. The man who'd always been so strong and capable was now lifeless and weak. She knelt by his side and tried to get a few sips down his throat. "Father?"

No response.

He hadn't spoken to her for several days. She didn't know what to do. Didn't know what to pray anymore. "Lord. . ." Words failed to come.

"When you don't know what to pray, Mary Elizabeth, pray the words Jesus taught us. . .pray scripture." Mother's words floated over her, and a single tear slipped down her cheek. Mary Elizabeth sat beside her father and closed her eyes.

"Our father which art in heaven, hallowed be thy Name. Thy kingdom come. Thy will be done even in earth, as it is in heaven. Give us this day our daily bread. And forgive us our debts, as we also forgive our debtors. And lead us not into tentation, but deliver us from evil: for thine is the kingdom, and the power, and the glory for ever, Amen."

When she opened her eyes, Father was staring at her. "Father?"

"I'm here, child. . . . Th. . .thank you for praying." As his breath washed over her, Mary Elizabeth couldn't help but worry. The putrid smell was what the ship's surgeon, Mr. Heale, called the beginnings of scurvy.

"Father?"

He closed his eyes again, and his deep, steady breathing told her that he was once again asleep.

Mary Elizabeth couldn't be thankful enough for the chance to hear her father's voice. But the concern of scurvy was now firmly implanted in her mind. Her father wasn't the first case. And that was what scared her most. What chance of survival did they have? She tucked the blanket around him tighter and stood up. Oh, to be able to see him walk around again. *Lord, please let it be so.*

"Mary Elizabeth! Come quick!" David called to her.

She slipped through the curtain as fast as she could and found David, Dorothy, and William hunkered down over a sopping wet form near the companionway. "What happened?"

"It's John Howland." William looked at her. "We need a warm blanket."

She ran to John's little area and grabbed the blanket off his make-shift bed. When she brought it back, he was upright and sputtering. Handing the blanket to William, she knelt down with the rest of them. "John, are you all right?"

A huge smile lit his face as he shivered. "Heavens, I'm thankful to be alive! But let's not do that again."

"What happened?" This time it was William who asked the question.

"As we lay at hull, I thought that perchance the storm had calmed. . .and I was desperate for some fresh air."

Dorothy gasped and covered her mouth.

Mary Elizabeth couldn't believe it. "You went out there? On purpose?"

"Aye." John nodded, his teeth chattering. "As soon as I was top deck, I knew the storm was indeed fierce. . .and the captain had rigged the ship just so to keep her upright." He pulled the blanket tighter around him. "Before I knew it, a huge wave blasted me, and I went sailing overboard. The ship almost turned on her side, and I was able to grab hold of the topsail halyards."

William's eyebrows shot up. "Unbelievable, man! Go on."

"I held on as tight as I could, but the sea took me way down into its depths and I was afraid I was done for until the sailors pulled me up by the rope and then grabbed me with a boat hook. After they saved me, Mr. Coppin tossed me down the steps and told me not to go on deck again during a storm." John's laugh turned into a scratchy cough. "I'll say it again—I'm thankful to be alive."

Mary Elizabeth shook her head. "Let's get you to your bed, Mr.

Howland. You've got to get warmed up and dry."

Dorothy smiled. "Why don't you let David and me help him, Mary Elizabeth?" She helped the man to his feet, and David took a spot under John's arm. "I'm sure we will need something for Mr. Howland to drink and eat."

William caught Mary Elizabeth's elbow as she turned. "How can I help?"

"Could you get a ration for John to eat?"

The look on his face showed disappointment.

Just like she felt. If only the circumstances were different and they could spend time together.

"Certainly." His nod made her heart ache.

Reaching out, she grabbed his hand. "Thank you, William."

❧

William worked to keep steady as the ship thrashed about. There was so much to record in his journal. While seasickness had laid most of the passengers ill, the signs of scurvy had begun to set in on some of the sickest passengers. Mr. Heale had warned them all, but what could they do? Everything was rationed daily, even though many complaints were heard. A lot of people feared they would die anyway, so why couldn't they have more food?

William knew what it felt like to retch after each tiny meal and then feel half-starved to death. With no land in sight and no end to the tumultuous seas, he feared people would start to revolt. If they found the energy to move.

The Saints made it clear at the beginning of the voyage that they wanted the rest of the ship to follow their rules and religious practices. The Strangers didn't want much to do with the Separatists and their strict rules, so the trip hadn't started off in a congenial manner. Then came that awful sailor and his insults. When the seas turned on them all, as well, the storms came one after another. Then came the sickness. Between that and the stench, they'd all just about gone mad.

He stopped writing and held the quill above the page. What could he report truthfully? How could he honor this job for Mr. Crawford and the other investors? Right now, the outcome of the *Mayflower's* voyage appeared grim. But William had come to care for their small band of travelers—these colonists who all shared a common goal. There had to be a way to gain a positive result.

The more he thought about the quandary, the more his heart felt heavy. It wasn't just the storms, the horrendous seas, or even their great delay—a greater problem existed.

The rift between the people on board. Saints and Strangers.

The thing was, William was a Stranger. Yet he found himself drawn increasingly to the ways and beliefs of the Separatists. His time with Elder Brewster had made him question his thoughts of God and examine his previous doubts. The valiant sacrifice each of these people made to stay true to their beliefs was beyond question.

To sum it all up? At the root of it all was the faithfulness to scripture.

That's how Paul had believed. For years, he'd tried to convey the same thing to William.

The chance to meet with Mr. Brewster had been enlightening, but how could he ease the misery of the fellow passengers when they didn't even trust one another?

The problem seemed too difficult to solve by himself.

Crack!

The sound was of wood splintering. And not just any wood. It had to be some large beam. The ship shifted hard to the right and William lost his balance. Righting himself, he grabbed the journal and tucked it back into the trunk and locked it.

As he ran up to the main deck, William spotted Master Jones at the main mast. A giant crack ran down the post into the deck of the ship.

"Get me the carpenter!" Jones yelled into the wind. Sailors ran in every direction.

Rain splattered William's face and dripped down his chin. "Sir! Might I be of assistance? I'm a carpenter."

"Aye. I remember you, Lytton. We will need every hand and mind that can help." The master waved his hand. "Follow me."

William walked with several of the crew into the steerage room that housed the whipstaff. The tiny room couldn't hold many, but at least they were out of the rain and wind and would be able to hear each other.

Master Jones cleared his throat and held a hand up in the air. "Men, we need to determine the extent of the damage down into the ship from the crack that is in the main mast, and then we need to know how to fix it. We're already too far into the voyage to turn back, if we could even make it. We are low on supplies and rations and too many are sick."

"Sir." John Clarke—the ship's pilot—spoke up. "The crack goes down into the gun deck, but not into the cargo hold. It's created a good-sized leak."

"Can we stop the leak?" Jones stood with his hands behind his back.

"If we can fix the crack." Clarke nodded.

"How is she under water?" The master looked to Coppin.

"She's holding firm, sir."

"Good."

The faces around William showed fear, uncertainty, and questions. Even the master of the ship seemed concerned with their great problem. But what were they to do? Then it hit him. "Master Jones?"

"Yes, Mr. Lytton."

"I recall seeing a great house jack being loaded onto the ship."

"House jack?"

"Yes, sir. It's like a great iron screw to help raise up beams and such when building houses."

The master's eyebrows raised. "Go on."

"If we were to use it to raise the beam into place, we could secure the mast with another post." William could see it in his mind but wasn't sure the captain of their ship would understand. After all, he was a skilled carpenter on land. Not at sea.

The ship's carpenter and John Alden joined them in the steerage room. "What needs to be done?" John's voice was always one of action.

Jones nodded to his carpenter. "Mr. Lytton here thinks that if we use the machinery he called a house jack, we could hoist the beam into position and brace it. Do you think it can be done?"

The smaller man nodded and drops of water splashed around him. "Aye, sir."

"Then you two get to work on the plan. The rest of the men will do whatever needs to be done to help. Once the mast is repaired, I'll need the carpenters to caulk everything they can and stop the leaking."

William followed the ship's carpenter out of the room. "Do you think it will work?"

"We better pray for a miracle, because if it *doesn't* work, we'll all be on the bottom of the sea by morning."

The *Mayflower* groaned and creaked with each plunge into the swells. William had lost count of how many times he'd been thrown to the deck by the crashing waves. But they had to fix the main mast, or all their hopes were lost.

John Alden worked next to him as they cranked the house jack to lift the beam back into position.

Master Jones yelled above the raging storm, "We need more hands on those supports!"

It didn't help that with every wave another man fell down. If they could keep everyone upright at the same time, they might make some progress.

"Lord, we could use some divine assistance." John's voice as he prayed and worked next to William had lost its usual confidence.

Dripping wet and weary from their efforts, the men stayed at it. No one wanted to go down with a ship.

"Heave!" Coppin yelled. "Just a few more inches."

Grunts and moans echoed around him as they worked to correct the beam. The house jack was working. Now if they could just get it back together and secure the supports in place.

Thunk! The beam snapped back into place.

"Secure the supports!" Master Jones eyed the men from his perch atop the poop deck.

Water sprayed over William's shoulder as another large wave shook the boat and rolled it larboard.

William held his support in place as John secured it.

"Get those women below deck *now!*" Jones sounded angry.

Women? What women? Looking over his shoulder while he held the support, William spotted Dorothy's and Mary Elizabeth's heads peeking out the opening of the companionway. Worry etched their faces as rain pelted them from above. He shook his head. Why weren't they going below?

The *Mayflower* rocked hard to steerboard, and William's feet flew out from under him. Water rushed over his head and body as he was washed to the bulwark.

Grasping for anything he could get his hands on, William felt panic rise up in his throat. It couldn't end this way. He wasn't ready.

"Help!" The cry was drowned by water filling his mouth.

But the waves were too strong and too tall, the ship was almost on its side as it heaved up onto another swell. When it came down, he'd be tossed overboard.

Lord, please save the ship and her passengers. . .

William closed his eyes as the seconds stretched, and he tried to grab for a hold. When he opened them, he was tossed upside down and then bounced off the bulwark and over the side.

"*William!*" Mary's scream was filled with anguish, and he could do nothing to comfort her.

This was the end.

CHAPTER 13

"N o!" Mary Elizabeth choked on the word. Tears blurred her already watery vision. Turning into Dorothy's arms, she wanted to jump into the water and save him. Why William? *Why, Lord?*

This couldn't be happening.

Thunder rumbled above their heads.

She sobbed into her friend's shoulder.

Dorothy gasped. "Mary Elizabeth. Look." Her friend grabbed her shoulders and made her turn.

As the ship shifted and rolled to lean to the other side, John Alden hung over the bulwark at his waist, his legs kicking in the air. Mr. Coppin jumped to grab John's legs and then sat on the deck and pulled.

Could it be?

"I've got him!" John's shout could be heard from the other side of the bulwark.

Mary Elizabeth let out the breath she'd been holding. Was it true?

Several other men went to assist in the efforts, and John was pulled up so only his arms hung over the ship.

He grimaced as they all strained to pull until a booted leg appeared grasped in John's hand. Within seconds, a sputtering William Lytton lay on the deck of the ship. He reached up for John's hand and nodded.

Mary Elizabeth couldn't wait any longer. She climbed up the rest of the steps and half ran, half slipped her way to William. "Are you hurt?"

The smile that stretched across his face melted her heart. He reached up a finger to touch her cheek. "I couldn't be better."

His brilliant blue eyes bore into hers. She wanted to relish his touch on her face for all her days.

"Get below deck. Now!" Master Jones's command was not to be disobeyed.

Nodding, she raced back to the companionway and looked back at William. Oh, how she loved that smile. . .

Mary Elizabeth woke with a start. The stench below deck reminded her that she was no longer watching William be rescued. But he was alive, and she would be forever grateful.

She sat up and scooted next to her father. When she touched his brow, it felt warm. But as she was still chilled from her adventure top deck, Mary Elizabeth couldn't gauge if he was *too* warm. One thing was certain—he'd gotten weaker and slept almost around the clock. What could she do for him?

As the waves continued to toss the *Mayflower* about and thunder cracked and sounded like cannons above them, Mary Elizabeth prayed. For Father's health. For the men working on the main mast. Were they done? For William and John. For the seas to calm and for the leaks to be stopped. And most fervently—that their journey would be over soon.

They all desperately needed to see land. To smell fresh air, and to be dry and warm. No water seeping in through the gun ports. No dark and smelly confined quarters.

After this journey, she would never complain about her circumstances ever again. She would be joyful and praise the Lord.

Father's favorite song from the psalter they used in church back home came to mind. As she sang softly to her father, the words ministered to her own burdened heart:

All people that on earth do dwell,
Sing to the Lord with cheerful voice.
Him serve with fear, His praise forth tell;

Come ye before Him and rejoice.

The Lord, ye know, is God indeed;
Without our aid He did us make,
We are His flock, He doth us feed,
And for His sheep He doth us take.

O enter then His gates with praise;
Approach with joy His courts unto;
Praise, laud, and bless His Name always,
For it is seemly so to do.

For why? The Lord our God is good;
His mercy is forever sure;
His truth at all times firmly stood,
And shall from age to age endure.

To Father, Son, and Holy Ghost,
The God whom Heaven and earth adore,
From men and from the angel host
Be praise and glory evermore.

The drippy, leaky ship couldn't take away that God's mercy was forever sure. The winds and the rain couldn't deny that His truth would endure. No matter if the mast was fixed or not. Nor if the ship even sank.

God's truth would endure.

The words that the apostle Paul wrote to the church in Philippi came to her, and she said the words aloud. "I speak not because of want: for I have learned in whatsoever state I am, therewith to be content. And I can be abased, & I can abund: every where in all things I am instructed both to be full, & to be hungry, & to abund, & to have want. I am able to *do* all things through the help of Christ, which strengtheneth me."

The depth of the words struck her heart. She could be content in whatever circumstances she faced. . .because she had the help of Christ. What a powerful thought.

Bolstered by the words of scripture and the song, Mary Elizabeth leaned over her father and kissed his forehead. She looked at little David and smiled. Everything would be all right because God was good, and she would rejoice. No matter what happened.

As she stood to go check on the others, Mary Elizabeth realized how much she'd changed over the past few weeks. The tragedy of losing Mother had almost broken her. Or so she thought. But she'd needed to learn how to give it over to God the Father. She needed to know that His strength and peace were always with her. For so long, she'd thought of herself as timid and afraid. Never courageous. But now, somehow, her thinking had changed.

Reaching the companionway, Mary Elizabeth had to slosh through an inch or so of water. As she looked up through the opening to the deck above, rain poured down on her and on the men working so hard on the ship.

William was one.

She crept back up the steps. Just to see his face again. Watching the men, well—if she were honest—watching William, made Mary Elizabeth all too aware of his masculinity. Moving away from the opening, she knew her mind needed guarding above all else. What would Father say if he knew she'd been watching William not out of curiosity or worry, but with appreciation and attraction?

Yet after his harrowing fall and rescue, Mary Elizabeth's heart knew the truth. She cared for him. Far more than she'd admitted to herself.

She shook her head and went to check on Mrs. Hopkins and the new baby. Best to keep her mind on other things. If only Mother were still alive, she could talk to her about the struggle.

Dorothy was holding the baby when Mary Elizabeth reached the Hopkinses' quarters. "Oh, Mary Elizabeth. Isn't he just the most gorgeous baby?"

She nodded. "He is." Kneeling down beside her friend, Mary Elizabeth watched the little fingers move. They were so tiny. What a miracle.

"Would you like to hold him?" Mrs. Hopkins tilted her head and smiled.

Mary Elizabeth loved babies and ached to hold the little guy again. "I'd love to."

Dorothy leaned toward her in slow, gentle movements. As she placed the tiny bundle in Mary Elizabeth's arms, Oceanus opened his eyes and looked up.

"Oh my. . ." Mary Elizabeth breathed.

Little Oceanus studied her face for a moment and then closed his eyes again.

"Mary Elizabeth, you have the touch." Mrs. Hopkins shifted on her bed. The woman grimaced as she moved.

Swaying back and forth with the baby, Mary Elizabeth let the rolling of the ship guide her rhythm. "Are you feeling all right, Mrs. Hopkins?"

"A bit sorer than the last one, but that's to be expected when giving birth in the middle of a storm."

Dorothy stood. "Perhaps some food sounds good?"

The woman sighed. "That sounds lovely, thank you."

"You'll need to build up your strength. Especially after the seasickness." Mary Elizabeth stared down at the wee one as she spoke to his mother. "This little one will need his strength too. He has lots of growing to do." The soft fuzz on top of his head reminded her of velvet.

"Here we are." Dorothy's singsong voice made the baby squirm. "I've got some dried meat and cheese."

"Thank you." Elizabeth Hopkins sighed. "Won't it be nice to cook something different once we reach the new land?"

Mary Elizabeth stifled a laugh. "Yes. I don't even care what we have, as long as it is something different."

"When we first set out"—Dorothy sat back down—"I didn't

know if I could handle any more fish after weeks of it. But now I would love to eat it again."

Mary Elizabeth laughed at her friend's dramatic expression. "I agree. The men haven't been able to fish in these storms, but I'll take fresh fish over dried meat every day."

Mrs. Hopkins nodded as she chewed the dried food.

A new thought struck Mary Elizabeth. "We sound a lot like the Israelites, don't we? The Lord provided manna for them, yet they asked for something else."

The ladies laughed together. And Oceanus woke up with a cry.

"I believe someone is hungry as well." Mrs. Hopkins reached for her son.

"We'll be back to check on you later." Rising up, Mary Elizabeth smiled down. "Dorothy or I will make sure the children are fed."

"Thank you."

As she and Dorothy made their way toward another family, William and another man came down the steps.

"Good day, Mr. Lytton." Dorothy tugged on Mary Elizabeth's arm.

"Good day, ladies." He smiled at Mary Elizabeth.

"I'm so thankful you're safe." Mary Elizabeth couldn't keep the words inside. "I was so worried when I saw you go over."

"Well, I'm a bit bruised from the tumble and soaked through to my bones, but God spared me, and for that, I am grateful." He stared into her eyes.

She stared back, unwilling to break the connection.

Dorothy cleared her throat.

"Yes, well. We have the mast secured, and now we must caulk as much as we can to seal off the leaks." William looked at Dorothy.

"That sounds like a big job." Her friend continued the conversation and poked her elbow into Mary Elizabeth's side.

She stopped staring and looked to her feet. What could she do with these feelings? When William went over the side, she thought her heart would wrench in two. This was all so new, and she didn't understand it. "It is a large task, and we must get to it." The other man with William ducked and headed toward the bow.

William nodded to them. "I'd better get to work, as well." He turned toward the stern.

The thought of the strong, tarry scent of the oakum cords they would need to stuff into the cracks didn't sound appealing. But then again, that smell would be better than the stench of sickness. Dorothy pinched Mary Elizabeth's arm.

"Ow. What was that for?" Mary Elizabeth watched William work his way to the back of the gun deck.

"You were staring. What's going on?" Hands on her hips, Dorothy squinted her eyes.

Mary Elizabeth wasn't sure what to say. "I. . .well. . ."

"I noticed the way he smiled at you. Mary Elizabeth, you can talk to me."

"Hush your words, Dorothy. I don't need everyone listening in." Mary Elizabeth grabbed her friend's elbow and walked over to the companionway. They'd get wet, but at least there weren't as many listening ears. She took a deep breath. "I've been thinking about William a lot."

"Aye. And. . .?"

"I realized a little bit ago that I've been. . .well. . ."

"Go on. . . ."

"Appreciative of his looks." There she said it.

Dorothy put a hand to her mouth. When she uncovered it again, a small smile at the corner of her mouth appeared. "Mary Elizabeth, I already guessed that you liked the man. I think it's a bit more than an appreciation for his looks. You nearly clawed your way across the deck when he went over. I think you need to be honest."

Heat rose to her cheeks. Her friend was correct. "It's difficult for me. I don't. . .well, I haven't felt this way before." What was she trying to say? And what would Dorothy think?

"It's plain to see that you care for him, Mary Elizabeth." Dorothy touched her arm. "And I'm happy for you."

"But don't you understand?" She lowered her voice to the barest of whispers. "I can't be unequally yoked. He's a Stranger. And it's not pure to have such thoughts."

"What kind of thoughts are we talking about?" Dorothy's smile turned into a frown.

"Just that. He's very handsome. And masculine. . .and strong. He's also smart and caring. He appears to be a very good carpenter and a hard worker."

Dorothy released her breath in a big sigh. She put a hand to her chest. "For a moment you scared me. Little, innocent Mary Elizabeth—my mother told me it was fine to find a young man attractive, but we can't allow our minds to"—her voice lowered and she looked around—"*lust* after them."

Mary Elizabeth's heart beat a little faster. While she hadn't allowed her thoughts to go past her admiration of William, she wished her mother were still alive. These were the kinds of things she should be talking of with her. Mary Elizabeth sat on one of the wet steps. "Did your parents speak to you about marriage?"

"Why yes, of course."

"Did they talk to you about arranging a marriage?"

Dorothy nodded.

"But have they ever spoken of love?"

"No." Her friend shook her head. "My parents' marriage was arranged, and they seem very happy."

How could she explain what she was pondering? She sighed. Dorothy had been her dearest friend and confidante. Maybe she'd have some sort of advice. "Before my mother died, she told me that things have been a certain way with marriage for a long time. Marriages were arranged for good matches and for procreation—the continuation of family lines. The world has tainted that by so many husbands and wives being unfaithful—all in the name of love." She bit her lip. "The way mother explained it is that marriage became a duty, and they sought their affection. . .elsewhere."

Dorothy raised her brows.

"I know. I was a little shocked too. But my mother and father were different. She told me that even though their marriage was arranged, she'd asked her parents to arrange it because she was in love with Father. She told me she wanted the same for me, but that I was to seek God first. Marriage was His design in the first place."

"And so, you wish for love in a marriage from the very beginning." A smile lifted Dorothy's lips. She reached over and grabbed Mary Elizabeth's hand. "I've had the same desire. Perhaps every young woman seeks that deep down in her heart."

"I know. But that is why I'm conflicted."

"I'm not sure I understand."

"I find William fascinating. Not to mention, *very* appealing." She sucked in a breath. "But to honor God in marriage, I need to honor my father and our faith and what we stand for. . ." She let the words drop off. What was she trying to say? Her thoughts were like a tangled ball of yarn.

"It sounds to me like you're afraid."

Once again, her friend was right. But she hadn't wanted to admit it. "Yes, I'm afraid. The future is so uncertain. And I want to be a Godly young woman."

"I understand, Mary Elizabeth, I do. You spent a lot of time caring for him while he was sick. Your heart is already attached to him, and you're worried. But have you seen William lately? He's been studying with Elder Brewster. Isn't that encouraging?" She tilted her head. "Don't run away from this because you're frightened. You need to give him a chance."

CHAPTER 14

Tuesday, 24 October 1620

The seas hadn't given up their fight, and William wondered if they would ever see land again. It seemed each day a new storm appeared to torment them. The crew was worn out. The passengers were worn out.

Their ship was worn out.

While the posts they'd installed against the main mast beam held, the ship had hardly been able to use its sails for days on end.

People sat or lay in misery in the damp, rocking vessel.

The only bright spots to his day were seeing Mary Elizabeth and studying with Mr. Brewster. Mary Elizabeth had been busy taking care of people and feeding them, so he'd only seen her a few times a day in passing. They'd exchange a brief word or a smile—and once he'd been able to hold her hand and assist her down the stairs to the cargo hold below. The warmth that spread up his arm and into his chest again confirmed that what he felt for Mary Elizabeth Chapman was true. But how could he ever deserve her? And would her father ever approve?

Before meeting her, he'd thought all his dreams were to start a new life in Virginia Colony. To be a successful carpenter—a well-respected member of society.

But now it had all changed. He'd begun to seek God.

And he hoped for love.

As he found his way to the Brewsters' quarters, William wondered what it would be like to have a wife and family.

"Ah, William. . . I'm glad you could join us again." The Elder's kind smile welcomed him.

"Thank you, Mr. Brewster."

The older man opened his Bible and looked to the two other men who were strong enough to sit up and join them. "We've been studying in the book of Matthew, chapter five. I'd like to start where we left off, verse eleven."

William moved closer so he could read over the man's shoulder.

"'Blessed shall ye be when men revile you, & persecute you, & say all manner of evil against you for my sake, falsely. Rejoice and be glad, for great is your reward in heaven: for so persecuted they the Prophets which were before you.'" Brewster read and then looked up at the men. "We've had to deal with some of this on the voyage, haven't we? Being reviled and persecuted for our faith."

The others nodded.

William thought of the nasty sailor who had said such awful things to the group of Saints. "Elder Brewster, might I ask a question before you continue?"

"Of course."

"When it says, 'revile you, & persecute you,' did you find it hard to *rejoice* when the sailor came down here and harassed everyone?"

Brewster's brow furrowed. "That's a good question, young man. It's difficult to be persecuted for our faith—especially when people say horrible things, like he looked forward to throwing us all overboard—but Jesus is saying here that yes, we need to rejoice in that. Because we are storing up treasure in heaven, not on earth."

William nodded as another man asked a question. The words hit the depths of his heart. He'd spent the majority of his life being reviled by others. Taunted and teased and ridiculed for being an orphan. This passage of scripture confused him.

"Mr. Lytton." Elder Brewster's voice brought him back to the moment. "If we go back to the beginning of the passage, we see Jesus say, 'Blessed *are* the poore in spirit, for theirs is the kingdom of heaven.'" William looked down to the page where Brewster pointed.

He nodded. He'd always been poor until recent years. That was something he understood all too well. But what did it mean to be poor in spirit?

"I can see you are puzzled." The man didn't mock him or make him feel uncomfortable. He reminded William of Paul. "Let me try to explain. To be 'poor in spirit' means to know the depth of our lacking—to know we are broken and unusable as we are. That we are sinners in need of a Savior and can't possibly attain anything on our own. When we come to that place of understanding and are truly 'poor in spirit,' then we acknowledge Jesus as our Savior—that it is only through His sacrifice that we can be saved—and then we can be cleansed and transformed. Then—oh what a beautiful thought—then the kingdom of heaven is ours. To live eternally with our heavenly Father."

William looked down to his hands. He understood the depth of lacking that Brewster spoke about. His whole life he'd felt empty— like something important was missing. When Paul took him in, that was the first time he'd ever felt any kind of love or belonging. It took a long time for that frightened and hurt boy to love back, but he had. Did Paul know before he died how much William cared? How thankful he was?

His eyes burned with the thoughts. Prayerfully, his friend and mentor knew.

The fact remained that William knew he needed God. The undeniable truth was in front of him, but the process seemed illusive. Was it really so simple as faith?

Monday, 30 October 1620

The small space was getting tiresome. David had done everything he could to help take care of people, but they were all tired of being stuck in a storm on a ship.

Father was sick.

Mary Elizabeth was busy.

She'd been short with him that morning when he asked her to play bowls with him. He'd kept his toys packed up in the trunk all this time. After he'd begged her to play, she scolded him about how she didn't have time and the balls rolling around could make someone trip and hurt themselves. He would never want someone to get hurt.

But he was bored.

It was hard growing up. Trying to be a man. Think like a man. Act like a man. Some days he just wanted to be able to play and be a child.

There was nowhere to run and play on a ship. Not when they had a hundred people crammed into a space smaller than their house in Leyden.

Guilt began to fill his gut. These thoughts weren't fitting for a God-fearing young man. He shouldn't be complaining. Father said that lots of children would love to have the chance that he had. He wasn't old enough to have a share in the Adventurers' and Planters' agreement, but Father said the children under ten years of age would have fifty acres in their name once the debts were paid and the company liquidated.

Land was worth more than anything else in David's mind. He needed to be grateful.

Especially that he wasn't sick like the majority of the people. Although, every time he had to empty a chamber pot, he thought he might get sick.

David decided to go check on each of the other children. There were about thirty of them aboard, but most of them were really sick.

As he made his way through the gun deck, he visited each family and said hello, asked if they needed anything. Not knowing what else to do, he wandered around the deck and looked for things he could help with.

Mary Elizabeth stopped him under the companionway. "I'm sorry, David. I shouldn't have responded to you this morning in such a harsh manner."

Peering down at his shoes, David shrugged. "It's all right, Mary Elizabeth. I knew you were busy."

She took his shoulders in her hands. "I know. But even though the journey has taken its toll on all of us, I shouldn't have spoken to you that way. Papa is still very ill, and this morning I was feeling guilty for leaving him. . .failing him."

"You haven't failed him, Mary Elizabeth. Almost everyone is sick, and you've been needed. Papa sleeps all the time anyway. I know he appreciates all you've done." He reached up and kissed her cheek.

A small smile lifted her lips. She laid a hand on his shoulder. "You've grown into such a sweet young man, David. I'm very proud of you. Would you like to help me bring food to people?"

"Yes, very much." Finally, another job. Something to keep his mind off the confining quarters.

Handing him a small cloth, she tucked some dried meat and dried vegetables inside. "This is for Mr. Fuller and his servant—young William Butten. Will you be able to help them sit up?"

"Yes, Mary Elizabeth. I can do it." He took off to see Mr. Fuller. The man had been a doctor back in Leyden but hadn't been able to help anyone on the ship because he'd suffered from seasickness since they set out to sea.

"Mr. Fuller?" David found the man sitting on his bed, his face pale.

"Aye."

"I've brought you some food. For young William too."

"Thank you, son." He leaned forward. "But I'm worried about the youth. He hasn't moved much the past couple days."

David looked down at the young man. Several years his senior, the boy appeared very ill. "Is there anything else I can do for you, sir?"

"No, thank you." The man sighed. "I wish there was something I could do to help all these people." He wiped a hand down his face.

"I'm sure we will be very appreciative of your assistance once we're in the new settlement, sir."

"If we make it there alive. . ." Mr. Fuller's face fell. "I'm sorry, son." Lying back on his bed, he closed his eyes.

All David's earlier thoughts rushed to his mind. Now he was

ashamed. So many of the people were fighting to stay alive, and he'd been complaining that there was nowhere to play. He could change that.

He'd just have to find a way to put his plan into action.

CHAPTER 15

Monday, 6 November 1620

Mary Elizabeth's heart thundered in her ears. She couldn't wake Father. For hours he'd been motionless, and she couldn't rouse him.

"Mary Elizabeth, why isn't he waking?" David's voice sounded so small. The poor dear had found Father this way earlier.

She closed her eyes and sent a quick prayer heavenward for wisdom. "I don't know, David. But I need for you to see if Mr. Heale can come down and see him, all right?"

Her little brother flung the curtain aside and took off at a run, leaping over obstacles and buckets.

Lord, please help me to know what to do.

"Father, please, I need you to wake up."

Several moments passed, and then she heard footsteps. Mary Elizabeth turned just in time to see Mr. Heale approach. "Thank you for coming." Pulling back from Father, she gave the surgeon some space. "He's not responding to me."

Giles Heale put his head to Father's chest. "His heart is very slow. How long has he been sick?"

She swallowed the tears building in her throat. "Weeks."

He nodded. "That's what I thought. I brought some smelling salts with me. We can only hope the intense ammonia will make him take a deep breath. Maybe then we can bring him out of this deep sleep."

"Please. Let's try."

The surgeon nodded to her and put the potent concoction under

Father's nose. It took a couple seconds, but then Father inhaled sharply. His eyelids fluttered. "Talk to him, Mary Elizabeth." He stepped back.

"Father, please, wake up."

Her father moaned.

"Please, we need you to wake up."

Mr. Heale stepped forward and tried again.

With a jolt, Father's eyes opened as he took a deep breath. He blinked several times and then locked eyes with her. "Mary Elizabeth?"

Tears streamed down her face. "Oh, Father. I was so worried."

"Miss Chapman?" Mr. Heale summoned her with a finger. "Might I speak with you for a moment?"

"Of course." She grabbed David's hand and pulled him close. "You talk with Father for a bit, all right? See if you can keep him awake."

Her little brother knelt beside their father and Mary Elizabeth exited the curtained off area.

"Thank you, Mr. Heale." She swiped at her face to dry the tears.

He shook his head. "I'm sorry, Mary Elizabeth, but I'm afraid your father is still very ill. Try to keep him awake as long as you can, but his heart is weak, and I'm certain he will fall back into that deep sleep."

"Isn't there anything we can do?"

"Whatever it is that has taken hold has weakened him. Unless we can get him to eat and move about, he won't be able to gain strength—he'll only lose it." The surgeon nodded and bowed slightly. "I'm sorry."

As the man walked away, Mary Elizabeth didn't know what to think of his words. What did it mean? Was he implying that Father would die? She shook her head. No. She was worrying too much.

She stepped back into the curtained off area and saw Father give David a tiny smile. "It's good to see you smile, Father."

"Aye. It's good to see your faces." He lifted his hand a few inches. "Would you get me something to drink, David?"

"Yes, Father." He dashed off.

"Mary Elizabeth, there's something I need to speak with you

about." His voice was raspy and light.

"Yes, Father?"

"I may not make it through this. And I'm at peace with God about it."

"Please, don't talk like that." A tear slipped down her cheek.

"No, child. I need you to listen. I'm tired already, and it takes too much energy to speak."

Mary Elizabeth nodded.

"If something happens to me, promise me that you will look after your brother." A horrible cough wracked her father's frame. "You have a share in the venture. . .since you are over sixteen, and you will inherit my share. . . . David is too young to receive a share, but he will receive acreage. Mr. Bradford. . .and Mr. Brewster have copies of all the contracts, and I have papers in the trunk." The cough returned, and he closed his eyes.

"No, Father. Please don't go back to sleep. You need something to drink, remember?"

He nodded. "I know I haven't been myself since your Mother died—God rest her soul—but if it's my time, I will gladly go. I just regret not taking the time to. . ." His voice sounded so weak.

"Father, there's nothing to regret." She held his hands.

"No, I neglected you and David in my grief. This trip to the New World gave me something new to think about, but I didn't realize what it did to you. For that, I am sorry."

"Oh, Father. . ."

"More than anything, I hope you know how much I love you."

She nodded as more tears collected at the corners of her eyes. "I love you too." She needed to be strong. David would return at any moment, and she didn't want him to see her falling apart.

"Did I tell you that young Mr. Lytton has come to see me?"

A gasp took her breath away. She leaned back. "Mr. Lytton? When?"

Her father nodded. "A day or so ago, I guess. I don't know. It appears he is quite fascinated with you, my dear. He's come to check on me several times while you were taking care of the others."

She didn't know what to say. What did her father think of the handsome Stranger?

"He's been sharing with me what he's learned in the scriptures. Most of the time, I'm not very good company... I tend to drift in and out..." Father's head bobbed to the right and his eyes shut.

David entered with a cup in his hand.

Mary Elizabeth took it and lifted her father's head. "I need you to drink, so don't go to sleep on me yet."

He moaned but took a few sips.

"Is he all right?" The squeak in David's voice made her want to hug him tight.

She laid her father's head back down. "He wore himself out talking, David. That's all." She didn't have the heart to share what the surgeon had spoken.

"Will he get better?"

"We'll just have to pray and keep helping him, aye?"

David nodded and ducked his head. Standing, he wrapped his small arms around Mary Elizabeth's neck as she knelt beside their father.

Someone cleared their throat.

Mary Elizabeth peered out the curtain and saw William hunched outside. "Oh, William, please come in."

He shook his head. "I'm sorry, Mary Elizabeth, but I think you need to come. It's Dorothy. She's taken ill."

All sound around her diminished as Mary Elizabeth went to see the Raynsfords. They'd swapped places with another family before everyone got sick. Around the gun deck lay the sick, the weak. Very few sat or stood or walked. Taking in the faces, she felt like time had slowed. What would become of them?

She felt William's presence as he walked right behind her, and she wished she had some of his strength.

The entire Raynsford family rested on their makeshift beds. Still. Pale. Silent.

"What has happened? Why are they all sick?" She sobbed into the blanket covering her dearest friend in all the world.

"We don't know. The surgeon was here, but he's just as confused as the rest of us. The seasickness has made many people weak, and now scurvy has set in. But just like that young sailor, there seems to be something else afflicting people."

"No...no...no..." Mary Elizabeth shook her head. Dorothy had been her lifeline. Her steady encourager.

The thoughts made her stop.

That wasn't true. She sniffed and sat up a little. Gazing down at her beloved friend, she realized that through all the loss of Mother, Leyden, and her church family, she'd grown up and learned a lot. It wasn't Mother, or Father, Dorothy, or David who had been her strength—had kept her going. It had been God working in her life through those people.

The words from the eighteenth Psalm flowed over her and exited her lips. " 'The Lord *is* my rock, & my fortress...' " As she spoke, her voice grew stronger... her heart grew stronger. "...& He that delivereth me, my God & my strength: in him will I trust, my shield, the horn also of my salvation, & my refuge.' " God was indeed her strength. She would trust in Him.

New determination filled her heart. She would rejoice in this time of trial because trials made a person stronger. Didn't James say something about that? What was the verse? The words came out in a rushed whisper. " '...Count it exceeding joy, when ye fall into divers tentations, Knowing that the trying of your faith bringeth forth patience. And let patience have her perfect work, that ye may be perfect and entire, lacking nothing.' "

All her life she'd been timid. A worrier. A doubter. Yet now she knew she was made to be strong in the Lord. Her mother had always exuded such joy and confidence. Mary Elizabeth understood now.

"Mary Elizabeth?" Dorothy's voice was just a whisper.

She looked back down to her friend. "I'm here."

"I'm sorry I am. . .sick."

"Me too."

"I know this creates more work for you." Dorothy closed her eyes. "Please take care of Mother and Father." Her head lolled to the side.

"I will." Mary Elizabeth put a hand on her friend's forehead. It was way too hot. "Dorothy? Dorothy?"

"Hmm?" Her eyes stayed closed.

"Can you stay awake?"

"No. . .so tired."

William laid a hand on Mary Elizabeth's shoulder. "It's all right. Let her rest. She's been working so hard and probably not getting enough rest."

She nodded and blinked back tears. William helped her to her feet, and she just stood there, shoulders hunched, staring at the floor. The Lord was her strength. She could do this.

"Is there any way we can go up for some air?"

William took a deep breath and let it out. "I don't know, Mary Elizabeth. The waves don't feel as treacherous right now, but we don't know what we might face up top."

She nodded and walked to the companionway. The steps were wet, but the skies weren't as dark as they had been in previous days. Sitting on one of the steps, she put her face in her hands.

A creak next to her made her think that William had sat as well. "I'm just going to sit here with you for a while, if that's acceptable to you."

"Yes." The words sounded muffled against her skin. There wasn't anything else to say.

And so they sat in silence.

Above them the sounds of the crew shouting back and forth to one another blended with the creaks and groans of the *Mayflower* as she cut through the water for yet another day. Two months had passed since they'd left Southampton. More than three months since they'd departed Leyden.

Her back ached from sleeping on the floor and not being able to stand up straight for all this time. Her hands were dirty, her clothes stank, and her shoes were wearing thin.

"You know, Mary Elizabeth, Mr. Brewster has been allowing me to read his Bible." William's voice soothed the frayed edges of her heart. "Lately, I've enjoyed the Psalms, and today I read through several. My favorite was the seventy-first. I memorized one of the verses. It says, 'But I will wait continually, & will praise thee more and more.'"

She lifted her head and looked into his beautiful blue eyes. He was so close she could feel his warmth and see the light reflected in his eyes.

"I just wanted to share that with you. In case it could help."

"It does help. Very much." She sucked in a breath. "Thank you."

Boots appeared in front of them. "I'm sorry, Miss Chapman. But I'm afraid I have some bad news."

Mary Elizabeth looked up into the surgeon's face and held her breath.

"Samuel Fuller's young servant has died."

"William Butten?" William grabbed her hand. "But he was just a child!"

She closed her eyes and slowly exhaled.

"Aye. A mere youth. But he's gone. I have a man wrapping and weighting the body. We'll have to get him overboard as soon as we can."

Mary Elizabeth didn't know what to think. There wouldn't be any prayer service or funeral procession. The boy would be tossed into the sea. And that made her ache even more.

The surgeon walked away, and William pulled on her hand. "Come, let's go up before they bring up the body."

The tiny thread that kept her emotions in place felt like it was frayed to the very last strand. But there was nowhere to run.

William kept hold of her hand as he led her to the bulwark on the larboard side. "I'm so sorry, Mary Elizabeth. There are no words."

Elder Brewster made his way up the steps, followed by the men with the body of William Butten. The crew joined their little group as Mr. Brewster prayed.

Two of the crew heaved the bundle overboard, and Master Jones barked his commands as soon as it was over.

Mere seconds had passed, and it was done.

The crew went back to work.

Mary Elizabeth took a deep breath of the salty and damp air as the wind whipped her hair from beneath her cornet. " 'But I will hope continually, & will praise thee more and more.' " The words came out on a great sob, and she threw herself into William's arms.

Chapter 16

The arms around his waist and the head against his chest were unlike anything William had ever felt before. Mary Elizabeth sobbed into him, and he wrapped his arms around her.

Never had he held a woman. Or anyone else, for that matter.

Never had anyone held him.

Words couldn't express the emotions that ran through him. He wanted to relish this moment forever. He longed to protect this woman he held, ease her pain and her fears.

She shook in his arms, and he remembered the grief and agony she must be feeling. The utter exhaustion. The overwhelming pain.

William understood loss.

The last thing he wanted was to lose this. This woman. This new faith and group of people he was beginning to trust.

But as he held Mary Elizabeth, he thought of all the bickering he'd heard between the Saints and the Strangers. The Saints wanted the others to follow their rules. The Strangers thought the Saints were sanctimonious and self-righteous.

The only reason the bickering had stopped was because the storms made everyone sick. God had essentially shut them up.

William banished the thought. That's not what God wanted for them. Nor was it the way He worked. If he'd learned anything from Elder Brewster, it was that God loved them more than anything else. So much that He sent His only Son as the sacrifice for all.

But there had to be a way to bring these two groups of people together—especially if they were going to survive as a new colony.

Mary Elizabeth sniffed, and his thoughts returned to how wonderful it felt to hold her in his arms.

"I'm so sorry, Mary Elizabeth."

She pulled back and wiped the tears from her face. A deep flush filled her cheeks, and she ducked her head. "No. It should be me who is apologizing. That was totally inappropriate for me to. . .well. . .to. . ."

"You were grieving." William looked around the deck to see if the crew was still watching them. "Besides, it was nice." When all else failed, it was best to be honest.

She lifted her chin, and he got a look into those deep brown eyes. They twinkled in the daylight. "Yes, it was." Lowering her head again, she gave him a curtsy. "And now I must go back down below."

He smiled as he watched her walk away. He needed to talk to her father again. And soon.

⚜

Thursday, 9 November 1620

"Just a few sips. You can do it." William lifted Mr. Chapman's head.

The older man struggled to swallow and held up a hand to stop. "That's enough."

William nodded and laid the man back down. "Is there anything else I can do for you?"

"No. Thank you." He grabbed William's hand—the grip was weak and clammy. "It has been good to get to know you."

"And I, you." William gave the man a smile.

"Mr. Bradford is a man of keen perceptions and delicate sensibilities. He will be a good adviser."

"Thank you, sir."

Mr. Chapman closed his eyes, and his breathing deepened. Again. The man didn't stay awake very long, and he appeared so very weak.

William stayed with him until he was certain the older man was asleep. Since the ship didn't seem to be rolling quite as much, he hoped to get top deck and take in some fresh air.

As he made his way to the companionway in the early morning hours, a ray of sunshine broke through the clouds and cast a beautiful glow on the steps. William couldn't pass up the chance. He climbed the steep ladder and stood at the top with his chin lifted to the sky.

How glorious to feel the sun on his face!

"Land, ho!" The shout from above his head shocked him. Had he heard correctly?

"Land, ho!" With the second shout, confirmation was made.

Master Jones strode purposefully across the deck to the forecastle. He leapt up the steps and pulled out his spyglass. "Indeed! Land, ho, Mates!"

William ran to the steerboard side and peered over. Squinting toward the horizon, he saw it. They'd made it! The New World was before them.

Making his way back down the companionway, William couldn't wait to tell Mary Elizabeth. And John Alden. And Elder Brewster! They'd seen land.

He found Mary Elizabeth sitting with Dorothy. "Mary Elizabeth, they've spotted land."

She jumped to her feet and hit her head on the ceiling. Rubbing the offended spot, she smiled up at him. "Truly?"

"Yes." He grinned back. "I need to tell the others."

He found John asleep on his bed, the poor man had been repairing barrels throughout the night. "John." He shook his friend. "Wake up, man. Land!"

Without waiting for an answer, William went to find Mr. Brewster. But he found several of the men already congratulating each other. They all headed toward the steps.

While the seas weren't anywhere near calm yet, they had slowed to a deep roll. So many people couldn't join them on deck for this historic moment, but William would tell them all about it as soon as he could.

Back on the main deck, William marveled at the sight of seagulls and the tiny edge of land on the horizon that grew in size as they inched closer. Several other people chattered on in excitement while Miles Standish spoke with Master Jones. It was good to see people standing, even though most appeared exceedingly weak as they leaned on one another for support. The rest of the passengers were still abed, and William prayed for them to recover. They would need everyone healthy and strong if they were going to build a settlement and survive.

He watched in fascination as Master Jones held up a cross-staff—a calibrated stick with a sliding transom—and spoke to Standish. They studied it, and Standish nodded. Leaving the ship master's side, he approached Mr. Brewster and Bradford. The men talked for a moment, and Standish called the remaining people on deck to come closer.

Standish wasn't a tall man, so he stood on a crate. "It appears, folks, that we are well north of our intended destination of the Hudson River, which as you know is in the northern corner of the Virginia territory. Where our patent lies."

Murmurs echoed through the small group as the reality of the situation settled upon them with Standish's last statement.

Standish held up both his hands. "Master Jones believes he has calculated our latitude to that of Cape Cod."

"Where is Cape Cod?" John Carver voiced the question most everyone probably thought.

Standish sighed. "It's in New England. North. Too far north."

Gasps were heard, and then several people shouted questions.

William listened to the discussion and watched the faces around him. Land was before them. But it wasn't where they were supposed to be. This could present a huge problem.

Elder Brewster quieted the people. "Let's not panic. When we reach the shore, if it is indeed Cape Cod, then a decision will be made about what to do."

"What's going on?" Mary Elizabeth's voice beside him drew William's attention.

"I'm so glad you made it up." He led her over to the bulwark and pointed. "Look."

She clasped her hands under her chin. "Oh my. Isn't it a beautiful sight?"

"Indeed." He watched her face light with excitement.

"What is all the commotion about?" She nodded toward the group of people speaking with Mr. Standish.

"We're not in Virginia. Apparently the storms blew us far north. We're somewhere in what Mr. Standish called New England."

"Oh." Her brow furrowed. "I saw that map when we headed out. Are they certain?"

"We'll know more when we reach the shore, but I believe they are pretty sure." He turned to fully face her. "How is your father?"

She sighed. "Very weak. But now that we are close to land, he must get better, right?"

"We can hope and pray." The wind held a sharp chill. "How is Dorothy?"

"Worse, I'm afraid." Mary Elizabeth shivered. "Her parents have been battling whatever illness it is for a long while now. It makes me worry."

John Alden joined them at the bulwark. "I just heard that we are too far north."

"Yes." William nodded at his friend.

"Well, I guess we will have to wait and see what they decide to do." John bowed to Mary Elizabeth. "It's good to see you again, Miss Chapman."

"Thank you, Mr. Alden."

"How's our little David doing?"

"Quite well, thank you." She looked around. "I'm surprised he's not up here."

William watched her face turn from joyous expectation to a worried frown. "Would you like me to go look for him? You look like you could use some more fresh air."

A small smile lit her face. "I should be the one to search for him."

"Nonsense. You stay up here for a bit and enjoy the view. I'm sure John won't mind keeping you company—you deserve it after all you've done to take care of everyone." William backed away a few steps. "I'll be back in a jiffy."

"All right." Mary Elizabeth's laugh was exactly what his heart needed. To see her truly happy was a wonderful sight, and William hoped he could be the one to keep her happy for the rest of their lives.

"Father?" David knelt beside Father and reached out to touch his pale face.

"Da. . .vid?" The voice was soft and scratchy. Not at all like the normal, strong voice of his parent. "My boy. . .it's so good to see you."

"It's good to see you too. I wanted to tell you that they've spotted land."

"Praise. . .God."

"Today we'll be at the New World. We'll find fresh food and start to build a house." Even if David had to build it by himself, he would do it. He was almost a man now. And it had to be done. For Father and Mary Elizabeth.

A smile started, but Father's face went lax again. His eyes closed.

Fear and uncertainty flooded his mind. *Why couldn't Father stay awake?* He began to cry. *What could he do?* "Once we're ashore, we'll find a way to get you better." Tears dripped down his nose. David laid his hand on top of his father's. David's seemed so small in comparison. But there wasn't any warmth to Father's hand. It just lay there. He sucked in a breath. He couldn't be childish anymore. "You'll see. We're at the New World, and it will be everything you hoped for." He bent over and laid his head on Papa's chest. What he wouldn't give to hear the booming voice and feel strong arms around him again.

"David?" A voice outside their quarters made David sniff and wipe his eyes.

"I'm in here."

William came through the curtain. "Your sister was worried about you."

"I just wanted to visit my father and give him the news."

"That was a wonderful idea. Did you get to tell him?"

David nodded and took a deep breath. "He was awake for a few moments."

"That's good." William turned his body toward the curtain. "Have you been up to see it yet?"

He shook his head. Looking down at his father, he knew the man was in a deep sleep. David stood. "Is Mary Elizabeth up there?"

"She is. And she's excited to share it with you." Mr. Lytton placed a hand on his shoulder and led him out of the quarters.

"Mr. Lytton, could I ask a favor of you?"

"Of course."

David clasped his hands behind his back like he'd seen so many of the men do as they discussed important topics. "Would you help me build a house for my family?"

CHAPTER 17

As the *Mayflower* drew nearer to the shore, a new sense of delight made Mary Elizabeth smile. After so many days at sea, they were finally here. No matter what they faced next, it couldn't be near as horrifying as what they'd been through already. She was sure of it.

With David at her side, she watched the approaching land.

"Look at the birds, Mary Elizabeth!" David pointed up. "There's a lot more of them now."

"Aye. There are." She looked down at her little brother and wrapped an arm around his shoulder. "It's exciting, isn't it?"

He beamed a smile up to her.

"Mary Elizabeth—I've got some news." William walked up beside them. "They've determined that it is indeed Cape Cod before us, and so we will begin to head south."

"We can't stay here?" Her brother chimed in.

William tilted his head. "Well, you see, we don't have the documents that we need to stay here. Our patent is for Virginia territory—near the Hudson River."

"Ugh." David slouched and smacked his forehead with his hand. Then he looked up to her. "Does this mean we have to stay on this boat for a lot longer?"

Laughter started in her stomach and bubbled up as she watched David's dramatic disgust with this new information. "Hopefully not a great deal longer. Just enough time for us to reach Virginia."

"And Master Jones will no doubt keep us close to shore as we travel, so we'll get to see lots of new sights."William nodded to David.

Her little brother furrowed his brow. "How will he know where it's safe to sail?"

Mary Elizabeth grimaced. "I don't know." She looked to William—hopefully he knew more about sailing than she did.

William took David by the shoulder and pointed. "See that man standing on the forecastle?"

"Aye."

"That man's job is to let the ship master know the depth."

"How does he know?"

Mary Elizabeth was just as curious as David, and she stepped forward too.

William chuckled. "He's got two different lead lines. So he's called the leadsman. One is a shorter line called a hand lead, and the other is called a dipsy lead or deep-sea lead. There's a large weight on the end of a long line that the leadsman heaves overboard. He measures the depth by how much line goes out."

"Oh. That makes sense." David nodded.

William pointed behind them to Master Jones standing high up on the aft castle poop deck. "From up there, Jones can see everything that's ahead. The leadsman shouts the depth, and then Master Jones can direct the helmsman who's in the small steerage room below him."

"Do you think we'll get there today?"

"Probably not."

"Well, that's no fun. I was hoping to run on shore today." David turned to Mary Elizabeth. "Don't forget about our race. You promised."

"I won't." The little imp. Of course he'd have to bring that up now.

William raised an eyebrow and smirked at her. "What's this?"

David rolled his eyes and sighed. "Mary Elizabeth says she's gonna race me when we get to the new land. She made a deal with me when I was sick. But you know girls. They're not very fast. Especially when they're old like she is."

William's laughter echoed over the whole deck.

It made Mary Elizabeth smile. "That's quite enough, David. You never know, I just might beat you in that race."

"I don't know." William gave her a wink. "You're awfully *old*."

Peter watched Lytton talking to those Saint people. Well at least he was occupied for the time being.

He looked around the deck. John Alden was on the other side, talking to some of the other passengers. Enough people were top deck that maybe Peter wouldn't be noticed if he snuck down below.

Making his way down the steps, the dim interior of the gun deck was in stark contrast to the sunlight from above. No one had thought to open up the gun ports yet today. Probably because they were all too worried about seeing land and how they would get to the right place.

It offered him the perfect opportunity to snoop.

As he came to Lytton's bed and trunk, he noticed the lock. Now why would a man lock his trunk unless he was hiding something? He'd have to make note of that to anyone who would listen when he brought all this to light. Another reason why Mr. William Lytton couldn't be trusted.

Peter dug around in the bed and came up with nothing.

The book he'd seen Lytton so diligently write in must be in the trunk.

Well, he wouldn't be able to keep it hidden forever.

The disagreements between the Saints and the Strangers would play right into Peter's hand. If he could keep them from working together, then he could accuse William of sabotage for his own gain, and the man would lose the trust of everyone.

Once word got back to the Merchant Adventurers, Peter could ask for the job.

Then all would be as it should.

The sunshine, the cold, crisp air, and the shore on the steerboard side of the *Mayflower* made William smile. They were here.

Soon they'd find a place for the settlement and begin to build. This first winter might be hard since they'd arrived so late, but the days of being stuck on a ship with no land in sight were finally over.

Mary Elizabeth had gone down below with David to help feed people too sick to move. But as the day progressed, many more of the weakened passengers made their way to the main deck. The calmer seas along with the knowledge that land was in sight was enough to rouse many from their beds.

William watched several people lean on the larboard bulwark. With all the excitement of the morning behind him, he had to admit there was gravity in their situation. This wouldn't be easy. The sixty-plus day journey had taken its toll on all of them. Most were weakened and on the verge of scurvy and who knew what else. Still many were bedridden with disease. Rations were low, and the beer barrels were almost empty.

"Avast! *Yaw, Yaw, Yaw!*"

William jerked his head toward the leadsman on the forecastle and then back to Jones on the aft castle. The leadsman pointed ahead.

Jones looked through his spyglass and barked commands to the crew.

Men climbed the masts like monkeys and began to work the five square sails. One man climbed out on the bowsprit to tame the sprit-sail. The *Mayflower* shifted its bow larboard, and William got a look at what lay ahead.

Roaring breakers and white-capped seas tumbled over one another. This was what the ship master had been worried about. The uncharted seas between Virginia and Cape Cod held dangers they knew nothing about.

Apparently, they were about to find out how dangerous.

Footsteps sounded behind William.

"What is it? What's going on?" Mary Elizabeth tugged on his arm.

"There seas ahead of us appear to be quite tumultuous." William pointed.

Mary Elizabeth gasped and put a hand over her mouth. "What should I do?"

"Make sure everyone is secure below and make sure all the gun ports and hatches are closed. . .just in case." William gave her hand a swift squeeze. He didn't have the right, but they'd been through so much together already and he wanted her to know his comfort. "And we really should pray."

Brewster stood on deck, directing his parishioners back below. His calm voice was reassuring and gentle. But William wondered what the man was thinking.

He looked heavenward. *Lord, You've brought Your people this far. They sure could use Your help.*

William wasn't sure about how to pray, but Mr. Brewster had told him just to talk to God. For now, that would have to do.

The wind was from the north pushing them south—which had been lovely and aimed them in the correct direction until they'd hit the breakers. Now they didn't have a way to turn around or break free from the dangerous water ahead.

Master Jones yelled commands that William didn't understand. How would he be able to get them through? The ship sat sideways dangerously close to getting swept into the current and tide that seemed to go every which direction.

As they were sucked into the waves, William got a closer look. These weren't just treacherous tides and breakers, there were shoals just below the surface that could cause them to shipwreck.

Lord, help us.

CHAPTER 18

After hours of fighting the seas and much prayer below decks, the *Mayflower* freed herself from the peril. Mary Elizabeth sat with her father and told him all about what had happened. She wasn't sure if he could hear her or not, but it soothed her heart to be able to share it with him.

The only problem now was that Master Jones had made a decision and turned them back toward Cape Cod.

"Father, I don't know what is going to happen. We don't have permission to settle there, but Mr. Jones fears it is too dangerous for us to venture on. We don't have enough food nor drink." She sighed and looked down at the frayed handkerchief in her lap. "While most of us are eager to have the sea journey over and be on dry land, there's still the problem with our patent. And so the bickering is back. Elder Brewster and Mr. Bradford are doing their best to calm everyone, but I am afraid it will be a mess."

"Miss Chapman?" The sound of William's deep voice made her stomach do a flip.

"I'm in here with Father."

He entered through the curtain and knelt beside her. "How is he doing?"

"He hasn't been awake for some time, but I was just telling him all about the adventures of the day." Mary Elizabeth smiled. She felt such a strong pull—a connection—to the man beside her. Even though she knew little about his past—and so many other things.

William covered her hand with his own. "I try to visit him often."

She ducked her head and felt the heat rush to her cheeks. "I know. Father told me."

"I don't wish to make you uncomfortable." He touched her cheek with his knuckle.

Mary Elizabeth shook her head. "Not at all. I'm glad you're here."

"I saw David a few minutes ago. He was entertaining the younger More children."

"He's been such a big help." She looked back down at the handkerchief. Awkward silence spread between them. Why couldn't they just share their hearts?

"Well, I thought maybe you'd like me to sit with your father while you go see Dorothy." William rescued her from saying something silly.

"Thank you. I know Father would like that." She hurried out through the curtain and put her hands to her cheeks. This was exactly why she'd never spent time with a young man before.

She had no idea what she was doing. William probably thought she was an ignorant and naive little girl.

Shaking her head, she went to see Dorothy. Her friend had gotten worse, and the Raynsfords weren't improving either. If only she could have a heart-to-heart chat with her friend right now. She needed guidance.

Dorothy opened her eyes a hair's breadth when Mary Elizabeth sat next to her. "Hi."

"Oh, my friend. How are you feeling?" Mary Elizabeth took Dorothy's chilled hand into her own.

"Not very good." Her lips were chapped, and was that blood between her teeth?

Mary Elizabeth worked to keep the tears at bay, but her eyes stung. "We'll have you better in no time. We should be in a safe harbor soon."

"They've spotted land?" Dorothy's voice cracked.

"Yes. And it's a glorious sight."

"God is good, isn't He, Mary Elizabeth?" She closed her eyes.

"Yes, He is, my friend."

"How's William?" Dorothy's lips stretched into a slight smile. "Are you betrothed yet?"

"Dorothy Raynsford, hush your mouth." Mary Elizabeth looked around to make sure no one was listening.

A half groan, half laugh escaped her friend's lips. "I have to tease you. You're my dearest friend."

"And you're mine. So I need you to fight whatever this is so you can tease me some more and keep me on my toes."

Dorothy gave a slight nod. "Give my little King David a hug."

"I will." Mary Elizabeth leaned down to kiss her friend's forehead. It was still so very hot, but Dorothy's hands were like ice in contrast. "I love you." Her whispered words floated in the air.

Dorothy was already asleep again.

Standing up, Mary Elizabeth left her friend's side and checked on a few of the sickest. Little Jasper More hadn't spoken in days, even though his siblings seemed to be improving. Then there was the beautiful Priscilla Mullins who'd been the first person to get seasick. As Mary Elizabeth went to check on her, she found the lady sitting up.

"Miss Mullins." Mary Elizabeth was shocked. "It's so good to see you up."

"Thank you, Miss Chapman. I hear you are the one I need to thank."

"For what?" Mary Elizabeth sat down next to her.

"For taking care of all of us." The young woman had to be around Mary Elizabeth's own age. But her cheeks were pale and thin.

"It was the Christian thing to do." Mary Elizabeth had never been good at taking compliments. She ducked her head.

"I hope that we can be friends." Priscilla's hand touched Mary Elizabeth's.

She nodded. "I'd like that very much. Is there anything I can do for you?"

"No. That is not unless you want to take me up the steps for some fresh air." Priscilla laughed. "I don't think I can walk yet, but I sure would love to see the sky."

"I don't think I could manage it on my own, but let me recruit some help."

"That would be lovely." Priscilla's smile lit up the dim area.

"I'll be back." Mary Elizabeth left with a lift to her spirits. Even surrounded by all these people for months on end, she'd felt alone in so many ways. And now God had seen fit to give her new friends. William, John, Priscilla. . . The future seemed very bright.

When she made it back to her quarters, William was still beside her father. "William, could you find John Alden for me?"

"Of course." He stood. "Can I be of assistance in any way?"

"Well, I was hoping John could carry Priscilla Mullins top deck, and then the four of us could see the stars together."

His smile filled his face.

"That sounds like a wonderful idea."

The brilliance of the night sky couldn't compare to the woman beside him. William watched Mary Elizabeth's face as she gazed at the canopy of stars above them.

"Do you know many of the constellations?" She looked at him, a sweet smile parting her red lips.

"Sadly, no." He pointed to the one he knew. "That's the Big Dipper. And that's the extent of my knowledge in the area." How could he tell her that he lived on the streets of London as a child and didn't have much schooling? Paul had helped him learn the basics. How to read and write quite well, and to work with sums. But there hadn't been time for anything else as he'd apprenticed as a carpenter. Would she think he was uneducated?

"That's all right. I don't remember many of them either. I guess I would make a paltry sailor." Her light laughter sounded like chimes in the air.

"What are the things you love most, Mary Elizabeth?" William leaned on the bulwark and stared at her profile as she looked into the sky. She was beautiful.

She turned her face to him and blinked several times. "Well. . .I'm not sure. No one's ever asked me that before."

"What do you love to do? What are your hopes and dreams?"

More blinking. But she didn't look away. "Love to do? Hmmm. . ." She bit her lip. "I enjoy cooking. And sewing. . . Is that what you mean?"

He smiled. "I just want to know more about you. Is that all you love to do? You also didn't answer about your hopes and dreams. . ."

"Well, I guess, I don't know what I love to do. I enjoy many things, but I've always been pretty. . .occupied with chores and work. As to your other question, I want what I presume every young woman wants. . .to marry and have a family." Her cheeks turned pink.

"Anything else?"

"To raise my children so that they love the Lord." She looked back to the sky. "What about you?"

William's heart pounded in his chest. "I always thought I wanted to do something important and be somebody influential. But now, my dreams have changed."

"In what way?" She turned back to him.

"I want to find love. Real love. Get married and raise a family." He gazed deep into her eyes. "And I want to help orphan children. Not just take them in and work them as servants, but show them that they are important too. That they are. . .loved."

"Oh, William." She took a step closer to him.

"Good evening," John called from the top step of the companionway. William took a deep breath and glanced at his friend.

"Would it be all right if we join you?" His friend carried a lovely young woman over to the steerboard bulwark.

Mary Elizabeth waved her arm. "Of course, that was the whole plan." She moved a crate closer to her. "Here's a place for Miss Mullins to sit in case she can't stand for very long."

"Oh, thank you, Mary Elizabeth." The other woman nodded.

John set her down on the crate. Then Mary Elizabeth wrapped

her in another blanket.

"Thank you, Mr. Alden."

John bowed. "It was my privilege, miss." He clapped his hands together and rubbed his arms. "It's a might chilly."

"I hadn't noticed." William gave Mary Elizabeth a smile.

"So…" John looked between William and Mary Elizabeth. "What are we talking about?"

CHAPTER 19

Saturday, 11 November 1620

As the sun rose in the east, the *Mayflower* rounded the top of the hook-shaped land that they'd all come to know was Cape Cod. William gathered with the other men to finalize the document that they all hoped would allow them to go ashore legally and with combined purpose.

The past day hadn't been a fun one.

Once the bickering started when Master Jones turned back to New England, they all knew some order would have to be made. Without the patent for their location, they wouldn't have land distributed to them once their obligations to the company were fulfilled. And without that same patent, the company had no right to govern. They either had to join together for the good of the settlement, or they would perish in disharmony. Everyone's livelihood depended upon them coming together.

Finally, a decision had been made and a document created. The men would all sign the document to create a government together. They would choose a leader together, work together, and get word back for their fellows in England to obtain the patent for the land they chose.

As the ship readied to lay anchor, each able-bodied man came forward to sign:

In the name of God, Amen. We whose names are underwritten, the loyal subjects of our dread Sovereign Lord King James, by the Grace of God of

Great Britain, France, and Ireland King, Defender of the Faith, etc.

Having undertaken for the Glory of God and advancement of the Christian Faith and Honour of our King and Country, a voyage to plant the First Colony in the Northern Parts of Virginia, do by these presents solemnly and mutually in the presence of God and one of another, covenant, and combine ourselves together in a civil body politic, for our better ordering and preservation and furtherance of the ends aforesaid; and by virtue hereof to enact, constitute and frame such just and equal laws, ordinances, acts, constitutions and offices from time to time, as shall be thought most meet and convenient for the general good of the Colony, unto which we promise all due submission and obedience. In witness whereof we have hereunder subscribed our names at Cape Cod, the 11th of November, in the year of the reign of our Sovereign Lord King James, of England, France and Ireland the eighteenth, and of Scotland the fifty-fourth. Anno Domini 1620.

Signed. . .

John Carver, William Bradford, Edward Winslow, William Brewster, Isaac Allerton, Myles Standish, John Alden, Samuel Fuller, Christopher Martin, William Mullins, William White, Richard Warren, John Howland, Stephen Hopkins, Edward Tilley, John Tilley, Francis Cooke, Thomas Rogers, Thomas Tinker, John Rigsdale, Edward Fuller, John Turner, Francis Eaton, James Chilton, John Crackstone, John Billington, Moses Fletcher, John Goodman, Degory Priest, Thomas Williams, Gilbert Winslow, Edmund Margesson, Peter Browne, Richard Britteridge, George Soule, Richard Clarke, Richard Gardiner, John Allerton, Thomas English, Edward Doty, Edward Leister

William watched as the men shook hands with John Carver, who'd been chosen as their first governor.

Now they could finally go ashore.

Master Jones had the *Mayflower* secured in the harbor just within the hook of Cape Cod, and the crew took care of the sails and rigging.

Governor Carver called the group together.

"Our first objective should be to get the shallop put back together. Master Jones has offered to use their longboat to take people back and forth to the shore, and the ship's carpenter will begin work on reconstructing the shallop."

William lifted his hand. "I'd be glad to assist with that, sir."

"Aye, and me." John Alden raised his hand.

"Good, good." Carver chose several other men who were able to stand more readily. Since most everyone had been sick, there weren't many who had strength to chop wood. "We will need you to go ashore and secure firewood." He turned to a couple other men. "I'll need you to search for a source of fresh water. Tomorrow is the Sabbath, so we must accomplish everything we can today."

The men nodded and set to work. Instead of being cooped up on a ship, they finally had a purpose. William followed John down to the gun deck, where the shallop was stored in pieces. Several people had been living within the pieces, and it had all taken a bruising during some of the fiercest storms.

Once the ship pieces were top deck, they were lowered into the long boat. "Go get your tools, men," Carver shouted.

William raced down the steps one more time. At the bottom, he ran into Mary Elizabeth. "I'm so glad to see you. I have been assigned to go ashore and work on the shallop. As soon as we can get it back together, we'll be able to explore the whole shoreline and find the spot for the settlement."

Her eyes twinkled as she gave him a small smile. "That's wonderful news, William. I'll be praying for you."

"Thank you. Now, I need to go fetch my tools." He turned to go to his quarters and then spun back around. He couldn't leave without saying one more thing. "Mary Elizabeth?"

"Yes?"

"I'll be thinking of you. . ."

"Aye." She ducked her head. "And I you."

The Sunday morning dawned bright and cheerful. Their first day ashore had brought them plenty of wood to burn, and many thankful prayers had been offered heavenward. The passengers who were strong enough stood gathered together on the main deck for their day of worship.

Even the Strangers who had been most against the Saints' rules and regulations gladly stood alongside and joined in on the praise to God and study of scripture. William was amazed.

God *had* been good to them. And now they were working together.

The only knot in the workings was the shallop. It would take days—possibly even weeks—to repair all the broken pieces and reassemble the small sailing vessel. While they had the longboat, it could only carry so many, and Master Jones was encouraging them to find a settlement as quickly as possible so he, his crew, and his ship could return to England. That meant the longboat would go with them.

Myles Standish decided to organize some groups to explore what they could on foot. But all that would have to wait. Because Sunday was their holy day.

Elder Brewster stood up on a crate and led them all in prayer. As William bowed his head, he felt a hand in his. After the *amen*, he looked beside him to find Mary Elizabeth. The beautiful red cloak was wrapped around her shoulders, and her eyes shone.

She released his hand and smiled. "Good morning."

"Good morning," he whispered, and his heart soared. She'd sought him out and held his hand. Before she appeared, William wondered how he would stay warm during the whole service, but now the cold couldn't touch him.

The people all sat down around the deck as their leader read from Psalm sixty-seven. For the first time in his life, William discovered a church service that wasn't boring. The words came alive and ministered to his heart.

" '...Let the people praise Thee, O God: let all the people praise thee. *Then* shall the earth bring forth her increase, & God, *even* our God shall bless us. God shall bless us, & all the ends of the earth shall fear him.' " Elder Brewster lowered his head for a moment in silence. When he raised it back up, his eyes held the sheen of tears. "My brothers and sisters, our God has indeed blessed us. And we will pray for the Lord to anoint the earth to yield her increase to us as we work in His name."

Several amens sounded around the deck.

"Let's look at Psalm seventy-one now. 'In thee, O Lord, I trust: let me never be ashamed. Rescue me and deliver me in thy righteousness: incline thine ear unto me, and save me. Be thou my strong rock.' "

The same psalm that Brewster had taken William through awhile back. It washed over him like a cleansing stream. *Yes, Lord, in You I put my trust.*

As he sat next to Mary Elizabeth, the meaning became even clearer. If he was going to be an honorable man worthy of her love and affection, he'd have to continually put his trust in the Lord. For the first time in his life, all the pain and despair of his past melted away. He didn't have to carry it around anymore, for the Lord was his refuge. The Lord was his strength. The Lord had given him hope.

Last night as he'd recorded all the day's happenings in the journal, he'd thought of Mary Elizabeth. Maybe it was time to tell her everything about his past. Maybe it was time to tell her how he cared for her.

He looked at the beautiful lady next to him. Could he deserve such a love?

Taking her hand in his, he gave it a squeeze. She may not understand now, but he would explain it to her one day.

Hopefully soon.

CHAPTER 20

Wednesday, 15 November 1620

Mary Elizabeth stretched her back and stood at the bulwark, watching the men go ashore. For two days, she'd done nothing but help the women with their laundry. Lots and lots of laundry. Two months' worth. While most of them wore the same clothes the entirety of the voyage, they now had a newborn aboard in addition to the younger children who needed changes of clothes more often than the adults. But her heart ached a bit watching the men leave. Even though the work of laundry had been grueling, it gave her the chance to go ashore and stand on solid ground again for the first time in weeks. And it didn't hurt that she'd been able to see William as he worked on the shallop.

Shaking her head, she tried to focus on something else. Thoughts of William seemed to invade her mind a lot these days.

And she wouldn't be seeing him at all today since they were separated, so there was no use wallowing in that. Mary Elizabeth turned her gaze back to the ship's deck. Looking around, she placed her hands on her hips. What could she be thankful for?

They made it across the ocean and didn't shipwreck.

There was access to land and prayerfully they'd find fresh water.

But so many were still sick. Her heart sank.

Shaking her head, Mary Elizabeth closed her eyes. She wouldn't allow her thoughts to go there. Father and Dorothy would get better now that they were anchored and safe.

And at least the horrific stench was finally going away on the gun deck. Since they'd been at anchor for several days and the weather was relatively calm, the seasickness had finally stopped. Many still suffered from disease which she could only assume was scurvy. That's what she should concentrate on. Helping the sick.

She'd been doing it for weeks, and it was a useful occupation of her mind. Turning back to the bulwark, she determined to see the men reach shore and then get back to work. It was the least she could do to help the surgeon.

Poor Mr. Heale. Mary Elizabeth found out that he'd hired on as the ship's surgeon and it had been his first contract on a ship since he'd only finished his apprenticeship the August prior. With so much sickness and two already dead, it had to be difficult for the poor man. Several of the sailors had been injured during one of the storms, and now he had this scurvy problem.

They'd relied on him a lot. But he was just as anxious to get back to England as the rest of the crew because he'd filed his intent to marry Mary Jarrett back in London. New resolve flooded through her. She would do whatever she could to help.

If only Mr. Fuller could fully recover. The man was a doctor but had also been too sick to help anyone else. They'd definitely need him if they were to survive the winter.

The men reached the shore and waved back to the *Mayflower*. The longboat would come back for another group of men to scavenge for food and water.

She turned from the bulwark and headed for the steps. Every muscle in her body ached from all that scrubbing, but at least it had kept her busy and her mind off William.

She would miss seeing his face.

She shook her head. Time to get her mind off of her handsome carpenter. Dorothy needed her and so did Father, along with the many others who still suffered.

When she reached the gun deck, the gun ports and hatches were all open and a nice, crisp breeze helped to air out the tight space. David sat in the middle of the floor spinning his top for several of the younger children.

The voyage across the ocean had changed him. He'd not only grown in stature but also in maturity. Helping with everything from emptying chamber pots to feeding those too weak to feed themselves, David was a bright spot on the ship. It made her heart swell to think of her little brother bringing joy to others around them.

She worked her way back to their little, curtained-off area that had been home for so long. While it had been safe and secure on the ship, she couldn't help but look forward to the day when they had a home again.

"Mary Elizabeth, is that you?"

She raced to Father's side and knelt down. "It's me. I'm so sorry I wasn't here when you awoke."

"Don't worry, child. I just opened my eyes when I heard your footsteps."

"It's good to hear your voice." She couldn't help it; the tears sprang to her eyes unbidden.

He reached up to touch her cheek. "Don't cry on my behalf."

She pasted on a smile. "Would you like me to open the curtain so you can see some of the light coming in?"

Father nodded.

Pulling the curtain aside at his feet, she hoped the light shining toward his face would be pleasant.

"That's nice, Mary Elizabeth. Thank you for thinking of that." He patted the spot beside him. "Come, sit." His breaths came in short gasps when he spoke.

Taking her place, she placed a hand on his forehead. "Is there anything you need or that I could get for you?"

"No. I just need to speak to my daughter." His eyes turned sad. "I miss your mother."

"I do too."

He laid a hand on hers. "What I'm trying to say is that I think it's time for the Lord to. . .take me home." A single tear slipped down his cheek. He swallowed and took a shaky breath.

Mary Elizabeth shook her head. "No, Father, don't say—"

"Hush, child. Let me speak. I will want to speak to David while I still have the energy, but I need you to know. . .that I trust you to raise him up in the Lord."

Emotion swelled into her throat. No. He couldn't be dying, could he?

"The papers in the trunk are in order." He paused for a moment. "Elder Brewster saw to that yesterday. . . . You will inherit my share. . .along with yours and the property allotted to. . .David." He closed his eyes for a moment and took several long but shallow breaths. "The seven-year contract should go by fast and. . .you will be well set for your future."

"But Father. . ." Great sobs shook her shoulders as the tears streaked down her face.

"No, Mary Elizabeth. It's time. . . I know it is. I only asked the Lord for enough energy to speak to you one last time." He took another shaky breath. "That young Mr. Lytton is a good man. Elder Brewster speaks highly. . .of him."

She nodded.

"Do you love him, Mary Elizabeth?"

"I. . .I don't know. . .but I think I might."

Father lifted his lips in a slight smile. "Your mother and I always wished that. . .you would marry for love as we did. . . . We were ready to arrange a marriage for you. . .if that was what you wanted." He patted her hand and then put his arm back across his chest. His breaths were rapid and short. "If William joins the congregation, you have my full blessing, my child."

"But Father, I want. . .no I *need* you to be there for my wedding. Can't you please fight this disease?"

"You have no need but that of a relationship with your Savior, my child." He closed his eyes again. It seemed to take all his strength just to speak.

"Father, please, don't waste all your energy on me."

He shook his head. "It's not a waste. . . . I would want nothing more than to see my daughter wed, if. . .I wasn't called home to the Lord. . . . You have to let me go, Mary Elizabeth. You have to be strong. . . . For David. For William. . . For the colony."

She sucked in a breath and nodded her head.

"I love you, my beautiful, precious daughter."

"I love you too, Papa."

"Go get David, I don't have much left in me."

Mary Elizabeth stood and kissed her father on the forehead, then called down the deck for David.

"Mary Elizabeth?"

"Yes, Father?"

"Would you ask one of the elders to come pray with me?"

"Of course." She stepped out of their quarters.

David ran toward her and stopped short when he saw her face. "Is everything all right?"

She hugged him tight and crouched down in front of him. "I need you to be very brave. Father wants to speak to you, and he doesn't think he'll be with us for much longer. Can you be strong for him?"

"Yes, Mary Elizabeth. I'm a man now." He strode purposefully toward Father's bed.

Her heart squeezed with emotion for her little brother. So much heartache at such a young age.

With a deep breath, she swallowed her tears and went to fulfill her father's request.

William climbed aboard the *Mayflower*, exhausted and sore. Night had fallen, and they expected the crew of explorers would stay ashore as they'd journeyed a great distance down the cape. The shallop was in such sad shape that it would take them weeks to put it back together again. If they had the right materials, they could construct it faster, but they had to work with what they had. No matter the time involved, he was willing to do whatever was necessary to help their group accomplish its goal. The barren wilderness surrounded them in this unoccupied territory. It would probably take a long time to explore it all and find a decent spot to settle. Winter was already upon them.

He longed for his bed and something to eat. But more than that, he hoped he could see Mary Elizabeth. It would be a lift to his spirits.

A good fire was going in the firebox as William stepped onto the main deck with the other men who'd been working on the smaller ship. He moved closer to it and warmed his hands from the damp ride over.

"William?" Mary Elizabeth appeared around the mast in her red cloak.

"Aye." He moved toward her. The firelight shone on her face. It was streaked with tears. "What's happened?"

"It's Father. He spoke to me earlier." She swiped at a cheek. "Told me that he didn't think he would be here much longer and asked to speak to David."

"Is he. . . ?"

"He fell back to sleep but hasn't moved since."

"May I go see him?"

She nodded.

When they reached the top of the steps, William took her in his arms. "I'm so sorry, Mary Elizabeth. I'm so sorry I wasn't here."

She pulled back and with a nod headed down the steps.

William knelt next to Mr. Chapman's bed with Mary Elizabeth beside him. David sat on the other side holding his Father's right hand. The man was so still. So peaceful looking. If it wasn't for the slight rise and fall of his chest, William would've thought that he was already gone.

After they'd been by the man's side for about an hour, William was at a loss for what to say or do. *Lord, I don't know what to do. But please comfort Mary Elizabeth and David.*

Mr. Chapman gasped and opened his eyes.

"Father?" Mary Elizabeth leaned forward.

He blinked several times and looked over to William. "Mr. Lytton."

"Aye, I'm here. Please call me William."

"I'd like to call you. . .son."

"Sir, I'm honored."

Mr. Chapman gasped again. "Take. . .care of them. . .for me."

"Yes, sir. I will."

Mr. Chapman closed his eyes. A long, last tremor of air left his body.

Mary Elizabeth put a hand to her father's chest. She shook her head. "No. He can't be gone." Sobs shook her body.

David sniffed, and a single tear slid down his cheek.

Reaching out a hand to David, William wrapped his other arm around Mary Elizabeth's shoulders. The road before them just became tougher than he could have ever imagined.

CHAPTER 21

David watched the men carry his Father's bundled body up the companionway. It wasn't supposed to be this way. They were supposed to all come to the New World together and start a new life.

Wasn't it bad enough that Mother had died?

He swiped a hand under his nose and sniffed. He wouldn't cry. He had to completely be a man now. He was the only Chapman male left.

The sun wasn't up yet and probably wouldn't be for a good hour. But Mary Elizabeth stood straight and tall next to him. She'd cried a lot during the night, and now she just stood there.

Mr. Brewster came up to them. "We are here for you two if you need anything. The colony is your family. Trust in the Lord for His strength to carry you through."

Mary Elizabeth nodded.

David sniffed.

The men came to the side, and David sucked in a deep breath.

Mr. Brewster prayed.

They dropped Father into the sea.

Mary Elizabeth shook beside him and grabbed his hand.

More than anything, David wanted to run. But there wasn't anywhere to go. Nowhere to hide. And there were people everywhere.

This wasn't how it was supposed to be.

"Mary Elizabeth, I. . ." William stood in front of them, his hat in his hands. "I don't know what to say."

"There's nothing to say, William, but thank you."

David looked up to the man who had tears in his eyes. "It's not fair, William. It's not *fair*." He threw himself into the older man's arms.

"Oh, David." Mary Elizabeth put a hand on his head.

William held him for a few minutes and let him cry. "There's nothing wrong with a man shedding tears, David."

He nodded against William's coat. He wanted to curl up in a ball and cry in his bed, but he couldn't do that to Mary Elizabeth. She needed him.

William pulled back and crouched down in front of him. "Why don't we sit down for a minute and talk. There's something I want to talk to you both about."

David sat on the deck while William pulled up a crate for Mary Elizabeth. His heart felt ripped apart.

"My parents died when I was a baby." William paced for a moment and then sat next to David.

Mary Elizabeth started to cry.

He reached out and took her hand. "I was given to family members to raise me. And I'm sad to say they weren't very nice. When I was nine years old, they threw me out into the streets of London to fend for myself."

David leaned forward. *He* was almost nine. "What did you do?"

William shrugged. "I scrounged for food, worked every job I could find, and slept under people's porches, bridges, in abandoned buildings—you get the idea."

"How long did you do that?" Mary Elizabeth chimed in as she wiped tears from her cheeks.

"About four years. Until a really nice man named Paul Brookshire found me in an alley one day digging in the garbage for food. He took me home, cleaned me up, bought me new clothes, and told me I could stay for as long as I wanted.

"I wasn't very nice to Paul at first, because I had been treated badly by adults and teased by other kids. But Paul wore me down with his kindness. Over time, he taught me everything I'd missed in school, and he began to train me as a carpenter."

"What happened next?" David couldn't believe that tall, strong William had gone through all that.

"Well, I apprenticed for him and worked in his shop until Paul had this grand idea for me to go to the New World. You see, I was still miserable. Didn't think that anyone would ever think anything of me except I was an orphan, and orphans were looked down upon. But Paul had been talking to me about God. He'd taken me to church. Told me how valuable I was to God and to him. I couldn't understand a loving heavenly Father because I'd never had an earthly father who loved me.

"At the time, I couldn't see that Paul had loved me like a son for all those years. That he had been trying to share with me the love of God through how he cared for me."

"Why isn't Paul with you?" David furrowed his brow. The Paul fellow sounded like a good man.

"Well, I was just getting to that. You see, Paul was sick, and the doctor told him he was dying. So he bought me passage on the *May-flower* and purchased shares for me in the venture. Before he died, he made me promise to make the most of my life, throw off the baggage of the past, and seek God."

"Paul died too?" It didn't seem fair. William had never had anyone in his life who cared, and then when that man came along, he died. David didn't know what to think about that.

"Yes, he did." William took a deep breath. "But that's not the end of the story. I came on this voyage to do what I'd promised, 'make the most of my life,' but what I didn't know at the time is that I couldn't do that without seeking God first. I've faced a lot of loss, David. I've had people treat me poorly. But it wasn't until I found salvation through Jesus Christ and my new faith that I was able to let go of the past. Paul knew I'd been carrying it around like heavy baggage. He loved me enough to set my feet on the path, but he knew I had to find this out for myself."

"Is that why you've been talking to Elder Brewster?"

"Yes, David." William chuckled. "I've asked him to teach me. And then I went to your father."

"You did?"

"Aye. And soon I will spend time with Mr. Bradford, because your father arranged for him to be an adviser to me, and I have a lot to learn still. But the point I'm trying to make is that for twenty years, I've thought I was alone. But I'm not. God's always been right there."

David looked at Mary Elizabeth and the way she looked at William. Then he looked down at their hands. They were intertwined.

"God is right here with you too, David. You're not alone. And your sister and I will be here for you, and the whole congregation. . ."

Hot tears streamed down David's face. No, he wasn't alone.

William opened his arms, and David ran into them.

He missed Father, and he didn't understand why God had to take him to heaven, but William was right.

He wasn't alone. If only it didn't hurt so much.

The sight of her little brother clinging to William made Mary Elizabeth's heart melt. She'd had no idea of what William had been through. All this time, she'd thought of him as a strong and capable man. She'd never known that inside he'd been so hurt and alone.

Although she should have guessed.

The nightmares he had during his fever had made her heart ache. Now she understood.

David pulled back from William and then hugged Mary Elizabeth. He whispered in her ear. "I love you."

"I love you too."

"Do you think Elder Brewster would have time to talk to me, Mary Elizabeth?"

She lowered her brows. "Well, of course, he would. Do you need me to go with you?"

"No. I want to do it alone."

"All right."

Her little brother walked off, a deep sag to his shoulders. The normal spring in his step was gone, but he'd just said goodbye to his father. Could she blame him?

William stood and held out a hand to her. "We will be getting ready to go ashore soon so we can work on the shallop."

"Aye." She looked down at the deck.

"I wish I could stay with you, Mary Elizabeth."

Tears pricked her eyes again. "I wish you could too. But they need your help, and I can't be selfish."

"Mary Elizabeth." He took both of her hands in his and pulled her closer. The deep blue of his eyes seemed darker in the early morning hours. "I know I don't have any right to be saying this—especially on today of all days—but I can't let another minute go by without sharing what's on my heart."

She held her breath.

"I care for you a great deal, Mary Elizabeth Chapman. And I intend to court you and seek you as my wife."

"Truly?" The words left on an exhale.

"Your father and I spoke of it often toward the end. And I want to honor him. . .and David too."

The love in his eyes overwhelmed her, and she had to look down at their hands.

Releasing one hand, he lifted her chin back up. "I need you to look in my eyes, Mary Elizabeth. Tell me the truth. Do you care for me too?"

"I do."

He crushed her against him in a great hug and whispered, "You've made me the happiest man alive." He released her once again and stepped back. "Forgive me." He smirked.

"There's nothing to forgive, William."

He took another step back. "I should be off. I need to gather my tools and such for the day."

"All right." She gave him a smile.

"May I see you tonight?"

"Of course. We can look at the stars together."

"I'd like that." With a wink, he turned on his heel and headed down the companionway.

Mary Elizabeth turned back toward the bulwark and looked at the sea below. Somewhere in the depths, the earthly shell of her father was laid to rest. But she knew he wasn't there. The scripture from 2 Corinthians, chapter five, she'd heard Pastor Robinson speak over her mother's grave came back to mind. *'Nevertheless, we are bold, & love rather to remove out of the body, and to dwell in the Lord.'*

Father dwelt with the Lord and would see Mother again. The thought gave her a little joy. The coming days would be difficult, and she had no idea how it would all work out. But she would rest in the Lord, as well. Because He was her rock and her strength.

Two tears dripped into the sea, and she lifted her face toward the sky. "Goodbye, Father. We'll be all right."

CHAPTER 22

Monday, 20 November 1620

The weather was bitter and dreary. Since Father's passing, Mary Elizabeth hadn't seen William much, and David had gone ashore to help stack wood while the men chopped. He'd insisted that he do his part, and Mary Elizabeth couldn't deny him wanting to work for their survival. While he was still small for his age, he'd begun to grow and build strength.

The weight of finding a settlement rested on every man, woman, and child's mind. It needed to happen fast. But circumstances weren't cooperating.

As she stirred the fire in the fire box, she worked to keep the grief and doubt from overwhelming her. What could she be thankful for?

Wood. She was very thankful for wood. They'd gone so long without it on the voyage over that she never wanted to take it for granted again. She'd be able to cook fish for everyone today, and that would be a treat.

David. Another bright spot in her life. It may have been the Lord's will for Mother and Father to leave this earth, but at least she wasn't alone.

Oh, and William. She was very thankful for him. She'd never been in love, but she assumed this was what it felt like. New understanding of the emotion helped her to understand the fervent love between first, Christ and His church, and second, a husband and wife—ideas that were shared in scripture. Although she'd never want to admit to the elders that she had spent some time studying Song of Solomon.

Thoughts of love made her cheeks heat. She missed William. He spent his days on the shore working with several others to rebuild the shallop that they desperately needed if they were to explore farther. It was difficult not getting to see him—especially after his declaration—but she knew it was for the best.

The first group of explorers came back with a tale of seeing six men and a dog that ran for the woods. The stories had been circulating for days that it must have been Indians and the *Mayflower* voyagers weren't here alone. Everyone thought of it as good news. They would need help farming in this new land, and it would be very advantageous to trade with native people. A few naysayers, though, kept churning up worry about the dangers the Indians could present.

But explorers also came back with dried corn they found buried in mounds in the ground. Mary Elizabeth wasn't too sure why they did what they did—other than the thoughts of their own survival—but she didn't say anything when the group returned. Unsure of what she thought about them "stealing" from other people, she prayed that their leaders would make good choices. The men insisted they were borrowing it for the good of the colony and they would pay the owners for it. Mary Elizabeth could only hope that it would be true and the owners wouldn't hunt them down in retaliation.

The men had gotten lost in vast thickets and woods and had trouble finding drinkable water until they finally found some fresh-water ponds.

Something else to be thankful for—they finally had access to fresh water.

Overall, the expedition didn't seem to result in much. No. She couldn't resort to negative thinking again. She needed to stay positive.

After everyone had listened to the men relay their experiences, the stories took on new life as they were shared from group to group. One version even stated that the corn seed that was dug up was found in graves and the natives would certainly come in the night and kill them all for such desecration.

Mary Elizabeth shook her head. The men said they had found

a grave, yes, but they'd put it back to rights when they knew what it was. They really needed to settle somewhere soon and get off this ship. Maybe that would help keep the gossip at bay.

Cleaning the cod a couple of men had caught that morning, Mary Elizabeth took a moment to look around her. While so many were finally up and about again and recovered from their seasickness, just as many had become sicker. Samuel Fuller was on his feet again and tried to help the people with his doctoring skills as much as possible, but disease had taken hold.

And this worried her. Winter was upon them. They had no shelter other than the ship they'd been living on for months already.

Without Father, she wondered what would happen to her and David. Would they need to live with the Raynsfords until they could build their own home?

The smell from the fish in her hand brought her back to the task at hand. It didn't do any good to worry about the future. Right now she had mouths to feed.

After their luncheon of fish, Mary Elizabeth went to check on each person who was still bedridden. Maybe she could do laundry for those who couldn't do it themselves. Clean clothes might help them feel better. Armed with a new plan, she went to Dorothy's bedside to check on her friend.

"Mary Elizabeth." Her friend's voice was weak in the greeting.

"How are you feeling today?"

Dorothy shook her head, and tears came loose at the corners of her eyes.

"I am so sorry." Mary Elizabeth sat and took Dorothy's hands in hers.

"I'm scared."

Closing her eyes, she searched her mind for the words to say. *Lord, guide me.* She thought of Psalm fifty-six. " 'When I was afraid, I trusted in thee. I will rejoice in God *because* of his word, I trust in

God, & will not fear what flesh can do unto me.'"

Dorothy relaxed a bit. "Thank you, I needed to hear those words. 'When I was afraid, I trusted in thee.'"

"I wish I could do more for you, my friend."

"You've been taking care of me for so long. You're doing everything you can."

"I still wish it was more."

"You've changed, Mary Elizabeth." Dorothy's voice crackled. "You're so much stronger and braver now. I'm proud of you."

"I owe much to you. Because you believed in me."

A faint smile lifted Dorothy's lips. "And I always will." Her eyes closed. "'I will not fear what flesh can do unto me. . .'" She squeezed Mary Elizabeth's hand. "Keep praying for me, Mary Elizabeth."

"I will."

"So. . .what can you talk about while I rest? I know. . . . Tell me about William."

"He's doing well. He's working on the shallop, so I don't get to see him very often. But it's for the best of the settlement. We all have to do what we can." She looked down. It appeared Dorothy was asleep, but she'd keep talking just in case. "It gets tedious, taking care of people and feeding people. I have to say, because of the change of scenery, it's nice to go ashore and do laundry. But I'm really looking forward to the day when we have houses built and can start to live off this new land.

"William is a wonderful carpenter. He's talked about building furniture and houses, and I can't wait to see the beautiful work he'll do in the colony. He spoke to my father, you know. And he declared his intentions to court me. I can't tell you how much that thrilled me to hear those words. But this is all so new. I don't know what I'm doing."

"It's all right, because I don't know what I'm doing either." William's voice startled her.

She put a hand to her throat and once again felt the fiery heat fill her cheeks. "You surprised me."

"I had to come see you. They were bringing a load of wood back to the ship, and I needed a few more tools."

Pulling herself together, she looked down. Goodness, what had he overheard? "I'm glad you did."

He knelt beside her. "I didn't mean to intrude on your private conversation. That's why I made my presence known." Lifting her chin with his finger, he ducked his head and looked into her eyes. "Will you forgive me?"

"Of course." His eyes drew her in and whisked the world away.

"Mary Elizabeth. . .I. . ."

"Yes?"

"I love you." Leaning in, William kissed her softly.

❈

Peter followed William to his quarters. Lytton opened his trunk and pulled out the journal and several other things and set them aside. He dug around and pulled out a couple of tools.

He placed the other items back in and shut the lid.

"Mr. Lytton?"

"Yes?" William turned, his brow furrowed.

"I'd like to speak to you about training as a carpenter."

The man relaxed. "Go ahead. But I need to get back to the longboat."

"Let me walk with you then." Peter headed for the steps to the upper deck. "Have you ever considered taking on an apprentice?"

"Hmmm. . ." He raised his eyebrows. "Can't say that I have."

"Do you think—after the settlement is established, obviously— you might think of taking me on?"

William walked over to the longboat. "It's definitely something I'll need to pray about."

Peter offered his hand to shake. "I appreciate that."

"Good day." William nodded and went back to the other boat.

Pasting a smile on his face until the boat was lowered out of sight, Peter congratulated himself. If his eyes hadn't deceived him, he'd interrupted Mr. Lytton before he had a chance to place the lock back on his trunk.

He took the steps back down to the gun deck and snuck over to where William kept his trunk.

Indeed. The lock wasn't in place.

Peter glanced around and then opened the lid and pulled out the journal. Flipping through the pages, he saw just what he needed.

And it fit with his plan.

Perfectly.

William shivered in the cold as he climbed onto the deck of the *Mayflower* and gazed back out to the shore. The shallop had been finished, and they'd taken it out on another exploration with Master Jones accompanying the group. Other than finding more corn and beans—along with several other graves—they'd only come to the conclusion that the whole area they'd surveyed wouldn't work for their settlement. They needed good land and a safe harbor and plenty of fresh water.

Discouragement had taken over several of the men. It hadn't helped that half a foot of snow had fallen one night and made it that much harder to trudge through the thick terrain. A few men developed bad coughs and deep colds. That fact didn't boost matters or morale, either.

God, I don't understand what You are doing. I don't want to complain, but we sure could use Your assistance.

Before he left a few days ago, he'd noticed the decline in the Raynsfords as well as a few others. Mary Elizabeth rarely left Dorothy's side as her friend suffered with an illness that Mr. Heale could only describe as a bad case of pneumonia compounded with scurvy. And William didn't want to pull her away from the Raynsfords. They were the closest thing to family—other than David—that Mary Elizabeth had left.

Once again, the feeling of loneliness took up residence in his heart. He didn't have any good reason for it, and when he took the time to examine it, he knew it wasn't true. But they all were desperate for some good news—something encouraging and uplifting. And he was tired.

Young David Chapman ran across the deck and greeted him. "William!"

"It's good to see you, David." He hugged the boy and crouched down in front of him.

"Did you find where we can build?"

"Not yet, I'm afraid." William let out a sigh.

"Well, we've got some exciting news." The boy bounced up and down. "Susanna White had her baby. It's a boy, and they named him Peregrine."

"Now that *is* good news." William stood and lifted his face to the sky. Guess the good Lord was listening after all. Maybe he needed to work on his attitude. "How are the Raynsfords doing?"

David shook his head. "Not very good, I'm afraid."

Movement and shuffling behind him reminded William that he needed to help. "How about you catch me up on the news later this evening after I help unload the shallop?"

"We can sit by the fire and look up at the stars?"

"Absolutely, as long as you stay warm enough. Please tell your sister I'm back and I will come see her as soon as I'm done."

"All right, I can do that."

"Thanks, David."

"I'm glad you're back."

"Me too."

William went over to where the men were working and hefted his tools and an armload of wood. Funny how a simple conversation could change his outlook. He needed to fight the discouragement and loneliness. The Lord had blessed him, and he would be thankful.

Now all he needed was to see Mary Elizabeth.

Monday, 4 December 1620

"Dorothy. . .please. . .no. . ." Great sobs wracked Mary Elizabeth's body. Her face was wet with tears, and she didn't think she could breathe as her throat clogged with grief. She shook her friend's shoulders again, but Dorothy didn't respond.

Mr. and Mrs. Raynsford had passed sometime in the night. Their bodies were white and stiff. Now Dorothy's breathing had slowed, and Mary Elizabeth knew deep in her heart that her friend was leaving.

This couldn't be happening. Not after all they'd been through. Dorothy had never even stepped foot in the New World, and she'd been the one so excited about this new adventure. *God, why?*

"You've been the best friend I could have ever asked for." Mary Elizabeth sucked in a deep breath. "This was *your* adventure. I was just along to be by your side. You can't leave me now. . . ." Sobs overtook her, and she cried out her anguish over Dorothy's still form.

"Mary Elizabeth. . ." A warm arm wrapped around her shoulders.

She sat up and found William kneeling beside her. "Oh, William. . ." Her grief washed over in great waves of pain. She went into his arms. How was this possible? Vibrant and joyous Dorothy? No. It couldn't be happening. No.

Pulling back, she looked into William's face. "Thank you for coming down here. I just can't bear it. First Mother, then Father. . .and now. . ." She buried her face back in his shoulder.

"I want to be here for you, Mary Elizabeth."

All she could manage was a nod as she pulled back again. Wiping the tears from her face, she looked back to her friend. "She's been my best friend. . .all my life. I was always the hesitant one, she the adventurer."

"Her spirit will live on though. You can keep her memory alive and honor her through how you live your life."

"I know that it's selfish of me to want her to stay here when she has heaven waiting for her, but I wish she could be *here*. . . ." Tears poured from her eyes as she leaned over her friend and kissed her forehead. "Go with God, Dorothy."

Her friend took a short breath, and Mary Elizabeth felt the air brush her face.

Dorothy didn't breathe again.

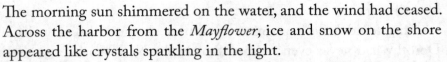

The morning sun shimmered on the water, and the wind had ceased. Across the harbor from the *Mayflower*, ice and snow on the shore appeared like crystals sparkling in the light.

Dorothy had always loved the snow. She'd loved winter. It was a pity she hadn't seen the beauty in the winter here. She'd never even been top deck to see the land.

And now men carried the bodies of the entire Raynsford family and young Edward Thompson, who'd also died in the night, out into the glorious sunlit top deck. All to see them buried at sea. Mary Elizabeth's heart broke a little at the thought.

William's steady presence at her side gave her the strength to stand. But there were no words. Her heart felt like it had been broken into a million pieces. How was she ever to put it back together again?

Elder Brewster spoke a brief prayer, and several people cried. No grave would be dug. No marker. Nothing to commemorate these people's lives.

Only the memories that the Leyden congregation would carry with them.

The little group of Saints and Strangers had banded together in hopes to build a thriving colony across the ocean away from everyone and everything they'd known. Now those numbers had decreased, along with their supplies and so much of their strength.

The men lifted a body.

Mary Elizabeth looked down. She couldn't watch.

Splashes of water told her when it was over. The mood on deck was quiet, somber. Sickness seemed to have hold of too many, and it created an unspoken fear among the passengers.

Would *any* of them survive the winter?

Wednesday, 6 December 1620

As the shallop left the *Mayflower* again, William hoped it would be the last expedition needed. This one had to prove profitable or they'd have no hope of getting anything built before spring. Already the weather had turned worse with rain, sleet, and snow a constant companion. Master Jones also voiced his displeasure and encouraged the passengers to search daily for a place so he and his crew could return to England.

William had great hopes that he'd be able to speak to Elder Brewster about what he needed to do to become betrothed to Mary Elizabeth on this trip. He'd already asked to join the Saints' congregation but would have to wait to be baptized until the water warmed. His new faith had given him so much joy, and he looked forward to the future with great anticipation. Mr. Bradford had been a wealth of wisdom and knowledge, and William found that studying the scriptures daily was his favorite part of the day.

But with the deaths of the Raynsfords so fresh, he didn't want to intrude on Mary Elizabeth's grief. He wanted to give her time. It didn't stop him from longing for the day when he could plan for building their own house in the settlement. He wanted her to know that he loved her and David and would do everything he could to give them the best life he could offer.

Waiting was not his favorite occupation. He'd already waited so long to get this far, and now he was ready for his new life to begin. Tension filled the air around him. It must be heavy on everyone's minds. The need to move forward with life. To locate a settlement and start building.

The *Mayflower's* pilot—John Clarke—and master's mate—Robert Coppin—led their expedition, along with the master gunner and three other sailors. Sickness and the freezing temperatures kept many of the other men aboard the main ship, so they only had half the men they took on the last expedition. But William was hopeful.

They would find a good place for the settlement. He was sure of it.

They hadn't journeyed far when the salty spray began to freeze on the men's clothes. But they pushed forward with their sail and watched the coastline for people, another good anchorage, or a good river. When the evening came with nothing to show for it, they anchored and went ashore to build a barricade and sleep.

The next morning, they were certain they had seen people, and a few men set out on foot to explore while some went in the shallop. But the natives weren't to be found.

William and the others found several more graves but no sign of anyone alive. Were they truly alone in this vast wilderness? He understood that it would be good to connect with others, but it distracted them from their purpose. Besides, William wasn't too sure the natives would like to find out that some of their corn had been taken.

The men trudged on in icy conditions, and again no suitable site was found. After a good deal of discussion on the shallop, they finally went ashore again to call it a day. William helped build a fire, while Mr. Coppin talked with some of the leaders. He talked of a harbor around the bay and north up the coast that he called Thievish Harbor. Since he had sailed to this area before, they all agreed it would be good to head in that direction the next morning. Maybe they would have better luck, or Providence would guide them to a suitable location. The weary men once again barricaded themselves and slept ashore.

The cold and lack of progress wearied William. He was a man of action, and here it was December and they hadn't even decided where to build. Sleep was hard to come by, but he finally drifted off with thoughts of Mary Elizabeth.

Horrible screams brought him out of his sleep. Were they being attacked?

The screams sounded again. This time closer.

Having no experience with a musket, William watched as the other men scrambled for their weapons. The fog of sleep still hung over his head, and he wasn't sure if this was a dream. But as he crawled behind a rock, an arrow hit the sand beside him.

Indians!

Fascination drove him to peek around the rock, but he couldn't see a thing. He swiped a hand down his face. What could he do?

Arrows flew and musket fire sounded in the air. Several of their company took off after the native warriors, chasing them into the thick growth.

William's heart pounded. It definitely hadn't been a warm welcome. Did the Indians know that their group had taken corn and beans from their stores?

He wasn't a leader or anyone important, yet he felt the need to make peace. If these were going to be their only neighbors, shouldn't they try to befriend them rather than shoot them? Maybe the Indians were just afraid of an attack and they shot arrows as a warning. Or maybe other travelers from afar had been unkind to them. Hadn't Coppin told them all that he'd been here before? Perhaps other ships had too.

William and another man waited back at their barricade. But without anything to defend themselves, they would be easy targets if the Indians came back before the other men.

A shiver raced up his spine. He couldn't think that way. Peace had been his previous thoughts, and no matter the fear in his mind, he needed to focus on that.

The minutes dragged by. William sat close to the fire, attempting to stay warm. When the other men ran back into their little barricade, a sigh of relief rushed out of him upon learning none were hurt. But what of the Indians?

Too many things were unknown. Many of the men were uncertain about what even happened. Roused out of their sleep by the screams, no one could remember who struck first.

William shook his head. One thing was sure: they hadn't made a friendly impression on the Indians, and hopes of building trade with them dwindled.

The icy wind did nothing to help Mary Elizabeth's mood as she stood at the bulwark and stared out at the water. *Why* had they left Holland? Why were they here? The burdens had been too much for her to bear. Seven-year-old Jasper More died of sickness the day the expedition team had left; William Bradford's wife, Dorothy, fell off the ship and drowned in the icy waters with no one to help her; and then James Chilton, the oldest man among the passengers, passed away.

In three days' time, they'd lost three more people.

Added to those dismal facts, they'd all heard the musket fire the other night. As it echoed across the water, they had no way to determine where the men had gone, much less discover if the men were injured or even alive.

Sickness and disease affected more than half of the people remaining on the *Mayflower*. Fear reached into her mind and tried to spread its icy fingers throughout her soul. Closing her eyes, she shook her head. Fear was not of the Lord. It didn't do anyone any good for her to sink into despair.

Lord, help me. I'm not strong enough for this trial, and I'm afraid. Please keep the men safe—keep William safe. Help them to locate a safe place for us to settle. We need food and water. We need for people to get well. Her thoughts drifted to all she'd lost. Holland, Mother, Father, Dorothy, the Raynsfords—the list seemed endless. Tears streamed down her cheeks.

This wasn't at all what anyone had expected.

"Mary Elizabeth?"

She turned and wiped tears off her cheeks. Tears she hadn't even realized she'd shed. "Hello, Priscilla. It's so good to see you up and about."

Her new friend strode over and reached for her hands. "You've been crying. What can I do to help?"

Mary Elizabeth ducked her head. "I'm ashamed of it, really. Discouragement attacks me every day—and I know that we have so much to be thankful for." She took a deep breath and looked back up at her friend. "But I believe God sent you at just this moment so I wouldn't be overcome with loss. I really should stop this nonsense and get back to work."

Priscilla's beautiful face lit up with a smile. "Well, I'm glad to be of use. Please. . .you always have someone to talk to if you need me."

"I appreciate that. It's all a bit overwhelming. Especially with Father gone. And little Jasper. . ." She choked on a sob. "He was so young." Shaking her head, she closed her eyes to pull herself together. "I'm not sure what the future holds. Or what I'm supposed to do. My parents are both gone now, and there's David to think about."

Priscilla squeezed her hands. "It seems Mr. Lytton has taken quite a fancy to you. Do you feel the same for him?"

Mary Elizabeth felt the heat rise up into her cheeks and couldn't help but smile. "I do. He's talked of the future, but I don't wish to be a burden to anyone."

That made Priscilla laugh. "I don't think *you* can be a burden to a man who's so clearly in love with you."

She felt her jaw drop. Truly? Was it clear that William was. . .in love with her?

"My apologies. I've embarrassed you." Priscilla leaned close and giggled. "If you need an alternative to life with Mr. Lytton, I could talk to my father for you. He's a shoemaker, and he brought over 250 shoes plus thirteen pairs of boots." She sat up straight and wiggled her eyebrows. "I'm sure he'll need help polishing them."

Laughter bubbled up from Mary Elizabeth's throat. "I'll be sure to remember that. But let's not speak to your father just yet."

Priscilla winked. "I thought you might say that. So why don't we get some food for everyone?"

Even though her heart was heavy, Mary Elizabeth had new strength and encouragement to face her grief. All through a precious new friend. *Thank You, Lord.* "I think that's a marvelous idea."

The weary men spent the day traveling up the coast on the west side of the bay, looking for the harbor that Mr. Coppin told them about. But so far they hadn't found it.

William looked to the sky. The sun was setting and soon they would lose all their light. He sent a prayer heavenward that the men would be wise in their decisions and get to safety, but the leaders pressed on, determined to find Coppin's harbor.

As darkness settled upon them, the winds picked up, and Coppin was unsure of their location. It had been many years since he'd sailed these waters.

William watched the men's discussion turn into an argument. He couldn't let it escalate anymore. He stood to his feet. "Gentlemen!" He raised his voice above the wind. "This bickering will get us nowhere. Right now, our main concern should be getting to safety, not who is right and who is wrong."

John Alden was at the other end of the ship and nodded. Several of the others followed suit.

Coppin lowered his head. "William is correct. We can continue searching for the harbor in the morning. My apologies."

A few grumbles echoed through the men, but they all nodded.

"Which way do we head?" one of the men at the sail shouted.

"To the west, we need to get to shore." Coppin nodded in that direction, but as soon as the words were out of his mouth, a large gust of wind pushed them in the opposite direction.

Water began to slosh into the small ship as the waves threatened to overtake them.

It took every man on the shallop to work the small sail and keep it upright.

William was at the stern of the boat when he heard an awful *thunking* sound. He peered over the edge and his heart sank.

"What is it, William?" Coppin shouted.

He closed his eyes. "It's not good. I think the rudder has come unhinged."

Wind blew them sideways, and William spotted the oars in the bottom of the boat. "We're going to have to steer her manually."

"Aye." Coppin grabbed an oar. "It'll take all our strength, men!"

Oars were passed out and directions were given. They'd have to attempt to keep the boat upright as they worked against the wind. William didn't want to voice his fear—that the wind could push them straight out to sea. That thought was a bit too much to swallow. He looked at John and saw the tinge of fear in his friend's eyes. But he knew what he had to do. Best to bring his concerns to the Lord.

God, I don't know how we will manage this. The wind is getting too strong, and the waves are big enough to take this small ship over. We need Your help. Please give us the strength to push against the wind, and guide us to safety. In Your holy name I pray, amen.

Coppin yelled commands above the roar of the wind, and the men took turns battling the waves with the oars. When one man would get tired, another would take his place.

Time passed in the oblivion of battling the elements. A deep darkness descended upon them as exhaustion took its toll. Hours must have passed, but William couldn't tell the time other than by his own weariness. As the wind picked up again, his heart sank. *Lord, help!*

Another large blast hit them and sent them all falling to the larboard side of the shallop.

Crack!

In an instant, the mast of the small ship snapped into two pieces. Despair descended on the men like a thick blanket. William looked from one drenched face to another.

Bradford stood up against the wind and rain. "Gentlemen, this is no time to fear. Our trust remains in the Lord—He will take care of us."

Coppin nodded and yelled for every man to row as hard as they could.

Another gust of wind blew and the shallop plowed forward. It shook as it struck something hard. They all jolted forward.

"Land! I believe we've hit land!" Coppin turned back to the men, and they cheered.

William woke up in the middle of night and shivered. His mind spun with the hardships they faced. True, they'd hit land, but the damage to the boat could be devastating in the daylight. They knew the rudder wasn't functioning, and the mast had clearly snapped into several pieces. On top of that, they didn't even know where they were.

Elder Brewster's words came back to him: *"It's in the toughest of times that we are challenged to trust Him. Because He is almighty God."*

Trust.

It wasn't an easy thing for William to do. Never had been. People had let him down all his life. But deep down, he knew he could trust God. Putting it into practice was the hard part, but he had to try.

Lord, the men have told me that I can come to You with anything. Well, I need to know how to trust You, and so I'm asking for You to teach me, show me. . .whatever it takes. I want to trust You.

As he gazed up into the sky, stars twinkled between the clouds. God had put all of them into place. He had put William in London and had led Paul to him. Without God, he wouldn't be here in the New World. He wouldn't have met Mary Elizabeth.

Yes, he could trust God. He closed his eyes and thanked the Lord one more time for saving him.

Saturday, 9 December 1620

The sun peeked in and out of the clouds as the men worked to put the shallop to rights. It was a good thing William had brought all his tools with him. John worked by his side as the other men waited for orders on what they needed to fetch to help with repairs.

William checked the new mast in the shallop to make sure it was ready to go out on the water again.

His arms ached. It took an entire day to fix the boat, but tomorrow was Sunday and they would be able to rest, worship, and study the scriptures together. And he desperately needed the encouragement. After all, they were shipwrecked on an island and needed to find the harbor and a good place to settle.

William was tired of mishaps and horrible situations. It was almost mid-December. Since he'd left England, it seemed like he'd faced one catastrophe after another. Everything except Mary Elizabeth.

When Monday dawned bright and beautiful, William was refreshed by the rest from the day before.

Today was a new day.

As the men assembled at the shallop, Mr. Bradford led them all in a prayer. "Father God, we ask for You to grant us Your mercy today as we seek to find a settlement. . . ."

William prayed it would be true. Even though they were on an island, they now knew that they were within a good-sized inlet—a bay—and they would explore it to find what they were looking for.

The men loaded into the shallop and, with renewed energy, started sounding the bay with the lead lines. They discovered the harbor could handle a ship the size of the *Mayflower* and were encouraged.

Myles Standish pulled out Captain Smith's map of New England and figured out that the island they'd run into was within the sheltered harbor. As he showed the men where they were, he shook his head. "Look. Smith named this area over here Plimouth."

The men scoured the shore and decided that Plimouth would be a good place to investigate. In the dead of night and the midst of those terrible winds, God had blown them directly into the place they had been trying to find. A safe harbor.

When the shallop reached shore, William was pleased with the area. Affirmations rang through the group of men. Maybe this was it.

They split up into several groups and spent the morning exploring. William was grateful to be with Mr. Bradford. Mr. Chapman had been correct—the man was full of wisdom and was sensible and level-headed.

He took a deep breath. This was the moment he'd been waiting for. "Sir, might I ask you a question?"

"Of course, William. Why don't we rest over here on these rocks for a while?" The older man sat. "Now what is it you'd like to discuss?"

"I'd like to inquire about Miss Chapman." But where did he begin?

"Ah, yes. The elders have discussed your interest in the lovely Mary Elizabeth."

"Prayerfully, sir, you know my heart now. When I boarded the *Mayflower*, I was indeed a Stranger. Not only to your congregation, but to God. It's been a difficult journey, but I feel firm in my faith now, and you've already heard my request to join your congregation."

"Indeed. You are most welcome to join us." He held up a hand so William didn't say anything else. "And we all know that you wish to court Miss Chapman."

"I do." He took a deep breath. "But I'd like to go a step further and know what your church's rules are on betrothal?"

Bradford laughed. "Son, we don't have set rules on the subject. Even though I appreciate you asking and your sincerity in the matter. I will say this: since Mary Elizabeth's father approved and gave his blessing, we are most eager to follow his lead and will not stand in the way."

William let out his long breath. "Truly?"

"Aye, son."

"So what do I do next?"

"Well, you should start by telling her your intentions. Then ask her if she is willing."

That sounded straightforward. And Mary Elizabeth already knew his intentions. He sure hoped she was willing, but the only way to find out was to go ahead and ask her. He couldn't wait.

Friday, 15 December 1620

William dipped his quill in the ink and sat on his bed to fill in all the details of the last few days. While his mind spun with all the happenings, words couldn't express the utter despair that hit the explorers when they returned to the *Mayflower*. Learning of the deaths of little Jasper, Bradford's wife, and Mr. Chilton had shaken them all to their cores.

Even the news that they had found a suitable harbor and place for a settlement couldn't break the grip of grief that had descended.

The sick were expanding in number, and the weather wasn't pleasant. It was winter in New England in the New World.

As the *Mayflower* cut through the water toward her new anchorage, William thought back. A month ago, hopes had buoyed. They'd reached land so the worst was behind them. Certainly there wouldn't be more loss.

But now he wondered how many more would die. How did the settlement have any chance of surviving—much less paying back the debts owed?

If they didn't have enough people to labor, they wouldn't be able to produce what was needed.

At this point, the outlook was dim. William hated to record his thoughts in such a foreboding manner, but he'd promised to be faithful in his job. And he didn't see any other truth.

The investors would have to understand what a difficult journey they'd had so far.

He looked up from the journal and waited for the ink to dry. It had begun to press on his heart that maybe he needed to share with Mr. Brewster and Bradford what he'd been asked to do for the company. Crawford hadn't wanted to alarm the people when they didn't know and trust one another, but William didn't believe it was supposed to be kept a complete secret. The whole point had been to build trust and be good stewards. He also wanted to tell Mary Elizabeth.

There was no reason he shouldn't since he'd hoped to ask her to be his wife.

Mary Elizabeth.

What he'd hoped to be a joyful reunion had been a time of sorrow as the news was shared. She still grieved her father and the Raynsfords, and each death took its toll. The only remedy William could see? Time.

William needed advice, but Elder Brewster had spent the days praying over each sick person, and Mr. Bradford had hidden himself away for a time after the news of his wife was shared. He couldn't blame the man.

He longed to spend some time with Mary Elizabeth and share his heart, but the circumstances seemed to dictate patience. So he'd waited. She looked worn out from caring for all the sick, and he knew how much she had come to care for the More children. Another blow like this could devastate her heart for some time, and William was unsure how to proceed.

Lord, I need help. Everyone on this ship needs help. Please give us Your wisdom and discernment as to how to proceed.

William tucked the blotter, journal, and quill back into his trunk. Perhaps he could be of some service to Master Jones on deck.

As he climbed the steps, he forced his mind to look forward. Past all the grief, past the building and settling. He could see himself thriving here for the rest of his days. God willing.

With Mary Elizabeth by his side, he felt he could do anything. He would cling to that—dreams of the future—and pray they would survive.

Saturday, 16 December 1620

The ship sat in its new harbor, and David watched the shallop and longboat take all the able-bodied men to shore. They were going to scout and find a place to build. Soon he'd get to run on dry land, and he couldn't wait.

Once they'd reached the New World, it hadn't been anything like he'd expected. He'd seen a lot of sandy shores and woods, and they'd had to stay on the *Mayflower* for all these weeks. Other than getting to go and help stack the firewood, there hadn't been much excitement for him.

Mother and Father were gone, and now Mary Elizabeth was needed again to help with the sick around the clock. She fell into bed for short naps each day but hardly had anything to say.

David felt like he'd lost everyone.

The boats reached the shore, and he wished he was with them.

"There you are, David. I've been looking for you." His sister's voice made him turn around. "Do you think you could try and catch some fish for us today?"

He nodded.

"What's wrong?"

"Nothing."

She stepped closer. "It doesn't look like it's 'nothing.'"

With a sigh, he looked into her eyes. "You haven't been yourself lately."

"There's been a lot to take care of, David." Her words sounded weak. . .defeated, as she looked off into the distance.

He couldn't take it anymore. "But don't you understand? You barely eat. You barely sleep. And you never talk to me anymore. . .or even William."

Tears filled his sister's eyes. She ducked her head.

He didn't mean to make her sadder.

"It's been very hard losing Father and then Dorothy"—she sniffed—"and all the others."

"I know, Mary Elizabeth." He didn't want to cry, but hot tears burned at the corners of his eyes. He threw himself into her arms. "That's why I'm scared. I don't want to lose you too."

CHAPTER 25

I *don't want to lose you too.*" David's words had pierced Mary Elizabeth's heart. As she leaned over Solomon Prower, she realized that she had allowed her grief to cover her in a fog. She wasn't the only one to face great loss. Everyone on board the ship had felt tragedy in one way or another. They'd all left behind family and friends and everything they knew.

"Take a sip, Solomon." Mary Elizabeth encouraged the man to drink. She needed some fresh air, time away from caring for the sick in the belly of the ship. Time to lift her eyes toward heaven and pour her heart out to God.

It'd been too many days since she'd allowed herself to feel anything. David was right to be concerned, and Mary Elizabeth should've seen this coming. She should've been strong enough to fight off the melancholy and sorrow. They couldn't afford to wallow in their anguish.

"Mary Elizabeth, how is Mr. Prower doing?"

She turned to see Mr. Bradford kneeling beside her with his Bible clutched to his chest. "He's just had some sips of water."

The man nodded. "I guess that's the best we can hope for now."

She bit her lip. Dare she speak to the man about his loss? "How are you doing?"

He took a deep breath and let it out. "I keep thinking of Job and his words, 'Naked came I out of my mother's womb, & naked shall I return thither: the Lord hath given, & the Lord hath taken it: blessed be the Name of the Lord.' " His eyes appeared teary as he gave her a sad smile. "While it doesn't take away the pain, it encourages me to praise the Lord even in this time of sorrow."

Mary Elizabeth blinked at him. The man had lost his wife, whom he seemed to love dearly, yet he was able to cling to God and his faith so beautifully.

"You look like you are struggling, my dear."

She nodded. "It has been pretty trying the last couple of weeks." Mary Elizabeth ducked her head. The only happy moments she could remember were with Priscilla and seeing William again, but then they'd had to share about the losses, and she'd tumbled back into her own grief.

While Mr. Bradford wasn't quite as old as her father had been, she still looked up to him as a father figure and one of the elders for their church. "I understand that, Mary Elizabeth. I do. And I wish I could take away the heartache you've had to endure. That everyone has had to endure on this voyage. I don't think any of us imagined it to be this way." He sighed and shook his head. "In the book of First Peter, we are reminded to 'rejoice, though now for a season (if need require) ye are in heaviness,' and indeed the times have been heavy with trials and loss. I keep asking the Lord for wisdom in how to rejoice through this, and even though I don't know the answer fully, I am encouraged to keep living one moment at a time. To keep serving Him. That's what this whole journey was about, my dear. To free ourselves from other restraints and be able to worship Him wholly. If we lose sight of that and dwell on our grief, we will tarnish the memories of those who've given up their lives on this venture."

The words sank deep into her mind and heart. "Thank you, Mr. Bradford. I haven't had enough rest, I know that, and I've allowed the sadness to drag me down. Had David not told me his heart earlier— his fear of losing me too—I might have gone further into the depths of despair. And I know that's not of the Lord."

"No, my child, it's not. Neither is fear. And I know many are fearful of the future right now. We must do our best to encourage them." He stood up and patted her shoulder. "How is Mr. Lytton doing? I thought you fancied him."

Mary Elizabeth felt yet another blush rise to her face. "I do. He's a good man."

"Aye. He is."

"But I'm afraid I haven't had much time with him, either, of late."

"Maybe you can change that."

She smiled. "Yes, maybe I can."

As she watched the man walk away, she resolved to do just that.

She stood up and went to their quarters. The lid of the trunk opened with ease, and she pulled out Father's Bible. It was hers now. And she would treasure it.

Making her way to the main deck, Mary Elizabeth hummed one of the psalms they sang from the psalter. If she wanted to lift the fog, she'd have to fight it. That meant getting enough rest to have the strength to fight it too. Something she'd neglected for far too long. It took David's scolding to help her to see it.

On deck, she positioned herself at the bulwark where she could see the boats on the shore. "Lord, I commit to You my heart and mind. Please help me to release this darkness that I've allowed to take me captive. David needs me, and I haven't been much of an encouragement and light to him lately. Please guide the men ashore as they seek to do Your will and find a suitable settlement for us all. I ask all these things in the holy name of Jesus, amen."

Her prayer left on the wind, and she closed her eyes and let the winter sun shine on her face. Letting go was hard to do. Losing people you loved, even harder. But she needed to keep her focus on the source of true joy—the Lord.

What could she praise Him for today?

Opening her eyes, she looked at the shore. William was her biggest source of praise. He gave her a hope for a future that she'd dreamed of since she was a little girl—to be married and have a family. Then there was David. Her precious brother. There was still so much growing for him to do, and she needed to help guide him in the right path.

This new land was another thing worthy of praise. And the fact that the long sea journey was over. Then there were new friends.

As she counted up the things to praise God for, she felt the heaviness begin to lift. She went over to a crate and sat down. Opening up the Bible, she went to the very first Psalm and began to read:

'Blessed is the man that doeth not walk in the counsel of the wicked, nor stand in the way of sinners, nor sit in the seat of the scornful: but his delight is in the Law of the Lord, & in his Law doeth he meditate day and night.'

'For he shall be like a tree planted by the rivers of waters, that will bring forth her fruit in due season: whose leaf shall not fade: so whatsoever he shall do shall prosper.'

She wanted to find her delight in the law of the Lord again. Not wander around in this blackness. The people needed her, David needed her. . .and William did too. Closing her eyes again, the weariness from lack of sleep hit her. She'd neglected her own health to care for the others.

Maybe the best idea she had right now was to get some rest, and then she could look forward to seeing William tonight.

The day of exploring had gone well, and William was exhausted. His bed sounded exceedingly welcoming, but more than anything, he wished he could see Mary Elizabeth. To look into her eyes and see her smile.

That hadn't occurred much of late. And he knew he shouldn't expect it, but he could still hope.

When they reached the deck of the *Mayflower*, Master Jones was waiting for them. "Any news?"

William nodded. "It appears we are close to making a decision."

"Good, good." The man's stern expression with his hands clasped behind his back seemed to be his normal posture.

"William!" That was Mary Elizabeth's voice, and it lifted his spirits, just hearing it.

He turned toward the sound. "Mary Elizabeth."

She came to him with a smile and took his hands in hers. "I'm so glad you're back."

"It's good to see you as well." Better than he even imagined. Especially with her bright smile. "To what do I owe this wonderful pleasure?"

Ducking her head, she squeezed his hands. "I didn't realize how much I had. . .neglected you."

With the crook of his finger, he lifted her chin. Something he'd had to do often. "Look at me, Mary Elizabeth. There's no reason for you to feel guilt or shame—or hide your face from me. Do you remember what I told you?"

Her cheeks turned pink. "Aye." The smile grew.

"I meant it, Mary Elizabeth. I love you. I want to know everything about you. I want to spend every moment the Good Lord gives me with you."

The look on her face did funny things to his heart.

"I know you've had your hands full taking care of all the sick—and that makes me love you even more. You have a beautiful, tender heart. But I have missed you a great deal."

"And I you." Her brown eyes shimmered. "There's something else. I'm very sorry for my distance. I didn't realize how much hurt I had caused until David spoke with me this morning."

"It's understandable, my love. I had resolved to give you time in your grief."

"I didn't do it intentionally. I guess I just didn't realize how weary I had become."

He ran a finger down her cheek. "But you look quite rested and happy now. It's good to see color in your cheeks again."

She lowered her eyes to his chest and smiled. "I slept a good part of the morning after I spent some time in prayer and in the scriptures. The happiness you see is because of you, William."

He put her hand to his chest. "You make my heart overflow, Miss Chapman."

"You do the same for mine." She smiled, and then her brow furrowed. "Mr. Bradford spoke to me after David did, and I was very convicted by his words. It's amazing to me that he's resting in God's will and yet just suffered so much. He mentioned Job this morning, and I think I might like to study that book."

"His faith astounds me every day."

"Aye. And his wife has only been gone a few days. It breaks my heart for him." She looked toward the water.

"Maybe we could study Job together?"

"I'd like that." The light was back in her eyes. "We could ask Mr. Bradford for help if there's something we don't understand."

William dared to step closer and lifted their joined hands to his chest. "Bradford has been my mentor and adviser at your father's suggestion. I think that's a wonderful idea." Was this the right time? He had no experience in this area, but he forged on ahead. "I know I don't have much to offer you, Mary Elizabeth, and there's no place or time to court you properly. But the elders have approved my request anyway." He took a deep breath. "What I'm trying to say is that. . .I'd like to ask you to be my wife."

She took a slight step back and smiled. "Aye. William Lytton, I'd be honored to be your wife."

"Hoo, hoo!" William threw his hat in the air.

Everyone on deck turned toward them and stared.

"She said *yes!*"

Chapter 26

Thursday, 28 December 1620

William climbed the hill where they planned to build a platform for the cannon. It would serve well as a lookout and help protect their settlement. His job was to get the structure started with John Alden's help while the others worked on the common house.

They'd hit one problem after another. First, the decision couldn't be made about where to settle. Several of the men said the island on which they'd almost shipwrecked would be a good place because it would keep them safe from the Indians. But even the pilot John Clarke—who'd had the island named after him since he'd been the first to step on it—argued that being on the mainland would be more beneficial in the long run. So a vote had been cast, and they'd settled upon what Captain John Smith had dubbed on his map, "Plimouth." And they decided to spell it Plimouth.

The last port they'd left in England was Plymouth, so it seemed providential.

Then the weather had turned stormy and they'd lost three more lives—one a stillborn baby. By Sunday, December 24, many members had lost hope of having anything accomplished by January.

William had shared his hopes and dreams for a house with Mary Elizabeth but had to wait on the rest of the men to decide how they would approach the planning of their town. If he'd ever prayed for patience, he knew now not to do it again. Learning how to be patient was proving to be his greatest enemy.

But on Christmas Day, they'd finally erected the first frame of their buildings. It was to be the common house and would measure twenty feet square.

Today they were supposed to plan out their town and get this platform built.

As he stood at the top of the hill, William looked out on the area around him. A good deal of land had been cleared by presumably some native people. And at one point, corn had been planted. The remains still stood in the fields. But when they'd scouted, they'd only found abandoned hut-like structures. William hated to say it out loud, but it did appear that something catastrophic had happened to whoever had lived there.

A beautiful brook ran by the hillside and provided them with plenty of fresh water. They had affectionately named it Town Brook. And at the mouth of the brook was a great place to harbor the shallop and other small boats.

From the top of the hill where he stood, he could see the tip of Cape Cod—where they'd first anchored—across the bay. As he turned, he saw plenty of trees in the distance to provide wood for them.

They had chosen well. This land should provide for them for years to come.

William pulled out his satchel of tools and set to work. Hopefully he'd hear soon about the plan for the town and he'd be able to work on that as well.

Anxious to get started and get the people situated on the land, William worked fast with his hatchet.

After he'd trimmed about ten logs, he heard rustling in the grass.

"Hello!" John Alden called from the side of the hill.

"Good day to you, John!" William took the opportunity to catch his breath and drink some water he'd brought up from the stream.

"And to you." John crested the hill and walked up to him. "Looks like you've made a lot of progress."

"Aye. When you have good motivation, it tends to keep you going."

"That is true." His friend patted him on the back. "Where would you like me to start?"

William pointed to the pile of trees he'd felled. "The rest of those need to be trimmed and sized."

John took his hatchet and went to work. "I have some good news."

William nodded and kept working.

"They've laid out where the houses will be built."

"Aye. That is indeed good news." He split another log.

"There will be a street down the middle with nineteen plots—one for each family unit—on either side. Fifty feet will be their depth and eight feet per person will be the width determining each for their house and garden." The repetitive *thunk* of John's hatchet accentuated his words. "Once we get the common house completed, each family will be responsible for building their own house."

It sounded great to William. At least it was a good start.

They worked in silence for a good while, the hard work keeping them warm in the frigid temperatures.

John let out a groan and stretched. "I think I got soft being on the ship for so long."

"It feels good though, doesn't it? To get back to work?"

"Aye. It does." John moved around a bit more. "Although tomorrow, I'm sure my body will protest."

William chuckled at the thought.

"So. . ." John raised his eyebrows. "Have you and Mary Elizabeth decided when you will have the wedding?"

"We've been discussing it with Elder Brewster. I think we will wait until we have a house built and most of the sickness is past. That way, the whole community can celebrate with us."

"When do you think that will be?"

"Hopefully by the end of January. That gives us plenty of time to plan and build."

"We'll be praying for you every day, William." Mary Elizabeth held David's hand on the top deck. How she hated goodbyes. He'd only be on the mainland, but she'd hardly seen him as it was. When the weather was decent enough, the men had worked long and hard to fell trees and build the common house.

"Thank you, Mary Elizabeth." He touched her cheek, his blue eyes almost gray today. "It won't be long." He leaned forward and whispered in her ear. "I love you."

Heat filled her face as he pulled back, and she gave him a smile.

With a nod, he walked away and joined the few other men who were to go ashore and live in the common house and work on the fort and the houses.

The original plan had been a good one, but no one had counted on the storms growing worse and the sick growing in number by the day. Some had gotten better and then succumbed again—this time much worse.

They needed men to hunt and fish so they would have food, and then thatch had to be gathered for roofs, timber needed to be chopped and hauled. It wouldn't be so bad if everyone were well and strong.

A tickle in her throat made Mary Elizabeth pull her cape up to her nose. She didn't want to cough in this cold, damp air. Last time she did, her lungs felt like they were on fire.

"Mary Elizabeth, I don't feel so good." David shivered and tugged on her hand.

"Let's get you closer to the fire, all right?" Weariness rested on her shoulders once again. No. She couldn't allow it to take over again. She would delight in the Lord. He would be her strength. They'd made it this far; He would see them through. She sat David down on a crate by the fire box. "How's that?"

"Much better. But my throat hurts, and I can't breathe through my nose."

She nodded and crouched down beside him. "Let me see if I can find anything to help you with that." Taking off her cape, she wrapped it around her brother's shoulders. "I'll be back."

She went down the steps to find Samuel Fuller. He had been taking care of the ones who were the worst that morning.

"Mary Elizabeth, I'm so glad you're down here." Mr. Fuller waved her over. "We need some extra hands—is David with you?"

"That's why I was looking for you, as well. David is complaining of a sore throat and that he can't breathe through his nose."

"It sounds like his humours are out of balance."

"So what should I do?" Mary Elizabeth followed the man to the next bed.

"I believe there is a little dried mint left in my satchel. Boil it in some water and have him breathe it in and then have him drink it. That's the best I have to offer. Everything else has been depleted." He squeezed her arm. "When you're done, could you come assist me?"

"Of course. I'll be quick."

Gathering what she needed for David, she sent another prayer heavenward. She hoped it wouldn't turn into another case of pneumonia for her poor brother. It had started the same way.

Climbing the steps to the main deck, she tripped over her skirt. There wasn't need for reckless behavior. Now would not be a good time to injure herself. She found David asleep by the fire. "Wake up. We need to get you to bed."

"I don't feel good, Mary Elizabeth." David's head lolled back as she lifted him up.

"I know. That's why I'm going to take good care of you. But I need you to walk; you're too big for me to carry."

She barely managed to get him down the steps when the tickle came back to her throat. A horrible cough wracked her chest as she led David to bed.

Mr. Fuller appeared at their curtain. "Was that you coughing, Mary Elizabeth?"

She nodded as another coughing spell came over her. "I don't know what's come over me."

The man shook his head. "It looks like it's not going to be just David going to bed. You are too."

The snow, sleet, and wind hammered the men in the common house. William stayed close to the fire to watch for embers flying—they didn't need any more fires to burn thatch roofs—and prayed for divine help. The storms had been so bad the past few days that there was a good amount of damage done to the structures they'd been working on. They were already behind, and now this would set them back even further.

Word had come from the *Mayflower* that Mary Elizabeth and David had both gotten sick but were finally on the mend. That news was better than most. The little Plimouth colony was already beginning to disappear, and they hadn't even truly settled. The few that were strong and healthy enough lived on shore and helped build, while the rest were cared for on the ship.

William didn't even want to think about the number who'd died.

If truth be told, the only thing that kept him going was his newfound faith. If he hadn't found the Lord on the journey over, William would've wanted to quit and head back with the crew to England.

But Master Jones wasn't even sure when he could leave. There weren't enough places to house the people who would be staying, and a good portion of his crew had fallen sick.

The times continued to oppress them.

Was this what it was like for the early believers? The past few days had given William lots of time to read God's Word, and he found that there were so many different passages that spoke on suffering for the sake of Christ and how to rejoice in the midst of suffering. Since it was addressed so much, he could only assume that there was a good reason.

There'd obviously been a lot of persecution—William knew of it from the bits of history that Paul had taught him—and he'd been learning of the persecution so many had suffered from the Church of England. From Bloody Mary to King James, differing beliefs could put lives on the line.

Last night while the winds howled around them, Elder Brewster talked about when their congregation had first fled England. It took years and several tries to get everyone together. They'd been betrayed, robbed, and imprisoned.

All for their faith.

While William had joined the journey to the New World for a fresh start and what he hoped would be a grand adventure, it had turned into so much more than that. He'd found life. And he'd found Mary Elizabeth.

But the price had been high. For everyone.

The thought of losing Mary Elizabeth and David struck his heart. It was a good thing he hadn't learned of their sickness until they were on the mend. Who knew what he would have done to get back to them and help. The doubts of his past plagued him on a daily basis, and he felt battle weary from the attacks.

But prayer was a beautiful thing. As soon as he laid his burdens down at the heavenly Father's feet, he knew he'd done the right thing.

His thoughts returned to the colony. And his journal. Would they be able to recover from such hardship? At this point, it would be a miracle if they survived, and they hadn't even thought about how to repay the company. The *Mayflower* would need to return to England, and even after all this time, the colonists had nothing to send back to put into the company's coffers. In fact, they needed more help— which would put them into greater debt.

John Carver had a heavy burden to bear—to be sure. As elected governor of their group, he was the leader and the one ultimately responsible for the decisions made.

The Compact they'd signed would ensure that the people would have their say. That's why votes had been cast about the settlement location and also about the layout of the town. But they still needed a strong leader.

In the glow of the firelight, William flipped through the pages of the Bible Elder Brewster let him borrow. The book of Acts fascinated him. Reading about the early church and how they cared for one another. Whether rich or poor, station or no station, they pulled all their monies together to clothe each other and feed everyone.

No wonder the Saints wanted to be separate from the Church of England. It had gotten away from what scripture demonstrated a church should do.

It was full of rituals and readings and ceremonies. While people's hearts might be in the right place, they were following man-made rules and mandates rather than scripture.

Paul had taken him to church the whole seven years he'd lived in the older man's care. But Paul seemed to believe very much like the Separatists—that scripture was the final authority. But they'd gone to the church in London, anyway. When William was younger, he'd asked a lot about the rituals they seemed to go through because he'd been bored. Paul's response was that it wasn't right to forsake the fellowship of the brethren. There would never be a perfect church because it was filled with imperfect people.

William never understood that until he read Hebrews, chapter ten: *"And let us consider one another, to provoke unto love, & to good works, Not forsaking the fellowship that we have among our selves, as the manner of some is: but let us exhort one another, & that so much the more because ye see that the day draweth near."*

Paul had been raised in the church of England, and even though later in life he disagreed with some of the practices, he still found the fellowship he needed there. It might not have been what he wanted in a church, but he had remained faithful.

The difference between Paul's faith and the Saints' wasn't great—if there was any at all. But now William began to understand why Paul had urged him to go with the Separatists.

"He wanted to go himself but couldn't." As he said the words aloud, a moment of comprehension struck him.

William remembered a conversation he'd had with Paul before he died. At the time, he hadn't understood it at all. . .

"If only I'd had the courage to do it long ago, things would be different. Maybe I could help you more. But I stayed in my comfortable place—even though the Lord prodded me on."

"You've helped me more than you will ever know. There's nothing for you to regret."

"Oh, but there is, my boy. I can't let you make the same mistake. It's time for you to make the most of your life. Throw off the past and follow God. The Separatists have done it right."

A rush of emotion filled his chest as he remembered the dear man's words. At the time, William was still too hardened and bitter to understand. But now he did.

The man had loved him like a son and wanted him to serve the Lord.

As all the events of the past few months filled his memories, William knew one thing to be true.

God was in control. He had directed their steps thus far. William would trust Him the rest of the way. No matter the cost.

Hunting for fowl was not Peter's choice of labor, but it was better than chopping and trimming logs or gathering thatch.

And they all needed food. He felt like he could eat an entire goose himself.

Today had not been a productive day, though. He missed every bird he'd shot at. If he could just kill one, he'd build a fire and roast it up. Forget about sharing with the rest of the men.

Several deer passed by his hiding spot. Venison had never been popular in England, and he had no idea what to do with it, but the thought of a big steak sure made his mouth water. None of the men had experience hunting the game, but maybe he could show them all by snagging one.

Crouching down into the grass, Peter took aim. A twig snapped under his elbow, and the deer skittered off into the trees.

This whole trip had been a waste of time. It was miserable, they were almost out of beer, and he'd been sick twice. More people died each week, and he determined he wasn't going to be one of them. He had no desire to work his fingers to the bone and live in some tiny thatched hut. That might be good enough for the others, but not for him.

No way was he going to stay here unless the company paid him a lot of money. And right now the job belonged to someone else.

Something he needed to change. And soon.

Wednesday, 28 February 1620/1

Twenty-five people were dead. Just in the past two months. William thrust his pick into the ground on the small hill they were using as their burial ground. He'd almost spent as much time burying people as he had building the small buildings the rest would soon live in. The thought made him shake his head.

As he'd spent more time with the elders and men of the Separatist congregation, he'd come to find that memorizing scripture was a vital part of faith. That way he could keep it on his mind and heart just like Psalm 119:11 read.

The verse he'd memorized this morning was from 2 Corinthians. Chapter four, verse nine. He said the words aloud to banish the discouraging thoughts as he dug another grave. " 'We are persecuted, but not forsaken; cast downe, but we perish not.' "

Many of the men had shared the same verse with him—they probably all needed the encouragement and reminder.

Their flesh might perish. They might all die and the little colony return to dust. But their souls wouldn't. Eternity in heaven looked better each day.

The physical labor kept his mind focused on the work ahead. They needed to get everyone off the ship and living in suitable housing. The cramped quarters for all these months had to breed the disease in some way that had infected all the people. It was the only thing that made sense to him.

He was just thankful that Mary was again healthy and recovered. All the time she'd spent with the sick made him worry.

Had it really only been two days since he'd seen her last? Ever since they'd anchored off Cape Cod, laundry had been done on Mondays, since that was their first opportunity. The tradition continued all these weeks, and now he wished that Monday was closer. Or maybe there was another reason he could give for going to see her.

The thought made him smile. Several of the other men teased him about the upcoming wedding. It was good to have the camaraderie and a topic that brought smiles and laughter rather than tears and sadness.

But would he make a good husband? A good father? He'd never had any real example other than Paul. And the Leyden men had been good to him, but he realized that he didn't know the first thing about being a husband or a father.

Maybe that was the next subject he should broach with Mr. Bradford and the elders. Before he said his vows, he should probably study what a Godly husband looked like and if there was any way he could be one.

CHAPTER 28

Monday, 12 March 1620/1

Spring was just around the corner. The thought brought a smile to Mary Elizabeth's face. They all needed a smile after the past few months. Even though she didn't have a house finished yet, she was anxious to be able to start the garden. The lettuce and peas could go in, and that thought thrilled her. Something fresh instead of hard tack, dried meat, and dried vegetables. They enjoyed the occasional fish and fowl if the men had time to hunt or fish, but with so few healthy, the majority of them worked on the construction of the town.

Because Master Jones had made it clear that the *Mayflower* would leave. And soon.

If half of the crew weren't sick, he would've left already.

Everyone who was able had come to shore this morning. The ladies had to do mounds of laundry, and the men were working on the houses.

She'd had a brief moment with William when they'd first made it to shore. He had prayed with her, which made her heart soar. Her dreams of a Godly husband to be the head of their household were coming true.

Perhaps she'd get the opportunity to see him again when they broke for the meal. That was enough encouragement to see her through the grueling hours of scrubbing clothes.

David ran up to her side. "Mr. Carver said I can help stack wood again. Is that all right with you, Mary Elizabeth?"

Anything was better to a young boy than helping with laundry. "As long as you aren't the one wielding the ax, you have my permission."

He took off running down the beach. The cold temperature didn't seem to bother him one bit. Mary Elizabeth laughed and went back to her scrubbing.

A couple of the other ladies chattered about what they planned to plant in their gardens. A few children played on the beach. But what caught Mary Elizabeth's eye was the sight of two girls sitting on a rock together. They didn't seem to be talking. They just sat.

Setting down the skirt she'd been scrubbing, Mary Elizabeth headed over to the two and realized it was Elizabeth Tilley and Mary Chilton. No wonder they were sitting together in silence. They'd both been orphaned this winter.

"Good day, Elizabeth, Mary." She nodded at them.

"Good day, Miss Chapman." Miss Tilley threw a small shell into the water.

The other girl didn't speak.

Maybe she should try another tactic. "Would either of you know how to fish?"

The girls shook their heads.

"What about hunt?"

Elizabeth giggled. "Girls don't hunt; only the boys do that."

"Oh, I guess you're right." Mary Elizabeth tapped her chin. "What about a game of bowls? Do you know how to play that?"

The quiet Mary shrugged. But Miss Tilley nodded. And there—that was a spark in the girl's eye. Progress!

"Well, I happen to know where a set of bowls are. And if we get the washing done, I think we should all play."

"Oh, could we, Miss Chapman? It's been ages since we've done anything fun." Elizabeth jumped off the rock.

"I'll say we have a plan. But I need to get the laundry done first, agreed?"

Mary followed her friend and nodded. At least that was something.

The little group went to work on the clothes, and Mary Elizabeth realized the girls were only a few years younger than herself. If she remembered correctly, they were both thirteen. On the cusp of womanhood but still longing for the happiness of childhood. She couldn't blame them—especially with their futures unknown. Prayerfully, the girls could stay together with one of the families. They were going to need each other's friendship.

Like hers with Dorothy.

The thought of her dear friend made her heart clinch. It didn't hurt as much as it had, but she had a feeling the ache would never truly go away.

When they'd finished the wash, Mary Elizabeth went to the common house and pulled the bowls out of their trunk. They'd gradually moved a lot of the cargo to the shelter in hopes that they'd all be living in Plimouth soon.

She walked back to the beach and began to play with the girls. It took her a while to find her footing—it had been far too long since she'd played. But the hour of laughter was well worth it.

Making her way back to the common house, she looked forward to standing by a fire. Her toes had gotten quite cold.

Then she'd have to check the laundry and see if there was any chance it was drying. Several times she'd had to bring frozen pieces of clothing back to the ship to warm them up so they could dry.

A commotion by one of the new houses drew her attention.

William stood with his hands on his hips. "That doesn't belong to you, Peter."

Mary Elizabeth wasn't sure what he was talking about, so she moved in closer.

Most of the elders and men were now gathered around the two.

Peter held a book up in the air and shouted. "This book proves that William Lytton is a spy."

Everyone started talking at once.

Mr. Carver held up his hands. "Calm down, Peter. Exactly what are you trying to accuse Mr. Lytton of? Who would he be a spy for?"

"The company." Peter held up a little pouch and shook it. "And here's the proof. He was paid to keep records on all of us."

William shook his head.

Their governor spoke again. "Exactly why would they need a spy?"

Peter glared at the crowd. "To ensure that we failed."

Gasps and murmurs filled the air.

"That is not true." William took a step forward.

Peter opened the book and read. "The explorers stumbled upon mounds on their first trip and, after digging, discovered baskets of corn. Although it didn't belong to them, the men took the corn for themselves."

This time Mr. Carver stepped closer to William. "Why would you write that, William?"

William stood tall and lifted his chin. "Because it was true, sir. But that's not the whole part. Of course it sounds negative when read in this manner."

Peter turned to another page and read, "The death toll rises. At this rate, there is nothing to show for the settlement except graves and debt. I fear the investors will be disappointed with our efforts."

"That's enough, Peter." Mr. Carver held out his hand. "Kindly hand me the book."

The young man stood there for a moment and looked at the faces around him. "We can't let him get away with this." Handing the book to the governor, he crossed his arms over his chest and frowned. "Surely you all can see that he's been working against us—so that we'll owe the precious investors more money."

Several others murmured their agreement.

Mr. Carver went to the front of the group and held both his hands in the air. "I think we all understand why Peter is so upset, but we haven't given William the chance to explain himself. Now please, quiet down so we can get to the truth of the matter." He turned back to William. "Did the company hire you to spy on us?"

"No, sir. But the company *did* hire me to keep accurate records."

Mary Elizabeth took a deep breath. *What?*

"Exactly what kind of records?"

"Everything. The work we did, the land we chose, the house we built, the timber we cut, fish we caught, everything for the settlement. Since the investors didn't have a representative here, they asked me to be it."

Mr. Carver sighed. "When did they ask you to do this job?"

"The day I was loading my things on the *Mayflower*, sir."

"So you had already planned to journey with us."

"Yes, sir." William held out his hands in front of him. "It was a good job for me, a good opportunity—and it seemed like an honorable thing to do to make sure we were all good stewards of the investors' money."

"I understand that, Mr. Lytton." Mr. Carver took off his hat and ran a hand through his hair. "But what I don't understand is why you didn't tell any of us."

It was at that moment that William noticed her at the edge of the crowd.

Oh, William. Her heart sank. Why hadn't he said anything?

William held her gaze as he spoke to the crowd. "I was one of the Strangers at the beginning. I didn't know any of you, and you didn't know me. I wanted to build trust so that you would know I was an honorable man in my dealings."

"So why didn't you tell us after we'd gotten to know you?" Mr. Bradford put the question forth.

William's shoulders sagged. "I'd thought about it many times, but the timing never seemed to be right. Especially with all the loss."

Mr. Carver nodded, even though several negative comments were made in the crowd. He paced back and forth for several minutes.

Mary Elizabeth couldn't handle it any longer. She walked to the center where her betrothed stood. "William hasn't done anything wrong. It's understandable that the Adventurers would have wanted to know what was going on here—it was their money, after all."

David walked through the crowd and stood by William. "I caught Peter snooping in William's things awhile back. I thought he was stealing, but he tried to convince me that he had loaned William something. Did anyone think about how he had to sneak around to find that book and the money? Isn't *that* stealing and spying?"

Mr. Carver continued to pace. Mr. Brewster and Mr. Bradford went over and spoke with the governor.

Whispers went through the crowd.

But Mary Elizabeth couldn't listen. She didn't care what the people were saying or what they thought. William was a good and honorable man. The elders would see that, and this foolishness could be put behind them.

The men turned back toward William, but Mr. Bradford looked at Mary Elizabeth.

"We need to ask you a question, Miss Chapman."

She straightened her shoulders. "Of course."

"Did William—your future husband—tell you anything about his job for the company?"

The air left her lungs in a great sigh. She looked at William.

He nodded to her and put his hands on David's shoulders.

The truth was her only answer. "No. He did not."

CHAPTER 29

Friday, 16 March 1620/1

The past few days had been torture. Other than Mary Elizabeth and David, everyone in the settlement treated William differently. The elders and Governor Carver stated they needed to pray about their decision, and he respected that. He just wasn't expecting for everything to change. For the men he'd come to admire to doubt him.

He worked on his house alone, hoping that soon this would all be a distant memory. He would give the money back in a heartbeat if it ensured the people's trust.

As William shoved clay between the logs of the west wall, John Alden joined him. "Are you going to the ceremony today for Standish?"

William shook his head. "I don't think the people want me there." As much as he wanted his friend's trust and missed the camaraderie, he didn't think John could do anything to make things better.

"That's just your pride talking." John grabbed a clump of clay and started working it into another crack.

"No. It's the truth."

"William, why didn't you tell me about the job? I noticed you scribbling in the journal often enough." His friend's tone wasn't accusatory. It sounded more hurt.

"I've asked myself that a million times since Monday."

John continued to work. "I'm sure you have. I trust you, William, and I don't believe you've done anything untoward."

"Thank you, John."

"But these people—the Saints especially—have been hurt by so many people in the past. They've been completely betrayed and lost everything."

William had forgotten about that. No wonder they wouldn't take him at his word. And he couldn't blame them.

"Give it time. They'll come around."

"My only thoughts were to do the right and honorable thing."

John nodded. "I know, my friend. The others will see the truth."

They worked in silence for a good while until John told him it was time for the ceremony. The military service was to name Mr. Standish the captain and head of their protection.

William cleaned up as best he could and decided to join the rest of the people.

Governor Carver stood and held up his hands. "Welcome, everyone. We are here today to honor—" The man blinked several times, and his jaw dropped. Several moments of silence passed.

William turned to see what the governor was looking at. Up their lone street strode an Indian.

Gasps were heard behind him, followed by complete silence.

The native man was tall with long black hair and a clean-shaven face. Most astonishing was that he was naked except for a span of leather with fringe about his waist.

Several of the women gasped and looked down at the ground. No one was accustomed to seeing that much skin, and wasn't the man cold?

He carried a bow and arrows, and he walked right up to them. "Welcome, Englishmen."

"Why, he speaks English!" One of the elders moved forward.

As the men moved in toward the Indian, William stepped back. The conversation was broken and stilted.

The people didn't trust him right now, and they had been hoping to connect with the natives since arriving. It would be better for everyone if he just went to work on his house.

He walked back to his little plot and went to work with the clay.

The process was time consuming, but if he worked hard, he could finish this wall today while it was still light.

"I guess you're not fascinated with our new guest?"

William shifted his gaze from the wall to his betrothed. She stood at the corner of what was supposed to be their home. "I figured I would stay out of the way."

Mary Elizabeth stood with her hands behind her back. "May I help?"

The sight of her—so sweet and beautiful—made him smile. "Of course." And it made his heart ache.

"You haven't said much lately, William. I'm worried about you." She worked twigs and leaves in with the clay.

He shoved the thick mud in a little bit harder than necessary. "There's nothing to worry about." But there was. She hadn't thought it all through like he had.

"Don't you want to talk about it?"

"Not particularly. It's in their hands. I will have to wait for them to decide what my true intentions were, and then they will decide my fate."

"They will see the truth. I have faith that God will work all of this out."

He let out a heavy sigh. "But what if they don't? That's the part you refuse to acknowledge. Do you still want to marry a man who's been accused of spying? On your own people?"

"William, it's not going to come to that."

"Mary Elizabeth, you've got to face facts. This could very well go in a direction that neither of us wants. Everything I've worked for could be lost. But what's worse is I could lose *you*."

She stomped her foot. "You are not going to lose me, Mr. Lytton."

"You can't know that." Shaking his head, he knew what he had to do. "Where would we go if they find me guilty? How would we survive? It's not possible."

"With God *all* things are possible."

Her optimism made him want to believe her. But the nature of people had proven she was carrying around false hope. He knew the people had been hurt a lot. But he'd also seen his share of misery. People let him down every time.

"William? What's wrong? Please talk to me." She laid a hand on his arm.

"I'm sorry, Mary Elizabeth. Truly, I am. But I think our betrothal needs to come to an end."

❦

After shedding a bucket's worth of tears and walking along the beach for hours, Mary Elizabeth asked to be taken back to the *Mayflower*. Only a few sick were left on the ship, and they were hoping to finish moving everyone by the end of next week. The least she could do was to help pack up their belongings. It would give her something to do with all her frustrated energy since she knew that sleep would be long in coming.

How could William hurt her like that? It didn't make sense, and it wasn't like him at all. Besides, she didn't believe it. She knew that he loved her.

Climbing aboard the ship that had been one of her seafaring homes for eight long months, she realized that it was on this ship that she'd fallen in love with handsome William Lytton. On this ship, she'd grown to be strong and brave.

On this ship, she'd lost her Father and her best friend.

The good had come with the bad. Just like this awful situation for William. He'd wanted to do the right thing. She knew that.

But she also knew her future was with him. No matter what happened. How could she convince him?

Taking the steps down to the gun deck, Mary thought of their first meeting. It had been on a set of steps just like this. And William had reached down a hand for her. His touch had ignited a flame of new life for her—and she never wanted to go back.

"Mary Elizabeth." Mr. Bradford stepped aside at the bottom of the companionway.

His voice startled her and brought her back to the present moment. This time, the steps held her broken heart. "I'm sorry, Mr. Bradford. I guess my mind was on other things."

"Would you like to talk about it?"

"I'm sure you're quite busy. I wouldn't want to delay you."

He sat on one of the steps. "Actually, at the moment I'm not." He looked around the dim and dirty area. "This will be my last night to stay here. My house is finished thanks to help from your William, and I was just gathering up the remainder of my things."

William had helped with Mr. Bradford's house? Her mind fought the urge to cry and scream all at the same time.

"Now tell me, what's on your mind?" He folded his hands on his knee. "Is it the Indian visitor today?"

"Oh my, I completely forgot about that!" She covered her mouth for a moment and then let her hand fall. "No, it's not that, although I'm sure David will want to tell me all about it. I'm actually worried for William."

"Ah yes, I see."

"He tried to end our betrothal today because he says that I haven't thought through what will happen if the town finds him guilty of spying."

"And have you?"

"Well, no. I hadn't until he brought it up, but it really doesn't change anything. I love William, no matter what. I don't believe that he's done a thing wrong, and I will stand by that."

Mr. Bradford nodded.

"But it's hard for me to understand why he would want to push me away in all this. And it exasperates me."

"Have you thought of the fact that William may be doing this because he thinks it will protect you in some way?"

She frowned. "Well, no. Not really."

"That's what strong, Godly men do. They protect the people they love. By sacrificing themselves and ultimately their own happiness."

"So he'd rather be miserable and just let me go?"

"If he thinks it's best for you."

"But how does he know what's best for me if he won't listen to me?"

He sighed. "That's the tricky part. Men are good at convincing themselves that they know what's best. We are the protectors and providers. But my wife, Dorothy—God rest her soul—reminded me that God gave the woman to be a helpmeet, and that meant that I had to learn how to listen to her wise counsel rather than always try to fix it all. It took years for her to teach me, but she was a very patient woman."

Mary Elizabeth stared down at her hands. Maybe he was correct. Her relationship with William was so new, she didn't understand a lot or truly understand how it should work. But how could she get William to see? "What do you suggest I do?"

"Pray."

She nodded. That should have been her first response.

He laid a hand on her shoulder and stood. "He loves you, Miss Chapman. Of that you can be assured."

While her heart knew the words were true, it still hurt. Would William turn his back on her forever?

The air was finally getting warmer. Maybe Mary Elizabeth wouldn't make him wear his heavy cloak everywhere now.

But she probably would. She didn't want him to get sick. That was what big sisters did.

The fact that she'd allowed him to stay with Mr. Alden in the new town the past few days was pretty impressive. She'd helped move the rest of the people from the ship and would come on the last shallop today.

David couldn't wait to tell her all the exciting news.

As he stood on the shore and watched the smaller boat make its way in, he thought about William. His sister's future husband hadn't been too happy lately. The governor had yet to decide what to do about the accusations Peter had made, but there wasn't any foundation for them to find him guilty. William was a good man. And he loved Mary Elizabeth.

The shallop reached the harbor, and they began to unload. It was pretty interesting to think about. They were finally all ashore. No longer living on the *Mayflower*.

More than fifty of the passengers had died, and Master Jones had lost half of his crew. It was a sobering thought.

"David!" Mary Elizabeth ran toward him. She hugged him tight. "I've missed you."

"I've missed you too."

She kissed his cheek. "So I hear you know all about our visitor?"

"His name is Samoset." He puffed out his chest. "I talked to him, and he let me look at his bow."

"Did you now?"

"Aye. And he knew some English words."

"I heard that."

"Well, did you know that he stayed the night?"

Mary Elizabeth's eyes widened. "No. I didn't know that."

"Yes, with the Hopkins family. Then he went back to the Wampanoag people—they're the ones that live a little ways away—and they came back to trade the next few days."

"That's exciting news for the colony, isn't it?" She lifted a few blankets from the pile at her feet. "So where are we staying?"

"William is giving us his house right now. He's going to stay with John Alden in the common house. A lot of people are sharing since there's only seven or eight houses built."

"That's fine. I'm sure we will do just fine. And once William and I are married, we should probably offer a place to stay for John, don't you think?"

"Sure." David shrugged. He didn't care too much, as long as he didn't have to live on the smelly ship anymore. "Hey, you know what else Samoset told us?"

"What?"

"That this place used to be called Patuxet. But a few years ago all the people died. There was a really bad plague."

"A plague? What kind of a plague?" Mary Elizabeth had that worried tone again.

"I don't know. One of the ships brought it over. It killed a lot of people, Samoset said. All the way up north to his tribe."

Mary Elizabeth slowed her steps. "So there's a lot of Indians around here?"

"Aye. He said the Wampanoag wish to be good neighbors, and it must have been the Nauset that attacked the men on shore that night."

"Oh." Her brow was all wrinkled.

"Don't worry. Samoset said they don't want to kill us anymore."

The plan hadn't gone as Peter had hoped.

And maybe he hadn't thought about what would happen if they all agreed that William *was* a spy.

What would they think of a new company employee then? Or would he be able to convince them that he was trustworthy since he'd discovered the man who wanted them to fail? He would be up front about it from the beginning instead of hiding the secret away. The people had to respect that.

He'd have to send word back with the *Mayflower* to his cousin. Maybe his family could pull some strings and get things expedited.

The worst part was that he would just have to wait and see.

And he hated waiting.

But he still had the money. No one had even thought to ask him for it after he'd confronted William with the journal.

Maybe he would just keep it. He'd earned it, after all.

Thursday, 22 March 1620/1

Mary Elizabeth woke to the sound of birds chirping and singing. For the first time in eight months, she'd slept on dry land—not on a ship. And it was wonderful.

Stretching on her bed, she looked up at the roof. William had done a good job with the thatch. It was so thick she couldn't see any holes, which would be good for when it rained.

Another thought sent a thrill through her. She stood up. All the way. Stretching her arms above her head, she still didn't touch the ceiling. No more crouching and bending to fit into the short space of the cramped deck they'd lived on. Laughing out loud, she covered her mouth so she wouldn't wake David. She'd never been so thankful to stand up straight. And inside.

Amazing what a few months of hardship could teach. To find joy in even the smallest matters.

She wanted to accomplish so many things today. Work in the garden. Unpacking all the possessions that had been stored in the hold for all these months. And goodness, she'd love to make some bread if she could scrounge up the ingredients. They had foodstuffs stored in some of the barrels that were now in the common house, but she couldn't remember how much flour they'd rationed.

Before any of that, Mary Elizabeth wanted to speak to William. This had gone on long enough, and now that Mr. Bradford had explained the "why" behind William's behavior, she was ready to talk to him about it and convince him that she would love him no matter what.

Tightening the strings of her shift, she prayed for guidance. Certainly the Lord would bless her efforts to honor her future husband by sticking by his side.

She put on her green shirtwaist and adjusted the laces at the shoulders. She'd lost a good deal of weight between the hardship of the voyage and sickness. Holding out her hands in front of her, she noticed her wrists appeared exceedingly bony. It wasn't the greatest appearance for a bride-to-be, but she'd just have to eat more in the coming weeks.

Slipping on the matching green skirt over her shift, she hoped the extra effort would impress William. He hadn't seen this dress on her before. Would he appreciate it?

Doubts filled her mind as she walked to the common house. She wasn't normally a confrontational person. Other than her spat with the sailor on board the *Mayflower*, she'd never confronted anyone. Ever.

She took a deep breath and entered the common house. Now or never.

William sat in the corner with John as they broke the fast over a barrel.

"Mr. Lytton, could I speak to you for a moment?"

His head snapped in her direction. "Of course." Standing up, he nodded to John.

"Thank you."

William took her elbow and walked her outside. "You look lovely this morning." His blue eyes seemed sad.

Unsure of the best way to handle it, she went straight to the point. "William, I can't let you end our betrothal. I've made a commitment to you, and you can't brush me aside so easily." She twisted her hands in front of her. "I understand you are trying to protect me in some way, but this is not the way to do it."

His face turned toward the hill where the cannons now sat. The muscle in his jaw twitched. "I can't risk your well-being along with my own—"

"But isn't that what marriage is all about? The two—side by side?"

"We're not married yet, Mary Elizabeth."

The words stung. She fought back tears.

"Until we know the outcome of their ruling, I can't even consider putting you in a scandalous situation. Your reputation is on the line along with mine. That's not fair to you or to young David."

"But it's not true! You aren't a spy. You haven't done anything wrong." Tears slipped out from under her lashes.

William took her hands in his own. "I love it that you think that, Mary Elizabeth, I do. It lifts my heart to the heavens to know that you believe in me. But I have to do this. It's for the best." He squeezed her hands while he gazed at her. Those blue eyes burning with sorrow.

Then he let go and walked away.

Mary Elizabeth stood in the middle of their street and cried.

CHAPTER 31

The hurt look on Mary Elizabeth's face stuck with William all morning. And he was the one who'd put it there. It was bad enough that people didn't trust him anymore and half of them thought he was a spy, but now he'd tossed her aside. A little more of him died with the thought. It didn't matter that he had to do the noble and right thing by her. That he had to protect her reputation from tarnish. He'd never get that look out of his memory.

After leaving her in the street, his decision became even clearer. He'd have to pack up his belongings and leave with the *Mayflower*. Mary Elizabeth would stand by his side no matter what, but if the people rejected him, didn't trust him, then her reputation would be linked with him. What future did that give her? And little David?

It didn't take him long to pack his things. All that was left was to secure passage with the master. It was best this way. The people of Plimouth could carry on and not have to worry about who to trust.

As he left the shelter of their fort—the fenced-in little group of buildings—William headed to the trees. The little colony of Plimouth would be having their ceremony for Captain Standish today, and while he wanted to be a part of it, he didn't think the people wanted him. Since he couldn't be much use anywhere else, he could at least chop some wood to make furniture.

The walk gave him a chance to pray. *Lord, this isn't going the way I'd planned. But I want to trust You. I just don't know if I'm doing the right thing. I didn't feel like it was wrong to take the job, but I should have listened to Your prodding and shared with my friends.*

Everything had changed. But he wouldn't trade his new relationship with the Lord for anything. He just wished that he could change some of the other circumstances.

They were finally all living in the new settlement. It should be a time of rejoicing, yet William's future wouldn't be here.

As he smashed the ax into a large tree, it felt like all his hopes and dreams were smashed as well.

Discouragement tried to strangle him. *Lord, what do I do?*

With each swing of the ax he prayed. Over and over and over again.

The verse from 2 Corinthians came back to him. " 'We *are* persecuted, but not forsaken; cast downe, but we perish not.' "

The words soothed his anguish a bit. And so he said it again.

" 'We *are* persecuted, but not forsaken; cast downe, but we perish not.' "

He swung the ax again and decided to quote every verse he'd memorized. If he couldn't think on anything but the doubt and discouragement, he would change that by thinking on what was good—God's Word.

As a second tree fell, William looked back toward the settlement. Breathing hard, he leaned on his ax. God was in control. He knew that and trusted in it. He'd have to leave his fate in the Almighty's hands and simply do the best he could. Even returning to England.

Would he ever get over Mary Elizabeth? No. The thought of her brown eyes made him want to cry. He'd never loved anyone but her. And there wouldn't ever be anyone else.

Movement down by Town Brook caught his attention.

His eyes widened. Indians!

And not just one like the other day. There were at least forty—no fifty!—men.

The ceremony for Captain Standish should be taking place now. Were these men readying an attack?

William picked up the ax and wound his way through the trees to get a better look.

What if he was the only one who could warn them? Those natives looked like warriors. They could kill everyone in a matter of minutes.

He couldn't let that happen.

Mary Elizabeth waited outside the door. Peter had gone in, and eventually he would have to come out. And when he did? She'd be waiting.

The ceremony would start any minute, and she wanted this over with.

The door opened, and Peter stepped out.

Mary Elizabeth stepped in front of him.

"Excuse me, Miss Chapman."

"I don't think I will, Peter."

His smile looked pasty. "I'd like to go to the ceremony." He offered an elbow. "Would you like me to escort you?"

"No. I would not." She placed her hands on her hips. "But I would like to know why you still have William's money."

His eyes shifted around and then stared at the ground. "I don't know what you're talking about."

"Yes, you do." John Alden exited the house behind Peter. "It's right here. Along with a few other things that don't look like they belong to you."

Running as fast as he could, William took a longer trek back to the fort by going around the back side. If he could just warn someone, maybe they could prevent a disaster.

When he made it to the assembly, he noticed Mr. Bradford standing near the rear. "Bradford!"

Several people looked in his direction, but he didn't care.

"Yes, William?" The man turned to him.

"There's Indians at the brook."

"How many?"

"At least fifty." By this point, half the crowd had turned to stare at William.

Governor Carver stopped his speech and walked toward him. "Where did you see them?"

"They're across the brook. I don't know what they're intentions are, but I felt I needed to warn you all just in case."

Their leader furrowed his brow and then rested a hand on William's shoulder. "Thank you. You did the right thing. Let's hope they are the Wampanoag that Samoset told us about."

As William caught his breath, he noticed Mary Elizabeth with David and John across the crowd. She smiled at him.

His heart ached to go see her, to hold her hand. But he knew he couldn't.

"Samoset!" Governor Carver's exclamation made everyone turn the other direction. "Welcome!"

The tall native man walked straight down the center of their street again, and this time he had a friend. They carried some skins and fish and didn't seem to be bothered by all the staring.

"We're glad you came back." Governor Carver smiled and bowed.

Samoset nodded. "This. . .Tisquantum."

The governor moved closer. "Do you know anything about the men at the brook?"

He nodded again. "That. . .Massasoit. Sachem of Wampanoag."

"And he's here for what reason?"

Silence covered the crowd as they all waited for the Indian's response.

Samoset poked Governor Carver in the chest. "You talk."

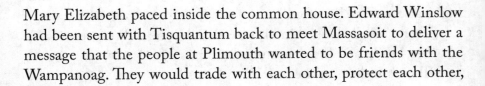

Mary Elizabeth paced inside the common house. Edward Winslow had been sent with Tisquantum back to meet Massasoit to deliver a message that the people at Plimouth wanted to be friends with the Wampanoag. They would trade with each other, protect each other, and be at peace with each other.

Winslow stayed at the brook with Massasoit's brother while the sachem and twenty of his men came into town. Governor Carver, Captain Standish, and Elder Brewster were all in a house, speaking with the chief at that very moment.

And so everyone waited.

As much as she wanted to have peace with the natives, she had another matter of urgent business. She couldn't wait for this meeting to be over so she could speak to Governor Carver about William.

The door to the big room opened, and the governor walked in with Massasoit. "We have a treaty!" Mr. Carver smiled.

The crowd clapped and cheered while Massasoit raised his eyebrows and simply nodded.

Mary Elizabeth had to admit the man was quite striking and an imposing figure. Thank the Lord a treaty had been reached.

Elder Brewster brought forth a parchment. "I shall read you all the terms." He cleared his throat. "One: That neither Massasoit or any of his, should injure or do hurt, to any of our people. Two: That if any of his, did hurt to any of ours; he should send the offender, so that he might be punished. Three: That if anything were taken away from any of our people, he should cause it to be restored; and we should do the like to his. Four: If any did unjustly war against Massasoit, we would aid him; if any did war against us, he should aid us. Five: He should send to his neighbors confederates, to certify them of this, that they might not wrong us, but might be likewise comprised in the conditions of peace. Six: That when their men come to us, they should leave their bows and arrows behind them. Likewise, when we visit them."

The men in the room all nodded.

Mary Elizabeth did too. It sounded like a wonderful peace treaty.

Massasoit turned away and left the building. Everyone watched as the noble-looking man walked down the street with his men.

Governor Carver held his hands up again. "I do believe we need to praise the Lord for this historic event today."

Amens were heard throughout the room, and people began to

talk over one another. The excitement of having so many Indians in their midst was thrilling.

Mary Elizabeth walked up to the governor. "Mr. Carver, I think it's high time that you and the elders discuss William Lytton and the accusations against him."

Peter walked forward, his head ducked.

"I believe that Peter has something to say to all of us."

The room quieted.

The man who'd accused William stared at his shoes. "I should probably tell you that I had planned on accusing Mr. Lytton from the beginning of the voyage."

"Why would you do such a thing?" Elder Brewster moved toward the young man.

"Because I wanted the job that had been offered to him. It was only after I saw Mr. Crawford offer him the job that I came up with the plan. If I could tarnish his reputation, then you all would believe that he was a spy and out to see us ruined."

Mr. Bradford also moved forward, his brow deeply creased. "What made you come forward today?"

Peter glanced up at Mary. "Miss Chapman came to me and said that if I didn't tell the truth, she would. And she would. . ."

"Yes, go on," Governor Carver pushed.

He sighed and ducked his head again. "She would present the evidence that I have been stealing from you all. She said I deserved the opportunity to confess first."

CHAPTER 32

The room erupted in a jumble of words. Maybe it was better for William to exit now. He could grab his belongings and go speak to Captain Jones. Even with Peter's confession, the people would still consider him a spy and would feel betrayed by him. There wasn't any other course of action for him. But at least people knew the truth now.

As William walked toward the door during the ruckus, John caught his arms. His friend whispered in his ear. "You aren't going anywhere."

Governor Carver raised his arms. "Please, everyone." He turned to Peter. "What have you stolen?"

Peter ducked his head and laid the items out in front of everyone. William felt sorry for the young man—something he wouldn't have felt before he came to know his Savior.

Several gasps were heard, and William spied the coin pouch he'd been given by Mr. Crawford. Oh, if he could only go back and tell people the truth.

Governor Carver worked to get everyone's attention. "Settle down, settle down. We need to conduct ourselves in an orderly manner." He turned to Peter. "What do you have to say for yourself, Peter?"

Peter apologized and confessed to everything—his plan to accuse William and stealing from the others.

"Mary Elizabeth?" Governor Carver turned to the beautiful woman William wished he could marry. But that dream would have to die.

She tried to convince everyone that he was a good man. Then John Alden vouched for him. Several men spoke up next of the good work William had done and how he'd helped others. And Mr. Bradford reminded everyone that William had warned them all about the fifty warriors that showed up unannounced.

Peter walked up to him and returned the pouch with the money.

William looked out at the crowd. These people that he'd lived with and worked with for all this time. They might not trust him, but he could at least do the honorable thing. He held the bag aloft. "I know that my actions have made many of you distrust me. It was never my intention to spy on anyone or to be dishonest in any way. So in an effort to ask for forgiveness, I'd like to donate these funds to put toward the debts owed by the colonists. This should help." He tossed the bag to Governor Carver and strode toward the door.

The governor asked for other testimonies so they could vote.

William couldn't bear to see Mary Elizabeth any longer. His departure would be best for all of them. If only he'd learned this lesson earlier—before he'd lost his heart to her. He snuck out of the common house and headed to the stream. His future was in God's hands. Exactly where it should be.

❧

The brook was beautiful this time of day with the sun shining down on its clear water. It made William think of being washed clean.

The rustling in the grass made him look across the brook. Captain Standish escorted Peter and looked to William. "This young man would like to speak with you, Mr. Lytton."

"I know you probably hate me after what I did, and I don't blame you. But I'd like to ask for your forgiveness, William." Peter's hands had been bound once he'd admitted to stealing. While William wanted justice done, he hated to see that.

William stood and faced his one-time accuser. "You are forgiven, Peter. Just as Christ has forgiven me." He turned to Standish. "What will happen to him?"

"Master Jones has agreed to take him back to England. The company will decide what to do after that."

He turned back to Peter. "I wish you well, Peter, and do not wish any harm to come to you." At one time, he wouldn't have been able to say those words. But God had done a mighty work in him.

A call from the fort reached his ears. William looked out across and saw John Alden waving his arm in the air.

"You better go. We will be right behind you." Captain Standish nodded.

William walked back to the little town. Dread lodged in the pit of his stomach. He'd have to find a way to say goodbye to Mary Elizabeth and David. The thought made his stomach turn.

John shook his hand as William reached the fort. "They've voted."

"And?"

"Well, you have to go inside and hear from them."

They walked toward the common house, and the crowd met them outside.

Governor Carver came forward. "It was unanimous, William. There are no charges against you."

Relief flooded his chest, and he felt like the weight of the world had been lifted off his shoulders.

"It's quite unfortunate that we've put you through this difficult time." Mr. Bradford came forward and shook his hand. "We're all very grateful that you have been part of our community, and we'd like to ask you to stay and *remain* a part of our community."

William blinked several times. Had they known he was leaving? "You want me to stay?"

Faces around the room were filled with smiles.

Mr. Bradford clapped him on the back. "Of course we want you to stay!"

John Alden was the next to come forward and whispered in his ear. "They knew you had packed to go, and that impressed many of the offended—that you would sacrifice your future for their trust."

William looked around the room again.

Elder Brewster came forward. "There is no hesitancy in our trust of you, Mr. Lytton. Rest assured."

The words touched his heart, and he let himself look for Mary Elizabeth. She stood in the back with David, a teary smile on her face.

John put a hand on William's shoulder and shouted to the crowd. "Looks like it's time to have a wedding!"

William walked to Mary Elizabeth as the crowd hushed. "Are you willing?"

Her eyes sparkled. "Aye, William Lytton. Always and forever."

※

Tuesday, 3 April 1621

The day was warm in the gorgeous sunlight. Mary Elizabeth walked down the beach toward the long sandbar and thanked the Lord for all that He'd done and provided. After so many months of hardship and devastation, they were looking forward to a brighter future.

Many trials were sure to be ahead, but most of the colony was beginning to rest in the fact that the worst finally seemed to be behind them. Tisquantum had stayed in their little town and taught them about planting corn and using fish as fertilizer to help it grow. Word traveled quickly around the native peoples, and Tisquantum was a wonderful asset to have as a translator. It didn't take long for the people of Plimouth to come up with a nickname for the tall and strong native man in their midst—Squanto.

He'd also been very handy teaching everyone—women included— how to fish in the brook. Mary Elizabeth thought of her conversation with Mrs. Hopkins aboard the ship—and no matter how much fish she ate, she would be grateful.

When she reached the sandbar about a mile down from their set- tlement, Mary saw David and William already there. She placed her hands on her hips. "Are you two plotting against me?"

"Us?" William put a hand to his chest and looked down at David. "We would never do that."

"Are you ready to race, Mary Elizabeth?"

"I just walked all the way down here. You could at least be a gentleman and let me catch my breath."

"You're just worried because you're going to lose."

She eyed her little brother. "I may be 'old' and a girl, but I'm still fast."

"How do you know? It's not like you ever run anywhere." David shook his head like she was out of her mind.

Mary Elizabeth laughed. It was true. She hadn't run in a very long time. But this was for David, and she'd do anything for the little imp. "All right. Do we have any rules?"

William stepped forward. "I'm so glad you asked, milady." He bowed. "This log right here marks the start line. There's another one way down there for the finish line. That's where I'll be waiting to see who crosses it first." He winked at her. "Now there will be no pushing, no shoving, no tripping, no biting—"

David started giggling.

"Honestly, William." Mary Elizabeth shook her head but couldn't resist smiling up at him.

"All right, there will be no cheating. How's that?"

"Run in a straight line. Win. I think I've got it." She nodded.

"Are you ready for me to head down to the finish line?"

"Yes!" David jumped up and down.

"Good. You'll know when to start when you see my arm lower, like this." William raised his arm high and dropped it down.

"Well, you need to hurry before anyone sees what we're doing. I don't think I want to be seen the day before my wedding in a footrace. I'm supposed to be a proper young lady, you know."

William's laugh was his response as he ran down the sandy bar.

David and Mary crouched down a little as they waited for the signal.

William dropped his arm.

She took off. Halfway to William she realized she should have made David wear a heavy skirt to make the race fair. But she pressed on.

William held out his two hands as they drew near.

Her feet pounded the sand, and she crossed the line of finish.

"Mary Elizabeth wins!" The shout made her laugh and raise her arms in triumph.

As she turned around, David barreled into her and tackled her to the ground. "You're pretty fast for a girl."

Breathing hard, she hugged her little brother. He wouldn't be little for much longer, and she would treasure every moment she had with him. "You're getting pretty fast yourself, little man."

He crossed his arms over his chest. "I guess you're not as old as you look."

William's laughter followed them the entire walk home.

❧

Wednesday, 4 April 1621

The deck of the *Mayflower* no longer held crates of chickens and pigs or other animals. It had been swept clean for the festivities of the day and now held the survivors of their first winter. As she looked around at the faces, she realized how wonderful it was to be a part of this group. Through joy and sorrow, they had triumphed. They were here today for a very special reason.

Mary Elizabeth's heart thumped in her chest. Today she would marry William.

Dressed in her finest dress of red wool, she checked her sleeves and the tucks of her skirt. She closed her eyes for a moment and breathed a prayer for peace and calmness for her spirit. She hoped that Mother, Father, and Dorothy knew that God had brought her a wonderful husband.

A tug at her arm made her open her eyes. "Are you ready, Mary Elizabeth?"

"I am." She looked at her younger brother. So handsome in his blue breeches and coat. "I'm so proud of you, David."

"As I am of you. I'm glad you're marrying William. He's a Godly man and he loves you. And he's a lot of fun."

"He is fun, isn't he?" The smile that stretched across her face felt like it might reach her ears. "And you're correct: he loves me. I love him too."

"As long as you're happy." Such grown-up words from little David. Time was moving far too fast. If she blinked, he might be grown and gone.

"Very much so."

"Well then, let's get you married." David took her arm and walked her to the center of the main deck.

Mr. Bradford stood there with William and smiled. "You look lovely, Mary Elizabeth."

"I agree." William winked at her.

Mary Elizabeth's stomach tumbled over itself as Mr. Bradford talked about the holy union of marriage and how it represented Christ and His bride—the church.

William's eyes were riveting. She could spend the rest of her life just gazing into their blue depths.

After reading some scripture, Mr. Bradford looked at her. "Are you ready?"

"Oh, yes." She determined to stay focused this time. Of course, who could blame her for being focused on her husband-to-be?

Mr. Bradford had them repeat some simple vows and then took William's hand and her hand and raised them in the air. He placed them together and quoted Matthew 19:6 in a loud, booming voice, " 'Let not man therefore put a sunder that, which *God* hathe coupled together!' "

Cheers broke out around the small crowd, and William took her hands in his. They walked to the longboat together where two sailors would row them ashore while the rest would return in the shallop.

William climbed down into the boat first, and he reached up for her. She couldn't take her eyes off his as she found her way in the small craft.

When he placed his hands on her waist, she placed her hands on the side of his face. This man was hers. And she loved him with all her heart.

He leaned in with a twinkle in his eye. "I love you, Mrs. Lytton." Before she could respond, he captured her lips with his own, and Mary Elizabeth didn't think anything in the world could be better than that.

Epilogue

1 August 1665

The wildflowers in William's hand put off a heady scent as he looked out to the harbor. Mary Elizabeth was sure to love the bouquet he'd brought her. In his old age, he was getting to be quite the romantic. The thought made him chuckle. Twelve children and forty-two grandchildren might get a kick out of hearing William Lytton was a softy.

A massive ship in the distance showed off her great sails as she entered their beautiful bay. Forty-five years ago today, he'd left England. For where and to what was uncertain at the time, but he was ever so thankful he had climbed the gangway to the *Mayflower*.

They'd suffered great losses, and it had taken much more than the original contracted seven years to pay off their debts, but they'd survived through all the ups and downs of life. He'd come out victorious with his God and his bride.

He snuck in the door to their kitchen and crept up behind Mary Elizabeth. Wrapping his arms around her, he whispered in her ear, "I love you."

Mary Elizabeth turned around and gasped. "Flowers! You dear man." She hugged him and whispered back. "I love you too."

Her eyes were still that beloved shade of deep brown, but her hair had turned gray under her cap. It was very becoming.

Taking her hand, William led her to the door and then out onto the path where they could see the harbor. "Forty-five years ago, I started a journey. It hasn't been easy, but I feel very blessed. I found

God. And I found you."

"Aye, my love. We are very blessed." She sent him a wink.

All around them, life bustled and bloomed. What had started out as eight meager buildings became a town full of buildings and activity.

Their congregation had grown, and so had their family.

Mary Elizabeth had been faithful at his side through it all.

And whatever the future held for their little colony and this brave New World, he couldn't wait to share it with her.

His *Mayflower* bride.

What could now sustain them, but the Spirit of God and His grace?

May not, and ought not the children of these fathers rightly say, "Our fathers were Englishmen which came over this great ocean, and were ready to perish in this wilderness, but they cried unto the Lord and He heard their voice, and looked on their adversity," etc.

"Let them therefore praise the Lord, because He is good; and His mercies endure forever. Yea, let them which have been redeemed of the Lord, show how He hath delivered them, from the hand of the oppressor.

When they wandered in the desert wilderness out of the way, and found no city to dwell in; both hungry, and thirsty, their soul was overwhelmed in them."

"Let them confess before the Lord His loving kindness, and His wonderful works before the sons of men."

–William Bradford, *Of Plymouth Plantation*

Note to the Reader

It's exciting to trace our lineages back. Many people are able to trace their family history all the way back to the *Mayflower*—I've had fun tracing my roots to 1659, Virginia, Colonial America.

I found it interesting in my research that the majority of Americans think of the *Mayflower* as the actual beginning of our great country. And it's true. The settlers that landed at Plymouth Rock and established Plymouth Colony are the foundations of this great land.

Take for instance, John Howland. His escapade falling overboard really did happen. How he managed to grab the topsail halyard is truly a miracle in and of itself. The most interesting tidbit to me about his whole story is that he ended up having ten children, eighty-eight grandchildren, and now almost two million of his descendants live in the United States. (Several presidents of this great country are in his line—including Franklin D. Roosevelt, George H. W. Bush, and George W. Bush—as well as many famous people, such as Alec Baldwin, Humphrey Bogart, Christopher Lloyd, and Sarah Palin.) That's incredible. Imagine what would have happened if he had been lost to sea that day.

Then there's John Alden—hired as the cooper on the ship and given the option to stay in the colony or return to England. He chose to stay and marry Priscilla Mullins. His line extends down to Dick Van Dyke, Orson Welles, Marilyn Monroe, former Vice President Dan Quayle, and Henry Wadsworth Longfellow. The lines of William Brewster and William Bradford are just as fascinating, as well as the lines of all the other passengers who lived through the great ordeal that was the *Mayflower* and her journey.

It was shocking to me to discover that out of all of the *Mayflower* passengers, only five adult women survived that first winter. Only five. Astounding, isn't it?

While we know the dates the *Speedwell* and the *Mayflower* left Leyden, Southampton, Dartmouth, and Plymouth, the rest of the dates for the voyage aren't exact. When dates weren't known, I used my own discretion and creativity with the time stamps. It's also important to note that during this time period, the Julian calendar was still in use—unlike the Gregorian calendar we use today. This makes for about a ten-day difference. The new year didn't start until March 25 (instead of January 1 like it does now). But to keep this consistent with history and to keep from confusing you as a reader, I've shown the year as 1620/1 starting in January.

It may be shocking to know that these strict Separatists—so staunch in their faith—drank beer for their staple beverage and considered it good for their health. During this time, beer was a brew watered down so that the alcoholic level was 0.05–1.0 percent. Strong enough to kill any bacteria in the water but drinkable by all—including infants and children.

The profane sailor's torment of the Separatists and his subsequent death are true events, although we don't know exactly when it happened, nor is he named (the nickname I gave him is purely fictional). According to William Bradford's *Of Plymouth Plantation*, "There was a proud and very profane young man, one of the seamen, of a lusty able body, which made him the more haughty; he would always be contemning the poor people in their sickness, and cursing them daily with grievous execrations, and did not let to tell them, that he hoped to help to cast half of them overboard before they came to their journey's end, and to make merry with what they had; and if he were gently reproved, he would curse and swear most bitterly. But it pleased God before they came half seas over, to smite this young man with a grievous disease, of which he died in a desperate manner; and so was himself the first that was thrown overboard; thus his curses light on his own head; and it was an astonishment to all his fellows, for they noted it to be the just hand of God upon him." So this unnamed man went down in history as the first to die on the *Mayflower*.

The story of the four More children is tragic, but how fascinating that Samuel More paid for their passage to give them a chance at a new life away from their mother's reputation and their own as illegitimate children.

Several sources state that Mr. Reynolds—the master of the Speedwell—sabotaged the ship so he wouldn't have to make the trip to America and potentially starve to death. A couple of sources state that the ship began leaking immediately (or that Reynolds complained of it leaking) after departing Holland, while others show that the leaking began after their departure from Southampton. Since the *Speedwell* after this adventure was "trimmed" and made many other voyages, it was believed that she was "overmasted and too much pressed with sail." William Bradford wrote in his journal, *Of Plymouth Plantation*, that once they returned to Plymouth, England, the leaks were never verified or truly found, but they kept taking on water. "No special leak could be found, but it was judged to be the general weakness of the ship, and that she would not prove equal to the voyage." He also wrote, "But it was partly due to the cunning and deceit of the master and his crew, who had been hired to stay a whole year at the Settlement, and now, fearing want of victuals, they plotted this stratagem to free themselves, as was afterwards confessed by some of them." How different would our history be if both ships—the *Speedwell* and the *Mayflower*—had journeyed to America on time with all the people who set out? Would they have reached their intended destination earlier in the year (which would be the area of modern-day Manhattan)? Would there have been as much death that first winter? We will never know, but the Saints and their expedition to the New World is indeed fascinating—not only for the beginnings of our great country, but also for the beginning of democracy because of the Mayflower Compact's impact on government over the years. Its influence on the framers of the Constitution alone is astounding.

Since our hero—William Lytton—is a fictional character, please note that he was not historically one of the forty-one signers of the

Mayflower Compact, but for the sake of the story, I had him sign. There also was obviously no espionage—there's no record of anyone being hired by the company to keep a journal or records or to spy on the Planters.

While there are many resources on the history surrounding the *Mayflower*, the best source I found was through Caleb Johnson and his fabulous website: www.Mayflowerhistory.com. You can find a complete list of the passengers and the crew (the ones that we know the names of) on his site, as well as much other information about this historic event. Mr. Johnson also granted us permission to quote from his edited version of William Bradford's *Of Plymouth Plantation*.

ACKNOWLEDGMENTS

No book ever just happens. So I'd like to thank those who have been so instrumental in bringing this novel to fruition.

First and foremost to my Lord and Savior, Jesus Christ. This is all for You.

Second, my amazing husband, Jeremy, who puts up with crazy author research and deadlines. I love you more than I could ever express. After more than a quarter of a century of marriage, it just keeps getting better, and I'm looking forward to spending decades and decades more with you. You are amazing.

Third, Becky Germany. What fun to be a part of this series! You are wonderful. Thank you. And to my agent, Karen Ball—what a journey we've been on! Thank you for your wisdom and guidance. Becky Fish, you were a joy to work with! Thank you for your diligent work even in the midst of wedding and eclipse craziness!

Fourth, my beloved crit partners: Kayla Woodhouse, Becca Whitham, and Darcie Gudger. You're all so brilliant and very unique in your insight—each book has been better because of you.

Fifth, to all the team at Barbour. Thank you!

Sixth, to Caleb Johnson, *Mayflower* historian and an incredible help during the writing of this book. Thank you so much. www.Mayflowerhistory.com

Last, but definitely not least, my readers. Thank you for journeying with me on yet another wonderful historical novel. I couldn't do this without you!

Kimberley Woodhouse is an award-winning and bestselling author of more than twenty-five fiction and nonfiction books. Winner of the Carol Award, the Holt Medallion, The Reader's Choice Award, Selah Award, and Spur Award. A popular speaker and teacher, she's shared her theme of "Joy Through Trials" with more than two million people across the country at more than two thousand events. Kim and her husband of thirty years have two adult, married children. She is passionate about music and Bible study and loves the gift of story. You can connect with Kimberley at www.kimberleywoodhouse.com and at www.facebook.com/KimberleyWoodhouseAuthor.

The
Pirate
Bride

KATHLEEN Y'BARBO

DEDICATION

To the survivors:

As I type this, my beloved Texas has been drenched by the
Historical flood waters of Hurricane Harvey.

May God richly bless those who waded through water,
Either away from a flooded home or toward one.
May He allow His blessings to shine upon the heroes
And His mercy on those who mourn.

From the tip of the coast at Port Aransas to
Galveston where my youngest son lives,
To Houston where two of my children and I call home,
And to Port Neches and the rest of Jefferson County,
The place where I was born and raised,
To any place on Texas soil where rain and tears have fallen this week,
We are Texas Strong.

God bless Texas!

For where your treasure is, there will your heart be also.
MATTHEW 6:21

Daughters of the Mayflower

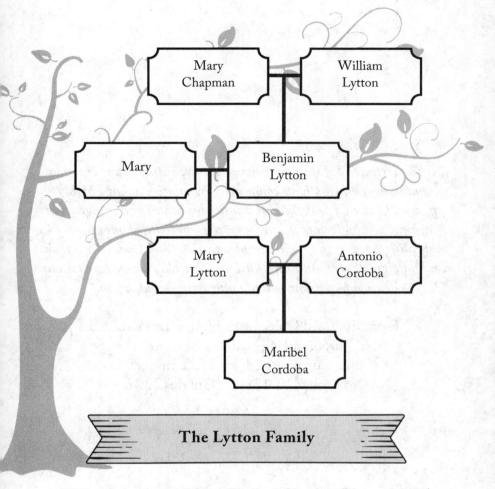

Mary Chapman — William Lytton

Mary — Benjamin Lytton

Mary Lytton — Antonio Cordoba

Maribel Cordoba

The Lytton Family

William Lytton married Mary Elizabeth Chapman (Plymouth 1621)
Parents of 13 children (one son is Benjamin)
Benjamin Lytton married Temperance (Massachusetts 1668)
widowed then married Mary (Massachusetts 1675)
Born to Benjamin and Mary
Mary Lytton who married Antonio Cordoba (Spain 1698)
Born to Mary and Antonio
Maribel Cordoba

"As the Testimony of your Conscience must convince you of the great and many evils you have committed, by which you have highly offended God, and provoked most justly his wrath and indignation against you, so I suppose I need not tell you that the only way of obtaining pardon and remission of your sins from God, is by a true and unfeigned repentance and faith in Christ, by whose meritorious death and passion, you can only hope for salvation."

From the Lord Chief Justice Judge Trot's speech
pronouncing sentence of death
upon the pirate Major Stede Bonnet,
November 10, 1711, at Charles Town

Maribel and the Privateer

Part I:

In the waters of the Caribbean Sea
April of 1724

He sent from above, he took me,
he drew me out of many waters.
PSALM 18:16

Chapter 1

Aboard the Spanish vessel
Venganza near Havana

M ama may have been named for the great-grandmother who
traveled from England on the *Mayflower*, but that fact certainly did not keep her in the land of her birth. Twelve-year-old
Maribel Cordoba sometimes wondered why Mama refused to discuss anything regarding her relations in the colonies beyond the
fact that she had disappointed them all by marrying a Spaniard
without her papa's blessing.

The mystery seemed so silly now, what with Mama gone and
the father she barely knew insisting she accompany him aboard
the *Venganza* to his new posting in Havana. Maribel gathered the
last reminder of Mary Lytton around her shoulders—a beautiful
scarf shot through with threads of Spanish silver that matched
the piles of coins in the hold of this magnificent sailing vessel—
and clutched the book she'd already read through once since the
journey began.

Though she was far too young at nearly thirteen to call herself
a lady, Maribel loved to pretend she would someday wear this
same scarf along with a gown in some lovely matching color at a
beautiful ball. Oh she would dance, her toes barely touching the
floor in her dancing shoes. And her handsome escort would, no
doubt, fall madly in love with her just as Papa had fallen in love
with Mama.

Her fingers clutched the soft fabric as her heart lurched. Mama.

Oh how she missed her. She looked toward the horizon, where a lone vessel's sails punctuated the divide between sea and sky, and then shrugged deeper into the scarf.

Nothing but adventure was ahead. This her papa had promised when he announced that, as newly named Consul General, he was moving her from their home in Spain to the faraway Caribbean.

She had read about the Caribbean in the books she hid beneath her pillows. The islands were exotic and warm, populated with friendly natives and not-so-friendly pirates.

Maribel clutched her copy of *The Notorious Seafaring Pyrates and Their Exploits* by Captain Ulysses Jones. The small leather book that held the true stories of Blackbeard, Anne Bonny, and others had been a treasure purchased in a Barcelona bookseller's shop when Papa hadn't been looking.

Of course, Papa never looked at her, so she could have purchased the entire shop and he wouldn't have noticed.

But then, until the day her papa arrived with the news that Mama and Abuelo were now with the angels, she'd only seen this man Antonio Cordoba three times in her life. Once at her grandmother's funeral and twice when he and Mama had quarreled on the doorstep of their home in Madrid.

On none of these occasions had Señor Cordoba, apparently a very busy and very important man, deigned to speak to his only daughter. Thus his speech about Mama had been expectedly brief, as had the response to Maribel's request to attend her funeral or at least see her grave.

Both had been answered with a resolute no. Two days later, she was packed aboard the *Venganza*.

She watched the sails grow closer and held tight to Mama's scarf. Just as Mama had taught her, she turned her fear of this unknown place that would become her new home into prayer. Unlike Mama—who would have been horrified at the stories of Captain Bartholomew Roberts and others—Maribel's hopes surged.

Perhaps this dull journey was about to become exciting. Perhaps the vessel on the horizon held a band of pirates bent on chasing them down and relieving them of their silver.

By habit, Maribel looked up into the riggings where her only friend on this voyage spent much of his day. William Spencer, a gangly orphan a full year older and many years wiser than she, was employed as lookout. This, he explained to her, was a step up from the cabin boy he'd been for nigh on seven years and a step toward the ship's captain he someday hoped to be.

Their passing annoyance, which began when she nearly pitched herself overboard by accident while reading and strolling on deck, had become something akin to an alliance during their weeks at sea. To be sure, William still felt she was hopeless as a sailor, but his teasing at Maribel's noble Spanish lineage and habit of keeping her nose in a book had ceased when she discovered the source.

William Spencer could not read. Or at least he couldn't when they set sail from Barcelona.

He'd been a quick study, first listening as she read from *Robinson Crusoe* and *The Iliad* and then learning to sound out words and phrases as they worked their way through Shakespeare's *Julius Caesar*. By the time she offered him her copy of Captain Jones's pirate book, William was able to read the entire book without any assistance.

She spied him halfway up the mainmast. "Sails," she called, though he appeared not to hear her. "Over there," Maribel added a bit louder as she used her book to point toward the ship.

The watch bell startled her with its clang, and the book tumbled to the deck. A moment later, crewmen who'd previously strolled about idly now ran to their posts shouting in Spanish words such as "*pirata*" and "*barco fantasma.*"

"Pirates and a ghost ship?" she said under her breath as she grabbed for the book and then dodged two crewmen racing past with weapons drawn. "How exciting!"

"Don't be an idiot, Red." William darted past two men rolling a cannon toward the *Venganza*'s bow then hurried to join her, a scowl on his face. "This isn't like those books of yours. If that's the *Ghost Ship*, then you'd best wish for anything other than excitement."

Shielding her eyes from the sun's glare, Maribel looked up at William. "What do you mean?"

"I mean they're bearing down on us and haven't yet shown a flag. I wager when they do, we won't be liking what flag they're flying."

"So pirates," she said, her heart lurching. "Real pirates."

"Or Frenchmen," he said. "A privateer ship is my guess if they're not yet showing the skull and crossbones."

She continued to watch the sails grow larger. "Tell me about the *Ghost Ship*, William."

"Legend says the ship appears out of thin air, then, after it's sunk you and taken your treasure, all twenty-two guns and more than one hundred crewmen go back the same way they came."

"Back into thin air?" she asked.

"Exactly. Although I have always thought they might be calling Santa Cruz their home as it's near enough to Puerto Rico for provisioning and belongs to the French settlements." He paused to draw himself up to his full height. "And care to guess who the enemy of the men aboard the *Ghost Ship* is?"

Maribel leaned closer, her heart pounding as she imagined these fearless men who chased their prey then disappeared to some mysterious island only to do it all over again. "Who?"

"Spaniards, Red. They hold license from the French crown to take what anyone flying under the Spanish flag has got and split it with the royals. And they don't take prisoners."

She looked up at the flag of Spain flying on the tallest of the masts and then back at William. "No?"

William shook his head. "No. They leave no witnesses. Do you understand now why you do not want that ship out there to be the *Barco Fantasma* as these sons of Madrid call it?"

She squared her shoulders. "Well, I care not," she exclaimed.

"There are no such things as ghosts. My mama said to pray away the fear when it occurred, so perhaps you ought to consider that."

Of course, if she allowed herself to admit it, Maribel should be taking her own advice. Much as Mama reminded her of her status as a woman not born in Spain, her father's lineage and the fact a Spanish flag waved in the warm breeze above her head would seal her fate.

"I'm not scared," William said. "If those fellows catch us, I'd rather join up with them than stay here. Wasn't asked if I wanted to sail on this vessel, so I figure I might as well invite myself to sail on theirs."

"You wouldn't dare. You're not the pirate sort."

"Privateer," he corrected. "And who says I'm not? I read those books of yours. Sure, I'm not one for breaking the law, but if Captain Beaumont offers honest work for my share of the pay, then I'd be better off than I am here. Besides, I can always jump off at the nearest island and stay there like Mr. Robinson Crusoe did. If I tried that now, the Spaniards would come after me and beat me senseless."

She recalled the bruises she'd seen on the boy's arms and nodded. "If you go, I'm going with you. I'll join up with this Captain Beaumont and climb the riggings just like you do."

"You're just a girl," he protested. "Don't you know girls are bad luck on privateers' ships? It was right there in the book."

"It was indeed," she said as she cradled the book against her chest. "But I don't believe in luck. If the Lord allows, then it happens. If He doesn't, then it doesn't. That's what my mama says, and I believe it is true. So I'm going to pray that Captain Beaumont is a good man."

"That's ridiculous, Red."

"The praying?" she said in a huff. "Prayer is never ridiculous."

"No, of course not," he hurried to say. "But to suggest that Captain Beaumont might be a good man—"

"You there, boy," a sailor called as he jostled past William.

"Back to your post and look smart about it."

William fixed her with an impatient look. "While you're doing all this praying, go down to your cabin and hide," he told her. "Bar the door and, no matter what, do not let anyone inside except me or your papa, you understand?"

"Papa," she said as she looked around the deck. "I need to find him."

"Likely he's helping prepare for the attack and won't want a child bothering him," William said. "Do as I said and make quick work of it. Oh, and Red, can you swim?"

"I can," she said even as his description of her as a child stung. "My mama taught me but said we couldn't tell my papa because he thought swimming was undignified and beneath our station. Why?"

"Then if all else fails and you're faced with being captured or the threat of death, jump overboard. It's a known fact that most pirates cannot swim, so you'd be safer afloat in the ocean than aboard a sinking ship." He nudged her shoulder with his, a gesture that reminded her once again of their friendship. "Now off with you, Red. I've got work to do."

"But what about privateers and Frenchmen?" she called to his retreating back. "Can they swim?"

"You better hope you don't find out," was the last thing William said before he disappeared into a crowd of crewmen.

Maribel stood there for a full minute, maybe longer, surveying the chaos unfolding around her. Though she was loath to take William's advice—he was always such a bossy fellow—she did see the wisdom in making herself scarce until the fuss was over.

Oh but she'd not run to her cabin where she would miss all the excitement. There must be a place where she could stay out of the way and still watch what was happening on deck.

Pray away the fear.

She raised up on her tiptoes to look over the men gathered around the cannon. The sails of the approaching vessel were much closer now, their pristine white matching the clouds on the horizon.

A roar went up among the men of the *Venganza*, and then the cannon fired. Covering her ears, Maribel ran in search of the nearest shelter and found it behind thick coils of rope and stacked barrels. Only when she had successfully hidden herself inside the coil did she realize she had dropped her prized book. She had to retrieve it; nothing else would do.

She rose slowly, clutching the ends of Mama's scarf just as the vessel made a turn to the right. With the tilt of the deck, the book slid out of her reach. Braving the throng of people, she headed toward the book, now lodged against the mainmast.

Pray away the fear.

She removed the scarf from her neck and tied it around her head like the pirates whose likenesses filled her books. The ends fluttered in the breeze, and if she thought hard, she could remember Mama wearing this scarf.

She did that now, thought about Mama. About how she loved to tie the scarf around her waist when she wore her pretty dresses. Someday she would tie this scarf around her waist like Mama did.

Someday when she was a grown-up lady.

A cannon sounded from somewhere off in the distance, and then the vessel shuddered. Stifling a scream, Maribel took a deep breath and said a prayer as she grasped the edges of the scarf.

Smoke rolled toward her as Maribel struggled to remain upright on the sloping boards beneath her feet. She reached the book and then slid one arm around the mainmast to steady herself against the pitching motion.

Pray away the fear. Pray away the fear. Pray away. . .

The cannon roared again. A crack sounded overhead and splinters of wood and fire rained down around her.

Then the world went dark.

CHAPTER 2

Captain Jean Beaumont took ownership of the *Venganza* before any man aboard had given it up. He did so simply by claiming it for the crown and glory of France. From that moment, according to the rights granted him in the Letters of Marque, the issue was not whether but how the Spanish vessel would be turned over to its new owner.

Predictably, the Spaniards had resisted all efforts to be peacefully overtaken. A pity, for it was obvious these men stood no chance against his well-trained crew. Now they were paying the price.

All around him his men worked as a team to corral the ship's crew and passengers and prevent any brave souls from seeking retribution. Those assigned to document and remove all valuable items from the vessel had begun their work as well.

Of these men, Jean was most proud. It was a badge of honor to be known and feared by reputation but also to be considered fair in his execution of the privileges extended to him as a privateer.

Each item taken from the vessel would be accounted for, with a list being sent back to the king along with the crown's portion of the spoils. The remainder would be divided among the crew with Jean forgoing his own share.

If the crew thought it odd that their captain took no profit from their voyages, none had been brave enough to say so. This voyage, however, was different. He would take his share, but not in the supplies and silver coin that were now being carried across the deck.

With command of the ship now his to claim, Jean stepped over a fallen Spaniard and kept walking. He sought only one man: Antonio Cordoba.

His second-in-command, a mountain of a man who had escaped slavery to pledge his allegiance to Jean, stepped in front of him holding a man by the back of his neck. It was Israel Bennett's job to go straight to the man in control of the vessel and subdue him.

He did that job well.

The gentle giant offered no expression as he held his quarry still with seemingly little effort. "Claims he's the captain, sir."

Jean looked down at the pitiful captain, taking note of the terror in his eyes and the spotless uniform. Revulsion rose. There was only one reason a man's clothing would be spotless on an occasion such as this. The coward had hidden himself and allowed his men to do the fighting for him.

"See that he understands we have boarded under Letters of Marque on behalf of France and King Louis XV. We wish him and his crew no harm, but we must confiscate what now lawfully is ours."

Israel Bennett dutifully repeated the words in flawless Spanish, saying exactly what Jean would have had he wanted the captain to know he spoke the language fluently. Jean nodded when the message had been delivered.

"I thought he would be older," was the Spaniard's muttered response. "It appears the ghost captain has ceased to age. I claim sorcery."

Israel chuckled, his laughter deep and resonant. "He is of sufficient age to best you and your ship, and I assure you no sorcery was used."

This captain's response was a common one. Though Jean would soon see his twenty-fifth birthday, he was often mistaken for one of his crew rather than the man in charge.

Perhaps this was due to the legend that had grown up alongside the reputation of the vessel that had been dubbed the *Ghost Ship*, not by him but by those who hadn't seen the ship coming until they were close enough for the cannons to reach them. Or perhaps it was because he felt twice his age most days.

"One more thing," Jean added as he looked up at Israel. "Tell him I wish him and his crew no further harm. However, I demand he produce Consul General Antonio Cordoba immediately so that he and I might have a private discussion."

The captain's eyes cut sharply to the left at the sound of the nobleman's name. Jean recognized this as a telling sign of acknowledgment without the man having spoken a word.

While Israel repeated the demand in Spanish and clutched tighter with his massive fists, Jean looked over in the direction where the captain had glanced. Under the watchful eye of one of Jean's crewmen, a dark-haired man in fine clothing knelt at the base of the mainmast. The man's attention was focused on what appeared to be a puddle of cloth.

Then he looked up.

When his eyes met Jean's, he slowly rose. Every muscle in Jean's body went on alert, and his eyes never moved from the man across the deck.

Jean was vaguely aware of a spirited conversation between Israel and the captain, but he kept his attention on the stranger. His last memory of Antonio Cordoba was etched in his mind, although it had been two decades since he had seen the man.

Two decades since the Spaniard pirate and his murdering crew had accosted an innocent French passenger ship. Two decades since they sent every passenger aboard except for a five-year-old boy to the bottom of the sea.

Why he had been saved, Jean had long ago stopped asking the Lord. Every day he awoke alive and healthy, he did so with the realization that he had a debt of gratitude to repay.

What he would do when he found Antonio Cordoba, however, he had long ago decided. Two decades, and now the time had come.

Everything around him ceased to exist in that moment, leaving only Jean and Cordoba. Jean rested his hand on the grip of the jeweled cutlass he'd chosen for the occasion, the same weapon left behind on the deck of that French ship twenty years ago.

The cutlass that had been used to cut down his mother and baby brother.

Jean walked toward the Spanish murderer, stepping over fallen men and stepping around debris that tilted with the list of the ship. All the while, the man Jean knew must be Cordoba merely stood his ground and stared.

"Antonio Cordoba?" Jean called when he was close enough to make his move.

"Who is asking?" the Spaniard responded.

Jean's heart thudded against his chest, every muscle in his body taut and his nerves on alert. "The only survivor of the sinking of the passenger ship *Roi-Soleil.*"

Cordoba's expression never changed as he lifted one shoulder in an almost disdainful shrug. "The *Sun King*, eh? No, the name means nothing. Perhaps I have forgotten," he finally said with a dismissive sweep of his hand.

Forgotten.

The murder of his mother and brother.

Forgotten.

Jean's own brush with death and the long journey to be reunited with his father and brother. All of it as meaningless as a sweep of a Spaniard's jeweled hand.

Something inside Jean snapped. His tight rein on control slipped even as his fingers held tight to the cold metal of the grip. Something akin to a fog blocked out everything except the motions he wished to take.

He lifted the cutlass and held it up. The next blood that stained this weapon would belong to Antonio Cordoba.

Forgotten no more.

A fist grasped his shoulder and held him in place. Jean

attempted to break free but failed.

"This is not how you want to do this, sir," Israel said evenly, his deep baritone cutting through to gain Jean's attention. "Let the Lord handle that man His way. Revenge is His, not yours."

This from a man whose entire family had been separated and sold at the whim of others. Who had been beaten and chained and sold into slavery in Africa by kinsmen bent on revenge.

And yet his words had no effect on Jean. He'd been waiting for this day too long to be dissuaded.

"It is exactly how I want to do this," Jean managed as he kept his attention focused on the arrogant expression on the Spaniard's face.

"Fair enough. But it is not how this should be done." Israel released him and then moved to stand between Jean and Cordoba. "If you proceed, then you'll have to get past me first."

Not since the day Israel Bennett walked out of the hold of a slave ship that had just been taken by Jean and his men and announced he was joining the crew had he seen such resolve on the big man's face. Then, in an instant, his expression contorted and Israel crumpled to the deck.

Jean crumpled with him, dropping the cutlass as he ripped away the rough cloth of Israel's shirt to see blood pouring from a wound on his shoulder. Israel had been shot.

He removed his own shirt to use it as a bandage. "Connor," he shouted above the din. "Someone find Evan Connor. This man needs a doctor's attention."

Israel turned his head to look up at Jean, his face etched with pain. "And you, Jean Beaumont, need the Lord's attention. Do not do this thing you have planned, whatever it is. It will not bring you the relief you seek."

He looked up past Israel's prone body to where Cordoba now lay on the deck. One of Jean's men had wrestled a flintlock pistol from the Spaniard and held him in place with a foot to his back.

Connor arrived in the company of several other men and

pushed Jean aside. As he rose, he felt Israel's hand on his leg.

"Revenge will not be as sweet as you think," the big man said. "It is the Lord's alone and not yours or mine."

Several responses occurred to him. Jean said none of them.

Instead, he rose to cross the deck and removed the flintlock pistol from the sailor's hand. Giving the order for his men to leave them and not intervene, Jean stared down at the man who had haunted his nightmares.

"Stand and face me, Cordoba," he said through clenched jaw. "It is time to look reckoning in the eyes."

Antonio Cordoba climbed to his feet with what appeared to be some measure of difficulty. Jean watched dispassionately as the older man stumbled and required the use of the rail behind him to finally stand upright.

Standing in insolent silence, the defeated enemy dared to smile. *Forgotten.*

Jean advanced on the man, reaching for his cutlass only to realize he'd left it on the deck beside Israel. No matter, he decided, as his fist landed the first punch. Cordoba responded with a blow that glanced off Jean's shoulder.

Immediately his crewmen surrounded them to pull the Spaniard away. "Release him and leave us," Jean called. "No matter what happens, do not intervene."

The last man to leave released the nobleman. Cordoba made a show of straightening his coat and adjusting his sleeves. Still that infernal smile remained.

When they were alone—or at least left alone with wary crewmen grudgingly watching from a distance while they pretended to work—Jean moved closer. Though Cordoba's smile wavered slightly, it did not disappear.

"Something you wish to say?" the Spaniard asked.

"Much," he managed through clenched jaw. "But I would have you speak first in hopes you'll say something that will convince me not to dispatch you to the place you belong."

"Ah," he said slowly. "I see your dilemma. You wish revenge for something so inconsequential to me that I no longer recall it. That must upset you greatly."

Forgotten.

Jean managed a ragged breath. His fingers clutched air and wished for his weapon.

"Oh," Cordoba continued. "It does. I see it. I also see you've left your weapon with your unfortunate friend. A pity I missed when I was aiming for you."

Jean hit him again, and this time the Spaniard went down hard. As he lay on the sloping deck, Antonio Cordoba had the audacity to laugh.

"Feel any better?" he taunted as he lay there. "Go find a weapon and come back. I will wait. Then you can finish me off and be done with whatever revenge you've been seeking."

Everything in him wanted to do as the older man said. And yet Jean remained in place.

"Vengeance is mine; I will repay, saith the Lord."

"No?" Cordoba said with a lift of his brows as he sat up to rest on his elbows. "Ah, well, fine then. You're one who wishes to exact pain before vengeance. You wish me to hurt as you have hurt. Go ahead." He stood and held out his arms. "I'll not fight back. I no longer have it in me. Just be done with it."

Again Jean found he could not move. Could not do the one thing he'd plotted and planned for all these many years.

"Oh, I see," Cordoba continued. "You wish to make me remember those I've killed. I did kill someone you loved, yes?" He shrugged. "Well then, let me relieve you of that burden. I choose not to remember any of them because they were of no consequence."

Something inside Jean broke open, and all the hate he had held in check was released. What happened next was a blur of motion wrapped in blind anger. Despite his claim, the Spaniard fought back like a man half his age.

A burning pain seared across Jean's bare chest. He looked down to find a slash of blood and then at the dagger in Cordoba's hand.

Dodging a sweep of the blade, Jean landed a swift but sure kick to the center of the Spaniard's chest, sending him tumbling backward. Cordoba dropped the dagger, and Jean reached for it.

The deck tilted and Jean missed his chance to steal the knife. Instead, he toppled overboard with Cordoba right behind him.

Debris littered the water around them and the salt water stung, but the battle continued.

"Let him go."

Jean froze, his hands on the Spaniard's throat. He looked at the man in his grasp and saw nothing. No fear. No anger. No recollection of his sins against the family Jean had lost. Against Jean himself.

Just nothing.

"Let him go."

His feet treading water to keep himself and the Spaniard from slipping beneath the waves, Jean looked around to find the source of the words he'd once again heard so clearly.

"Who is there?" he called.

"No one." Cordoba sneered even as he gasped for breath. "You've called off your men. No one is there."

"Who is there?" he called again.

"I AM."

"Let him go."

So he did.

CHAPTER 3

Mary Lytton Cordoba stood in the foyer of her home in the most fashionable part of Madrid and willed herself to remain upright. Two words echoed in her head: *they're gone.* She gripped the stair rail, its newel post covered in pure gold, and tried to understand.

How could Antonio just take her? And more important, why? He'd rarely spared their daughter a moment since her birth.

"And where is my granddaughter?" Don Pablo Cordoba called from the front steps.

Antonio's father, a man closer to Mary than her own father had been, stepped inside and handed his hat to the cowering maid. The girl skittered away from the elegantly dressed nobleman, her head ducked as if he might strike her.

Don Pablo turned his attention to Mary, his ever-present smile in place. "In all the times I have paid visits to this home of yours, Mary, my sweet Maribel has never failed to greet me at the door."

"Oh, Papa," she finally managed when she could speak. "Our Maribel is gone."

"Gone?" Horror etched his features. "Impossible. I saw her only last month and her health was outstanding."

"No," she said as she moved toward Don Pablo to reach for his hand. "She has gone away. With Antonio." Despite her best efforts to calm herself, Mary's voice rose along with her fears. "He has taken her from me. He sent me off on an errand, and when I returned, he had her things packed up and she was gone."

The nobleman reached for Mary's hands and cradled them in his. He inhaled deeply and then let out a long breath before looking down into her eyes.

"I thought by securing this assignment for him in Cuba that he might be safely away from you and my granddaughter."

"As did I," she said. "You know I married for love, Don Pablo, but sadly I was the only one who felt that love. I was a fool."

"Do not believe that of yourself. My son, he is many things, but a man who would marry without thought of love? No, I do believe Antonio loved you, at least as much as he could."

He looked away as if attempting to collect his thoughts. Mary swiped at her wet cheek and gave thanks that the Lord had provided such a kind and loving man in the absence of her family.

A family she should never have left.

"My darling," the older man said gently as tears shimmered in his eyes. "If my son has taken our Maribel, then the duty and responsibility falls to me to go and get her."

Her hope soared for the first time since she returned home to find her daughter, her world, gone. Don Pablo held much power, both here in Spain and elsewhere. If anyone could find her Maribel, it would be him.

"Would you do that?" she asked, her voice soft as a whisper.

The old man looked into her eyes, his expression somber. "You have my promise, Mary, that I will not rest until our Maribel is found."

❈

"Nothing but a scratch, Connor." Jean stepped back aboard his ship with victory achieved and a stream of crewmen behind him carrying the spoils of the battle. "How is Israel?"

Stepping aside to allow his well-trained men to do their jobs, Jean turned his attention to his father's dear friend, a physician of great wisdom and advanced age. Though his hands were steady, he had to concentrate to keep the sword's grip from falling through his fingers.

"Our second-in-command is a hardy fellow, and the wound was not deep. He'll be fine soon with just a scar and a story to tell." The doctor fell into step beside him. "You're bleeding. I will have a look."

Not a question but a statement. Only Evan Connor would dare speak to the feared privateer in this manner.

Jean glanced up. The sails caught in the afternoon breeze as Jean's men carried the last of the cache of silver coins into the hold. The Spanish frigate *Venganza* had been cut loose and was drifting away, its smoking hull too badly damaged to claim as a prize but still seaworthy enough to limp to port somewhere before those who chose to remain aboard starved.

By far the most precious possession taken among the spoils of battle was the cutlass found among Antonio Cordoba's belongings. The heavy silver weapon bore a scabbard encrusted with precious stones and had obviously been made by a craftsman with great skill.

He secured the cutlass to his waist and felt the weight of the weapon against his side. Yes, this would do nicely. The men could divide his portion among themselves and he would keep this in return.

A heated argument caught Jean's attention, and he quickly headed in that direction. On a vessel of this size, any disagreement could quickly become more than a small inconvenience, especially one that began after a prize had been taken. He'd learned this the hard way and would allow nothing of the sort on his ship.

In the center of the circle of men were two children of barely more than a decade, one male and the other decidedly female. The prisoners were bound together with a thick rope, each of them wearing a gag and struggling to free themselves. The girl wore an absurd scarf tied around her head, with a bloodstain the size of a doubloon decorating the part that covered her forehead.

"What's this?" he demanded of those under his command. In

an instant, the braying crowd fell silent.

"The men found them," the doctor said as he easily caught up to Jean. "Because you were otherwise occupied, I made the decision to have them brought aboard."

"Did you now?"

When Jean took over this ship some three years past, he instituted a policy that any man who stepped aboard was free to join and free to go as he pleased. Jean cared not for the man's nationality or past but rather determined his worth by the work he was willing to perform.

However, he also refused to harbor fools. Thus, there had been many a man set adrift with provision enough to reach shore in relatively good health.

Unlike the man he had sought, he refused to harm innocents. Without exception, should he overtake a vessel carrying women or children, they were not to be accosted. Nor were slaves or the aged. The policy served him well and allowed his conscience to remain clear.

Until now, however, he had never had to decide what to do with children aboard his ship. Worse, his vessel now harbored a female.

The ship's carpenter was a bald fellow missing most of his teeth, and yet Sebastio Rao's smile was broad as he nudged Connor. "The boy there says he's ready to join up with us."

A smattering of chuckles followed this statement. "The young lady was found in the Consul General's cabin. She also wishes to join us." Evan Connor leaned closer to Jean. "Apparently the gag was deemed necessary due to the girl's insistence on telling anyone who might listen about the books she's read on pirating and how she knows their jobs well enough to do all of them." Humor rose on the old man's face. "She's a spitfire, that one. Watch yourself near her."

Jean regarded the girl sharply as the men burst into hearty laughter. She couldn't be more than eleven or twelve, not much older than his little sister. Even so, the child showed signs of one day becoming a great beauty. Her copper-colored hair fell in thick waves over her shoulders and spilled onto her once lovely but now bloodstained blue dress.

"What is the cause of this blood?" he demanded.

Evan Connor leaned toward him. "She sustained a crescent-shaped cut on her forehead during the battle, likely before we boarded given the look of the wound. Nothing of any consequence, though she may bear a scar."

Oh, but those eyes. Deepest emerald green, they were, and staring at the assembly of misfit sailors with a loathing that was palpable. Even as she seemed to express her opinion about her current situation, the girl stood tall and showed no fear. Indeed, she seemed willing to run him through should someone give her a weapon.

Jean couldn't help but be impressed.

"Consul General Cordoba's daughter as a privateer," Jean said as he stepped into the circle and allowed his gaze to sweep the length of the contemptuous young lady. "Now this is interesting. And we have a young man also wishing to gain our company, do we?"

The fellow tied to her offered a nod of deference. Jean nodded to the nearest sailor. "Remove his gag."

He looked over the lad, a gangly fellow who'd already reached the height of an average grown man despite not appearing much older than the Cordoba girl. Though his hair was dirty and his clothing stained and mended, there was something about the boy that seemed almost aristocratic.

"Name is William, sir, William Spencer," the boy said when he could speak. "I meant what I said. I'll join ye happily."

"And slit my throat soon as you're trusted with something sharp," Jean said with a laugh that held no humor.

"Not hardly," the boy insisted. "I know who you are. And I know this is the great *Ghost Ship* what scares the life out of the Spaniards."

Had he held an interest in doing so, Jean might have corrected the lad on his statement that the boy knew who he was. Only two men aboard this vessel could claim this, and William Spencer was not one of them.

"So you know all this, do you now?" Jean paused to allow another cursory glance at the lad. "Tell me why you believe you belong on this ship, and I'll have nothing but the truth or I'll send you overboard."

He would do no such thing, but the boy did not yet need to know this. Rather, a healthy fear of the captain was always a good thing in a new recruit. If, indeed, the lad could convince him of his sincerity and usefulness.

"The truth is, me pappy and brother, they died at the hands of the Spanish. Rest of my family's dead and buried too. That's how I got where I was on that ship what's thankfully sinking. Straight to the bottom with it, if you ask me."

"We are privateers, not pirates," he said, as much to inform the lad as to remind his crew. "We operate legally under Letters of Marque, and we conduct ourselves with honor and in accordance with the laws of France. This ship accosts only those vessels we are allowed to capture based on these letters, and each man aboard gets his share. More if he's earned it and less if he's new and only just joined up. I am in charge here, and no other man controls this vessel. So, if you're looking for a pirate ship, you'll not find one here."

"No, sir," he said. "I'm looking to join up with you and your men and no other. You can ask Red here. I told her exactly that when we spied your sails on the horizon. I told her I'd join you if you'd let me." He glanced down at the girl. "Didn't I now, Red?"

Jean nodded to a deckhand. "Remove her gag so she can speak for William Spencer here, if she so chooses."

The deckhand did as he was told and then jumped back when the girl aimed the point of her boot in his direction. Several crew members shouted jibes at the jittery deckhand while the remainder laughed at his expense.

"Watch her, Captain," the hapless fellow said as Jean walked past him. "Almost took out my knee, she did. And worse, mayhap I hadn't been so swift in dodging her."

"Duly noted," Jean said as he stopped in front of the girl. "Go ahead, Red. Answer the lad."

For a moment Jean thought she might not say anything. Her face remained unreadable, a feat he could only admire. Faced with this group of misfits and fearsome louts, he might not have been so calm at her age.

His attention went to the scarf around her forehead and the stain of blood there. He would have Connor see to whatever injury was hidden beneath that cloth, but for now he had a defiant child to deal with.

"Speak, or have the gag returned to your mouth," Jean snapped, his patience growing thin.

She let out a long breath but kept her attention focused solely on Jean. "So I'm to vouch for this fellow when he did no such thing for me when these ruffians were making their decision to gag me?" she said with a shake of her head. "Just what sort of arrangement would that be? Not a good one for sure."

"All right, then. Sir, what Red here said about the books she's read is completely and positively true. Why, she taught me to read, she did. I can't help it if I told the truth when those men over there asked me if I thought she might ever tire of speaking about it. Because in truth, the answer is she will not. Or at least in my experience, she has not."

Jean stifled a chuckle. Apparently the girl was not the only one who had difficulty tiring of speaking.

"Too little, too late, William Spencer," the girl called Red said. "Next time respond in my favor when you're asked and perhaps you and I will stay on good terms."

William Spencer rolled his eyes, although the gesture was accompanied by a patient smile. It appeared he and the girl sparred frequently.

"Now that all of that's been cleared up," Jean said as he gave the girl a wide berth as he returned to standing in front of the lad, "I believe we were discussing whether you were fit to join us, lad."

"Where do I sign up?" he said. "I can climb sails, do carpenter work and whatever else needs doing on a ship. Oh, and thanks to Red, I can read too, so maybe there's a job that would require that. And most of all, I'd be grateful to be here. I'd say that's all the fitness I need."

"You're certain?" He gave the boy a sideways look. "It's not an easy life."

He squared his shoulders and drew himself up to his full height. "I told you I was."

"You might be called on to work alongside people not like you." He paused to watch the boy's face. "People who are from other places. People who care not to have their identities discovered. Perhaps men from Africa taken from their homes against their will."

"Slaves?" the lad asked.

"Former slaves," Jean corrected. "Or men who were bound in that direction but relieved of that burden before they were sold."

William Spencer seemed to give the matter a moment's thought, and then he nodded. "Long as they don't mind working alongside me, I'd say we'd get along just fine."

Jean met the boy's gaze and saw he told the truth. He saw, too, a determination in those youthful eyes that reminded him of himself at that age.

"You'll do, then," he said before stepping around to the girl.

She, too, offered a look of determination, although it was likely she'd determined to do him whatever harm she might manage. "And you, Red?" He met her even gaze. "What do you propose we do with you?"

"You'll allow me to join you. I'm just as useful as William."

"Ain't no woman going to join us, is she, Captain?" someone called.

"It's bad luck and ye know it," another said.

Jean waved his hand and the crowd fell silent. He had no intention of allowing this female child to join their ranks, though he had no belief in luck, either good or bad. However, it wouldn't do to let the girl or his crew know that just yet.

"I am the captain of this vessel," he said to her. "As such, I regret to inform you that a woman will never be fit to join my crew."

"And why not?"

A few of the sailors chuckled, while the rest seemed to be watching to see what would happen next.

"Because you'd be a burden, Red, and a danger to the men. Should we be called upon to engage in battle, having you aboard would be a distraction. Someone would have to be assigned to protect you, and that could cost valuable time and lives. And ultimately, as captain, I am the one responsible for protecting all of you."

She met his gaze. "That's ridiculous. I've done a fine job of fending for myself."

Jean shook his head. "I doubt that. Do show me what you would do should someone accost you." He shrugged. "Please wait. I'm terribly sorry. Someone already did and managed to tie you up. You being bound by ropes proves my point exactly."

Before Jean realized what was happening, the young lady kicked him solidly with the pointed toe of her shoe. Pain shot up his wounded leg as he stumbled backward. Peals of laughter were quickly replaced by stunned silence when their captain let out a blistering yell.

CHAPTER 4

A nd that, sir, proves mine," Maribel said. "Although I hope you'll forgive me. See, I have been praying you would be a nice man."

"Keep praying, then," Jean snapped. "Because that is not the case as of yet." He looked over at the doctor, who appeared to be having difficulty keeping a neutral expression. "Mr. Connor," he managed through clenched jaw. "Put the girl in the brig and set the young fellow free."

"The brig? You're certain of this?" the older man asked, concern now etching his features.

Ignoring the quiet stares of the men around him, Jean focused on the man who had known him practically since birth. "I am. If Red wants to be a privateer, then we will show her what happens when a crewman accosts his captain."

Connor shook his head. "But, lad, surely you do not mean to—"

"Surely I do." He then turned to address his crew. "William Spencer here is to be afforded the rights and share of a new crew member once he proves his worth, and as such he is not to be harmed. Anyone who does not comply with this will feel the full fury of my wrath and join the girl known as Red in the brig until a suitable punishment is carried out. Is that understood?"

A low murmur of agreement permeated the crowd. Jean nodded and then continued. "The girl is to be considered under my protection, even though she is to remain a guest in my brig. Should I hear of any maltreatment against her, I will take it as a personal affront to me and deal with the perpetrator accordingly as well. Is that clear?"

This time the murmur of agreement was much softer and appeared to be reluctantly given. Jean locked eyes with the girl called Red, who now stood as if ready to run despite being held in place by two of his largest men. The lad had wisely moved away into the crowd and now stood silently watching.

"It appears there is no solid agreement to this command," he said. "Perhaps someone wishes to challenge me?"

He allowed his attention to sweep the crowd, enjoying them shrinking back, before returning it to the girl. Jean had allowed his temper to best his good judgment and he knew it. Still, he refused to back down.

"No," Jean said. "I thought not. Take her to the brig, and the rest of you mind my warning. And, Connor, see to whatever is hidden beneath that wretched scarf she is wearing. I warrant she will need one of your vile potions."

With that, he turned and walked away, secure in the knowledge that his orders would be followed. No one aboard this ship would dare do otherwise.

Once in his cabin, Jean closed his eyes and settled onto his cot. He took a breath and let it out slowly as he tried in vain to get comfortable even as he also worked to tame his temper.

The wound he'd received two months ago in a skirmish with a slaving ship off the coast of Jamaica ached thanks to the girl's assault on him, but that was the least of his concerns. The thought of the lives saved during that battle—the men who were freed to go back to home and family—was not enough to erase the ones lost today.

Unbidden, Antonio Cordoba's face appeared before him as he had looked before he slipped beneath the waves for the last time. Jean shook his head to rid himself of the vision.

Cordoba was dead, an enemy vanquished, and justice had been served. Calling him back, even in his thoughts, served no purpose.

He should have felt relief. Cordoba was nothing but a cold-blooded murderer.

Jean pounded his fist against the wall. The deaths of Jean's mother and baby brother had been avenged, yet all he felt was a vast emptiness.

"There should be more," he whispered in the French language of his childhood. "Vengeance should feel much sweeter than this."

He sighed. Perhaps Israel was right. Jean managed the beginnings of a smile, though he felt no humor. Indeed, Israel almost always was.

The thought of Israel sent him in search of his friend. He found the man asleep in the doctor's cabin, his legs far too long for the bunk where he lay. Still, he appeared to be sleeping comfortably, so Jean left him there and returned to his cabin to attempt some rest of his own.

Sometime later, Connor opened the door without any pretense of knocking. "I've come to bind your wounds," the doctor said as he crossed the brightly colored Persian rug—bounty taken so long ago Jean couldn't name the vessel from which it came—and dropped his bag of ointments and bandages beside the cot then knelt with a heavy sigh.

Jean removed his boot and let it drop. Bright red streaked the bandages.

"You've gone and opened it again. I could blame the girl for this, but we both know you had it coming when you taunted her."

Refusing to admit what he knew to be true, Jean remained silent. Outside, the watch bell rang indicating that sufficient time had passed that he must have managed to sleep. Why then did he still feel so very tired?

Connor opened his bag and began searching through its contents before looking up at Jean. "Now that you've got your revenge, will you be taking my advice and laying low awhile? I wager you're needed back in New Orleans."

"A wager you would likely win," he said, as they both knew his life there put demands on him that never seemed to cease. "Yet there are details left to handle before I can return."

Connor looked up at him. "Such as?"

He met the old man's even gaze. "Such as what to do with Cordoba's child."

"Ah, yes. That." The doctor went back to work swabbing the wound with a clean piece of muslin then applied a foul-smelling poultice.

Though he wanted to cry out in pain, Jean remained stoic. Finally he'd had enough.

"Can you not treat this with something that smells less like the garbage heap? Truly I've smelled dead animals that were more pleasantly fragrant."

Connor leaned back on his heels and regarded Jean with a look that told nothing of his thoughts. He rose. "Do you know what would please your father greatly, lad?"

Jean forced himself to smile. "There are many things that would please him, chief among them things I have no interest in doing."

"Therein lies the problem," Connor said as he settled onto a chair nearby.

"I know that look." Jean grimaced as he shifted positions. "You're about to tell me what to do, and then I'll ignore it."

"That is generally how it goes with us, isn't it? You avoid the difficult questions I ask."

"As do you," Jean reminded him. "Else I'd know why you don't leave this leaky tub of a ship and make your living doctoring a better lot of people than are found aboard."

Connor chuckled as he leaned down to hand Jean his boot. "Why would I leave? With all the trouble we manage to find, I keep up with my doctoring skills. Now get that boot on, and then I'll look at that scratch of yours."

"That scratch" was the slash across the muscles of his chest made by the murderer Cordoba just before Jean sent him tumbling into the sea. Jean eased his boot on. The long gash had ceased bleeding, but Connor insisted on treating it with more of his vile potion.

"A few inches deeper and you'd not be with us, lad. You won't need stitching up, but do try to stay out of trouble until you can heal proper." He shook his head as he returned his doctoring supplies to their case. "What am I saying? Trouble finds you."

Ignoring the comment, Jean climbed to his feet to retrieve a clean shirt. "I paid a visit to Israel. He appeared to be sleeping in comfort. Will he recover?"

"Completely and swiftly, I do believe. Had he not been standing between you and the flintlock, you would not be alive, my friend. However, his constitution and the fact he carries much more muscle than any of us has saved him yet again. It's been all I could do to keep him immobile and allow some measure of healing."

"So you gave him a sleeping draught."

Connor chuckled. "Not that he is aware of, no. But, yes, it was all I could think of to keep him from returning to the deck and seeing to your safety."

Jean smiled. Indeed Israel had appointed himself to that task. A pity it was proving so difficult. Another thought occurred. "How does our prisoner fare?"

"She's holding her own down in the brig. Other than a cut on her forehead, she bears no marks from her ordeal." He paused. "Don't you think it's a bit harsh to lock up someone so young and innocent, especially so soon after the loss of her father?"

"Innocent? Did you see what she did to my leg?" he said as he donned his shirt. "I wager she can hold her own anywhere."

"Perhaps you're right. Seems she can certainly stand up to you, lad. 'Tis a brave thing to kick a ship's captain when you're bound and gagged." Connor paused. "She puts me in mind of a younger version of you, Jean Beaumont."

"Perhaps," he said slowly, "but my accommodations in the brig can only be temporary. Women are not allowed about my vessel, and there's certainly no friend or relative of mine who would accept her. Not that I'd risk the exchange, mind you."

"I understand your dilemma," the doctor said. "And yet despite her parentage, she's innocent in all of this. We cannot exactly put her off somewhere without friend or family to look after her."

"Then we contact Cordoba's family and settle on a price for her return." He let out a long breath, his body aching. "Surely there's someone willing to ransom her."

"The girl says she's not Cordoba's daughter," Connor said. "She won't tell me who she is, only who she isn't."

"Of course she's his daughter. Why else would she be on a Spanish merchantman with a king's ransom in silver in its hold, all of it belonging to the new Consul General?"

"A worthy question," Connor said. "I do not disagree. Perhaps the lad should be questioned. He appears to know her well enough."

"Agreed. Would you have that handled, Connor? I do not wish to intimidate the lad into answering in a way that isn't truthful out of fear."

"You do have that effect," the doctor said. "I'll see if perhaps we can get to the truth without terrifying the lad."

"Thank you." He paused to think a moment. "Connor, no one with any sense would bring a child on such a risky voyage except for a fool like Cordoba. Have you seen what the Spaniard had hidden away in the belly of that ship? A fool's errand it was to bring such wealth on the same vessel with his own child. He mistakenly believed he was invincible."

The doctor nodded. "Apparently his daughter has inherited the same attitude, although she does execute the behavior with a much more charming demeanor."

"Has she caused more trouble already?"

Jean steadied himself as he carefully put more weight on his injured leg. The wound already felt better, a testament to the doctor's medical skills. Still it did plague him.

"Doctor?" he said when he realized Connor had not yet responded to his question. "What is our prisoner up to down in the brig?"

The older man shrugged. "I did check on the young lady before coming up here to dress your wounds and found a perplexing situation afoot in the brig."

"Perplexing?" He shook his head. "Elaborate, please."

Connor nodded toward the door. "Perhaps you'd best see for yourself," he said. "If you're fit for the walk, that is."

"I am easily fit for the walk." Jean straightened his spine and marched past the doctor without limping, a feat that took concentration.

Stepping out into the starry night, he nodded to the young man posted to the watch and then headed down the sharply descending stairway that led below the deck. Navigating the dark-as-night passageways with skill learned through years of experience, he turned a corner and heard, of all things, laughter.

Several of his fiercest sailors, men whose penchant toward ill temper was well known, were standing outside the open door of the brig while a circle of men gathered inside on the straw-covered floor. It appeared the men inside the brig were wagering on something. Laughter filled the close space and spilled out into the passageway where Jean stood.

The ship lurched, parting the men and allowing him to see what was causing all the uproar. Situated cross-legged in the center of the men was the Cordoba girl, a blanket spread out beneath her as if she were at a picnic instead of being held prisoner in his brig. Her copper-colored hair and fashionable dress set her apart from the attentive crew, as did the sound of her childish laughter.

Though she still wore the stained scarf, the ends of a length of muslin showed. Apparently Connor had been able to doctor the girl's wound without sustaining bodily harm.

Seated directly across from her was the burly carpenter, Rao. As he stepped closer, Jean realized Rao and the girl were playing a board game that looked deceptively like draughts.

Jean frowned. Surely not.

And yet that is exactly what he saw. Grown men, brutal men of war, encircling a child's board game while the toothless carpenter entertained their prisoner. To make matters worse, Swenson, chief rigger, seemed to be leading the cheers in favor of the girl.

The girl moved her game piece over the carpenter's last two black pieces and then looked up at him and grinned. "I win, Mr. Rao."

"Best three out of four?" Rao inquired.

A small roar erupted. Jean let out a long breath, his temper at its peak.

"Gentlemen," he said with as much sarcasm as he could manage. "Am I interrupting something?"

A hush fell over the crowd. Slowly those nearest to Jean pressed past him to slink away, their eyes downcast.

"Not at all." The Cordoba girl looked up at him with a smile and no appearance of fear. "Would you like to play? We don't wager, although it's awfully fun to win anyway."

"This is a privateer's ship and not a gaming vessel."

"I've only heard the *Ghost Ship* called a ship for pirates," she said, her face a mask of innocence.

At the word *pirate*, any man still remaining nearby turned to disappear down the passageway. The distinction between piracy and privateering was what allowed Jean to keep his conscience clear and the coffers of his vessel full, all under the protection of the French crown. Any man who used the word in his presence swiftly felt his wrath.

But this was a child, and a female child at that. Still, his blood boiled. "Privateer," he said.

She shrugged. "Same thing."

Jean took a deep breath and let it out slowly. "Your ignorance is understandable," he said as gently as he could manage. "Given the fact you know nothing of the subject of which you speak. But one is most definitely not the same as the other."

"I am not ignorant on the subject of pirates," she protested. "As William Spencer attested, I have read *The Notorious Seafaring Pyrates and Their Exploits*."

Jean met her stare with an impassive look that defied his temper. "And this book, of which I am well aware, makes you an authority?"

"I read that book two full times, going on three except that I dropped the book on the deck when the pirates shot at us, and then I retrieved it but lost it again when I—"

"Silence!"

CHAPTER 5

To Jean's surprise, the girl actually ceased her chatter. He decided to take the opportunity to change the subject rather than dwell on her persistent need to argue this one.

In order to achieve his goal of having her confirm what he felt he already knew, Jean took a gentler approach. "What is your name, child?"

She climbed to her feet and crossed her arms over her chest. The girl he'd heard called Red was a skinny thing, barely a wisp of a girl with innocent eyes big as saucers, and yet he wouldn't dare trust her given the result of their last encounter.

"Your name?" he repeated.

"I see no need to tell you unless you plan to allow me to join your crew. And then, I would most likely prefer to change it to a pirate name," she responded matter-of-factly. "However, I suppose I could admit that my mother named me Maribel."

"Maribel Cordoba." Her eyes narrowed, but Maribel said nothing, so Jean continued. "You were found in the cabin belonging to Consul General Antonio Cordoba, so do not bother to try and convince me otherwise."

"As you wish," she said with a shrug. "But I am still trying to decide on a pirate name, so I cannot comment as to what I will eventually be called."

"Privateer," he corrected.

"Yes," she said sweetly. "My privateer name. I welcome your

advice, of course, since you will be my captain."

"I will be no such thing," he snapped. "Stop this. You are Maribel Cordoba, and you belong with your family. My dilemma is how to best reunite you."

"You cannot," she said softly. "My mama is gone."

Jean paused. Until now, he hadn't thought about the child's mother.

"I see," was the only response he could manage. "Is there another family member somewhere who would take you in?"

"I have a grandfather," she told him. "He is an important man, so I only see him sometimes. Although I've seen him more than my papa, and Grandfather Cordoba is certainly more important."

"Cordoba, is it?"

She shrugged. "Yes, you've caught me. But I still plan to change it once a proper *privateer* name is chosen for me."

The bravado she attempted with these words seemed brittle and nothing like her previous attitude. His heart lurched, but Jean held his feelings—and his words—in check.

"You are the ward of your grandfather now," he said. "Any change of name for you will be his choice, not yours or mine. How do I find your Grandfather Cordoba?"

"He is dead too." For the first time, the girl's lip quivered. "Papa told me they're both dead, Mama and my grandfather. I pretend they're not, but. . ."

"What else?" he encouraged, even as his heart broke for this motherless child. "Surely there are others with whom you can stay."

Maribel plopped back down on her blanket, her face a mask of defiance. "There is not," she said. "My mama had no one else, and when any member of my father's family wishes to appear, they appear. I cannot call on any of them, nor can I tell you a place where I am welcome because my mama's home in Spain is being sold so I had to go and live with my father, only. . ."

"Only?" he asked.

She paused only a moment then began again. "That is truly

all I know, and all the torture in the world will not get anything further out of me."

"Torture?" Jean laughed despite his heartbreak at the tears shimmering in the girl's eyes. "What kind of man do you think I am? You're perfectly safe here."

"Am I?"

A smile rose, and so did the girl. She wrapped her arms around Jean to envelop him in a hug. "I knew you would turn out to be a nice man. I prayed for that, you know. William told me I shouldn't bother because privateers are not supposed to be nice men, but I told him I was going to pray anyway, and he said—"

"Maribel. Stop. Talking."

She closed her mouth and took a step back to look up at him. He waited for a word or two to come tumbling out, but the girl remained silent.

Then slowly a smile tried to wobble into place as she reached out to grasp his hand. "You're alone too, aren't you?"

Jean looked down at the girl with the eyes of a man who had seen too much for the amount of years he had lived. He tried to form an answer to her question, but no words would come.

Her coppery hair flamed around her dirt-smudged face as she waited for him to speak. Though the wound on her forehead was small enough, as Connor had said, for the rest of her life she would bear a reminder of the day her father died.

For a brief moment, he felt a bond growing between them.

A bond he could not allow, for the girl could never be subject to a privateer's life. He would find another solution.

He must.

Jean slipped his hand from her grip and took two steps backward. "Are you hungry?"

"I prefer to work for my food," was her response.

Stubborn girl. "That is not possible at the moment. Are you in need of anything else?" he continued, still grasping for words that would release him from the obligation of remaining here with her.

"To join your company and be put to work on your crew just as you allowed William Spencer," she said. "Beyond that, nothing more."

"And you know my answer to that," he said evenly.

"It is the wrong answer," she quickly responded.

"Miss Cordoba, I will remind you that I am the captain of this vessel. As such, any answer I give—should I determine a question is worthy of answering—is not only the correct answer, it is the only answer."

"I understand," she said. "But I also disagree."

"The first rule for a crew member in my employ is that he never disagree with anything I say. Thus, you have just proven yourself unfit to join us."

He turned then to walk away, his verbal victory temporarily won. She would continue to argue the point, of this he had no doubt, but for now he could claim a small victory.

Jean left the girl in her cell but did not bother to lock the door. Should she try to escape, there was truly nowhere she could go. Besides, unless he missed his guess, there were several of his crewmen hidden in advantageous places along the corridor listening to their exchange.

"Rao," he said as he spied his crewman lurking just around the corner. Likely he was eavesdropping and not just lurking, but Jean gave him the benefit of the doubt. "See that Miss Cordoba is moved into a cabin of her own. Also, see that she is fed properly and looked after so that she is not bothered by the crew."

"Aye, Captain. Will you be giving her a job too?" he asked, his toothless grin broad.

The humor Rao offered grated on what little good temperament Jean had gained. "I suppose I could give her yours," he snapped and then continued walking.

Even reaching the deck and finding a nice breeze in the ship's sails did not repair his mood. Several more of his crewmen appeared to be waiting for him to leave the brig, as witnessed by the group gathered near the mainmast.

"Whoever was next on the list of opponents at draughts should be advised that Miss Cordoba will be available to best you as soon as she is installed in a proper cabin and fed a meal."

Though no one nodded or even acknowledged his statement, they all scattered to their posts with smiles on their faces.

Maribel watched the captain go, taking note that he was limping. Whether the cause was the shot Papa fired at him or something else that happened while aboard the *Venganza*, the result had been that the pirate captain had been harmed.

"Privateer," she said under her breath.

Captain Beaumont was mighty proud of his distinction as a privateer, and her stating otherwise was something she would need to remedy. Apparently there was some sort of honor among men who acted like pirates but followed the rules of the Letters of Marque.

If she had her favorite book, she might be able to read up on the subject. However, with nothing but quiet this deep into the belly of this ship, she had plenty of time to try and remember what Captain Jones said on the matter.

She leaned back against the wall, the straw making for a soft spot to do her thinking. Back on the Spanish ship, she had shared a cabin with her father but had never felt as comfortable there as she did here.

Papa.

His face came to her, and she banished it just as she had done when she was a young girl. Missing Papa had become so much a part of her life that the word *missing* ceased to have meaning.

He was the man who married Mama, and he gave Maribel her name. Beyond that, Papa was the man in the painting over the fireplace and the man who caused Mama's tears when she thought Maribel wasn't listening.

She had seen him take aim at the captain. Heard him curse when she kicked his leg to ruin his aim as he fired and the African went down in the captain's place.

Maribel closed her eyes. She would have to beg the African's forgiveness for causing him to be shot. That hadn't been her intention. At the same time, she gave thanks that the Lord had spared Captain Beaumont.

For she truly knew in her heart that someday he would be a good man. He had to be, for God always answered prayers.

That's what Mama told her, and that's what she knew to be true.

Mama.

Oh, Mama.

A wave of sorrow so deep and dark that she had no name for it or control over it rolled up from some bottomless place inside her.

Mama. "What will I do without you, Mama?"

Pray away the fear.

She tried, really she did. But every word that rose in her heart died before it reached her throat. Though she knew prayers were not useless, at this moment they just seemed impossible.

Mama would tell her to pray anyway, so she did. When she opened her eyes, the big African man who she'd been certain her papa had killed was standing before her.

"Are you an angel?" she said softly as she climbed to her feet. "Because you sure do look real, and I see you've got a bandage on your shoulder where my papa shot you, and my mama told me that God heals every wound, so if you're an angel and you've still got need of that bandage, then either my mama was wrong or you need to go back and remind God He forgot to take that wound away."

Out of words, Maribel stood very still waiting for the African angel to speak. In the Bible, Mary was visited by an angel and she ended up with the baby Jesus in the manger after she rode on a donkey a long way then had to sleep in a barn on straw just like this. Surely the Lord would be sending a different message to her through this angel.

One that didn't involve donkeys, a husband, or sleeping on straw.

Slowly the corners of his mouth lifted into a smile. Then, without saying a word in regard to her question, he began to laugh.

Whether or not the man with the bandage was indeed an angel, Maribel decided this is exactly how an angel's laughter ought to sound. When the laughter stopped, silence filled the small room.

"Mr. Angel?" she finally said. "I want to ask you to forgive me for what my papa did. He shouldn't have shot you like he did, although to be fair he wasn't aiming at you. Though he was aiming at Captain Beaumont, and that was also wrong. But I did try and stop him, and when I couldn't, I hit his leg and he got mad at me so I ran and hid in his cabin, but I saw he still shot you anyway, so I'm very, very sorry."

"Little one," he said gently, his voice so deep and beautiful, "I am no angel. I am just a man, and a flawed one at that. But you need to learn right now that the sins of your father are his alone. Do you understand?"

She studied his brown skin and eyes the color of the dark coffee her grandfather loved, and then smiled. "I suppose, but if I had been able to stop him, then you wouldn't have that bandage."

He nodded and seemed to consider her statement. "That is true, but if you had been able to stop him from taking that shot, who is to say that the next one might not have killed someone? You and I will never know the answer to that question. Only God knows, and we cannot possibly know everything He knows."

"That's what my mama says too." She pushed back a thought of her mother and the big Bible that filled her lap as they read it together. "So if you're not an angel, then who are you and why are you here?"

"Israel Bennett is the name I am called on this ship."

Her eyes widened. "You got to pick your own name? Captain

Beaumont told me that wasn't allowed." She paused to think about her conversation with the captain. "But he also told me I couldn't be on his crew because I disagreed with him, and I guess he's right because when I read the book about pirates that is my favorite, all the captains insisted that everyone do what they said. So since I told him he was wrong about something and didn't do what he said, I think I understand why he told me I couldn't be on the crew."

Israel Bennett nodded. "It is important to follow whoever God has put in charge of you."

"Unless what he is doing isn't right?" she said.

The big man's expression softened. "You're a very wise person, Miss Maribel. If you ask me, you've got a fine name and ought to be proud of it. What purpose would it serve to change your name just to become a member of this crew?"

She thought about the question then offered one of her own instead. "What purpose did it serve you?"

"Ah well," Mr. Bennett said as he nodded. "My new name kept me and the captain out of trouble."

Maribel shifted positions and looked past him to where Mr. Rao seemed to be trying to hide from them. "I don't understand."

"No," he said gently, "and I hope you never do." His face brightened. "But right now I need to get you out of here. Did you bring anything with you?"

She shook her head. "I had a book with me, but I dropped it on the deck of the *Venganza*. It was my favorite. The pirate book. But maybe the captain would be happier if I didn't have a copy of that book, what with the fact he seems particularly sensitive to the use of the word *pirate* on this ship."

"Would that happen to be *The Notorious Seafaring Pyrates and Their Exploits* by Captain Ulysses Jones?"

Again her eyes widened. "Yes. How did you know?"

Mr. Bennett chuckled. "Because I've read it. Twice. Now come with me and let's get you out of here."

CHAPTER 6

I've read it twice too," Maribel said as she followed Mr. Bennett out of the cell. "And part of a third time until I lost it on the deck. I might have finished reading it more times than two, but I loaned it to William Spencer so he could practice his reading." She stopped short. "How is William? Is he faring well as a crewman?"

"Hasn't been long enough to say for certain, but I do believe he's going to make a fine ship's doctor." He nodded toward his shoulder. "The lad helped our Mr. Connor to patch me up, so I'm told."

"A doctor?" she said softly. "I had no idea he possessed doctoring skills. Although, there was quite a good chapter on medical attention at sea in the pirate book. I suppose he may have taken an interest in the study of medicine by reading that chapter."

Mr. Bennett took her hand and started her progress down the corridor once again. "Or, he was assigned the job of doing what Mr. Connor told him and he did it."

"Yes," she said thoughtfully. "I would guess that's the correct answer. It pains me to say this since I have been the one teaching him, but I suppose I could learn something from William Spencer."

"Considering what I've heard, I'd agree, Miss Maribel." He nodded toward the corridor ahead. "Now follow me or you'll get lost. And remember you just decided you'd follow orders from now on."

"Yes I did, Mr. Bennett, but I feel like I ought to warn you about me. See, what I decide to do and what I turn out to do is not always the same thing. So if I don't follow orders very well right now, I would like you to know I will only get better at it the longer I keep trying. I'm working on it, but I've got a long way to go."

Again he chuckled. "Miss Maribel, you and me both. You and me both."

Rocking at anchor in the warm turquoise waters of Havana, Jean's ship was taking on supplies for the trip back to New Orleans. The time had come to lay low for a while.

Jean walked down the sandy street in the direction of the town square. If anyone could help him with the problem of what to do with Maribel Cordoba, it was Rose McDonald.

She spotted him before he saw her, and hurried to greet him with a warm embrace. "Welcome back, love. Have you changed your mind about sweeping me off my feet and marrying me?"

He laughed at the joke, an old one but one that never ceased to bring a chuckle. Though Rose was a beauty, she was twice his age and the widow of a former crewman.

"You'd not have me and you know it," Jean said. "However, I do have a favor to ask. It concerns a situation I find myself in that is in need of your assistance."

Rose gave him a serious look and then nodded toward her home, a cottage perched on the edge of the hill overlooking the harbor. "Come in and let's talk about this, shall we?"

Jean followed her inside and then produced a heavy bag of coins from his coat. "I have a business proposition, Rose, but I want you to think carefully before you accept it."

"What is it you want me to do?" she said as she studied him carefully.

An hour later, the talking was done and it was time to introduce Maribel Cordoba to her new home. Rather than tell her what he intended to do, Jean coerced Israel into bringing the girl to Mrs.

McDonald's cottage for what she believed was a tea party.

"Just us girls," Mrs. McDonald said as she shooed the men out the door.

"You will take good care of her," Israel said. A statement, not a question.

"Yes, of course," Mrs. McDonald said softly. "I shall treat her like my own daughter." She turned her attention to Jean. "You have my word she will be treated well."

Those words were little comfort when he and Israel returned to the ship without Maribel. Ignoring the silence of his crew, Jean stalked to his cabin and slammed the door with a resounding thud. A short time later, a timid knock sounded at the door.

"Enter," he said and then looked up to see Israel standing in the door. "The ship is fully loaded up and ready to sail, sir."

He took note of Israel's woeful expression and decided to ignore it. "Weigh anchor and head for New Orleans then."

Israel did not move from the doorway. Rather, he appeared to be considering what to say or perhaps whether to say anything at all.

"Will there be anything else?"

"There would be, yes," he said slowly. "Are you sure this is best, leaving the girl here? I know you can vouch for Mrs. McDonald, but is it the best thing for the girl to be raised here in Havana? And should we not have said good-bye to her? Seems wrong to just walk out the door as if we were coming back then sail away."

He felt the same way, but his position as captain would not allow him to admit it to Israel. Or perhaps it was his fear that if he did admit such a thing, he would be forced to go fetch the girl and haul her back on board.

"Wrong?" he said instead.

"Nothing, sir," he said. "I'll give the order."

"Thank you, Israel."

It did not escape Jean's notice that his second-in-command slammed the door a little harder than necessary. Nor did he miss the four solid days of silence his crew offered him on their sail back to New Orleans.

Finally, Jean could condone the silent protest no longer. He called a gathering of the entire crew and then climbed the quarterdeck to speak to them when they had assembled on the deck below.

"Let any man who would challenge my decision to leave the girl in a safe home in Havana rather than subject her to the rigors and dangers of sailing with us step forward and speak up."

The startled crew gaped and a few even laughed as one lone sailor broke through the line of men and presented himself to the captain. "I offer my challenge, sir."

The youth was small in stature and wore a pair of trousers that had been made for a much larger man. A thick leather belt appeared to be the only thing that kept the threadbare garment in place. The lad's dirty muslin shirt was knotted at his waist, and a length of blue muslin covered his head.

"Draw your weapon, sir," the small voice squeaked as he held a stick of wood aloft.

Jean stared down at the angry young man and tried not to laugh. "Do I know you, lad? Perhaps you were misinformed as to how we conduct business on this ship, so I will take your obvious youth and inexperience into account." He allowed his gaze to travel across the men assembled on the deck, and then he returned his attention to the boy. "Whomever vouched for this cabin boy and is responsible for bringing him aboard, please silence him now."

Jean waited, but no one came forward. "All right, then. What do you wish, boy? Shall we duel to the death with pistols, or would you prefer to feel the bite of my cutlass?"

Before the impudent youth could respond, William Spencer stepped in front of him. "This is none of your concern, young man," he told the new recruit.

With a swift move of his hand, Spencer pulled the length of muslin off the youth's head, revealing fiery curls that could only belong to one person. The crew began to applaud.

Maribel Cordoba faced him with a broad smile on her face and then bowed deeply. "Now can I be a pirate, sir? If I swear to follow your orders from now on, that is?"

"How did you get here?" he demanded, ignoring her questions and the cheering crew.

Her pale face held the innocent expression of a child at play. He noticed the crescent-shaped wound was on its way to healing.

"I told you I wanted to join this crew," she said as the men crowded around her. "Mrs. McDonald was a nice lady, but I am much happier here. This is where I belong, not in Havana."

If esteemed Widow McDonald had taken his money knowing she had no plans to keep her end of the bargain, he would be very disappointed. He was usually a decent judge of character, and he'd truly thought she would raise the girl as her own and not let her slip away like this.

"Does Mrs. McDonald know you're here? And I'll have the truth."

"Oh no," she said. "Miss Rose thought I was waiting for her at the mercantile. We had gone there after tea, and she let me pick out sweets while she ordered new dresses for me. I slipped out while she was looking at unmentionables for herself." She paused and shrugged. "She told me to make myself busy, so I did."

Peals of laughter erupted among the men. Jean grabbed the girl by the elbow and relieved her of her weapon.

"Back to work, all of you," he shouted at the crew. Immediately the men scattered.

Dragging her back to his cabin, he seated her on a chair and glared at her. "How did you get aboard? I will have the name of the man or men who brought you back aboard my ship, and I will have those names now."

"It was none of them," she said. "I did it myself."

"Your friend William Spencer helped you, didn't he?"

"He most certainly did not."

Jean paced the room, sorting through possible scenarios for how the girl got past his men. Then he stopped in front of her, his arms crossed over his chest. "No, he's a rule follower. I don't see him amenable to breaking the rules for you."

"Nor would I ask that of him."

"So," he said as he gave the matter more thought, "was it Rao? He has a certain fondness for you. I warrant he would gladly do your bidding if you asked him to bring you aboard without my knowledge."

"I told you, I did it myself. I climbed into a barrel of silk cloth that bore a label with your name on it and hid myself inside. It was quite comfortable, and I did fall asleep for a short time, but that is how I ended up back aboard this vessel."

Jean let out a long breath. He knew the barrel to which she referred, for it was meant to be a gift for his stepmother, long considered his mother, and sister. To think the girl rode onto his vessel in that barrel was almost funny.

Almost, but not quite, because someone allowed her to climb into that barrel. Someone else missed finding her when he inspected the barrel's contents. He had an idea of who that someone was.

"You don't believe me, do you?"

He paused. "I'm not sure if I do or if I do not. Where did you get the clothes you are wearing?"

"I found them myself," she answered proudly. "I just looked around the hold until I found something appropriate to my new life. A privateer cannot be seen parading around in a dress."

Jean tried to keep a serious expression, but his laughter got the better of him. "Yes, I do see the dilemma. And I am willing to strike a compromise, at least for the remainder of this voyage."

"And what would that be?" she asked.

"You are welcome to remain with us until we reach New Orleans. Once there, proper arrangements will be made for you."

She shook her head. "I want to remain on the ship. I'm not

interested in whatever arrangements you think you'll be making for me in New Orleans."

"You've no choice in the matter," he told her. "The vessel will be dry-docked for repairs and the crew released from their duties until such time as the vessel is ready to sail again."

Her haughty expression fell. "Yes," she finally said. "I do see the dilemma."

He wouldn't dare tell her yet that his plans involved turning the troublemaking girl over to his mother for her assessment. Either Maribel would end up spending the remainder of her childhood under a New Orleans roof or Abigail would find a more suitable solution such as taking her to the Ursuline convent.

Of course, there were serious complications in allowing the girl to be privy to a side of his life that Jean shared with very few people. He would have to give this plan serious consideration before he decided a course of action. In the meantime, it appeared he was now the captain to his first female crew member.

"I'm sure a solution can be found," he told her. "But for now, do I have your word that you will abide by the rules of my ship and cease your infernal arguing with me?"

She grinned and offered a smart salute. "I promise."

"Then there is one more requirement." He ignored her exasperated expression to continue. "You will write a letter of apology to Mrs. McDonald asking her forgiveness for running away from her. Likely she has the constables searching for you. I'm sure you've given her a terrible fright."

Maribel looked contrite. "I didn't think of that," she admitted. "I will write a very nice letter and be sure to tell her how wonderful her tea and cookies were and how very much I enjoyed getting to know her for the hour we spent together. How's that?"

"That is a good beginning." Jean could stifle his amusement no longer. His laughter filled the room as he looked down at the newest member of his crew. "Welcome then, Maribel."

The loud boom of a cannon and the sudden pitch of the ship

punctuated his words. The vessel momentarily righted itself before another blast tore through its hull.

"Get under that bunk, and do not come out until someone comes for you," he snapped. "That is an order."

He waited just long enough to be sure Maribel complied and then strode out toward the deck. Israel met him in the passageway. "What is going on?" he bellowed over the noise and chaos unfolding on deck.

"Over there." Israel pointed toward a low, fast schooner heading toward them. "Her French flag claimed her for a friend. Until she started firing on us."

The gunners had already begun to return fire, but the ship listed heavily to port and its torn sails hung uselessly in the breeze. The schooner continued to approach, its hull cutting swiftly through the waves.

"I will have the necks of the cowards who refuse to strike a proper flag," Jean shouted as he took his place behind one of the port cannons. Because of the dangerous incline of the deck, he had to hold on tight to avoid slipping into the water.

"Hold our fire," he shouted above the din. "Wait for my signal."

The acrid smell of smoke burned his lungs as Jean watched the schooner's swift approach. Waiting until the last possible moment to adjust for the sharp angle of the listing ship, he finally shouted the order.

"Fire away."

The schooner was hit broadside by eleven cannonballs at once. The vessel burst into flames and immediately began to founder. A rousing cheer went up on the deck as the schooner began to disappear below the water.

"Good work, Captain," Israel said when he caught up to him.

"Too early for celebrating," he said as he rubbed his sore leg. "Get the carpenter and our sailmaker up here."

Jean squinted his eyes against the setting sun. The holes in the deck were large but reparable, and the mainmast still stood sound. He would not celebrate until his hunch was confirmed, but it appeared that the damage below would be minimal.

"Send a party to search for survivors," he told Israel. "I want to know who is behind this unprovoked attack."

"Aye, sir," Israel said, though he lingered just a moment longer than expected. "Regarding Miss Maribel. . ."

"If you're about to confess some transgression regarding how the girl was able to slip aboard my ship and remain here for several days, I advise you to wait until we've reached land and I have had sufficient time to decide if whatever decisions were made were the correct ones."

Israel studied him a moment and then nodded. "Agreed," he said.

Jean paused to give him an assessing look. "Go and carry out my orders. I'll be in my cabin. I left our newest crew member there."

To his surprise, Maribel had not only followed his orders but remained under the bunk exactly where he told her to go.

Chapter 7

U sing the blankets she found on the bunk, Maribel had snuggled herself into a cozy spot.

She watched the boots walking toward her. Thankful as she was
that the captain had survived whatever happened, she made no move
to leave her hiding place. In fact, she liked where she was hiding
just fine.

The boots stopped inches from her. "You are unharmed?" the
captain said.

"Yes," she managed.

Later she would add that somewhere between the cannon fire
and the fear that William Spencer and the captain might die she
had decided to give up on the life of a privateer. To lose her father
was awful. To lose people who treated her as if they cared. . .

She bit her trembling lip and turned her face away. The last
thing she wished to do was allow Captain Beaumont to see his
newest crew member shedding tears.

"So you wish to sleep, then?" he said. "I'll not keep you from it,
although I can report that your companion Mr. Spencer showed
himself admirably during the battle. You were correct in vouching
for his abilities as a sailor."

Maribel let out a long breath. She hadn't dared think of William,
because to think of him would mean to worry about him while the
cannons were firing and the noises of battle were sounding. She
hadn't managed the same ability regarding the captain. Instead,

she'd kept up a prayer that he would survive.

The boots stepped away to stop at the desk where the captain's log was kept. She knew this because she might have peeked at what was in this cabin while the captain was away taking care of whatever disturbance was unfolding outside.

But she only peeked for a moment and only long enough to see that Captain Beaumont was much more than just captain of this vessel. Not that she would ever tell.

The cabin door opened and another pair of boots stepped inside. These she recognized as belonging to the kind doctor who reminded her a little of her grandfather.

Her heart lurched just a little at the recollection of the man she called Abuelo. Only knowing that he and Mama had been together when their lives were lost kept her from being completely devastated.

Now that she was an orphan and unfit for service as a privateer, what would she do?

"She is sleeping," Captain Beaumont said. "What news have you brought me?"

"Rao reports the repairs to our ship are minimal and will be completed before sunset. Piper sends a similar message in regard to the sails."

"Then we lift anchor as soon as we are able." He paused. "And what of the vessel that attacked us?"

"We fished a man out of the water, but the rest of the fools aboard were not so lucky. The crew voted to burn it rather than surrender. Israel is with him in the brig. I've been to see to him, and he's told quite a tale."

Maribel's ears perked up at that statement. She'd read something similar in *The Notorious Seafaring Pyrates and Their Exploits*. Though she hadn't understood why men would rather go down on a burning ship than submit to their captors, she did admit it was an effective way to keep a vessel from being used in illegal trade.

"What is his condition?"

"Burns are nasty injuries to treat, and as extensive as his were, it is unlikely he will live beyond a day or two."

She clenched her eyes shut against the image of a man on fire. Still she could not stop thinking of what that must be like. More proof she was not suited for life aboard a privateer's ship.

The doctor spoke for a moment in a voice too soft for Maribel to hear clearly. From the few words she could make out, the discussion had turned to pirates.

The captain shifted positions as Maribel opened her eyes. While the nice doctor was still standing by the door, the captain seemed poised to jump from his chair at any moment.

"Is he talking?" Captain Beaumont asked.

"Indeed he is. I suggest you hear the story directly from him."

The boots moved again, and this time the captain rose. "I will have the abbreviated version first, please," he said with the tone of a man most unhappy with whatever he'd been hearing from the doctor. "Then I will decide if I wish to pay him a visit."

"The abbreviated version is there is a bounty on us all, but more specifically, there is a bounty on your head."

Captain Beaumont took a step to the side and laughed. "Connor, you had me worried. Of course there's a bounty on us. We've made quite a few Spanish ships' captains unhappy when we've relieved them of their cargo in the name of France." He sat back down. "I thought this would be of interest to me."

"It should very well be," the doctor snapped. "That ship was just the warning. They've got a much bigger and well-provisioned vessel coming along behind her, and the man in the brig believes that's the one that will take us down."

"A strategy that does not surprise me," the captain said far too lightly, in Maribel's opinion. "We will be long gone before the companion ship can find us. Have Rao and Piper double their efforts. Take every man off his duty to assist them if necessary."

"I will pass on your order," he said. "However, there's more, and I'd like you to hear it from me first."

"As you know, last year the regent died and Louis XV has ascended to the throne. With that change of events comes a change in the leadership on many levels, albeit a slow change."

"Get to the point," Captain Beaumont snapped.

There was a moment of silence, and Maribel wondered if the doctor would continue. Finally he cleared his throat.

"Yes, well, the result of all that tumult is that after the passage of a year's time, those who were friendly to us in the higher levels of government have been replaced with others who do not take lightly the death of a Spanish nobleman at your hands. We are technically at peace with Spain, you know, and perhaps this particular nobleman had French friends in high places."

"More likely French friends to whom he owed vast sums of money. As to your statement regarding Spain, I agree we are technically at peace," the captain echoed, his sarcasm thick. "But still charged with carrying out the duties our Letters of Marque allow."

"I will call upon your own use of the word *technically* to respond. Yes, we technically are still charged with carrying out these duties."

The captain pounded his fist on his desk, resulting in a small glass object falling to the floor. The crystal shattered into a thousand pieces of sparkling debris.

"And has anyone accused me of being derelict in these duties or holding out profits that rightly belonged to the crown?" the captain asked.

"To my knowledge, they have not."

"I wager those same men would not take it lightly if I were to surrender my letters and walk away from the enterprise that has lined their pockets these past few years."

"I doubt you'll be given the chance," Mr. Connor said. "That ship was sent to kill you by men who hold the purse strings of the king's coffers and are capable of ordering any vessel in the Royal Navy to fire against us. Likely the next attempt will not be such an abysmal failure."

"So I am now a pariah and my friend is now my enemy?"

"You are a wanted man, yes." The doctor moved toward the captain. "But this is not completely unexpected. That is why we made the plans to. . ."

The rest of the doctor's words were lost as Maribel's heart thumped hard against her chest. How she hated the privateering life.

Please, Lord, just put me on solid ground somewhere and leave me there. Anywhere.

"Then we sail for New Orleans," Captain Beaumont said.

"We cannot do that, lad," the doctor countered. "Where do you think these French vessels call their home port here? If you were to attempt to sail into the city, you would be immediately arrested as a traitor to the crown."

"Which crown?" the captain quipped.

"Truly, lad, it could be either, if you really think on it. Though the French are after you, I warrant the Spaniards would like to see you strung up as a pirate."

"And the rest of you along with me," he said thoughtfully. "Yes, I see the dilemma. Then we sail for another port, and along the way we make plans to find another vessel. Would that solve the issue?"

"It would solve one of the issues," he said. "The other, you and I have discussed at length on more than one occasion."

"I will not consider it."

The room fell silent for a moment. "You may not be given the option."

Seven weeks later

Don Pablo Cordoba paced the confines of the vessel and paused only occasionally to look outside at the stars that shone above them. Word traveled fast in his world, and knowledge of a nobleman's death at the hands of a man who held French Letters of Marque could spell disaster for those in power in France.

Thus Don Pablo had stepped in to mediate what could quickly have become more than just an unfortunate situation. He had done so, not letting any of the parties know he had motives other than keeping peace between the country of his birth and the country where his roots went deep.

While he had never held much love for the place where his grandmother was born, he did have numerous relatives scattered across the positions of power in the French capital. Relatives who were happy to prove loyalty to him by seeing that the death of his son was avenged.

Not that he had any particular interest in avenging Antonio's regrettable demise. Like as not, the son he hardly knew deserved whatever had happened. At least his Isabel was not here to see what had become of her only son. A mother's love transcended the truth of her child's true personality. Don Pablo, however, had a very clear idea of just what Antonio had become.

Sadly, his attempt to remove Antonio from the lives of Maribel and her mother had turned into a disaster that he must remedy. Of course, he would not tell Mary about Antonio's death until he could also tell her what happened to her daughter. To his granddaughter.

At least he could count on the silence of his friends on that matter. And for those who were not friends, he could count on allegiance. To cross him was something few dared to do.

None now that the regent was no longer in charge.

He took up his pacing again, this time walking out a solution to how best to retrieve a girl he prayed with each step would be found alive. Testimony freely given by men who he believed were truly witnesses to his son's murder led him to believe the girl was spirited away aboard a vessel known to sailors as the *Ghost Ship*.

All agreed the girl was very much alive and unharmed when she was taken. Thus, he would continue to believe this until the moment he held her in his arms once more.

So as to keep her from learning she was a widow, Mary was installed in the cabin next door and would be traveling with him to

New Orleans. The appointment he had secured would provide for him a home and a salary that would hardly compensate for all he left behind in Spain.

However, it would provide a base of operations that would allow him closer access to the ruffians who saw fit to steal his precious Maribel. And as he had promised Mary, he would stop at nothing until she was returned.

What he did not tell Mary was what he planned to do with the men when they were found. That was certainly not a fit conversation for a woman of her delicate disposition.

One room past the door to Don Pablo's cabin, Mary Cordoba leaned against the wall and stared up at the stars overhead. The night was clear, eerily so since their passage had met with such terrible weather until they reached the warm waters of the Gulf of Mexico, or *Seno Mexicano* as the crewmen had been calling it since they reached this latitude just before sunset.

Somewhere her Maribel was looking at the same stars. She had to be. The alternative was unthinkable.

Mary turned her back and closed her eyes. It was her fault. Had she not defied her mother and father and fled to Spain to marry Antonio, life would not have taken her to this place of desperation.

She let out a long breath and opened her eyes once more. If she had not married him, there would be no Maribel.

That was also unthinkable.

CHAPTER 8

From her place in the lookout post high up in the rigging, Maribel studied the stars overhead. Though to most of the sailors on this vessel, duty in the lookout post was considered the worst assignment, it was her favorite.

Not only could she see for miles in all directions during the day, but she could also dream beneath the stars at night. Dream with her eyes wide open and her senses finely tuned to detect any approaching vessels, of course.

Seven weeks ago, the captain had sailed their other ship—the one people called the *Ghost Ship*—into a secluded bay somewhere off the coast of Mexico and burned her to the waterline. Waiting for them was this sloop, a fast ship with a low draft that allowed them to slip in and out of narrow channels and bays.

It also allowed for a much smaller crew, which displeased those who were not chosen to rejoin them. Those men were much happier when they discovered the amount they would be paid for remaining behind.

Several storms had kept them from sailing out into open waters, but Maribel did not mind. With the vessel rocking at anchor in the shallow green waters of the Caribbean Sea, life aboard the ship that had been christened the *Escape* was idyllic.

Though they were all under orders not to leave the ship, the captain did allow for plenty of time for Maribel to read when she was not otherwise assigned to a task. Thus, in the past seven weeks, she had begun the task of reading every book in the captain's library.

Maribel had also convinced the captain to allow her to bring whatever book she might be reading up to the post with her, although she had to prove to him after many weeks of work that she could read and remain alert at the same time. Oh, but prove it she did.

However, that was the only negative to the night watch. No matter how hard she tried to convince him, the captain refused to allow her a lamp or even a candle up in the watch post, so her reading was limited to nights when the moon shone at its brightest. She understood the reason behind it, of course, but the night watches seemed so much longer this way.

"Are you trying to read up there?"

She peered down in the direction the voice had come from. "No sir, Captain," she said.

"Good," came his good-humored reply. "Reading in the dark will damage your eyes, you know."

The same thing the captain said almost every night when he came to check on her. "Yes, sir," she responded as usual.

The ship rocked and swayed over seas that were only slightly more choppy than usual. The moon was a mere fingernail in the southern sky, so she would not be reading tonight.

In the east, lightning skittered across the clouds from east to west, as it often did on warm nights like tonight. She had learned to tell the difference between what the men called heat lightning and the other type, which indicated a squall was present.

William Spencer told her he'd once seen a book with pictures in it that showed different types of clouds and gatherings of stars called constellations. Someday she would find that book and read it from cover to cover, memorizing all the patterns of stars so she could recognize them up in her watch post.

Likely she would have plenty of time to search and even more time to read and remember what was in the book. No one aboard the ship wanted this job, likely because she was the only one who did not get sick from the rocking motions.

What Maribel would never admit is that the first time she was assigned to this task, she nearly lost her breakfast of porridge on the heads of the men working on the deck below. Pride alone kept her from embarrassment, and pride taught her how to remain that way.

Lightning flashed again, this time zigzagging west to east. Something on the horizon caught her eye. Was that a sail?

Her heart lurched. In all the nights she spent on watch, she could count on one hand the times she thought she had seen something out on the water. Only once had there actually been another vessel, and it had turned out to be a stranded merchantman flying the English flag.

She lifted the spyglass to her eye with trembling hands. The sky remained dark with only tiny pinpoints of light to remind her there were stars overhead.

"Calm down," she whispered. "It's probably nothing. Probably not sails at all."

Maribel lowered the spyglass and waited with more patience than she thought she could possess. As each second ticked by, she wanted to scream. Wanted to have an answer to the question that was causing her heart to race and her hands to shake.

There! Lightning once again showed in the clouds, winding its way parallel to the horizon. A horizon where three sails had gained on them.

She opened her mouth to shout a warning and found her breath frozen in her lungs. *Pray away the fear. Pray away the fear. Pray away. . .*

Trying again, she managed to cough out a cry. Nothing like words but a noise all the same.

"What's that?" William Spencer, who always seemed to be assigned to a watch below her post, called from below.

"There is a ship," she managed with more strength. "I see sails! Due east."

William sounded the alarm as Maribel gripped the edge of the watch post with one hand and lifted the spyglass up to her eye with the other. This time she held it still, and after what seemed like endless moments of blackness, she saw the sails again.

Having learned all the vessels by name, she called out what she saw. She counted the masts and made sure there were two and that they were square-rigged. The next time the lightning illuminated the vessel, she confirmed there were two sails on the mainmast. Yes, there was the topsail and the gaff sail.

"Brigantine," she called. "No flags showing."

Probably British in origin, she decided after considering the drawings of vessels she had seen in the captain's books. Rather than be wrong, however, Maribel kept her opinion to herself.

From what she knew of the brigantines, they were swift and easily maneuvered in all types of seas. They were a favorite of pirates and as a naval vessel.

She took a deep breath and let it out slowly to calm her racing heart. Whoever was at the helm, this was no stranded merchantman.

She remained still, watching and waiting until the sails were once again illuminated. Or should have been.

Maribel lowered the spyglass and swiped at the glass on the end to see if perhaps it was smudged. There was nothing on the eastern horizon.

Swinging her attention across the horizon, she spied the sails now tacking to the west. After taking a moment to calculate, she called out the new coordinates. She continued to repeat this process, forgetting her fear. Down below on deck, the crew was going about the business of preparing to engage in battle, all the while remaining silent and working under cover of darkness.

Finally she became aware that someone was climbing up to join her. "William Spencer?" she called as she trained her spyglass on the horizon. "What are you doing up here?"

"Captain sent me to fetch you. Said he doesn't want you up

here in harm's way."

"You know you cannot spend five minutes up here without getting ill. How in the world will you manage to continue to call out coordinates if your supper is on the men below?"

"That is not. . ."

She turned around to spare her friend a glance. Even in the dim light, she could see from his expression that the motion of the vessel was already causing him discomfort.

"I told you I can manage this. I know the captain won't like what you have to tell him, but I will take the blame once this kerfuffle is finished, all right?"

Maribel waited for William to speak or even nod, but he said nothing. Instead, he stood very still and gripped the edge of the lookout post.

"For goodness' sake," she told him. "Get out of here before you keep me from doing my job. If I am worrying about you, I cannot be tracking that brig."

At that, William complied. She imagined he carried a mixture of relief and dread with him as he shimmied back down the mast, but at least he did not carry the remains of his supper on the front of his shirt.

She returned to her task, lifting the spyglass to her eye. What was it about some men, especially the ones aboard the *Escape*, who held the opinion that in times of danger they ought to protect her? There was nothing she couldn't do just as well as they could.

Maribel let out a long breath as she waited for the next lightning to dance along the clouds. Indeed, there were some tasks she could do better than any of them, chief among them the job she was doing tonight. William had just proved her point.

Lowering the spyglass, she glanced over the edge to make sure William hadn't fallen due to his impending illness. Behind her something cracked with a noise so loud it deafened her.

Something white tangled around her. Her ears rang as she fought to find fresh air again.

Another crack, something she felt rather than heard.

Then came the sensation of flying.

Or falling.

And then the world went black.

"I can't find her, Captain," Israel said. "We've all looked, and she just isn't anywhere."

Jean looked up at his second-in-command, exhaustion tugging at the corners of his understanding. They'd outrun the French ship, but only after they disabled their opponent by taking out the vessel's mainmast.

"That cannot be," he said as he let out a long breath and scrubbed at his face. The smell of blood, gunpowder, and smoke clung to him, and he wanted nothing more than to fall into his bunk and sleep. "She would not leave her duty. Go look in the top of the mainmast. And if she's fallen asleep, wake her and tell her she'll spend time in the brig the next time she is derelict in her duties."

Israel's face wore a stricken look. "That's just it, sir. The lookout post is gone. Shot through by a cannonball, I'd guess. Missed the mainmast but got. . ." He shook his head. "I can't say it, sir."

Jean stumbled to his feet, his exhaustion gone. "Turn the ship around and go back to where the first shot from the French brigantine was fired."

"Consider it done," Israel said, moving much faster than a man of his size should have been able to move.

The sloop had been a wise choice, for this vessel was easily able to maneuver around and head back toward the scene of the battle at a fast clip. With all its sails unfurled, the *Escape* practically flew toward their destination.

At some point during the voyage, Connor came to stand beside him at the wheel. They remained in silence, watching the waves with Jean preferring not to speak. Apparently the doctor felt the same, for he remained stoic with his attention focused straight ahead.

"Lad," he finally said. "I would be remiss if I did not remind you that we are taking this vessel back into waters where a French Navy vessel may be nursing her wounds." He paused. "And not only nursing a grudge against us but also likely aware of the bounty on your head."

"I am aware of that," Jean said through clenched jaw. "And if there was a way for me to search for Maribel without the rest of you, I would certainly exercise that option."

"You are once again taking on a responsibility that is not yours alone to bear," he said.

"I'll not have another of your lectures, Connor. Not tonight, and certainly not on this topic."

"So you do not wish to hear that I believe you are a fool for risking your life to go back and try to find that girl?"

"I do not," Jean said evenly as he concentrated on the horizon.

"Good," he said. "Because I do not believe that at all."

"No?" Jean spared him a glance. Slowly a smile dawned. Connor answered the smile with a nod.

No more words were necessary. As he always had, and as he had done for Jean's father before him, Evan Connor would follow him into battle and remain at his side.

When Israel called out that they had reached their destination, there was no sign of the French vessel. Jean ordered the anchor dropped. Though the danger was there, so was the opportunity to retrieve the child.

A loud splash announced that the skiff had been lowered down into the inky water. Evan held the lamp as Jean slid down the rope to land in the craft.

"Send down the lamp, then release the ropes," Jean told him.

"Not yet," came the booming voice of Israel Bennett.

His second-in-command tucked the rope into the crook of his

arm and slid down with his free hand. The skiff rocked as Israel landed.

"I'll row," Israel announced. "You hold the lamp." He paused, obviously realizing he had overstepped his position. "Unless you prefer it the other way around, sir."

"No," Jean said as Connor released the rope. "Head us off in that direction. I will let you know if I see any sign of her."

"You worried about those Frenchmen coming back after us?" Israel asked.

"Not my concern right now," Jean said.

"Mine either, sir," was his swift response. "I figure I do my part and the Lord'll do His. That generally works best for me."

Jean gave the statement some thought and then discarded his responses. No need to comment on something he struggled to understand. Israel was generous in sharing his faith, although Jean understood that even less.

How was a man who was taken prisoner at the hands of his enemies and sold into slavery able not only to forgive those men but to rise above it all to still hold on to his faith in God? It made no sense.

"You got questions, then you go ahead and ask them, Captain," Israel said as he continued to row.

"Don't know what to ask," Jean said.

Israel gave a thoughtful nod. "Well then, when you do know, that'd be the time, sir."

Jean nodded. A comfortable silence fell between them as Israel rowed and Jean searched the waters for even a scrap of sail or piece of the lookout post.

Though they remained on the search well beyond the time when the sun rose, there was no evidence that Maribel had been lost here. Jean ordered the anchor lifted, and they moved to another location where the lookout thought he saw debris.

The process continued throughout the day and into the night. Still nothing was found that would offer any idea as to where the youngest member of the crew had gone.

The crew of the *Escape* was lifting anchor to move to yet another location when Connor intervened. "Israel, please call Mr. Rao up to take your place. I will stand in for our captain while the two of you get some rest."

Both men argued the point, but the doctor refused to back down. Finally Jean nodded. "We are of no use to Maribel if we can hardly hold up our heads or keep our eyes open." He turned his attention to the doctor. "I will have four hours' rest, and then we go out again. I've given the coordinates already. I trust you to find that location and drop anchor there."

"It will be done as you ask," Connor said as he handed Jean a dipper of water. "Although as your doctor I would suggest more sleep than just four hours."

Jean regarded his old friend with an icy stare and then took several grateful sips. Though he understood why Connor would make such a suggestion, the idea of any rest at all while Maribel might be floating in the ocean was appalling to him.

A stronger man would not need such a thing. And yet as he looked at Israel, he knew the thought was absurd. No man could live long without sleep.

"Argue with me," he finally said to Connor, "and I will make it three hours. Perhaps two."

"And what do I do to make it six, Jean? Or eight?" The doctor returned Jean's stare, his expression showing concern.

"Nothing," Jean said as he turned to walk away. "Connor, send someone to wake us in four hours' time."

"Aye, Captain," he said. "And I'll have Cook prepare a meal for you to take with you." He held up his hands as if to fend off any response from Jean. "When you find her, she will likely be hungry."

A point he could not argue, so he made no attempt to try. For as much as he held out hope that Maribel Cordoba was floating nearby and awaiting discovery, serious doubts had taken root. Given the time that had elapsed and the distance she would have had to fall, human logic and reason told him survival was unlikely.

Something else, though he was unwilling to call it faith, told him otherwise. So in four hours he would rise from his bunk and commence the search again. He would continue to search until whatever it was inside him that sent him out called him back in.

Jean allowed his eyes to fall shut, but still sleep eluded him. Never once had he allowed himself to reconsider any decision he made as captain of a vessel. To do so could cripple his ability to lead.

But tonight, in the darkness of his cabin, Jean let his mind sort through the steps on the path that led him here. The choices that sent an innocent if exasperating girl out into open water during the blackness of night.

He slammed his fist against the wall beside him and sat up. There was just no sense to any of it.

Then it came to him, the knowledge of his fault slamming against his chest with enough force to knock him backward. Jean Beaumont, the notorious privateer with a bounty on him, hung his head and cried.

❈

The green water was pretty and warm, just like what Maribel had imagined in the books she read about the Caribbean Sea. Her head hurt and her eyes wanted to close, but every time she tried to sleep she fell off the piece of wood that kept her floating along.

If she tried hard, she could remember a disagreement she had with William Spencer. To be exact, she could remember that she and William exchanged words, although the particulars of the discussion were unclear. If only he were here to remind her. And maybe to continue the discussion.

Looking up at the stars, she had counted more constellations than she thought she knew. When she could find no more familiar star patterns, she began to create names for her own until the sun peeked over the horizon and ruined her game.

Maribel rolled over onto her stomach without sliding off the board, a skill she had developed with practice in the hours since she woke up from whatever nightmare landed her in the water. Until now she hadn't thought about how the water turned from inky black to deep purple and finally to red, gold, and then green as the sun rose, even though she must have seen it happen from the watch post.

The seas were calm now, with only a slight wind to propel her over the waves, putting her in mind of Robinson Crusoe. Maybe she would find her own island and live there.

Maribel gave that some thought even though her head hurt so much that it became hard to string ideas together. Yes, she could live on an island, but no, she would not like to live there without friends. And certainly she would miss reading her books.

Oh, but a nice island where she had friends and books? She smiled even though it hurt her lips. Now that sounded just right.

Sound.

She opened her eyes but closed them again because they were too heavy to control. Yes, there it was again, a sound that wasn't the waves or the wind or the occasional seabird squawking.

But what was it? People talking?

"Captain?" she called.

Still the talking continued, but she could say nothing more. Not right now. Just a little nap, and then she would call out so Captain Beaumont would find her.

Because he would find her. She knew it.

She absolutely and positively knew it.

CHAPTER 9

Evan Connor walked down the passageway toward the captain's cabin. Jean Beaumont may believe himself to have superhuman endurance, but as his doctor and longtime friend of his family, Evan knew otherwise. He'd patched up the man since he was a lad, and likely would continue doing so until the Lord took him home.

Thus, Jean might eventually forgive him for not following the specific command to awaken him after four hours of rest. He took a deep breath and let it out slowly. And because Jean would probably not forgive him for the sleeping draught Evan slipped into the dipper of water he'd offered the captain, that information would not be mentioned.

He opened the door slowly and was greeted by the sound of the captain's rhythmic snoring. Though he was sorely tempted to let the man sleep even longer, a full seven hours had elapsed since Jean laid his head on his bunk.

Israel and Rao had resumed the search two hours ago. A second boat had been made seaworthy and was heading off in the opposite direction with two more crew members.

The carpenter's assistants were working on a third boat, but it might be another hour or more before the craft was ready for use. That news would be delivered gently and only if the captain asked.

Evan closed the door and let out a long breath as he set his medical bag on the floor beside him and then lit the lamp he'd brought along for this task. Where had the time gone? Only yesterday the man in the bunk had been a lad on his papa's knee.

When he swore an oath to his best friend to protect this son of his, Evan had not expected where that oath would lead. Nor had he questioned it.

The snoring had ceased. "Who's there?" Jean demanded, his speech slurred.

"It is I, Evan Connor," he said. "You wished me to let you know when it was time to awaken."

Silence.

"Jean? Are you awake?" he said as he crept forward.

Loud snoring met his question. Perhaps he underestimated the amount of sleeping draught he had slipped into the water dipper.

A roar of noise went up on the deck overhead. Evan froze. The men's shouts echoed in the cabin, but their words were undecipherable.

Jean shifted on the bunk, but his snoring continued. As the noise persisted on deck, Evan debated whether to leave him there or to wake him up.

The warning bell rang, and his decision was made. "Wake up, Jean. Your crew needs you."

Whatever was happening above them, the situation was urgent. Shouts of the men competed with the sounds of the bell that foretold an emergency.

"Jean," he called as he walked toward the bunk.

The sound of something crashing and a flash of light sent him reeling backward. Smoke engulfed him as he choked to find his breath. Beneath him, the ship listed heavily to starboard.

When he could manage to climb to his feet, Evan looked around to survey the damage. What must have been a cannonball had burst through the wall next to Jean's bunk, splintering the wood planks.

The bunk where Jean had been sleeping only moments before was practically gone, its wood splintered and the mattress destroyed. Seeing the oil lamp dangling precariously on the edge of the table, he caught it just as it fell.

The force of the blast had thrown Jean away from the place where he had been sleeping. Upon closer inspection, he found the captain lying on the floor beneath the ruins of his desk. His ever-present cutlass glittered in the lamplight as it slid away from reach.

A moment of grief pierced his heart rendering Evan immobile as he viewed the tangled wreckage. Had he not given Jean the sleeping draught. . .

He quickly pushed the guilt aside to allow his medical training to take control. Though he had to move the lamp to haul away heavy boards and debris, he managed to free Jean and pull him to a place where he could more readily assess his injuries.

First he felt for a pulse. Yes, there it was. Faint but still a pulse.

Evan went back to the spot where he'd left his medical bag only to find it gone. After a lengthy search, he found the bag—its contents spilled—in the opposite corner of the room. He managed to collect his medicines and tools and return them to the bag despite the pitching of the ship.

Screams pierced the air as another round of cannonballs hit the foundering vessel. The French, for likely that was the source of the attack, obviously wanted the vessel dispatched to the bottom of the sea.

Those same Frenchmen would want the man laid out on the floor before him dispatched as well, first to a French prison so their bounty could be collected and then to the hangman's noose.

"Can you hear me, lad?" Connor shouted above the din.

No response.

"All right, then," he said, keeping the panic from his voice lest the lad hear him. "I'll make do. Probably best you're not awake to feel this. I warrant it will hurt."

Removing the captain's shirt, he saw injuries that were a threat to the lad's life. Evan reached for the brandy to cleanse the wounds and found the contents of the bottle empty and the glass shattered. He tore strips of linen and fashioned rudimentary bandages to stop the bleeding and splinted the arm he knew must be broken.

Evan swiped at the sweat on his brow and saw blood on his sleeve. He felt nothing, so either the cut was minor or shock had already set in.

In either case, it would not hinder his ability to care for his patient. He continued to bind wounds and assess Jean's condition despite the sounds of shouting and metal clanging that indicated the battle had moved from the sea to above him on the deck.

The bleeding was profuse, and it appeared Jean might not survive. All Evan could do was continue to pray as he dabbed at wounds and administered treatment that in all likelihood would be futile. He'd seen men in much better shape die of their injuries. Only the Lord could intervene and keep the lad with the living.

Footsteps sounded in the hallway, but there was no way to tell whether they were from friend or foe. When the door burst open, the question was answered.

"In here," a French sailor called.

Evan ignored the men to continue to administer more of the sleeping draught to the dying captain. If he could not save Jean, at least he could keep Jean from remembering his death.

Three French sailors stepped aside to allow a man of middle age and exceptional girth to enter the cabin. A lieutenant by the looks of him.

"What is this?" The lieutenant kicked debris out of the way to move closer in a manner that told Evan he must be their leader. "It appears your man is not doing well, sir. Who is he, and who are you?"

Evan ignored him. The head wound he thought he had closed was open again, and he would need more bandages. He reached into his medical bag for linen and continued the process of treating his patient.

"From what I see, it appears this is the captain's cabin," one of the sailors said. "See over there on the floor? That's the captain's log."

"Yes, I see that," their leader said as he nodded to one of

his men. "And somewhere in that desk would be the Letters of Marque, I would assume. You there." He nodded to one of the sailors. "Search the desk until the letters are found. If other items of value are there, take those as well." He offered Evan a smile that held no humor. "Confiscate them for the crown."

One sailor headed for the desk while the other fellow picked his way toward Evan and yanked him to his feet. Jean's head fell to the floor with a sickening thud.

The captain's eyes fluttered, but he remained unconscious and unaware of what was happening around him. Evan gave thanks for that mercy even as he prayed for a miracle. Prayed that somehow God would save them both or, failing this, that He would save his best friend's son.

There was more to this lad's life. More than this. Evan knew this with more certainty than any other living person other than the lad's father as he wrenched free of the Frenchman to once again cradle the man's head and apply pressure to the most troublesome of the wounds.

Please, Lord, give him another chance to go back to who he was.

"Which of you is the captain of this vessel? The man called Jean Beaumont?"

He stared into the eyes of the sailor who towered over him and said nothing. Blood flowed freely now and clouded his vision, but Evan held his ground and did not move.

Screams from somewhere above them tore through the silence. The ship heaved furiously as the smell of smoke once again filled the room. As the floor tilted, the sailor at the desk lost his footing and skidded into the wall.

In his hand, the sailor held up a document. "Got those letters, sir," he said. "Looks like we got our man."

"We're going down with this ship if we remain much longer," the lieutenant said as he nodded toward Evan. "Take the old man out and feed him to the fish. Those letters from this vessel will be enough to prove our victory and gain the bounty on Beaumont's head. And you," he said to the nearest sailor, "take the dead man on the floor and do the same."

Something inside Evan snapped. "Do not touch this man," he said.

The sailors pushed Evan aside to jerk Jean to his feet. His limp body hung between them, his eyes closed. The steep incline made for slow going as the men carried Jean toward the door. Behind Evan, the third sailor grasped his arms and held him in place.

"Wait! That man is innocent!"

As soon as the words escaped Evan's mouth, the men stopped. Their leader frowned. "What do you mean?"

"He is not part of our crew, sir," Evan said, affecting a deference he did not feel. "He is a hostage. A lawyer from New Orleans held against his will."

"Well now, that is interesting," he said. "Can you prove this?"

Evan squared his shoulders and stood straight despite the shifting floor beneath him. "His father will attest to what I say and likely provide a handsome reward for his return."

"How can you expect me to believe this?" their leader said.

With a shrug, Evan affected a casual expression. "I don't suppose a man of your intelligence could be fooled. I will give you the name of the man's father and you will tell me if you've heard of him. Perhaps that will convince you that you are better off delivering him to New Orleans and his family than dispatching him to his death."

"Go on," he said, and Evan knew he had him.

"Perhaps it is better I write a letter to his father. Give him an explanation of how he came to us so that he will not have you arrested on the spot when you bring his son home in this shape."

The Frenchman's thick brows rose. "Surely you cannot mean to threaten me with that sort of thing, sir. My reputation is impeccable."

"As is Monsieur Valmont's," he said as he looked down at Jean, his heart breaking but his face stoic. "Perhaps you have heard of his family? His father, Marcel, is well known in New Orleans as well as back home in France. And his uncle is Jean Baptiste Le Moyne."

Evan made this statement in French, all the more to impress the haughty sailor. Apparently his ploy worked, for the older man's thick eyebrows rose at the mention of the Valmont name.

"Valmont and Le Moyne, did you say?" The man's voice gave away that he was impressed by the names. Then abruptly his expression went serious.

"Perhaps you realize Le Moyne is once again the governor of Jeaniana? And no Frenchman could claim he did not know Marcel Valmont. He has the ear of the king, you know."

He shook his head. "Impossible. What would the son of Monsieur Valmont and the nephew of the *Sieur de Bienville* be doing here in the company of a wanted man? Take them both to the deck and throw them over. I have no more time for such foolishness."

"I doubt that is what his family would call this. They would deem it murder, of course."

"Murder? I call it service to the crown. Good riddance to bad men."

Mustering the last of his strength and every bit of his courage, he laughed. The ruse worked, as the Frenchmen stopped in their tracks to look at him as if he had lost his mind.

"You find this funny?" their leader said as he stormed toward him and slammed his fist into Evan's gut and sent him doubling over. The older man wrenched Evan's head up, forcing him to look into his eyes. "If he is a hostage, then who are you?"

"Captain Jean Beaumont at your service."

It was the leader's turn to laugh. "You expect me to believe an old man is the cause of all the trouble this ship's given our country? Not likely."

"Any trouble attributed to this crew is a lie told by those who wish to better themselves at our expense. This vessel has Letters of Marque from the king himself, and those letters have been followed exactly." He paused. "Perhaps you wish to dispute my statement?"

"Oh, so that is how it will be, then?" The man in charge laughed. "We are of a certain age, are we not? And men of our age, we are proud and brave until perhaps we are confronted with the shortness of the remainder of our days." He retrieved his flintlock pistol and made a show of loading it. "But what do we do when our days can either be lengthened or shortened by the mere response to a question? To tell the truth may be to lengthen your days, or perhaps a lie will save you. What to do?"

He refused to look away. His hands trembled, but as a physician Evan knew the response to be medical and not panic. In this moment, he felt absolutely no fear.

Evan returned his attention to Jean, who he hoped was still alive. He was broken and bloody but recognizable. Blood trickled down his forehead despite the bandages placed there. Still, his father would know him if he saw him, and Evan hoped he would also know that his old friend had tried his best to keep the lad safe.

"I am a man of honor, so I choose to tell the truth."

"Why should I believe you?"

"As I said, I tell the truth." He refused to blink as he stared down the barrel of the flintlock pistol. "That man is Jean-Luc Valmont. Take him to his father or his blood is on your hands. Either way, should he die before you reach New Orleans, the Valmont family will see that you all will hang for murder."

"We are protected by the French government," the lieutenant snapped.

He gave the older man a steely look. "Sir, I do hope you are extremely confident in that fact."

"Why wouldn't we be?" he asked, his tone haughty but his expression showing the slightest bit of discomfort.

"If you know the name Valmont, then you know the power Marcel Valmont wields in the higher levels of the French government and the power his brother-in-law has in the city of New

Orleans." Evan shrugged. "I am not certain the king or his men will stand behind a man of your rank should they be informed you chose to go through with this execution."

The lieutenant turned his attention to the sailor still rummaging through the desk. "Leave it and bring me those letters."

Obliging his commanding officer, the young man did as he was told. After reading the Letters of Marque, the lieutenant looked back over at Evan.

"So you say the young man is Jean-Luc Valmont?"

"He is indeed, and if you hope to get him to New Orleans without hanging for his murder, I will go with you to treat him. I am a physician. Make haste, though. He needs a soft bed and clean bandages."

"If he is Valmont, then that would make you a doctor, a ship's captain, and a fugitive with a bounty on his head." He gave Evan a sweeping look and then shook his head. "How do you manage it all?"

"We are wasting time, sir." Evan pressed past him, not caring that he'd pushed away a fully loaded flintlock. The only way off this sinking ship was to convince these men that they were more valuable alive than dead.

Before Evan could reach the door, one of the sailors had stepped up to block his exit. The young man grasped him by the arm and hauled him out of the way.

"Make way," the lieutenant said as he gave the order to remove Jean from the cabin. "See that he is given a bed and medical care," he added as two of the sailors carried the lad away.

A man came running down the passageway. "Sir," he called. "There are skiffs in the water. Our men saw two with men aboard heading this way. Shall we go after them?"

Evan schooled his expression so as not to give away his thoughts. "You have no time," he told them. "If you chase after small boats, you may be putting Mr. Valmont at risk of dying before he can reach the city. Do you want to explain your decision to his father?"

The lieutenant seemed to consider his statement a moment, and then he nodded. "Captain Beaumont is right," he said as he tucked the Letters of Marque under his arm and followed his men out into the corridor.

Gathering up his medical bag, Evan hurried to catch up to the sailors. He kept his attention straight ahead, knowing if he looked at any of the fallen crewmen, he would be unable to keep from stopping to help.

The walk across the deck seemed to take an eternity. It took everything he had not to be swayed by the cries of the men who needed him. But he had made a promise to his friend Marcel Valmont to deliver his son safely home, and he would stop at nothing, and for no one, until he kept that promise.

Evan watched while the lieutenant supervised his men as they hauled the lad over onto the French vessel, and then waited for his turn. Around him, French sailors were fleeing back to their ship, some of them with items they did not appear to own.

All the cannons on the *Escape* had either been moved to the other ship or tossed into the sea. Around them in the green waters, debris and bodies floated.

Finally the lieutenant gave one last sweeping glance around the vessel and then returned his attention to the last few members of his crew still aboard. "Burn this tub to the waterline and shoot anyone who tries to flee."

Then he lifted his flintlock and shot Evan through the heart.

CHAPTER 10

Jean Baptiste "Bienville" Le Moyne had been pacing the confines of his home near the river ever since news arrived that his sister's son had been found aboard the vessel of a notorious privateer. Captain Jean Beaumont was well known, both in France and here in New Orleans, and the news that there was now a French bounty on his head had come as a surprise to many.

A Spanish bounty, of course, but for the king of France to turn on a man who allegedly brought much in the way of coin and supplies into his royal coffers? There had to be more to the story than what he'd gleaned from those few Frenchmen willing to speak to him.

The door opened and his aide stepped inside. "They've got him down at the dock, Governor."

"Thank you," he said as he hurried to greet the man he hoped would someday follow in his footsteps.

Bienville had been reluctant to bless the marriage of his sister to a much older man, but theirs had been a love match. And though the Spanish pirates had taken her when their sons were but babes, she had not been forgotten in the Valmont household.

The crowd parted ways as his aides alerted them that their governor was en route to the docks. A blustering fool in the uniform of the French Navy came hurrying in his direction.

"What an honor it is for you to be visiting my ship, Monsieur Bienville. Please come with me and I will show you to where we have kept your nephew in comfort."

He gave the vessel a cursory glance, offering a brief nod toward the men assembled on the deck in his honor. "My nephew, please," he instructed the officer.

"Yes, of course. Please follow me."

Bienville attended the captain until they reached the room where Jean-Luc was being kept. Nodding to his aide, he pressed past the officer. There a man lay on a cot, a sheet covering him. Where there once had been a handsome and strong young man, a broken and bloody image of Jean-Luc Valmont stared back at him with unseeing eyes.

Bienville dropped to his knee beside the cot. "How long has he been like this?"

"Since the men brought him aboard," the captain said.

"Do not let this man leave," he told his aide as he nodded toward the man in charge. "His father will have questions, and I will have the answers."

"Yes, of course," the Frenchman said, his head nodding in obedience. "When the old man told us he was your nephew, of course it was my privilege to deliver him back to you in a suitable condition."

"If that is your definition of suitable, I am grateful he was no worse than this," he snapped. "What have you fools done to him?"

"I assure you, sir, we have given him the best of care," he protested. "Any injury to his person can be attributed to the pirate Beaumont. The old man claimed this Monsieur Valmont was his prisoner. I found nothing to dispute this."

The Frenchman wrung his hands as perspiration dotted his brow. This man knew more than he was saying.

"As soon as he has been given a cursory medical examination, I will authorize his transport to his father's home for further care." He looked to the captain. "Send a man you trust to arrange for a litter and men to carry it. And if you botch this job, it will go even worse for you."

"Even worse?" He tugged at his collar and then removed his handkerchief to dab at his damp brow. "I do not understand."

"Of course you do," he said evenly. "And I wager every man on this ship understands as well. You attacked the ship where my nephew was being held. During that attack, the fact he suffered serious injuries is obvious to—"

"Forgive me, sir, but I must protest. We were fired upon."

"You, sir, are a liar. Find a better story and tell it to someone who might be more easily deceived. There was a bounty on Beaumont's head, and you went after him without caring who else might be on his ship. Did you sink it? And tell me the truth, because I will read the report myself when you claim your reward."

"We did, I believe," he said, "although the vessel was still burning when we set off. At that point we were more interested in making haste to New Orleans to see to your nephew's restored health than we were in following some protocol regarding pirate vessels."

"Privateer, sir, and if you don't know the difference, I can certainly see that you are taught."

"I do know the difference," he said, looking quite displeased.

"Your physician has arrived, sir," his aide told him.

"Send him in."

Bienville stepped back so his nephew could be examined. Once the sheet was pulled away from Jean-Luc's body, the extent of his injuries was obvious. A jagged red scar traversed the muscles of his chest while another snaked down his leg, ending just above the ankle. One arm had been bound with a rudimentary bandage from his fist to his elbow. Thick strips of muslin covered his forehead, allowing only wisps of his black hair to show beneath the bloodstained fabric.

"What matter of heathen. . ."

Bienville shook his head. Giving way to his temper would serve no purpose. He moved back to allow the physician to complete his examination and then called for the litter to retrieve the lad and bring him to his father's home.

"Will he live?" he demanded of the physician.

From the man's expression, he had his answer. Still, he needed to hear the words.

"You may speak freely," he told him.

"Then if I speak freely, I would have to tell you that this lad is as near to death as I have seen a man with breath still in his body. Whether he lives or dies, it is in God's hands."

Bienville clasped his hand on the physician's shoulder. "Go with him and see if you can explain to God how very much his family wishes him to live." He offered a smile that held no humor. "And I shall do the same."

The task of moving him to the litter and removing him from the vessel had been completed, and the litter carrying Jean-Luc was on its way toward the docks when a young French soldier hurried toward him.

"Monsieur," he said as he glanced around and then returned his attention to Bienville. "What the captain said, well, it is not completely correct. You see, there was a threat to throw both men off the ship until the old man, Captain Beaumont, he convinced the lieutenant that he was the one who deserved to die that day."

"So the man your superior officer killed saved my nephew?"

He seemed thoughtful and then finally nodded. "That's about the size of it, sir, although there was more to it than that. Talking and arguing and such before the shooting. Not Monsieur Valmont, of course. He was in no shape to argue."

"I see."

"But your man there, he was indeed as you see him now, although I have no way of knowing if the injuries were sustained before we overtook the vessel. He was in a bad way when we got to the captain's cabin, although there was one thing odd."

"What was that?"

"The privateer, he was doctoring Monsieur Valmont when we found them. Said he was a physician. Now, I've wanted the reward much as the next man on our ship, so I've studied up on the *Ghost Ship* and its captain. That wasn't the *Ghost Ship*, and not once did I hear anything about Captain Beaumont being a physician."

"I appreciate your candor, son. One more question: How did you overtake the vessel?"

He looked sheepish. "The usual away. We used our cannons, and then, once we had control of the ship, we. . ." He looked away. "Suffice it to say, the privateer's vessel was under attack when our men arrived on its deck, and that attack continued until such time as Jean Beaumont's life came to an end. And as to that not being the *Ghost Ship*, our lieutenant had word from fellows he knew in the navy who pointed out that ship as belonging to Beaumont. Beyond that, I do not know any more."

"I see." He paused. "Thank you." Noting the man's expectant look, he added, "Is there something else?"

"There is," he said. "Would you come with me? It'll only take a minute, but it is important."

Bienville nodded to his aide, and the three of them walked with the sailor to a spot in the rear of the vessel. There the lad opened a barrel and pulled out a heavy silver cutlass with a jeweled scabbard and presented it to Bienville.

"For what purpose would I wish to take this weapon?" he asked.

"We took it off your nephew," he said. "I thought it only right that it be returned to his family."

"You're certain Jean-Luc was wearing this cutlass when he was found?"

"Absolutely certain," he said. "Took it off him myself before the men could get him out of the captain's cabin."

"So my nephew, a lawyer by trade, was wearing this cutlass when he was found in Beaumont's cabin?"

"That's the whole of it, sir."

He nodded to the aide. "Reward this man for his diligence." He moved closer. "And see that he understands we wish this story to go no further."

Bienville held the magnificent weapon up to the waning sunlight and watched the jewels sparkle. The craftsmanship appeared to be Spanish, the stones exquisite. It was a ferocious instrument that should belong to a man of war, not a man of the law.

"Lock this in my library," he told his aide. "Someday I will have a conversation with Jean-Luc about this."

As he said the words, he knew they would not speak of it. And not because he believed his nephew would not be around to have this talk.

Rather, he had long ago learned there were things men did not discuss. Things that would lead to information best not given.

This cutlass and its provenance was most certainly one of those things.

It was better the girl did not recall when they found her. Had she opened her eyes or given any indication she recognized them, neither of them would have been able to leave her with the Mother Superior.

She was safe there. Much safer than she would be with them.

Had he not held a deep belief in the Lord, Israel might have believed their spying the floating plank on the vast green sea as some accident of nature. As a coincidence.

But there were no coincidences. Not when God directed paths and sent boats floating in just the right direction and at just the right time to arrive in just the right place.

They were meant to find her, just as they were meant to set aside their selfish wishes and see that she had a proper raising on the island of the nuns and orphan children. The island where his old friend, the Mother Superior, would keep her safe.

As the island appeared on the horizon, Israel cradled the girl while Rao did the rowing. It was only right given his higher rank aboard the vessel they'd served upon together. Anyone who might think it odd that a slave outranked a man whose skin was pale would never dare say it to the captain.

At least not more than once.

He and Rao prayed over that child as the skiff slid along toward Isla de Santa Maria. Prayed that the Lord would spare her.

Prayed that He would see she grew into a fine young lady.

And selfishly, they prayed that they would both see Maribel Cordoba again, even if she was never to know who they were or their connection to her survival.

When wood slid against sand, Israel held tight to the girl so as not to jostle her. Had he thought walking barefoot might keep from waking her, he would have tossed his boots into the skiff and headed off toward the chapel, caring not for what brambles and rocks pierced his feet.

But Maribel seemed unable to wake, something that concerned Israel greatly. Though he was no expert on medical conditions, he knew sleeping through all that had happened could not be a good sign.

He would be certain to tell Mother Superior of this.

"Bring her to the chapel," a soft voice said.

Of course Mother Superior had seen their approach. Nothing and no one arrived on this island without first being noticed.

Israel spied the nun coming around the corner, her dark gown hiding her from all but the closest inspection. He followed her instructions—and her—until he arrived in a small building that had obviously been converted to a chapel.

"I had a bed put in for her," she said, indicating that Israel should leave her there.

He would have. Should have. But he just could not.

Not yet.

Instead he told her of the girl's condition when he found her. Then he answered the nun's questions, all the while holding the sleeping girl in his arms. Finally, they arrived at a depth of silence that told him he was expected to leave her.

"A moment first?" he said as he carried her back outside under the last purple minutes before daybreak.

Here the light was just sufficient to take in her features and memorize them. "I want to know you when I see you again even if you do not know me," he told her, though she made no response. "Rao and I, we will find you someday, although you'll likely not know us."

"The captain too," Rao added solemnly. "He will want to find her."

"No," Israel said. "That is impossible."

CHAPTER 11

"If the captain is alive—and I believe the Lord has spared him—he cannot know about her. And she cannot know about him," Israel said.

"Why not?" Rao asked.

"Can you not see? There are two of us who were saved from the hands of the French attackers. Possibly there are two more, if the other skiff was launched as planned and had not returned. Four people who recognize the face of Jean Beaumont, and all of us are loyal to him as if he was our own blood."

"That is true."

He nodded at the girl in his arms. "But she also can recognize the captain, and she is but a child. She will someday grow to be a woman. Who can say then?"

"Aw, come on, Bennett," Rao said. "Surely the girl wouldn't do or say anything to harm the captain. He didn't take to her at first, and I know her being there broke the rule for females aboard ship, but he and she were fast friends by the end of it all."

"Fast friends, yes, between a young captain and a girl with her nose in a book and her mind carrying silly ideas of wanting to sail the seas as a privateer." He paused to look down at the sleeping girl. "But time will pass and she will grow to be a woman. Then who will she be? What will her allegiance be then?"

"I reckon I see your point, but it's awfully sad to think those two will never meet. He did save her life when he let her stay aboard. Might be good for her to know this."

"I warrant she will remember it," he said. "She will know there was a brief period of time when she was held in high esteem within the company of a crew of privateers who no longer live. It is good to allow her to have that memory. Not so good to believe more than this, I think."

"Are you certain?"

"As certain as I am that there is a bounty on all our heads." He paused to look Rao in the eyes. "Do you wish that bounty to extend to this girl? Because it will if she is considered to be associated with us."

Rao seemed to be sorting the thought out in his mind. Finally he nodded. "Then we agree to leave her be and let these nuns raise her."

"We do," Israel said. "And we agree should we ever have the occasion to come to this island, we will not give up our identities to her."

Rao nodded. "Agreed."

Israel looked up to see Mother Superior in the doorway. "It is time," she told him. "You have overstayed your welcome."

He nodded but still made no move to release the girl to the nun or to bring her in and settle her on the cot in the corner of the chapel. "She will be safe. You give me your word?"

"Yes," the old nun told him. "You have my word."

"And the other matter," he said firmly. "I will not have the man who saved me from slavery lose his life over what this girl might remember. The two can never meet, and she cannot know who he is. Promise me you will not allow this."

"I heard your conversation with Mr. Rao and can see that she might offer evidence that could harm your captain," she said. "I will tell no lies to her or your captain, but I will do my best to guide the girl away from those memories that might put them both in danger. Perhaps I can convince her to stay with us once she's grown. Is Miss Cordoba an intelligent girl?"

"Very," he said with pride. "Before the attack on our ship, I was teaching her to read Homer in the original Greek. She was a quick study. I warn you, though. Her favorite spot to read was up in the masts in the lookout's perch. More than once I found that a man who was assigned there had been convinced to give up his duties to her so that she could be up there with her book. You may be searching the treetops looking for her."

Mother Superior smiled. "Then we will discourage climbing as not appropriate for a lady but continue encouraging her to read so that someday she might become a teacher, although I do not believe our little library has such an impressive volume."

He smiled. "Then it will when I can manage it. And every time I am able, I will send more."

"We would accept your gift with thankful hearts, but you do realize we cannot allow anyone to know from whom this gift comes. To do so would be to lose all protection of your identity. I cannot protect the girl if she has any connection to you or your captain. Are we in agreement?"

He nodded. "We are."

"And there is one other requirement of accepting the child. She is the child of the deceased Antonio Cordoba and his late wife?"

"Yes," he said.

"It is my solemn vow to the Lord and to these children that I do all in my power to reunite families and see them returned to the homes where they once belonged. Should Miss Cordoba's extended family—perhaps grandparents, uncles, or siblings— search for her and find her here, I will not keep her from them. If that goes against my promise to you, then that promise will be broken."

"I understand," he said. "And I will not hold you to the promise should those circumstances occur. However, the girl believed herself to be an orphan, having watched her father die and claiming her mother and grandfather already deceased. She mentioned no siblings. I believe St. Mary of the Island will be the only home she knows."

"Very well, then," she said and then nodded at the girl. "I believe it is time, Mr. Bennett. These partings are best done swiftly else they might not be done at all."

"I suppose."

"Or there is another option," she said with that half grin she affected when she was teasing. "You could stay with us. I am certain a place like St. Mary of the Island could use a man of your intelligence, and I do enjoy our spirited discussions of literature and the Bible. Have you considered taking up the profession of teaching? You would have to give up your other endeavors, of course."

"As you likely expect, I must decline your very generous offer."

She met his gaze with an understanding look and then nodded to Rao, who had been standing in the shadows. "And you, sir? What say you about remaining with us here on Isla de Santa Maria? We could always use a strong man like you to do carpenter work and other tasks around the orphanage. Have you an interest in remaining with us?"

His eyes widened. "Thank you, but no, Mother Superior. Although my mother would be most pleased if I were to give up the seafaring life for work in a more godly location."

Mother Superior's attention lingered on Rao and then returned to Israel. "Then the offer shall remain open for both of you as long as you shall live, and you two will get on your way." She touched Israel's hand. "But first we pray for the girl, and we pray that your captain has survived. Then you will go and allow us to care for her while you search for him."

With a heavy heart, Israel carried the girl to the place the nuns had prepared for her. Rao said his good-byes and hurried past, likely ashamed at the tears in his eyes.

But Israel cared not whether anyone spied his sorrow.

The last time this gut-wrenching pain had taken hold of him he'd been in chains and saying good-bye to his bride Nzuzi under the shade of the judgment tree in Mbanza Kongo. Just as he promised her, he now promised the girl.

"You may not remember me, but I will find you again."

❋

The weeks that followed were a blur of sounds, pains, and deepest black nights of endless slumber. Faint snatches of memories would rise up only to fade before Jean-Luc could make sense of them.

Faces appeared before him, but they swam in the filmy seas of uncertainty between life and death. None meant anything to him, and yet each one meant something. Their images blurred; the sounds they made, both loving and insistent, were only an echo in his head.

His mother spoke to him often, as did Jean-Luc's baby brother. Even in the depths of his slumber, he knew they were no longer alive. And yet in his fevered state, they appeared no less real than the parade of persons who attended his bedside.

Jean-Luc longed to ask his mother if she knew that the man who killed her had been dispatched to his death, but his mouth would not form the words. Instead, he listened to his mother tell her stories of French Canada where she and her dozen Bienville siblings enjoyed an idyllic life.

He heard his name being called, but Jean-Luc ignored it to give in to the tug of his mother's voice. To hear more of the stories she told. To be a child again at his mother's knee.

"It is no use," he heard another voice—perhaps belonging to his father—say. "He is beyond our reach. We must give him to the Lord and pray the Lord gives him back to us again."

A figure peered into the fog, her red hair visible even in the swirling grayness that surrounded her. She called his name. No, she called him the captain. Yes. Captain.

Jean-Luc tried to follow, but the girl was gone. Still the girl was calling to him. Reaching out and then oddly, telling him to go home. To return to those he loved.

Once again there was nothing but darkness. The girl was gone.

He tried to follow, tried to call out to her so he could tell her how sorry he was that he had somehow lost her to the ocean. Sorry that she would never grow up and never get another chance to sail again or read another of her ridiculous books.

But hard as he tried, Jean-Luc could not divest himself of the invisible chains that kept him in place. Could not make his legs work to chase her or his voice work to call out to her.

"Where is she? Where did she go?"

At the sound of his own voice, Jean-Luc sat upright. The shadows were gone, and his eyes stung as he looked into a blazing fire.

It was different here.

No gray swirling fog.

No feeling of being wrapped in chains.

Jean-Luc blinked again, believing the fog would return and so would the girl. Instead, a commotion sounded around him. Someone moved between him and the fire. A face he knew. A name that was just beyond the realm of understanding.

"Welcome back, Jean-Luc," she said in a silky voice that was warmly familiar. "We have been waiting for you to return to your family."

Abigail. His father's beloved wife. Yes, he remembered now. A second mother to Father's two grateful motherless sons and the mother of. . .

Of whom? He didn't know. Exhausted from the effort of trying to sort it all out, he allowed her to return him to his pillows.

"It is true."

Father.

Jean-Luc wrested his eyes open and then lost the battle to keep them that way. Even behind his closed eyes, Jean-Luc was aware of his father's presence, of his tight grip on his hand, and of the sobs that came from deep inside.

Whether they were his sobs or Father's, he could not say.

Then came the sounds of voices in the distance. They were

arguing, or perhaps it was good-natured debate he heard. Twins, yes. A brother and a sister.

Then the voices were gone and only Abigail and Father remained, although neither of them appeared to be looking at him. Rather, their heads were together—his silver hair mixing with her midnight curls—and they seemed to be praying. Beside them, a fire flickered in the fireplace.

Jean-Luc blinked and saw them clearly now. Remembered the moment his father introduced Jean-Luc and his brother to the woman who would take their mother's place.

Though she was a full two decades younger than Father, theirs had been a love match. Life had become good again when Abigail came to them. And she loved Father as much as he loved her.

All of this he remembered, and yet he could not recall what happened to the girl who eluded him in the fog. "Where did she go?"

Father and Abigail jolted, both climbing to their feet at the same moment. "He's asking for someone," she told his father, although their images had begun to swim again. "Who are you looking for, son?"

"Red," he managed before his eyes closed again.

"She is here," Abigail said from somewhere far away. "If the woman with the red hair is who you're looking for, she is here with us."

"Girl," Jean-Luc corrected, though he could not be certain he had managed to speak the word aloud.

Later, when he could manage it, he opened his eyes once more. The flames had died down to glowing embers. Embers that matched the hair of the woman who now sat in the chair beside the fireplace.

CHAPTER 12

M aribel?" Jean-Luc managed through lips that refused to
cooperate. "You?" was all he could add.

But it was enough, for the woman with the red curls stumbled
to her feet, tucking her hair beneath a scarf as she hurried to him.
"Hello, Mr. Valmont," she said as she knelt beside the bed. "Can
you hear me?"

He reached to grasp her hand and then struggled to sit up
as the room spun around him. He was weak, so weak. "I thought
you were lost."

"Hush now," she said. "I've been with you all the while. I will
just go and fetch your father. He asked to be alerted if you were to
awaken."

"No, don't go," he said, but his grip was too weak to make her
stay. His legs refused all demands to follow, and his eyes continued
to be unreliable when commanded to remain open.

Finally, he awakened and found the room flooded with sunshine. There was the red-haired girl again, back in the chair by the
fireplace after chasing him through the fog of his dreams.

Abigail was there too, her hands deftly working knitting need-
les as she created some object of clothing that would be far too
warm for the New Orleans winter. The itch of last year's Christmas gift, a sweater made from wool taken from her family home,
had been a source of much jesting between Jean-Luc and his
younger brother Quinton.

"I sincerely hope that sweater is not for me."

"You are teasing me, Jean-Luc," Abigail said. "I refuse to jump and run to your bidding."

With that one comment, Jean-Luc knew he was fine. Knew he would live.

For as fiercely protective as Abigail was of him and his family, she would not make light of his situation unless she knew him to be safe. Though he wished to allow tears at the knowledge he was not being taken to heaven just yet, instead, he matched her humor with teasing of his own.

He shook his head and instantly regretted the action, all the while keeping his attention on the woman holding the yarn for Abigail. "Have I been much trouble?"

His father's wife laughed, a pleasant sound that reminded him of good days and smiles shared with this family of his. "A bit," she said, "although as the months went by, we did despair of hearing your complaints ever again. I am very happy to be wrong about this."

The red-haired woman looked away as if she might be uncomfortable with him watching her. Clearly the situation had been reversed for some time, because he could see now that the woman was obviously in the employ of Abigail, possibly as a companion or nursemaid.

No, that could not be right. The twins, Michel and Gabrielle, were beyond the age of needing that sort of supervision.

"Who are you?" he finally asked the woman before turning his attention back to Abigail. "Why is she here?"

"Back to your charming self, I see. I wonder if you will remember this conversation. You and I have had many these past months, but you rarely seem to recall them."

"In fact, I recall none," he said. "Not because what you say isn't worth recollection. I think there might have been some other trouble that caused me to be less than attentive."

"Yes, quite." She folded her knitting into the basket at her feet and cast a sideways glance at the woman beside her. "This is Kitty. She has been invaluable to us during your inconvenience."

"Kitty," he said as his gaze went back to the woman who now returned his smile. "Then I must offer you my most sincere thanks and an apology that I have not been able to fully appreciate your beauty until now."

She looked at Abigail. "Is he always like this?"

"No, dear," she said with a laugh. "Sometimes he is worse."

Jean-Luc almost managed a chuckle, though the effort pained him through his chest. "I don't know if I ought to be offended or not."

"You ought to be thankful that this lovely young lady gave up a good portion of her time over these past months to see to you. She was trained at the Hospital St. Louis in Paris. You could get no better care than in her hands."

Red hair, green eyes, and a smile that lit her face. Despite his current situation, Jean-Luc was intrigued. "I was fortunate to be visiting when this need was made known to me."

"Months?" he said as he tried to remember the last time he had been on his own two feet. Though he failed miserably, he somehow knew that when he did remember, he would not like what he recalled.

Her voice was heavily accented with her native French tone, but the words were beautifully spoken. "Indeed I do thank you for your care," he said in French.

"*De rien*," she responded easily as she looked away, a coquette in nurse's attire.

"Come," Abigail said abruptly, "and let's send up his butler to handle his needs. You and I are no longer needed here."

She sent Kitty out first and then lingered until the young woman was no longer nearby. "You've given us quite a start, Jean-Luc Valmont," she said, her mock scolding light but her meaning clear as she grasped his hand and held it tight. "First, know that I am more grateful to God than I knew was possible that He chose to spare you."

"As am I," he said.

She released his hand to kneel at his side. "Then I will have two promises from you."

He leaned back on his elbows and offered what he hoped was a charming smile despite cracked lips and who knew what else. "And what would those be?"

"First," she said as her eyes held his, "you will never put your father in this position again."

Not knowing exactly what had been discovered regarding his last weeks at sea, Jean-Luc decided to let Abigail tell him exactly what she referred to rather than offering anything of his own. "I'm afraid you'll need to be more specific."

Her eyes narrowed. "Held prisoner by a wanted man and then nearly dying aboard a French Navy vessel?" Abigail shook her head. "I fail to see how you managed any of that. You are a lawyer, for goodness' sake. You manage your father's business interests in the territory and see to the details of trade agreements. How in the world does that translate to putting yourself in such danger?"

"I wish I had an answer for you," he said. "I do not."

"You do not remember or you do not want to tell me?" She held up her hand. "No, do not respond. Just understand I will not have you upsetting your father needlessly in his condition. Should you ever come back to my home battered and bleeding again, you had best have a good reason for it."

"I promise."

"I am not finished, Jean-Luc. Your father adores you, and I love you like my own flesh and blood. It was pure torture to watch you move between life and death for months on end. Your fever broke and you will live, but I do not want your father to have to endure this again. Do you understand?"

He stifled a smile. Though Abigail was barely older than him by a decade, she had taken to mothering him quite well. She also knew how to get her point across so that he comprehended clearly. And then there were the tears shimmering in her eyes. Indeed he must have frightened them all greatly.

"I do understand," he said, "and I shall endeavor to keep this promise."

"Don't you endeavor me, Jean-Luc Valmont. I am not some woman you can fool. I know whatever you were doing that landed you in this fix is likely something you will do again."

He let out a long breath. Sadly, she was right.

"But I will not do it in the same way," he said. "On that you have my word."

She gave him an even look and then nodded as she swiped at her damp eyes. "I will accept that as a promise and move to my next point, but not before I give you this book. It was a gift left on our doorstep some months ago."

"Thank you," he said as he lowered himself back to his pillow to look at the thin volume of Homer's *Odyssey*. As expected, inside there was a message from Israel letting him know he survived and where he would be waiting.

"How long ago did this arrive?"

She shrugged. "Not long after you were brought to us," she said. "So several months ago."

Several months. He let out a long breath. Israel could be anywhere by now. But what of the others?

"This doctoring that was done," he said. "Do I have Evan Connor to thank?"

She looked away and then rose. Trouble etched her beautiful features. "No," she said gently.

"Then he. . ."

Jean-Luc could not complete the question. Stupid, for he already knew the answer. Any man who did not step aboard the French vessel alive went down with the ship. Grief compounded with guilt coursed through him.

"Though I cannot blame you for this, Abigail," he said, all good humor gone, "my head is beginning to hurt again."

"No doubt you'd like me to call for your nurse," she said. "And that brings me to my second point. Do not toy with that girl's affections."

He looked up sharply. "What do you mean?"

"A woman knows things, Jean-Luc, and she has been by

your side for months. You may not be aware of this time passing together with her; she has been acutely aware of it. You are all she has known for months, and because of this I believe she has formed a bond with you."

Jean-Luc shook his head. "Yes, of course. I will proceed with caution."

"You will proceed with the intention of marrying her or keeping your relationship on a completely platonic level. I have promised her mother and father I would look after her, and that is what I will do."

He looked down at his broken body and then back up at Abigail. "I doubt she wants a weak man with the scars I bear. So your nurse is safe from me, I promise."

This was a promise he should never have made.

Four months later, with all weakness gone, he had fallen hopelessly in love and married the red-haired nurse whose care had brought him back from the grave. Eleven months after that, Kitty and his unborn son were buried in the same grave.

He was beyond inconsolable. When he finally realized the Lord had not meant him to die alongside them, he retrieved the book from the shelf where it had been hidden all those months ago and found Israel again.

With that reunion came news that others had survived, which made him grateful but could do nothing for the guilt he bore.

If he could not find happiness of his own, then he would turn back to the life he led before. The promise he made to Abigail would be kept, for this time he planned to do the same thing in a different way.

It took Maribel the better part of three years to realize the secretive man who sometimes did work for Mother Superior was the same man who once sat in a cell and played draughts with her. The carpenter kept to himself and never allowed anyone near while he was working, and no one considered it odd.

Then came the day when she was reading in the guango tree and he passed beneath it in conversation with Mother Superior. "As always, we at the orphanage appreciate your help in this matter, Mr. Rao. We've despaired of how to repair the trouble with our window in the chapel, so you've arrived at just the right time."

Mr. Rao.

Maribel was a young lady of almost fifteen now, and running to hug a man of Mr. Rao's age was not considered appropriate. Neither was plopping down from the guango tree to chase Mother Superior and her guest.

So she waited until the pair had parted ways, and then she edged up to him as he was repairing the window in the chapel. "Excuse me," Maribel called from the other side of the chapel. "Might I have a minute of your time?"

"Sure, miss. Something else that needs fixing?" He looked up from his work as she approached, and then froze.

"Hello, Mr. Rao," she said. "Do you remember me? I'm Maribel."

The mallet fell from his hand and barely missed landing on his foot. Mr. Rao dipped down to retrieve the tool and then took his time straightening again.

"What is this?"

Maribel jumped at the familiar sound and knew from her tone of voice that Mother Superior was displeased. Children were expressly forbidden from interacting with any adults other than the nuns, so she knew she was in deep trouble.

Slowly she turned to face the nun. As expected, Mother Superior wore an expression of irritation. "You know you should not be here. I will insist you leave at once."

"But Mother Superior, you see, I have a very good reason for being here."

She shook her head. "I will not hear excuses made when rules are broken. Go directly to your classroom, and I will come and get you once I have decided what your punishment will be."

"But I was just..." She had no good explanation other than the truth. "I am not excusing my behavior, and I will accept any punishment I have been assigned. However, I believe I know this man."

"What man?"

Maribel turned back around to see that Mr. Rao and his tools were gone. All that remained to show he had been in the chapel was the fresh repair to the chapel window.

"But Mr. Rao was here." She ran to the window to look out onto the grounds of the orphanage but saw no one fitting his description. "I know he was just here."

Mother Superior came to stand beside her and then lightly wrapped her arm around her shoulder. "Miss Cordoba, it is obvious we've had a carpenter on the island working on the chapel, so of course he was here."

"But he just left." Tears began to swim in her eyes, but she refused to cry in front of Mother Superior. "He didn't answer me and he didn't even say good-bye. But I know it was him. It just had to be him because nobody else smiles like he does, and he was so nice to me when I was on the boat. Did you know he built my own room for me? And Mr. Piper used a sail and made a hammock."

Mother Superior led Maribel out of the chapel and into the courtyard. "Collect yourself and go back to your classroom. And please exercise more control next time."

"But he didn't remember me," she said, hating how her words came out sounding so pitiful. "I remembered him and he didn't remember me."

"Miss Cordoba," she said gently, "you are assuming the man you saw was the man you believe him to be. You do not know this for certain. If this man was your old friend, then he certainly would not have left without acknowledging you."

She shrugged. "I suppose. So you think it wasn't him?"

"I think he is not the man you wish him to be," she said. "And I think you are now late for your class and likely earning an extra punishment from your teacher in addition to whatever I decide to assign you."

Several protests arose, but she kept them to herself as Mother Superior walked away. Abruptly, the nun stopped and turned around once more. "Miss Cordoba?"

"Yes?"

"Have you been having those dreams again?"

Maribel was reluctant to reply. Indeed she had experienced recollections of her days on the ship and the time leading up to her arrival on the island many times over the past few years. However, she had stopped asking questions of Mother Superior regarding their authenticity because her answer was always the same: it was a dream.

"No, Reverend Mother," she told her, "I have not had any more dreams."

Because they aren't dreams. They're memories.

Maribel and the Pirate

Part II:

Isla de Santa Maria
Near Port Royal, Jamaica
and New Orleans, Louisiana
May of 1735

When I consider thy heavens, the work of thy fingers, the moon and the stars, which thou hast ordained; what is man, that thou art mindful of him? and the son of man, that thou visitest him? For thou hast made him a little lower than the angels, and hast crowned him with glory and honour. Thou madest him to have dominion over the works of thy hands; thou hast put all things under his feet: all sheep and oxen, yea, and the beasts of the field; the fowl of the air, and the fish of the sea, and whatsoever passeth through the paths of the seas. O Lord our Lord, how excellent is thy name in all the earth!

PSALM 8:3–9

CHAPTER 13

St. Mary of the Island Orphanage

Y ou have a visitor, Miss Maribel."

Maribel Cordoba looked up from her reading to offer a silent chastisement. All the children knew she was not to be disturbed during her hour of respite. Furthermore, the boys and girls should be resting and not gadding about the orphanage to pop up unannounced in her place of solitude.

"Miss Maribel?"

She debated offering a response. After the last time she was found reading in a guango tree, Mother Superior threatened to relieve her of her teaching duties. It wasn't seemly for a lady, apparently, or at least that is what Maribel was told after she had endured a scathing lecture on propriety.

Of course she agreed with Mother Superior. It was not seemly to be caught reading in that guango tree. So she moved to a different tree and determined not to be caught.

She also made sure the sticky seedpods did not adhere themselves to her in places where the students and faculty might spy them but she would not. Of course, that humiliation had only happened once, but it had been quite terrifying to sit down on something that she had not expected to be there.

The children did enjoy her reaction, however.

So yes, it was a bit sly to climb a tree to hide and read, but it was not meant to be rebellious. As much as she loved teaching these beautiful children, she also loved having time to herself to escape to those books that had become her favorite.

With the orphanage being run on a strict schedule, these stolen moments were precious. Those and the other rare occasions when she managed to slip off to the other side of the tiny island a few miles across the bay from Port Royal to enjoy a swim or the view from the mahogany trees.

Owing to the risks involved in such an activity—and the fact that Mother Superior would fire her and banish her from the orphanage on the spot—Maribel rarely attempted this anymore. Oh, but perhaps someday soon.

"Really, Miss Maribel," little Stephan said as he jumped from one bare foot to the other. "Mother Superior, she said I should find you and see that you get to her office with the upmost speed."

"Utmost," Maribel corrected as she closed her well-worn copy of *Robinson Crusoe*.

Stephan gave her a gap-toothed grin. "Yes, that's what I said."

"Thank you, Stephan," she told him. "I'm curious. How did you come to meet with Mother Superior when you should have been resting in the classroom with the others?"

He looked down at his feet then back up at her. "I might have seen her while I was out and about."

"I see." Maribel stifled a grin.

It was well known that Stephan loved to hurry down to the little tributary that ran through the orphanage grounds just beyond Mother Superior's office when he thought no one was watching. She saw no harm in it as the stream was shallow and slow moving, but the knowledge was useful. The fact the boy's dark hair was slick with water gave him away.

"Then if you do not mention to Mother Superior where you found me, I will conveniently forget that you have been swimming instead."

She tucked her book into her pocket and waited until the boy had scampered off. When the coast was clear, Maribel carefully climbed down and straightened her skirts then adjusted the scarf that she wore tied around her waist.

Woven through with threads of silver, the scarf was not part of the uniform Mother Superior prescribed for her teachers. Thankfully, Mother Superior did not require her to remove it once she learned the length of cloth was all Maribel had left of her mother.

Taking a deep breath, she let it out slowly as she made her way toward Mother Superior's office. Though the distance was short, it felt much farther as she walked toward the front of the orphanage.

The afternoon sun slanted across the avocado trees that marked the boundary between the orphanage and the path that led to the beach. Out of habit, she cast a glance at the sparkling green water and then let her attention rest on the horizon.

There she spied white sails off to the northeast. "Sloop," she whispered under her breath. Another set of sails fluttered some distance away to the west. "Brigantine."

Her fingers curled involuntarily as she felt the imagined grip of the watch post. The sensation of standing so close to heaven that she could almost touch the stars had never left her. Nor had her curiosity as to what had happened to the kindhearted men who she often prayed had survived the battle that plummeted her into the sea and deposited her at this place.

When she first came to St. Mary of the Island, she was very ill. This she had been told by others. How she got here was a mystery, however. Someone brought her, but she had asked Mother Superior who that someone might be so many times and received no answer that she had eventually given up. Though she owed her life to a person she may never be able to thank, she nevertheless offered up a prayer for him daily.

"Miss Cordoba, do join us."

The sharply enunciated tones of Mother Superior preceded her as she glided around the corner. How this tiny woman always seemed to know where her students and teachers were without actually standing in sight of them had unnerved Maribel when she first arrived at the orphanage. Only later did she discover the old nun was blind.

"Yes, Mother Superior."

She picked up her skirts and followed Mother Superior's brisk pace around the corner and into the low-roofed building that served as offices, classrooms, and the chapel. Hurrying behind the woman who finished raising her and then hired her to teach, Maribel once again attempted to affect the elegant gliding gait of the older woman and the other nuns.

It was useless, of course. Rumor had it that Mother Superior had been a great beauty in her youth, trained and educated in the highest levels of society. Though the country of her birth varied depending on who was doing the telling, all the stories agreed: the loss of her sight sent her here to this remote corner of the Caribbean where the children and teachers took the place of whatever social life she left behind.

"Do keep up," Mother Superior said as she turned sharply and disappeared into the office she had carved out of this corner of the building after it was rebuilt following the hurricane last year.

The room was small but not at all dark, owing to the floor-to-ceiling windows that spanned the length of one wall. If anyone thought it odd that a woman without sight would insist on putting in a wall full of windows, no one dared approach Mother Superior about it.

Rather than take her customary place behind the rather simple desk in the center of the room, Mother Superior held the door open for Maribel and indicated she should take a seat. There behind the desk was a rather stern-looking bespectacled gentleman wearing the formal attire that marked him as one who had not spent much time in this climate.

Before she could turn around to ask Mother Superior who this man might be, the door shut and the nun was gone. Maribel returned her attention to the desk and the stranger.

He indicated with a sweep of his hand that she should sit. In deference to the behavior she always exhibited when called to this room, Maribel obeyed.

Perched on the edge of the hard wooden chair, she rested her palms on her knees. Out of the corner of her eye, she saw Stephan float past in the creek.

"You are Maribel Cordoba?"

The question caused her to jump as she swiftly returned her attention to the stranger. Her fingers clutched handfuls of her scarf as she tried not to allow his stare to unnerve her.

"Yes," she finally said. "I am."

"Yes, of course you are." His expression softened. "Forgive me, but I expected you would be a nun."

Maribel laughed despite her nerves. "I assure you it was not for the lack of trying. Mother Superior had hopes that I might join the novitiate, but unfortunately I am apparently quite unsuitable. She despaired of me ever learning to be still and quiet, but beyond that I read the most unsuitable books."

One silver brow rose above his spectacles. "Is that so?"

Horrified, she shook her head. "That just sounds terrible. Please understand I do not read books that are bad, I promise. Rather, I prefer stories of pirates and such, and Mother Superior believes that tales of adventure on the high seas do not qualify me for the more sedate and cloistered life of a nun."

He looked away, and when he returned his attention to her, the beginnings of a smile rose. "Yes, I do see your point." The stranger's expression sobered. "I'm sorry. You are likely wondering who I am and why I am here."

"The thought did occur," she said. "I assume you aren't here to learn why I was not accepted as a nun in this fine establishment."

"No, that is true," he said. "I will get to the point, Miss Cordoba. My name is Rafael Lopez-Gonzales. I have been sent to find you and bring you back with me."

"I don't understand."

"Yes, well, the matter is of the utmost urgency, but since you have no family here on the island, I did speak to Mother Superior before I broached this topic with you. After much spirited discussion, we are in agreement that you should take leave of your position here and—"

"I'm sorry to interrupt, Mr. Lopez-Gonzales, but I must stop you right there," she said. "I have no idea who you are or why you believe I should leave my teaching work here and just go off with you. St. Mary of the Island Orphanage has been my home for some eleven years now. Perhaps we should call Mother Superior back in to explain this urgency to me because you have not done a decent job of it as of yet."

"You are correct." He removed his spectacles and regarded Maribel with a smile. "Forgive me. Miss Cordoba, you are exactly as you were described."

"Again, Mr. Lopez-Gonzales, you have me at a disadvantage. Please speak plainly. I assure you I will not faint. What is the urgency that sent you searching for me and that apparently requires me to leave everything I know and love to follow you to. . ." She shook her head. "Where was it?"

"New Orleans," he supplied.

"Yes, well, all right. To follow you to New Orleans." She gave him the look she generally reserved for her most unruly pupils. "Do please continue, sir. My time is limited, and my students will be wondering where their teacher has gone."

"Mother Superior has assured me she will assign another teacher to see to your students so that you might have the remainder of the afternoon free to make your arrangements."

"Sir, forgive me, but you truly are maddening." She rose. "Your reticence to provide me with pertinent information leads me to believe you have something to hide, which also leads me to believe you very likely have not been honest with Mother Superior. Thus, our conversation is at an end. Now if you will excuse me, I have preparations to make for my afternoon class."

"If I am reticent," he said as he also stood, "it is because the news I bring is not easily delivered. You grew up here, so you have been raised an orphan."

"I believe it is obvious, given that fact, that I have, sir."

She crossed her arms over her waist and determined to give him no more than a minute longer of her time. He had already interrupted her precious reading time. Soon he would be interrupting her class time.

Mr. Lopez-Gonzales removed his handkerchief and dabbed at his forehead. "That is unfortunate because, despite the fact your convent dowry and maintenance has been paid by a donor who Mother Superior assures me is not a family member of whom you are aware, you are not an orphan at all, Miss Cordoba."

She heard his words, but they made no sense. Maribel shook her head. "Excuse me?"

"Please be seated," he said. "There is more to tell, and you will likely want to sit down. This heat is rather unbearable."

"I will do nothing of the sort, and as I said, I will not faint. How is it possible that I am not an orphan when my mother died and then I saw my father drown in front of my eyes?"

"Your mother is very much alive," he said gently. "As is your grandfather."

The breath slammed from her chest, and spots danced before her eyes. Despite her protests to the contrary, she did feel as though she might faint at any moment.

"Impossible," she managed as she gripped the back of the chair with both hands in order to remain upright. "Completely impossible."

"I assure you it is not." He nodded toward the stack of documents in front of him. "Your mother is the former Mary Lytton whose late father Benjamin descended from William and Mary Abigail Lytton. Your late father Antonio Cordoba did indeed drown at sea, and your name, I believe, is a mixture of your mother's name and your maternal grandmother's name—both Mary—along with your paternal grandmother's name, which was Isabel. I am told Isabel descended from Spanish royalty, but there has been no time to make a determination of this."

"Anyone could know these things," she said as she gripped the chair tighter, achingly aware that she had not known most of these facts until now. If, indeed, what he said was true.

"Fair enough. Your grandfather has anticipated your reluctance and has provided this as proof."

He shuffled through the documents until he retrieved a letter that bore a red seal adorned with what appeared to be her grandfather's coat of arms. His expression solemn, Mr. Lopez-Gonzales handed it to her.

Maribel accepted the letter and tucked it away with her book, refusing to even look at the handwriting on the outside. Not with this stranger watching her.

"Thank you, Mr. Lopez-Gonzales. I will read this and give it the consideration it deserves."

If her response flustered him, the stranger did not offer any indication of such. "Yes, all right. Might I then let you know that I will be sailing tomorrow on the tide and I wish you to join me? Your family has been most encouraged that I have been able to find you and are very much hopeful that I can bring you home to them as soon as possible."

Your family.

Maribel shook off the strong urge to think the man's search might have culminated with her. Instead, she took a deep breath and allowed the reality of the situation to sink in. This very kind man had mistaken her for someone else. Yes, that was the likely scenario.

And yet he knew her name. Knew Mama's name, though she could not vouch for the string of ancestors he quoted in relation to her.

Along with all of this, he offered hope that the people she had mourned so many years were alive. It was too much.

"Thank you," she managed. "I will give the matter serious consideration, but I do have an allegiance to this orphanage."

"I do understand." He returned his spectacles to his nose. "However, I will need an answer before I sail. And should you decline to accompany me, might I request a letter in response to the one you've tucked away? Your mother and abuelo would then at least have some measure of comfort in knowing you have been found and are alive."

Her heart lurched.

Somehow Maribel managed to keep her dignity intact as she responded in the affirmative and then walked slowly out of the room. She managed to continue to maintain that dignity until she reached the hedge of avocado trees.

There the temptation to run toward the beach and cast herself into the surf almost overpowered the good sense the nuns had taught her. Instead, she straightened her spine and walked past the avocado trees with only the quickest of glances at the sea beyond.

"Gaff-rigged schooner to the northeast," she said almost without realizing the words had escaped her lips.

❈

A gaff-rigged schooner was not his vessel of choice, but today it was Jean-Luc Valmont's vessel of convenience. From his post at the wheel of the ship he called the *Lazarus*, Jean-Luc spotted the old convent and orphanage, a landmark he had used many times before to navigate his way into port.

Not the port where ships of the line rested anchor. That was Port Royal over on the island of Jamaica. Rather, he pointed the schooner toward the inlet he preferred that kept all but those he trusted from knowing where he was.

Though Isla de Santa Maria sat within view of Port Royal, the presence of the nuns had discouraged any of the undesirable element of the city to relocate there. Whether it was the prayers of the nuns or the fiercely protective Mother Superior that struck fear in otherwise fearless ruffians, the end result was that the little island—easily walked around in a few hours—was a haven for the orphans in their care and off-limits to just about anyone else.

They sailed past the orphanage with its line of avocado trees and center courtyard marked with a cluster of guango trees rising above the center spire of the chapel. A small boy played in the stream that ran past the chapel, likely hiding from the classroom where the other children would be at this time of day. Beyond the orphanage, a forest of mahogany trees hid an inlet and a small sandy beach.

He called out the order to prepare for docking then turned the wheel over to his second-in-command. "Take us in, Israel," he said with a smile.

If anyone thought it odd that a former slave held such a position of honor on a vessel that was reportedly engaged in the slave trade, no one dared say it. For in his world, the name Valmont opened doors and closed mouths.

It always had.

As was their habit, Israel guided the *Lazarus* past the intended spot for docking. He would order the schooner to circle back around once the man in the watch post indicated he had not spotted anything—or anyone—problematic awaiting them onshore.

Jean-Luc looked up at the forward mast to watch for the signal to land. After all these years, this still brought back memories of a wisp of a girl with flaming hair who was better at spotting and naming vessels than any man with whom he'd sailed then or now.

"All clear," the man on watch called, drawing him back to the task at hand. Two other men on lookout shouted their agreement.

"All clear, Mr. Bennett," he said. "Take her in and let's get on with it."

CHAPTER 14

Maribel tucked her feet up under her damp skirt and tried to make herself as inconspicuous as possible. From her perch in the mahogany tree, she'd hoped to evade Mother Superior—or whichever of the children might be sent to fetch her—while she read her grandfather's letter yet again.

She hadn't planned on evading pirates too.

Past memories that she generally kept in check arose as Maribel heard the slap of sails and the sound of men shouting commands. When the craft bypassed the inlet and continued on, she let out the breath she did not realize she had been holding and retrieved Abuelo's letter from between the pages of *Robinson Crusoe*.

Age showed in the spidery handwriting, but enough of her grandfather's unique script and signature remained for Maribel to know that Mr. Lopez-Gonzales had spoken the truth. According to Abuelo, Mama was very much alive and distraught that she was not allowed to travel with their representative to Isla de Santa Maria to greet Maribel herself.

> *Your mother and I came to this city we now call our home in hopes of being closer to the place where you were last seen. It was our hope, a hope we never once gave up on, that our precious Maribel would somehow return to us. No expense has been spared in our search for you, my sweet granddaughter. And now at last you have been located.*

*We give thanks to God that what we believed to be
forever lost has now been found. Please come home to us,
sweet child. Make an old man happy in his last days.
I am your adoring Abuelo.*

Maribel traced her grandfather's signature with her forefinger, noting the swirl of the oversize *C* that she always tried to imitate in her own handwriting, and wondered about Abuelo's statement regarding his last days.

She sighed. Of course she would go. There was no doubt. But why had Papa told her something that was not true?

Her grandfather had not broached this topic in his letter, but it was a question that would someday need an answer. Had her father truly sought to separate her from Mama and Abuelo? Obviously he had, and yet it made no sense that a man who barely paid her any heed would somehow fabricate a situation that would require him to become her caregiver.

But those were questions for another day.

Maribel folded the letter and tucked it back into *Robinson Crusoe* and then held the book against her heart. From somewhere deep inside her, a gut-wrenching sob arose.

She had a home. And a family. She was no longer an orphan.

An answer to a prayer Maribel had never possessed faith enough to pray.

Thank You, Lord. Oh, thank You.

Her expressions of gratitude continued until the tears that went along with them finally dried. Resting her head against the rough bark, Maribel closed her eyes. In her dreams she saw the sea all around her, heard the splash of a wooden hull through waves and the slap of sails in the breeze.

The sounds engulfed her, growing louder until she opened her eyes to realize it wasn't a dream at all. The gaff-rigged schooner she saw earlier was now sliding into the inlet.

Maribel secured her book and prepared to climb down. If she

failed to get away, she would be stuck in this tree until the vessel lifted anchor and sailed away.

The alternative was to reveal herself to be hiding in a mahogany tree on an island populated with only nuns and children to protect her. Maribel sighed. While Mother Superior might very well take on an entire ship of pirates, it was best she did not.

She moved down lower in the tree, but the schooner was too fast. Scampering back into place, she resolved to hide as best she could.

Moments later, another ship of similar design docked slightly behind the vessel that was already there. Though leaves obstructed her view, it appeared a skiff was being lowered from the first ship.

Leaning forward, Maribel was able to see that skiff when it came into view between the vessels. She gasped. "Slave traders."

While she watched, the boatload of humanity was brought up against the other vessel, and the men, women, and children were hauled aboard. The process was repeated multiple times until finally the skiff no longer emerged from behind the schooner.

After a while, the vessel that was now loaded with slaves lifted anchor and sailed away. However, the other vessel seemed to be making no move to leave.

When Maribel could no longer feel her legs, she had to act. Stretching slowly to bring feeling back to her limbs, she made her plans to escape.

She gave thanks that she'd chosen a dress of drab brown today, for it did help to keep her from being visible to the slave traders. However, her hair would most definitely be a problem should anyone glance in her direction.

Improvising, Maribel removed the scarf from her waist and tucked her all-too-noticeable curls underneath just as the novitiates did. Should the slave traders spy her, perhaps they would think her a member of the convent.

Placing the tree trunk between her and the ship, Maribel began to climb down. Just when she expected her feet to touch solid ground, she felt hands on either side of her waist. A moment later, those same hands swung her about and set her down on the sand.

Maribel whirled around, her fists raised and her heart thudding. Instincts from long ago kicked in, and she swung her fist to connect with a dark-haired stranger's jaw.

The man stumbled backward, and Maribel seized the opportunity to run as fast as she could back to the convent walls. Only when she reached the garden did she realize she had dropped her copy of *Robinson Crusoe*.

Going back was not a consideration, but telling Mother Superior was. Maribel hurried toward the office but found the door closed. She knocked, but her way was blocked when Mother Superior came to the door.

"Not now, Miss Cordoba," she said, as she slammed the door shut once again.

"But Mother Superior," she called. "I really must speak to you. It is of the utmost importance."

"Upmost," a small voice corrected.

She turned around to see Stephan grinning up at her. "That's what I said."

Maribel returned his grin and then affected her most serious expression. This child certainly should not be running freely with slave traders on the island.

"You should be in the classroom."

He made a face. "I would rather not."

Maribel knelt down to speak to the little boy. "I want you to listen carefully and do exactly as I say. You must go into the classroom very quietly and stay there. If you do not, I will see to it that you are not allowed to swim in the creek ever again. Do you understand?"

His eyes began to tear up. "Ever again?"

Maribel shrugged. "Well, for a very long time anyway. You see, if I cannot trust you to do what I ask you to do, then I cannot trust you to have the privilege of swimming in the creek. Do you understand?"

Stephan maintained his stubborn look. Maribel rose.

"All right, then. I am very sorry you have chosen not to be allowed to swim. Now I will have to march you into the classroom without your cooperation." She reached for his hand, but Stephan took a step backward.

"I'll go, but I was just trying to tell Mother Superior about the bad men in the harbor."

"You saw bad men?" She looked around and then knelt again. "Tell me what you saw."

He related a story similar to what Maribel had seen unfold. "And then the man with the scar on his face saw you in the tree and I told him to leave you alone because you were a teacher and you were a nice lady and he said he didn't want to hurt you."

Maribel gasped. "It was very dangerous of you to speak to him, Stephan. You have no idea who he was. He might have been a criminal."

"Oh no," he said. "I've seen him here before."

So slave traders had been using Isla de Santa Maria as their base of operations for a while then. Maribel frowned.

Certainly Mother Superior would have an opinion on this. And a remedy for it.

"All right, Stephan, off to class with you. And promise me you will not speak to any strangers you see on this island unless I or one of the nuns give you permission."

"I promise," he said. "Does that mean I can go swim in the creek again?"

"Not today, and not as long as the strangers are sailing into that inlet. It is too dangerous."

Stephan stuck out his lip but remained stoic as he trudged off to the classroom. Maribel waited until the boy had safely gone into the building before she turned away, her heart racing.

Until she knew whether St. Mary of the Island Orphanage was

safe, how could she leave tomorrow on the tide?

The answer was she could not. Much as she wished to be reunited with her mother and the grandfather she had not seen in eleven years, her current allegiance was to the second family that had raised her. Once she knew this second family was safe, then she could go home to her first family.

And if that meant standing at Mother Superior's door until first tide tomorrow, then she would.

Maribel marched back over to the office and lifted her hand to knock. "Come in, Miss Cordoba," Mother Superior said in that uncanny way she had. She was seated behind her desk, her expression slightly exasperated. "And how may I help you this afternoon?"

She shut the door and returned to the chair she had vacated earlier in the day. "I must warn you about something terrible going on here on our island."

"Oh?"

"I chanced to learn that there are slave traders using our island for their nefarious deeds. If Stephan is to be believed, and I think he is, then this dreadful behavior has been going on for a while."

"I see." Mother Superior paused as if choosing her response. "And other than the testimony of a small child with a penchant for escaping the classroom to lounge about in whatever body of water is available, exactly what proof do you have of such an accusation?"

"I saw it with my own eyes, Mother Superior. There were two schooners, and a man rowed slaves from one to the other and then the vessel with the slaves aboard sailed away. It was absolutely horrific."

"Ah," she said. "And exactly where were you when you witnessed this alleged slave trading?"

Oh. Maribel studied her skirt as she worked out a proper response. There was no way to answer without giving away the fact that she had defied the older woman's edict to cease reading in trees.

"Miss Cordoba," Mother Superior said. "Where exactly is your scarf?"

Maribel touched the edge of the scarf that now was wrapped around her hair. "Well, I covered my head with it."

"And it is usually at your waist." She paused. "You are fond of toying with the ends when you are nervous. For what purpose did you decide to cover your head?"

"Mother Superior, please forgive me for my impertinence, but I don't understand why you are asking questions about my scarf when we have a serious threat to the orphanage happening at this very moment. I absolutely cannot think of leaving Isla de Santa Maria for New Orleans until I am certain you, the nuns, and the children are safe from these awful ruffians."

The old nun sat very still, and Maribel knew for sure she had said far more than she should have. Finally, Mother Superior rose.

"I sincerely thank you for your loyalty, Miss Cordoba, and I applaud your dedication to our safety. You will be greatly missed here at St. Mary of the Island, but you must go with Mr. Lopez-Gonzales tomorrow."

"I simply cannot until I am certain—"

"That an old blind nun and a handful of nuns and novitiates can fend off slave traders bent on harming us?" She chuckled. "Miss Cordoba, do you really think that will happen?"

Maribel perched on the edge of her chair, her nerves taut and her passion for this topic rising. "I really think that men who are willing to trade in the sale of humans would not care if they harmed other humans, be they nuns or children, who might interfere with their commerce. I cannot allow that to happen."

"Admirable, but the Lord has kept this island safe from all threats for some time now. I am merely His steward, but I do like to think that my reputation among the criminal element is such that they do not bother us. Have you noticed that?"

"Until now, yes."

Mother Superior sighed. "I insist you are on that ship to New

Orleans tomorrow. I have given my assurances that you will be."

"But, Mother Superior, I cannot possibly—"

"Miss Cordoba, you have no choice. Leave the handling of these men you call slave traders to me. Go and pack your things and prepare for your journey tomorrow." She rose. "That is my last word on the subject."

Defying Mother Superior was something she never thought she would do, but if it took defiance to be heard, then so be it. "I simply cannot," she said as she stood with shaking knees.

"I am sorry you feel that way." She paused, her expression solemn but without any hint of anger. "Then I must make a correction to what I previously told you. That was not my last word on the subject. These are: Miss Cordoba, you are fired."

CHAPTER 15

Jean-Luc slipped out of his meeting with the Mother Superior—where she once again asked him to thank Israel for whatever was in the package he had sent to her—in the same way he always did. He climbed out the window.

Skirting the edge of the beach, he kept a brisk pace until he reached the inlet where the *Lazarus* waited at anchor. Only when he reached that spot did he look back to be sure he had not been followed.

Given the behavior of the young nun, Jean-Luc preferred to take all precautions.

Mother Superior assured him the novitiate he'd interacted with in the mahogany forest would not pose a threat. However, a woman who wished to become a nun should never be that good at causing a man pain.

Out of curiosity, and possibly to warn the old nun that one of her charges was a danger to others, Jean-Luc retraced his steps to find the tree where the woman had been spying on them. He assumed she had been spying, although Mother Superior indicated this particular female had a past history of hiding herself in trees in order to read her books without being interrupted by the children.

"And you are certain there is no danger because she has seen us?"

He watched the old nun's wrinkled face for any evidence of what she might be thinking. As always, hers was a face that was unreadable.

"I am certain. As I said, she is harmless. Just a girl who grew to a woman who has not yet forgotten childish things on occasion." She paused. "Had I any concern that you and Mr. Bennett's enterprise would be endangered, do you think I would not warn you? I stand to lose much should any of you be caught."

It was a plausible answer, although in his business, plausible answers were not good enough. He would not risk his men's lives over a supposition. And if the girl were to tell anyone what she saw, many lives would be at stake.

He walked down the narrow path, pushing back the foliage as he went. Just around a bend in the path, he tripped on a thick mass of exposed tree roots and went sprawling forward.

As he climbed to his feet, Jean-Luc spied a rectangular object—a brown leather-bound book—wedged into the sand at the base of the tree. He retrieved the book and dusted off the sand to read the title.

And then he laughed.

"Of all the lost books in the world, I would find *Robinson Crusoe* abandoned on a tropical island." He glanced up at the sky through the filter of mahogany leaves and smiled. "Thank You, Lord. I needed some good humor today."

After going in search of the girl who had obviously lost this book, he encountered Mother Superior hurrying down the path. Somehow the blind woman managed to step right over the tangle of roots that had caused him—a man with completely good eyesight—to stumble.

"I must insist that your ship depart immediately," she said as she turned him around and set out down the path toward the inlet beside him.

"Have we overstayed our welcome, Mother Superior?" he asked in jest.

"In a way, you have," she responded with her characteristic lack of humor.

"I was on my way back when I found an item I believe one of your novitiates dropped." He offered her the book.

If the old nun realized he had offered the book to her, she gave no indication of it. "Did the book or she happen to fall out of a tree? Perhaps both?"

"The book might have," he said. "She did not, but only because I caught her first. However, I'm sure she would like her book back. I found it on the path back there."

For the first time since Israel introduced him to the nun, Jean-Luc found something akin to shock in her normally placid expression. He studied her a moment, trying to figure out just what he had said that upset her.

"Please accept the book as a gift from St. Mary of the Island Orphanage and go," she told him, urgency in her voice.

"Are you certain? I don't mind doing a search to find the book's owner, although I do not relish repeating the sort of greeting she offered the last time."

"I am certain," she said. "And make haste. I wish you no offense, but you truly have stayed too long."

"Then in that case, I will accept your gift and take my leave." Tucking the book under his arm, Jean-Luc made his way back to the *Lazarus* with that same smile still in place.

"What's got into you?" Israel asked when he arrived on deck.

"Cast off for home, my friend," he said. "I'm going to go see a man about an island." At Israel's confused look, he gestured to the book under his arm. "*Robinson Crusoe*," he said. "I found it. Can you believe that?"

Apparently the humor was lost on his second-in-command. Israel just shook his head. "How many times have you read that book, Captain?"

"I've lost count," he said. "But when I do get a tally, I'll add one to it. I've needed something to think about other than the mission that brought us here, and now I have it."

"You wound me, Captain," Israel said with a broad grin. "I had hoped to challenge you to finally read Homer's *Odyssey* in the original Greek."

Jean-Luc shook his head. "You, sir, are the expert in the scholarly languages. I keep to English, French, and Spanish."

"A pity," Israel said. "There's just something about reading the philosophers' words exactly as they wrote them. No translation measures up."

"And I would counter with the statement that there is something about reading a book about a man who finds peace alone on a deserted island." Jean-Luc used the book to gesture to the bow. "We've completed this endeavor successfully and our hold is empty. Order the anchor raised, and let's go home, Mr. Bennett."

Once in his cabin, he placed the book on the corner of his desk and then went to work updating the log. Just as he was reaching for the novel, a warning bell rang. In his surprise, Jean-Luc knocked the book onto the floor.

He reached for it and banged his head on the edge of the desk as the schooner tilted. Leaving the book where it landed, he went up to the deck in search of the reason behind the warning bell and found a squall churning ahead of them.

Setting to work alongside his men, they fought the weather. By the time the crew had steered the ship through the storm, exhaustion sent him to his bunk for much-needed sleep.

He awoke during the night as wide awake as if he'd slept until daybreak. Swinging his legs out of the bunk, Jean-Luc retrieved the sandy copy of *Robinson Crusoe* with the intention of reading. The light was not sufficient to see the pages, so he placed the book on the bunk beside him and lay there until sleep finally overtook him.

The next morning he awakened to the book on the floor and a letter with the seal of the Cordoba family beside him on the bunk. Jean-Luc snatched up the letter and then looked around the cabin to see if perhaps it was some kind of joke.

Only one man aboard this vessel knew of his connection to a certain red-haired girl. Surely Israel felt that loss as keenly and would never make sport of anything in relation to her.

Still, what else could be the explanation?

"Come out and show yourself, Israel Bennett," he called to the man he hoped would have a guard posted outside to report back to him. "Your pitiful attempt at a joke at my expense has failed."

Silence.

He called out again but met with the same reaction.

"Truly, your joke has gone too far," he added as his temper rose. "You and I both know what the girl meant to us. To make this sort of jest is not like you, my friend."

Once again, there was no answer. This time his curiosity got the better of his temper. The letter looked real enough, the wax on the seal certainly giving it an official appearance.

And though the seal had been broken, indicating someone had already read it, the letter was intact and appeared to have been recently written. He turned the letter over and then set it beside him on the bunk.

Finally, with shaking hands, Jean-Luc opened the letter. When his eyes reached these words, his heart felt as though it had stopped:

> *Your mother and I came to this city we now call our home in hopes of being closer to the place where you were last seen. It was our hope, a hope we never once gave up on, that our precious Maribel would somehow return to us. No expense has been spared in our search for you, my sweet granddaughter. And now at last you have been located.*

Located.

He let the letter fall to the floor and then picked it up to read it all over again. Located where?

Jean-Luc's eyes went to the book. Surely this letter hadn't been inside.

He breathed in. Breathed out. Forced himself to calm his thoughts.

A man in his position did not allow speculation to rule him. He took action.

"Israel," he shouted as he stormed out of the cabin. "Israel Bennett, where are you?"

He emerged onto the deck and called to the first crewman he saw. "You there. Have this ship turned around. We are headed back to Isla de Santa Maria, and see that we get there as swiftly as possible."

"Aye, Captain," he said, hurrying away.

Jean-Luc found Israel at the wheel, standing in the same place where he had left him last night. "Did you not sleep?" he asked.

His old friend smiled. "I sleep enough when I need it. So what is this I'm hearing about turning the *Lazarus* around?"

Rather than respond, he handed Israel the letter. After reading it, Israel looked up at him. "Where did you get this?"

"It was on my bunk this morning."

He thrust the letter back in Jean-Luc's direction. "An odd place to find a letter from Don Pablo Cordoba, don't you think? I say ignore it. It cannot be authentic."

"I did wonder for a passing moment if you might be playing a joke on me."

Israel's expression showed he took great offense at the suggestion. "Surely you're not serious. Why would you think I would joke about the girl?"

"I wouldn't," he said, tucking the letter away, "but that was my first thought."

Israel, too, bore some measure of guilt over the loss of their youngest crew member those many years ago. But then he also bore guilt that he had not been aboard the ship when the French took them down.

In all these years, Jean-Luc had not managed to make Israel realize none of these things were his fault.

"And your second thought is what?" he asked, his expression now tender. "That somehow returning to the island we just left will answer the question of what happened to Maribel Cordoba?"

"Yes," Jean-Luc said with a smile. "Remember the book I brought back with me to the ship?" At Israel's nod, he continued. "I found that book at the base of a tree. Earlier a young novitiate had been climbing down that very same tree, so I assumed it might belong to her. When I attempted to return the book, Mother Superior insisted I take it as her gift and go quickly because we had overstayed our time."

"All right," Israel said slowly. "So how does all of that relate to the letter from Cordoba?"

"I don't exactly know except that I believe the letter was inside that book."

Something in his old friend's expression changed. "And the owner of the book is on Isla de Santa Maria? I see no reason to believe this, Captain."

He gave Israel an even look. "I don't want to get my hopes up, but possibly. The only way to know is to go back and see if she is there."

Israel nodded to the crewman nearest them and indicated the man should take the wheel. "Stay the course for now," he told the man, and then he ushered Jean-Luc to a spot away from any crewmen. "Think carefully about this, my friend. Do you really want Maribel Cordoba found?"

"Of course I do. Don't you?"

"For my own sake, perhaps. I do miss the girl." He paused and looked past Jean-Luc toward the horizon. "But for your sake? No. I do not." Israel swung his attention back to him. "Think, Captain. Everything you worked for, your reputation and perhaps even your father's could be gone if that girl tells anyone who you were. The Valmonts could lose everything."

"You're assuming she remembers any of it, or that she would connect Jean-Luc Valmont to a privateer working under an assumed name."

"Maribel is a smart girl. I say it because I do know she is out there alive. Just like the Lord spared me and those other three, I have no doubt He spared our Red."

Jean-Luc leaned against the rail. "I know I have hoped He did."

"However, the four on those skiffs who were spared slaughter at the hands of those French dogs, we took an oath."

Not only did they take an oath, but also those four men had made guarding him and his reputation from anything and anyone that might tarnish it their sole mission. To these men he owed his life and everything he had in this world.

Them and Evan Connor.

"I am forever in your debt," Jean-Luc said.

"Between us we have no debts that have gone unpaid, Captain," Israel said. "If you go after that girl, you just may find her. Then you'll have to deal with what happens next. We will not be able to protect you."

Israel was right, of course.

Jean-Luc shook his head. "There's nothing in what you've said that I can find disagreement with."

"And yet you will not rest until you have found her."

He shook his head. "She found me, Israel. That letter did not come to me by accident of fate. There is a purpose behind me knowing our Maribel is alive, and yes, I will not rest, but you are wrong about one thing."

"And what is that?"

"I don't have to find her, but I do have to find out what happened to her."

"Then let me do this. I will go ashore and inquire," Israel said.

He looked up into the concerned eyes of his best friend. "I must do this myself. You will not change my mind, but I do respect your concern. I wish to do this together, though."

Israel stuck out his hand to grasp Jean-Luc's, though the reluctance was still showing on his face. "Then we do this together, my friend."

"Together it is." Jean-Luc caught the attention of the crewman at the helm. "Turn back for Isla de Santa Maria, and make haste about it."

"We'll be weathering the storm once more," Israel reminded him.

"Then so be it," he said. "I doubt it will be our last."

"Of this, I have no doubt," Israel said as he turned to his work, his shoulders noticeably slumped as if in defeat.

"Take heart, my friend," Jean-Luc said as he clasped his hand on the bigger man's shoulder. "You cannot protect me from everything."

Israel turned around to face him. "I wear the scar of a flintlock's wound that proves this point. You wear more scars than that."

Only his friend knew how he hated the fact that first the Spaniard and then the French had marked his body. Every time he looked at the lines etched in his skin—some so deep he'd been told the physician could see bone—he was forced to remember the hands that put them there.

And every time he remembered those hands, he had to release them to the Lord for His revenge. Because Jean-Luc had learned the hard way that seeking one's own revenge was often the true source of those scars.

Israel reached out to place his palm over Jean-Luc's heart. "So when you ask me to take you down a path where you will very likely add more scars to the ones you've collected? I follow your lead because you are my friend and my captain, but I do not follow that lead willingly."

Jean-Luc nodded. "I often say the same thing to my heavenly Father, and yet I do follow Him all the same."

※

Maribel paced the deck of the *Paloma*, not caring that rain threatened. Half the day was now gone and the vessel had not left port. If it was going to rain, then get on with it. If not, then get on with that as well.

She shook her head. Never had she allowed her nerves—or

perhaps it was fear—to control her. At least not in a very long time. Nor had she thought herself an impatient person until this very moment.

Had Mother Superior not chosen her path, Maribel might still be back at the orphanage trying to decide what to do. Now, with that decision made for her, there was nothing left to do but somehow manage to pass the time until she arrived in New Orleans.

"Fired indeed," she muttered as her fingers toyed with the ends of Mama's scarf.

Of course they both knew why Mother Superior did what she did, but that did not remove the sting of having her choices limited to only one. She had packed her few meager belongings with tears in her eyes.

All the books she read had come from the little library that seemed to grow by a book or two almost monthly. And though the volumes that appeared were often classics such as the works of Homer or other philosophers, Maribel found it curious that the occasional volume of seafaring adventures found its way onto the shelves despite Mother Superior's edict that the books were not fit for young ladies and gentlemen.

Stepping onto a sailing ship after all those years on land had been exhilarating, despite how her last trip at sea ended. Her cabin offered a level of comfort she hadn't expected, but then her comparison was to the hammock she'd had slung between two posts in a tiny space no bigger than a prison cell.

But that prison cell had been a special courtesy to her privacy and a labor of love from Mr. Rao, who fashioned the space in a far corner of the hold, and Mr. Piper, who fashioned a hammock from sailcloth.

Maribel turned her back on the horizon and its ominous black clouds to take another long look at the home that had sheltered her these last eleven years. All the children had come to the dock this morning to see her off, accompanied by the sisters and Mother

Superior. It had been a tearful farewell, made all the more so by Stephan's declaration that he would always have the upmost respect for her.

She had been crying too hard to correct him.

Then, when Mother Superior had tucked the package into her hand, the crying paused only for a moment. "A book?" she said as she looked into the old nun's eyes.

"Two," she said with tears shimmering. "A book of the Psalms and another I've been told is a favorite of yours. I thought perhaps you might make some time to further your education while you are en route to your new home."

Now as she allowed her gaze to drift across the buildings that made up St. Mary of the Island Orphanage, across the avocado trees that lined the beach side and the copse of guangos that filled the center of the structures, she was struck by how small it all looked. Her gaze lifted to the cross decorating the chapel as her mind returned to the first time she arrived here.

Surely the Lord brought her to Isla de Santa Maria. There was no other explanation. And where He took her, she would go.

Even if that meant leaving her home to find another in a strange land.

Oh, but Mama would be there, so all else was of no consequence. Her heart soared even as she felt tears fill her eyes. And Abuelo too. Soon she would see them both and they would be a family again. How terribly had she missed them.

Maribel let out a long breath and said a prayer of thanks for all God had done for her. And then she said one more for the safety of the people who lived in this wonderful place.

The warning bell rang and crewmen took their stations. The man assigned to lifting the anchor began the process. Up at the wheel, the captain stood at the ready, his second-in-command at his side.

But it was not her captain—not the terse but oh-so-kind Captain Beaumont—who would be guiding this vessel. Nor would the gentle African giant Mr. Bennett be assisting him.

Another tear fell, this one for friends lost. And though the light was still quite good, Maribel could bear looking at her island home no longer.

To the north, the black cloud bore down on them. Over on the deck, the sails were being adjusted to turn the vessel out into open water at an angle designed to sail around the coming storm. Overhead the lookout was doing his job, likely wondering when the captain would warn of lightning and send him back down onto the deck.

She smiled. On those few occasions when Captain Beaumont had called her down to a place of safety from the storm, she had not gone willingly. Unlike the others on the captain's ship, she loved to watch the lightning zigzag across the sky.

This much she did remember.

Maribel's heart thudded as an image rose. Sails. Yes. Black night and sails that were only revealed when lightning danced across the clouds.

A memory buried so deep that she wondered whether she had imagined it. She willed her heart to slow its rapid beating. Imagination, that's what it was.

After all the books she read, of course she would begin to see things she hadn't seen at all. Hadn't Mother Superior said as much every time a thought such as this occurred?

She'd told the old nun all about how she got to the island. About the planks of wood that had become her floating home for an interminable amount of time. About the explosion of light that led to her landing on those planks, and ultimately about awakening from a deep sleep on a soft cot in the back corner of the chapel. Somewhere in between were voices and strong hands. Embraces and promises too, but nothing that she could recollect with any assurance.

Mother Superior had listened patiently, her unseeing eyes never leaving Maribel's face. And then, at the end of it all, the old nun patted Maribel on the head and told her it was likely that it had all been a dream.

It wasn't, of course.

She knew very well that Captain Beaumont, Mr. Bennett, Mr. Rao, and Mr. Piper were all very real. But the rest of her memories? Those she'd been unable to sort into real and imagined, so eventually she had ceased to try.

But the lightning? That was a new memory, one she could not recall reading about in any of her novels.

As if on cue, fat raindrops began to plop around her. Maribel gathered the ends of her scarf tight in her hands, gave a cursory glance toward the horizon, and then made her way to the passageway leading to her cabin.

"Sloop to the northeast," she said out of habit just as she disappeared inside.

CHAPTER 16

Maribel froze.

Sloop to the northeast?

She raced back onto the deck. There it was, a gaff-rigged schooner.

Taking a calming breath, Maribel watched the vessel continue its approach. Surely this was not the same vessel she had seen in the inlet. Also, there was no proof that this ship was headed for Isla de Santa Maria. More likely, the schooner would tack around to lay anchor at Port Royal to the west. Most of the ships in this part of the Caribbean Sea were headed there.

Very few ever made a stop on the tiny island where orphans and nuns awaited.

"Yes, of course," she whispered as the rain pelted her. There was nothing of concern in a gaff-rigged schooner sailing toward Port Royal. "It will tack soon."

But the schooner did not tack, nor did it veer off a course that would take it directly to Isla de Santa Maria. That just would not do.

And yet there was nothing she could do to stop it.

She could, however, get a good look at the ship and its crew so that she could report them to authorities. Which authorities she would work out later.

Ignoring the rain that pelted her, Maribel raced to the rail and remained there as the schooner drew nearer. The seas roiled, and the deck heaved beneath her feet. Still she kept her attention focused on the gaff-rigged schooner.

"Excuse me, miss." A crewman came to stand beside her. "The captain has asked all passengers to please return to their cabins until the weather improves."

She spared him a quick glance. "I'm sure I'll be fine here. I've had experience sailing, and you may tell the captain this."

"I do appreciate that you've sailed before, but I am afraid the captain's request applies to everyone and not just those who do not have as much experience sailing as you do."

His sarcasm was evident, but she ignored it—and him—to return her attention to the white sails silhouetted against the black clouds. The vessel still had not made the adjustments to its course that would take it to Port Royal.

"Miss, forgive me, but I must insist," he said as he reached for her arm. "I am only following orders."

She shrugged out of his grasp. "I do see the predicament, but I am in the process of attempting to identify a vessel that is suspected of criminal activity on Isla de Santa Maria. Thus, I am certain your captain will understand if I decline his request that I return to my cabin."

The young man gave her a frustrated look and then nodded. "Be that as it may, you will have to explain this to the captain. I will just go and fetch him."

The schooner tacked and seemed to be changing course. Maribel smiled. Perhaps she was wrong about the vessel's destination.

Still, she wanted to be certain.

"Do as you must," she said as she squinted against the impending darkness. "And I will do the same."

Yes, the vessel was tacking. Then, abruptly, the vessel veered off in the opposite direction and made a straight line for Isla de Santa Maria.

Now the schooner was close enough to see the men running about on deck, the spot where the watch would be, and the wheel where the captain or one of his crewmen would be steering the ship.

There. Now she could almost make out the looks of the man behind the wheel. He was tall but not as tall as the man beside him. That man was dark, possibly African.

Something in how the dark man stood as he weathered the storm sparked a memory. Something buried deep. Not a dream but a memory.

Mr. Bennett. Yes, although surely not. He was long ago lost to the sea.

Yes, this man surely just resembled him.

Turning her attention to the captain, if that was the captain of the schooner, she could make out less of his looks because he had his back to her. They were almost side by side now, separated by a distance no farther than the avocado trees on the beach to the mahogany trees at the inlet.

Slowly, the captain turned toward her. Now they were almost close enough to see facial features. Maribel spied dark hair, broad shoulders, and an expression of surprise on his face.

She leaned closer, her perch precarious as the waves buffeted the ship. But there was something in that face. . .something that she remembered. Surely that was not the captain.

Her captain.

The world upended and tilted. A moment later, Maribel realized she'd been hauled up into someone's arms.

"Begging your pardon, miss, but the man with whom you're traveling, Mr. Lopez-Gonzales? He gave the captain permission to carry you down to your cabin if you would not go peaceably. He says he is charged with delivering you safely to your family, and I do see his dilemma what with you hanging over the side of the ship like that. Common in those who haven't traveled by sea much, though."

"Of all the nerve," she said. "I will have you know I sailed with the best of the best during my time at sea. My job was as lookout up high on the mast, and I only fell off once, but that was not my fault. You see, we were being shot at by the French."

"Shot at by the French," he said in a tone that clearly conveyed the fact he did not believe her. "That does make for a troublesome voyage. I, myself, have not had that experience, so I would not know for sure."

"You're patronizing me," she said as she squirmed against his grip.

"I am stating facts, Miss Cordoba. Never have I been shot at aboard a ship, be it French, Spanish, or any other."

The young man avoided any eye contact as he walked toward the passageway. Only when they reached the corridor heading down to the cabins did the crewman realize he would need Maribel's cooperation to traverse the remainder of the distance to her lodgings.

Though she considered putting up a fight, Maribel knew the vessel had passed behind them by now. Besides, to think the man at the wheel of the schooner could possibly have been the captain she knew eleven years ago was ludicrous.

"I can find my way from here," she told him.

Looking skeptical, he lowered her to her feet. "I'll just watch until you've gone into your cabin then," he said, and he did just that.

Reluctantly, Maribel returned to the tiny room that served as her bedchamber for this voyage. The accommodations, consisting of a bunk, a pitcher and bowl for washing, and a hook to hang her clothes, were much more comfortable than Mr. Rao's makeshift space.

Given the choice, however, Maribel would once again pass the time during this sea voyage in that sailmaker's hammock with the sound of Israel Bennett and Captain Beaumont bellowing orders overhead.

Her gift from the nuns and children was still where she left it atop the traveling trunk Mother Superior had provided. She retrieved the package and then went over to the bunk to open it.

When the wrapping fell away, her breath caught. Beneath a beautifully bound copy of the Psalms was *The Notorious Seafaring Pyrates and Their Exploits* by Captain Ulysses Jones.

Maribel traced the edges of the book and then ran her hand over the words of the title, embossed onto the cover in gold script. "Oh," was all she could manage as she cradled the book to her chest. "Oh," she said again and swiped at the tears shimmering in her eyes.

When she could finally see the pages without the words swimming in tears, Maribel turned to the first page and smiled. It had been a very long time since she'd read this story, since she had traveled the world of pirates and privateers through these tales.

Eleven years, to be exact.

Once she discovered the treasure that was her copy of *The Notorious Seafaring Pyrates and Their Exploits* and the lovely poems that were the Psalms, Maribel was content to do nothing but remain in her cabin and read these two books.

Then one evening as she arrived at the page containing the Eighth Psalm, Maribel felt the words come alive in her heart.

> *When I consider thy heavens, the work of thy fingers,*
> *the moon and the stars, which thou hast ordained;*
> *what is man, that thou art mindful of him? and the*
> *son of man, that thou visitest him? For thou hast*
> *made him a little lower than the angels, and hast*
> *crowned him with glory and honour. Thou madest him*
> *to have dominion over the works of thy hands; thou*
> *hast put all things under his feet: all sheep and oxen,*
> *yea, and the beasts of the field; the fowl of the air, and*
> *the fish of the sea, and whatsoever passeth through the*
> *paths of the seas. O Lord our Lord, how excellent is*
> *thy name in all the earth!*

"The fish of the sea, and whatsoever passeth through the paths of the seas," she read aloud as she heard the gentle sound of waves hitting the ship as the sails slapped above. "Thank You, Lord, for that reminder."

For as the day drew near for their arrival in New Orleans, Maribel had begun to worry about something that until now she hadn't considered. What would Mama and Abuelo think of her now?

When she last saw them she was a girl of twelve years, a child really. And now here she was a grown woman of three and twenty. Educated by nuns and kept from all but the simplest of pleasures, she would be nothing like the girl they knew.

Would they still want her?

More important, would they still love her?

Maribel carried these worries in her heart until the morning the ship's lookout called out that land had been spotted. Unable to sleep, she had long ago prepared for their arrival by packing her belongings into the trunk, including her books. If Mother Superior was correct, a bookish girl was one thing, but a bookish woman was altogether a different sort of creature.

She wished for a mirror so that she might smooth her unruly hair yet again. The next moment, Maribel gave thanks she did not have one, for she would not be treated to the sight she had become after all this time at sea.

A soft tap at the door indicated the time had come. She allowed Mr. Lopez-Gonzales into the cabin but remained standing at the door.

"What will happen next?" she asked as she toyed with the frayed edges of Mama's scarf.

The older man offered a kind smile. "You are nervous," he said. "Do not be. Your family is most anxious to be reunited, so there is absolutely no need for concern."

"All right," she said. "So once we dock, then what? Will my mother and grandfather be there to greet us?"

"Probably not," he said. "The city is young, and its riverfront is a place where proper ladies and gentlemen do not belong. I expect a representative of your grandfather's household will meet us, and you will be taken to the Cordoba home. It is quite nice, by the way. A beautiful new residence within view of the river."

"You said that I would be taken," she said. "Won't you be coming with me?"

"Oh no," he said gently. "I was retained to find you and bring you back to your family. Now that my job is done, I will bid you good-bye."

"I see."

Though Maribel had not developed any feelings of friendship to the older man, she certainly had not expected to continue on to the final destination of her journey without him. Indeed, he was the only person who had the benefit of knowing both her family and her.

"I do wish you would accompany me," she said, "but I do understand. Perhaps you would consider escorting me to their door?"

"Yes, I believe that would be appropriate."

"Thank you," she said. "And just one thing more. Would you be willing to tell me more about my grandfather and mother? There is so much that must have happened in the eleven years since I've seen them. I would like very much to hear whatever you might be able to say in that regard."

He seemed to consider her request for a moment, and then he nodded. "Yes, all right. I don't suppose it would hurt to tell you a few things, but keep in mind if I do not share something it is because that is a tale that your family must tell. Agreed?"

"Yes, of course."

Mr. Lopez-Gonzales smiled. "All right, then. I first came to know your grandfather in Spain when he had been searching for his missing granddaughter some two years, perhaps three. I was recommended to him as someone who might be able to assist him in his search. We determined it would be best for him to move to New Orleans to be closer to the places where we believed you might be living. When I suggested this, he immediately put the plan into action."

Maribel nodded. "My grandfather always was a man of action."

"Any man who leaves all he has in the way of power and influence and moves to a foreign land. . ." He shook his head. "Your grandfather is a very good man, Miss Cordoba. He is fair but honest, and for that reason he and I have worked well together over the years."

She returned his smile. "Then that much has not changed. And my mother?"

"A great beauty, your mother, well liked and highly sought after." He paused. "Beyond that, I will allow her to tell the story."

Above them the warning bell rang, and a moment later, Maribel felt the familiar tugging motion of the anchor catching hold.

"We'll be off soon," he said. "I will send a man down for your trunk."

"A moment more and I will join you," she said. Reaching once more for the book she'd left inside the trunk, Maribel turned to the page that had caught her attention previously. *"When I consider thy heavens, the work of thy fingers, the moon and the stars, which thou hast ordained; what is man, that thou art mindful of him?"* She took a deep breath and let it out as she returned the book of Psalms to her trunk. "What am I that You are mindful of me, Lord?" she whispered. "What indeed? Oh, but thank You all the same."

CHAPTER 17

Maribel's first impression of New Orleans was not a flattering one. Though the town had been established as the capital of the French territory, the condition of the city left much to be desired.

Water and waste ran from the street into the river, and persons of questionable intent loitered about as if waiting to snatch her or her belongings at any moment. One moved too close and was met with her elbow in his midsection.

As the ruffian went tumbling, Mr. Lopez-Gonzales looked back at her. From his calm expression, he had obviously not noticed the impending attack and its swift resolution.

"Miss Cordoba, the carriage is just up there. I hope all of this is not too much for a lady's delicate constitution."

Maribel stifled a smile as she glanced over her shoulder. "No, nothing I cannot handle, Mr. Lopez-Gonzales, but thank you for asking," she said, straightening her gloves.

Behind her the man groaned but remained on the ground. Maribel returned her attention to the older man's straight back and followed him all the way to where her grandfather's carriage awaited.

Though Maribel had not been used to such fineries while at St. Mary of the Island, she certainly recalled the conveyances her grandfather used back in Spain. In comparison to those carriages with their plush interiors and the Cordoba crest on the doors, this one was certainly no match.

Either Abuelo's fortunes were no longer what they once were, or the luxuries he enjoyed back in the old country were not available here. In either case, Maribel gave thanks that she had any means of transportation at all.

For as much as she disliked trudging through the filth on the docks, the mud that filled the streets of the city was even worse. Between the droppings left behind by the animals that pulled the carts and carriages and the heat of the Louisiana sun, the smell was abhorrent.

How could Mama and Abuelo possibly be happy here?

Then it came to her. They were only here for her. And they had endured this for years in anticipation of her arrival.

Mr. Lopez-Gonzales helped her into the carriage and then joined her. "Would you like me to tell you about the buildings we will see along the way?"

"Yes, please," she said, as much to learn about this city as to have something to discuss that would keep the silence from falling between them.

Silence gave her time to think, but discussion about buildings such as the Place d'Armes, the Director's House, and the Ursuline convent kept her occupied until the moment the carriage lurched to a stop in front of an elegant home built of brick and plaster with a broad porch across the front and four gables across the second-floor roof.

The older man leaned forward to nod toward a rather large building with a two-story towerlike structure next to it. "As you can see, your grandfather's home is just across Dumaine Street from the observatory and the governor's house."

"The observatory is the tall building?"

"It is, yes," he said. "Its owner, Mr. Baron, designed those terraces on the second floor so as to be able to make scientific observations with his telescope. You see, he is a scientist of some renown who—"

The imposing front door opened, interrupting the older man's speech. Expecting a dour servant to step outside and greet them, Maribel was stunned when a lovely woman of middle age and great beauty appeared in the doorway.

"Mama!"

Maribel couldn't get out of the carriage fast enough. When she reached her mother, time fell away as they embraced. The years had been kind to Mama, adding only the slightest touch of silver at her temples and lines at the corners of her eyes.

But those lines meant she had smiled. At least that is what Mother Superior always said.

"My baby," Mama repeated over and over until Maribel knew she would never tire of hearing the words. Their tears fell, and laughter sounded.

The reunion she dreaded had become one she did not want to end.

Gradually Maribel became aware of someone else nearby. She looked up to see her grandfather standing in the doorway.

The years had been less kind to Abuelo than they had to Mama, but he still wore that same smile and had the same gleam in his eyes when he looked at her. He still had the posture of a soldier and the presence of a man used to getting his way.

Mama released her and offered Abuelo a smile as she swiped at her tears. "Look, Don Pablo," she said. "You have succeeded in bringing our girl home."

"My Maribel," he said, his voice quivering with the same emotion that caused a tear to slide down his wrinkled cheek. "Is it really you?"

"It is me, Abuelo," she said as she fell into his arms. "And I am home."

"Come inside," he said when she would allow him out of her embrace. "We have much to discuss."

"Don Pablo," Mama said. "Don't you think you need to rest first? Normally at this time you are—"

He waved away the remainder of Mama's statement with a

sweep of his hand. "Nonsense," he said. "Normally at this time I am wondering where my precious grandchild is and asking the Lord to bring her home. He has answered my prayers, so I have no need of praying them again." He winked at Maribel. "You only thought I was taking my morning nap."

Maribel giggled and followed her grandfather through a beautifully decorated foyer and into a parlor that faced the front of the home. Here and there were pieces that must have been brought from the family home in Spain, but they had been mixed with other furnishings that Maribel did not recognize.

Abuelo took a seat in a chair nearest the window and then indicated that she should join him. Choosing the settee for its proximity to her grandfather, Maribel settled on one end and waited for her mother to seat herself on the other.

A uniformed servant hurried in with refreshments, but Abuelo waved them away. "Nothing for me," he said. "But my granddaughter will likely not feel the same. She's been on an ocean voyage, you know."

"Several of them," Mama said softly as she reached across the distance on the settee to grasp Maribel's hand. "My sweetheart, I cannot believe you are actually sitting here. So many years I hoped and prayed and waited. . . ." She shook her head. "And so many times I wished I hadn't allowed Antonio to make a fool of me."

Her grandfather leaned forward and rested his elbows on his knees. "What did your father tell you about us?"

Recalling the conversation as if it had happened just yesterday, Maribel took a deep breath and let it out slowly before responding. "That you were dead," she managed. "He said you and Mama had been in an accident and neither of you survived."

Silence fell. Outside on the street, a wagon rolled by with two plodding horses pulling it.

"This is my fault," Abuelo finally said. "If only I had not decided my son would be better off sent to Cuba. He was given a nice placement in the colonial office, you know. I thought I had done well by him."

"You had, Don Pablo," Mama said. "But he did not do well by us."

"No, he did not." Her grandfather turned to Maribel. "I do not wish to stir up unpleasantness, but some say my son drowned. Others claim he was murdered. I hope you did not see him meet his demise, but if you have knowledge of this matter, I wish to hear it."

"I do have knowledge," she said. "And those who tell you he drowned are correct. There was a fight. My father shot a man in the back."

Abuelo winced but said nothing further. Maribel continued. "He fought a man on the deck. Their battle sent them over the railing and into the sea. The other man lived, but my father did not."

She let out a long breath and waited for the tears to come. Not since she was a child had she relived that moment at sea. Other moments, yes, but not that one.

"So the question is answered, then," he said as he leaned back in the chair. "I am very sorry you saw this, my dear. I would give anything to have spared you of it all."

Maribel managed a smile. "You know, Abuelo, it was not the childhood any of us expected, but it was a good childhood. I missed you both terribly, but not knowing you were alive and looking for me made the situation easier to bear."

Mama's hand fluttered. "When you are ready, I would love to celebrate your return with a proper party. So many of my friends here are aware of your impending return, and they will be asking for introductions. My dear friend Abigail is begging to host a small gathering."

"Oh, I don't know, Mama. Will they think it odd that I was rescued by privateers and lived among them for nearly two months before spending eleven years at an orphanage in the Caribbean?"

Neither Mama nor her grandfather spoke for a moment. Finally, Mama shook her head. "Maribel, I don't understand. Mr.

Lopez-Gonzales said he found you at an orphanage. He did not indicate anything other than that. Your grandfather and I assumed. . ." She sat back seemingly unable to continue.

"What your mother is saying, my dear, is if any of that did happen, then we are only just hearing of it. Please tell me about this privateer who rescued you. Is he someone I might know?"

The thought of her very proper Spanish grandfather knowing someone like Captain Beaumont made her smile. "No, I doubt you know him. He was a kind man, young for the profession he chose, and loyal to his crew. For the time I was on board, I was treated with kindness."

"I see," he said. "And his name?"

"Captain Beaumont," she said.

Her grandfather looked over at Mama, who shook her head. "I wondered if he might be enemy of Antonio."

"If he was, I was not told of it," she said.

"Tell me about the orphanage and how you came to live there," Mama said. "I want to hear every detail."

Maribel smiled. This was a topic she could easily discuss at length. And discuss they did until it appeared Abuelo's eyes were fighting to remain open.

"You see, you stubborn man," Mama said to him. "You've missed your morning rest and now you can barely stay awake to entertain our granddaughter."

He chuckled but did not disagree. Instead, he looked over at Maribel and smiled. "I will sleep well knowing you are under my roof, child." He paused. "Although you are no longer a child, are you?"

"I fear not," she said. "But I am not so old that you should despair of me. I taught the children at the convent for several years now, and if it is possible, I wish to continue teaching. Perhaps the Ursulines are in need of someone with my abilities."

"Are you considering joining the convent?" Mama asked, concern etching her voice.

"Oh no," Maribel said with a giggle. "I tried that at St. Mary of the Island and was deemed most unsuitable. Apparently reading adventure novels and climbing trees is not appropriate behavior for a novitiate."

From the look on her mother's face, it apparently was not appropriate behavior for a young lady in the Cordoba household either.

"Yes, well," Mama said. "I can see there have been some lessons on proper social behavior that might have been missed during your time with the nuns." Her expression brightened. "No need to worry. I am here to see to your continued education, Maribel. And once you are ready for society, then I will allow dear Abigail to throw the grandest welcome-home party this city has ever seen."

"Wonderful." Maribel stifled a groan. Gone were the days when she would be allowed to run barefoot across the courtyard or slip off to swim in the ocean. The return of her family had certainly been more wonderful than she expected. It also brought with it a few concerns she had not considered.

"You know, Mary," Abuelo said as he rose, "I think we could all benefit from some rest. Perhaps a siesta and then later we can discuss evening plans?"

Mama rose and nodded in agreement. "I will have refreshments brought to your room, Maribel. Come, it is right this way."

Maribel followed her mother down a corridor that led to two rooms. Ushering Maribel into the room on the right, Mama paused in the door to smile.

"I still cannot believe you are home with us," she said. "I thought you were. . ."

Tears fell, and Maribel caught them with her handkerchief. "Oh, Mama," she said when she could manage words. "I was afraid you wouldn't want me."

"Wouldn't want you?" She held Maribel at arm's length. "After all we did to find you, why in the world would you think we wouldn't want you?"

She shrugged. "I'm not like you. My life, it was different. I thought perhaps that would make me unsuitable."

"My precious child," she said softly. "You could never be unsuitable in my eyes."

"Even if I have climbed a mainmast and acted as lookout for ships on the horizon?"

Mama grinned. "Especially if you have done those things, and do you know why?"

"Why?" she said through happy tears that had Mama dabbing Maribel's cheeks with her own handkerchief.

"Because now I am extremely jealous and want to know every detail of what that was like." She pressed her forefinger to Maribel's lips. "But not now. Rest and have something to eat and drink. Later I will send in a tub for your bath and fresh clothing." Mama's gaze swept the length of her. "Tomorrow we will see to a new wardrobe and perhaps pay some calls, but today?" She paused. "Today I am keeping you all to myself."

Maribel surprised herself by doing as she was told and actually resting rather than reading her book or slipping out to explore her new home. When the maid and her helpers came to prepare her bath, she happily gave over her soiled traveling clothes in exchange for warm, clean water and fragrant soap she remembered from her childhood in Spain.

The dress that appeared in her bedchamber was breathtaking. Like nothing she had ever owned—or seen—during her time at the orphanage, the gown was constructed of a soft floral material and fit Maribel as if it had been made specifically with her in mind.

When she finished dressing, Maribel took up her book and settled onto the chair nearest the window to make the most of the afternoon light. It was there she found herself the next morning, having fallen asleep right where she'd been sitting.

Mama despaired of the wrinkled gown the moment she saw Maribel. "You were exhausted from your voyage. I could not bear to awaken you, even if it meant that your dress would be ruined."

She smiled. "Don't worry, though. I've had the maid prepare another dress for you to wear. Now just go on and let her dress you, and then we will get started on the day's events."

"But, Mama, I haven't had breakfast yet."

"No time," she said. "Perhaps later. After our visit to the dressmaker."

Maribel complied and somehow ended up in the carriage dressed in a floral gown and feeling as though she hadn't eaten in a week. As the carriage turned down Chartres Street, Mama gasped.

"Do put a smile on your face, Maribel," she said as she nodded toward a carriage coming toward them from the opposite direction. "That is Bienville approaching. He's the governor of all of the territory of Louisiana and a representative of the king and Versailles here, you know."

She did not know, but he sounded very important. Maribel did as she was told and offered the older man a smile when his carriage slowed to a stop beside them. The man Mama called Bienville appeared to be a fellow almost as old as Abuelo.

And quite distracted.

"Lovely day, Governor," Mama said with the languid tone of a woman who hadn't just indicated her excitement at receiving the governor's attention.

"It appears your daughter has arrived, Mrs. Cordoba," he said, moving his attention from Mama to Maribel. "Welcome to New Orleans, young lady. We have prayed for your safe return."

"Thank you, sir," she obediently responded.

The governor's attention had already returned to Mama. In truth, he seemed quite interested in her. "Have you called on my nephew yet? He returns to the city as of today, and I do believe he might be able to help you with that bit of trouble you're having."

Mama cut her eyes at Maribel, but her broad smile never wavered. "I have not yet paid him a visit," she said. "Perhaps next week I will find the time to set an appointment. Do you truly think he can help?"

The older man matched Mama's smile. "At my word, of course he can." He made a great show of retrieving his pocket watch and checking the time, and then he returned his attention to Mama. "Please forgive me, but I'm to send my carriage to the docks shortly. I'll let him know you will be paying him a call next week."

"Do think of me fondly, Governor, and know my father-in-law always does enjoy your friendly conversation."

"Then please convey a message to Don Pablo that I wish to engage him in friendly conversation very soon."

"He will be pleased," she said as she lifted her fan and instructed the driver to proceed.

"Mama," Maribel said when the carriage was in motion again. "Do you have a romance or a marriage planned with that man?"

"Oh, dear," Mama said. "That is not how a woman goes about marriage, nor do we plan romance. The proper question is whether I have plans to convince that man he ought to marry me. And the answer to that question is maybe I do and maybe I do not."

Maribel shook her head. "Because you do not want to admit which it is?"

She shrugged. "Because I do not yet know which it is. Bienville is a busy man and a confirmed bachelor. I'm not certain I wish to be wed to such a man, even one as nice as he."

"Then perhaps you can tell me what this trouble is that the governor mentioned." She gave her mother a sideways look. "Is there something wrong?"

Mama waved away the question with a sweep of her hand. "Nothing is wrong, sweet daughter. Just a little wrinkle that needs to be ironed out next week."

CHAPTER 18

As it turned out, there were other wrinkles to be ironed out. Wrinkles in the silk gown that Mama insisted was properly fitted for the celebration of her homecoming. And wrinkles that appeared at the corners of Mama's eyes when she grinned at the seamstress and asked her to send the bill to Don Pablo's home.

Then came the wrinkle of getting from the seamstress's shop to the carriage without getting wet from the rain that had begun falling during the grueling fitting session. Back on Isla de Santa Maria, Maribel would have ignored the rain to allow her gown a soaking.

Not if she had to teach, of course, but during her own time it was nothing to take a stroll in the rain. But here in New Orleans, it was quickly apparent that a proper lady did not do such things.

Nor did a proper lady complain about paying visits or taking tea. She did not complain about the heat in stiff gowns or the sore feet that came from wearing what Mama called proper lady's shoes.

And she did not complain when her mother planned the event of the year in her honor.

Even if the last thing she wished to do was to be paraded among the ladies and gentlemen of her adopted city so they could watch closely to be certain she behaved like a proper lady. Because, apparently, being a proper lady was Maribel's new role.

This last fact Maribel learned as Mama was chattering about

the party that her friend Abigail intended to give. They were to pay this woman a visit, and all Maribel could think of was the faint hope that Mama's friend might offer some sort of sustenance to keep her from evaporating into nothing.

Even as she held out hope, she knew it was unlikely. Apparently ladies did not eat in this city. So she decided to make one last attempt to avoid the visit altogether.

"Mama, I know you wish me to meet your friends but perhaps another day?" she said as her stomach complained loudly. "It has been a busy morning, and I am quite exhausted."

"You slept enough for two days, Maribel," she said as she adjusted the lace on her sleeve. "Abigail has been my dearest friend ever since Don Pablo and I arrived in the city. If you were to visit anyone else before you visit her, she would be heartbroken."

"Then I will take a vow not to visit anyone else," Maribel said. "And tomorrow she can be the first on our list."

"Don't be ridiculous." Mama shook her head. "We are practically on her doorstep. You will behave like a proper lady and enjoy this visit. Do you understand?"

"Yes, Mama," she said, although the events of the morning had been a fair indicator that she did not yet completely understand how to behave like a proper lady. But if that sort of thing was important to Mama—and it appeared that it was—then she simply would have to learn.

"Mama," she said as an idea occurred that just might buy her some time before she was required to be paraded about in public. "Perhaps I need a tutor."

"Tutor? Whatever for?"

"Well," Maribel said as she slowed her speech to allow the idea to properly unfold in her mind, "if I am to navigate the perilous waters of society, perhaps someone of my own age could be of service in showing me exactly how to accomplish this. Of course I do understand you are fully capable of repairing my social deficits, but wouldn't someone of my age group be more likely to give advice that would be relevant? Also, she might know others with whom I could become friends."

At that statement, Maribel almost visibly cringed. The last thing she wished was to join a social circle of proper ladies. Not when Abuelo's home had a library full of books just waiting to be read.

Mama seemed ready to speak and then closed her mouth. Apparently something in what Maribel just said had made sense to her.

"Yes," her mother finally said. "Yes, I do believe you came up with a wonderful idea, Maribel. Much as I would love to tutor you in the ways of a proper lady, a girl of your own age would be much more appropriate." She smiled. "And besides, you know no one in the city."

"Other than you and Abuelo," she reminded her, still wishing she hadn't gone down the path of making Mama believe she wanted to gain a circle of friends.

"Yes, of course," Mama said. "But no one of your age and social standing. Yes, I know exactly the girl who can help you."

"You do?"

The carriage pulled to a stop in front of a large house that stood two stories high and spread out quite a distance in both directions. Before Mama could emerge from the carriage, a footman was there to assist her. Another footman in matching attire aided Maribel.

"But, Mama," she said. "I thought perhaps we would begin my training before I was subjected to any visits."

"Nonsense," Mama said as she allowed a maid to usher them inside. "Abigail doesn't care about any of that. She just wants to meet you after all these years of praying you would come home. And, of course, I will want to discuss your idea with her."

"Whatever for?" Maribel asked as she took in the elegantly carved furniture and crimson silk drapes that filled the expansive parlor.

"Because the young lady I have in mind for tutoring you is

Abigail's daughter, Gabrielle. What better time to ask this favor of her than now? For if there is to be a welcome-home celebration, it makes no sense to wait a lengthy amount of time before holding the party."

"While I do agree," Maribel said as she perched on the edge of a settee covered in navy-striped silk, "wouldn't it make more sense to just let me learn how to conduct myself in public first?"

"My dear daughter," Mama said, her tone soft but firm. "When you were very young, I realized how intelligent you were. There was not a skill presented to you that you failed to master. I despaired of keeping you occupied until your tutor taught you to read." She slid Maribel a knowing glance. "You were not yet four years old."

A horse plodded past, its rider oblivious to the spirited conversation going on inside on the other side of the window. She watched the hooves kick up muddy tracks in the road until she finally could manage a response. Because unfortunately she knew where this conversation was leading.

"Yes, well, while I will agree, I don't follow how this has anything to do with my ability to adapt socially to this new city."

"You do follow," she said. "You are the same now as you were eleven years ago. Anything you put your mind to you can master, and, my darling, you require very little time to master it. Just as now when you believe you have mastered me, but you have not. For you see, I have no doubt that if allowed, you would put off these lessons or fail miserably at them so as not to have to be introduced socially at all."

Of course, Mama still knew her quite well. Thus there was no need to protest. Just to make another plan.

"Mama," she said softly as she gave her a sideways look. "Why did that seamstress seem upset when you did not offer payment? Is it customary here to do such a thing? Back in Spain proper ladies did not handle money. Are things different here?"

Mama's smile went south and was replaced by the neutral

expression Maribel recognized from her childhood. The expression that would let her know just how displeased she was with the question.

"Mary, dear," came a voice from just outside the parlor.

"That will be our hostess, Abigail," Mama said, her voice now taut with irritation. "There will be no more discussion on this topic, either here or once we are back home. Should you make the attempt, you will regret that you did not heed my warning. Do you understand?"

Before Maribel could respond, a voluptuous dark-haired woman a full decade younger than Maribel expected burst into the room. "Please forgive the delay. I was upstairs supervising the opening of Jean-Luc's chambers and up to my elbows in...oh!"

Her hands went to her cheeks, revealing sparkling jewels on several fingers and a clattering collection of bracelets dotted in pearls and diamonds. Matching pearl-and-diamond earrings sparkled beneath inky-black hair that had been swept away from her face with jeweled combs.

The effect was both stunning and intimidating. Then she smiled, and her deep brown eyes lit with joy.

"You must be Maribel," she said as she approached her in the same way one would approach a delicate vase or fragile flower. "You are everything your mother said you would be and more." She looked toward Mama, and her smile rose higher. "She's home, Mary. Can you believe it? She is home."

And then this lovely creature—this proper lady—began to weep.

"Abigail, my dearest friend, meet Maribel Cordoba," Mama said with a tremble in her voice. "Maribel, this is Mrs. Abigail Valmont."

The lady of the house shook her head and swiped at her eyes with a lace-edged handkerchief. "I am so sorry for these silly tears," she said. "I am just so overcome with how very good our Lord can be to us on occasion. When I see the efforts of our prayers standing before us, well, it is just all too much."

"It is indeed," Mama said. "Her grandfather and I are beyond grateful that she has been found. And we are, of course, indebted to you and Marcel for your generosity as well."

She shook her head. "It is nothing. Oh, but, Maribel, you are quite something. Look at you." Her attention went back to Mama. "For a girl who grew up outside of a city with modern conveniences, she seems remarkably well settled here and quite sophisticated."

"She is still learning our ways, but I believe she is happy to be home, are you not, Maribel?"

"I am," she said, even as she knew that happiness came with an equal amount of regret at what she had left behind on Isla de Santa Maria. "And I am thankful for the prayers that kept me safe while I was lost and then brought me here."

"But as to learning our ways," Mama said, sliding a warning glance toward Maribel before facing their hostess once more. "There is much yet to be taught, I'm afraid. You see, Maribel was still but a child when we lost her, and eleven years have passed."

"Eleven years," Mrs. Valmont said as if that number held some significance. She paused a moment, her expression hinting that her thoughts were far away. Then the smile returned and she turned her focus to Mama. "Yes, that is a long time to wait for a child to return."

"I have had the most interesting conversation with my daughter, and I would like your opinion, Abigail."

"Of course," she said with an expectant look as she settled onto the chair nearest Mama.

Mama shifted positions and gave their hostess her full attention, leaving Maribel to take in her surroundings. Although this was a fine home, it was very much a family home as witnessed by the gilt-framed painting over the fireplace.

The artist had captured the family of six seated in this very room. A man easily as old as Abuelo sat next to a younger Abigail on the settee, his expression that of a proud father and happy husband. Positioned on either side of them were a boy and a girl barely old enough to sit alone—who must be twins. Standing behind the couple were two young men in their teen years, one slightly taller and possibly a little older than the other.

While the elder Valmont looked straight ahead, Abigail had her attention focused on her husband, their hands entwined. Maribel's gaze went from the little girl beside her mother to the little boy next to his papa. Then she studied the young men behind them. Very much alike in their facial features, the younger-looking of the two wore a broad smile. The elder one, though he. . .

Maribel leaned forward. There was something familiar about the elder son. Something in the way he looked directly at her as though he could jump out of the painting and stand right in front of her. Something in those eyes, beautifully silver, and that insolent expression—not unhappy but not completely happy either—that struck a memory.

Or perhaps her imagination.

She sat back and let out a long breath. Mother Superior was right. Her imagination made her think things were real when they were, in truth, imaginary. How could a stranger in a painting on some woman's wall in New Orleans possibly be someone who was part of her memories?

And yet she could not look away from that painting. Could not relieve herself of the notion that she had looked into those eyes before.

"Maribel?"

Mama nudged her, and Maribel tore herself from the painting to return to whatever reality awaited in Abigail Valmont's parlor. She found both Mama and their hostess staring at her.

"Yes, Mama. I'm sorry. I was distracted by that painting." She looked past Mama to Mrs. Valmont. "It is lovely."

"Thank you, Maribel," Mrs. Valmont said. "My husband would like another painted, but I do like this one. The children were all so much younger then. Such an innocent time for all of them. And for us as their parents. But as they grow, well. . ." She shrugged.

"My mother used to say little children, little problems. But as they age, it becomes big children, big problems. I suppose that truth has been borne out more times than I wish."

"Isn't that the truth?" Mama said. "Oh, but what blessings your children are all the same."

"Depending on the day, yes," she said with a grin.

"So, Maribel, you likely missed our conversation regarding the subject you and I discussed in the carriage."

"I did, and I am terribly sorry for my inattentive rudeness."

Even Mama looked suitably impressed at her apology. So much so, she actually smiled.

"Oh, darling, I know there are so many new things here that you are unused to. Being inattentive is understandable in the short term." Her smile evaporated. "However, my darling, I must insist that you do pay attention now. Abigail and I have come up with the most brilliant plan, haven't we, dear?"

"Oh, we have," Abigail said, her hands pressed together as if she might soon begin applauding the two of them and their strategies. "While your mother despaired of a way to help you learn our ways here, I did think perhaps I had a solution. You see, my daughter, Gabrielle, is in dire need of a new friend. Suffice it to say, she has not spent her time as wisely as I wish and needs to be redirected to a cause that is worthy."

"And I am that cause."

Soon as she said the words, Maribel wished to take them back. The very tone of them sounded rude at worst and ungrateful at best. Before she could speak to remedy the situation, her hostess laughed.

"Oh, Mary. She is so quick-witted. She and Gabrielle will get along famously, and I will make the introduction right now." Mrs. Valmont rose. "You two just wait right here, will you?"

"Of course," Mama said sweetly. As soon as the parlor door closed behind Mrs. Valmont, Mama's expression changed. "What am I going to do with you, Maribel Cordoba? The moment I think

I have finally gotten through to you regarding the behavior of a proper lady, you prove me wrong."

"I'm sorry, Mama. Truly I meant no offense," Maribel said as she rose to walk toward the painting, now mesmerized by the young man with the fearless look and the memorable eyes.

"You're doing it again," she said. "What is so important about that painting that you have to lose all ability to respond to anyone else in the room?"

"I don't know," she told her. "There's just something about. . ."

Maribel paused. Had Mother Superior's warning about her imagination not been echoing, she might have admitted to Mama that there was something about that one fellow in the painting that seemed familiar. Instead, she chose to keep that to herself.

Mama came to stand beside her, grasping Maribel's hand. She turned away from the painting to face her mother. "I owe you an apology," Mama said gently.

Not at all what she expected to hear from her mother. "Why?"

Her expression softened. "Because I have expected far too much from you. My darling, you have barely been in the city for one day. How in the world would you know how to conduct yourself after so short a time?"

"Yes, well, I was taught manners by the nuns, so I will not allow them to accept the blame for behavior they did not cause," she said, suddenly feeling the need to defend Mother Superior and the others who toiled at the orphanage.

"Of course," she said. "I am a complete fool. Will you forgive me?"

Maribel shook her head. "Again, why?"

"I lived through eleven years' worth of days spent wondering where you were. Eleven years of nights when I fell asleep praying or crying—sometimes both—because my daughter had vanished. I refused to believe you died when the *Venganza* was sunk by those horrible pirates and—"

"Privateers, Mama. There is a difference. And those privateers did not sink the *Venganza*. The idiocy of those in charge of that vessel is what sunk it. The crew had Letters of Marque from the king of France, and they did not seek anything other than the treasure in the *Venganza*'s hold. No violence was spent against the Spanish vessel and yet they fired against us."

Mama's eyes widened. "Daughter, tell me exactly who is *us*?"

She had said too much, this Maribel could easily tell. Though the truth of her life was there for her family to know if they wished, it was becoming quite clear that Mama did not wish to know it.

"*Us* would be the crew aboard the *Ghost Ship*, although Captain Beaumont did not prefer that name for the vessel," she said. "I tried to tell you of how I arrived at the orphanage. Did you not believe I spent time aboard a privateer's vessel?"

Mama released her hand and walked away only to return. "There will be an appropriate time to continue this conversation," she said, her voice barely above a whisper. "But that time is not now."

"I tried," she said again.

"Perhaps you did, but there will be questions regarding at what point this *Ghost Ship* became *us* to you, and you have not yet tried to tell me this. This captain, he had a bounty on his head, and not just from the Spaniards who did not take kindly to him accosting their vessel."

"I was on that vessel, Mama," she said, her temper rising. "I can tell you exactly what happened."

Mama's eyes narrowed. "There is no need, Maribel. You can be sure that the father and widow of the late Antonio Cordoba were told the facts surrounding these supposed Letters of Marque and how the *Venganza* came to land at the bottom of the Caribbean Sea. The one fact they got wrong, however, was that you were very much alive and not dead like your father."

"Well, Mama, it appears you will believe strangers over your daughter," she snapped as she heard a conversation out in the foyer, "but I was there, and I can tell you that the facts you were told are absolutely and positively wrong."

CHAPTER 19

Jean-Luc walked into the foyer of his family home and then stepped into his sister's open arms. "You are finally home!" Gabrielle exclaimed. "You promised you would be back days ago. More than a week, actually, and you had us all very worried."

He grinned and spun the spirited girl around then set her back on her feet, slipping a small package into her hand as she tried to find her balance. "There," he said with a grin, "am I forgiven?"

Gaby hurried to open the package. "I am not a child that you can distract with pretty things. I was worried about you. And worse than that, I have been given the most vile of punishments, and all because I dared sneak out of the house to pay a call on a friend. Can you feature it?"

She retrieved a strand of pearls from the package and tossed the wrapping behind her. "Oh, Jean-Luc, they are exquisite."

"As are you," he said. "Turn around and let me see how they look on you."

"Mama will not be pleased if she sees me wearing pearls during the daylight hours." Her grin rose, making her look so much like her mother. "But I am already in trouble, so what can it hurt?"

Jean-Luc held the pearls away from her and frowned. "Oh, I don't know then. I have seen your mother when she's displeased with one of her children. I do not want to be in the line of fire." He pretended to slide the pearls back into his pocket. "I'll just give these to her so that I will be the favored child and you can stay in trouble."

"No," she said as she snatched them out of his hand. "You will do no such thing. Put these on me now so I can see how they look."

He did as she told, but then most everyone gave in to the brown-eyed charmer's demands. It had been that way since her birth, the only daughter in a house full of brothers, and likely would always continue.

"So this friend you went to visit?" he said as he held both ends of the strand and began the process of closing the clasp. "What was his name?"

She whirled around, eyes blazing. He nearly dropped the pearls. Thankfully, the clasp held, or else she would have been throwing the tantrum he knew was coming amid several dozen exactly matched pearls from the Orient rolling around on the marble floor.

"If I didn't adore you so much," she said evenly, "I would be insulted that you would assume such a thing of me."

"I will rephrase the question then," he said.

"Thank you." Her smile returned, just as he knew it would. *Brat*.

"What was his name?"

"Jean-Luc," she exclaimed as she shook her head. "Oh all right. He's a very nice fellow, but Mama and Papa are being ridiculous about the whole thing. It's Mama, I know it, because Papa trusts me."

"Papa trusts Mama to keep you in line," he said with a laugh. "Because if it is left to Papa, he will tell you yes no matter what you ask."

"This time he actually agrees with her." She leaned against his shoulder in mock horror. When she looked up at him, her expression was pitiful. "It is a fate worse than death. I am to be a tutor."

"A tutor?" Jean-Luc laughed. "That is your fate worse than death? Oh, my darling Gaby, you really should tell Papa you're running away to join the theater. I'm sure he would let you, because as we have established, he does tend to do that, and of course, I will vouch for your flair for the dramatic."

"Flair for the dramatic? I will have you know that—"

"Gaby, is that you I hear out in the foyer?" Abigail called from somewhere upstairs. "Where have you gotten off to?"

Gabrielle's eyes widened, and then her gaze darted about the room as if searching for the best place to escape her mother. Jean-Luc nodded toward the closed parlor door.

"I generally hide in there." He shrugged. "The curtains are quite handy if you stand behind them. Or at least they were when I was seven."

"Stop teasing me," she said. "I am not a child playing hide-and-seek. This is serious. And besides, the person I am to tutor is in the parlor with her mother, so that will not work at all."

He nodded toward the room on their left. "Then I would try Father's library. If you climb under the desk and gather up your skirts, she may not find you. Although beware, when she does find you, you'll have to answer to her."

"I'm just trying to buy some time until she changes her mind. I absolutely cannot be stuck teaching some girl from the outer banks of nowhere how to fit in here in the city."

Jean-Luc shook his head. "The outer banks of nowhere? You and Michel were born in this city, true, but I was born in Paris, as was Quinton. Compared to us, *you* are from the outer banks of nowhere, so be careful when casting stones."

"I heard you talking, Gabrielle Valmont, and I will not be ignored," Abigail called. "Where are you?"

Gaby made for the open door to the library, but Jean-Luc grasped her wrist. "What is his name?"

She struggled against his hold on her even as her mother's footsteps echoed above their heads. "Let me go," she demanded. "You truly do not want her to find me right now, and if she does because of you, then I will exact my revenge."

"How?" he said with a laugh. "By forcing me to tutor someone?"

"Perhaps," she said as her expression went penitent. "Please, just let me go."

"Not until I have a name."

Stubborn to the end, Gaby continued her attempt to break free. Finally, as Abigail's tread hit the stairs behind them, she leaned up on her tiptoes and whispered, "Louis Gayarre."

Jean-Luc let her go just in time for Gaby's skirts to disappear inside the office. As Abigail reached the bottom of the stairs, he saw his sister scurry under the desk.

"Jean-Luc, you're home!" Abigail enveloped him in a hug, temporarily distracted from her search by his arrival. She smelled like lavender and hugged him like he'd been gone for months and not weeks.

She released him to hold him at arm's length. "I will never get used to the trips you take, my son. I always worry, and then you come home and all is well again."

"And I am always glad to be home." He cut his eyes toward the library where Gaby had done a poor job of gathering her skirts out of sight. "I understand all is not well, however. What is this about my sister and a young man?"

Abigail let out a long breath and shook her head. "I am at my wit's end, Jean-Luc. She has been sneaking out to go and meet this fellow, and your father and I are plenty worried about this. I've told her if he wishes to court her, he must first discuss his prospects with her papa. She claims courting is not what they're doing, but if that's not it, then I cannot imagine what it is. I am worried sick about her. And now she's gone and disappeared."

Jean-Luc winked and then nodded toward the library. Abigail followed his gaze. She must have spied the skirts showing beneath the desk, for she shook her head.

He kept his voice just low enough to prevent his sister from overhearing. "Tell me about this tutoring punishment that has been inflicted on her. Is it as awful as she claims?"

Abigail laughed. "Not at all. She's a completely lovely girl and the daughter of a dear friend. She's recently arrived in New Orleans and is lacking in some of the social graces needed to establish friends and make a good match. I merely offered Gabrielle as someone who would be willing to assist the young lady in making the transition. If she indicated it was anything more than this, she is being overdramatic."

"Is that even possible?" he asked as he stifled a smile.

The daughter's penchant for these types of antics had definitely come from her mother. Not that he would ever tell Abigail that. Or Gaby for that matter.

"Who is this young lady? Perhaps a rival for her male friend's affections?"

"I am not at liberty to give the young lady's name, nor would I if I were. I do not wish to cause any embarrassment to her mother. It is not my friend's fault that her daughter's education is lacking in certain areas. As to a love rival? No, that's not possible. She's only just arrived here, as I said. She knows no one."

Abigail watched as Gaby gathered up her skirts so they no longer could be seen from the foyer. Shaking her head, she leaned close to Jean-Luc.

"Honestly, I am hoping your sister learns as much from this young woman as the young woman learns from Gaby. Our daughter is a good girl, but there is a level of maturity that I wish was a bit higher than it currently is. She is eighteen years old, for goodness' sake. When I was her age, she and Michel were already on the way."

"Given the fact Gaby is currently playing hide-and-seek with you by climbing under Father's desk, I tend to agree." He paused. "How can I help?"

Abigail tapped her foot on the marble floor as she considered his question. "I suppose something needs to be done about this young man of hers. We've tried for weeks to get the name from her, but she refuses to tell us."

"Louis Gayarre." At Abigail's look of surprise, he shrugged. "I am more convincing than you are, I suppose."

"I don't even want to know how you managed it," she said. "Unless you think I can replicate the process the next time I try and get information out of her."

"I don't know, Abigail." He gave her a sideways look. "How strong is your grip?"

She gave him a playful swat. "Stop teasing me and go tell your sister her father is on his way downstairs and has need of his desk. She will have to find another piece of furniture to hide under."

"Yes, ma'am," he said.

Abigail gave him a grateful look. "Thank you. Some days I truly despair of what I would do without you, Jean-Luc, and not just in the management of your siblings." She nodded toward the closed door of the parlor. "I am being a terrible hostess, so I must go and apologize. Will you be staying with us tonight?"

"For a few days, yes." He had an obligation that would take him out of the house later tonight, but the family would be long abed by then.

"Good." She clasped his shoulder and smiled. "I am very glad you are home, Jean-Luc Valmont. Very glad, indeed. You are good for all of us in this family," she said over her shoulder as her hand touched the knob of the parlor door.

He offered her a broad smile. "And my family is good for me."

The parlor door opened, revealing the backs of two women who stood in front of the fireplace. Both were dressed in gowns that looked very much like the clothing Abigail and Gaby wore, thus he assumed these two were not another of Abigail's charity projects.

From time to time, the woman who raised him would cause Father much concern with the projects she took on. Sometimes these projects were as ordinary as a food drive for the hungry or a knitting circle that donated scarves and mittens for the nuns at the Ursuline convent to distribute.

Then there were the other times when Abigail's good intentions overruled her good judgment. Such as the day she brought home an opera singer from Bavaria who mistakenly thought he had been signed to perform at the New Orleans Opera House. Only after he arrived did the poor man discover there was neither an opera house in the city nor a ship that would accept him as a passenger without payment.

Father had complained for days about the noise emanating from the room at the end of the hallway. Terms like "strangling a wild goose" and "murdering a squealing pig" were tossed about as the men of the family plotted to remove their houseguest from beneath the Valmont roof.

The consensus was that the Valmont family should buy the singer a ticket back to Bavaria, but Father refused. If word got out that the Valmonts would pay for this, there would likely be no end to the itinerant musicians who might darken their doorstep. Not only that, but Abigail would welcome them.

While the men were making their plans, Abigail took action. She organized a week of performances and took donations. After the first show, there was enough to send the man home to Bavaria that evening.

When asked how Abigail managed it, she admitted that before the performance she allowed her friends to compete for places on the list of homes that would host the illustrious singer each night of the performance series. The largest donors to the fund were the ones who had won the right to have him as their houseguest.

Jean-Luc chuckled as the parlor door closed. Since he hadn't heard any inappropriate yodeling or music coming from the parlor, he had to hope that these two ladies might be a project that would require no intervention from him beyond seeing that Gaby understood she would be required to participate.

He found his sister still hiding beneath the desk and reached down to pull her to her feet. "Is she gone?" Gaby asked as she straightened her skirts.

"If you mean your mother, she is no longer in the foyer. If you mean the young lady you will be tutoring, she is in the parlor." He paused to give her a stern look. "Now stop playing at the game of behaving like a child at home and then demanding we all treat you like an adult."

Gaby opened her mouth, likely to complain. Jean-Luc shook his head.

"If you cannot do as your mother asked, then you will not see the Gayarre fellow."

"You cannot stop me," she said as he walked away.

"No, you're right," he said when he stopped to turn around and face her. "But I will stop the Gayarre fellow. In fact, he will be so afraid to be anywhere near you that he will likely find another girl." Jean-Luc nodded. "Perhaps the new girl in the parlor."

"You are cruel, Jean-Luc," she said.

"I am nothing of the sort and you know it," he told her. "Now go do the right thing before I change my mind about allowing that Gayarre fellow access to my sister and do the wrong thing."

He watched Gaby skitter inside the parlor. As the door closed, he still wasn't certain this fellow would be allowed even five minutes' time with his sister. He would never tell Gaby that, though.

Jean-Luc was still contemplating this when he spied Father coming down the stairs. "You're home. Excellent. A moment of your time, if you have it, son," he said.

"I do." He followed his father into the library and took a seat on the opposite side of the desk.

Father sat and then opened a desk drawer to retrieve a stack of documents. Placing them on the table, he glanced over at the open door. From there, women's laughter floated toward them.

"Would you like me to close the door?"

He shook his head. "As long as those two are occupied, I have no further need of privacy." Sliding the topmost document across the desk, he nodded for Jean-Luc to read it.

Jean-Luc scanned the document, a letter from Versailles regarding losses sustained in attacks against vessels flying the

French flag. He handed it back to his father.

"A pity this is happening, but I fail to see why this would be addressed to you."

His father leaned back in his chair, his expression unreadable. "It is addressed to me because I own the trading privileges in the territory. With this privilege comes the responsibility for what happens to the French vessels that come into our port on my behalf. If vessels are being stolen from, then it is my job to investigate and determine who is doing the stealing."

"The letter says nothing of the kind," he protested.

"No, it does not. Nor does it say anything of the kind in any of the other letters that came from Versailles." Father leaned forward and rested his forearms on the desk. "But your uncle has recently returned from Paris. He brought the message back personally. It seems as though rumors of pirates have reached the king."

At the word *pirate*, Jean-Luc looked away. "Again, why is this your concern? Do the French not have a navy to handle this anymore?"

He flexed the knee that still plagued him on occasion, the same leg that had been laid open by a French fleet's weaponry. "How can I help with this?"

"I need names, Jean-Luc. The crown wants men who have come up against the French, be it as pirates, privateers, or simply common thieves. I know we swore an oath to never speak of a time when you were more connected to this sort of trade, but forgive me. We must speak of it. The alternative is to provide no answers to the king and risk losing our trading privileges. If that happens, it will ruin us."

Letting out a long breath, Jean-Luc returned his attention to his father. "What do you want me to do?"

"As I said, give me names. However, I have a plan. I believe I can offer a compromise. If there are enemies of the king doing business in his territories, I believe we are within our rights to go after anything of value that enemy might have. Would you agree?"

"I would," he said. "It has certainly been done before."

Father nodded. "To that end, I have made inquiries into a resident of our city who may have profited from a family member's illegal activities. For reasons I cannot go into at this moment, I cannot tell you that name." He slid a look at the closed parlor door. "Perhaps later once our guests have gone home. However, if the facts are as I suspect, I will have a name to give to the king along with a substantial amount of money for his coffers."

"That should fix the problem," he said. "Or at least buy some time to get the issue of theft under control."

"About that," Father said. "I would like your thoughts on what can be done."

"I have told you," he said with a lift of one shoulder. "Arm the merchantmen well enough and the problem goes away."

"I want you to handle that."

Jean-Luc shook his head. "Give that responsibility to Quinton, please."

Unused to hearing no from anyone, Father frowned. "I assume you will add an explanation to that request."

"If I add an explanation, then you will be party to information you may be required to surrender to the authorities. Do you still want me to add that explanation to my request?"

Once again feminine laughter drifted across the foyer and into the library. "No," Father finally said. "I don't believe I need to have an explanation. I do have a question I would like answered. This thing you are not telling me, does it involve something I would advise you not to do?"

Jean-Luc thought for a moment. "It does involve something that you would likely advise me not to do. However, it is something that you would do without caring what you were told."

His father smiled. "Exactly the answer I expected."

CHAPTER 20

At the sound of raised voices, Maribel crept down the hall to find out the cause. Mama and Abuelo were in the library, and their argument seemed to be over money.

"I must present her as a young lady of the proper social set, Don Pablo," Mama said. "And to do that she must be properly outfitted."

"You must stop," Abuelo said. "These inquiries have progressed to the point where I expect we will soon be paid an official visit to answer questions."

"Do you think so?" Mama asked, her voice suddenly much quieter.

"I cannot imagine that we will not. Our credit is being questioned, and men who were my friends suddenly cross the street to get away from me. What other reason would there be?"

"After all these years," Mama said. "How is it that Antonio can still bring us harm?"

"This time the charges against him are false," Abuelo said. "I cannot imagine anyone would have such proof as the law requires. And you know why this is happening, don't you? Your friend's husband is in trouble and looking for someone to blame."

"You cannot lay the fault on Abigail. She and Marcel have been very kind to us. Nor can you blame the French. Abigail and the governor have both suggested I make an appointment with the younger Valmont to plead our cause. He does much of his father's work for him."

"It matters not who does what work, Mary. Of course, when a Frenchman is looking to make trouble, he picks his fight with a Spaniard. Your friends may treat you well now, but at the first sign of trouble, they will disappear and leave you—leave all of the Cordoba family—alone. Isn't that always how it—"

Her grandfather began coughing and seemed unable to stop. Maribel ran to fetch something for him to drink and then hurried into the library.

"Here, Abuelo," she said as she handed him the glass. "Drink this."

She watched her grandfather take small sips until the cough subsided. "Thank you, sweet girl," he told her. "You have always been a great help to me."

"If I am of help to you in this little thing, perhaps I can also help elsewhere." She paused to look at Mama before returning her attention to Abuelo. "I heard what you and Mama were saying. If someone is making trouble here because you are a Spaniard, then why not just leave? Go back to Spain. Your letter said you moved closer to the search for me. Now that I am found, should we not just all go home?"

"It is not so simple," Mama said. "It took a fortune to move here and settle in. There are debts here we cannot pay." She looked past Maribel to Abuelo. "And your grandfather, he is not as young and healthy as he was all those years ago when we traveled to New Orleans. If we were to attempt a journey back to Spain, I fear it might be too much for him."

"Bah," he said. "If I am to die, better it is on Spanish soil, Mary. And if I die on the way, then at least my bones will reach Spain. I say the girl is right. We should consider this."

"But, Don Pablo, there are obligations. . ."

He waved away her statement with a sweep of his hand. "I am a man of honor, so I will agree that debts are owed." He paused to take another sip from the glass. "However, we must consider the possibility that repayment of certain portions of our debts might need to be delayed."

Mama looked away. Clearly she did not agree, but there was no disagreeing with Don Pablo Cordoba. Not under his roof anyway.

"Then it is settled. We make arrangements to return to Spain. I will speak to those men who have been most generous and execute a document promising I will repay our debts at a time in the future."

"Are you certain that is wise?" Mama asked.

"I am certain this is the only chance we have to leave this city." He set the glass aside and rose. "Mary, I would like you to decide which of our things we will need to bring with us. Perhaps what is left can be sold to settle some of the monies owed."

"Yes, of course." Mama looked troubled. Finally she rose to follow Abuelo out into the hall. "A word with you, please," she said to him before turning to Maribel. "Just your grandfather and me, please."

Maribel complied as the door closed with her still in the library. Of course, she tried to remain close enough to the door to listen to the conversation going on in the hallway.

"You'll find the safe empty," Mama said. "I know I told you that Marcel Valmont did not require any repayment, but do you recall when you awakened from your siesta and I was hosting Mr. Valmont in the parlor?"

"I do," he said. "And I found it strange then, just as I find it strange now."

"Well," she said slowly, "he was here in his official position as a representative of the king. He explained there had been an inquiry and there was a need for us to make good on some portion of the repayment."

"I do not follow," he said. "What did you do?"

"Marcel is a friend, Don Pablo. He wished to help us."

"He wished to help himself," he snapped. "Likely there is something in this for him. A threat to his exclusive trading privileges, perhaps? How much did you give him?"

"Everything," she said. "But do not let this upset you. You know what the physician said about getting overwrought."

"Everything? The coins and the jewels?"

"Yes, but I have an appointment to speak with his son regarding the matter in the coming week. The governor believes at his word the issue may be dropped and the coins and jewels will be returned. I am quite hopeful of this."

Before any more words could be spoken between them, Mama called out. Maribel came running and then froze when she reached the door to the library.

Her grandfather lay prone on the floor.

Jean-Luc left his home that night under cover of darkness, making his way down Dumaine Street without being detected. Though the meeting place was isolated, nevertheless, he took the usual precautions. By the time he reached the bend in the river, the moon was high overhead, but a cloud obscured its glow.

"Is that you?" a decidedly male voice called out. "It seems like I've been waiting for hours."

Circling around with the tangle of brush and trees as his cover, Jean-Luc easily came up behind the fellow and wrapped one arm around his throat. Though the man fought, he quickly gave up.

"I have money in my pocket but not much," he said. "Please, don't kill me. I have a rich fiancée who will pay you whatever you ask for my safety."

"Do you now?" Jean-Luc turned Louis Gayarre around to face him. "Tell me about this fiancée of yours? Is it my sister and you have not told the family yet, or is it someone else and you have not told my sister yet?"

Silence.

"Do not answer yet," Jean-Luc said. "I have a more important question. Why is it you are not paying proper visits to my sister in her home under the supervision of her parents? Is there a particular reason for that?"

Once again, the lad said nothing.

"Well, now," he continued. "Is it because you don't like the supervision of her parents? Because if that's so, then that would also indicate that you do not care about my sister's reputation and what might be said about her if anyone caught the two of you out here together. Is that possible? I hope not, because no man would dare think so little of my sister and then stand in my presence and not expect to be greatly harmed."

The cloud moved away, revealing the terrified face of a man who knew there was nothing he could say to get himself out of the trouble he'd gotten himself into. So he ran.

"Gayarre," Jean-Luc called to the fellow's quickly disappearing back. "I require an answer."

The Gayarre fellow kept running. Jean-Luc shook his head.

"Truly you vex me," he said. "I do not want to chase you down, nor have I brought any weapon that could touch you from this distance. Stop and face me like a man and tell me whether you plan to stop seeing my sister voluntarily or because I have told you to."

Gayarre paused to turn around. "Does it matter? You'll never see me near her again."

Jean-Luc grinned. "If you have met my sister, then you know it matters whether I am guilty in ruining her romance with you or not. So which is it, am I to blame or not?"

"You are not to blame," he said.

"Thank you, now please do continue running. I was so enjoying it."

He heard a noise and smiled. "How long have you been watching, Israel?"

"Long enough to know I don't want to be caught anywhere near your sister."

Jean-Luc laughed. "What report do you have?"

"There is not much notice, but I am told of a vessel making port tonight. Very quietly and without the knowledge of the authorities." Israel paused. "There is time to intercept this ship, my friend. But there will not be time to make the usual preparations."

He thought only a moment. "I will need to make arrangements."

"There is no time." He gestured toward the river. "Your ship is there, as is your crew. What say you?"

Abigail would be frantic and Father would be furious once they learned he had sailed off again. Then there were the issues with the crown that his father should not have to handle alone. None of those issues, however, were as important as the men and women aboard that vessel.

Jean-Luc looked up at Israel, his decision made. "Let's go."

❧

Maribel walked into the offices of Marcel Valmont & Sons and demanded to see the man in charge. The three Monsieurs Valmont were unavailable, she was told by the aide who ushered her back outside.

Of course, she followed the aide right back in and took a seat at his desk. "Then I will wait," she told him.

"Monsieur Marcel is not expected in today, and Monsieur Quinton has sailed to Paris on business that will keep him occupied until the end of the month." He regarded her with lifted brows. "And thus, that leaves only Monsieur Jean-Luc, who is obviously not here."

She shrugged. "Then I will await Monsieur Jean-Luc's return."

"I'm sorry, Miss Cordoba, but I cannot say when that might be. His hours are often irregular." He gave her one last long look and then returned to his work, obviously dismissing her.

Maribel remained seated as long as she could stand it and then rose and began to pace. Eventually someone from the Valmont family would have to come through the doors and speak to her.

She hadn't counted on that someone being Gabrielle Valmont.

"I know he is here, Mr. Landry. Do not cover for him." Gabrielle stormed past Maribel without taking notice of her and threw open the doors to what Maribel soon realized was an office. "Where are you, Jean-Luc Valmont? I know you're here. You do not just leave for nearly a week without telling anyone, so you cannot fool me into believing you aren't here." Doors opened and closed and then opened again. Maribel watched Gabrielle pace back and forth, her anger evident.

"Miss Valmont," the aide called. "I must object. You'll need to leave now."

"I am ignoring you, Mr. Landry, because I know my brother is paying you to keep me from bothering him. I know you're here, Jean-Luc. Don't you dare try to hide from me."

Mr. Landry looked over at Maribel and shrugged. Though he returned his attention to Gabrielle, he did nothing to make her cease her search.

"I know what you did to my Louis," Gabrielle continued. "How dare you try and frighten the love of my life away? Why, he will not even give me the time of day now. I was walking down the street with William Spencer on our way to his shift at the charity hospital, and Louis actually crossed over to the other side of the road. Do you know why? I am certain I do."

She continued to search, even looking beneath the massive desk that decorated the center of the room. Finally she gave up and sat on the corner of the desk, her face crestfallen.

Maribel stepped into the room and waited for Gabrielle to notice her. Such was the younger woman's upset, that she had managed to make a fine mess of an office that once appeared to be quite nice.

"Oh," the Valmont girl finally said as she kicked a pillow out of her way. "It's you. I didn't know we had a lesson today."

"We don't," Maribel said as she looked around at the destruction. "I'm looking for your brother. I assume you haven't seen him."

"Obviously no. If I had, I would have punched him by now." She reached over and another stack of papers went flying off the corner of the desk. "I wouldn't have, actually, but I do want to. He's such a pest and a bother. He's run off another fellow who might have been the one."

"Why would he do that?" she asked as Gabrielle pushed away a stack of papers to make room for her on the desk.

"Jean-Luc will tell you it is because he loves me, but secretly I think he just doesn't want me to be happy." She shrugged. "Oh, who am I kidding? He wants me happy but thinks he knows exactly what that takes." She slid Maribel a sideways look. "Why are you trying to find him?"

"I am keeping an appointment my mother made." She avoided Gabrielle's intent gaze. "Mama was unable to attend the meeting, so I am here on her behalf. Something in regard to a business matter between the Valmonts and the Cordobas."

"That sounds quite official. You are young to be handling family business, aren't you?"

"Not so young as you," Maribel said. "But it isn't what I wish I was doing."

"What do you wish you were doing?"

She offered a half smile. "The truth? I would like very much to find a place to read a book undisturbed and without worrying what a proper lady would do or about whether a dressmaker needs to be paid or whether a reputation is about to be lost. That is what I most wish for today. What about you, Gabrielle? What do you wish you were doing?"

"Please call me Gaby. And what I wish I was doing is. . ." She seemed to be considering a response. Finally she shook her head. "Truly I do not know. I have been told what to do for so long that I have forgotten what it is like to do whatever I wish."

"Oh, Gaby," Maribel said. "I can tell you what that is like. It is the most glorious feeling. I have climbed trees, read books under the stars with just an oil lamp for light, and even managed a swim once or twice in this little inlet where no one else goes."

"It sounds heavenly." She linked arms with Maribel and then leaned back on the desk so that they both were staring at the cherubs painted on the ceiling above. "Tell me more."

"What in the world has happened to my office?"

Gaby looked over at Maribel, a smile on her face. "Jean-Luc," she said with no small measure of glee. "Your appointment is here."

CHAPTER 21

This time Gaby had gone too far.

My appointment, indeed. Jean-Luc stood in the doorway of his office and surveyed the damage. She and her friend were currently lying on their backs on his desk, apparently enjoying themselves by giggling rather than feeling remorse at the mess they made.

Important documents, many of which carried the seal of the crown on them, were scattered like confetti across the floor. He picked up several and then his temper got the better of him.

"Even for you, Gabrielle, this is juvenile. The man was beneath you and not worth the trouble you've gotten yourself into."

She raised up on her elbows and regarded him imperiously. "Truly you are no fun at all."

"Truly you have no concept of the trouble you have caused. Someone will be here for days making order out of this mess, and it will not be me." His attention went to his sister's friend. "Who is she?"

The girl sat bolt upright and regarded him with wide green eyes as a lock of red hair escaped her braid.

"She is your appointment, Jean-Luc." Gaby lowered herself off the desk and then straightened her sleeves. "Truly develop a sense of humor. It will aid you in your old age."

"Go home, Gaby," he said through clenched jaw as he turned to his sister's friend. "I advise you to go too."

"No," she said. "I have business with you."

Something in her haughty demeanor caught his attention. That upturned nose, the way she looked at him as if she and not he was in charge. She shifted positions and another stack of papers fell.

"Truly, just go," he said. "If you do have an appointment, it will have to be rescheduled."

"No," she said as her feet landed on the floor and she straightened. "It cannot be rescheduled. I do see your point about the office, and I am sorry your sister decided to take her anger out on your papers." She looked up at him, her expression somewhere between fearless and fierce. "But my issue cannot be put off."

"I see," he said as something deep inside him began to sound a warning.

He knew her.

Knew of her.

Had been bested, perhaps, in an argument with her.

Something was familiar. Something was. . .

Jean-Luc shook his head. The memory was there just beyond his reach. But what was it?

"Mr. Valmont?" She indicated that he should take a seat behind his desk, and he did.

"Thank you," she said. "Now, it has come to my attention that a sum of money has been put on account for the benefit of my family. I do believe it was in the form of coins and jewels, although my mother is quite distraught and cannot be counted upon for any sort of reliable facts in her current state."

She gave him an expectant look. Somewhere in all the words she just said were facts he should have understood. Or perhaps not. Either way, all he could manage as she began talking again was to look at her and try to think of where he might have seen her before.

Indeed, she resembled his late wife, although only slightly. Kitty had never been this animated or this passionate about a topic. If only he knew what in the world she was talking about.

"Miss," he finally said, holding his hand up to slow her incessant conversation to a halt. "I am having trouble following you. Thus far I have determined that your mother claims something that requires my assistance in regard to a sum of money, that you may or may not have participated in the destruction of my office, and that I have no idea who you are."

She regarded him with a patient look. She even appeared to roll her eyes, although he could not reconcile that sort of behavior with the perfectly proper woman seated on the opposite side of the desk.

"All right, then," she said. "I will clarify."

"Thank you." He sat back and reached for a pen and paper. Thankfully, they had been hidden in his desk drawer and were still within reach. "All right, please do clarify," he said as he prepared to listen to another lengthy diatribe, and this time he would take notes.

She smiled. Then she gave him a curt nod.

"Yes, no, and Maribel Cordoba."

The breath went out of him. Spots appeared before his eyes. The pen fell from his hand and landed somewhere. The blank page in front of him remained pristine. No notes were needed.

"Repeat, please," he managed.

"Yes, no, and Maribel Cordoba," she said, and this time he saw it.

Saw the tilt to her nose and the gleam in her eye when she gave him an answer that she found to be quite clever. Saw the red color of her curls and the emerald color of her eyes.

"Maribel Cordoba."

He hadn't said those words in years. Eleven years. Saying them now felt wrong, as did seeing a grown woman in the place where a child had been.

"Yes," she said. "And to be precise, I also am here in regard to my mother's claim, and I did not participate in what has happened to your office. However, a word of warning. Your sister does have quite a temper, so you might think twice before you interfere with her romance. Was the fellow really not the right sort for her?"

"He seduced her into meeting in an open field near the river rather than courting her properly at her home, and when cornered he offered her up as someone who would pay his ransom. So I would say yes, he is not the right sort. But truly, you are Maribel Cordoba. The Maribel Cordoba from Spain?"

She gave him a sideways look. "Yes, but then you know that because my mother brought you money some two weeks ago, and she definitely would have mentioned that this was regarding an issue between the French and a citizen of Spain. Are you trying to hedge on this? Because I have brought a receipt."

She handed him the paper, and he read it then pushed it back across the table toward her. "Look at the signature. That was signed by my brother Quinton. I was away two weeks ago." He shook his head. "You are here, aren't you? I never thought I would see you again, but here you are."

Color rose in Maribel's cheeks. She was lovely when she was angry, much more so than when she was a girl aboard his ship. How old must she be now? Two and twenty perhaps, possibly older.

"If this was not an urgent matter, I would leave and return with my grandfather. However, he is ill and cannot come himself. As I said, my mother is distraught and cannot be relied upon for her facts or, quite frankly, for her behavior. Thus, I am the only remaining member of the family with whom you can discuss this matter." She viewed him primly. "You have seen the receipt. I wish a refund at once."

"You don't know who I am, do you?"

Her gaze swept the length of him and then returned to his face. "I know you are a Valmont and you are apparently not Quinton. Your sister calls you Jean-Luc, so I will answer by saying I believe you are Jean-Luc Valmont."

"Yes, I am," he said slowly as he decided how to proceed.

It was apparent Maribel did not recognize him. He knew all the arguments against revealing his identity, and he could not disagree.

Gradually he became aware that she was speaking again. "So," he heard her say as his focus returned to the woman seated before him, "I will expect to have the items listed on that receipt returned to me immediately."

"I, well. . ." He shook his head in hopes that he could dislodge something appropriate to say. "Since my brother signed the receipt, he is the one who would have to verify what has been left with us, and he would be the one who would return it. Unfortunately, he is in Paris and not expected back until the end of the month."

Yes. That ought to buy some time.

"That is unacceptable," she said as she rose. "Your father is the man in charge of this endeavor. It says so on the sign beside the door. Marcel Valmont & Sons is what I read. So, since the son who took my grandfather's money is unavailable, Marcel Valmont himself should easily be able to stand in his stead and handle the transaction."

Jean-Luc stood and stuffed his shaking hands in the pockets of his coat. "Under normal circumstances I would agree. However, since I know nothing about this case, I will have to investigate further and—"

"Sir, excuse me." Mr. Landry stood at the door. "Your next appointment has arrived. I put him in Mr. Quinton's office. Shall I tell him you'll be right in?"

Jean-Luc managed a nod before he turned his attention back to Maribel Cordoba. "I'm sorry. My next appointment is here."

An appointment that certainly hadn't been on his calendar this morning. But then, neither had meeting Maribel Cordoba again.

She gave him another of those looks he remembered from their time at sea. "I am leaving reluctantly, and only because you have made a decent case for rescheduling this appointment. I can see that you will need time to look over the transaction documents."

"Thank you," he said, hoping his relief did not sound so obvious in his voice.

"I will see you tomorrow, then. Same time." She cast a glance around the room and then turned her attention back to him. "Although I would suggest we meet in your brother's office. You seem extremely distracted, and I wonder if it is because of this mess. Do consider it, won't you?"

Jean-Luc left the question unanswered, holding his breath until the redhead was safely outside the building. He was still staring at the closed door when Landry stuck his head into the office.

"Your next appointment, sir?"

"Oh," he said, "I thought you were just trying to help me get rid of Miss Cordoba." He straightened his jacket and walked over to Quinton's office, throwing the door open as he stepped inside.

"Good morning, Mr. Valmont."

❧

Maribel was nearly home when a carriage caught up with her. Gaby Valmont climbed out and hurried to fall into step beside her.

"I am so sorry for all the trouble I am sure I have caused you." She stepped in front of Maribel. "Please let me make it up to you."

"Don't be silly," Maribel said as she stopped to keep from running into her. "What makes you think you've caused me any trouble?"

She shrugged. "Maybe because I listened to the conversation and I know you didn't get what you came for."

"Oh. That." She stepped around the Valmont girl and kept walking. "It was a simple matter of scheduling a meeting with the wrong Valmont. I'm sure he will read the documents and have my money for me tomorrow."

"Yes, I hope so." They walked in silence until Maribel reached her doorstep. "Would you like to come in?"

"Thank you," she said, "but I don't think your family would like to have a Valmont pay a visit right now."

"Your mother and mine are close friends," Maribel protested. "I see no trouble in it."

"Perhaps, but I will decline all the same." She paused. "I'm sorry your grandfather is ill. Has he been seen by a physician?"

"My mother is attending him," she said. "But perhaps a physician would be a good idea." She shook her head. "No, forget I said that. Until your brother refunds my mother's payment, we have nothing with which to pay a physician."

Gaby grinned. "What if I were to tell you that I know a physician who would come and see your grandfather at no cost? He's a very nice man and often practices at the charity hospital so that he can be of help to those who cannot pay."

"Who is he?"

"Well," Gaby said, "he is sort of my brother, only not. We grew up as siblings from when I was very young. My parents adopted him." She paused. "Sort of, but not."

Maribel gave the matter a moment's consideration. "Yes, then, please do send for him."

She smiled. "I can do better than that. I was on my way to fetch him home for lunch. Come with me. As long as you've got something to feed him, I'm certain he will allow the detour to examine your grandfather."

"I would be forever in his debt. And yours." Maribel paused. "However, I have been away all morning and I'm sure my mother will be concerned by now as to what is taking me so long to return."

Gaby smiled. "Of course. You go and see to your family, and I will bring him to you."

"Thank you." She lingered a moment and then gave her new friend a direct look. "Your brother," she said, "can I expect him to be fair with me?"

She laughed. "Oh, Maribel, he is so fair it is ridiculous. In fact, my brother believes there isn't a rule in existence that is worthy of being broken. If your business affairs require Jean-Luc to administer them fairly, then you have nothing to concern yourself with. Truly, I have never met a more exasperating and boring man."

"Thank you," she said as she made her good-byes and watched the Valmont carriage drive away.

Exasperating and boring.

Maribel let out a long breath. Funny, because in her imagination Jean-Luc Valmont was a pirate standing at the wheel of a gaff-rigged schooner, his hair tossed like the sea-green waves beneath the vessel and his giant of an African friend by his side.

He was a man who slid beneath the rules in a vessel that could escape even the fastest enemy. And he was absolutely anything other than boring.

Exasperating? That she could agree on, however.

Certainly Gaby's version would be much easier to deal with. Why, then, could she not get her version—the imagined man that came from the same creative mind that Mother Superior warned against—out of her head?

"Is that you?" Mama called when Maribel closed the door behind her.

"It is," she said, following her mother's voice to find her in Abuelo's library. The room looked to be in much the same condition as the office she had just left.

"What happened in here?" She reached down to gather up a pile of papers that had been carelessly strewn across the carpet. "Have we been robbed?"

"We have," she said, "but not by thieves outside the family."

Maribel set the documents on the desk and bent down to reach for more. "These are Abuelo's, Mama. You shouldn't be looking through them, and you certainly should not be tossing them about as if they have no meaning."

"Well, they don't have much meaning," she said, clutching a paper with a seal that looked important. "Not to me, anyway. I despair of this, but I cannot make sense of why our family has all of this and yet we are destitute."

"Destitute?" Maribel released the pages she held and watched them flutter to the ground then sat down behind the desk. "That is impossible, Mama. I will get the valuables you've put on deposit with the Valmonts for you. Then we will be fine."

Mama sank onto a chair without bothering to clear off the papers that it held. "So you succeeded, then? What a relief." Her smile rose quickly and then became laughter. "What a mess I have made and all for nothing. Here, help me pick all of this up before your grandfather surprises us by recuperating enough to walk down here and see this."

Maribel opened her mouth to correct her mother. To tell her that while she had not yet had assurances from the Valmonts that the valuables would be returned, she certainly would get those assurances tomorrow.

Perhaps not certainly, but likely.

Instead, she closed her mouth, rested her palms on the desk, and watched her mother transform from frantic and distraught to practically dancing around the library as she set the room to rights again.

And she said nothing. She could not. Tomorrow she would keep that appointment with Jean-Luc Valmont. She would get all the things back that had been taken from the family, and then the Cordobas would no longer be destitute.

What she could not do was explain why Mama thought that the threat to their financial security came from within the family. Surely Abuelo had nothing but their best interests in mind.

It made no sense.

Neither did the ledger beneath her hand. Ignoring Mama altogether now, she allowed her gaze to slide down the list of entries, some with dates going back more than ten years.

Each entry was written in her grandfather's familiar handwriting. The same handwriting that had been on the letter that brought her home to New Orleans. It was the name in the other column that stopped her cold.

"Is Abuelo awake?"

She shook her head. "He has not awakened since he fell. Is

there something there that needs his attention?"

"Nothing that cannot wait until he is able to provide answers," she said as she gathered up the ledger and stuffed it into Grandfather's leather valise. "I must go out. Gabrielle Valmont is bringing a physician to look in on Abuelo. Would you make my apologies for not being here?" She took three steps toward the door and then turned around. "And the doctor will expect lunch. I promised Gaby," she said. "Is that a problem?"

"Of course not," Mama said, her smile still in place. "I will see to everything. You just go on and handle whatever it is. Nothing urgent, I hope."

"As do I," Maribel said just after the door closed behind her.

CHAPTER 22

Antonio Cordoba sat behind the desk and looked up at Jean-Luc as if he owned the place. "Sit down, won't you? I believe you and I have some business to discuss."

Age had not been kind to the Spaniard, but he would have known the man anywhere. "So you lived after all," he said through clenched jaw. "I suppose it's true that you cannot drown the devil."

The Spaniard laughed. "Well, not this one," he said as he picked up Quinton's jeweled letter opener, fashioned in the style of a small cutlass, and studied it. "Truly though, sit. Your refusal to accept my hospitality is most annoying."

"Why are you here?"

"I am a man of business now, as are you." He shrugged. "I find we have business in common. Namely, my father's estate."

"Your father is very much alive," he said evenly as his mind struggled to reconcile what he now knew of this man with the death he thought he caused. "If I have business with any Cordoba, it is he and not you."

"Oh, but it is me," he said, pointing at Jean-Luc with the letter opener. "My father is an old man. He believed he was protecting my wife and child from me, so he made certain decisions on my behalf. Unfortunately, he has met with reduced circumstances of late. Most unfortunate."

Protecting his wife and child.

Maribel.

Jean-Luc let out a long breath as he tamed the temper that was rising. Anger would never work against a man who thrived on that very emotion. Rather, he must be smart. Calm. The better man.

Help me, Lord.

"What do you want from me, Cordoba?" he managed.

"Much less than you want from me." He dropped the letter opener and threaded his fingers together, resting them on the desktop. "I merely want what is in your vault. Had my wife not been so stupid as to bring the coins and jewels to you instead of keeping them at home as I instructed, none of this would have been necessary."

"You are assuming I have possession of these things."

"I know you do." He shrugged. "I have seen the receipt."

The same receipt Maribel had in her hands this morning. "Who else knows you are alive?"

He laughed. "Are you worried about my daughter? Trust me, Valmont, she is oblivious to my existence. My father insisted that be part of the terms of our agreement. So far I have seen no reason to break that agreement. And my wife? She has known all along, but Mary always did know how to look after herself. The old man had the money, so she joined him here in New Orleans and played the part of the grieving widow and hostess to the old man. Perhaps you've met her. She's quite stunning."

Had he met anyone named Cordoba, Jean-Luc would have remembered. As he avoided any social circle to which his parents might belong—by his own preference and against theirs—it was possible he had not seen her, although he might have, owing to the size of this city. Impossible, though, that they would have been introduced and he not recall.

"Make your point or leave," he told the Spaniard.

"My point is you have items in your possession that were not meant to be here. They are mine, and my wife had no ownership in them or any right to distribute them elsewhere. You and I are both men of business. I say we complete this transaction and then go our separate ways."

"You're right, Cordoba," he said. "We are men of business, but I conduct my business in a very different way than you do. I will look into your claim and speak with my father to make a decision on the ownership of anything that might be in our vaults."

"I see." He rose. "You know, the last time I saw you I tried to put a bullet through your heart."

"I remember it well."

Cordoba smiled. "I did not miss."

"No," Jean-Luc said slowly, "you did not. Nor were you successful."

"I am older now, and wiser," he said as he came around the desk to stand in front of Jean-Luc. "And I have eluded you and everyone else for eleven years," he said as he walked to the door.

"Only because I was not looking for you," Jean-Luc said to his retreating back.

Maribel set off walking with no idea exactly where she was going. Returning to the Valmont offices was one option, but so was going off by herself to look over what she had found and make a plan. She certainly hadn't been able to think with Mama around, and it was unlikely she would fare better in Gaby's brother's presence.

So she set off toward the river and the stand of live oaks that had intrigued her since she arrived in the city. Thus far she had been practicing the art of being a proper lady and had not fallen back into her old ways.

Today, however, she would make an exception. For where better to be alone and read something as important as this ledger?

After looking around to be certain she had not been followed, Maribel tucked the strap of the valise over her shoulder and hiked up her skirt just enough to allow her to climb into a welcoming spot out of sight of anyone who might be passing by.

How long she remained in the tree, Maribel could not say.

However, when the light began to fail her and her stomach pleaded for her to eat something, she folded the ledger back into the valise and rested her head against the oak tree's gnarled trunk.

She had long ago given up wearing Mama's scarf at her waist. In fact, Mama had taken it from her and declared it unfit for a proper lady to wear. But as she sat here quietly mulling over what she had read, Maribel wished for the gentle comfort of the scarf that tied her to a home she thought she knew.

Though she preferred to remain exactly where she was rather than return to what she'd left in her grandfather's home, Maribel nonetheless stretched her legs and then reached for the branch that would aid her in climbing down.

A loud crack split the air and the world tilted. The valise slid from her shoulder and landed with a thud on the ground.

She, however, did not.

Rather, she landed in the arms of a man with silver eyes and a broad smile. "Reading in the dark will damage your eyes, you know."

The same thing the captain said almost every night when he came to check on her. "Yes, sir," she responded out of habit.

The captain. Maribel's heart soared. The captain!

"Captain," she finally managed to say aloud. "When I saw you in the office this morning, I knew it was you," she said. "Well, not exactly *you*, but someone *like* you. You see, Mother Superior told me that what I thought were memories was just my imagination, but I never was certain if she was correct. I mean, she is a nun and I am sure she would never tell me anything but the truth, but it always seemed as though I was reliving something that had happened and not making something up. Anyway, I knew you would turn out to be a nice man. I prayed for that, you know, and I have been for all these years, and now—"

"Maribel. Stop. Talking."

She clamped her lips shut against the torrent of words still demanding escape. Still, she could not look away from those eyes. From that smile.

"I just should have known it was you," she said. "I sat in that office and made all sorts of demands on behalf of my family and all the time I was in front of the one person I had always wished I would find again. I never really stopped hoping you were alive, you know."

"I looked for you," he told her. "Looked everywhere. We sent out boats and search parties and scoured every inch of any place we thought you might be. When you walked into my office, I couldn't believe it was you. I thought you had died out there on that ocean. The cannonball took out the entire lookout post and part of the mainmast. How could you have survived?"

"Captain. Stop. Talking," she said as she nestled her head against his chest and felt, for the first time since she left the island, as if she was once again in a familiar place.

"You can't call me Captain here in New Orleans," he finally said as he set her on her feet.

She looked up at him. Really looked this time instead of ignoring the fine details of the once-familiar face that had aged very little. "Why not?"

"It would compromise certain things and complicate others," he said, apparently reluctant to go into any further detail.

"Are you still a privateer?"

The captain ducked his head and then lifted it again. "When the French set a bounty on my head and then nearly killed me, I decided it was time to leave that part of my life behind, so no, I am not."

Her face must have registered surprise, because he shook his head. "No, I don't suppose you would have known any of that."

"You were working for the French," she said. "Why would they want you dead?"

"It all comes down to politics, I suppose. Or maybe it was just God's way of letting me know that it was time to stop and follow Him instead of trying to do things my way," he said as he reached down to retrieve the valise. "This is heavy."

She nodded, but when her gaze collided with his, she found words nearly impossible. "Important papers."

"That's what you were reading in the tree? So have you given up your adventure books?"

"Of course not." Maribel shook her head, as much in response to his question as to dislodge the fog that was surrounding her now.

The captain lived, and he was standing right here in front of her. All those prayers, all those times she wondered if he lived, wondered if it had all been something her imagination conjured up, and now here he stood.

"Is there something wrong?" he asked.

"No," Maribel said, tears now shimmering as the realization hit her with full force. "It's just that. . ." Again she shook her head. "You're real and you're alive and you're not just someone I imagined."

His chuckle was exactly as she recalled. "Yes, I am very real."

She fell into his arms again, and this time she held on tight, until he stepped back to drop the valise. "I don't want to let you go," she said, reaching for him again. "I am just so very happy you're alive."

After a while, the captain held her at arm's length. "You're not a little girl anymore, Red."

"It has been eleven years since we parted, so I would hope not," she said. "You, however, look exactly the same."

"And that, Miss Cordoba, is your imagination speaking. I am eleven years older and many decades wiser." Jean-Luc retrieved the valise. "Walk with me. I would prefer to escort you somewhere that is more secure so we can speak without being seen. I have a few things to tell you that I prefer not be overheard."

She shook her head. "There is nowhere more secure than up in that tree."

"You're joking."

"I am serious." She nodded toward the valise. "Would you like me to take it up with me, or do you think you can manage it? What with your advanced age and all."

"Pick the limb," he said as he threw the valise over his shoulder.

CHAPTER 23

W hen Jean-Luc managed to settle himself on the limb beside Maribel without doing anything more than minor damage to himself, he made a solemn vow. He would never climb a tree again.

Yet here he sat quite a distance from the ground with a leather valise in his lap and a beautiful redhead beside him. So, overall, he could not complain.

Much.

Though he would likely pay for his exertion with sore muscles later.

"All right," she said. "Which of us is to go first?"

"You," he said, not because he had any particular interest in hearing all the details of the past eleven years but because he did enjoy looking at her when she talked.

The girl had become a woman in their time apart. And though she still rattled on incessantly at times, he found he rather enjoyed listening to her now.

"And so when I arrived at the orphanage on Isla de Santa Maria, Mother Superior despaired of convincing me that the things I recalled were not real. She said they were just products of my imagination and that a girl like me couldn't have possibly been on a privateer's ship or watched for approaching vessels in the top of the mast or even—"

"Wait," he said as he shifted the valise off his lap and hung the strap over a sturdy limb. "Are you telling me you were at St. Mary of the Island Orphanage this whole time?"

"Until recently, yes," she said. "Why?"

All the warnings he'd been given by Israel, Rao, and the others rose up in his mind. Every time he brought a ship into the inlet he had risked Maribel Cordoba recognizing him. And to recognize him was to jeopardize everything.

Jean-Luc shook his head. "No reason. I'm just surprised."

"Yes, well, apparently my grandfather was not surprised at all." She nodded toward the valise. "I found his ledger. He has been paying my maintenance since the second year I was at the orphanage."

"Who paid the first year?"

She gave him a strange look. "I never thought of that. I don't know. But still, don't you find it strange that my grandfather would know where I was, pay for my upkeep, but only send for me recently? When I arrived, he behaved as if I were his long-lost granddaughter returned. Yet he knew where I was all along."

"Not so strange when all the facts are known," he said. "I wonder if your grandfather might have been protecting you from something. Or someone."

"You mean my father?"

Maribel asked the question in such a matter-of-fact manner that it took him aback. "Yes," he said. "I assume there are payments in the ledger to him as well."

"You assume correctly." She looked away. "Apparently my father is very much alive and has been draining my grandfather dry." Her gaze returned to him. "It is not what I had hoped when my mother told me Abuelo was destitute."

"What did you hope?" he said gently.

"Oh I don't know. That he had spent all his fortune searching for me, maybe, although that would bring its own guilt too. Or perhaps he was just a man who did not have as much as I remembered, and he had outlived his funds." She shrugged. "Anything but what I saw there."

Jean-Luc let out a long breath and then chose his words carefully. "Never judge a person's heart by what you see on a balance ledger. And never assume you know the motivation behind someone's actions by that measure either."

She nodded. "I understand. But the truth is there."

"The truth is, you cannot go back to your grandfather's home. It is too dangerous."

"I must warn my mother," she protested.

"She knows, Maribel. She has known from the beginning."

The breath seemed to go out of her. Finally she shook her head. "Yes, I believe you. Mama is capable of many things, but being unaware of what is going on around her is not one of them. She has always been a strong and intelligent woman. I assume my father has either charmed her or frightened her."

"Have you sensed that your mother is frightened lately?"

"Only of not being able to retrieve the valuables placed in your care."

Jean-Luc gave the statement a moment's thought. "But she does not fear for her safety?"

"Her comfort, yes," Maribel said, "but her safety? I would say no."

"That answers your question in regard to how your mother feels about your father. You will not go back to that house," he said. "I won't allow it."

She shook her head. "I have nowhere else to go."

He reached to take her hand in his. "Not as long as I am here to protect you. It is my job as your captain."

"I do remember you saying that a time or two, oh, about eleven years ago." She smiled even as tears shimmered in her eyes. "I am never supposed to call you that, remember?"

"That doesn't mean it isn't true," he said. "As long as I draw a breath, you will be under my protection. For eleven years I have believed I failed you when I lost you to French cannon fire. I will not fail you again."

Maribel smiled and then she leaned toward him. "While I am

perfectly capable of taking care of myself, I do very much thank you," she said as she briefly touched her lips to his cheek.

The action, obviously spontaneous, seemed to surprise her. Then a beautiful pink color rose in her checks.

"I'm sorry. That was terribly presumptuous of me."

"No, Maribel," he said as he gathered her closer. "It was wonderfully presumptuous. I wonder if you would mind doing it again."

She leaned in, and Jean-Luc was ready. As soon as she got close enough, that kiss on the cheek would be a kiss on the lips.

"Wait a minute." Maribel leaned back, her eyes wide. "If my grandfather knew where I was, then who in the world is Mr. Lopez-Gonzales, and why did he pretend to be the person who found me and brought me home to my family?"

"I don't know," he said as he struggled to change his focus. "Who did he say he was?"

"When he came to the island, he told Mother Superior that he had been employed at great expense by my grandfather to find me. He said he was the one who encouraged my family to move to New Orleans so they would be closer to the place where I had last been seen."

She shook her head and gave Jean-Luc a look that said she was still mulling over the facts in her mind. Silence fell between them as he allowed her to continue thinking this through.

"Only here is what I do not understand. How could anyone know where I was last seen other than my father? Was there ever a location given for where the *Venganza* went down?"

"I am sure dispatches were sent from Cuba once the news arrived that the ship was lost," he said.

"Yes, likely," she said, warming to her topic. "But the ship was headed from Spain to Havana. Why relocate to New Orleans, which is a French territory, not a Spanish one, when there are a number of other cities in the Caribbean that would have been much closer and friendlier to a Spaniard?"

"Perhaps the answer to that question will provide the clue as to who this man Lopez-Gonzales is," he offered.

"And for that matter," she continued, "why not Havana itself? Abuelo obviously had friends there if he was able to secure a position for my father in the city."

"Perhaps he had friends here too."

A thought occurred, but he would not be sharing it with Maribel. There was a connection to this city that might explain it all, especially in light of Father's complaints of pirates operating in the region.

"You need to be taken to safety," he told her. "Once I know you cannot be harmed, then I will solve this mystery."

"*We* will solve this mystery," she told him. "You have a poor memory if you think I am going to run and hide when I am confronted by something unpleasant. I did not do that when I was twelve, and I will not do that now."

Jean-Luc ignored her attempt at argument in regard to who would do the solving. "Never did I use the word *run*. I am simply stating that we need a place of safety for you so that a plan of action can be developed."

"I am a grown woman, and as such, I will take complete responsibility for figuring out just what has happened and remedying it."

He chuckled. "And yet we are having this conversation while sitting in a tree."

She offered him the beginnings of a smile. "You do have a point."

"I do," he said, "and so does this branch where I have been sitting. If I am still able, I would very much like to climb down to solid ground. You and I have work to do, and we cannot do it up here."

"What kind of work? It is obvious what these entries are."

"Is it?" He shrugged. "Often there are patterns in these things. Entries that repeat and others that are possibly encrypted so that their true purpose or recipient is not evident. I would like to take a look at the ledger to see if any of those things might be true."

"Yes," she said. "There were a few things that made no sense. I think that's a brilliant idea."

Much more brilliant than allowing himself to be convinced to climb a tree. Although if he examined his actions closely, Jean-Luc had to admit that it had not taken much in the way of convincing to get him to follow the redhead up into the branches of the old live oak.

Somehow he managed not to make a fool of himself as he climbed down. His only explanation for this miracle was that the Lord had taken pity on him, because his knees were aching and his legs had very little feeling at all.

He was, indeed, an old man.

Twelve years older than the beauty who easily slid down the tree trunk to land nimbly on her feet. Apparently his thirty-five years to her twenty-three made a huge difference in how well a person might scale a tree.

However, with no plans to repeat that performance, he felt decently secure in offering her his arm and taking the heavy valise with the other. "Surely all of this weight cannot be the valise and ledger."

She shrugged. "I put nothing else in."

He adjusted the leather strap and continued on, glad to finally set the thing down on his father's desk. Abigail and Gaby were thankfully absent as he shooed away the servants and closed the library door.

If Father was around, he would soon find them. If not, they would manage nicely without him.

Setting the valise aside, they opened the ledger on the desk between them and began looking over the entries. At some point, a servant came in and lit the lamps. Awhile later, Cook brought a tray of food. By the time the noise of female voices sounded outside, they had made substantial progress.

"What will I tell them?" Maribel said as the front door opened and the voices of Gaby and Abigail drifted through the closed library door. "If we are to decipher all of this, I need a reason to spend time here."

"I, um. . ." His usual wit failed him, as apparently did his brain.

The door flew open with Gaby leading the way. An instant later, Maribel leaned over the desk and kissed him soundly.

On the lips.

"Oh," Gaby said. Out of the corner of his eye, Jean-Luc saw his sister stop so quickly that Abigail ran into her.

"Oh," Abigail added as she adjusted her hat to peer around Gaby.

"Oh," Maribel said sweetly as she removed her lips from his and smiled at his family. "We didn't expect you home so soon."

"Apparently not," Abigail said, her attention squarely focused on him and not on Maribel. "Might I have a word, Jean-Luc?" She gave Maribel a look that might have been interpreted as sweet and welcoming by anyone who did not know her. "Please excuse us for just a minute, won't you?"

He spied Maribel's expression and couldn't believe what he saw. The redhead actually looked amused. Did she not realize she had practically ruined her reputation in this city if either of these two chatty women decided to speak of their little adventure in falsifying a romance?

Apparently not, for she was still smiling when Abigail led him from the room.

Though he expected she would give him a brief lecture in the parlor, Abigail bypassed the welcoming front room to grasp his elbow and haul him back through the house and out into the courtyard.

Sticky evening heat remaining from the afternoon enveloped them as they stepped out into the evening shadows. There she finally released her grip, but she was only just getting started on showing how she felt about what she had seen. "Your sister's friend? Truly, Jean-Luc, could you have found anyone more unsuitable?"

"Yes," he said. "I could have. I fail to see what the problem is with Maribel."

"The problem is twofold. First, you hardly know her. And second, she is Spanish."

"Abigail," he said, his eyes narrowing. "I will concede the first point, although I do have evidence to the contrary. However, I never figured you for an elitist who would care about a person's country of birth."

"Do not be so judgmental, Jean-Luc. I don't give even a passing interest in where she was born. I don't even care where she lives or of what social class she is. Why, did I say a word when you married Kitty? And she was a poor nurse whose family depended on her to provide for them."

She hadn't mentioned his late wife since the funeral, so to hear the name from her lips surprised him. "I do remember you warned me not to toy with her affections. But, no, I do not recall any objections of that sort."

"That is because Kitty suited you, and you needed each other. She had cared for you, and truly, Jean-Luc, she had fallen in love with you before you were ever aware she existed. That you cared for her in return was something I would never have offered comment on."

"Then what is wrong with Maribel?"

The question was ludicrous because the answer truly did not matter. Still, he felt a responsibility to defend the woman Abigail apparently thought he loved. Or, more likely, thought he was toying with.

"Maribel is a lovely girl. Perfectly lovely," Abigail said as she reached for her fan to chase away the heat. "In fact, were she not Spanish, I would highly recommend her." She paused. "For Michel."

"For Michel?" Outrage rose. "You would recommend her for my brother and not me?"

"Yes," she said. "You are far too old for a vivacious young woman like her. What in the world would the two of you ever have in common? It is ridiculous."

"Not so ridiculous as you think, Abigail," he said, even though he knew the comment strayed into dangerous waters where he ought not go.

"Well, you have offered no reason that I should think otherwise, so I have given you my opinion of the matter."

"Thank you, Abigail, for your opinion," he snapped. "I will concede your point on age only because it is based on observation alone. However, I still fail to see what her Spanish heritage has to do with making a good match for me."

"Oh, darling, are you so blind?" She gave him an appraising look. "Yes, you are. You've had that look ever since I walked into the room. You are so in love with that girl that you absolutely cannot see that it is not her who is unsuitable but rather you."

In love? Hardly, although her kiss did take him off guard and he had found it difficult to breathe when she reached for him. Then there was the strong desire to march right back into the library and repeat the entire event, this time with anyone who cared to watch in attendance.

But love? Hardly.

"Jean-Luc?" Abigail said. "Have I said something that made sense?"

"The opposite, actually. Now I truly do not follow."

Abigail sighed. "Oh, darling," she told him as she touched his sleeve. "I so want to be wrong about this, but should her grandfather and my friend Mary learn that you are pursuing Maribel, I fear there will be much opposition to the match."

He shook his head. "Correct me if I am wrong, but her mother is not a Spaniard. I do not detect any evidence of it."

"True. My understanding is she fled home to marry Antonio. He's deceased, you know. I believe she is originally from somewhere in the colonies. Virginia, perhaps?" She shook her head. "But her grandfather? Don Pablo Cordoba will never agree to a marriage between the two of you."

Marriage. He tried to keep his expression neutral. "And why do you assume that is where my relationship with Maribel is leading?"

"Because if you have moved from calling her Miss Cordoba to Maribel and you feel it appropriate to bring her into our home and kiss her in front of me and your sister—"

"Excuse me, Abigail, but we were not kissing in front of you. You and Gaby walked in on a private conversation."

"Excuse me, Jean-Luc," she said as she returned his neutral look. "But there was absolutely *no* conversation going on when we walked in. Did I miss something?" she added sweetly.

"Nothing that we intended for you to hear," was his impertinent answer. "Truly, Abigail, you worry for nothing."

"I worry because except for the fact I did not actually give you life, I am your mother in all ways and in my heart. So you, my beloved son, worry me terribly."

He leaned over to kiss her forehead. "Stop worrying. I am fine."

"The last time I heard that, a French lieutenant brought you home in bandages and on death's door. You were up to something before you left on that voyage, and you're up to something now. And you know what?"

"What?" he said, half amused and half touched at her fervor.

"I think both times it involved Maribel Cordoba."

"Stop worrying," he told her. "I am fine. Now I'm going to go back into the library to see if Gaby has had any more luck getting information from Maribel than you have had getting it from me."

Abigail hurried to catch up to him. "If she has, she better be prepared to tell me."

Jean-Luc laughed as the coolness of the house enveloped him once more. "If she has, she will be prepared to tell everyone."

CHAPTER 24

Jean-Luc returned to the library to find Maribel alone. "Where is your inquisitor?" he said with a grin.

"Likely off to spread the word of our engagement," she said as she returned her attention to the ledger in front of her.

"You're joking, right?"

She lifted her head to regard him with a look that told him she was not. "I doubt she will go far. She headed out the back door, not the front."

"That is because the back door is nearest the carriages. No doubt she's working her way down the street announcing our betrothal to everyone who is anyone in New Orleans."

"Why bother telling the rest?" she said with obvious sarcasm. Then her expression went serious. "Oh. I'm sorry. I've ruined a courtship you're having with someone, haven't I?" She sat back in her chair and shook her head. "I was raised by nuns. I have no idea how any of this works, but I am fairly certain I have caused you trouble. My thought was to break the engagement once a proper time had passed."

He had to laugh at her serious expression. "There is no court-ship other than the one Abigail believes we have been carrying on without her knowledge. And as to being unused to the way courtship works, I promise your lack of knowledge at the feminine airs that are put on during this ridiculous ritual is refreshing."

"I have been learning," she told him. "Your sister has been a great source of knowledge on how to be a proper lady. My mother and Abigail insisted she tutor me."

He groaned. "I do hope you haven't been paying attention."

"Well, I did try, but somewhere between which fork to use at the table and which way to hold a fan to signal an intention, I gave up." She paused. "She has no idea, though, so please do not tell her. Gaby does have such enthusiasm for the topic. I would hate for her to know that I do not."

"Your secret is safe with me." He glanced down at the ledger and back at Maribel. "But neither you nor that ledger are safe here. I have a place I can take you, but you will have to trust me."

"I trust you," she said. "But what about my mother and my grandfather? Won't they be worried if I do not come home? Or suspicious?"

"Let me take care of that." He looked up at the clock over the mantel as the front door opened. "And here is the man for the job."

Jean-Luc stepped out into the hall and motioned for him to come into the library. "Maribel," he told her. "I think you might find this fellow familiar."

She looked up from her study of the ledger to fix her eyes on the young man who had spent the last eleven years as a ward of the Valmonts. "William Spencer?" she said on a soft breath. "My Will Spencer!"

The physician's expression froze. "Red?" He looked over at Jean-Luc. "Is it really?"

"It is," she said before he could respond.

And then Maribel practically launched herself into the young doctor's arms.

Over her head, William gave Jean-Luc a stricken look.

Likely William Spencer could climb a tree, remain there all day, and still climb down without any aches or pains to show for his effort. And he could certainly pass Abigail's test of appropriate age.

"Maribel was raised by nuns," he said, irked that he felt even the slightest amount of jealousy rising up inside him. "She doesn't realize her enthusiasm at seeing you again is inappropriate."

"Then I hope she never figures that out," he said as he returned the embrace. "You look prettier than a picture," he told her when she finally let him go.

"There is nothing inappropriate in letting my friend know I am happy to see him again." She offered William a smile. "I thought you were dead."

"And I thought the same of you."

"And yet you both are obviously very much alive," he snapped before catching himself and changing his tone. "As much as I know you two have to discuss, it must wait. There's a situation brewing, and we need to take evasive action."

Will knew exactly what he meant, for he had used the words they all agreed upon. "Aye," he said. "But first I should bring news of her grandfather." He focused his attention back on Maribel. "He is of decent health as of today," he said. "I prescribed a change in his diet and indicated that he should be taken from his bed to be allowed to walk more. I find that does a body more good than lying there with the fireplace going."

"So he will be fine?"

"These determinations are never exact," he said. "But he is strong and appears he will recover."

"And my mother?"

He shook his head. "Was I supposed to evaluate her too?"

"No," she said, "but I wondered what your impression was of her current state?"

"Oh," he said, "well, she seemed happy that your father was home."

"He was there?" she asked Will.

"Not at the moment, but she did mention that fact at least twice during our conversation. I thought it odd she spoke of him so much." He paused. "Now that I've seen you, is it also true, then, that your father survived the *Venganza*?"

"He did," Maribel said. "Although I have only just learned this."

Jean-Luc looked to Maribel. "What do you think of your mother's mentions of your father to Will?"

"I believe I can answer," Will said. "Perhaps she then would expect me to convey the news to Abigail?"

"She might," he agreed. "Can you think of another reason?" he asked Maribel.

"No," she said. "In looking through this ledger, have you seen any expenses that my mother might have benefited from?"

"Not directly," he said. "Why?"

"It is as much a hope as a theory, but perhaps she and my grandfather are both afraid of what my father will do if they do not cooperate. If she and Abigail are so close, perhaps Mama wanted Abigail to know my father had finally come for her."

He thought a moment. "You may be right."

Jean-Luc addressed Will as he nodded toward Maribel. "I will see to her safety. You alert the others."

"So soon?" Abigail stepped into the room, her smile intact. "Yes, I know. You didn't think I realized what was going on here."

"If you'll excuse me," Will said. "I'm just going to go and wash up for dinner now."

"Stay." A command, not a suggestion. Of course Will obeyed. When Abigail used that tone, generally they did.

"Maribel," she said gently. "Please accept my apology for the way I am about to speak of your father. I understand we are all given our parents and have no choice in the matter, so do not think his behavior reflects on yours or your family."

"Thank you," she said.

She turned to Jean-Luc. "There is a man out there somewhere who has been terrorizing my friend for the better part of ten years. Don Pablo has paid to keep him away from Mary and has paid dearly to keep this girl hidden away and safe. The money has run out." She paused to look at Jean-Luc. "It ran out three years ago, actually."

"Three years ago?" Maribel shook her head and then closed her eyes. "Oh," she said when she opened them again. "You and Mr. Valmont. . ."

"Have been helping," she offered. "Yes, although that would just as well be our secret, thank you very much. Your grandfather is a proud old man and it would kill him if he knew, and I did tell your mother that information would not be disclosed publicly."

"How does he think money has gone into his coffers, then?" Jean-Luc asked.

"It is my understanding that he believes his son has finally come to his senses and contributed his share." She paused as if considering her words carefully. "The ruse worked until Antonio had the audacity to arrive on their doorstep. I cannot prove it, but I believe his presence in that home is what caused that old man's illness."

"It is possible a shock of some sort would contribute," Will said. "But impossible to say for certain."

"Jean-Luc," she said. "I engaged you in a spirited conversation regarding this young lady because I needed to see what your intentions were. And I had to know if she is safe with you." She paused. "Given factors and situations we do not discuss, I have reason to believe she may be in only slightly less danger with you than she would be at home with her mother."

He said nothing, allowing the accusation to hang in the silence between them. Sadly, she was likely speaking the truth.

But then Abigail usually did, even if the truth was not welcomed.

"I will spare you my opinion of this supposed relationship between you and Miss Cordoba. However, I stand by what I said in the garden. And, you," she said to Maribel. "I have no doubt you kissed him first as a diversion so that we would not know why you two were conferring at that desk."

Maribel slid Jean-Luc a glance and added a smile. "I like her."

"Just wait," he told her. "We like her too, but her honesty can be a bit brutal."

Abigail stifled a smile. "However, both of you enjoyed that kiss far too much for my comfort. I suggest once this trouble is behind you, the two of you should have a serious discussion about whether the marriage plans you have tormented Gaby with should in actuality take place."

"See," Jean-Luc said. "Brutal."

"But honest," Abigail said. "Now, I need no knowledge of whatever plans you've made for situations like this, but I have no doubt there are plans. Go on about it all, but do one thing first."

"What is that?" Jean-Luc asked.

"Get that young lady's mother and grandfather out of his house and back here so we can keep them safe."

Jean-Luc glanced over at Will. "Send Rao and Piper. Tell them they'll need at least two extra men, and make sure they know they could be facing danger."

Will hurried away but then stopped just short of the front door. "Maribel," he said. "It's great having you back." And then he was gone, leaving Jean-Luc and Maribel alone with Abigail.

"Now, as for you two," she said. "Something happened between you that has bound you together." She nodded to Jean-Luc. "You spoke of her constantly during your recovery. She has meaning in your life." Then she turned to Maribel. "You were a child and now you are a woman. Do not confuse how you felt about him when you were a child to any feelings that may grow as an adult. They are not the same. Do you understand?"

"Yes," Maribel said. "But there is nothing—"

"There will be." She shook her head and then reached for Jean-Luc's hand. "I have done all I can do here. Please, Jean-Luc, take care of her."

"You have my word," he told her. "Now if there's nothing else you wish to say, then we must go."

Abigail smiled. "Oh, there is plenty more I wish to say, but I best keep my mouth shut."

"Will wonders never cease," he said as he kissed Abigail on the cheek. "Do tell my father I have seen a miracle and will report back on it when I return."

"Watch your manners, son," she told him. "And yourself."

"I promise," he told her then caught Maribel's attention. "We should go now. It'll be best if you don't ask for any details. Just know we're going and your family will be safe."

She nodded as he retrieved the ledger and returned it to the valise. "Thank you," Maribel told Abigail. "The words seem so very inadequate."

Abigail offered an embrace and Maribel accepted. Apparently Abigail whispered something that caused the redhead to lift her head in surprise. A moment later, they stepped apart and Maribel followed him outside.

"What did she tell you?" he asked.

"That when you asked what she told me, I should tell you it is something you already know."

Of course. All Jean-Luc could do was laugh.

❧

Maribel followed the captain's lead as they traveled under cover of darkness toward the river. Bypassing the docks, they climbed into a small skiff that had been tied up not too far from the live oaks where they spent the afternoon.

A man wearing a dark cloak awaited them. He revealed his face only after their journey downriver was under way.

"Mr. Rao," she said softly. "It is you."

"Always was me when you thought it was," he whispered. "Sure wish I could've admitted it sooner, but promises were made, and, well, I was always one to keep my promises."

"I do understand."

"Quiet, both of you," Jean-Luc said.

They were in the skiff so long that Maribel's eyes began to drift shut. When the skiff thudded against something, her eyes opened and she found herself cradled in Jean-Luc's arms. The skiff was now tied to a larger vessel.

"Gaff-rigged schooner," she said out of habit, and both men looked at her oddly.

Maribel shrugged. "A habit I acquired during my youth," she said with a grin. "I just can't seem to break it."

Jean-Luc helped her onto the schooner and then climbed over the rail, the valise slung over his shoulder. "Cast off," he said as Mr. Rao reversed his rowing and pulled away from the vessel without boarding.

"Isn't Mr. Rao coming too?" she asked as she watched the skiff disappear into the night.

"Not this time." He crossed the deck and indicated she should follow. "Your cabin is at the end of the passageway. Take this valise and hide it."

She did as he instructed, following the passageway until it stopped at a door. Opening the door, she saw she was given the captain's cabin. Although luxurious, the room was not exceptionally large.

Given the choices of where the valise might fit, she picked the least obvious and stuffed the leather bag into the hole between the wall and the bunk. Returning the loose plank, Maribel stood back to admire her handiwork.

Her next order of business was to find the captain's library, for surely he had books stored in here somewhere. She opened one cabinet only to find a change of clothes and a pair of boots. The other cabinet held tools and rain gear.

The desk had three drawers. Two were unlocked and void of any reading material. The third, however, was locked tight.

Maribel sat back to examine the lock and then removed a hairpin from her hair. Such was the benefit of teaching a group of children from diverse backgrounds. Occasionally they were taught the most interesting skills. And of course children did love to brag about what they could do that no one else could.

The lock turned with a satisfying click. Like picking the occasional lock.

She tucked the pin back into her hair and opened the drawer carefully.

Inside she spied two books. One was the captain's log.

Her fingers stilled as she reached for the log. Hadn't she chastised her mother for looking through Abuelo's papers? And yet, the information those papers contained had proved of great value. So, too, could whatever had been written on the pages of this log.

Maribel tucked her guilt aside and opened the log and then scanned the entries. Nothing of any interest here.

But the other. She reached for the book, bound in dark leather and edged in gilt.

Footsteps echoed in the corridor, warning her that she might be sharing this book with a visitor if she kept the drawer open. Returning the log to its place above the book, she closed the drawer and hurried to perch innocently on the bed just as the door opened.

"Captain wishes to see you, Miss Cordoba," a crewman said.

"Yes, of course," she said, rising to follow him. Pausing in the door, she cast around at the secrets hidden there and smiled. This room's secrets were safe.

For now.

CHAPTER 25

Closing the door, she hurried to keep up as the man led her to the deck.

"Over there, miss," he said as he indicated two men standing near the bow.

Maribel crossed the deck and then froze. The man standing beside Jean-Luc...

"Mr. Bennett!"

She cared not for propriety as she closed the distance between them. "Oh, Mr. Bennett!" she said as she buried her face in his coat. "I am so glad to see you."

"I did notice that," he said with a chuckle. "And I am so glad to see you."

He held her at arm's length and studied her. "Oh my, you did grow up to be a beautiful young lady, didn't you?"

"Oh, I don't know about that, but I did grow up."

"Trust me," Jean-Luc said just loud enough for her to hear. "What my friend says is correct."

Mr. Bennett reached up to slide her hair off her forehead. "Yes," he said with a nod. "No doubt it is you."

"Why did you do that?" Jean-Luc asked him.

"She has a scar," he told him. "Right there." He indicated a spot on her forehead. "Happened aboard the *Venganza*. Connor treated it, but she would only bind it with that infernal scarf of hers. Whatever happened to that scarf, Miss Cordoba?"

"I wore it every day until my mother confiscated it. Said it was ratty and belonged in with the rubbish. Truly she was right, but I do miss it." She paused. "I missed you too, Mr. Bennett. I spent my childhood with the nuns on an island near Port Royal. Did you know that?"

His expression went neutral. "I believe I did hear something about that. Did you enjoy it?"

"Immensely," she said. "The nuns treated me well, and when I got too old for the orphanage, I was hired as a teacher." Maribel smiled. "I even taught the children how to read Homer in the original Greek."

His laughter filled the night air. "Perhaps someday you will teach our captain that."

"Hush now," he told them. "I will learn eventually."

Mr. Bennett shook his head. "I have things to do. You two behave."

And then he was gone, leaving them alone on the deck. A comfortable silence fell between them as the river carried them downstream. Finally Jean-Luc turned to her.

"Did you really have such a good childhood? With the nuns, I mean? It sounds lonely."

"Lonely?" She shrugged. "Hardly. Not when you're on an island filled with children and nuns."

He nodded. "I felt responsible, you know. When I couldn't find you, I didn't want to go on. Abigail is right. I did call out for you. I still do. Or did. I always felt you were out there and I was supposed to find you."

She smiled. "And then you did."

"No, I think it was you who found me. This Lopez-Gonzales fellow was the one who found you." He paused. "Or did he? I've been wondering about that, and I think he and your father were in league with each other."

"Do you?"

"Unless you have another opinion. Did he indicate any association with your grandfather that you were able to prove? Such as seeing them converse?"

"He had a letter from Abuelo when he arrived on the island, but he elected not to go with me inside my grandfather's home when I arrived in New Orleans. In fact, while my mother was greeting me on the front steps, he seemed to just slip away."

"And you never saw him again?"

She thought a moment. "No, but can we change the subject?"

"Of course," he said as he rested his hand on the rail. "What do you want to talk about?"

"You," she said. "Tell me what I missed in your life."

He looked away. "You don't want to hear all that."

She moved her hand over to rest atop his. "I do. Tell me, please."

"Not here. Come with me, then."

Maribel followed him to a quiet spot away from the men who were working. "You're sure?" he said. "Much of my story is not pretty."

His eyes went soft when she nodded. "Tell me, but only what you wish to say."

And then he did. And she cried, especially when he got to the part where he told her about his wife and his son and the awful fever that took them both. About how he, too, had the fever, and although he begged the Lord to take him, He did not.

"And until now I did not know why He saved me," he said.

He held her then, and she went willingly into his arms. "It is late," he finally said, his voice gruff.

"I suppose," she said as she looked up into his eyes.

"No one knows me as you do," he told her. "I haven't told anyone the things I've told you."

"I don't find that odd at all," she said. "What I do find odd is that you haven't kissed me yet."

At his look of surprise, she smiled. "What? Remember I was raised by the nuns and I was not taught the social graces."

He laughed. "And for that I am forever grateful."

And then he kissed her.

"Did you mind that?" he asked after.

"Not at all," she said. "But to be sure, might we try that again?"

Once again Jean-Luc laughed, but he did not argue.

Later when Maribel found her voice again, she asked him, "Why Beaumont?"

"What?" He shook his head. "Oh, that. Well, it was not my idea. In order to have Letters of Marque, I had to make application to the crown. My father was enthusiastic about the endeavor—to tell the truth, it was his idea—but my uncle would have been horrified."

"The governor? Why?"

"Depending on the year, sometimes the month or day, the Spaniards were either friend or foe. Uncle Bienville had friends from both countries. Father was still making his fortune and had not yet secured the exclusive trade agreement, so his idea was for both his sons to set sail, and possibly him too. He never liked the Spaniards ever since my mother and brother were killed."

"By my father," she said. "I am so sorry."

He touched her cheek with his palm and looked into her eyes. "That sin is his to bear, not yours. So when the time came to make application, he chose familial names that were close but not ours. Thus, I was Jean Beaumont after my paternal grandmother's maiden name. I was young, about your age, and I was allowed no opinion. Looking back, I see it was advantageous not to have my name known."

"Because there was a bounty on your head."

"Still could be," he said with a shrug. "I have no idea whether that has been rescinded. Far as I know, Captain Beaumont was reported killed and some French lieutenant claimed the glory." He shrugged. "End of the story."

"That is a story I am glad to see end."

He traced her jawbone with his finger and she shivered. "Cold?"

"No," she said as she snuggled closer. "Are you too old to fall in love with me?"

He chuckled. "According to Abigail, yes and no."

"What do you mean?"

"Yes, apparently I am too old for you. She would prefer for you to be spending your time with Gaby's twin, Michel. However, she feels I have already fallen in love with you."

"What do you think?" Maribel said.

"If I didn't know you grew up with the nuns, I would believe you're flirting with me."

It was her turn to laugh. "How exactly does one flirt?"

"By doing exactly what you're doing, Maribel Cordoba."

And then he kissed her again.

"Captain," Mr. Bennett called. "You're needed up here."

Jean-Luc stretched out his legs and frowned. "Duty calls."

She smiled. "I am tired. It's been quite a day."

"That it has," he said as he helped her to her feet.

"I can see myself to my cabin. You go find out what Mr. Bennett needs."

He walked her down the corridor anyway and stood on the other side of the door until she proved to him that it was locked. When she was certain he'd gone, Maribel went to the drawer and removed the leather book.

An hour later, she stuffed the book into the valise and slammed the drawer shut, anger pounding in her temples. By the time she found Jean-Luc and Mr. Bennett, she was so mad she could barely control her words.

"So," she said to the two men, now standing together at the wheel. "I have a question."

Jean-Luc grinned. "For both of us or just for me?"

"I suppose since you are the captain, I should ask you."

He moved around to stand beside her and then wrapped her in his arms. She looked up into his eyes, her own arms held tight at her sides.

"Exactly when were you going to tell me that you and Mr. Bennett were slave traders?"

When neither man spoke, she had her answer. Maribel turned her back and walked away, tears stinging her eyes. Jean-Luc stepped in front of her just before she reached the corridor.

"It isn't what you think."

"I saw you," she said, angry now that her tears were falling. "You and he were at Isla de Santa Maria. You pulled your boat into the inlet and loaded slaves from your ship to the other. I watched you do it."

"From a tree?" he said, sarcasm touching his voice.

"Actually, yes," she said.

"Then you should not base what actually happened on what you think you saw."

She let out a long breath and looked up into his eyes. "I saw it, Jean-Luc. I saw you and I saw him." She nodded toward the wheel where Mr. Bennett stood. "And I saw the slaves leave a gaff-rigged schooner very much like this one. Are you now telling me that did not happen?"

"Captain," Mr. Bennett called. "We've got a ship coming up behind us."

Maribel moved toward the rail so she could see. "Brigantine to the south," she said.

"Brigantine? You're certain?"

At her nod, he smiled. "Raise the French flag," he told Israel. "It appears my uncle would like a word with me."

Sure enough, the vessel carrying the governor came alongside and greetings were exchanged. When Jean-Luc was invited aboard, Maribel asked if she could go along and was allowed.

Only when Jean-Luc spied her carrying the valise did he seem to realize her voyage with him was over. "Might I have a moment of your time, Governor?" she asked the older man.

Though his brows raised, he did smile and agree to a meeting. When she retrieved the leather book and handed it to him, he seemed confused.

"That is evidence that your nephew is a slave trader," she told him.

The governor shook his head. "I do not understand, young lady. Why give me this?"

"Can you not stop him? This is piracy of the worst kind."

The older man rose and left Maribel alone in the room, the book still on the table where she put it. A short while later, he returned with Jean-Luc and left them together without a word.

"My uncle wished to let us know your father has been captured. Apparently the word of a French spy was good enough to give away his dealings."

"A French spy?" She shook her head. "Who?"

"One Mr. Lopez-Gonzales." He shrugged. "Though your grandfather was not a well man, he was a smart man. He was able to feed information to those who were eager to prove whether the Spaniard who had been stealing from French ships was indeed Antonio Cordoba."

"And it was."

Jean-Luc nodded. "It was. Your mother and grandfather are safely back home, and your grandfather's valuables have been returned to him along with a substantial reward for helping to capture an enemy of the French."

"I see." She thought a moment. "So I can go home now?"

"Aboard this very ship," he told her. "My uncle is returning tonight. He could see you home safely. By the way, he told me you've accused me of piracy."

"Thank you," she said, those stupid tears returning. "And, yes, I have." Why had she thought she cared about this man? She hadn't even known him.

"Maribel," he said gently. "I asked you if you would trust me and you said you would." He pressed his palm over the book that sat on the table between them. "Will you trust me when I tell you this is not what it seems?"

"Why should I?" she demanded. "I see nothing but proof here. Proof that lines up perfectly with what I saw on Isla de Santa

Maria. What possible evidence would you offer to refute it?"

"The word of a nun and more," he said.

She shook her head. "You're making no sense."

He reached beyond the book to take her hand. "Trust me, Maribel. Come with me and I will show you. Look at me." When she did, he continued. "Do you truly believe that Israel Bennett and I would be involved in something as vile as slave trading?"

She sighed. "No," she said. "But the book. . ."

"But the book proves something entirely different." He nodded toward the vessel still tied up beside the brigantine. "Come with us and I will show you."

"All right, although for the life of me I cannot tell you why."

"Because we were always meant to be a team, Red. I just didn't know it when you first tried to join up with my crew." He gave her a broad grin. "I'm older and wiser now. Welcome to my crew, Maribel."

She gave him a frown that she had a hard time maintaining. A short while later, they were back aboard the schooner and headed into open waters. Maribel avoided Jean-Luc during the voyage, preferring to remain in the cabin below.

Thanks to the generous contribution of books from Mr. Bennett's library, the time flew past and soon the lookout was calling for land. Maribel emerged onto the deck to see the familiar beaches and structures of Isla de Santa Maria coming closer.

"Home," she said softly, and for certain she knew it to be.

Though New Orleans was nice and reuniting with her family had been God's own miracle, this sleepy island with the children, the nuns, and the sandy beaches was her home.

By the time the ship neared land, all the children and the nuns were waiting for them. Strangely, they bypassed the docks and continued around the island, only returning to dock at the inlet after a roundabout pass through the open ocean.

Maribel waited on deck for the skiff to be lowered. When Jean-Luc came to stand by her, she froze. There had been nothing in the way of conversation between them for almost a week, and now he stood close enough to touch.

"What you are about to witness is what Israel and I have done for years. More years than I can count. When the Lord spared me after my privateering days, I made a promise I would use the remainder of my life for His purpose. Israel and I believe this is His purpose. His piracy, if you will."

A bell sounded, and then Maribel heard a door open and footsteps heading toward them. Out from the hold came dark-skinned men and women, boys and girls, dozens of them.

"Jean-Luc, no," she said softly as another schooner slid into place behind them. "They were with us all along?"

Without sparing her a glance, the unexpected passengers filed into skiffs that were lowered into the water. She stepped into the line and grasped the arm of a young woman carrying a baby. "You don't have to do this," she said.

The woman gave her a confused look. "She doesn't understand what you've told her," Mr. Bennett said. He said something to her that she understood, and the girl smiled.

"Going home," she managed in broken English. "To Kongo."

"What does she mean?" she asked the men, but no one answered.

The girl returned to the line and disappeared into a skiff. Once they were all gone, another bell sounded and the other schooner departed.

Jean-Luc moved closer and wrapped his arm around her. "I tried to tell you. We are sending them home. That's the sort of pirates we are."

"When we can, we intercept vessels carrying human cargo," Mr. Bennett said. "Just as the captain did for me when he freed me from a vessel like the one we found these people on. Sometimes Rao and Piper come along. Spencer, he's a doctor now, so we bring him when we can, but mostly he's with those who need him at the charity hospital in New Orleans."

"Is he telling the truth?" she asked Jean-Luc.

"He is," he admitted.

"It started out as a search for my wife, Nzuzi," Mr. Bennet said. "We started doing this regularly because after a while of working for the captain, I earned enough to go back and get her. I went back to find out she was gone—captured by traders and sold off, so every ship we stopped for years, I held out hope she was on it."

"Oh," she said and then found herself incapable of saying more.

Tears were flowing and Maribel could barely speak. All she could do was turn around and allow Jean-Luc to wrap her in his arms. "I'm so sorry," she finally managed. "I—"

"Hush," he told her. "If you don't collect yourself, we will be late for the celebration."

"Celebration?" She shook her head. "What do you mean?"

"Your homecoming," he said. "Apparently there is quite a party being held, and we are missing it."

She swiped at her eyes and laughed. "But how did they know?"

"How does Mother Superior ever know?" He nudged her. "By the way, use of the inlet has always been at her discretion. And she has never failed to know when we would be arriving. You may not have noticed, but there is a signal that goes up when we bypass the inlet. Once we are given the signal, we know it is safe to land."

"I would ask what that is, but there's no point, is there?"

"Not really."

He laughed and escorted her off the ship. A few minutes later, she found herself surrounded by laughing children. Standing at the edges of the circle were the more soft-spoken nuns.

Mr. Bennett pressed past them to disappear into the chapel. A moment later, he returned carrying a tiny dark woman. The children giggled as the woman's good-natured complaining drifted toward them.

Finally the pair reached Maribel and Jean-Luc. "Miss Cordoba," he said as he returned the lovely lady to a standing position. "May I present my wife, Nzuzi?"

"You found her," Maribel said as tears welled in her eyes.

"He did," Mr. Bennett said, nodding toward Jean-Luc. "And thanks to him we have two sons now. Named Evan Connor and Jean-Luc." He grinned. "I felt I ought to honor both men."

Evan Connor. The name should have meant something, this much Maribel knew. And yet like so much of her childhood, the memory had been lost. "Do I know this Connor fellow?" she asked.

The men exchanged looks and then Jean-Luc's expression softened. "That is a story for another day, but suffice it to say that Evan Connor is a greater man than I ever could be." Jean-Luc smiled at Nzuzi. "And what will you name the next one?"

Mr. Bennett looked down at his wife, who did appear to be expecting. "She says this one is a girl, so it will be up to her."

"So very pleased to meet you," Nzuzi said in softly accented English. "I have heard much about you."

"Do not believe all of it," Maribel said, and they both laughed.

Off in the distance she spied Mother Superior. As the old nun approached, everyone else parted to allow her to walk through. Even little Stephan gave way as she moved past him.

"Welcome back," she told Maribel. "I knew you would return."

"You did?"

"I did," she said. "In fact, I have taken the liberty of preparing the cottage for you and your husband. And one for your mother and grandfather when they come to visit."

"I have no husband," she said, shaking her head.

"I wish to remedy this," Jean-Luc said as he came to stand beside her. "In the absence of her parents, might I ask you for her hand?"

Mother Superior laughed. "My boy, I think you'd best ask Miss Cordoba. She always was the independent type."

"Maribel?" he said as he took her hand. "Will you marry this pirate and sail the seas with me now that you know what our mission entails? I cannot promise you smooth sailing, but I can always promise you my love."

"And a cottage on Isla de Santa Maria," Mother Superior added.

"And that is of the upmost importance," Stephan called from the crowd.

"Let me think about it," she told him with a grin.

She would marry him, of this she was certain. But for now, she would let him guess whether she would become this pirate's bride.

And then he kissed her.

Author's Note

and Bent History:
The Rest of the Story

As a writer of historical novels, I love incorporating actual history into my plots. As with most books, the research behind the story generally involves much more information than would ever actually appear in the story. In truth, I could easily spend all my time researching and not get any writing done at all!

Because I am a history nerd, I love sharing some of that mountain of research I collected with my readers. The following are just a few of the facts I uncovered during the writing of *The Pirate Bride*. I hope these tidbits of history will cause you to go searching for the rest of the story:

The opening quote of the novel from Stede Bonnet's sentencing speech by Judge Trot is part of the transcript of a lengthy speech actually given by the judge upon this occasion. Throughout the speech, which spanned a number of manuscript pages in my resource book, the judge liberally refers to scripture and salvation and calls on the name of Christ to save the sentenced pirate's soul.

Maribel's favorite book, *The Notorious Seafaring Pyrates and Their Exploits* by Captain Ulysses Jones, is loosely based on *A General History of the Robberies and Murders of the Most Notorious Pyrates* by Captain Charles Williamson, which was first published in London in 1718.

The position of Consul General is a fictional one. Havana, Cuba, was a Spanish colony ruled by the king of Spain. As such, Spanish noblemen were regularly posted to this and other colonies.

Speaking of the king of Spain, in January of 1724, Louis I of Spain became king upon the abdication of King Philip V. When Louis I died from smallpox just over seven months later, Philip V returned to the throne and reigned until his own death in 1746.

An interesting side note: Philip V was the grandson of Louis XIV of France. Thus, there were times during the tumultuous history of Spain and France when the two countries were allies. For the purposes of my story, it is assumed that during the periods the novel takes place, the two were once again at odds.

Letters of Marque are essentially licenses issued by an entity—usually a country—that allow their holder to capture and claim ships or their cargo, or both, for that country. Holders of these letters are generally referred to as privateers although some might incorrectly call them pirates. Essentially, these privateers had a license to steal from one country's vessels as long as they followed the rules—very specific rules, including appearing before admiralty courts to report and receive shares taken from vessels—and only chose to seek out ships flying the flag of countries covered by their letters. Even when those rules were followed, privateers were still occasionally branded pirates and hung for their "crimes." Letters of Marque have been used throughout history—including by our own American government—and are a fascinating topic for study outside the scope of this novel.

Although Captain Beaumont considers that Maribel may end up at the Ursuline nuns' convent, in truth, the Ursuline nuns did not arrive in New Orleans until 1727, and their convent was not completed until 1734. An interesting fact associated with this building is that although France owned the land upon which the city of New Orleans was built at the time, the designer of the building hailed from Bavaria and held the honor of the King's Master Carpenter.

Upon the death of King Louis XIV of France in 1715, King Louis XV succeeded his grandfather to the throne at the age of five. Because of the new king's young age and due to political struggles among those closest to the crown, the Duke of Orleans—namesake of the city of New Orleans, Louisiana, and closely related to Spanish nobility—acted as regent until the new king came of age in 1723. Because the French and Spanish royal families consisted of marriages between the two royal houses, there were many noblemen from one country who claimed relatives in nobility in the other country.

Though you would think that wars among folks who were related would be less likely, the countries of Spain and France continued to be either friend or foe depending on the day, month, or year. When relations with England is factored in, suffice it to say that at almost any given time for the past few centuries, one or all of these three countries were at war with one another. Because of this, it was easy to imagine a scenario where my poor hero gets in trouble with politicians who previously encouraged him. However, this scenario is completely fictional.

Jean Baptiste Le Moyne, Sieur de Bienville, was a French-Canadian explorer and the founder of New Orleans. Jean and his brother Pierre founded New Orleans on the banks of the Mississippi River on March 3, 1699. As a fun fact, for those of you who know of Louisiana culture, this date coincides with Mardi Gras, which, similar to modern convention, was the day of celebration before Lent in that year. Bienville was governor of Louisiana from 1706 to 1713, 1717 to 1723, and 1733 to 1743. The last period, he returned as the ambassador of the king during French rule. History does not record the names of the children of his siblings (there were more than a dozen children born to his parents), but I promise my hero Jean-Luc is not really one of them. That association is completely fictional.

Isla de Santa Maria is a fictional island I created and plopped down in the Caribbean Sea near the island of Jamaica. It is not to be confused with the actual Isla de Santa Maria in the Azores chain off the country of Portugal. The orphanage and nuns are also a figment of my very active imagination. However, any mention of the city of Port Royal or the island of Jamaica is based on my understanding of the history of the area at the time my story is set. And, yes, there really was a hurricane that hit Jamaica in September of 1734.

The real-life city of Mbanza Kongo, first settled in the 1300s, was a city of substantial size and sophistication during the time of this story. The name was changed by the Portuguese to Sao Salvador in the 1500s. When Angola received independence in 1979, the city's name was changed back to Mbanza Kongo, which means city of Kongo. Kongo is the original spelling of the current version, Congo. The judgment tree I mention in my story is real and can still be seen in downtown Mbanza Kongo. It is the site of a rectangular ground-level structure where local tradition claims the king's body was washed before burial.

The character of Marcel Valmont is loosely based on a real French merchant named Anthony Crozat who, in 1715, was given the exclusive privilege of trading in the Louisiana Territory. Upon signing this contract, Sieur de Bienville was dismissed from office and replaced by Lamothe Cadillac. While Crozat had no luck with the venture, I have allowed my fictional character to be much more successful. I also allowed him to be married to the fictional sister of the real man who lost his job after the contract was signed. As you have read above, however, Sieur de Bienville got several more chances to be governor of the territory, so everything did work out fine for him.

The city of New Orleans is very old. By the 1700s, a number of buildings had been erected, including the ones described by the fictional Mr. Lopez-Gonzales as he escorts Maribel to her grandfather's home. The streets were laid out in 1721, and the Director's House was built on the corner of Levee (now called Decatur) and Toulouse Streets facing the river. Like most of the early buildings in the city, it was built with wood timbers directly touching the soggy ground. To be certain, the house did not last long. The governor's house was built two years later on the corner of St. Ann and Chartres Streets. Governors Perier and

Bienville lived in the home during their administrations. Scientist Pierre Baron built the observatory in 1730 on a lot adjacent to the governor's house, and he did make accommodations to the building that would allow him to study the stars with his telescope.

Bestselling author **Kathleen Y'Barbo** is a multiple Carol Award and RITA nominee of more than eighty novels with almost two million copies in print in the United States and abroad. She has been nominated for a Career Achievement Award as well as a Reader's Choice Award and is the winner of the 2014 Inspirational Romance of the Year by *Romantic Times* magazine. Kathleen is a paralegal, a proud military wife, and a tenth-generation Texan, who recently moved back to cheer on her beloved Texas Aggies. Connect with her through social media at www.kathleenybarbo. com.

The
Captured
Bride

MICHELLE GRIEP

DEDICATION

To my wilderness-loving daughter
and her redheaded mountain man,
Callie and Ryan Leichty.
And, as always,
to the Lover and Keeper of my soul, *Iesos*.

ACKNOWLEDGMENTS

While writing is a solitary profession, a novel is never written alone. My hearty thanks go out to the critique partners who held my sweaty hands on this story: Yvonne Anderson, Laura Frantz, Mark Griep, Shannon McNear, Ane Mulligan, Chawna Schroeder, and MaryLu Tyndall. And also an honorable mention to Dani Snyder, my first-reader extraordinaire.

A huge thank-you to historical reenactors everywhere, but especially those who perform an awesome three-day event at Old Fort Niagara in upstate New York. If you ever get the chance to see the French and Indian War Encampment (usually held near the Fourth of July), it's totally worth the effort.

And as always, my gratitude to Barbour Publishing for taking a chance on a girl like me. Waving at you, Becky Germany.

Readers, you make this writing gig all worthwhile. And guess what? I love to hear from you! Follow my adventures and share yours with me at www.michellegriep.com.

French Language Glossary

Chiens Anglais: English dogs
Démissionner: Stand down
La fin: The end
Merci: Thank you
Regardez: Look
Rien, monsieur: Nothing, sir

Mohawk Language Glossary

Aktsi:'a: Older sister
Ehressaronon: Wyandot
Iesos: Jesus
Kahente: Before her time
Kahnyen'kehàka: Mohawk nation
Kanien'keha: Native name for the Mohawk language
Kaia'tákerahs: Goat
Ó:nen ki› wáhi: Farewell for now
Ó:nen: Goodbye
Onontio: Big mountain
Rake'niha: My father
Sachem: Leader
Skennen: Peace
Skén:nen tsi satonríshen: Rest in peace
Tsi Nen:we Enkonnoronhkhwake: I love you forever

Mohawk Lullaby

Ho, ho, Watanay.
Ho, ho, Watanay.
Ho, ho, Watanay.
Ki-yo-ki-na.
Ki-yo-ki-na.

Sleep, sleep, my little one.
Sleep, sleep, my little one.
Sleep, sleep, my little one.
Sleep now.
Sleep now.

Daughters of the Mayflower

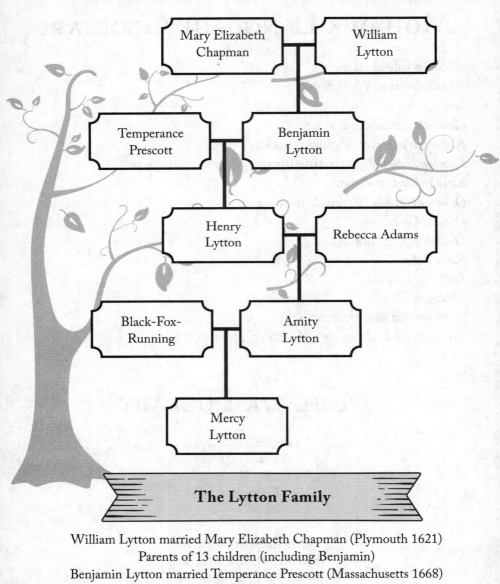

Mary Elizabeth Chapman — William Lytton

Temperance Prescott — Benjamin Lytton

Henry Lytton — Rebecca Adams

Black-Fox-Running — Amity Lytton

Mercy Lytton

The Lytton Family

William Lytton married Mary Elizabeth Chapman (Plymouth 1621)
Parents of 13 children (including Benjamin)
Benjamin Lytton married Temperance Prescott (Massachusetts 1668)
Children included Henry
Henry Lytton married Rebecca Adams (New York 1712)
Children were Goodwill and Amity
Amity Lytton married Black-Fox-Running, a Mohawk warrior (New York 1737)
Only child was Mercy Lytton (Kahente)

I t ain't right. *You* ain't right."

Mercy Lytton brushed off Captain Matthew Prinn's comment as easily as she rubbed off the dried mud marring her buckskin leggings. Too bad she couldn't so easily rid herself of the bone-deep weariness dogging her steps. Matthew had a point—somewhat. Going from a scouting campaign and on to the next mission without a few hours of sleep wasn't right.

She glanced at her self-appointed protector as they crossed the Fort Wilderness parade ground. " 'Tain't about right. 'Tis about duty."

Despite the blood under his nails and bruises on his jaw, Matthew scratched at three weeks' worth of whiskers on his face. "Seems to me by now your duty ought to be raisin' a troop of your own littles."

And there it was. Again.

She bit back one of the many curses embedded in her head from a life amongst warriors. A bitter smile twisted her lips, yet she said nothing. It was a losing argument—and she'd had her fill of loss.

So they walked in silence, save for the guffaws of a group of soldiers nearby, smoking pipes just outside a casement doorway. A late March breeze skimmed over the top of the palisade surrounding the outpost, and she shivered. She could forgo rest for a few more hours, but changing out of the damp trade shirt beneath her hunting frock was mandatory.

As they neared the brigadier general's door, a grim-faced Mohawk strode out and stopped in front of her, blocking her path.

"There is ice in that one's veins." Black-Fox-Running spoke in *Kanien'keha*, tipping his head back toward the general's quarters. Afternoon sun flashed like lightning in his dark eyes. "Return home, *Kahente*. We are done here."

Captain Prinn bypassed them both and disappeared inside the rugged log building. Ever the quick-witted strategist when it came to fighting, he clearly sensed a coming battle between her and her father.

Mercy widened her stance yet bowed her head in deference. Searching for the right words, she studied the fine layer of gray dirt hardened on the toes of her moccasins. Appeasement was never a clever policy, but sometimes a necessary evil. "Your wisdom is unequaled, my father."

He grabbed her chin and lifted her face. His black gaze bored into hers. Even so, a hint of a curve lifted the edges of his lips. "Wise counsel or not, you will do as you will."

She stared at him but said nothing. A survival tactic—one her mother should have learned.

"The best *sachem* is not the one who persuades people to his point of view. He is the one in whose presence most people find truth." Releasing her, he squared his shoulders. "There is no truth left in the English father Bragg."

She sighed, long and low. He needn't have told her what she already knew. But this wasn't about General Bragg or Black-Fox-Running—and never had been. Reaching out, she placed her hand on her father's arm, where hard muscle still knotted beneath four decades of scars. "I respect your insight, *Rake'niha*. I will consider it."

His teeth bared with the closest semblance of a smile he ever gave. "That is the most I can expect from you, for you will land wherever the wind blows. *Ó:nen Kahente*."

"No!" Her breath caught. Why use a forever goodbye? She tightened her grip on her father's arm. "Only until we meet again."

Shrugging out of her grasp, he stalked past her, leaving behind his familiar scent of bear grease and strength. She watched him go, tears blurring her sight. While she hated yielding to the will of any man, for him she would almost bend.

Proud head lifted high, Black-Fox-Running called to a group of warriors, her brother amongst them, clustered in front of the pen with their horses. Without a word, they mounted. She turned from the sight, unwilling to watch them ride off, and focused on the task at hand. Better that than second-guess her decision.

She shoved open the brigadier general's door, and the peppery scent of sage greeted her. Across the small chamber, a few leftover leaves were scattered on the floor in front of the hearth. She bit her lip, fighting a sneeze. Did the man really think he duped anyone with this ruse? Even if she couldn't detect the smell of whiskey on his breath, his red nose betrayed his daily indulgence. He rose from his seat at her entrance.

She strode past a silent private on watch near the door and joined Captain Prinn, who stood in front of the commanding officer's desk. Matthew raised his brow at her—his silent way of inquiring after her conversation with Black-Fox-Running—but she ignored him and greeted the general instead.

"Pardon my appearance, sir. Captain Prinn and I only recently returned, and I had no time to make myself presentable."

"No pardon needed. It is I who am keeping you from the comfort of a hot meal and a good rest. God knows you deserve it." The general swept out his hand. "Please sit, the both of you."

General Bragg fairly crashed into his seat, knocking loose a long blond hair that had been ornamenting the red wool of his sleeve. Apparently the man had visited the supply shed with Molly the laundress as well as imbibing until he wobbled.

He coughed into one hand, clearing his throat with an excessive amount of rattling. "Now then, Captain Prinn has filled me in on the intelligence the two of you gained. It is my understanding you had quite the adventure keeping hidden from a Wyandot war party. Between Prinn's tactical strategies and your keen eye, I daresay we will win this war."

She shifted in her seat. Praise always prickled, for it usually meant she'd be asked for more than she was willing to give.

The general folded his hands on the desktop. No calluses thickened his skin. No ink stained his fingers. What did the man do all day besides chase skirts and drink?

"Normally I'd give you both some leave, but these are not normal days. There's been a recent development in your absence." Reaching for a stack of papers, the general lifted the topmost parchment.

Next to her, Matthew stretched out one long leg and leaned forward. "What would that be, General?"

"The Frogs are running scared, and that is good. Many are scuttling back over the border. A sortie of our men captured a group of them shorthanded, traveling with a load of French gold. We've got hold of one of them now. . .or I should say one of ours." He squinted at the parchment, then held it out to Matthew. "You recognize this name?"

Matthew's eyes scanned the paper before he handed it back. "No, sir. It means nothing to me. Congratulations on your fine catch, but what has any of this to do with us? Miss Lytton and I have done more than our fair share of *duty*." Emphasizing the last word, he flashed her a look from the corner of his eye.

She flattened her lips to keep from smiling. The rascal. Using her own sentiment of duty.

"I needn't tell you our position here is tenuous, especially now with Black-Fox-Running pulling his aid. Fickle natives." Shoving back his chair, the general stood and planted his palms on the desk. "That gold's got to be moved into secure British lands. I want you and Miss Lytton to be part of that team. You will leave first thing come morning."

Matthew shook his head. "Why us? You have stronger, younger, more bloodthirsty men in the garrison. Why send a worn-out soldier like me and a young lady who spots trouble a mile away but can't fire a gun to save her life?"

"It is precisely for those reasons I chose you."

Mercy rubbed her eyes. Something wasn't right here. She lifted her face to the general. "Excuse me, sir, but what's to stop the French from simply taking back the gold as we move it, just as you took it from them?"

His wide mouth stretched ever wider, and a low chuckle rumbled in his chest. "That is the beauty of my plan. It won't be a shipment of gold."

Matthew cocked his head. "Come again?"

"We'll hide the crates in plain sight, under the guise of two wagonloads carrying naught but homestead belongings. The longer this war drags on, the more families are pulling up stakes and escaping back to civilization. You shall simply be yet more of those tired settlers who've had their fill of frontier life."

Matthew shifted in his chair, the scrape of his tomahawk handle against his seat as offsetting as the lowering of his voice. "You want us to move that gold overland instead of by river? Do you have any idea how long that will take?"

"A fortnight, if luck smiles on you."

A frown weighted Mercy's brow, and she glanced at Matthew. The hard lines on his face were unreadable. Scouting out danger from the safety of forest cover was one thing, but rolling along on a wagon in the open was quite another. Suddenly her words of duty tasted sour at the back of her throat.

She shot her gaze back to the general. "Captain Prinn and I hardly make up a family, sir."

"Indeed. And so I've enlisted a few others to add to your numbers. You shall have a recruit to play the part of your nephew. Captain Prinn here"—he aimed his finger at Matthew—"will pose as the kindly father figure in your life, as he always does. And you, Miss Lytton, will no longer be a miss."

She tensed. If she ran out the door now and saddled a horse, she could catch up to her father in no time. She gripped the chair arms to keep from fleeing. "Pardon me, General, but what are you saying?"

"Why, my dear Miss Lytton." A grin spread on his face. "You will be wed by tomorrow."

CHAPTER 2

Mercy bolted out the general's door, heedless of the stares of milling soldiers. Without slowing her stride, she crossed the parade ground and raced to the sanctity of the women's tents. This being an outpost garrison, the men were afforded timbered shelters. The women got canvas, unless they were an officer's wife. There were only six ladies living in the tents—three who refused to leave their husbands, herself, and two who stayed simply because they had nowhere else to go.

Flinging aside the door flap, she ducked inside and closed the stained canvas behind her. Three empty cots were lined up before her like fallen soldiers. The farthest one called her weary bones to lie down and forget the world. Pah! As if she could. The general's words boiled her blood hotter with each pump of her heart.

"You will be wed by tomorrow."

"We'll see about that," she muttered, glad her tentmates were either out washing regimentals or nursing sick soldiers. "Men! Pigheaded, the lot of them."

Reaching up, she fumbled at her collar and pulled out the locket she never took off. She ran her thumb over the center of a ruby heart, surrounded by gold filigree, and slowed her breathing. Years ago, she'd worn the necklace out of rebellion. Now the heavy stone was a weight of penance and—oddly enough—comfort.

Oh Mother. . .

Wind riffled the canvas walls. She felt more alone now than she had in years.

With a sigh, she shrugged off a man's trade shirt that hung to her knees, untied her leggings and peeled them off, and lastly loosened the breech-clout at her waist. She'd have to hang them up to dry before packing them away, but for now, she gave the heap a good kick, tired of straddling the line between male and female, native and white. Tired of everything, really.

Shivering, she knelt in front of her trunk and opened the lid. Pulling out a clean gown and undergarments, she frowned at the feminine attire as fiercely as she'd scowled at the hunting clothes. Why was she so different? Why could she not be like other women?

She blew out a sigh and slipped into a dry shift and front-lacing stays, knowing all the while there were no answers to be had. She'd been born different, and there was nothing to be done about that.

After retrieving a hairbrush, she closed the lid on her trunk and sank onto its top. For the moment, she set the brush in her lap, then began the arduous process of unpinning her long hair, her thoughts every bit as snarly. Why must everyone push her into marriage, as if she were some precious bauble that required protection? Little good it had done her mother. Brushing her hair with more force than necessary, she winced. In a man's world, survival came by acting and thinking like a man.

With deft fingers, she braided her hair into a long tail and was tying a leather lace at the end when footsteps pounded the ground outside her tent.

"Mercy, come on out." Matthew's voice leached through the weathered canvas. "We need to talk."

She dropped her hands to her lap. What was there to say? She'd given her answer. Not even a war party of Wyandots could make her change her mind.

"I know you're in there," he growled. "And I won't go away."

Of course he wouldn't. She rolled her eyes. The man was as determined as a river swollen by winter melt. Tucking up a stray strand, she rose and opened the flap. "You're wasting your time. I will not entertain the general's suggestion."

"At least hear me out. Then make up your mind." He held up a blackened tin pot. "Besides, I've brought stew. Don't tell me you're not hungry."

Her stomach growled, and she frowned. Of all the inopportune times to remind him—and her—that she was human.

Matthew smirked.

She sighed. Ignoring him would sure be a lot easier with a belly full of hot food. "Very well. Give me a moment."

Darting back inside, she retrieved a shawl, then grabbed a horn spoon and wooden bowl.

Outside, Matthew already sat on a log next to a smoldering fire, dipping his spoon into his own bowl. She joined him. The rich scent of broth curling up to her nose nearly made her weep. And the first bite. . .aah. There wasn't much finer in the world than thick stew on a chill day—especially after going without for so long.

She shoveled in a mouthful before eyeing Matthew sideways. "What'd you trade for this?"

"Rum."

"Your loss. Much as I'm obliged"—she paused for another big bite—"I won't be bought for a bowl of pottage."

"'Course not." Afternoon sun glinted off the stew droplets collecting on Matthew's beard as he spoke. "You're worth far more than that."

The soup in her mouth soured, and she swallowed it like a bitter medicine. The man was forever prattling on about God's great love for her. "Don't start, Matthew. I can't bear a sermon right now."

"Fair enough." Lifting the bowl to his lips, Matthew tipped back his head and finished the rest of his meal. He swiped his mouth with his sleeve while setting down the dish, then angled to face her head-on. "Look, I don't like this any more than you do, but despite the danger of it, General Bragg's plan is solid. Like he said, with clear weather, it'll take but a fortnight to get the load over to Fort Edward."

"Fort Edward?" Her appetite suddenly stalled. The rangers were stationed out of that fort. Matthew's former cohort. Was this his way of saying goodbye?

She swallowed, the stew having lost its appeal. "I see."

His brows gathered together like a coming storm. "No, you don't. When it comes to that falcon eyesight of yours, you are unequaled. But in matters of the heart, you are blind."

"Matthew!" She spluttered and choked. After three years of scouting sorties with this man, surely he wasn't pledging troth to her. He was old enough to be her father!

"Certainly you are not hinting at. . ." She cleared her throat once more, unable to force out any more words.

For a moment his eyes narrowed, then shot wide. His shoulders shook as he chuckled. "No, girl. Nothing like that. Look at me, Mercy. Really look. What do you see?"

Lowering her bowl, she focused first on her breaths. In. Out. Slower. And slower. Sound was next. One by one, she closed off the hum of the camp—the whickering of a horse, coarse laughter from afar. The thud of men tromping about. Even the beat of her own pulse quieted until silence took on a life of its own. Only then could she see, and in the seeing, her heart broke.

Where whiskers were absent, lines etched a life map on Matthew Prinn's face. A chart of the years—decades—of toil and grief. Spent vigor peppered his beard and hair that were once raven. Even his eyes were washed out and gray now. In the three years she'd known him, he'd earned a new scar near his temple and a larger bump on his nose—all in the service of the king.

And her.

She set her bowl on the log beside her, no longer hungry. "What I see is a great man who faithfully serves the crown, relentlessly brings back intelligence, and keeps me safe in the process."

He shook his head. "That is what you want to see. The truth of it is I'm tired. This fight is winding down, and so am I." Pausing, he looked up at a sky as sullen as the furrows on his forehead. "I aim to go to Fort Edward, then keep on going east till I find me a nice patch of land and put down stakes."

"You're going to quit? Just like that?"

" 'Tis been a long time coming." His gaze found hers again. "You did not see it because you did not want to."

The accusation crept in like a rash, hot and uncomfortable. Of course she did not want to see it, because if she did, she'd have to look long and hard at her own life. She dropped her gaze and picked at the frayed hem of her shawl. He'd sacrificed time and again these past three years for her. Time now she returned the favor.

"I understand, Matthew. Truly."

A grunt resounded in his chest. "Good. Then we're agreed."

She jerked her face upward. "But that doesn't mean I will marry."

His teeth flashed white in his beard. "I did not say it did."

"But the general said—"

Matthew held up a hand. "If you'd have stayed long enough to hear the man out, you'd know we'll travel as a family unit in name only, not deed. Rufus and I—"

"Rufus *Bragg*?" She spit out the name like an unripe huckleberry.

"Aye. We will both have a cross to bear. He is to pose as my grandson, and he and I will man the rear wagon. You will ride the lead, scouting for trouble as always."

Picking up a stick, she stabbed at the coals in the fire, stirring them to life. "With my husband, no doubt."

"Like I said, in name only." His hand snaked out and stilled her frantic poking. "Why are you so skittish over this? I've never known you to back down from a request to serve. What of your high ideals of duty and honor?"

She pulled from his touch, wishing it could be as easy to shy from his question. But she couldn't, for truth once spoken could not be unheard. "You're right," she mumbled. Slowly, she lifted her face to his. "But what shall I do without you?"

"Time you took stock of your own future, girl. Where is it to be? What is it to be? With whom is it to be spent?"

She jumped to her feet, grabbing up her bowl and spoon. She'd rather run barelegged through a patch of poison oak than consider the answers to those inquiries, for she wanted nothing more than to remain unfettered and free. "If we are to leave at daybreak, I need to pack and get some rest."

She whirled toward her tent, then turned back. "Tell me, Matthew, who is to be my, er. . ." The word stuck in her throat, and she forced it out past a clenched jaw. "Husband?"

He stood, gathering the tin pot and his bowl. "Fellow by the name of Dubois, more than likely."

"Dubois?" The French name festered like a raw boil, the food in her stomach churning. "Pah! I'm to be *married* to a Frenchman?"

"Oh, he is more than that."

Her hands shot to her hips. "What aren't you telling me, Matthew Prinn?"

"Dubois," he drawled, leveling a cocked eyebrow at her, "is a condemned traitor."

CHAPTER 3

Light crept in through the cracks between boards. Pale. Lethargic. Morning, but not quite. As if the sun hovered just below the horizon for the sole purpose of tormenting Elias Dubois, forcing him to live his last moments on this earth stuck between night and day. No matter. It felt like home, this in-between, the threat of death a familiar companion. But this time, more than his life would be on the line. Other men depended upon him if he did not make it back to Boston. And that single, bruising thought stuck in his craw, sharp as a wedged bone.

"You are a disappointment."

Lifting his hand, he shoved away his grandfather's words echoing from the grave and probed his swollen eye. The chains hanging from his wrist rattled like a skeleton—a reminder of what he'd soon become. A slow smile stretched his lips. At least he could see. Face the noose head-on and die with dignity. His smile bled into a frown. Was there anything dignified about the last beat of a heart?

"Dubois! You ready to die?" A voice, as chilling as the spring air, blasted against the storage shed door.

Elias pushed up from the crate he'd called a bed. "Now is as good a time as any." The lie flowed a little too easily, and he winced, regretting the falsehood. . .regretting his failure. Because of his error, a deadly French weapon would kill countless English and Colonials.

Unless he made it out of here—alive and with that weapon—the tide of the war could once again turn back to the French. Ah, but his grandfather surely must be rolling in his coffin to know that the fate of an entire war hinged on his prodigal grandson.

A key scraped against metal. A wooden bar lifted. The silhouette of a red-coated grim reaper darkened the door.

"Then let's be about it." Captain Scraling stepped aside, leaving enough room for Elias to pass yet not escape, for another soldier stood outside, five paces away from the door.

His smile nearly returned. Where would he run to inside a palisade with guards at the ready?

Stretching a wicked kink out of his neck, he strolled ahead as if the request meant nothing more than a call to a hearty breakfast. But once past the threshold, he stopped and studied the sky—gray as a corpse drained of life. He shot the captain a scowl. "You are early. The sun is not up yet."

Scraling shrugged. "I have many things to do today. You are the least of them. Follow the private, if you please." He tipped his head toward the Colonial regular.

Elias smirked. "And if I do not?"

The captain's fist shot out. Elias's head exploded. Reeling, he plummeted backward, unable to stop himself from crashing to the ground. Blast! Just when his eye had started to open.

The next strike drove the air from his lungs. Groaning, he rolled over and gasped for air. An impossibility though when Scraling grabbed the back of his collar and yanked him to his feet.

"Move it!" The captain shoved him between the shoulder blades.

He stumbled forward, catching himself before ramming into the man in front of him. And a good thing too for the private stood ready to pummel him as well.

"Lead on, Private," the captain ordered.

They marched across the parade ground. Two wagons were being loaded near the front gate, not far from the rough-hewn gallows—a reminder to those arriving and departing that justice would be meted out, even here in the New York wilderness. Each step stole a breath from the few he yet owned, but he couldn't begrudge these men who prodded him onward. He was as guilty of the charges as Lucifer himself.

Birdsong trilled in the quiet of predawn, a pleasant accompaniment to the tramp of their feet. The shaking started then. First in his hands, working upward over arms and shoulders, diving in deep and spreading from gut to legs. It was always like this when the smell of death grew stronger—or was that his stench from being locked in a shed for two days without courtesy of a privy break?

He glanced skyward. *Is this it, Lord?*

A gentle morning breeze nudged the hanging rope. The movement was slight, barely noticeable, but enough to twist Elias's throat into a sodden knot. The hairs at the back of his neck stood out like wire. Was he truly ready to die? Was anyone?

Spare the lives of those men, God. The ones I failed. And forgive me for my lack.

Just ten paces more and—

The private made a sharp right, pivoting away from the scaffold. Elias's step faltered. Was this some kind of trick? He looked back to the captain.

A fist smashed into his nose. Double blast! His head jerked aside, the force knocking him to his hands and knees. The ground spun. Blood dripped over his top lip. The captain taunted from behind, something about his manliness or lack thereof. Hard to tell. Sound buzzed like a beehive that had been whacked with a stick—but even louder was the anger inside him, pumping stronger with each heartbeat. His fury strained at the leash. Staggering to his feet, he bit back a curse and spit out the nasty taste in his mouth, then lifted his face to the sky.

"Forgive these men too, Lord, for I surely am not able to at this moment." He spoke in French, not only to prevent the satisfaction the captain would feel at his admission, but more importantly to irritate the Englishman.

"Move along!"

Head pounding, he tromped after the private, unable to work up any more curiosity as to why they bypassed the noose and neared the officers' quarters. Likely a last interrogation—and his last chance to talk his way out of this mess.

Please, God. More than my life depends upon this. Have mercy.

The private knocked and, after a gruff "Enter" grumbled from inside, shoved open the door.

Elias advanced, swiping the blood from his nose and breathing in sage and rotgut rum.

Brigadier General Bragg did not so much as look up from his desk. He merely flicked out his hand as if the lot of them were blackflies to be swatted. "Captain, Private, wait outside."

With a final scowl aimed at Elias, Captain Scraling stomped off. Clearly he was not happy for being told to wait like a dog—and the thought of his inconvenience made Elias smile, despite the way the movement stung.

The general pinched a document in his fingers and held it up, skewering him with a glower of his own. "This is a warrant for your death."

Elias frowned. Why show him the document before draining the life from his eyes? This was not standard procedure. He'd fold his arms and stare the man down were his hands not weighted by irons.

"And this"—Bragg paused and held up a different parchment—"is a stay of execution."

A stay? What in all of God's great glory? A muscle jumped in his jaw, but he refused to gape, for surely the general expected such a response.

Though he'd regret it, the irony of the situation slowly unraveled inside him, and he chuckled. If only François could hear this. He laughed until the pounding of his skull could no longer be denied.

Bragg's brow darkened, as did the scarlet tip of his nose. "I fail to see the humor in this, Dubois."

"Are you seriously cutting a deal with a traitor?"

"I'd deal with the devil if I had to."

"Well, I suppose I am the closest thing you have to that." He angled his head. "What is your offer?"

Bragg leaned so far back in his chair, the wood creaked a grievance. "I have a shipment of gold needing safe delivery into British lands."

Elias advanced so quickly, Bragg reached for his pistol. Stopping short of lunging across the man's desk, Elias slammed his hands onto the wood, the chains adding to the startling effect. "Are you asking me to deliver the gold you stole from me?" The question echoed above the crackle of wood in the fire and the snort of the man in front of him.

"Yes."

Straightening, he lifted his face to the plank ceiling. "You never stop surprising me."

"We've only recently met."

He aimed his gaze back at Bragg like a loaded musket. "I was not talking to you."

The general shifted in his seat, laying his pistol in his lap. "My terms are these: You will be part of a four-person squad, traveling under the guise of a family moving back to civilization. Reach Fort Edward with the gold intact, and your execution will be pardoned, though the required jail time is nonnegotiable."

His stomach clenched—and not from lack of food. Something wasn't right about this. "Why me?"

"I don't think I need to tell you, soldier, that you will be crossing danger-ous ground. The chances of making it alive to Fort Edward are slim. You're a condemned man anyway. Expendable. And if you don't make it. . ." He shrugged.

Interesting—but completely implausible. Elias grunted. "What is to stop me from killing my companions and running off?"

"They will be armed. You will not."

No one could survive in the wilderness without a gun or a knife. Elias shook his head. "Then I might as well die here."

"With good behavior, you shall walk free. Eventually." Bragg held up both papers, shaking them so that the documents rippled like living things. "So, what will it be? Life. . .or death?"

Elias shifted his gaze from one to the other. Was this an answer to his prayer? Or a fiendish jest?

Reaching out, he snatched the parchment sentencing him to the gallows. He could end this here and now. Stop the running. Finish the vagabond life that he'd come to hate. Just a quick jerk from a tight rope, then a blissfully peaceful eternity with the only Father he'd ever respected.

Bragg's jaw dropped.

Elias smiled from the satisfaction of it.

Then ripped the document to pieces.

CHAPTER 4

Morning stretched with a gray yawn across the sky, unwilling to fully awaken. Mercy frowned as patches of rainwater, frozen to brittle sheets by last night's chill, crackled beneath her feet. If the cloud cover tarried and the earth held firm, at least they would make good time today. The sooner this journey was over, the better.

Across the parade ground, a curious sight snagged her attention. Three men filed past the gallows, then veered away from it. The raggedy one in the middle strode the proudest, shoulders back, gait sure, despite the shackles weighing him down. The man was so filthy it was impossible to see the true color of his coat or breeches. Was this the traitor who would play the part of her husband? But no, clearly he was in no condition to travel anywhere except back to the stocks.

The prisoner turned to the captain behind him, and a fist knocked him to the ground. Not an unusual sight given the nature of the fort, but what followed put a hitch in Mercy's step.

The man staggered up from the blow, turned aside and spit, and then, with as much grace as a buck, lifted his face to the sky. His sudden stillness reached across the distance and pulled her in. This far away she couldn't hear his words, but the sacredness of the moment stole her breath. Clearly he spoke to his God, and she got the distinct impression his God bent and listened with a keen ear. Growing up in a Mohawk camp, she was no stranger to the mystical ways of shamans, but this? Gooseflesh prickled down her arms, and she was unaccountably glad when the captain shoved the man forward into the brigadier general's quarters.

Shaking off the unsettling feeling, she shifted her hold on her bundle of belongings and upped her pace. The man was none of her concern. She had bigger wolves to slay this day, namely setting out on a journey with a husband she did not want—even if it were in name only. Maybe she could persuade

Matthew to let her ride with him instead. As a rule, she did not like working with strangers, and she especially did not pine for it when the man had a name like Dubois.

Drawing near the two wagons at the front gate, she caught Matthew's eye and hailed him with a tip of her chin. After so many years learning each other's ways, words were a hindrance.

He helped a soldier shove a crate up a ramp into the wagon, then strode her way. "Stow your pack. And you wanna check those supplies?" He hitched his thumb, indicating a box on the ground up near the other wagon. "Prob'ly ain't much."

"We've been through lean." She glanced past Matthew's shoulder to where another soldier had taken his place in the loading. Both men strained their muscles against the next trunk. She recognized one private, but not the other. Neither was a bowlegged effigy. "Where's Rufus?"

"I imagine he'll show when the work's done."

"No doubt. Is that man over there my. . ." The word *husband* crawled back down her throat. Thinking it was one thing. Speaking it into being, an impossibility.

Matthew shook his head. "He ain't showed yet either."

Relief hit her as sweet as the brisk morning air. It would be short-lived, but she savored it nonetheless. Her bundle clutched to her chest, she bypassed the length of the canvas-covered wagon with four horses hitched to the front of it and neared the back of the other wagon. She hefted her pack over the back gate and tucked it snug beside six fat trunks that rode shoulder to shoulder, close as friends huddled near a fire—clearly more comfortable at the prospect of the ride than she.

She turned from the sight and rifled through the contents of the remaining crate on the ground. A blackened tin pot. Several packets of hardtack. Dried beans and some strips of meat so old and shriveled as to be beyond recognition. There was one jug of watered ale and several handfuls of root vegetables, all as wrinkled as tribal elders. This far from civilization and after a winter spare of game, they were the best victuals to be had.

She secured the lid, then heaved the crate into the wagon, grunting from the effort. For such mean supplies, the box weighed heavy. Footsteps thudded on the hardened dirt, and she turned.

Rufus Bragg wasn't much of a man, for he barely held on to sixteen years. So gawkily built was he, his bones put up a fair fight to support his garments. Were it not for the knobs of his joints, he'd have to tie the shirt to his skin to keep it from falling off. Mouse-colored hair hung over one small, dark eye. The other one blinked at her. He said nothing. Not only did he own no manners, it seemed he never intended to purchase any.

But beyond looks and manners, the mark of wickedness was the young man's worst fault. She'd once seen him torture a rabbit kit just for the enjoyment of it. Were he not the brigadier general's son, he'd have been cashiered long ago.

She glanced over at the other wagon, where the men loaded the last crate, then pursed her lips and speared Rufus with a scowl. "Right on time, as always."

His mouth parted in a toothy grin. "Ne'er too late and ne'er too early."

"Never around to lift a finger, more like it."

He shrugged, and she feared the sharpness of his shoulders might cut through his shirt and coat. "Cain't be blamed if the men don't wait for me."

She clenched her jaw. Matthew was right. They would both be bearing crosses. Sidestepping Rufus, she strode back to Matthew. "As you thought, there's not much by way of food. Have to hunt along the way. Could slow us down some."

Matthew rubbed his jaw, clean shaven but not for long. "Now yer eager to be rid of me?"

"That is not what I meant, and you know it. The sooner we reach Fort Edward, the sooner"—she lowered her voice as the man-boy swung around the back of the wagon—"we'll be rid of Rufus. We ready to go?"

"Soon as your man shows."

She gasped. "My man?" The familiarity he awarded a known traitor and a French one at that roiled the bellyful of chicory coffee she'd swigged for breakfast.

"Quit yer chafing. Gotta play the part, *Daughter*." He rested a big hand on her shoulder. "If we don't swallow our roles now and trouble comes along, our lives are on the line."

"Fine. But I don't like it."

"You have made that quite clear." His hand fell away, and the rebuke in his gray eyes scorched like an August sun.

She dipped her head. "Very well. I will be the most obedient daughter ever to grace the wilds of upper New York."

"That don't worry me. I'm fretting over how you will manage to act the goodwife."

Elias shivered, naked and cold. Having just left the general's office, he'd expected to be outfitted for the upcoming trek—but not with an icy drenching.

He gritted his teeth to keep from gasping when the next bucketful hit. Captain Scraling and the private laughed—then the private picked up yet another bucket and did it again. Elias shook his head like a dog. He should be thankful for the washing, but Lord have mercy, this was humiliating.

"Get yourself dressed. I ain't no lady's maid and those wagons are itchin' to leave."

The private lobbed a ball of clothing at him. He caught it just before the bundle landed on the wet ground.

Scraling leaned against the general's quarters, gun at the ready. Did the man truly think he'd need it? Only a fool would make a stripped-bare run for it in the company of soldiers long deprived of a good fight.

Elias shrugged on a shirt too small and breeches better fitted to a scarecrow. His own clothes had been ruined beyond repair, thanks to men such as these. He shoved his arms into the sleeves of a linen hunting frock, and forgave the tightness of the garments beneath, for this coat with its long sleeves and longer hem covered a multitude of sins. He grabbed up his own leather belt and secured it, then jammed his feet into his moccasins, both mercifully unscathed save for a few nicks.

Once again he fell into step between the private and the captain, who led him around the building. Scraling rapped on the general's door and Bragg emerged. Daylight wasn't kind to him. Though dawn hardly grabbed hold of the day and cloud cover did its best to vanquish even that weak light, broken veins showed clearly on the fleshy parts of the general's face.

"So, there was a man beneath that filth." The general nodded at Scraling and the private. "Thank you, men. That will be all. Dubois, follow me."

Elias kept time with Bragg's hike across the parade ground. The noose dangling from the gallows waved as they passed, and Elias tugged at his collar. While this wasn't his day to swing by the neck, that did not mean death wasn't crouched nearby.

Narrowing his eyes, he studied the figures ahead. A tall man, silver-fox hair shooting wild from beneath his hat, conversed with a woman, who stood not much shorter. If it weren't for a long braid of dark hair tailing down her back and a dun-colored gown flaring out at her hips, he almost might have mistaken her for a man, so wide was her stance, so confident the stretch of her shoulders. Two soldiers strode away from the rear wagon, revealing a lank-limbed, scruff-faced younger man.

"If the weather holds"—Bragg's voice interrupted his assessment—"it should take you a fortnight to reach Fort Edward, though given the rain we've had, the going could be treacherous. You are adept at handling a wagon, are you not?"

He bit back a smirk. The man had no idea. "Are the loads weighed even?"

"Captain Matthew Prinn, your. . .er, *father-in-law*, will have seen to that."

He grunted. "Then yes. I am no stranger to hauling goods."

"With a name like Dubois, I thought as much."

Elias let the slur slick off him like water from a beaver's tail. With a French surname, he'd heard it all before. Most English thought him either a voyageur, a criminal, or a scalp-taker—and they were right on all accounts. Or at least he had been in the past. But if Bragg knew what British blood also flowed in his veins, the man would bend a knee and plead for mercy.

The general stopped just paces behind the woman. "Miss Lytton, Captain Prinn, allow me to introduce the last member of your team, Mr. Elias Dubois. Keep an eye on your weapons, for under no circumstance is this man to be given one."

Anger scorched a blaze up his neck, erasing any memory of his earlier cold dousing. A man couldn't survive without a gun and a blade, especially not in the company of this sorry-looking lot. They would be lucky to make it to nightfall. His hands clenched at his sides, itching for the feel of a musket stock or knife hilt. "That is a mistake, General. Unarmed, I am of no use to anyone."

"As I said, you're expendable if need be. Godspeed." The general wheeled about.

So did the woman. Brown eyes bored into his, just about level with his own. This close, she was taller than he'd first credited. Dark of hair, darker of gaze, with cheekbones high and eyes large and wide enough to dive in and swim around. He might almost place her as a native—were it not for skin so fair, it glowed soft and white. He sucked in a breath. By all the blessed stars above, how had he ever thought her to be mannish?

"Ma'am." He dipped his head in greeting.

Her lips parted, full and surprisingly deep in color, yet she said nothing.

"Mr. Dubois." The man behind her stepped forward and offered a hand. "I'm Matthew Prinn."

"Elias, please. If we are to pose as a family, it would be best to be on a first-name basis." He clasped the fellow's hand and measured his character by grip alone. Strong. Unwavering. Calloused and hard. But not overpowering, revealing a kind of stalwart humility.

"I s'pose you're right." The man let go and nudged the woman with his elbow. "This here is Mercy."

Elias clamped his jaw. An apt name, for Lord have mercy, she captivated like no other woman, and to his shame, he'd known quite a few.

She lifted her chin. "Daylight's wasting. We should be on our way."

She whirled so fast, her long braid slapped his arm. Her skirts swished as she stalked toward the front wagon.

Elias's brows shot up. There was nothing skittish about this one.

Prinn's gray eyes followed the woman while his jaw worked. "Mercy can be a little. . . Let's just say she is a fiddle string wound tight and about to break. Might wanna ride quiet for a while. If she snaps, it will leave a mark. She'll get over it soon enough. Rufus! Hike yerself up to the seat. I will take first scout." He turned, leaving Elias standing alone at the rear, caught between the empty gallows and the fort gates swinging wide, gaping open to a wilderness filled with danger.

Elias cracked his neck one way then the other. Had he escaped one sure death only to face another? He lifted a prayer as he hiked toward the front wagon. More than one life depended on his survival—and with the worn man, young buck, and fiery woman, he'd just added three more to that count.

CHAPTER 5

Mercy studied Elias Dubois as he swung up onto the wagon seat beside her. She had never thought this day would come. She sitting next to a man purporting to be her husband—real or not. She gripped the wagon's side to keep from pinching her skin to check if this was some kind of nightmare. After years of watching her mother being subdued so thoroughly by her father, she had sworn not to put herself in the same position. Ever. Not even as a farce.

To Mr. Dubois's credit, the man said nothing, merely spit out a "Get-up" and slapped the reins, lurching the wagon into movement. It was a small act, one she did not want to admire, but clearly he owned some sense—both in coaxing the horses to tow such a heavy load and in allowing her time to settle in silence.

Beneath a felt hat, his dark hair hung wet to his shoulders, stark against his colorless linen collar. One eye was purpled nearly shut. His good eye stared straight ahead. A fresh cut drew a red line on his cheekbone, just above the scruff of his beard. He sat tall, but not much higher than her. A bump rode midway down his nose, the legacy of a fighter, but not nearly as pronounced as the crooked bend of Matthew's. His skin was tanned to burnt honey—a rarity this time of year, unless one lived outside regardless of the seasons.

Her gaze shifted down his arms. While one hand gripped the reins, the other rode on his thick leg. His knuckles were grazed raw. Fighter, indeed. How many men had those fists struck? She stared harder. Worn grooves marked the flesh between his fingers—ruts worn by rifle balls, a testimony of years spent caressing a gun.

Yet despite his rugged exterior and the fact that he rode toward God knew how many years of imprisonment, he guided the horses as if he were on a Sunday drive. A strange contentedness flowed from him, as if he'd lived and walked around in hunger and need, then strolled out the other side a more peaceful soul for the journey.

"Your assessment?" He spoke without pulling his gaze from the narrow trace they followed.

His voice carried a strange mix of accents. French. British. And oddly enough, a throaty twang she couldn't place at first—and when she did, she narrowed her eyes at him.

Native. . .but which people?

"You're capable enough," she admitted. "Leastwise I don't think I shall have to be saving your hide."

"So, you think it is a hide worth saving then?" He flashed her a smile, one that did strange things to her belly.

"You tell me."

His grin faded. A shameful loss, that. His blue gaze—the color of an October sky—held hers with as much intensity as she might employ.

"You are a bold one," he said simply.

"And is that the sum of your appraisal?" At the quirk of his brow, she continued, "Don't bother denying it. Even without looking, you have been measuring my strengths and weaknesses since we left the fort."

He threw back his head and laughed, a warm sound, heating her despite the chill of the spring morn. He smelled of smoke—gun smoke, wood smoke, and the heated charge in the air left behind when lightning struck a pine.

Laughter spent, he faced forward again. "You are as much a riddle as me—and I think we both know it."

"At least I'm not a traitor." She bit her lip. Too late. An arrow once shot could not be re-quivered. If Matthew heard her, an ear-burning scolding would light her on fire.

But Elias—for yes, she ought to think of him as such, despite her misgivings—merely continued guiding the horses along the trail. "Judging on hearsay is a danger," he said in an even tone.

Her jaw dropped. This man, the one she'd seen shackled and dropped to the ground, was denying the accusation? She hitched her thumb over her shoulder. "Isn't this load of gold what you were moving for the French?"

"It is."

"But you have English blood."

"Indeed." He glanced at her sideways. "Sharp eye."

"Seems to me your loyalties are a-tangle, Elias Dubois."

His shoulders shook. For one beaten half-dead and parrying an earful of a woman's blows, he was generous with his humor.

The chuckle in his throat faded. "I would say my allegiances are no more conflicted than yours."

She smirked, then grabbed the wagon's seat as they bumped over a large rock. There was no answer to his remark—for he couldn't be more right.

"All right, here is my assessment then, since you asked." He turned to her, allowing the horses to find their own speed. "What I know is that you are fair to chafing in that gown, and lest you decide you are done with it, I had best keep an eye on my breeches. Your words are more crumpets than cowpeas, proving somewhere along the way you were raised by a proper lady, a curiosity considering you now travel with a ranger. But there is one thing I am hog-tied to figure out."

Don't ask. Don't do it. That was what he wanted. But the need to know, ever her downfall, swelled like snowmelt on the Genesee River. "What's that?" she asked.

"If that lilt to your voice is Mohawk or Mohican."

Scowling, she faced forward once again, ignoring the man and his questions. He could wonder about her heritage all he liked—for she had no intention of sating his curiosity.

They rode in silence until it was her turn to swap with Matthew on scouting duty. Only once did they break their pace to water the horses and gnaw on a hardened crust of bread and a pouch of pemmican Matthew had seen fit to bring along. Matthew commented to her that he was surprised Elias was still in one piece. She'd shot back that she noticed Rufus was too, to which he'd answered the day wasn't over yet.

And she couldn't agree more. Would this day never end? With no sun to gauge by, she figured there were maybe two more hours of travel time until they hit the clearing to camp for the night—but when they turned a bend in the trail, she revised that opinion.

An enormous oak lay sideways in their path. Why hadn't Rufus run back to tell them? The man was worthless as a scout, though it shouldn't have surprised her. The only thing he excelled at was shirking his duties and complaining.

Elias set the brake and hopped down. So did she.

Eventually, Matthew joined them in front of the felled blockade. "That is a big one."

He wasn't jesting. Laid flat, the trunk stood as high as her knees. She frowned at the barrier, fighting the urge to kick the thing.

Elias turned to Matthew. "How many axes have we?"

"Two."

Her frown deepened. A fool's task, an idea brought on by too much brawn and not enough brain. "If we backtrack a half mile or so, I know a way around this. 'Tis an old *Kahnyen'kehàka* trail but ought to be wide enough."

Elias shook his head. "Too dangerous. We stick to the route."

What gall! Why did this man—this *traitor*—think he owned the last word? She whirled to Matthew. "If we turn around now, we can—"

"Go grab the axes, Mercy." Matthew cut her off.

"Matthew!" His name shot past her lips like a hiss. Was he really siding with a man he barely knew over her—and a branded turncoat at that? "You know I can walk this land blinded. I'm telling you my way will be faster."

"I don't doubt your knowledge, girl. But this time of year, after a winter of holing up, those trails are a-swarm with braves keening for a fight. I reckon you know that too. So like Elias says, we'll bust up this tree and continue on. Agreed?"

Her hands curled into fists. Unbelievable! Why did men always think they knew better? The time it would take to clear a path would put them behind schedule on the first day out. But the cut of Matthew's jaw and the blue steel in Elias's gaze fairly shouted they would not be moved.

"Fine," she strained out. "I will scout up ahead."

She stormed along the length of the trunk, spying out the best place to heft herself over. It was a grand and glorious lie she'd told, for she couldn't scout a thing—not with the red haze of rage coloring everything.

❧

Night fell hard and fast in the forest. Elias worked quickly in the dark, spreading an old army blanket across the tops of the crates in the wagon. If anyone asked what he was doing, he could say he was preparing a place for Mercy to sleep—which he was. Now. But before darkness had eaten up the last of day's light, he'd rummaged to find the crate he'd notched and made sure the weapon he'd tucked safely at the bottom was still there.

"Dinner's ready."

Mercy's voice seeped through the canvas, competing with the low whirr of a few brave insects. Shrugging out of his coat, Elias added the extra layer to soften the bedding. It would make for a lumpy mattress, but if the sky's rumble held true, at least it'd be dry.

He climbed out of the wagon and headed back to the fire—the small flames of which were an allowance he and Matthew would abide for this night only. This close to the fort there likely weren't any scalp-takers on the prowl, not with soldiers frequently ranging this far out. But the farther they traveled into the backcountry, the more careful they would have to be.

Rufus and Matthew already sat cross-legged on the ground, holding out their bowls. Mercy stooped over a pot, stirring the meal. He took a spot opposite them all, the orange flames a barrier between him and the men, and held out his fingers to the warmth. It would be a cold one tonight, but late March was ever fickle in its temperament.

Mercy ladled out a watery broth with softened salt pork and root vegetables, the earthy aroma mouthwatering on the evening air. The stew hardly hit the bottom of Rufus's bowl before he moved to take a slurp of it—the beast.

"Hold off, Bragg." Elias skewered the young pup with a piercing gaze. Wilderness or not, a lady deserved respect, one of the few lessons from his mother that had ever taken root. "Wait for the lady to take the first bite."

Rufus spit out a curse. "Who died and put you in charge?"

"If you would act as a human instead of a beast, I would not have to tell you." Half a smirk twitched his lips. How many times had he heard that himself growing up? He could almost feel the swat of his grandfather's big hand across the seat of his breeches.

"You are a disappointment."

His smirk faded at the ghostly reminder.

Mercy scowled and sat next to Matthew, her own dinner in hand. "Such manners are for fine ladies at white linen tables. Neither are here."

Elias shrugged. The women he'd known back in Boston would've taken his words as a kindness. "A lady is a lady, no matter the setting."

"The man's just lookin' out for you, girl." Matthew nudged her with his elbow. "Take a bite so we can get on with it."

Silently, Mercy lifted the bowl to her lips, her gaze fixed on Elias the whole time. What went on behind those dark eyes of hers? She stared warily, as if he were a rattler about to strike.

The silence wore on until he could take no more of Rufus's slurping. Setting down his bowl, Elias swiped his mouth. "We will need to leave come first light to make up for today's loss of time."

Mercy set down her bowl as well, breathing out guttural words too fast and low to identify.

Matthew frowned at her for a moment, then met Elias's gaze over the fire. "I'm surprised you're eager to reach the fort. Seems a man in your situation might want to drag his heels."

He stared the captain down. "I never shirk a duty, even when it is not to my liking."

A chuckle rumbled in Matthew's chest. "You sound an awful lot like someone I know."

But there was no humor in the shadows on Mercy's face. "You seem to have no qualms about which side those duties are for. Do you, Mr. Dubois?"

Her challenge crackled in the air like the pop of wood in the fire. He clenched his jaw. There was no easy way to answer that, leastwise none that wouldn't give away his true colors.

Matthew broke the standoff by setting down his bowl. "Rufus, you take first watch. Mercy, grab second. I will take—"

"I will take third," Elias offered. A smile as thin as the stew twitched his lips. "But I will not be much of a guard without a weapon."

"By the looks of you, you're a scrapper. I have no doubt you can take down a man without a gun in your hands." Matthew stretched out on the ground vacated by Rufus, the younger man already having stalked off into the dark. "Besides, you got a voice, don't you?"

Elias grunted. His bellow wouldn't be much of a defense should someone decide to attack them in the blackest hours of the night.

Mercy gathered the bowls, wiping them out with nothing but moss and the hem of her apron. She lifted the pot from the fire with a large branch, letting it cool in the dirt. Elias was just about to ask her if she was finished when she plopped onto the ground and curled up next to the fire. Did she seriously think to sleep outside? What kind of woman did that without a mutter of complaint?

He stood and stretched out his hand to her.

She looked at his fingers, firelight making it impossible to read what went on inside that mind of hers. Regardless, she did not move.

So he lobbed his own challenge. "You are not afraid, are you?"

With a hiss, she grabbed his hand, allowing him to hoist her to her feet—but when her warm skin touched his, a jolt shot through him. Instantly he released her, shaken beyond reason. Of course he'd held women's hands before—and much more than that—but never, *ever*, had one left a mark on him like this.

And by the sound of it, she felt the same, for she sucked in a sharp breath.

He turned away, unwilling to ponder the strange sensation any further. Must have been the chill spring air getting to him in naught but a shirt. "Follow me."

Her feet tread silently behind him. Were it not for her musky sweet scent, he'd wonder if she followed at all. He led her to the wagon and nodded for her to climb up.

Her brow furrowed at him. "You need me to fetch something for you? Why not do it yourself?"

"Nothing of the sort. Just go on up."

She stood silent for a moment, only God knowing her thoughts. Then without another word, she hiked her skirts and climbed up.

He bit back a grin. She'd been surprising him all day, and the thought of surprising her right back warmed him as much as if he wore his hunting frock.

She ducked inside, and he hesitated. Should he wait here for her gratitude or go back to the—

A fury of dark hair and flashing eyes sprang down from the wagon seat, landing in front of him. If the woman could kill by glower alone, he'd already be bleeding out on the dirt.

"I may not be the kind of woman you're used to, Mr. Dubois, but I am *not* that kind." She whirled, the thick coil of her braid once again whipping his arm. Her feet pounded hard on the ground.

What in the name of God and country was she going on about? Couldn't she—

His breath hitched as her meaning sank teeth into his conscience. Did she think. . . ? He hadn't intended that at all.

He charged after her. "Thunder and turf! Rain is in the air. Most women would be happy to bed down in a dry space. I thought you would be pleased."

Her steps did not slow. "Stay away from me."

Instantly Matthew was in front of him, a deadly set to his jaw. "Is there a problem?"

"Yes!" Elias threw out his hands. "By the name of Mercy Lytton."

Matthew glanced over his shoulder to where Mercy whumped onto the ground, her back to both of them. Then he quirked a brow at Elias.

Elias stifled a growl. Somehow being locked in that stinking storage shed with shackles on his wrists seemed preferable to this drama. "All I did was make a dry spot for her to bed down. Alone. Nothing more. I swear it."

A slow smile spread on Matthew's face, then he tugged Elias's sleeve, leading him out of earshot of Mercy. Matthew's gray eyes, black now in the dark of night, peered into his.

"A word of advice. Mercy can't be prodded. She can be led, but only if she trusts the leader. You ain't earned that trust yet, and with what she knows of you, it might take a long time. A very long time. Same goes for me. While I appreciate your hard work today and that you have not tried to run off, just know that I've got my eye on you."

Elias blew out a breath, long and low, easing some of the tension but not all. Were the tables turned, he'd feel the same way. "Point taken."

"Good." Matthew turned to go but then doubled back. A peculiar glint in his gaze—like that of a freshly sharpened blade—cut through the darkness. "One more thing. You ever try to touch that woman, and she doesn't finish you off first, I will kill you."

CHAPTER 6

Rain tapped a tattoo against the canvas, trapping Mercy in the foggy world of awake-yet-not. Though the patter did its best to lull her back to sleep, she forced her eyes open. The soft light of a morning yet to come washed everything gray. For a moment she lay there, blinking, thankful she'd taken Elias up on his offer of dry bedding—though in the end it had been Matthew's words that had persuaded her. Yawning, she pushed up, the scent of Elias Dubois's coat still thick in her nose, peppery and smoky. A manly smell—one she did not wish to know so intimately. She snatched up his hunting frock and climbed out of the wagon.

Outside, water dripped everywhere. Heaven's tears, weeping life into the earth, made everything soggy. At least it wasn't snow. While not likely, a final strike of winter wasn't out of the realm of possibility.

Thick snores cleaved the predawn, tearing out from inside the other wagon. It must be Rufus, for Matthew had taken the final night watch. Ahead, Elias stood with his back toward her, fingers busy checking harness buckles on the horses. The linen fabric of his shirt stretched tight across his broad shoulders.

She advanced toward him with his coat outstretched. He had to be miserable without it, though the gleam in his blue eyes as she approached did not hint at such. In fact, he looked all the more rugged and thriving without it. She pressed her lips tight to keep from an openmouthed stare. The man was an enigma. Once she'd gotten over the fact that he'd meant no ill intent by making her a cozy shelter, she truly had been thankful. Not even Matthew would've provided in such a personal way. Why had Elias Dubois?

Elias nodded, the hair unprotected by his hat wet and curling at the ends. "Good morning."

"Morning. I think you will be needing this today." She thrust the hunting frock into his hands.

He grunted then proceeded to shove his arms into the sleeves. "I trust you slept well."

"I trust you did not," she shot back, but she added a half smile to soften her banter.

Tying his belt, he said nothing, yet the smirk on his lips acknowledged her attempt at levity.

Though the rain was light, the dampness of it soaked into her bones, and she removed her shawl from her shoulders to resettle it over her head as a mantle. She should've thought to grab her hat. "Thank you, for the shelter last night, I mean. I. . ."

Her words stalled as his gaze locked onto hers. The same queer rush of heat fired inside her from heart to belly like when she'd gripped his hand the night before. It was a new feeling, unexpected—and completely uninvited. What kind of magic did the man wield?

She forced the rest of her words out in a rush. "I appreciate your sacrifice."

With his forefinger and thumb, he ran his fingers along the brim of his hat, flicking off the water dripping onto his face. Then he jutted his chin toward the wagon where the next loud snore ripped through the air. "I have suffered worse than Bragg's wood sawing."

She cocked a brow. "And his stench?"

For a single, breath-stealing moment—and quite against her better judgment—she shared a grin with Elias Dubois.

He turned and pointed at a mug sitting on a rock, a flat biscuit atop it. "There is a cup of chicory and a square of hardtack, rain-softened by now. I figured you could eat on the road. We should head out."

Her smile flattened. Ought she be cross that the man had thought her incapable of keeping herself fed—or flattered that he'd set aside food for her? If she had to think this hard on every odd thing he did, she'd be addle-brained by the time they reached Fort Edward.

Pushing aside a pine bough, Matthew strode in from the cover of the woods and eyed them both. "We ready? Besides Rufus, that is. A nudge with a gun barrel will get him moving fast enough."

She flung the loose edge of her shawl over her shoulder, securing the fabric snug against her head for a venture into the woods. "I will be, after a moment. Go on ahead. Elias and I will catch up."

She pushed her way into the damp green of the New York wilds, breathing in the pungent odor of wet dirt and bloodroot crushed beneath her step. All the stress of the past few days seeped away the farther she ventured. This was home, this maze of trees and rock. A place where she was master, where the only one she had to be sure about was herself.

Surveying from trunk to trunk, she set a course for a private spot to answer morning's call. With a last look around, she squatted, unwilling to admit the convenience of a skirt for such a purpose. Breeches were nice for running, but cumbersome when it came to other necessities.

After a moment, she stood. She ought to rush back, but the pull of creation tempted too strongly. Closing her eyes, she gave in to the luxury of inhaling a few breaths of peace and moist moss. Soon this journey would be over, and she would return to. . .what? With Matthew wanting to settle, she'd be alone. No one would hire a woman to scout on her own. It was a shaky future, as uncertain as chaff caught by the wind. Where she'd land was—

Her eyes shot open. She froze, still as death, for her life might depend upon it. Senses heightened, she scanned the area. She should've thought to grab her gun, but the blue gaze and kindly manner of Elias Dubois had scrambled her normal thinking. How foolish.

Around her, rain tapped the same as always. Rivulets whooshed from rock to rock where the ground drank no more. The only movement was that of freshly sprouted leaves bending from the steady beat of droplets. At ground level, trillium quivered from the constant pelting. Nothing else moved.

Even so, she pulled out the knife she wore against her chest. Something wasn't right.

She sniffed, hoping to catch the scent of whatever it was that bristled the fine hairs at the base of her neck. She breathed in the same zesty aroma of a wet March morning—but this time something more muddied the air.

The rank tang of bear grease.

She whirled, knife raised.

And two eyes—darker than her own—stared into her soul.

Elias glanced over his shoulder from his perch on the wagon seat, studying the trees yet again. No buff-colored skirts broke the green monotony—and that rankled him. It had been too long since Mercy had hied herself into the woods to take care of her morning business. The grind and suck of Matthew's wagon wheels were nothing but a memory by now. Maybe that stew from last night hadn't set well in the woman's belly.

Or maybe she had met with trouble.

He swung down to the ground, heels sinking into the soft earth. Thunderation! What he wouldn't give for a gun to grip.

Following the route of flattened greenery, he worked his way into the woods. Every so often he spotted a small footprint pressed into the mud.

Only one set of prints though. No other humans or animals. He thought about calling softly for her, so as not to startle her if she really were just doubled over with cramps or such. The ways of women were and always would be a mystery.

But he changed his mind as he scented a faint whiff of bear grease. Alert to the slightest sounds, he crept onward, bent low, one thought burning white hot: *Kill or be killed.*

Oh God, for Mercy's sake, let me find her before it is too late.

Twenty yards farther he stopped and molded his body against a black-trunked hemlock. Ten paces to his left, Mercy stared wide-eyed at a mountain of an Indian, her face stricken. One swipe of the man's massive hand could split her skull. Yet she stood still and straight, God bless her, neither wilting nor swooning.

Elias's blood ran colder than the rain trickling in between collar and skin. He'd have to move fast and quiet, a panther on the prowl.

Step by step, drawing on all his experience of shadow walking, he advanced, edging in behind the warrior. Two paces more and he'd snap the man's neck—a sorry sight for Mercy to have to witness, but better the man's life than hers.

Her eyes widened, as did her mouth. "No!"

Elias lunged. Too late. The man had turned. Elias's grip slid into a mere chokehold. Blast! The man's feet scrabbled for purchase on the slick ground as he clawed at Elias's arm.

Elias choked all the tighter—until his own feet slipped.

They whumped to mud and rock, tumbling in a death roll. Whoever landed on top would hold the advantage. If he died here, what would become of Mercy?

Lord, give me strength.

With a feral growl, he tore into the Indian, riding atop him. His fist crunched into the man's nose and sank into cartilage, splitting his knuckles.

"Enough!" Mercy screamed. "I know this man!"

The words stung, making no more sense than the drone of hornets, nor did the following guttural language she spewed. For a single startled moment, he pulled back, hand still clenched and ready to strike. Was this some kind of foul trick?

The big man shoved him off and stood. Turning aside, he spit out a mouthful of blood.

Elias rose on jittery legs, the drive to fight still flexing each of his muscles. Keeping one eye on the Indian, he spoke to Mercy. "Are you all right?"

"Of course I'm all right." She threw out her hands. "Onontio is my brother."

Brother? He eyed her warily. "You are not in danger?"

She frowned. "I am not some fair maiden in need of saving, especially not from that one." She tipped her chin at the big man.

Words flew between Mercy and her supposed brother, and Elias tried to read their body language, so foreign were the words. Of only two things he was certain—they definitely knew one another, and the man was a Mohawk.

As if reading Elias's mind, the brute turned a savage glower toward him. Mercy laughed.

Elias shot his gaze to her. "What did he say?"

"He says for one so small, you hit like a fallen boulder."

"Small!" His hands clenched once again.

Mercy shrugged. "To Onontio everyone is small."

The man's eyes flashed back to hers. Despite her claim of kinship, there was nothing alike about them. He was night to her day, beast to her feline sleekness. More words passed between them until each held up a hand.

"*Ó:nen ki› wáhi*, Onontio." Her farewell was plain enough to understand.

"*Ó:nen ki› wáhi*, Kahente." The big man gave the slightest of nods, then stalked off into the woods.

Kahente? Was that her native name?

Mercy turned on her heel and strode back toward the wagon, not pausing a step as she called over her shoulder, "We should make haste."

Elias caught up to her and grabbed her arm, pulling her back. "Hold on. You cannot expect me to let this pass without first telling me what is going on."

A crescent dimple curved like a small frown on her chin. "Onontio"—she glanced at the man's retreating form—"is my half brother. He came to warn me—us—there are signs the Wyandot are on the move. The sooner we make Fort Edward, the better. . .unless you prefer to meet up with your French allies?"

Elias huffed out a low breath, spent and weary. He'd been at this duplicitous game far too long. He could more than hold his own with the Wyandot, but the woman in front of him and the ranger he was coming to respect wouldn't stand a chance. As for Rufus, well. . .better not to wish so horrific an end even to such a slackard.

He pulled back his hand and flexed his sore fingers. "You are right—it is best we move on."

Her brow raised with a flicker of skepticism, but she turned and trod through the wet woods on feet as silent as his.

He guarded her back the whole way, but each empty-handed step was a grim reminder that should a war party cross their path, he was no match unarmed. "I would be a lot more help to you and everyone if you would just give me a gun," he muttered.

"You could be a lot more dangerous too." She reached for the wagon seat and hefted herself up.

He snorted. "As dangerous as a Wyandot bent on a killing rage? You have no idea."

The woman blinked down at him. "And you do?"

He shook his head, fighting back memories of slaughter and carnage. He'd seen things, done things, no woman or man should ever have to witness, all for the call of duty. Sickened, he felt his gut twist. Save for God's grace, he'd still be such a monster.

Mercy bent down toward him. "I'm not afraid of Wyandots, Mr. Dubois. Nor am I afraid of you."

"Maybe you should be." He lowered his voice. "Because if killing any of you were what I was about, I would have done it by now."

He stomped to the other side of the wagon. If what her half brother had warned was true, they had best get a move on, for the Wyandots were ruthless killers.

A fact he knew far better than most, for he'd learned his skills from them.

CHAPTER 7

Five days of solid rain—and as many wet nights—yet still no sign of the danger Onontio had warned about. Mercy tugged the brim of her old felt hat lower, glad she'd brought it along. Though they had not run into any Wyandot thus far, she'd rest easier once they made Fort Edward.

"Cursed weather," she mumbled.

On the wagon seat next to her, Elias angled his head, moisture collecting like tiny diamonds on the ends of his beard. "There is no shame riding inside, especially after scouting in the rain. Go dry off."

She shook her head. " 'Tisn't that. It's just such blessed slow going. We won't reach the fort in two weeks. We've traveled six days already and aren't near to a third of the way there."

"You tired of my company?" He flashed an easy grin.

Too easy. Must the man be as bountiful in his humor as he was in good looks? And therein lay the problem—she *wasn't* tired of his presence, and in fact was beginning to develop an unhealthy appetite for it. She turned her face before he could read the truth warming her cheeks. Despite his claim of latent violence, Elias Dubois was far too good-natured.

"So tell me." His voice rumbled along with the wagon wheels. "What does it mean? Your name, that is."

The query tangled into snarls as thick as those she brushed from her hair each night. "You bow your head over meals and betimes steal off to bend your knee, and yet you ask me such a question? Clearly you know the meaning of mercy and believe in a God who grants it, elsewise you'd not go to so much trouble."

"Trouble?" His brows shot high. "Nay. 'Tis a privilege. An honor. Why is it you sound as if belief in such a God is a struggle?"

"I never said that." She tucked her chin, shrinking from the uncomfortable turn of conversation. It wasn't that she did not believe a merciful God existed, for truly, was not the first cry of a newborn babe or the way the mists rose on a summer morn proof enough? No, indeed. God was real, as close as the breath filling her lungs.

She just wasn't sure she could trust Him. Her mother's faith in a merciful God surely hadn't protected her. Absently, she reached up and fingered the locket through the fabric of her gown.

Elias clicked his tongue and slapped the reins, urging the horses through a slick of mud. "What I meant was your people's name—Kahente. I have been thinking on all the Mohawk words I know, which admittedly are few, and I cannot square it."

She clenched her jaw to keep from dropping her mouth. No sense letting the man know how often he surprised her, for that would only encourage him. "You speak Kanien'keha?"

"Just enough to get me killed." His white teeth flashed in the gloom of the day.

A smirk twisted her lips. That he knew any of the people's language warmed her heart in a strange way—though she'd not admit it aloud. "*Kahente* means 'before her time.'"

Rows of furrows marred his brow, but he did not prod her any further. Obviously the man's curiosity was as insatiable as her own, yet he shied away from forcing the matter.

She hid a smile, her esteem for him growing. "There's not much to it, really. I merely did not wait the nine moons to leave my mother's womb, but came at seven."

"A credible explanation." He flicked the reins, snapping the horses into a faster pace. "But I think whoever gave you that name had much more in mind."

How could he know what thoughts Black-Fox-Running had pieced together those many years ago? She studied Elias's profile as he drove, looking for some hint of what he meant. His strong-cut jaw did not so much as twitch, nor did he look at her. Was he baiting her for the sheer sport of it, or did he truly have another thought on the matter?

"What do you mean?"

"You speak your mind without pausing to listen to reason. You don't wait for danger to pass but run headlong after it. So in those respects, I would say you are before your time, for there's nothing patient about you." He slipped his gaze her way. "Kahente."

The anger that had been building from his stinging assessment melted away with the heat of his gaze. Her native name flowed so easily from his lips, she couldn't help but stare. His was a fine mouth. Wide and strong. Thick and full. What would it feel like to—

She jerked her face forward. So many queer feelings churned inside her belly that she had to be some kind of sick. What was wrong with her? Maybe a visit to a healer ought to be her first order of business when they did make the fort. Likely she had tick fever or some other such ailment.

"Who gave you the name?" he asked.

She frowned. Maybe she should have taken his suggestion and crawled back beneath the canvas, for he was getting far too comfortable with conversation.

"My father." She pressed her mouth shut. That was all she'd offer, no matter what inquiries followed.

But no more questions came. The wagon rattled along on slickened weeds. Rain fell slow and steady.

And blending with it all came the bass murmur of Elias's voice. "So your mother must be white. . .which explains a lot."

She cocked her head. What did this stranger think he knew of her? "Such as?"

"Your ability to speak two languages. Your ease among the British and their acceptance of you. Your uncommon knowledge of this land." He faced her head-on. "Your beauty."

"Beauty?" She flung the word back at him as a surge of anger shot through her. She'd heard that before, usually followed by an unsolicited touch. Why was it that once a man discovered her mixed heritage, he suddenly thought her easy prey?

She narrowed her eyes. "Better men than you have mocked me, Elias Dubois, only to find themselves flat on the ground."

"Oh, I assure you, Miss Lytton, I meant every word."

She went back to scanning the road. Better that than natter nonsense with a man who had an answer for everything.

Far in the distance, shapes thickened on the road. Scooting to the edge of her seat, she grabbed the wagon's side for balance and peered ahead through the wet veil. One by one she shut down all other senses save for sight. The slog of the wheels faded. The creak of leather and jingling tack disappeared. The jarring ride on the hard seat vanished as she focused far down the trail, beyond what should be seen.

Breathe. Breathe.

And there. . .rocks. Lots of them. A pile of stones had slid onto the road, blocking the route.

"There's a problem ahead." Her own voice pulled her from the trance.

Elias frowned at her, then narrowed his eyes into the distance. "I see nothing."

"You will."

With his free hand, he rubbed his eyes, then leaned forward and res-canned the trail. "No, nothing. . .or maybe. . ."

The wagon rolled along until the undeniable shape of a mound of jagged rocks came into view. It appeared to be a rockslide, the rubble having fallen from a steep bank on one side of the road. With so much rain, it was no wonder. But even so, she snatched up her gun and loaded the pan.

Elias pulled back on the reins and set the brake. He scanned the area as well, but breathed out in a whisper, "How did you see that?"

Was that awe or accusation roughening his voice? Not that she could answer, for she'd never come up with a suitable way to explain her keen sight even to herself. So she didn't bother. Her gift was as much a part of her as her hands or arms—and she never had to explain those away.

Hefting her leg over the side of the wagon, she scrambled down to the wet earth and probed the immediate area. On the other side, Elias did the same.

In time, Matthew's low, "Whoa," and the snort of his horses caught up. By now, both she and Elias had met and stopped at the edge of a four-foot-high pile of rocks, wide enough to lay five bodies head to toe across. She could feel the gaze of Elias's blue eyes hitting between her shoulder blades, but she did not turn, not even when he joined her side and asked her again how she'd seen the rockslide from so far back.

Matthew's footsteps tromped up to settle on the other side of her. A low whistle passed his lips. "This journey is cursed."

Rufus skittered up next to Elias, then bent and hefted one of the fallen rocks with his own curse. He lobbed the chunk of granite with another profanity.

In spite of the rain, Elias yanked off his hat and ran his fingers through his hair. "It appears Rufus has the right idea."

Mercy gawked at him. "We're to stand here and curse the rocks away?"

"No." He reset his hat and turned to her. "We will heft them out one by one."

Matthew hissed through his teeth. "There goes the rest of the day."

Mercy frowned. The thought of wasting more time pinched tighter than the stays digging into her ribs. If they backtracked to Megrith Crossing and headed west, they would meet up with a passage just wide enough to accom-modate their wagons, a trail riding on higher ground—ground not littered with a ton of rock.

She peered at Elias from beneath her hat brim. Would he listen this time? "I know another way. 'Tis a little narrow, but it'll do." She swung about to face Matthew. "What say you?"

Matthew looked past her to Elias. Some kind of manly conversation took place, but hard to tell what with naught but a grunt and a half shrug from either of them.

Rufus hefted another rock. "Listen to the half-breed, she oughta know——"

Elias moved so fast, air rushed past Mercy's cheek. He grabbed Rufus by the collar and hoisted him up, letting his gawky body dangle like a shirt pegged on a line. Rufus's face purpled to an ugly shade of dark, his feet kicking and his hands clawing at Elias's arm.

"Her name is Mercy—and I will have none of the sort for you the next time you call her otherwise." Elias's tone was deadly flat. For a breathless eternity, he held Rufus aloft; then his fingers splayed.

Rufus dropped. Gasping and rasping, he staggered like a soldier on leave.

Mercy glanced at Matthew to gauge his reaction, for she wasn't sure what to make of it. He said nothing, but his lips twisted into a wry smile.

Bypassing Rufus, Elias strode toward the wagon and called over his shoulder, "Remount. This time we will try Mercy's way."

It took all of Elias's resolve not to gape at the woman next to him as he urged the horses back to plod through the same mud slick they had slogged across before. He often marveled at God's great wonders. The pounding rush of spray at the bottom of a waterfall. A spiderweb dazzling silver in dawn's breaking light. The sacrifice of a mother's heart. But Mercy Lytton took his astonishment to a whole new level. His eyesight was keen—enough to shoot a lead ball through the eye of a raven in full flight at five rods off. Yet he hadn't seen that rockslide until a fair sight after Mercy spied it, and he couldn't fathom how she did.

Nor did he like it.

"There." She lifted a slim finger and pointed. "Just past that stand of sugar maples."

He slowed the horses as they neared the spot. Green growth, thick and wild from the rain, tangled as high as the horses' shoulders, in some places near to touching their withers. Easing back on the reins, he quirked a brow at her. "That is a road?"

She jutted her chin, eyes dark and unreadable beneath the brim of her hat. "I did not say it would be easy."

And it wasn't. Turning at such a sharp angle from a trail not much wider than the wagons was a miracle. Coaxing the horses to pull at an even speed so as not to foul the wheels with grabber-vine was another. But it wasn't until the trail took off up a steep incline that the truth of her words sank in like claws.

She was right. There was nothing easy about this.

Sweat beaded on his brow as he yelled, "Hyah!" then whistled through his teeth, calling upon every trick he knew to keep the horses plodding upward. If they stopped now, the weight of the cargo could yank them backward—right into Matthew's oncoming wagon. Picking rock would've been less work than this. To her credit, Mercy remained silent, leaning forward as if to will the horses onward.

By the time the trail leveled, sweat ran as freely as the rain on his skin from the toil of it. Once he cleared enough space for Matthew's wagon to rest behind, he stopped to breathe.

Reaching back, he massaged a cramp in his shoulder, knotted into a rock-hard bulge from the strain. "Well, that was some ride."

"Yet you managed it."

"Aye. Barely." He lowered his fingers, a half smile curving his lips. "Next time remind me to ask if there are any mountains involved."

"Oh, well. . ." White teeth nibbled her bottom lip, far too beguiling for a bone-weary moment such as this. She lifted one hand and pulled out a locket from beneath her bodice, then clutched it like some kind of amulet. He'd seen her do it several times throughout their journey. Clearly the thing gave her some kind of assurance. . .but for what?

"That wasn't the hard part," she mumbled.

His smile faded. "What do you mean?"

"This ridgeline runs about a half mile beyond that next bend."

He blew out a sigh. "And I suppose the decline will be just as treacherous."

"Not so much." Her coil of hair unraveled lopsided beneath her hat, and she tugged the long braid free of the felt, shifting it to trail down her back. "The slope is gentler going down, and it empties onto the trail we were on, bypassing that rockslide."

He scratched his jaw, his fingers rasping against a week's worth of stubble. Trying to track the logic of Mercy's words was sometimes as twisted as the trails they journeyed. "Then what is so hard about it?"

Footsteps tromped from behind, and Matthew's grizzled face appeared on Mercy's side of the wagon. He glowered up at her. "Blazing fires, girl! Don't tell me you just led us up to Traverse Ridge."

She stared straight ahead, as if the man were nothing more than a passing shadow. "We'd hardly be through a quarter of that rock pile if we'd stayed, and you know it."

"Traverse Ridge?" Elias repeated, hoping the voicing of it would shake loose some memory connected with the name.

A growl percolated in Matthew's chest. "Nothing to be done for it now. We sure as spit can't go back the way we came." His gray eyes burned into Elias's. "Take it slow, but keep moving, no matter what. Just keep moving."

He strode away before Elias could query him further. Mercy refused to meet his questioning gaze.

He gathered the reins and edged the horses forward. The trail was wide enough for the wagon before it dropped off to a maze of tree spires below. Surely Matthew did not think this was dangerous after what they had already ascended? Perhaps age had made him overcautious. Lord knew the older Grandfather got, the more he'd placed restrictions on him as a young boy. It seemed elders were ever skittish about taking risks.

But then the path curved, following the bend of the rise, and he sucked in a breath.

Ahead, the road continued straight and narrow, but at such an angle that all the weight of two tons of gold would be laid into the outer-edge wheels. If the load shifted or one of the spokes cracked from the pressure, there'd be no stopping a tumble down the steep drop of rock and trees. He scrubbed a hand over his face. He'd have to keep them in one piece for a whole half mile? A groan rumbled deep in his throat, mimicking Matthew's. No wonder the man had been so chary.

Holding a taut rein, Elias restrained the horses to a sluggish yet steady pace. Too fast and those wheels would snap like kindling. Mercy grabbed the side of the wagon to keep from falling out. At least the rain had let up some. A gift, that, but it did not make the wet ground any less slippery. If he lost this load now, more than just their lives would be at stake.

God, please.

Foot by foot, the wagon creaked along, so cattywampus that he and Mercy leaned hard to the left. The horses balked at the grade and weight of the wagon tongue pressing against their collars, but Elias held strong, never letting up on the steely tension of the reins.

Rocks plummeted, knocked loose from their passage. With the ground so saturated, no wonder that slide had let loose. The crash of granite chunks jarred like thunder as they collided with tree trunks, then rumbled off. An eerie sound. Like the breaking of bones—their bones if he gave in to his shaking forearms.

At last the road flattened. As much as he wanted to jump down and see how Matthew fared, there was no time, for the descent began as soon as the rear wheel evened out.

As Mercy claimed, the decline wasn't as extreme, but it made for perilous going nonetheless. By the time they finally met with the original road, his ribs ached from strained breathing.

Pulling far enough ahead for Matthew's wagon to clear the flattened trail, he halted the horses. Heart racing, he sank back against the canvas and closed his eyes, every muscle jittery.

"Well done." Mercy's words were quiet.

An offering, he supposed.

He glanced at her—and couldn't help but smile. Any other woman would be pale-faced and wide-eyed after that trek. Mercy's cheeks glowed pink, her brown gaze bright, as if her existence hadn't just depended on the strip of leather in his hands that he'd gripped for dear life.

"You just might be the death of me, Mercy Lytton."

He swung down to solid ground before she could reply and stalked over to her side of the wagon. Bending, he studied one wheel, shaking it to see how the spokes fared, then did the same with the others, praying the whole while he'd not see a problem.

But God was good. The spokes held true.

He strode to where Matthew squatted near his own back wheel, Rufus at his side, swearing down brimstone and damnation on them all for putting him through such a dangerous ride.

Matthew looked up at Elias's approach, his face as dark as the thickening black sky. "This wagon's not as stout as yours. One more trail like that, and these spokes will give way."

CHAPTER 8

Mercy rolled one way, then the other, seeking comfort where none would be found—certainly not on a bunched-up blanket laid on damp dirt. With a huff, she flipped onto her back, lying flat and staring up at the darkened cave ceiling. Finding this cavern had been a boon in the downpour, and she was thankful. Still. . .she flipped to her stomach. Guilt stole all the peace out of that gratitude.

Though neither Matthew nor Elias had disparaged her for their perilous trek along Traverse Ridge, Rufus had—when out of earshot of the other men. But he needn't have wasted his breath. Ever since she'd learned of Matthew's weakened wheel, she'd been flaying herself mentally. Sleep wouldn't come to call when such an intrusive visitor occupied her mind.

With a huff, she scooted over to what remained of the fire. On the side nearest the cave opening, Matthew stretched out on the ground, hat over his face and chest rising at an even pace. Rufus was gone—out on watch. On the other side, Elias sat cross-legged, the smoldering mound of embers casting a glow on his face. He looked like a god forged from the flames. Only his eyes acknowledged her approach.

She sat opposite him, pulling her shawl tighter at her neck. Not much warmth radiated from the dying fire, so she grabbed a stick and poked it, coaxing a few licks of red to life. All the while the man's gaze asked questions she did not want to answer—so she avoided looking up.

"Can't sleep," she explained quietly.

"There is no rain."

She quirked her head, listening. The shushing drone outside had ceased, replaced by stray drips looking for a home.

Elias's lips curved. "There is no pattering to lull you to sleep."

Would that were the only reason. A sigh emptied the air from her lungs, and she went back to poking at the fire. "No, 'tisn't that. I want to apologize for taking us up that ridge today. I did not consider the weight of the cargo. I could have gotten us killed."

"Well." His soft voice curled around her like smoke. "No real harm done. And we did make good time, better than if we had moved those rocks. That would have set us back a whole day."

A more than gracious response—but suspect. Ought not a criminal facing years in jail drag his heels instead of running into such a destiny?

Lifting her face, she studied the man. He sat so calmly still one would think him at peace with the universe. But how could that be, when he yet faced charges of sedition? And why had such an outwardly peaceful man decided to take up treachery to begin with? Was he a traitor of convenience, or did he do it for mere capital gain? Or perhaps his principles ran deeper and he was somehow proud to serve time for an action of conviction?

So many questions swirled in her head that she couldn't stop at least one of them from leaking out. "Why are you so bent on reaching the fort? You will be locked up, likely for years on end. There's no guarantee you will survive it."

Elias's blue eyes glimmered with some kind of knowledge, something she couldn't understand. He knew things of darkness and beyond, of blood and honor—which made her all the more curious.

She threw aside her poking stick. "Why did you trade loyalties in the middle of a fight? What made you turn?"

A muscle jumped in his neck, and he lowered his chin, hiding his face in the shadow of his hat. He was silent for so long, the drippings outside faded away.

She folded into her shawl, prepared to wait him out. She'd sat in more rugged conditions than this while holing up on a scouting mission.

Eventually, his low voice purled soft. "You are inquisitive tonight."

Obstinate man. Her lips pursed into a pout. If he thought to make her stray from her line of questioning, he'd be sorely disappointed. "And you're full of silence—a technique better used on army interrogators, not me. I have nowhere else to go and nothing else to do but wait for you to answer."

"Has anyone ever told you that you are a stubborn woman?" His tone changed, dark and cold as the cave. He leaned close to the fire, light riding the strong planes of his face.

She tensed at the formidable sight, both attracted and repelled, yet met him stare for stare. "Aye. I believe you have mentioned it a time or two."

He snorted. "What is it you really want to know, Mercy Lytton?" His query dangled like a rope from a gibbet. "Think carefully, for I shall only answer one question tonight."

"Why did you defend me against Rufus earlier today?" The words barreled out before she could stop them, and she bit her lip. Where on earth had that come from?

"Of all the. . . ?" Rearing back, he shook his head. Astonishment smoothed out the road-weariness from his face, making him appear as a wonder-eyed boy. "You never stop surprising me."

She squirmed, warmth spreading up her neck and onto her cheeks like a rash.

But just as suddenly, his jaw tightened and a storm cloud gathered on his face. "Men like Rufus are too ignorant to see who you really are."

She swallowed, afraid to speak, afraid not to. "Who do you think I am?"

"A beautiful creation of God."

His words were pleasing to the ear, but it was the reverent way he stared at her that became embedded deep in her heart. He meant what he said, but more than that, he knew what he said was as true as if God had come down and spoken to him alone. A staggering thought, one that stole her breath.

"You really know Him, don't you?" she whispered.

He nodded. "I do—and you can too."

She stiffened, the turn of conversation feeling like stays yanked too tight. This was too intimate to even think of, let alone talk about with a man. "I think I shall retire now."

His teeth flashed a knowing grin. "See you come morning then."

She scooted back to her corner of the cave, more painfully awake now than when she'd first left it. Flinging herself down to her blanket, she faced away from Elias Dubois.

How could she both love and hate the way someone made her feel?

Elias watched Mercy edge away from the fire, her pale skirts light against the darkness of the cave. She was a ghost in the darkness, one who would surely haunt his thoughts for the rest of the night.

He stared into the embers long after she disappeared, listening to the rhythm of Matthew's breathing and the rising chorus of insects outside. Ah, but the woman was spirited, an even match to his own willfulness. A slow smile lifted his lips. And if he were right, if she truly were like him, she had no idea of the fire about to blaze down and refine her.

He glanced up at the jagged ceiling. "So. . .You are working on her, eh, God? She could use it." Huffing out a breath, he bowed his head. "And so could I. Lord, make us both pleasing in Your sight."

The tromp of Rufus's feet drew near outside and pulled him from his prayer. He met the young man just outside the cave opening on a slick of gravel and mud.

Rufus eyed him as he might a wolf that could spring. Good. The young upstart needed his anger tethered to a taut rein—and Elias was more than happy to be the one to hold it. Scrubbing a hand along his jaw, he masked a grin. Rufus Bragg reminded him entirely too much of himself at that age. Would to God someone had kept him in line—not that Grandfather hadn't tried.

He tipped his head at the young man. "No sign of anything?"

Rufus stopped just out of reach and widened his stance, likely a show of power—but it did not work. The young man's knobby-framed body would break like a November twig were Elias to charge him.

A sneer curled Rufus's upper lip. "Nothing to worry your pretty head over."

The mockery hung in the damp air, and Elias left it right there, hovering. "Listen, Rufus, this is going to be a long journey if we do not work together."

Faster than he thought possible, Rufus swung up the muzzle of his Brown Bess, aiming square at him. From this range, a hole through the chest would kill him on the spot.

"Yer right." Rufus cocked open the hammer, the click of metal loud in the woods. "I could just shoot you now to save us both the trouble."

"You could." He eyed the barrel, noting the steady hold. The boy knew how to handle a weapon, he'd give him that. "But who is going to drive that wagon? Mercy or you? The way I see it, neither of you could manage such a haul, not on your own."

With a flick of his chin, Rufus spit to the side. "You think you got all the answers, don't ya, Frenchie boy? What do you care if we manage to reach the fort or not?"

"I care not whatsoever." And he didn't. Mercy and the boy were right to question him, for he had no intention of letting that gold reach Fort Edward—leastwise not one crate in particular.

But what would the boy make of his answer? He stared into Rufus's eyes, surveying his reaction. By the spare light of a sky now sprinkled with stars, it was still too dark to read with any accuracy what went on inside Rufus's head. Clearly the boy didn't see an unarmed man as a threat.

Elias threw back his shoulders, calling the boy's bluff. "Go on then, pull the trigger. You will be doing me a favor."

Once the challenge passed his lips, Elias sharpened his whole body into stillness, for his life teetered on the thin line of Rufus's integrity—if the boy had any. It would be a shameful way to go, breathing his last from the shot of an angst-filled boy-man. But at least he knew where he'd go, for he'd made his peace with God nigh on two years back. If only he could have settled things with Grandfather, a regret he'd take with him to the grave.

The boy stood fixed—the kind of rock-hard bearing only a seasoned killer would dare. Apparently Rufus had taken life before. Many, judging by his deadpan gaze.

Sweat beaded on Elias's brow. For the first time the thought crossed his mind that perhaps he had risked too much.

Metal clicked. The gun lowered. Elias let out a breath.

"You ain't worth my lead," Rufus hissed through his teeth, then turned and strode into the cave.

Once the boy was out of sight, Elias's shoulders sagged. His life had been spared. Again. Clearly it was God's will his delivery made it to Boston.

Nonetheless, it would be difficult with Rufus begging for a fight every blessed minute. A sigh deflated him, and he glanced at the sky. *How am I to do this, Lord, without bloodshed?*

CHAPTER 9

Bumping along in the wagon, Mercy lifted her face to the sun, strangely content after a night filled with dreams of a questioning blue-eyed man and a God who spoke to him face-to-face. She pulled off her hat and closed her eyes, soaking in the spring warmth. Tree silhouettes splotched black against the orange background, and she breathed in the freshness of the damp woods. By her reckoning, this was the finest first day of April since the year she'd surprised Black-Fox-Running with a basket full of wild garlic shoots. He'd praised her industry—but Mother had frowned. Her locket burned hot against her breast.

Mercy's eyes shot open. Better to face the present than live in a world of past hurts.

She gave in to the soothing sound of the wheels and the caress of a mild breeze, until loose hair tickled across her cheek. Working stray strands back into a braid that never stayed tight, she angled her head and listened. Something else pickabacked on that breeze. A shushing.

She peeked at Elias, only to find his gaze already studying her.

Despite the sunshine, his face darkened. "Did you not say the Nowadaga crossing was fair passable?"

"Usually."

His mouth drew into a grim line. "I have a feeling it is not going to be so fair this time around."

He faced forward, urging the horses toward the rushing sound. When the slope of the river came into sight, her own lips flattened.

Ahead, the Nowadaga overran its banks like a warrior gone mad with battle fever. The river was half again as wide as its usual spread.

Elias halted the horses with a low "Whoa." Behind them, Matthew did the same. Climbing down from the wagons, they all gathered on the bank—even Rufus. No one spoke. Not for a long time. Elias paced along the shore, blue eyes scanning from ripple to ripple. Mercy could only guess at his thoughts. Hers were a-tumble with danger, not for the depth of the water, but for the speed.

Eventually, Elias pulled his hat from his head and ran his fingers through his dark hair before slapping it back atop. "Daylight is wasting. We should get a move on."

Mercy reached for her locket. Surely he did not mean. . . "Don't tell me you're thinking of crossing this today?"

Elias looked down at her. "You have another back trail in mind?"

Swallowing the shame of yesterday, she averted her gaze. "No. The next ford is twenty miles off."

Matthew grunted. "I'm with Mercy. Crossing now ain't worth risking our load and our lives."

Rufus rolled out a string of curses—

Until Elias's dark glower ended the unraveling. "I've about had it with your vulgarities. Mind your tongue in front of a woman."

"She ain't no. . ." Whatever cutting remark Rufus had in mind ended when Elias took a step toward him.

"Nothing," Rufus mumbled and held up his hands. "I ain't saying nothin'."

Elias shifted his gaze to Mercy. "What do you know of this stretch of river? Any peculiarities?"

If she closed her eyes now, how many sweet memories would swell as strong as the rushing water? The glide of Onontio's canoe as she sat in the bow. The sting of December water on her fingers when dipping in a jar. The way autumn leaves bobbed. But that was farther up, near the headwaters, where the Kahnyen'kehàka camped.

She shrugged. "The Nowadaga is not usually deep. The current not strong. But I can't vouch for it while being this rain-heavy. I say we wait till it goes down some. A day. Two at most."

"No." The combined voices of Elias and Rufus thundered louder than the river.

Elias frowned at them all. "The longer we stay in one place, the higher our chances of ambush."

"Fair enough." Matthew rubbed his hand along the back of his neck. "And you, Rufus? Why you so breeches-afire to cross?"

Red spread over the young man's face like a bruise, his eyes narrowing. "Tired of yer company. Sooner we make the fort, sooner I'm done with you all."

Mercy held her breath. One of these times Elias or Matthew would be done with Rufus's yapping and bite down hard.

But Elias ignored him and instead faced Matthew. "Are you up for testing the depths with me?"

Matthew nodded. "Aye."

They strode back into the tree line, hunting for a straight limb long enough to plot the best possible route through the river. Mercy yanked her bonnet back on, tired of the string tugging at her neck, tired of strong-bent men, and more than tired of this journey.

Rufus turned aside and spit. "That man of yours is crazy."

She'd sigh, but Rufus Bragg wasn't worth that much effort. "He is not my man."

"Yeah? I seen the way you look at him."

Her hands curled into fists. Whether she looked at Elias cross-eyed or doe-blinking, Rufus Bragg had no call to be watching her in the first place. "If a fight's what you're after, Rufus, then go get yourself a prodding stick and tussle with the river."

He spewed out another foul curse. "Not me. Those fools will get themselves washed downriver."

"Those men have more courage than you will ever know."

"You don't know nothing 'bout me." A queer gleam in his dark eyes streaked like lightning. Then he turned on his heel and stalked to the wagon.

By now Elias and Matthew stood at the river's edge, ten paces apart. On Elias's mark, they stepped in, water passing over their feet. Pace by pace, they worked their way into the rushing river.

Midway through, water swirling thigh high, Matthew stumbled.

Mercy strangled a cry. To scream might set Elias off-balance—and he had his own step to care for. Yet even in the midst of fast-flowing water licking against his legs, he remained stalwart, exuding an unearthly kind of peace.

Thankfully, Matthew shored himself up with his big stick, and Mercy started breathing once again.

They waded to the far shore then back, landing dripping wet from the legs down in front of her.

"Well?" she asked.

Matthew eyed Elias.

Who eyed him right back. "I say we give it a go."

"Could be worse, I suppose." Matthew leaned hard on his stick. "We have a fair shot at it if the horses don't spook."

"Then we will make sure they do not. If you and I walk along with the lead animal, calm and steady, there will be less of a chance for them to go rogue. Mercy and Rufus can mind the reins."

Biting her tongue, Mercy turned on her heel and tromped back to the wagon, following Rufus's earlier route before she said something she'd regret.

This was a bad idea.

Elias hid a smile. Mercy hadn't said a word against his and Matthew's plan, but she didn't have to. The braid swishing at her back and furious swirl of her skirts said it all. Did she really think her silence wasn't shouting loud her opposition?

Hefting his stick onto one shoulder, he hurried after her. "Mercy, hold up."

She did not stop until she reached the wagon, and when she turned, he was glad he'd held on to the piece of wood, so lethal did her eyes spark in the afternoon sun.

"Just listen." He softened his voice. Iron against iron would only make for more sparks—a fact he wished he'd learned earlier in life. "Either we stand together, or we die together. If I did not think we owned a good chance of making a safe crossing, I would not ask this of you."

She tucked her chin like a bull about to charge. "The power of that water is more than we can fight. I saw Matthew stumble, and he is as sturdy as one of the horses. You have no idea—"

"Do not think to question me when it comes to the wiles of a river." Anger surged a rush of blood to his head, his pulse beating loud in his ears. He knew better than anyone the vicious clout of water gone wild.

Slowly at first, memories began to rise, then flash-flooded him all at once. Jacques, Henri, Arnaud. . .and François, his one true friend. His throat closed, and for a moment, no words would pass. All brawny men—and all lost to unforgiving currents, pulled under by greed, pride, and, in the case of his friend François, ignorance.

He sucked in a ragged breath. "I have seen men die—*friends* die—from lack of respect for water. Believe me when I say I would not take such a risk if I did not think it possible. Trust me, I know whereof I speak."

Red flamed on her cheeks. "Why should I?"

The question punched him in the gut. Exactly. Why should she entrust her life to a man she thought was a traitor?

Even so, he dared a step closer. "I respect your mistrust of me, but know this. . ." He stared deep into her eyes, as if by virtue of will alone he could impress upon her the truth of his words. "I will not let harm come to you. I vow it."

She looked away, her eyes hidden in shadow, obliterating any chance he might have of reading what went on in her mind. Did she believe him—or did she think he merely said what was necessary to get her to go along with him?

Eventually the hard line of her shoulders sagged, and she reached for her locket.

He pressed the advantage. "All you have to do is hold steady on the reins. I will do the rest. Mercy. . .please."

"Why?" She threw the question like a tomahawk. "Why is this so important to you?"

He clamped his jaw. Men's lives depended on his timely arrival in Boston—possibly the fate of an entire fort—but he couldn't tell her that. So he said nothing. Just stared her down, admiring and hating the pluck in Mercy Lytton.

"Pah!" She threw out her hands. "I can see there's no moving you. Stubborn *kaia'tákerahs.*"

He couldn't stop the smile tugging at his lips—nor the words that followed. "I do not know what you just said, but it sure sounds pretty coming from your lips."

She whirled and reached for the wagon seat. Scrambling upward, she put as much space between them as possible.

His grin widened, but it did not last long. Though that battle was over, an even bigger skirmish was about to ensue.

Craning his neck, he searched for Matthew. The man stood next to his lead horse, with Rufus holding the reins of the other wagon.

"Ready?" Elias shouted.

Matthew nodded. "Aye."

With a last glance at Mercy, Elias strode to the front of their team and grabbed hold of the headstall on the lead horse. He held the prodding stick in his other hand, ready to encourage a skittish mount or simply to use it for balance once in the water. "Onward!"

The first rush of water over his feet wasn't nearly as cold this time, for his skin was already clammy up to the top of his thighs. Pace by pace, the river rose higher, from ankle, to shin, to knee. Only once did the horse buck its head, but Elias kept his grip firm, letting the animal know he'd brook no nonsense. If the leader spooked, the rest would follow suit.

Halfway across, Elias's foot hit a hollow. He canted to the side, the rush of water yanking him from the team. He flung out his arm to counterbalance, desperately seeking a hold for his stick. No good. The current grabbed that too, and his legs shot out from beneath him. His grip on the headstall kept him afloat, yet he was no longer leading the team. The river led him.

And it was winning.

"Elias!" Fear shredded Mercy's voice.

Sensing the dilemma, the lead horse faltered a step. If the team stopped now, the river would gain the upper hand. . .and once those crates hit the water and broke open, there'd be no gaining back the weapon he'd taken such pains to transport this far.

There was nothing to be done for it then. *God, please give Mercy strength.*

"Keep going!" he yelled at her.

Then he let go.

The current dragged him along. With strong strokes, he fought against the pull, straining to swing his feet around. Careening headfirst down an unknown stretch of swollen river was never a good idea. His lungs burned with the effort. Gritty water slapped him in the face, filling his mouth and nose. He worked his way toward the shore, scraping and banging against rocks.

At last, the flow lessened, and his feet purchased a solid base. He shot up, some twenty yards downriver of the wagons, coughing and spluttering.

And when he caught his breath, he let out a big whoop.

Mercy, God bless her, laid into the horses and drove them right up the side of the bank. The rear wheels cleared the river, hauling up the load of crates to safety.

"Thank You, Lord," he breathed as he waded toward shore.

Matthew's wagon was at the halfway point now—but thankfully the man must've seen where he'd taken his fall, for the ranger led his team a hair more upriver. Smart man. Rufus's thin arms jutted out in front of him, reins wrapped tight in his hands.

Elias stopped in shin-deep water, watching the progression. To distract any of them now could mean the loss of the second wagon.

Little by little, Matthew advanced. His moccasins hit the bank. The first pair of horses cleared the water. The second pair. Elias held his breath. So close.

The first set of wheels rolled out of the river, slanting the wagon so that all the weight rested on the back two wheels.

And a crack split the air.

CHAPTER 10

Mercy eased back on the reins, bringing the horses to a slow stop. They deserved a rest. So did she. Every muscle in her arms jittered from the harrowing crossing.

Dropping her hands to her lap, she leaned back against the canvas and closed her eyes, just as she'd done before they had crossed the Nowadaga. The sun beat warmer, the air smelled sweeter. Life seemed less burdensome. Why was it that her gratitude heightened only after a vexing experience? How much peace did she miss out on by appreciating a rainbow instead of valuing the rain beforehand? Should she not thank God for both?

The questions chafed. She'd not thought this much about God in a long time, not since she'd left behind her childhood. And Mother. Mercy flexed her fingers, working out the last of her tension and fighting the urge to reach for her locket. Elias was far too much like her mother in his spirituality—yet there was nothing soft about him. Nothing cowardly. Maybe—just maybe—faith did not have to mean weakness.

A scream of horses ended her contemplations, followed by men's shouts. She set the brake and bolted from the wagon.

Dread pumped her legs as she tore back the way she'd come. Some kind of argument waged between Rufus and Elias, accompanied by the drone of Matthew, speaking calmly to squealing horses.

Her steps slowed as she descended the slope of the riverbank into chaos. Matthew held tight to the lead horse's headstall. The others snorted and strained at their harnesses, trying to break free. And she didn't blame them. Behind lay a cockeyed wagon, rear barely dragged out of the water and digging hard into the soft ground. Rufus had bailed from his seat and stood on the mucky bank, cussing at a half-drowned Elias.

She stopped, gaze fixed on the dislocated spokes—sticking out of the wheel weakened when they had taken Traverse Ridge. The peace of moments before vanished, replaced by a sickening twist in her belly.

This was her fault.

"Mercy!" Elias's voice shook through her, and she yanked up her head.

He stood soaked to the skin beside Rufus near the rear of the wagon. "Grab the horses. We need Matthew to help haul these crates from the river."

Without a word, she walked in a daze over to Matthew, the image of the spokes askew and the curve of defeat in Elias's shoulders strong in her mind.

All Matthew's shushings and "Easy now" murmurings had stilled most of the madness in the horses. Either that or the animals had figured out they no longer lugged a scrape-bottom, off-kilter wagon up a hill. But whichever, Matthew didn't let go until she wrapped her fingers around the leather band on the lead horse's head.

She peered into Matthew's gray eyes. "Are you all right? No one's hurt, are they?"

He shook his head. "No, girl. Thank the good Lord. Keep a firm grip—on this horse and yourself. They take off running, you let go, you hear?"

Swallowing against the tightness in her throat, she nodded. If she'd never suggested that ridge shortcut, if she'd just kept her mouth shut, they wouldn't be in this sorry situation.

Most of the crates had been strewn along the bank when the horses charged off in a frenzy. One crate remained on the wagon bed. Only three of the ten had landed in the water, so it didn't take long for the men to lug them up to the muddy shore. Pots and pans, gold bars, and some opened packets of trade silver sparkled in the shallows, contents they would need to collect before nightfall. The rest of the flotsam was likely already a mile downstream, pulled by the current.

Stroking the velvety nose of the horse to soothe the beast and herself, she waited until the men caught their breath. "Now what?"

Matthew pulled off his hat and flicked the sweat from his brow with the back of his hand. "We'll have to unload the other wagon and bring it back down to collect as much of this mess as we can."

Elias nodded. "After we unload that, we will come back for the broken wagon."

Turning aside, Rufus spit on the ground, then jabbed his finger her way. "This is your doin'. We get a passel of Indians breathin' down our neck, you remember that."

In two strides, Elias planted himself between Rufus and her. "Leave off. This is your only warning."

But it was too late. Rufus's accusation heaped another coal onto the fire of her own guilt, the shame of which would burn for a very long time.

Matthew jammed his hat back atop his head. "You're doing a fine job with the horses, Mercy, so just stay here. We'll be back with an empty wagon to collect the rest."

The men stomped off, but Rufus's indictment stayed. He was right. If Onontio's warning held true and a band of Wyandot came along, they would be easy to find and too small in number to fight back. But what was to be done for it now? How could she possibly make the situation better?

Slowly, she released her hold of the bridle, cooing all the while. She inched from the horse, testing the skittishness of the leader, but by now they had all discovered the green shoots breaking up the ground in patches. The pull and chomp of well-earned provender played an accompaniment to the steady rhythm of the rushing water.

From this angle, she viewed more clearly the devastation where the land sloped into the river. Contents from the crates littered a wide swath of mud—and what contents they were! She'd already seen the household goods that had been stored in the top half of each crate, but she'd not imagined so much gold, so many packages of trade silver. She couldn't begin to guess at the value. No wonder Elias and Matthew were so bent on getting this load to Fort Edward. If anyone discovered them with this much treasure, their throats would be slit before they could holler.

A shiver shimmied across her shoulders, and she forced her gaze to move on. Nearby, a fallen wooden box wasn't too damaged, though it was mostly empty. If she dragged it down to the water's edge, she could at least begin collecting what had spilled.

Treading on light feet so as not to scare the horses, she picked her way down the bank. Near the toe of her moccasin, a gold bar lay half-embedded in the muck. She bent to retrieve it—and was surprised at the weight. It took two hands to pry it out and heave it into the crate. The linen-wrapped packages of trade silver weren't any lighter or easier to free from the suction of wet earth. Eventually though, she rinsed each item off and filled the box. Now to drag it up a ways.

Planting herself uphill, she grabbed the edge with two hands and pulled. The thing didn't budge. If anything, the bottom edge dug deeper into the muck.

But she wouldn't be thwarted. Sucking in a huge breath, she grasped the crate's side yet again, and this time she lifted before she pulled. The wood moved, but not much, so she grunted and strained for all she was worth— which by now wasn't much.

The momentum did not mix well with the slick ground. The box lifted but her feet slipped. The crate crashed. Pain exploded in her left foot, shooting agony up her leg. One hundred fifty pounds of heavy metal smashed her toes against a rock, trapping her.

She let out a wail that wouldn't be stopped.

Elias trotted back to the river, leaving Matthew and Rufus to turn around the empty wagon. That broken wheel would set them back days. . .days he didn't have to spare. Hopefully Matthew was a better wheelsmith than him, for he had no experience. He was about to turn back and ask him when a cry keened from the river, loud as a scream from a red fox.

Mercy!

He sprinted, wishing to God he held a tomahawk in his grip. Even so, weapon or not, if anyone harmed her, he'd kill. Fury colored the world blood red as he scanned for movement.

Past the horses, by the end of the broken wagon, Mercy hunched on the riverbank, holding her leg. A crate hid the bottom half of her skirt from view.

Taking the bank half-sliding, he skidded to a stop next to the box—fully loaded. He crouched and lifted the crate. She lurched back. As soon as she was free, he dropped the box and scooped her up. Even with her wet skirts, she weighed hardly more than a feather tick. Cradling her against his chest, he hauled her up to level ground, then set her down.

Her eyes pinched shut, trapping her in a world of private pain. No tears cut tracks down her cheeks, nor did she cry out anymore. Still, the single scream she'd let out earlier would haunt him in nightmares to come.

"This is going to hurt, and I regret it, but it has got to be done." He hunkered down near her foot and, as gently as possible, lifted her mucky leg so that her shoe rested in his lap. Ignoring propriety, he pushed up her gown to gain a better look. Stockings, torn and dirty, covered a shapely leg, thankfully not bent or crushed. She must have taken the full brunt of the weight on her foot.

She didn't make a sound as he unlaced her moccasin. She didn't swoon or flinch. She just sat, grasping handfuls of her skirt into white-knuckled fists, eyes still closed but face resolute.

He tugged on the heel of her shoe and slid it off. When it caught on the end of her toes, she sucked in a breath—he did too. Blood soaked a stain into her gray stockings. That fabric had to come off. Now.

"Mercy, this is going be hard, but I need you to take off your hose."

Her eyes blinked open, either from shock or anger, he couldn't say. Without a word, she released her handfuls of skirt and reached for her bodice. A blade appeared, shiny and sharp in the late afternoon sun.

His brows rose. No wonder she hadn't feared traveling with him or any other man. Between her knife and Matthew's overseeing, the woman was thoroughly protected.

She bent forward and sliced a line through the fabric around her ankle. Breathing hard, she leaned back and tucked her knife away.

"Go on." Her voice shook. "Do what needs to be done."

He gritted his teeth. Would to God he could take the pain for her. Bit by bit, he peeled the fabric down from her ankle. No swelling there. No odd angles or broken skin. The weight must've hit farther on.

He pulled the thin wool past the arch of her foot, steady, using a constant force, and faltered only once—when the stocking stuck to the bloodied pulp of her last two toes.

His chest tightened. That had to hurt.

Horses' hooves plodded behind him. The grind of wheels. Matthew's voice. "What happened?"

Before Elias could answer, he heard the sound of Matthew's moccasins hitting the ground. "So help me, Dubois, if you hurt that girl—"

"Enough!" Mercy cried. "Your infighting is making me sick."

"Easy," Elias whispered to her as he would a skittish mare. Then he glanced over his shoulder. "I need some water here. Mercy crushed her toes."

Matthew loped off.

Elias turned back to the woman. Thankfully, now that her foot was free, color seeped back into her cheeks. A light wind teased a runaway lock of dark hair across one of those cheeks, and the urge to brush it back tingled in his hand. He curled his fingers tight, annoyed by the base response at such a moment.

"What were you doing?" His voice was flat, even to his own ears.

Her big brown eyes stared into his. "I thought to gather some of the spilled contents."

He frowned. "Gathering is one thing, but trying to move a full crate on your own? What were you thinking?"

Her eyes narrowed. So did her tone. "Clearly I wasn't."

"Well," he sighed. "It could have been worse. One—maybe two—toes look to be broken, but thank God it is not your ankle." He allowed a small smile. "You should be kicking Rufus's hind end in no time."

Matthew returned and handed him a canteen. "We'll start loading. Join us as you're able. But you"—he shifted a cancerous gaze to Mercy— "stay put."

She frowned at Matthew's retreating back. Though she said nothing, Elias got the distinct impression that any other man who'd just told her what to do would be wearing that knife of hers through the back.

He uncorked the metal flask. "How long have you two been together?"

"Three years," she murmured.

"Three? Have you been tangled in this war for that long?"

She nodded, loosening more hair in the process.

Setting down the cork, he shifted her foot so that the water would run off into the grass instead of his lap. Best to busy her tongue to keep her mind from the pain he was about to inflict. "Why did Bragg even consider taking on a woman?"

He poured a stream over her toes with one hand, the other supporting and rubbing off bits of mud with his thumb.

"I'm good at what I do." Her voice strained and her nostrils flared, but she kept talking. "My sight is a gift. And no one expects a woman scout. A messenger, yes, but never a scout."

He grunted. No argument with that, for he'd never run across such.

Dousing her foot afresh, he bent and studied her toes. Now that the blood was gone, the damage was easier to assess. The little toe, as suspected, was likely broken, already swollen to nearly twice its size. She'd lose the nail for sure. The toe next to it pulsed an angry shade of deep red, but it wasn't as puffed up. More like a deep bruise. She'd live to fight another day—and soon.

He set down the canteen and faced her. "War does not last forever, thank God. What will you do when the fighting is done?"

Her brown eyes glazed over, but this time he guessed it wasn't from pain. Gently, he resettled her foot on his lap and dried off what he could with the hem of his hunting frock.

"I suppose I shall cross that creek when I come to it," she said at last.

His gaze shot to hers. "There is no man waiting for you on the other side?"

Her lips curved, sunlight painting them a rosy hue. "I've been told I am a handful. . .not to mention stubborn. Even were I to want a man, not many are up for the job."

While spoken in jest, her words sank low in his gut, and a strange urge rose to meet such a challenge. He cleared his throat, then shrugged off his hunting frock and balled up the fabric. He set the lump on the ground and eased her foot to rest atop it. "Let this dry off while I help load those crates. I will bind that toe when I am finished."

Her chin jutted out. "I am fully capable of binding my own foot."

Proud woman, as stubborn as she was beautiful. He scowled. "Just promise me that when I am down there loading"—he hitched a thumb over his shoulder—"I won't turn around and see you next to me, lugging up a crate."

A small smile flickered on her face. "You have my word."

It was a small victory, her giving him her word—so why did it make his heart thump hard against his ribs?

Rising, he turned toward the task at hand. Would that fixing the broken wheel would prove as easy a conquest.

CHAPTER 11

Sun beat down surprisingly hot for an early April day. The afternoon warmth on Elias's back joined the heat from the heaping pile of glowing coals in front of him, and sweat trickled down between his shoulder blades. After two days of whittling spokes that never seemed to fit, the need to be on the move burned hotter than the sun and embers combined. Despite the threat of roaming Indians, they'd had no choice but to build a fire. Moisture dripped down his temple, and he shoved the dampness away with the back of his hand. Heat blistered off in waves from the coals, hinting the temperature was just about right—hopefully.

Throwing down his stick, he reached for the flat steel tire, then worked it flush into the fire so that all sides heated evenly. This would work. It had to. He glanced up at a cornflower-blue sky and lifted a prayer as the metal heated.

Please, God. A little help here.

Behind him, Matthew readied the wheel. Once the flat-tire heated through, they would have to work fast, especially since they labored without tongs or pincers. One wrong move and the metal would set cockeyed, or one of them could suffer a wickedly bad burn.

He faced Matthew. "Are you ready to give this a go?"

Matthew hoisted the wooden wheel, the new, crudely carved spokes fixed between axle and rim. He gave it a last once-over with his hawkish eyes, then set the thing down in the sandy spot they had created. "Aye."

Grabbing two stout sticks, Elias jiggered the flat-tire loose. He rushed the charred metal ring over to Matthew, and the two of them set to whacking the band over the felloes. Long before they could pound it on the wheel straight, it cooled and shrank, setting lopsided.

Frustration churned the blackened fish he'd eaten at noontide. If that metal rim weren't righted now, there'd be no prying it off without rebreaking the wheel, and they would have to start all over. *If* they could even get it off. He dropped one stick, hefted the other in two hands, and brought the end down with all his might. The stick hit the edge of the metal—and slid. The force of it lifted the opposite side of the wheel, shooting it into the air. He and Matthew dodged backward. Though the metal was too cool to fit as it should, it would still pack a flesh-searing burn.

The wheel juddered back onto the sand. The metal tire sat mostly on but partly off. If they attached that to the wagon, the first turn would crush it.

"You are a disappointment."

Elias yanked off his hat and slapped it against his thigh. "Blast!"

A laugh rumbled in Matthew's chest, as if nothing more than a game of stickball had been lost. Retreating to a nearby log, the ranger sank onto it. "You're a man of many talents—but wheelwrighting ain't one of 'em." He swept his hand toward the crooked wheel.

Elias blew out a long breath. No sense taking offense at the truth. Cramming his hat atop his head, he joined the man on the log. "You're right. I am surely no wheelwright."

Matthew's smile faded. "Then what are you?"

Elias tensed, the turn of conversation as troubling as the ruined wheel. "What do you mean?"

Sweat trickled down the older man's brow in rivulets. "Well. . ." He paused and pulled out a dirty kerchief, rubbing off the offense. "It seems to me you took to that water like an old friend. Dubois is your surname. And you're accused of consorting with the French. If I don't miss my mark, you have voyageur blood in you."

Elias stared him down, saying nothing. Clearly the man had been giving him some thought, and by the sounds of it, quite a bit. That was a danger. Nothing good ever came of too close a scrutiny.

But then Matthew elbowed him, an easygoing smile returning to his face as he tucked his cloth away. "There's no shame in it. I've yet to meet a harder working lot, and you have more than proved your mettle this past week—excepting the wheel, that is."

Matthew's good-natured teasing loosened the tight muscles in Elias's shoulders. The man was a honey-dipped hound on the hunt, he'd give him that. Yet for the most part, it was a pleasant way Matthew had about him, seeking information with amiable conversation instead of at knifepoint.

Unlike his own father.

Elias frowned. Normally he didn't think about the man, but Matthew's speculation had unearthed an ugly patch of dirt. He kicked at a rock with his heel as he spoke. "My father runs pelts up north of Kippising—or did, depending on if he yet lives. I traveled with him for a time. It was. . .an experience."

His throat closed, shut down by too many memories. Those years had been harder to bear than the tears in his mother's eyes when Bernart Dubois had left her alone with a young boy clutching her skirts.

As if sensing the turmoil, Matthew's grizzled face softened. So did his voice. "Why'd you leave?"

The question pierced straight through his chest, and he sucked in a breath. The man could have no idea of the wounds he prodded.

"It was my father's dream, not mine," he muttered. "The life of a wanderer is not for me."

"Yet here you are."

He shot to his feet. The stink of smoke and sweat clung to him, the odor of travel and toil—things he'd sworn to change.

Yet here you are. Matthew's words taunted him, especially with the end of his wandering within reach. It had seemed simple at the outset. One last trek to Boston and his drifting days would be done—if only that blasted wheel didn't lie in a broken heap.

He faced Matthew. The man wasn't the only one who had questions rattling around like rocks in a can. "And here you are. Judging by the way you send Mercy to scout for enemy tracks before we leave and your chafing at keeping to known paths, I would say you are a ranger, for those are two primary rules of rangering, are they not?"

Matthew angled his head, sunlight sparking humor in his gray eyes. "It appears you have been studying me as well."

Elias held the man's gaze. "You are pretty far afield for a ranger—and a lone wolf at that. Not a common sight. Mercy tells me you met up with her three years back."

All humor fled from the man's face. "She saved my life."

He couldn't stop the lift of his brows, picturing the lithe-limbed Mercy snatching the barrel-chested man in front of him from the jaws of death. "How did she manage that?"

"I did not mean it in that sense, though there is more strength in that girl than in most men I've known." For a moment, Matthew grew silent, his eyes glazing over with a faraway look. Deep ruts lined the parts of his face not sporting bristly scruff. How many years had this man seen?

Matthew scratched at the week-old growth on his chin. "I strayed out here, abuzz with a bellyful of anger. Sometimes those you fight alongside of aren't there for the cause, but for themselves. Meeting up with Mercy, well. . .would to God the rangers had more men like her."

The captain lapsed into silence for so long Elias wondered if he'd finish his tale or not.

At last, Matthew pushed up from the log, meeting him head-on. "Mercy reminded me that a few bad men are just that—few. That there's still a lot of good in this world. It was her zeal what breathed new life into these old bones. When that girl puts her heart into something, there's no holding her back."

He needn't close his eyes to imagine her, so branded in his mind her face had become. The way her long braid swung down to full hips. The determined gleam in her brown eyes. How she'd fit so light yet strong in his arms. "She is a rarity," he murmured.

As if by speaking so, the woman herself appeared from out of the tree line, at a sprint despite the hindrance of skirts and limp favoring her sore foot. Something urged her to such a pace—likely something bad.

A battle charge ran along each of his muscles, and he took a step toward her. So did Matthew.

"Someone's coming," she warned.

Sucking in air, Mercy caught her breath. Judging by the way Matthew's hand hovered over his tomahawk and by the icy blue streak in Elias's gaze, she'd better get her words out before they tore off on a killing spree.

"Two wagons," she huffed. "Three men, one leading on a mount, coming from the east." She shoved back the hair from her eyes, lungs finally filling. "There're two women, three littles. One's a babe in arms."

Matthew looked past her, where the route cut a path through the greenery. "How far out?"

"Two miles or so."

Elias narrowed his eyes at her. "You cannot see that far, not with the bend of the road and the scrub in the way."

A familiar rage flared in her belly. She had yet to meet a man who trusted her ability when it exceeded his own. Still, after twenty-five summers, ought she not have learned to master such anger? Black-Fox-Running told her so often, but that did nothing to change her on the inside.

She lifted her chin. "That is what scouts are for, Mr. Dubois. You told me and Rufus to keep a sharp eye while you had a fire going."

He folded his arms, looking down the length of his nose. "I also told you to mind your foot."

She rolled her eyes. The man harped on her more than Matthew. "My foot's near to better."

"You are still limping."

"Not as much."

Matthew stepped between them. "No time for bickering. We'll have company soon. I say we help 'em on their way across the river as fast as possible. We can't have so large a party staying the night with us. That many people attract too much attention—something we can't afford."

Elias nodded. "Agreed."

Matthew turned back to the wheel on the ground. Though his big shape blocked part of her view, from her angle she could see things weren't right. The metal rim choked the wooden frame, jutting off where it ought to lay flat. Her gaze strayed to Elias, his broad back toward her now as he crouched beside Matthew, conferring. No wonder he was so ornery. The wheel was no more fixed than when she'd set out hours earlier.

Beyond them, orange coals yet glowed. She might as well make the most of them. There'd been no sign of any Wyandots, and if any were about, they would have attacked by now. A pot of stew would lighten everyone's mood, especially since they had eaten nothing hot in over a week.

After rummaging in the provisions box, she procured some root vegetables. Chopping up the few turnips and potatoes didn't take long, so she cut up some salted venison as well. She tossed it all into a pot of water, and while that heated, she hunted the nearby growth for wild ginger shoots to add a tang. By the time the water boiled and the scent of pottage wafted strong, Rufus wandered in from his scouting.

Just as a man on a horse rode into camp, coming from the east.

Elias and Matthew advanced toward him, Rufus tagging their heels. Mercy hung back, staying near the fire. Holding the reins with one hand was the sandy-haired man she'd seen with the wagons. She'd detected he seemed to coddle one arm, but this close up, she saw why. His arm lay limp in his lap, bound with linen strips soaked through with a yellowy-orange discharge. Brown stained the edges of that mess. That kind of injury needed an open-air salve with a light pack of dried cottonwood batting at night, not a strangle of cloth—and filthy cloth at that.

He dipped his head in greeting toward the men. A single, garish peacock feather tucked into his hatband bobbed with the movement. "Good afternoon, gentlemen."

Her brows shot skyward. *Gentlemen?*

"'Tis a right fair one." Matthew tipped his head up at the man. Judging by his stance, all loose-legged and thumbs hitched into the front opening of his hunting frock, he didn't see the newcomer as a threat.

But when the man's gaze strayed past Matthew, beyond Elias, and lighted on her, she clenched the stir stick in her hand until her arm ached. Too much interest glimmered in his green eyes. Far too much curiosity. She knew that look, for she parried it often.

Elias sidestepped, blocking the man's view. "Are you looking to ford the Nowadaga?"

"I am. I have two wagons to guide across."

"Yer a guide?" Rufus turned aside and spit, then wiped a smear off his chin.

Even from yards away, Mercy saw the stranger's upper lip curl. For once she was in agreement with Rufus. This man was no guide, leastwise not an experienced one.

Ignoring the question, he slid down from his mount, taking care not to jostle his sore arm overmuch. "My name's Logan. Garret Logan, guide to the Shaw party." He offered his good hand to Matthew.

Matthew shook it. "Matthew Prinn."

Logan moved on to Elias. For a moment, Elias stood rock still, not taking the man up on his greeting. Did he sense something not right about this guide as well?

Finally, he gripped the man's hand. "Elias Dubois."

Rufus shot out his hand—the one he'd used to swipe away the spit. "I'm Rufus. This here's my grandpappy." He elbowed Matthew with far too much gusto.

Logan barely touched Rufus's fingers before pulling back and stationing himself in front of Matthew once again. He aimed a finger at the wagon with the broken wheel. "Met with hardship, have you?"

Though the man spoke to Matthew, Elias cocked his head toward Logan's arm. "Looks like you met with some of your own."

A smile lightened the man's face, teeth white in a mat of a sandy-colored beard—far too trimmed and smoothed for trekking through the wilderness. Perhaps if he'd paid closer attention to his surroundings instead of his grooming, he wouldn't have suffered such an injury in the first place. "I acquired a knife wound, I'm afraid, and it is festering more than I'd like."

By now the other two wagons had rumbled into the clearing, filling the space near to full. Two men, two women, and two children piled out. As they drew near, Mercy studied the men first. Both were tall and big-boned, giving the impression of competency, but each wore a sunburned nose, as if neither had the intelligence to don a hat during the heat of day. Strength without common sense was worse than dangerous. It was deadly. Shaggy haired, with shaggier beards, they were the opposite of Mr. Logan with their fine coating of dirt and travel grime. They sported similar noses and the same color eyes, the hue of a blue trade shirt washed one too many times in murky water. Were they brothers then?

Tagging one man's heels were two young boys. Mercy set down her spoon and folded her arms, shoring herself up for trouble. She'd once seen raccoon cubs destroy an entire season's worth of dried berries by sneaking into an impossibly small crack in a storage hut. These two boys were capable of far more than that, with their torn breeches, untucked shirts, and freckles scattered across their cheeks like a handful of pebbles tossed into a pond.

"Jonas! James!" A spring day of a woman caught up to them, surprisingly light of step despite her protruding belly large with promise. What on earth was a woman this close to birthing doing out here? Sunlight glinted off her spectacles as she bent to haul each boy back with a tug on his shoulders.

Joining the group last was another woman, holding a bundle of swaddling close to her chest. Her skirt hem was caked with filth, a queer contradiction to the pristine white baby wraps in her arms. While the two men introduced themselves, Mercy stepped around the fire to gain a closer look at the woman. Something wasn't right about her. . .but what?

"Wife, come over and meet the Shaws." Elias stretched out his hand toward her, an inviting smile curving his lips.

She bristled. Must he carry out this charade with such easy cheer? Unfolding her arms, she smoothed her skirts and joined his side. When he wrapped his arm around her waist and pulled her close, she clenched her hands, fighting the urge to yank out her bodice knife and end such a liberty here and now.

"This is my wife, Mercy. Mercy, meet the Shaws. Amos and his wife, Mary."

"Pleased to meet you." The older man tipped his hat, and the dark-haired woman next to him offered a tremulous smile, pulling her gaze from the babe in her arms only for a moment. Her face was like the moon, pale and round, one that could change in the night. A strange light shone in her eyes, hinting of madness, not a rabid savagery but the kind that caught a person off-guard with its stealth, like it might reach out at any time and snatch a bit of Mercy's own sanity.

Elias's fingers dug into her waist, reminding her to respond.

"Pleased to meet you, Mr. and Mrs. Shaw."

The other man and his wife stepped forward, both dipping their heads. "I'm Nathan Shaw and this here is my wife, Emmeline. 'Tis surely good to see some fellow travelers. We have not run across any since Fort Edward, and I know my wife and my brother's could use some womanly conversation."

Mercy sucked in a breath. Surely they did not plan on staying that long. Elias's forearm tensed against her back, and next to him, Matthew cleared his throat. Only Rufus seemed to ignore the suggestion of the Shaws remaining long enough to strike up companionship, for he ambled off with a whistle.

"Well," Matthew's voice rumbled, "we'll be happy to help you ford the river if you like. There's still enough light left to cross with time to spare for you to make camp on the other side."

"Very generous, but it seems you folks could use our help first. What do you think, Mr. Logan?" Nathan Shaw looked to where the man had taken up a silent residence at their flank. "Mightn't we stay here a day or two to help these folks with their wheel?"

The man opened his mouth, but Elias interrupted. "No need. We would not want to hold you up."

Nathan stepped nearer, turning his face away from his wife, and lowered his voice. "The truth is, the women and little ones could use a break. We've been pushing them hard. Too hard. We can spare a day or two, and that's a fact."

"No! You cannot stay here." The words tumbled out of Mercy's mouth before she could stop them. All eyes turned her way.

Elias chuckled, but compared to his usual good humor, this laugh sounded strangled. "You will have to pardon my wife. It seems she is a bit hard up for conversation as well. If you will excuse us, I shall have a word with her now."

He hustled her aside before anyone could question her and did not stop until they rounded their wagon and were out of hearing range.

The forced smile on his face fled, and a stranger stared out at her through his blue eyes. "Do not raise suspicion like that. A single misspoken word can ruin an entire mission. I have seen it happen."

She looked away, preferring to study the stained canvas of the wagon cover instead of the accusation in his gaze. He was right, and that shamed her more than her loose tongue. "I apologize," she mumbled, then she shot her gaze back to his. "But those people can't stay here, not with us. You know they can't."

He pressed his fingertips to his brow and rubbed. Was she giving him a headache, or were the Shaws?

"Listen," he said. "I do not like this situation any more than you do. But whether they move on or stay, we have to play the part, *Wife*."

He tossed the word like a knife to be caught. Should she grab the challenge with an open hand and work with him? Or not? Yet was it not her duty to carry out the assignment given her?

"Very well." The agreement she spit out tasted bitter, but even more sour was the smile she forced after it.

The sooner the Shaws crossed that river, the better.

CHAPTER 12

Daylight died a long and anguishing death. The time for the Shaw boys to bed down wouldn't be soon enough for Mercy's liking. Their whoops and chatter violated the peace even down at the riverbank. A nest of rattlesnakes wouldn't make as much noise or wriggle about so.

She threw another handful of wet sand into the stew pot and scrubbed the bottom, breathing in the damp evening air. Across the river, dusk smeared shadows together into a blend of ashy charcoal. The sky was on the verge of rolling over from indigo to onyx, and peeper frogs piped a chorus despite her presence. This time of day was holy, a reverent peace settling everything down for the coming night—or it would be without the Shaws' ruckus.

Dipping the pot into the water, she rinsed out the sand. The tin inside practically gleamed, she'd been at it so long. Never easy around women, she'd kept her distance from Mary and Emmeline. They were probably fine people if she'd give them a chance—which she wouldn't. Too risky. She had ever preferred the plain speaking of men. Women most often attacked sideways and upside down with their catty remarks whenever they felt threatened. She purposed to give the Shaw women no cause for such spite.

Heavy footfalls crunched at the top of the bank. She'd heard the approach long ago, but an irrational hope that whoever it was would go away kept her from turning, for it surely wasn't Matthew or Elias. They trod with ghost feet.

Garret Logan slid-walked down the slope, then stopped next to her. The tip of the peacock feather in his hatband riffled with a slight breeze. "Good evening, Mrs. Dubois. I hope I did not startle you."

Rising, she stretched her mouth into a small smile. "It takes more than footsteps to startle me, Mr. Logan."

His green gaze swept over her like an ill wind, and she shivered.

"Yes, I suppose it does."

Clutching her pot, she whirled to climb the bank, letting his first volley sail over her head. No sense asking what he meant. The hardened gleam in his eyes indicated he'd already summed her up to less than nothing—the usual reaction of men who couldn't look past her height and independent ways.

She'd just gained level ground when a grunt of pain back at the river's edge slowed her steps. The suppressed moan that followed stopped her feet. The third cry turned her around. Even a suffering wolf merited either a quick slit to the throat or some healing help to end its suffering.

Below, Logan kneeled near the water, his arm—now unbound—dipped in the river. The tight hunch of his shoulders screamed louder than his groans.

She blew out a sigh, unable to stop the softening of her resolve against the man, and retraced her steps. "I will leave out an onion from our stores, Mr. Logan. Mash it up and put the paste on that wound of yours for the night. Come morning, wash your arm again, then leave it air-breathing. The festering will stop, and it will heal."

He stood and faced her, arm dripping at his side. Darkness hid his face but not the revulsion in his voice. "An old Indian trick? I will not partake in such savagery."

This was the gratitude he showed for her compassion? She clenched the pot handle tighter. If she stood any closer, she'd swing it at his head. " 'Tis a common enough cure out here in the wild, known to whites and reds—and you'd know it too if you were a true guide. Tell me, Mr. Logan." She dared a step closer. "How much are you fleecing the Shaws for, and what kind of trouble are you running from?"

His head jerked back. A direct hit. "It is women like you, Mrs. Dubois, too independent, too free with your mind, who are a stain on the fabric of this land."

A slow smile tugged her lips. If Elias heard this conversation, Mr. Logan would have more than a festering arm to heal from.

"I am the land, sir—a land that will chew you up and spit you out. You won't make it to Fort Wilderness in one piece. Neither will the Shaws. Their blood is on your head." She turned to hike the bank and called over her shoulder, "I will set your onion out if you want it."

Though each step carried her farther from the hateful man, she upped her pace anyway, even if it did shoot pain from her crushed toe clear up to her shin. By the time she reached camp, she'd blown off most of her anger—but not all, apparently, for as she neared the wagon, Elias stepped out of the shadows and grabbed the pot from her.

His blue gaze held her as firmly. "What has you so riled?"

She swung her braid to trail down her back, loosening her shoulders and her ire. "Just needed a brisk walk."

"I could use one myself." He glanced over to where a fire blazed, lighting the faces of the Shaw men and one of the women—Mary, with her babe yet clutched in her arms. Did the woman never set the little one down?

Elias shifted his gaze back to her. "I have put out that fire twice now, but every time I turn my back, those men are hell-bent to kindle it again. I am surprised they made it this far from Fort Edward without being set upon."

Elias's low voice soothed in a way that wrapped around her shoulders—or mayhap not his voice, but the land-wise knowledge that was so much a part of him. She respected that. And more.

"I will see to this pot." He strode off on soundless feet—so unlike the earlier stamp and crunch of Mr. Logan's steps.

She followed. Better to get that onion out now and hole up in the wagon for the night until it was her shift to keep watch. "Where're Matthew and Rufus?"

"On first watch. We need two pickets at a time with this much noise and smoke." He winked down at her.

When they reached the wagon, Elias crouched and set the pot underneath, upside down, to keep it dry and clean. She stood on tiptoe over the back gate and rummaged in the provisions box.

"Need something?"

She stiffened at his nearness, his scent of horse and smoke far too alluring. Likely it simply reminded her of Onontio—though she'd never felt quite this tingly with her brother standing next to her.

"An onion," she answered.

He cocked his head. "Is your toe not healing properly?"

"The skin's mending fine." She grabbed the onion and faced Elias. "I told Mr. Logan I'd leave one out. That arm of his will do him in if he doesn't treat it soon."

Elias's jaw hardened. "When did you talk to him?"

"Down by the river."

The call of a whippoorwill worried the night air, mingling with Elias's grunt. "That man is trouble. Keep your distance."

This time his command didn't rankle nearly so much. Were she to hold his words in her hand and examine them by sunlight, they might almost sparkle with endearment. Flit! What was she thinking?

She set down the onion on a nearby rock, then straightened at the approach of swishing skirts and thudding boots. She and Elias turned at the same time.

Amos Shaw and his wife, Mary, drew near, his arm holding her close about the shoulders. "My wife here is weary-worn. We came to say good night before you two cozy up for the evening."

The innuendo stole her breath. Of course they expected her to sleep with the big man next to her. A reasonable enough assumption, but one that lit a fire in her belly.

Elias shook his head. "I am about to go put that fire out, then I shall take the next watch. Get yourselves to bed, and we will see you come morning."

Mary's amber eyes landed on Mercy, a frown dimpling her chin. Something wasn't right about the woman. She was like a beautiful china cup, turned so you couldn't quite see the ugly chip in the porcelain. What was it?

The babe in her arms lay deathly still and quiet. Another mournful *whip-poor-will* haunted the air—and then Mercy knew.

She pressed her lips tight to keep from gasping. In all the hours the Shaws had been here, that baby hadn't made one squawk—not a cry, a peep, or a movement. Nor had the woman set the bundle down. That was no baby. It was a swaddled mass of grief not even her husband could pry from her arms.

Mary's lower lip folded into a pout, and she looked at Elias. "Do not trouble yourself about the fire, sir. It is near to go out. Your wife is sorely in need of you." She lifted her face to her husband. "Mrs. Dubois doesn't have a little one yet, Amos. Surely we can spare them a night?"

A night? Mercy's pulse took up a war beat, and she inched away from Elias. His big hand caught hers before she could make a run for it.

Amos kissed his wife on the brow. "That is my girl." He beamed at them. "Mary is right. There's no need for you to take any watches tonight with us here, Mr. Dubois. There's plenty enough men to cover for you. How long has it been since you two have had some time to yourselves?"

Mercy's gasp collided with Elias's. Her gaze snapped to him. His dark eyes burned into hers, wide open.

Amos chuckled. "That is what I thought. Go on now. We'll relieve your men when they come in."

Elias let go of her hand. "No, I—"

"Go on now. I mean it." Amos shooed him off with his free arm. "The missus and I won't move a step till you settle."

"Not a single step," Mary repeated.

Beside her, Elias blew out a low breath and mumbled, "Much obliged." Then he pivoted and stalked off.

Leaving her alone. Blinking. Feet itching to tear off into the woods. But that was not what a wife would do, was it?

Grabbing handfuls of her skirt, she padded to where Elias waited at the front of the wagon.

His face was more shadowed than the twilight. "After you." He swept out a hand.

Surely he couldn't be serious. Yet there he stood, unmoving, a determined clench to his jaw.

Swallowing, she climbed into the seat, then worked her way through the opening of the canvas, more aware than she ought to be of the man following her.

Once inside, she immediately turned. Better to face a danger than be attacked from behind. If he thought to act upon that which the Shaws had hinted at, she'd gut him before he could holler for help.

But his blue eyes merely burned into hers, some kind of pleading bending his brow. "Mercy, I—"

His voice weighed heavy with an emotion she did not want to guess, for her own feelings surged in a dangerous swirl.

She backed over the crates and pulled out her knife, brandishing the blade for a quick strike if need be. "Keep your distance, Mr. Dubois."

The heat of a summer day warmed Elias's back. Small puffs tickled the hair at the nape of his neck, as feverish as an August breeze. His spirit quieted, so peaceful and calm the moment. It was a dream. He knew it. But he held on to the sweet sensations with all his strength. This kind of tranquility hadn't bathed him in years. Decades, were he honest. He rolled over, sinking deeper into such serenity.

Until a faint coo shot his eyes open.

A breath away, in the soft light of early dawn, an angel slept deep and even. Mercy's familiar scent of pine and woman instantly awoke his every nerve. Her dark lashes curved shut above high cheekbones. Her lips were parted, barely, issuing the warmth he'd felt on his neck—which now brushed against his mouth like a kiss. How sweet would that taste?

He should leave. Now. Crawl right out the canvas opening and let the cold air slap him in the face. He should. He swallowed. All the *should* in the world never had kept him from reaching for trouble. Only the grace of God had stayed his hand.

Give me strength now, Lord.

Slowly, his gaze moved from the sleeping eyes, to the full lips, to the hollow at the base of her bare neck where a gold chain hung heavy, weighted by a ruby heart. Her long hair, free of her braid, draped over her shoulder, spilling across her waist and highlighting the swell of her hips. A charge ran through him. If he moved, slightly, he could pull that body against his and—

He bolted up, not caring if his rash movements woke the sleeping beauty. He needed air, and lots of it. He dove out the canvas opening and scrambled to the ground.

Straight into the barrel of a musket. His hands shot up in reflex.

"There a problem, Mr. Dubois?" Matthew's voice, barely above a whisper, shouted a threat as cold and hard as the muzzle shoved into his chest. The man's eyes were hidden in the thin light of a morning just waking and the thick shadow of his hat brim, pulled low. Had he been out here all night?

Elias lowered his hands and lifted his chin. "Nothing to concern you."

Matthew looked past him, gun still trained on his heart. "You all right, Mercy?"

He didn't need to turn around to know a brown-eyed woman stared out from the canvas hole.

"I am fine."

Her words were sleep-laced and breathy, rekindling his desire.

Slowly, the gun lowered, and Matthew nodded at him. "Get yourself out on watch. A walk will do you good."

Bypassing the older man, Elias stalked off, glad for the task. Matthew couldn't have been more right. He did need a walk—a *very* long one.

By the time he returned, sun painted the camp brilliant. One Shaw woman sat on a log, fussing with the wrappings of her baby. Her sister-in-law hauled one of her boys with a firm grasp on his ear toward the wagon she shared with her husband. The other boy scampered too close to the fire. Matthew and the two Shaw men worked with the broken wheel. And Rufus, as usual, was nowhere to be seen.

Mercy stood on the far side of the clearing, red-faced and aiming a finger at Logan much the same as the muzzle he'd faced earlier this morn. What the devil?

He strode over to the pair, catching the tail end of Mercy's heated words.

"Stray near those belongings or me again, and your scalp will be swinging from my apron ties."

Elias's brows shot skyward.

Logan's face paled to an ugly shade of gruel. Without a rebuttal, he pivoted and trotted off like a hound from a cornered badger. Even the ridiculous feather in his hat seemed to droop.

Elias stifled a chuckle. "Remind me not to cross you."

She faced him and her hand flew to her mouth, her eyes wide. So she hadn't thought before shooting her word arrows.

This time he couldn't stop a laugh. "What did Logan do this time?"

Her hand fell, and red crept up her neck. "He was poking around our load. Said he was looking for a whetstone to sharpen his knife. A whetstone! You'd think we'd brought the whole of a fort's provisions with us. Why, I—" She cocked her head. "Why are you looking at me like that?"

Sunshine warmed her skin to a burnt-honey glow, highlighting every curve he'd appreciated earlier in the dark. The fire of her words reminded him all too much of the heat she'd radiated next to him in the wagon. His grin widened. If he answered her question, his scalp would be swinging from her apron strings right next to Logan's.

He wheeled about and retraced his steps back to where the men worked. Matthew and Amos Shaw pounded away on the iron tire ring. Nathan Shaw sat on a rock, whittling a new spoke.

Squinting against the sun, Nathan peered up at him. "Looks like you married a feisty one." His lips parted in a sloppy grin. " 'Tis worth it, though, especially once the younguns come along. Love's always worth the trouble, eh?"

Was it? He had no experience. Nothing to measure Nathan's words against. He cast a glance over his shoulder. A brown braid swished wide down Mercy's back as she darted toward the fire to yank away the Shaw boy.

Yet as he watched her pull the lad from danger, he had a niggling feeling that Nathan might be right. For the love of this woman, any amount of trouble might be worth the effort.

Chapter 13

Moisture trickled down Mercy's back as she darted toward the fire. She'd been chasing after fools all morning. First little James Shaw, unattended down by the river. Then Garret Logan, poking around their belongings as if he owned them. Now James's twin brother, Jonas, played an insane game of pitching rocks onto the fire, shooting up sparks and scattering the coals the men would need for the wheel. If one of those burning embers flew out and hit the five-year-old, the child could be branded or blinded. She upped her pace, unsure which provoked her more—the mischievous boy or Mary Shaw, who sat on a log nearby, ignoring all but the bundle of empty swaddling in her arms.

Jonas hefted another rock, raising it high. Mercy sprang, grabbing the boy's arm before he could swing.

"Enough!" She tugged him around, his brown eyes widening from the surprise attack. "Fire is not a plaything. You could get hurt—ow!"

Pain bit into her shin, and the rascal wrenched from her grasp. Jonas Shaw scampered off laughing while she sported the beginning of a bruise from where he'd kicked her. She clenched her fists, breathing out a string of oaths in Mohawk. The scamp reminded her far too much of Onontio when he was a boy.

The fuss broke the trance of Mary Shaw, who peered up from her perch on the log. "You shall make a fine mother, Mrs. Dubois."

She froze, breath hitching in her chest. What was she to say to that?

"Oh, don't fret." The woman smiled, clutching her blankets tighter to her chest. "I see the way your husband looks at you. It'll happen soon enough."

Despite the warmth of the day, a shiver ran across her shoulders. Mary Shaw was crazy, plain and simple. And she ought to know, for as a young girl she had frequently been in the presence of insanity. How many times had she sat cross-legged with a heart full of doubt, listening to the tribe's milky-eyed oracle spin crazy tales of fire monsters or talking trees?

Unbidden, her gaze strayed to where the men worked. Elias's broad back all but blocked her view of whoever it was he was talking to. His felt hat rode proud atop his tousled hair, the ends of which curled against his shoulders. A waft of breeze carried his scent, so well did she know it by now, for she'd breathed it in all night when he'd lain beside her, separated by only a blanket and her knife. Her mouth dried to dust at the memory, shame rising up. She'd meant to stay awake the night through, on guard against any untoward advances. But the peace of his steady breathing and the comfort of a warm body at her back fighting the chill of evening air had embraced her in a way she'd never known.

Without warning, Elias turned, his blue eyes seeking hers, pulling her close in ways that pulsed warmth to her cheeks. She gasped at the tangible connection. How had he known she was looking at him?

She spun back to Mary, then wished she hadn't, for the woman's gaze was every bit as canny as Elias's.

A smile beamed on the woman's face. "The only thing better than the love of a good man is bearing his little one."

Mercy turned and fled, following the earlier route of Jonas when he'd escaped her. She needed air, solitude, a lung-clearing scream, something. Anything but the strange allure of a traitor and the babble of an addlepated woman. She rounded the corner of the Shaws' wagon, intent on beating a path to the river, when Emmeline Shaw appeared, a wriggling boy in her grasp.

"Pardon me, Mrs. Dubois, but I saw what my son did to you, and Jonas here has something to say." She nudged the boy forward, planting him between herself and Mercy. "Go on, Jonas."

The boy kicked at the dirt with one toe. "Saw-ree-missus-do-bwa," he mumbled.

His mother thumped him on the head. "Jonas Shaw, you apologize proper, right this minute, or I will have your father take care of this."

His chin shot up, the threat flaring his little nostrils. "I apologize, Mrs. Dubois."

She pressed her lips together, making him squirm a bit, then offered the boy a smile for doing the right thing. "Apology accepted. Now, stay away from the fire, you hear?"

Jonas nodded then darted off before his mother could yank him back.

Emmeline's gaze followed the lad, a frown creasing her brow. "Those boys are like to be the death of—oh!"

A groan stole the rest of the woman's words. Emmeline Shaw bent, hand on her swollen belly, gasping.

Mercy shot into action, wrapping her arm around the woman's shoulders and leading her to a crate near the wagon. She guided Emmeline to sit, wishing she could drop onto a seat as well. Every time a woman in the village went into the birthing hut, Mercy ran the other way. Some women relished the process of bringing a new life into the world. Not her.

"Mrs. Shaw, tell me true." She crouched and peered into the woman's face, moisture dotting both their brows. "Is that baby coming?"

Emmeline sucked in a big breath, then straightened, color returning to her cheeks. "No, not yet, I think. Leastwise I hope not. It is too soon."

Though the woman appeared to be recovering, unease tightened Mercy's chest. If that babe came now, Mrs. Shaw would be likely to lose it—and possibly meet the same fate as her sister-in-law, clutching a heap of empty swaddlings and crooning lullabies to a nonexistent child. Blast that Mr. Logan for leading this family out at such a time—unless there was some reason she didn't know about.

She smoothed back a hank of blond hair from Emmeline's face, sneaking a feel of the woman's forehead in the process. Cool to the touch. That was good. She sank back onto her heels and smiled at Emmeline. "Tell me, Mrs. Shaw, why did you leave Fort Edward? Why did you not stay until the baby came?"

"Mr. Logan said we needed to reach the lake before the heat of summer."

"The heat of summer?" She cocked her head. "I never heard of such a thing. Usually guides are more concerned about winter snows."

Mrs. Shaw rubbed her belly, arching her back but not groaning. "Mr. Logan says heat is the bane of all travelers."

Maybe for that big skin of hot air, but a larger problem would be the war being waged on whites and reds alike—and these people were headed in the direction of land that was in the heart of it all. She frowned. "What lake are you talking about?"

"Lake Ontario."

She stood and smoothed her skirt with her hands, schooling her face to hide the horror the woman's words birthed. How could the Shaws have missed hearing about a war that'd been raging for near to five years now? "Surely you know, Mrs. Shaw, that there's already a post—a French post—at Fort Niagara, on the westernmost shore of Lake Ontario."

"Exactly." The woman nodded, eyes flashing bright. "We'll be the first to set up an English post in that territory. My husband and his brother say there's a lot of money in fur nowadays—more so than they could make in a lifetime had we remained in New York. We've scrimped and saved for a year now, selling all to purchase a load of trade goods. That is the beauty of it."

"That is the danger of it!"

"But Mr. Logan says this is the only way to gain an edge over the traders on the Mohawk River. We'll have first access to the finest furs before they travel from the Great Lakes on down to New York."

Mercy's hands curled into fists at her sides. Sure, they would have first access, but only if they lived long enough to establish a foothold in the trading industry—and with Logan leading them out beyond Fort Wilderness, that wasn't likely.

Splaying her fingers, she swung her long braid back behind her shoulder. "How did you say you met up with Mr. Logan?"

"Mr. Logan placed a post in the *Evening Gazette and Universal Advertiser*. Did you know he is one of the top ten guides listed in the paper? We were fortunate he took us on."

Ill fortune, more likely. She cleared her throat to keep from snorting. "Well, there's nothing to be done for it now, I suppose."

"How's that?"

"Look, Mrs. Shaw, you have not yet begun to face danger. Once you pass Fort Wilderness, you will be on your own with no one between you and peril but Mr. Logan. Mightn't your husband consider turning south, or better yet turning back? At least hiring a different guide at Fort Edward?"

"Turn back?" The lady worried her bottom lip with her teeth as if the words tasted bitter. "I don't understand."

Blood. Gore. Death and sorrow. It was a blessing Emmeline did not understand what was ahead of her—and far be it from her to tell the woman. "I'm thinking your Mr. Logan isn't as experienced as he claims."

For a moment, the woman's brows pulled in to a tight knot, then slowly loosened. "I appreciate your concern, Mrs. Dubois, and I sorrow over whatever misfortunes made you and your family head back east. But regardless of Mr. Logan, I trust my husband. Nathan's looking out for us as surely as Mr. Dubois looks out for you."

A sigh drained the rest of her fight, and she rose to her feet. The woman's trust in her husband was commendable—but completely naive. From what she'd seen of the Shaw men, they didn't have half the wilderness sense of Elias. Or Matthew.

She spun and stomped off, annoyed that Elias came to mind sooner than her old friend.

An early evening breeze blew away the chatter near the fire. Where he stood, yards away, Elias drank in the moment of relative quiet, save for the squawk of a jay on a nearby branch. He crouched in front of the newly constructed wheel, examining the workmanship for a last time before joining the others. Running a finger along every seam, he tested the strength of each new spoke, then squinted to blur the outline and gauge the shape. The thing appeared to be the picture of sturdiness, a testament to the value of many hands lightening the work. Not that the Shaws were expert wheelwrights, but they labored as a team—unlike Rufus and Logan.

"I've brought you something."

Startled, he shot to his feet, reaching for a gun he did not have, a reaction honed from years of experience—yet one unnecessary in this instance. He turned to face Mercy, who smirked at his obvious surprise.

He grinned in return. "Even with a toe on the mend, you move on panther paws."

"I wouldn't be a good scout if I banged around like the Shaws. Here"— she held out a mug—"I figured it a wifely thing to bring you some of this."

The rich scent of coffee hit his nose, as stunning as her words, and he took the cup from her. "Thunder and turf! Where did you find this?" He slugged back a mouthful of the brew, ignoring the burn and relishing the flavor.

"The Shaws have many unnecessary things. Mr. Logan's ideas of provisions are peculiar at best." She leaned against the oak trunk, scaring the jay off its perch. Her gaze landed on the wheel at his feet. "Matthew says you will be able to give that a go tomorrow."

"He is right." He savored another mouthful, appreciating both the coffee and the ranger. "Matthew is a good man. I see why you took up with him."

She nodded, still staring at the wheel. "I will miss him, for certain."

She'd miss the man? He grunted. What was Matthew—or she— planning? "Who is doing the leaving, you or him?"

"He is, when we reach the fort." She scowled up at him. "He says he will be turning in his ranger uniform and is bent on becoming a farmer."

The tone of her voice, the curve of her shoulders, the way the first shadows of night darkened her face all spoke of her displeasure. He lowered his cup, intrigued. Most women would think such a pursuit admirable.

He advanced a step toward her, pulled by such an anomaly. "You think he is making a mistake?"

Defiance glinted in her brown eyes. "I know he is. Plowing dirt's not the same as running footloose atop it, free to come and go at will."

He blew out a long breath, feeling the bone-crushing weariness of years on the run. What would she say if he told her Matthew's plans were exactly what he'd be about once he returned to Boston? "Running gets old, Mercy. Everyone realizes that at some point."

"What about you?" She cocked her head, much as the jay had earlier. "After you get out of jail, that is. I expect you will run far and wide, not tie yourself to a patch of ground."

Laughter rumbled in his chest. She would've been right even a year ago, but not now. His chuckle turned to ashes in his mouth. *Oh François*. Had his friend not been washed down the Petawawa River, he'd also planned on leaving behind the voyageur life and putting down roots. Would the knife in his heart ever get pulled out?

He gulped back the rest of the coffee, grounds and all, then swiped the back of his hand across his mouth and handed her the cup. "The truth is, Matthew's plan is the same as mine. I intend to settle on a little place down in Connecticut, near Hartford. Build a house, have some children."

She snorted. This close, he saw her nose bunch much the same as a rabbit's—altogether too charming.

"You might want to find a wife first, Mr. Dubois."

"I already have one. You."

Color rose on her cheeks, and he grinned. Teasing this woman was far too gratifying.

"Your sense of humor is as ridiculous as Mr. Logan's peacock feather," she shot back.

He studied her for a moment, questions sprouting up like a freshly seeded field. Was she never lonely, roaming the woods, always on the move? Did she not long for a home other than the trees overhead or a night in a cave? What kind of woman didn't yearn to dandle a babe on her knee?

He dared a step closer. "Do you never think of settling down?"

She shook her head. "Matthew does that enough for me."

"I find it hard to believe no man has ever struck a fancy for you." Why had no one pursued this rare woman?

A small smile lifted her lips. "More like I've never taken a fancy to any man."

She peered at him, a peculiar gleam deepening the brown of her eyes. The same charge he'd felt when first holding her hand sizzled in the air between them.

He edged nearer, almost breath to breath. Slowly, he brushed his knuckle from her brow to her cheek, then lower to rub against the softness below her jaw. She didn't lean into his touch, but neither did she veer back or run. She didn't move at all, save for the rapid rise and fall of her chest.

"What is it you want out of life, Mercy Lytton?" he whispered—then froze with a sudden realization.

Everything in him craved for her to say, *"You."*

Her lips parted. He leaned closer—any closer and she'd be in his arms.

"Peace," she murmured.

His hand lowered, and a grin rose. He was a fool. One didn't expect something as ethereal as star-shine to hunger for a man—especially one such as him.

"Well." He retreated a step. "Seems we are in agreement then, just going about it in different ways."

"I—"

A scream ripped through the air, cutting off whatever she'd intended to say. A keening scream, shot through with fear and pain.

Much pain.

CHAPTER 14

Mercy dashed after Elias, his long legs outdistancing hers—but not by much. They halted just about even at Nathan and Emmeline Shaw's wagon. Nathan stood at the front of it, gripping the kickboard, face drained of color and visibly shaking. Jonas and James held on to Nathan's legs, for once silent. Rufus and Mr. Logan were out on watch, so the footsteps pounding behind her had to belong to Matthew and Amos Shaw.

Another scream ripped out from behind the wagon, lifting the hairs at the nape of Mercy's neck.

Letting go of the kickboard, Mr. Shaw took a step toward her, dragging his boys along with him. "You got to help her, Mrs. Dubois."

She clutched her hands in front of her to keep from grabbing Elias's arm for support, feeling as unsteady as Mr. Shaw looked.

"I—" Her throat closed. How to explain she could gut an elk, elbow deep in blood and gore, but the thought of seeing a baby birthed turned her stomach inside out?

"Mercy." Elias's voice was hardly more than a whisper, but it was a command nonetheless.

She lifted her face to him. His blue gaze blazed strong and confident. What she wouldn't give for some of his strength right about now.

"You can do this, you hear me?" His words flowed with the power of a mighty river. "Go on."

Sucking in a breath for courage, she forced one foot in front of the other, then stopped cold when the next wail of agony rent the evening air.

Lord, give me strength.

The wailing ceased, and she pressed on.

"Emmeline?" Her voice trembled as much as she did.

Emmeline Shaw stood hunched over, shored up against the wagon, one arm cradling her big belly—with a bloody puddle at her feet. For now, the woman was quiet, but that wouldn't last long.

Mercy escaped back to the front of the wagon, gasping for air. This was beyond her. A normal birthing, maybe she could attend, but this? No. Most emphatically not. She scanned the gathering at the front of the wagon, looking for a blond woman clutching a heap of swaddling. Four pairs of worried eyes stared back—the same four she'd left. "Where's Mary? Emmeline needs her help."

Amos Shaw shook his head, avoiding eye contact with his brother Nathan. "My wife, well, she can't. She. . ." He retreated a step, tugging his hat brim lower. "No."

Nathan advanced, his face paler than a winter moon. "Can I. . . ?"

Her stomach sank. The man would be less help than her. She closed her eyes, wishing that when she opened them, this would all be nothing more than a nightmare. But another scream pried her eyelids open. There was nothing for it. Either she did this, or the blood of Emmeline Shaw and her baby would haunt her for the rest of her life.

"Tell us what to do." Elias's strong voice was a lifeline.

Swallowing back the acidic taste rising past her throat, she skewered Emmeline's husband with a stare she hoped looked imposing. "Boil some water. Keep it hot and bubbly all the while, and make sure to keep your boys with you."

Without a word, he pivoted and ushered his young ones toward the campfire.

"Mr. Shaw." Her voice yanked up Amos Shaw's chin. "Bring me whatever clean cloths you and your wife can find. Have them to me as soon as you're able. Can you do that?"

He nodded, then turned tail and ran.

Next, she sought Matthew's face, all the while fumbling in her bodice for her knife. "Here, sharpen this." She tossed him her blade.

He caught it with ease and strode off.

Elias stood alone, his eyes twin blue fires in the gathering shadows. "What about me?"

"Get me some kind of light—"

Another scream howled, ragged with desperation.

Mercy clenched her teeth, wishing to God she could trade places with him. "And pray. Just. . .pray."

She spun and ran back to Emmeline before she could launch herself into Elias's arms and bury her face in his shirt.

Behind the wagon, Emmeline arched and panted, one hand planted into the small of her back. The crazed sheen in her eyes looked far too much like her sister-in-law's. As Mercy neared the woman, Emmeline grabbed her by the arms. "Am I going to lose my baby?"

Mercy pinched her lips shut. By the looks of it, yes, the woman would—but she forced a small smile. "Of course not. We shall—"

Emmeline's head dropped and her grip tightened, her fingers digging deep into Mercy's flesh. A raspy groan tore from the woman's throat. This was going fast. Way too fast.

Mercy rubbed little circles on her back, wishing she could think of something better to do. "Shh, shh."

Surprisingly, Emmeline calmed. Not much, but enough to give Mercy an idea. Slowly, quietly, she sang—not a birthing song, for she knew none, but a lullaby. The woman wouldn't know the difference anyway.

> *"Ho, ho, Watanay.*
> *Ho, ho, Watanay.*
> *Ho, ho, Watanay.*
> *Ki-yo-ki-na.*
> *Ki-yo-ki-na."*

By the time her voice stilled, so had Emmeline. "Thank you," the woman whispered.

She wrapped an arm around Emmeline's shoulder and gave a little squeeze. "Come on. Let's try to walk a bit, shall we? I don't know much about birthing, but I know it is good to walk."

Between singing, mopping Emmeline's brow, and shifting the woman from walking to leaning against her, the hour wore on. Nothing seemed to work, not for long. Night fell hard, yet despite the cool evening air, Emmeline sweated and writhed as if the heat of a July afternoon bore down on her. Between her groans and moans, she called for her mother.

And Mercy did not blame her. She'd not missed her own mother so keenly since the day she'd walked away from her grave three years back. In between Emmeline's pains, Mercy fingered her locket. Her mother would have known what to do in this situation. She always knew when it came to matters of women. How to soothe. Ways to comfort. Methods of easing the hurt. For the first time in her life, she wished she'd listened to her mother rather than despising her soft ways.

Emmeline stilled suddenly. So did she. Was this it? Would the woman die in front of her? Blast that Mr. Logan for hauling the Shaws out to the wilderness.

"God, please," Mercy breathed out. "I'm not much for prayer, but save this woman and her child despite my lack."

During one of their treks around the wagon, Elias had set a lantern on the ground next to a pile of quilts at the back, giving them a privacy of sorts. In the soft glow of lamplight, Emmeline Shaw's gaze shot to hers and her mouth opened into a big O, but no sound came out. Suddenly the woman grabbed the back of the wagon and lowered into a squat, all air huffing out of her lungs.

Mercy's heart stopped—until a wriggling mass landed on the blankets.

Emmeline sank back, breathing hard. Mercy grabbed a clean cloth and scooped up the babe, wiping the newborn's nose and mouth.

A lusty cry broke out. This time the squall of a little one.

Mercy's arms shook as she rubbed the wetness off Emmeline's new daughter. She wrapped the girl tight in another cloth, then handed her to her mother.

"Ohh." Emmeline's one word—and not even a word at that—rang sweetly in the thick night air. It was a victory cry. A benediction. An all-is-well-with-the-world kind of coo.

For the first time in hours, the tension in Mercy's shoulders unknotted. The woman wasn't quite out of danger yet, but hopefully the worst of it was over. Giving Emmeline a moment to breathe, Mercy stood and stretched. It would be best to put everyone's mind at ease. But as she took a step forward, the lantern's glow highlighted a white face in the darkness.

Mary Shaw stood at the edge of the reach of light, glowering. Her arms empty at her sides. The swaddling blankets lay in the dirt.

❧

Elias's head bobbed to his chest, then immediately snapped up. He couldn't afford to doze off, not when those Shaw boys could awaken at any time and sneak off in the darkness. Rubbing a hand over his face, he leaned his head back against the tree trunk, then blinked over to where the boys lay sleeping on the ground. His frock coat, thrown over the top of them, didn't move a whit. Good. The rascals were still a-slumber in the quiet.

Wait a minute. . .*quiet?*

He jumped to his feet, instantly alert. Leaves shushed overhead. Night insects clicked. Across the clearing, the fire yet crackled—unattended. And not one groan or moan droned on the air.

Elias padded past the boys on silent feet, then lengthened his steps into a long-legged stride. Amos Shaw, arm slung around his weeping wife's shoulders, led her off to their wagon. Mercy stood in conversation with Nathan Shaw in front of the other wagon, but not for long. The man scrambled to the back side of the canvas, where Elias had earlier laid out blankets and a lantern.

Upping his pace, Elias clenched his teeth. By the looks of it, a whole lot of grief had broken wide open, and Mercy had been the one to have to deliver the awful news. It was his fault, the way she rested her hand against the wagon's side and propped herself up. Her long braid drooped. So did her shoulders. She'd not wanted to attend the birth in the first place—and he'd been the one to suggest it.

He drew up in front of her, the urge to pull her into his arms so strong, he flexed his fingers. "How is Mrs. Shaw?"

A weak smile curved her lips. Ah, but this woman was brave.

"Emmeline and her daughter are fine for the moment. But Mary Shaw—"

"Whoa." He shot up a hand. "The woman *and* the babe are doing fine?"

She nodded. Loosened hair—her hat dispensed of hours ago—fell onto her brow, and she pulled it back. "They are."

He chuckled. "Thank God. And thank you. You are a wonder, you know that?"

"Nature's a wonder, not me." She reached for her locket, this time already worked loose from her bodice. How many times had she clutched that thing for strength during Emmeline's arduous labor?

She peered up at him. "Would that I could do something for Mary Shaw. I fear she has lost whatever sense she had left."

The mournful wail of a screech owl sounded from the woods, adding a haunting quality to Mercy's words. Life could be harsh sometimes, downright throat-slitting harsh. . .and well did he know it.

So did Mercy, judging by the bow of her head.

He reached for her, wishing to soothe away all that she'd endured this night—then pulled back before his fingers touched her hair. He had no right to do so, no claim on this woman, so why the persistent desire to touch her? A strange fire burned in his belly, and he retreated a step.

"How do you fare?" His voice cracked at the edges.

She didn't seem to notice. She merely angled her face and stared off into the night. "You know that feeling after a breakneck run, when you're bone-weary but the excitement of it is still jittering through your body?"

He nodded. "I do."

Her gaze slid to his, and she smiled, so brilliant it shamed the starlight. "That is how I feel."

He couldn't help but grin back. "You did a good thing."

"Well, I'm not finished yet. There's more to be done." She turned to leave.

But he stayed her with a hand to her shoulder. "You want I should haul that boiling water over?"

Her brow scrunched and she cocked her head; then as suddenly, the look disappeared and she laughed. "No, it is not needed."

Her words chased circles in his head, never landing in a coherent line. "Then why did you have Mr. Shaw tend that water this whole time?"

She shrugged, taking her braid along for a ride on her slim shoulders. "He needed something to do other than worry himself over his wife and babe. Besides, we can use it to launder the soiled quilts."

He sucked in a breath. The woman was cunning, but not like most women. He'd had his fill of the conniving sort, always trying to gain what they wanted at the expense of others. But the brown-eyed beauty blinking up at him was nothing of the kind. Though he was her sham husband in a faux marriage, he suddenly understood some of what Nathan Shaw must've felt this night at the thought of losing the one he loved most.

"Tell me true, Mercy, if we had not been here—if *you* had not been here—would Mrs. Shaw and her baby have made it?"

She said nothing, just stared at him. But she didn't have to. The owl answered for her, chanting its woeful dirge.

Rage prickled hot up his spine. "Blast that Logan!" He wheeled about.

"Elias? Where are you going?"

"To have a word with the man," he called over his shoulder.

"Why don't you sleep on it? Save it for morning."

He left her and her questions behind. Too much pent-up anger simmered to a boiling point. Rufus's slights and grievances were nothing in comparison to Logan's. That fool led these honest people to their deaths. He tromped down the trail to the riverbank, where Logan should've been on watch, should've heard him coming—or at the very least seen him.

But the man sat with his back against a rock, eyes closed, head tilted and mouth open. Snores issued on the inhales.

Elias nudged the man's leg with the toe of his moccasin, hoping the restraint of not kicking the fool in the gut would please God—for it surely did not satisfy him. "Get up, Logan."

The man's head bobbed forward. "What? Who's—"

"I said get up." Bending, he grabbed a handful of the man's coat and yanked him to his feet. "That Shaw woman nearly died because of you tonight, and you sleep?"

Fully awake now, Logan glowered and batted at his arm. "Unhand me!"

He clenched the fabric all the tighter, wishing he'd grabbed higher and squeezed the man's neck instead. "I ought to string you up myself."

The man's face blanched in the darkness. "Put me down!"

"Fine." Using all his muscle, he whumped the fellow to the ground, flat on his back.

Logan gasped for air.

Elias widened his stance and stood over him, like the Grim Reaper come to call. "When you get these people to Fort Wilderness—*if* you can manage that—then you find them another guide. You are done. You hear me?"

"You cannot dictate"—he wheezed—"what I. . .or the Shaws do."

"True. I cannot." He folded his arms. "But if I hear you led these people out beyond the fort, what I can do is hunt you down. And that is a promise."

"As will I." Matthew's voice shot straight and true over his shoulder.

Elias stifled a smirk. No doubt Mercy had told the ranger about his murderous retreat.

Rolling to the side, Logan staggered to his feet. Without a word, he retrieved his hat where it lay on the ground, then scurried off toward camp like the rodent he was.

Matthew blew out a long breath and faced him, an odd gleam in his gray eyes. "Mercy warned me you were about to put the fear of God into that man. As much as I appreciate it, you know I can't allow you to hunt anyone down. Don't make me shackle you up just when I'm beginning to like you. I expect better than that from a man of your caliber."

He bit back a smile. Lord, but he admired this man. Maybe—*perhaps*—if Grandfather had used such encouraging words more often, he might not have strayed so far in rebellion. Who knew? But one thing he would bet on. Matthew Prinn would make the finest grandfather a boy could have. He clapped the man on the back. "I will take Logan's watch. You go on back."

Turning, he strode off along the riverbank, keeping to the weeds. Matthew and Mercy were good people. The best. And the longer he stayed with them, the harder it would be to leave them.

But even harder would be convincing his Wyandot contacts not to harm them.

CHAPTER 15

The squawk of crows jerked Mercy awake—but not fully. It took her a few blinks to attach meaning to the overhead branches and back side of a wagon. She pushed up with a yawn, thankful the long night of midwifery was finally over. She'd rather outrun a Seneca with a war club than attend to another birthing on her own, for Emmeline had bled thick and heavy after the delivery. Truly, it was a wonder Mrs. Shaw's heart yet beat after the loss of so much blood.

Mercy glanced down at the woman sleeping next to her. Emmeline and her new babe nestled together beneath a faded quilt, both breathing evenly. The woman looked hollow-cheeked and pale, but the babe, while impossibly tiny, held good color and slept soundly. Having made it through the night, the child stood a fighting chance of survival—as good as any of them could hope for in the middle of a war-torn wilderness.

She tucked the blanket snug where it had fallen away at Emmeline's back, then dared to run a light finger over the little one's cheek. Silky. Warm. With each stroke, a foreign yearning welled stronger. What would it be like to nuzzle a downy-headed babe of her own? To hold in her arms a child created in love, with a tuft of dark hair and eyes the color of an endless sky, blue as—

She drew back, stunned by the rogue desire. Lack of sleep and the strain of the journey were getting to her.

Taking care not to jostle Emmeline or the babe, she crawled out from beneath the shared blanket and arched a kink out of her back. Sun slanted lines of shadows from a stand of nearby hemlock, and she rubbed her eyes—then berated herself. She was no better than Rufus. Morning was already half spent and here she stood sleepy-lidded. A fine cup of the Shaws' coffee would be just the thing, if Mary were of a mind to share—or if she were of a mind at all. The woman might not yet have a grip on her senses.

Rounding to the front of the wagon, she neared the campsite and scanned the area. Elias, Matthew, Rufus, and Nathan Shaw huddled near the broken wagon, the repaired wheel at the ready to put back on. The Shaw twins each grasped a shovel and were furiously digging a hole—or trying to. Breaking ground next to a broad-trunked maple was near impossible. A small smile twitched her lips. Had that been Elias's idea to keep them out of mischief? Had he given that worthless guide Logan some busywork to do as well? For that man was conspicuously absent.

But so were Amos and Mary. Turning on her heel, Mercy headed to their wagon. If Mr. Shaw was with his wife, perhaps a request for coffee would be a possibility.

Rounding the back of the wagon, she slowed her steps. A low voice— one frayed to ragged threads—filtered out from the canvas.

"I can't take this anymore, Mary. I can't lose you too, not like our boys. Please, Wife, come back to me. Come on back. Don't do this to us."

The raw grief etched deep in Amos's words seared Mercy's ears. Would that she could brew a tea, blend a salve, do something for the man's wife. Broken bones, torn flesh, those things could be mended, but how did one heal a mind so ravaged by sorrow?

Mercy turned away from Amos Shaw's murmurings. Such intimacies should be left in private. Better she dip her feet in the river than interrupt such a moment for a trifling cup of coffee. Cold water would work just as well to fully waken her.

She retreated and strode across the campsite, bypassing the men shoring up the wagon. Elias and Matthew strained all their muscles into wielding logs they used as levers while Rufus and Nathan shoved a makeshift stand beneath the back edge of the wagon. She paused, heart swelling in a strange way at how well Matthew and Elias worked together. With the combined effort, bit by bit, the wagon rose. By tomorrow, they ought to be back on their trek to the fort.

Turning from the sight, she padded the rest of the way to the river with a soft step, a habit from years of walking invisibly. If her mother had learned to do the same, she would not have suffered such derision. *Oh Mother.* She sighed as she sank to the ground and unlaced her moccasins, shoving down the bitterness that still dogged her years after her mother's death. Would she never be free of wishing things had been different? Be released from the anger her mother's faith still bubbled inside her?

"Trust, Daughter. Trust in a God who is big enough to make the universe, yet kind enough to dry each of your tears."

She frowned. Would that God had never given cause for tears to be created in the first place.

Before she left the safety of the spring growth, she scanned the banks for any sign of danger. Black water flowed undisturbed, upriver and down. No canoes. No unexpected rustle of brush on either side. All appeared to be— No, wait.

One by one she shut down her senses, focusing on a pinpoint of blue that ought not be flashing against the muck left behind from receding waters.

She shoved her feet back into her shoes and gathered her skirts, trekking down twenty yards or so to the sight. Bending, she plucked a peacock feather from the mud. Why would Mr. Logan's treasured ornament be here? He was a proud enough man to take great care of his belongings. This was no accident.

Her gaze dissected the immediate area. Five paces farther, hoofprints marred the mud—headed toward the water. She hiked her skirts high, impropriety a thing she'd long ago learned to discard at a moment's notice, and waded into the Nowadaga. Thankfully the rain-gorged river had decided to calm into a proper stream, and she crossed without a tumble.

On the other side, curved gouges in the soft dirt led out of the water, heading straight into the trees. Never once in the days they had spent together had Mr. Logan ridden off in such a fashion. Why now?

Standing tall, she shaded her eyes against the sun and squinted into the woods. A thrashed path beat a trail as far as she could see. Clearly the man had ridden off toward Fort Wilderness, but— She pursed her lips. That he'd made it so obvious did not sit well in her empty belly.

She let go of her clenched skirts and worked her way south along the riverbank, scouring for any sign of disturbed ground. After a mile or so, the growl of her stomach urged her to turn around and break her fast, ignore the silly man who'd ridden into danger, and—

She stopped, gaze snagged on a depression in the muck from where a rock had sat. A stone that size wouldn't just up and march off like a soldier. Something had kicked it into the water. Shifting her gaze, she stared inland. Bent weeds, not much, but spaced wide enough to accommodate the leap of a horse. Her brow tightened. Why had Mr. Logan taken so much effort to show he'd ridden into the water, away from camp, then doubled back and hidden his return? Was he even now stretched out and snoring on his bedroll, having completed whatever harebrained errand he'd been about?

Pivoting, she tromped back to the crossing, angry with herself for having fallen prey to Mr. Logan's antics and even angrier with him for having put them all in danger by running off into the forest. She'd give him an earful and then grab an oatcake for breakfast.

She stalked back to camp, not caring if she had to wake the man for being such a dolt, but when she got to the spot where he'd set up his own lean-to, the ground beneath it was barren. No bedroll. No pack of belongings.

And no Mr. Logan.

Elias grabbed a canteen and sank onto the ground. Back propped against a hemlock, he stretched out his legs and swigged back a long drink before he joined Matthew and Rufus in loading the crates. Getting the wheel on took more grit than he'd reckoned. Still, God was good. How long would it have taken without the strong back of Nathan Shaw to help them?

As if he'd conjured the man, Nathan strode over and sat cross-legged next to him, handing over a strip of jerky. " 'Tisn't much, but you wouldn't want me to cook a meal."

"Thank you." He bit into the meat and tore off a chunk.

So did Nathan. As the man chewed, his gaze followed the movement of his boys, directly across from them beyond the trail. Their shovels forgotten, James and Jonas had dropped to their knees and were scraping up dirt using some rocks.

Nathan shook his head and faced him. "It is a sad shame you don't have little ones yet. The way you keep my boys in line, you will make a fine father. I've learned a trick or two from you."

The jerky stuck in his throat. Him, a father? And a fine one at that? He swallowed hard at the ridiculous notion. He knew nothing of little ones or their ways. No, his knowledge of human nature—be it younglings or elders—had been forged in the flames of experience. It took a scheming mind to know the function of another's, may God forgive him.

"No tricks involved." He swigged back a drink and swiped his mouth. "You cannot stop someone bent on mischief, but ofttimes you can redirect it."

Nathan cocked his head. "How so?"

"I told your James and Jonas a story I heard once, of an Indian cache of arrowheads buried at the base of a tree just like that one." He nodded his head toward the boys. "And they have been at it ever since."

Nathan chuckled. "My wife and I are beholden to you."

"There is no debt." Tearing off another bite of jerky, he shrugged. "You helped us make repairs. It seems we are even."

"Far from it. Emmeline is more valuable than a broken wheel. If Mrs. Dubois hadn't helped her, my boys and me might be digging something worse than an aimless hole right about now. Your wife is a fine woman, stepping in to help the way she did."

A memory of her pale face surfaced, the sheen of dread blinking at him from wide eyes, just before Mercy took on the delivery of the Shaw baby. She'd been terrified, but she'd done so anyway—and without complaint. Indeed, she was a fine woman, in more ways than one. He grunted in agreement.

"But you're not really married, are you?"

The question flew like an arrow in the dark, sticking him through the throat without warning of an attack. He forced his expression to remain as stoic as a Wyandot sachem while scrambling for a response that wasn't an outright lie. "What makes you say that?"

Nathan's gaze bored into his. "There's a tension between the two of you, a wanting and not having. Like a couple courting and being denied."

His gut clenched, and he was hard pressed to decide if it was from the fact that the man had been studying them far too keenly, or because there was some small measure of truth to his observation.

Regardless, he corked his canteen and stood. "My thanks for the jerky, but we'd best get on to loading our cargo."

Nathan shot to his feet, staying him with a hand on his sleeve. "No offense. 'Tain't none of my business."

He pulled away. "None taken."

They both turned at the sound of swishing skirts. Mercy drew close, pink of cheek and huffing. "Hate to tell you this, Mr. Shaw, but your guide is gone."

Logan gone? Though slipshod, at least the man was a guide, of sorts. How were the Shaws to manage with a newborn babe, a mother not yet recovered, and a woman who even now suffered so cruelly she'd not let go of her husband?

He stepped closer to Mercy, studying her face. Maybe she meant something different, though what, he couldn't imagine. "Gone where?"

"It appears Mr. Logan beat a clear path toward Fort Wilderness, but a mile downriver, he doubled back. I did not follow it any farther, thinking he'd likely come back here. But all his belongings are gone."

"Worse than that." Matthew's voice turned them all around. "He has taken some of our belongings along with him."

CHAPTER 16

The sunny day turned blood red. So much anger shook through her, Mercy retreated from Matthew and Rufus lest she strike them for Logan's thievery. She should've known the man was up to something when she'd caught him poking around their cargo yesterday morn. Across the way, the Shaw boys hollered at each other, and her own scream begged to join theirs.

Next to her, Elias turned to Mr. Shaw. "Go get Amos. This needs to be sorted out."

Sorted? She choked. The situation needed more than a peace talk. As soon as Nathan Shaw was out of hearing range, she growled out, "I should've knifed that man when I had the chance."

Matthew frowned at her. "Violence only begets violence. You know that as well as I."

"Not if I grounded him first. I should have—"

"There is no time for should-haves," Elias interrupted. "What did Logan take?"

"Gold. Near to half a crate." Rufus shot out a broad fire of expletives. "I'm with Mercy. We grab our guns and hunt him down for the skunk he is."

Rufus wheeled about, and for a half second Mercy considered joining him.

Matthew yanked him back by his collar. "Tracking in a rage makes for mistakes. Elias and I will set out. Logan can't have gone far."

Rufus sneered. "Dubois ain't even got a gun."

"Do you really think I need a musket to bring in Garret Logan?" His voice was a panther's growl.

"You managed to get hauled in while totin' one."

"Enough!" Matthew cuffed the young man on the back of the head. "Rufus, go run a scouting check on the area. Elias, come with me."

Matthew turned. Elias stalked after him.

And so did Mercy. "I'm coming along. You know I can see farther than the two of you combined."

Elias just kept on striding to where the horses were hobbled.

But Matthew stopped, his gray eyes kind yet firm. "I need you here, girl. Those Shaw men have to be talked out of going any farther into the backcountry, and you're just the one to do it."

Frustration roiled in her empty belly. "Why me?"

"Because you're the best one to remind them of their wives."

"But—" She clamped her mouth shut.

Matthew had set his jaw. Once he did that, there was no point in going any further, not even with a stick in hand.

She whirled, stifling a huff, and marched ramrod straight over to where the Shaw brothers rounded their wagons. Both had aged years in the space of three days.

She stopped in front of them. "My father and husband"—she paused, swallowing back the sour taste of the lie—"have gone off to bring back Mr. Logan."

Nathan Shaw nodded, his shoulders bent as if he alone bore the weight of the world. "We're much obliged, Mrs. Dubois. Seems we've brought more trouble upon you folks than any of us reckoned."

"Don't fret on our account. Life is trouble, and there's no stopping it. It is in the darkest skies we see the brightest stars."

Amos Shaw tugged at the soiled kerchief around his neck, his Adam's apple bobbing. "Wise words."

"Then I hope you will listen to what I have to say next. Come, let us sit." She bypassed the men and settled near the ashes of the spent fire. Even though no flames flared, the familiar position of working through issues at a fire pit was too ingrained to even think of sitting elsewhere.

She waited for the brothers to sink onto the ground across from her before she began. "You have already been cautioned on the dangers of continuing to Fort Wilderness and beyond."

"We have." The brothers exchanged a glance, then Nathan Shaw faced her. "Yet we're not to be moved. There's no going back east for us, with or without Mr. Logan's guidance."

She bit her lip. Willful men! How to upend minds plowed so deep into a rut? There could be no better outcome than the sharp end of a tomahawk if they journeyed west. But what about south? An idea began to unfurl, lifting her chin with the possibility of it. "I have an alternative."

Neither man spoke a word, but both their heads cocked.

"There is a closer fort you might want to consider. While I can't promise the route will be any safer, I can say for certain 'tis a lot shorter."

Nathan Shaw rubbed his jaw. "We ain't heard tell of no other garrisons out this way."

Of course not. There weren't any. But this was the next best thing—and the only idea she had left in her quiver. She forced a small smile. "It is more of a fortified house than a garrison."

"Speak plain, Mrs. Dubois. No need to fancy up your idea. I give you my word I shall consider it." He glanced at the other man. "Amos?"

His brother nodded. "Me too."

"All right." She leaned forward. At least they had given her a fair shot, which, despite Matthew's confidence, was more than she'd expected. "Not far past where the Nowadaga drains into the Mohawk River, there's a trading post set up by a man named Johannes Klock."

"But we—"

She held up her hand. "I know you aim to set up your own post, and you will. But for now, it might be best if you sheltered with a family who can teach you how to interact with the people of these lands. It takes more than slapping up four walls and hanging an 'open' shingle on your door. You need patience, understanding, and a fair amount of cunning. The Klocks know this."

Amos Shaw blew out a big breath.

Nathan shook his head. " 'Tain't what we had in mind."

She speared the man with a pointed stare. Sometimes a direct hit, while cutting to the bone, did the most good. "Neither was a babe come early with a mother still too weak to lift her head." She snapped her gaze to Amos. "Or a wife broken by grief."

Amos Shaw reared back as if she'd slapped his face. Nathan's lips folded into a grim line.

She held her breath. Had she pushed them too far?

For a long while, no one said anything. Only the chatter of the boys across the way—for they had given up their bickering—carried on the morning breeze, mixing with birdsong and the soft squall of a newborn.

Nathan ducked his chin. "Give us a few moments alone, Mrs. Dubois."

"Of course." She stood. "I will go check on Emmeline."

"Wait."

She turned back at the sound of Amos Shaw's quiet voice.

"Could you—*would* you mind checking on my wife too?"

She nodded, then swung around and grabbed up a mug of water on her way to Mary Shaw's wagon. Dread dogged each step. What would she find? Would the woman light into her for bringing a babe not her own into the world? Would there be tears? Screams? The swipe of claws or worse. . . gaping silence and hollow stares?

"Mrs. Shaw?" she called out as she neared the wagon.

No response.

"Mary?" Reaching for the seat, she hauled herself upward. Still no answer.

Sucking in a breath for courage, she grasped the canvas covering the opening. "I'm coming in."

Growing up amongst warriors, she'd seen things that had turned her blood to the chill of a winter night, but as she crawled into the Shaws' wagon and gazed upon Mary, she shivered.

Mary Shaw curled into a ball, naked as the day she graced the world. Wicked red scratches covered her arms and legs, everywhere her nails could've possibly ripped away skin. Most were dried scarlet, yet some still oozed. Her eyes followed Mercy's entrance, fiery and cavernous, but did she even see her?

"Just me, Mary. 'Tis Mercy." Another shiver shimmied across her shoulders, and she forced her arm to hold steady as she held out the mug. "I brought you some water."

Mary didn't move. Didn't blink. Didn't anything.

How to deal with this? A cornered badger could take down prey three times its size—and Mercy suddenly knew exactly how that prey felt. Keeping her movements fluid and steady, she set the cup down, then dared to inch closer.

"Mary? You all right?"

She reached out a tentative hand and rested her fingers on the woman's bare back. Sometimes a gentle touch calmed more than a soothing voice. Slowly, she rubbed a circle on skin prickled with gooseflesh, avoiding the scratched areas. Mary did not move, so she edged closer and rubbed some more.

What seemed like hours passed, and in that eternity, the sun slanted higher where it worked its way up the canvas back opening. Mary's shoulders sagged looser. The woman's grip around her knees loosened. Her eyes never closed, but the glassy sheen eased to normal. Perhaps this was working.

Quietly, for anything loud might shatter the tentative peace, Mercy hummed the same lullaby she'd sung to Emmeline the night before.

And a tiny sob gurgled in Mary's throat.

"Oh dear one." The words, her own mother's, slipped past Mercy's lips unbidden. "I don't know how many babes you have lost, and I don't need to, but what I do know is this kind of grief isn't made to fit inside your body. You must allow your heart to break so that the sorrow runs out. My mother used to tell me there's more love in Christ for us than there can ever be broken-ness. Only in turning to Him can you be healed on the inside."

Her hand paused, stilled by a sudden insight. Was that how her mother had survived the loss of her family? Her captivity amongst the Wyandot—and later the Mohawks? Was it her mother's continual turning to Christ that had given her such joy, her reason for not fighting against her captors?

Perhaps the weakness in her mother that she'd reviled all these years had really been strength—God's strength. Why had she never thought of that before? Shame withered her spirit, curling it up every bit as much as the woman shrunken before her.

"*Iesos*," she whispered. "Take this scorn from me, the pain from this woman, and heal the broken parts in both of us."

Mary stiffened. She did too.

For the warmth of a thousand suns suddenly filled the wagon.

※

Elias walked on silent feet in the water, his moccasins leaving no mark where the Nowadaga ran smooth along the bank. Matthew followed, gun in hand. It rankled to have his own fingers hanging loose at his sides, but there was nothing to be done for the injustice.

The sun beat warm and the river nipped cold as it leaked into the seams of his shoes. He frowned. Had he known he'd be so waylaid from his original course to Boston, he'd have taken extra care last time he greased the leather.

Five paces later, he stopped and crouched, studying grass barely bent, a slight indentation where a rock had once sat, and a river that flowed unre-lenting. Not much to go on.

Lord, but Mercy had a keen eye.

Satisfied, he straightened and nodded toward the opposite bank. Mat-thew shadowed his steps, neither of them splashing nor hardly rippling the water. The ranger knew how to track as silently as any brave—he'd give him that.

On the other side, they paused and scanned the rocks. Sand and shrub ran sparse up to the wood line, making it harder to distinguish disturbed ground. He shook his head, annoyed this foray was eating time he didn't have.

"I never should have threatened Logan last night." A sigh trailed the end of his words. "This is on me. He is running scared."

"He is running stupid to think he can get away." Matthew pointed five yards farther south, where the bank dropped off from the trees. Beside a row of tree trunks, a depression flattened the middle of a patch of wild ginger—not big, but enough to give away the tread of a horse.

Elias smirked. "Well, I never did credit Logan with much sense."

Climbing the bank, he grunted, pleased. The man had made no effort to hide his trail. Maybe this wouldn't take so much time after all.

"Truth be told"—Matthew pulled up alongside him—"I did not credit you with much sense at first either."

He glanced sideways at Matthew, as off-center as the statement. Why such a confession? "Sounds like you changed your mind."

"In most respects."

"And others?" Turning his head, he gazed at the man full-on.

Matthew shrugged. "It depends."

His step faltered. The ground rose and dipped, the uneven remains of a long winter's freeze—but the terrain had nothing to do with his sudden imbalance. A foreign longing troubled his step—a desire for Matthew Prinn's good opinion. "What would that depend on?"

"How much space you give Mercy."

Space? What was he to make of that? He paused, searching for a hint in the lines on Matthew's face. "I do not follow."

One brow rose. Was that mistrust or astonishment?

"Don't tell me you have missed noticing the girl's smitten with you."

He snorted. Unbelievable. Perhaps he'd credited Matthew with too much sense. He veered away from the man and his preposterous idea, following the angle of a hoof gouge pointed northwest. "Mercy would as soon knife me as she would Logan."

"No, you're wrong. I've seen how she looks at you. I've never known her to give any man a passing glance, but you? You she studies. Memorizes. I wager there's a battle raging fierce inside her that she can't begin to understand."

Heat as from a dying sun scorched through him, and he sucked in a breath. Was such a notion true?

He shot forward, prodded by a realization he dared not reach out and hold hands with. "You are sorely mistaken, Prinn. Mercy is of a sharp mind. She would not go wobble-kneed for the likes of me."

"I would have sworn she'd not go wobble-kneed for anyone—ever—knowing her history."

"Which is?" Elias turned back around, facing the man.

" 'Tain't really mine to tell, but—" Matthew rubbed his chin. "I s'pose 'tis common enough knowledge. Mercy's mother was a white woman, taken captive by the Wyandots."

He grunted. That explained her animosity toward the French, being they were practically one and the same. Still, something didn't sit right. He squinted at Matthew. "But Mercy is part Mohawk, is she not?"

"Aye." The man nodded. "Her Mohawk father stole her mother as part of a raid on the Wyandots' camp, taking her for one of his wives. Her mother never quite picked up the people's ways though, choosing instead to cling to her Christian faith, which of course the other women scorned. Mercy included. Troubles her to this day, whether she owns up to it or not. And I will not see her troubled further by the likes of you."

He held up his hands. "I have not touched the woman."

Matthew's gray eyes bored into his. "Good. Keep it that way. I will not see her heart pierced through, not by you. Not by anyone."

The thought of Mercy weeping over any man curled his hands into fists. "On that we are agreed."

Turning, he shrugged away from Matthew's intense gaze. Better they give the entire conversation concerning Mercy a good distance.

Matthew fell into pace beside him, and for a long while, they stalked quietly. Logan's trail was simple enough to follow. The fool had no idea how easily he could've been pursued by those bent on killing.

" 'Tain't none of my business, but I am a mite curious." Matthew shoved aside a swath of dogwood branches, allowing them both to pass. "Why did you switch sides?"

He blew out a long breath, disgusted more by the answer than the question. He'd known going into this he'd lose face with his countrymen. And in truth, before he'd met up with Matthew and Mercy, that had never bothered him. His brow tightened into a knot, for it surely did trouble him now. What would Matthew think if he shared his story of intrigue and espionage? Would the man believe him—or brand him a liar, bent on talking his way out of prison?

His shoulders sank. As much as he valued Matthew's esteem, he couldn't reveal his mission.

"It is. . .complicated," he finally said.

Matthew chuckled. "Good."

He jerked his face toward the man. "What?"

"That was no easy answer." Matthew clouted him on the back. "Enemy or not, I respect a man acting on conviction."

He pressed his lips flat, stifling an openmouthed stare. How much of a different man—a *better* man—would he be if he'd had this man for a father? No wonder Mercy fretted over parting ways with this ranger.

Ahead, sticks snapped. Tender young plants swished. Something moved. Fast.

Toward them.

He dropped. Matthew flattened against the trunk of a fat maple. Neither of them breathed. Matthew cocked his hammer full open.

A horse emerged. A black-tailed bay. Riderless—but laden with saddle and bulging bags.

Elias shot up and dashed after the horse, easing it with a low, "Here boy, good boy," on his advance. The animal slowed, and he snagged a loose rein, then led the mount back to Matthew.

Matthew pulled out a handful of dried berries and offered them over with a flat palm. "So, where's your master, eh, fella?"

With the horse occupied, Elias tied off the lead on a nearby branch. "I wager he is not far, being on foot—which begs the question, why? Logan would not willingly let a treasure roam far from his grasp."

"Aye." Matthew nodded.

They both plunged farther into the woods, then stopped short a quarter mile later, just before the ground gave way to a ravine with a sheer rock face. Were this a creek, the cut of it would make for a spectacular waterfall.

Elias peered over the brink. Below, a dark shape lay unmoving, head jutted at an unnatural angle.

Garret Logan.

CHAPTER 17

Twilight padded in from the wood's edge, silent, thick, and gray, like a great wolf on the hunt. A chill came with it, teasing curls of steam from the bowls in Mercy's hands. She handed them over to Amos Shaw.

"Thank you." He nodded.

She rubbed her hands along her apron, wiping off the moisture from a few drips. "You might want to save that thanks until you take a bite. I'm not much for cooking. How does your wife fare?"

"Better since this morning. I don't know what you said, but it got her dressed, and she is willing to eat." He held up the bowls. "No matter the taste."

"I am glad for it." And she was, truly, but in her belly a remnant of disappointment yet churned. After the strange sensation she'd experienced in Mary Shaw's wagon that morn, she'd felt certain the woman couldn't help but be as changed as she. As lightened of spirit. As freed. But Mary Shaw had yet to emerge from the confines of her wagon.

Still, the easier step of Amos Shaw and the lift of his shoulders as he retreated squelched that disappointment. He was pleased with his wife's progress. That would have to be enough.

Grabbing her own bowl, she turned to find a spot to sit. Nathan and his boys took up one log. Elias sat on another—with enough room to spare. She sank next to him and, for one blessed moment, relished taking the weight off her foot. Her toe was healed—mostly thanks to comfrey soaks every chance she could manage one—but it still felt good to ease up on it now and then. She sighed before digging into her pottage.

"You sound as weary as I feel." He flashed her a smile before tipping his bowl and draining the rest of his stew.

She cocked a brow. "I did not think you ever tired."

Swiping his mouth, he set down his bowl and faced her. "Retrieving

Logan's body out of that ravine was harder than either Matthew or I expected. He must have been riding at a good clip to have been thrown with such a force. Then there was digging a grave, reloading our cargo, mm-hmm. . ." He closed his eyes. "Sleep will come easy tonight."

"Tell us a story, Mr. Dubois?" Food flew out of Jonas's mouth, right along with his question.

"Yeah!" His brother bounced beside him, soup spilling over the bowl's rim and darkening his breeches in a wide splotch on his leg. "Tell us another one."

"Now, boys," Nathan interrupted, "let the man eat his supper in peace."

"Aww!" Their combined voices keened into a fine whine.

Mercy gritted her teeth, spoon hovering above her bowl. What those boys needed was a firm hand for such insolence. Mr. Shaw merely shoveled in another bite of his soup, ignoring the rascals and their complaints.

"Well. . ." Elias hunkered forward, resting his forearms on his thighs. From her angle, he was all shoulders and back, muscle and strength.

"Since I am finished with my supper, as long as you boys promise to finish your meal and pack right off to bed when I am done, I will tell you a story."

"Deal!" they said in unison.

"All right. There is a tale told by some northwoods trappers near Montreal, way up in New France. It goes like this."

The boys stilled. So did Mercy. Elias had a way of mesmerizing like none other—grasping her attention and pinning it down—and she wasn't sure how to feel about that.

Elias lifted his hat and ran his hand through his hair, shoving it back beneath the band, out of his eyes. "There was a woman who lived in those northern woods, a beautiful woman, so comely no one could figure out why Mademoiselle Delphine lived by herself in the wilds. Some say she was a witch, but surely you boys do not believe in witches, do you?"

Two sets of wide eyes stared back at him from the other log. No, three. Half a smile tugged her lips. Apparently Nathan Shaw loved a good story as well.

"I suppose that is neither here nor there though." Elias sniffed. "The fact is that Mademoiselle always carried with her a set of keys. Some say she used them to lock up lads who were naughty, but I do not think you boys have anything to fret about. Montreal is far off, and you two are not of a mind for mischief tonight, are you?"

A duo of undertakers couldn't have shaken their heads more solemnly.

"Good." Elias slapped his hands on his legs, making them all jump.

"Now where was I? Ah, yes, the keys. Early one morning, as Mademoiselle leaned against the rail of her pigpen, she spied a pig she'd never before seen. This swine was larger than the rest, grunting and rooting louder than any. When she slopped the trough, he crowded out the others, letting none but himself fill his belly. Seeing this, she grabbed her key ring and struck the big pig on the nose. Soon as she broke skin and the blood flowed, the pig disappeared—and a tall, handsome man stood in his place."

The boys stared, drop-jawed.

Mercy frowned, disgusted. Filling children's heads with happily-ever-afters only set them up for disappointment later in life. She knew that better than most. None of the stories her mother ever told her had come true.

She speared Elias with a stare. "And I suppose they shared a lifetime of bliss with scores of little ones at their feet, hmm?"

He winked at the boys, then smiled at her, his blue eyes twinkling. "No. The handsome young man tipped his hat, said, '*Merci*,' and walked away just like that." He lifted his hand and snapped his fingers, sharp on the evening air. "*La fin.*"

She blinked, stunned. Must he always keep her so off-kilter? Snatching up his empty bowl, along with hers, she stood.

"All right, boys." Nathan Shaw stood as well. "You have had your story and filled your bellies. Off to bed."

"Aww!" Jonas wailed.

Next to him, James glowered. "Just one more?"

"Your father is right, lads." Rubbing a muscle at the back of his neck, Elias rose. "We break camp just before dawn. You shall be crossing that river as the sun blinks over the horizon, so get yourself some sleep."

Like two pups, the boys scrambled up from the log and rambled off, chattering all the way. Poor Emmeline. Hopefully she and the babe would rest easy once the boys quieted, for no one could sleep with their ruckus. But perhaps she ought to check on the woman before night fell hard and they all settled down.

Before she could turn aside, Nathan approached her and Elias. "Once again, much obliged for the way you bear with my boys." Then he faced her. "And I thought I'd let you know, Mrs. Dubois. Amos and I talked a piece. We'll be heading down to the Klocks'. My thanks to you for the suggestion."

Relief filled her as much as the stew. When neither man had spoken of her idea all day, she'd thought for sure they were bent on going their own way.

Not that the journey would be any easier, but at least it would prove a mite safer and cover a lot less distance.

"No thanks needed, Mr. Shaw. If we do not work together, we die together." She pressed her lips shut, surprised at how easily Elias's words had slipped past them in the first place. It was as if part of the man had moved in and taken up residence inside her head.

Nathan Shaw tugged the brim of his hat then ambled off.

Elias stared at her. "So are you willing now to work with a traitor?"

"I did not say that." She collected all the dirty bowls, ignoring any response the man might make. Let him think what he would, for he often did the same to her. After giving the dishes a good scrubbing, she stowed them in a crate, along with a covered tin of leftovers for when Matthew and Rufus came in from watch.

With a yawn, she trekked toward the sound of a mewling babe's cry inside the Shaws' wagon. But as she rounded the front of it, she paused. Amongst the beginnings of a night chorus rife with scritches and rustlings and croaks, something more high-pitched whistled at the edges. She cocked her head.

A warbler trilled. Her pulse beat a rush of war drums in her ears. Warblers sang in sunlight, and twilight already darkened into dusk.

She dashed back to her wagon, retrieving her gun. Overkill for a small bird—but not for a man imitating such. After priming the barrel, she strode off on silent feet into the woods.

Shadows thickened. The loamy smell of earth, damp now in the evening air, filled her nostrils. She inhaled as she wielded her way past brush, praying to God she'd not smell the tang of bear grease or the musky scent of warriors, ready for battle.

Darkness grew. Night animals stirred. No more warbler trills. Had she been mistaken?

Pausing near a tree trunk, she studied the ground she'd already covered, checking to make certain no one had doubled back to sneak up behind her. Satisfied, she turned and strained to see ahead through the maze of trees and shadows.

Far off, a doe ambled by with a tentative step, nosing the air. Closer, left-over autumn leaves rustled as an opossum passed. She stood still for so long, the chirrups of tree frogs struck up a song around her.

Slowly, the tension in her shoulders slackened. No man-shapes emerged from the growing darkness.

But a hand clamped over her mouth.

Elias pressed his fingers against Mercy's lips, gentle yet firm, fighting the urge to throttle the woman. When he'd seen her grab her gun and slip off into the trees, his gut had twisted into a thick knot. Why must she run head-long into danger? She truly would be the death of him.

Beneath his hold, she stood rigid, neither weak-kneed nor quailing. Not a whimper. Not a sound. What kind of woman did that?

"Shh," he breathed into her ear.

He released her—then wished he hadn't. A musket barrel pressed cold against his chest, and he froze.

"Don't move," she hissed and widened her stance. "What are you doing here?"

Meeting her challenge, he stared right back. "Warblers do not sing at night."

Without pulling her eyes from him, she lowered her gun. "You heard it too." Her whisper was more a statement than a question.

He nodded, hiding a grin. Ah, but she was a picture, framed by the dark-ening woods. Her skin glowed soft in the last remnants of light as she stood at the ready, stance poised for a fight or a swift-legged escape. The musket in her hands was as much a part of her as the long braid tossed over her shoul-der. She'd knotted up her skirts, and her slim legs, hard with muscle, peeked out bare and stockingless from her knees down. Upon his soul, he'd never seen such a singular beauty.

A rogue desire to pull her into his arms coursed through his veins, but she'd only half-set her hammer, not fully closed it. Judging by the gleam in her eye, she'd as soon blast a hole in his chest than yield to his embrace.

The buzzing squawk of a woodcock cut into his thoughts—thankfully. This was no time for moon-eyeing a doe, not even a comely one such as Mercy.

"See anything?" he whispered.

She shook her head.

"Me either. Come on." On silent feet, he stepped past her and led the way farther into the woodland. It was a risk, bringing her along, but keeping her near seemed the lesser of whatever evil lurked in the growing darkness.

Ten paces apart, with her on his left, they stole from tree to tree, her tread as light as his. A marvel, that, for he'd never known anyone to move as a shadow other than himself. They scouted side by side for near a half mile, until night fell too hard to see beyond a few paces.

Mercy closed the distance between them, signaling with a tip of her head they ought to turn back. "Whatever it was, we lost it."

Defeat always tasted bitter, and he swallowed. "I do not like it, the not knowing."

"Nor I." Her dark eyes lifted to his.

"But you are right." A sigh deflated him. "There is too much darkness now. Maybe Matthew or Rufus got a lead. Whatever gave that call, it is not this way."

They stalked back toward camp, his mind buzzing with dangerous possibilities. He'd wager his lifeblood that he'd heard that warbler trill twice. Were they not leaving in the morning, he'd give this stretch of wood another good scouring come daylight.

"Could have been a hermit thrush," Mercy murmured beside him. "Makes sense. Still. . ."

A half smile twitched his lips. Apparently her thoughts swam the same direction as his.

She shifted her gun to her other shoulder. "Maybe I heard wrongly."

"Do not doubt yourself. It *was* high in pitch." The words came out gruff, a reprimand to himself as much as to her. They couldn't have both imagined the same sound, could they? Then again, how many unexplained screeches and growls had shivered down his backbone during murky nights while traveling with his father?

"Though I suppose"—he softened his tone—"I have heard stranger things."

She slanted him a glance. "You sound as if you clasp hands with doubt yourself."

"Not quite. Not yet. Let's sweep back along the other side of those boulders." He veered north, taking care not to trip over a downed maple. Mercy trailed him, close enough that the chill air curling over his shoulder carried her sweet, musky scent.

Twenty yards out from camp, they rounded the last of the rocky stretch. Leaving the light-colored lichen plastered against the boulders was a shame, for it proved a guideline for his steps, keeping his feet close to the line of rocks. The rest of the way would be dark-stepping on black ground, as black as the circles—

Circles?

He dropped into a crouch. Mercy gained his side and squatted next to him. Her sharp intake of air could only mean she understood exactly what he saw carved into the lichen at the base of the last boulder. The cut of the two spheres was fresh, connected by a line through the middle—a native sign denoting two days.

He lifted his eyes to the black woods and stared hard into darkness now so thick there was no telling if whoever left this sign remained behind a tree or not. Or worse, if there were more than one.

He shifted his gaze to Mercy. The same question creased her brow.

What would happen in two days?

CHAPTER 18

Night faded like a bruise, the predawn darkness lightening in increments from black to indigo, painting the world in deep blue. Mercy passed the cluster of men discussing the surest way to cross the river on her way to the front wagon—Emmeline and Nathan's, poised to venture across the Nowadaga. James and Jonas huddled on the driver's seat, likely scheming some kind of trouble despite the early hour. She hauled herself up and nodded them a greeting, though neither responded.

"Emmeline?" she called as she crawled through the canvas opening. "I came to say goodbye."

Inside, the new mother and her babe reclined atop crates heaped with blankets. Emmeline held out her hand. "I was hoping you would. I shall miss you."

"And I, you." The truth of her words hit a soft spot in her heart, and she sucked in a breath. She *had* enjoyed this woman's company.

Drawing near, she smiled and clasped the woman's cold fingers. "You keep that little one fed and warm, and she'll grow up just fine."

"Thank you. I will." Emmeline squeezed her hand. "I'm sure it won't be long till you hold a babe in your arms."

Her smile faded. Emmeline was wrong. Her arms would not cradle a wee one anytime soon, but maybe someday. . . Her lips flattened. What a ridiculous notion.

Leaning closer, she kissed the babe on her downy cheek then let go of Emmeline's grasp. "Godspeed to you all."

"I shall never forget you, Mercy Dubois."

As always, the false name went down sideways, and she swallowed. "Neither shall I forget you, Emmeline."

Working her way around in the confined space, she wriggled back out the front canvas hole and faced James and Jonas. "You boys behave yourself.

You have a mother and sister to look after, you hear?"

Jonas frowned at her. "Mr. Elias already told us that."

She hid a smile. As much as she hated to credit a traitor, Elias would make a fine father one day. "Then mind what he said, and mind your father as well. Go on inside now."

The boys scrambled past her, bickering over who got to peek out the back canvas hole. She climbed down, emotions swirling. In the few days she'd spent with Emmeline, she'd grown to like the woman. Given more time, they might've been great allies.

Matthew, Rufus, Elias, and the Shaw men still stood near the horses, though as she passed by, she noted the conversation had moved on to final route advice. None lifted their eyes to her. Just as well. When had a man ever taken a woman's word on directions?

Eight paces past them, she stopped even with the front of Amos Shaw's wagon. Mary sat atop, bundled in a gray woolen shawl and long-brimmed bonnet. She stared, as usual, but this time not unseeing. Had the real Mary Shaw left behind the netherworld of bleak sorrow and ventured back into her own body?

Mercy smiled up at her. Indeed, the woman's eyes shone clear, and a faint flicker of a smile curved the edges of her lips.

Lifting her hand, Mercy spoke a blessing, wishing with everything in her that it would come true. "*Skennen*, Mrs. Shaw. Skennen."

The deep blue light left over from night faded as the morning sun rose. Time for their own departure soon enough. With a nod to the woman, she set off up the road to camp, where their wagons sat at the ready, aimed east instead of west. It wouldn't hurt to scout ahead a bit, now that the coming sun lessened the shadows. She'd grab her gun, poke around, then swing back to rejoin the others as they returned from helping the Shaws cross the river.

Holding on to the wagon's side, she hefted herself up to the seat—then froze. Gooseflesh prickled hundreds of bumps along her arms. A scalp lock with a turkey feather yet attached to the bloody skin was draped on the bench.

She snapped into action, grabbing her gun from inside and hitting the ground with silent feet. A trail of moccasin prints led to the wood line, and she lifted her gaze. Shutting out the morning chill, the shush of wind, the trill of birds, she narrowed her eyes and stared, hard. A man stepped out from behind a sycamore trunk, armed with bow, arrows, tomahawk, and war club.

A mountain of a man.

She shouldered her gun and broke into a run. "Onontio!"

But her steps faltered as she drew near her brother. Beneath the red and black colors of war painted on his face, a gash split his flesh from temple to chin. One eye was purpled shut. Blood darkened his breechclout, spreading from thigh to knee on his deerskin leggings. By the looks of it, that scalp lock on the wagon seat had been bought at a great price.

"You're hurt!" she cried.

He lifted his chin, smelling of sweat and battle. "I live."

Proud man. Proud, stupid man. What had he gotten himself into? A frown weighted her brow. "What happened?"

"I came for you with a dark tale when a snake crossed my way." Murder glimmered in his eyes. "The Wyandot snake is no more."

"Only one?"

He nodded.

"Not a scout then." Shoving loose hair out of her eyes, she thought hard. A lone man. An enemy. Why would a single warrior venture so close to their camp when— Of course. The circles carved into the lichen. She stared up at her brother. "A messenger. What do the people hear? What do you know of what might happen in two days?"

"I know nothing." Onontio's face hardened to granite. "And our people are no more."

The words skittered about in the air like a swarm of gnats, ones she'd like to swipe away. "What are you saying?" she whispered.

"After warning you, I returned home." The cut of his jaw slanted grim. "To death and ash."

"But Father?" She shook her head, a useless act to ban the black thoughts that would not be stopped. "Surely not Rake'niha!"

She grabbed his arm, hoping, wishing, needing to know that what she suspected surely wasn't true. Couldn't be true. Not Black-Fox-Running. Never him.

Onontio nodded swift and sharp, the movement cutting like a razor-edged blade—slicing her heart in two.

No, this couldn't be happening. Grief slammed against her chest, seeking a crevice to breach, but she would not let it in. One tear, half a whimper, and she'd be undone.

She lifted her chin. "Who did this? Why?"

For a moment, Onontio's nostrils flared. Whatever went on in his mind could not be good. "After severing ties with Bragg, Rake'niha allied with Johnson, promising our men to fight against the blue coats' Fort Niagara. Before the traveling sun, a raiding party of *Ehressaronon* swept down from the north. None in our village survived."

Despite her hold on him, she swayed, and his other arm shot out, balancing her. The world turned watery. She blinked, fighting against tears, swallowing back thick pain. She'd always known there'd be graves coming. Darkness coming. Heartbreak. But not now. Not yet. Suddenly she knew how Mary Shaw felt.

After a few deep breaths, though everything in her screamed to plow into him and weep against his chest, she pulled away. She had to be strong, leastwise in front of her brother, for he shared the same hollow ache that carved a gouge in her breast.

She blinked up at him. "What will you do?"

"I will hunt them down." Blood marred his words, dripping from the slash on his cheek to his lips.

Another piece of her heart broke off. He didn't stand a chance. "You are but one man, my brother."

He flung back his shoulders, swiping away the blood from his mouth. "That is of no account."

"I can't lose you too!" Her ragged voice ruined the sanctity of the early morn, staining the birth of the new day with the portent of death.

He reached out, his big thumb running rough over her cheek, leaving behind the dampness of his own lifeblood. "Our paths were meant to split, *aktsi:'a*. You have walked between two worlds, but no more. You must choose life. Prinn is a good long knife. Go with him."

Her shoulders sagged. There was no way she could tell him Matthew had plans of his own to leave her. Her brother had enough to bear without the thought of what would become of her.

"*Ó:nen* Kahente." He pulled back his hand. "*Tsi Nen:we Enkonnoronhkhwake.*"

"Tsi Nen:we—" Her throat closed. Looking at her brother for what might be the last time on this side of heaven, she choked. He looked so much like a younger Black-Fox-Running, it was like speaking to her father. A sob welled up, begging for release. She'd never get another chance to tell her father she loved him forever. And in truth, this just might be her last shared endearment with Onontio.

She sucked in a breath and forced out a clear voice. "Tsi Nen:we Enkonnoronhkhwake, Onontio. Ó:nen."

Their gazes locked in a last goodbye; then he turned and stalked into the woods. As he walked away, a shiver blew through her soul like a cold moan. She stared, long and hard, until even her keenest eyesight could no longer distinguish his strong, broad shoulders. Would she ever see him again?

Loss stretched out bony arms and pulled her to its bosom, crushing her in a chokehold of an embrace. Despite her resolve to stay strong, to be brave, she dropped to the ground.

And wept.

Water squished between heel and sole in Elias's left moccasin. He'd have to ask Matthew tonight for some extra grease to stop up that leaky seam. But for now, he'd yank off the shoe and let it dry while he drove.

Morning light blazed a halo above the rear of the wagon as he approached. It hadn't taken long to help the Shaws cross the river, especially now that the waters ran low and slow. But it had still taken time—time they didn't have. Time *he* didn't have. If all went well and he stole off just before they veered north toward Fort Edward, he'd still have a hard go of it to reach Boston. Four days of tough riding. Possibly five. The enormity of the undertaking crashed down on him like a rockslide. So many things could go wrong. For a moment, he gave in to hanging his head with the weight of responsibility—

And saw fresh tracks leading away from the wagon.

He dropped to a crouch, his gaze following the indents of two sets of footprints. The first sank deeper into the ground. A big man, then, shod in moccasins much like the ones he wore.

He narrowed his eyes and studied the other set, but it didn't take long before his breath hitched. The length was short, with a sharp solid curve digging heavy on the right side. Mercy's step. Nearly on top of the other set of prints. Apparently she'd followed someone into the woods, but with no sign of struggle.

Rising, he stared into the maze of brilliant greens and browns. Wherever she went, she'd gone willingly.

He pivoted and faced the wagon behind his, lifting his palm toward Rufus. "Hold on."

Rufus turned aside and spit off the side of the wagon, then spit out a curse as well. "We ain't got time to be waiting!"

Elias frowned. He knew that better than anyone. Strange though to see Rufus ruffled up about anything other than the next meal.

"This will not take long." He strode off, glad to leave behind the sour-faced complainer. It was a wonder the young man had lasted this long as a regular without a cashiering.

The trail was easy enough to follow, with no trace of care being taken to cover the tracks. Ahead, twenty yards into the forest, a small shape took on form, bent low to the ground. At twelve yards, he distinguished a dark stripe splitting that shape—a long, dark braid—and he upped his pace. He stopped only steps away from where Mercy curled over in a patch of flattened trillium. Alone. Was she sick?

"Mercy?" he murmured so as not to startle her. "What ails you?"

She jerked upright, the cloth across her shoulders stretched taut. She said nothing, nor did she face him.

"Are you ill?" he tried again.

"I. . .I am fine. Give me a moment."

The hesitation, the stutter, the slight tremble shimmying down her backbone all twisted a knife in his chest. Something was wrong. Very wrong.

In two strides he bent and gripped her shoulders, pulling her to her feet. Before he could turn her around, she wrenched from his grasp and scuttled away, picking up her gun where she'd dropped it.

He froze, fully prepared for her to swing the barrel straight for his chest, but she did not. She just stood there, cradling her gun, breathing hard—and that kindled a fear in him more terrible than staring down a cold, gray muzzle.

"Mercy, look at me. I would see your face."

"Go." Her voice shook, throaty and unsteady. "I will take first scout."

"Matthew is already on it." Using all his skills at shadow walking, he approached her on silent feet, stopping inches behind her. "Now, turn around."

She whirled, eyes red, wet stains yet shiny on her smooth cheeks. "Go away!"

The tension in his jaw loosened. This she-devil he could work with. "Your brother brought news?"

She sucked in a sharp breath, her dark gaze narrowing. "What would you know of that?"

"I followed two sets of prints from the wagon to the wood's edge. Yours and those deep and long enough to belong to a big man, just like your brother. I did not figure you would go willingly with anyone else."

She sighed, mournful as a dove. The nod of her head looked as if it took all her strength—and more. Sweet mercy! What awful news had the man brought her?

He looked past her, expecting the painted shapes of warriors to spring out at any moment. "Are we in danger?"

"Life is danger." The emptiness in her tone chilled the sun's warmth. No one should sound so hollow.

He cut his gaze back to her. "What happened?"

Her lower lip quivered. A single fat tear fell, riding the curve of her cheek. "Our father—" Her voice broke.

So did his usual reserve. The woman was naught but a sorrow-filled waif, gripping a gun too big and a grief too great. He opened his arms, offering, hoping, and surprisingly willing to take on her pain instead of running the other way. He hardly knew himself anymore.

And that was a very good thing.

Mercy blinked, loosing a fresh burst of tears—then dropped her gun and plowed into him. He staggered from the force of her assault, her weeping, her ragged cries. Wrapping his arms around her, he held on through the storm.

"My father is gone," she wailed into his chest. "My village. . .and now my brother. There is nothing for me to go home to."

Her pain lanced through his heart, making it hard to distinguish from his own.

"I hardly know the meaning of the word *home*," he mumbled against the top of her head, more to himself than to her. He knew the horrid feeling all too well, the sudden ripping away of the ground he'd always stood on. The plummeting sensation of not knowing where to land, how to land. If he'd land. All the emotions of losing his mother as a young lad, the regret of not making peace with his grandfather before he died, barreled back, unexpectedly vivid.

He clung to Mercy every bit as much as she pressed into him.

Eventually her breathing evened, and she stilled. It wouldn't be long before she pulled away, but for now, he cherished the trusting way she leaned against him, drawing from his strength. Would that they might stand here forever, him bearing her up, her warming his arms. A perfect fit. Like none he'd ever known.

"Dubois! Where are you?"

Rufus's voice hit him from behind, shattering the moment. Mercy jerked away and retrieved her gun, the loss of her from his arms near to unbearable.

He blew out a sigh, letting go of the gift. He'd learned long ago that nothing beautiful lasted, save for eternity. "Did your brother know anything of that sign we found last night?"

"No. He killed the man before he could talk." She glanced at him as she passed by. "But he was a Wyandot."

Once again he gazed at the endless stretch of trees. Wyandot. Had that message been for him? Because if it was, then he really had trouble. Good thing they would put plenty of time and space between this place and themselves by the time two days were spent.

If the new wagon wheel proved roadworthy.

Chapter 19

M ercy ran, the gun at her back bouncing a rhythm against her spine. The strap dug into her chest, but that did not slow her. Driving herself hard and fast, she ignored the fatigue in her quivering muscles. She could outpace Matthew, who'd been tracking her for hours now, but it was impossible to outrun a demon—especially the one that gnawed to get out from the inside. Still, a trifle such as impossibility had never stopped her before.

And she wasn't about to show any more weakness.

So she pumped her legs faster and leapt over a downed maple, barely catching herself with a wild swing of her arms, then pressed onward. If the world had an end, she'd find it and fling herself off the edge, putting a stop to all the ragged emotions burning inside.

But as the afternoon dragged on, the futility of her race caught up to her. Lungs heaving, she slowed, body spent and near to ruin. Any farther and she'd collapse. Not a bad idea, but it wouldn't be fair to Matthew. She'd given him enough of a challenge.

She bent and planted her hands on scraped knees, gasping for air. It did no good. All the running. The distance. In spite of secluding herself yesterday and the better part of today, the ache was still there, raw and unrelenting. The same grief raged. The same humiliation churned. Nothing had changed save for the new rips in her hiked-up skirts and fresh gashes on her legs.

She sank onto a rocky ledge, letting her feet dangle. Below, the woods encircled a small glade where spring flowers sent up green shoots. Come the corn-planting moon, this patch of dirt and sun would yield a beautiful swath of purple and white, fresh and innocent. And for some odd reason, the thought of such magnificence was too much to bear.

With her remaining strength, she snatched up a rock and threw it, squashing a small patch of plants far below. A churlish thing, but unstoppable. She'd never been so out of control in her life.

And that scared her more than anything.

Behind her, ferns rustled, crushed beneath a heavy step. Labored breathing whooshed along with a slight breeze tickling the overhead maple leaves. The tangy odor of sweat wafted up to her nose as Matthew flopped down beside her. She ought to lower her skirts and cover her bare legs, but honestly, she just didn't care. Besides, it was only Matthew.

Yet when he opened his mouth, a stranger rebuked her. "I gave you plenty of space yesterday and most of today, but this stops here and now. You're officially off duty until my say-so."

The command was steel cold and just as hard. She jerked her face toward him. "You can't do that."

"You know I can." His gunmetal eyes sparked a challenge—one she'd best not meet. She'd seen only one man ever survive it, barely.

Tucking her chin, she sighed. "What I mean is you *can't* do that. How could you? I can't sit on a wagon seat all day, not with this burning inside me."

"Oh girl." He shook his head, the familiar Matthew peeking out through his softening gaze. "I know you're hurting, but it is time to quit running."

She peered up at him, drawn by the tenderness in his tone. More white whiskers than she remembered peppered his bristly beard. Weathered lines cut into his cheeks below a purple bruise that spread from his eye. She squinted, studying his face more closely. A cut marred his jaw and a scrape made a red stripe on his forehead. Were those wounds purchased at the expense of chasing her?

She slumped. He was right, as usual. All her running hadn't eased her pain but instead had given him some.

"Elias told me about your father. Unh-unh." He wagged a finger. "Don't get all puffed up about him telling me your business. I forced his hand. He said it was yours to tell, but after a tussle, he broke."

Her eyebrows shot skyward. "You wrestled with Elias?"

"Flit! I ain't in the grave yet." He rubbed his jaw, the rasp of it soothing in an odd sort of way. "But I admit he packs a powerful right hook. Truth is, I think he took pity and lightened up."

Unbidden, the feel of Elias's embrace wrapped around her once again, and just like all the other times she'd relived that moment, she was powerless to stop it. He'd stood there open-armed, inviting her in but at her own pace. Even now if she inhaled, she'd likely still breathe his scent of smoke and danger. Ah, but there in his arms, for the briefest of time, she'd experienced a release like none other when she'd wept into his shirt. He'd stood there, taking her sorrow, shoring her up like a great beam. Waiting her out until she settled. No one had ever done that. Not her father, her brother. . .not even Matthew. Elias was like none other. And if she dared to admit it, if he ever opened his arms again, she'd run into them headlong and unflinching.

She hung her head. What kind of daughter thought of another man when mourning her father? A weak one, that was what. She was weak as the woman she'd scorned for such softness all these years. With a sigh, she reached for her necklace.

Matthew's big hand patted her leg. "Grief never comes easy, girl. It never comes calling at an opportune time. I grieve for your loss."

She stared at the skin on the back of his hand, all leather and snaked with blue veins. "You're all I have left."

"Someday a man will steal your heart, maybe already has, and I won't be but a memory."

"No." She snapped her gaze to his. "No one will ever take your place."

He chuckled. "Well, I expect we'll always remember our times together."

The faintest of smiles whispered over her lips. "Does that mean I can be back on duty?"

He reared back and looked down his nose. "You are a wonder, Mercy Lytton. A full-out, stubborn-headed—"

His words cut off like a snuffed candle, and they both sat rock still, listening.

Mercy drew up her legs and flattened to her belly. Beside her, Matthew lay flat as well. Below, at the edge of the glade, a flash of blue and white marched in. Twenty. No, twenty-four. A full squad.

Of French soldiers.

❧

Tree line. Road. Tree line. Road. Elias pinged his gaze from ruts and rocks to the dark green of forest on either side, looking, hoping, praying for some sign of Mercy or Matthew. It'd been too long. Far too long. The twinge in his gut said so, as did the lengthening shadows heralding day's end.

"Hold up!" Rufus's holler bellowed louder than the turn of the wheels—which all held solid, even the one they had recrafted.

He pulled on the reins, slowing the horses to a stop, and waited for Rufus to jog up alongside him.

The young man swiped back a swath of stringy hair, then reset his hat and peered up at him. "It'll be dark soon. I say we stop for the night."

Elias pulled his gaze from the young man and scanned the area. Thick trees closed in on both sides—too thick to wedge a horse's rump through, let alone an entire wagon. Surely even Rufus knew they couldn't stop mid-road and spread out bedrolls in an occupied stretch of wilderness. He grunted. "Not here."

"Din't mean here, you half-witted—"

The deadly scowl he aimed at Rufus ended whatever tirade the man-boy thought to spew.

"What I meant was—" Sniffing, Rufus ran his sleeve beneath his nose. "We turn off past three-oak boulder, just a spell farther, and there's a nice patch o' land hidden by a ridge. That is where we camp."

Elias chewed on the information like an overly spiced piece of meat, the kind that had been smothered in strong flavor to hide rancidity. Something rotten was hidden in Rufus's words, for the young man was never that accommodating.

He narrowed his eyes. "Now how would you know that?"

One of the more colorful profanities flew out of Rufus's mouth. "That old man and Mercy aren't the only ones what know this countryside. I been to Fort Edward before."

Reaching back, Elias kneaded out a knot in his shoulder while he thought on Rufus's proposal. Judging by the slant of light, they had maybe an hour, hour and a half of day remaining. Since yesterday morning, they had put a good distance between themselves and the Nowadaga crossing, so whatever ill omen that sign had portended, they were far enough afield to miss it. Hopefully. And Lord knew Mercy could use a good sleep. Valid reasons, all.

So why the sudden prickles on his scalp? He lowered his hand. Other than the queer feeling, there was no other basis on which to turn down Rufus's suggestion.

Against his better judgment, he nodded. "All right."

Rufus scuttled back to his wagon, and Elias slapped the reins with a "Giddap." The horses kicked into a trot, and he went back to his tree line–road–tree line–road routine. Still no sign of a dun-colored skirt or a barrel-chested old ranger.

Just past a moss-covered boulder at the base of three oaks, the woods thinned on the south side as Rufus had predicted. Teasing the right rein with steady pressure, he turned the horses off the road and onto uneven ground. His teeth chattered as the wagon bumped over virgin growth, felled tree limbs, and rocks. Near to a half mile in, he wondered if the narrow path would ever open up—and when it finally did, if he were a swearing man, he'd have put Rufus to shame.

He drove the wagon into a grassy clearing, flat and wide, protected on three sides by a ridgeline of rocks, a perfect enclosure for a campsite—and for an ambush. He should've known better than to trust Rufus's suggestion.

Pulling hard to the left, he turned the wagon around so that once Rufus caught up, they were side-by-side and face-to-face. "This is your idea of a 'nice patch o' land'?"

"Unless you wanna camp on the road." He paused to pick at his teeth. "Next glade I know of is five miles off. Be dark by then."

"If you knew that, then why not say something back when we had a chance to pull off earlier?" The low-grade anger that had been simmering all day started to boil, shooting heat up his neck.

Rufus's bony shoulders merely jerked skyward in a sharp shrug.

Closing his eyes, Elias counted to twenty. First in English, then in French. It was either that or leap over and throttle the dunderhead.

Disgusted, he blew out a sigh and jumped off the seat, then resurveyed the area. He had to admit the flatland was suitable for bedding down, and they would be sheltered from the road. It could work—if three kept watch while one slept.

He frowned. It would be a long night.

"Well?" Rufus prodded.

"All right." He turned back to the man. "See to the horses. I will take a look around."

He tromped over to where grass met rock and climbed to the top of the ridge. For a while he scouted along the western edge, poking around for Indian sign. The most interesting things he uncovered were some bear scat and a rabbit warren. So he swung back around and worked his way eastward. More bear tracks, some wolf paw indentations, and then suddenly the crack of a twig.

He cocked his head, every sense heightened. No more cracks. No rustle of underbrush. Just that single, isolated snap.

That was no animal.

He dropped belly down in a thick patch of wild senna and held his breath.

A minute passed, then more, until his lungs burned—and the step of a foot crushed a swath of leftover leaves.

He lifted his gaze to see a pair of brown-legged breeches cross ten paces in front of him. Sucking in a breath, he rose.

In front of him, Matthew spun, musket leveled. Then his eyes widened, and he lowered his gun. "Might wanna think twice before you do that again. I can't be blamed if I put a hole in you for jumping out like that."

Though he was no longer a target, his pulse pumped loud in his head. Why was Mercy not with Matthew? "Where is Mercy?"

Matthew's gaze shifted just past his left shoulder.

Elias turned. Mercy stood, quiet as a shadow, staring at him with hollow eyes and even hollower cheeks. When was the last time she'd eaten? Torn skirts hung askew from her hips. Her braid was undone and wild to her waist, and a cut marred her jaw.

He took a step toward her. "What happened? Are you hurt?"

"I am well, but we may not be for long. There's a French squad, twenty-four men, five miles off."

The news rippled through him like a pebble thrown into a pond. French? Could he use this to his advantage? Possibly, but not without the capture of Matthew and Mercy. Or Rufus. He frowned. French captives were notoriously mistreated, especially women. The thought of Mercy enduring such brutality twisted his stomach. No, better to stick with his plan.

"Don't even think it, Dubois." Matthew's threat blasted him from behind.

Shaking his head, he turned to the man. "You have nothing to worry about from me."

Mercy's soft steps drew up alongside him. "You know these people. Why is there a squad here? We are not near a fort."

"If it is only one squad, they are more than likely men who have been replaced, on their way to Montreal for reassignment. I doubt they are looking for trouble. There were no Wyandot with them? No Seneca? Ottawa or Shawnee?"

Matthew shook his head. "None. All white."

"Like I said then, men on their way home. My guess is they will soon cut northward."

Matthew grunted.

Mercy shifted her stance, resettling the gun on her back. "Then we continue with our ruse of settlers returning east?"

The set of Matthew's jaw did not bode well—nor did the black gleam in his gray eyes. "I've got a few changes."

Elias stiffened. "Such as?"

"If any of those French soldiers recognize you, or take sport and rummage through one of our crates, this mission is over. We are captives. Or dead."

Elias threw out his arms. "Bragg's men already killed the men who knew me."

"You sayin' there ain't more?"

Blast, but the man was cagey!

"I cannot say that for certain, but Bragg knew that, even when he put me on this team. His orders were to travel as a family, keep my head low. That is what I aim to do."

Mercy advanced toward Matthew, peering at him all the way. "He is right, but what's your plan, Matthew?"

His gray gaze shifted to Mercy. "We hide the gold, tie up Elias, and move out in the morning. After the squad passes us, we double back and retrieve our belongings, then go on as usual."

Elias's breath hitched. If anyone unpacked that gold but him, they would discover his secret. He strode over to the duo and glowered at Matthew. "Are you mad? It will take too long to bury all that gold and repack the crates."

A muscle on the side of Matthew's neck jumped, and he deadlocked Elias with a stare, daring him to break away first.

But Elias held—a trait he'd learned from the best. His father.

"Bah!" Matthew spit out then stalked past them both. "Get a move on. That gold ain't gonna bury itself."

For a moment, Mercy looked at him with cavernous eyes, then turned aside and followed Matthew on silent feet.

Thunder and turf! The two were a pigheaded pair. He stalked after them. He'd have to make sure he was the one unloading the marked crate, or their lives could be in danger.

As he worked his way down the ridge, other possibilities surfaced. While he did not relish being tied up, this could be the perfect time to slip away once the wagons rolled off—providing Matthew didn't tie too awful a knot. He'd have to leave the gold behind. A loss, that. But if he could manage to hide the leather packet of metal tips between hunting frock and shirt, at least he had a fair shot of making it to Boston in time to help the men of Fort Stanwix.

He landed on the flatland, heels digging hard in the soft ground. Should he leave? Or stay? Both were risky.

Stifling a groan, he trudged toward the wagons. Lord, but he was tired of risk.

CHAPTER 20

Fighting a yawn, Mercy traipsed through shin-high wildweed, tired enough to drop in her tracks. Why was she doing this? Roaming free and outsmarting the enemy had always given her a thrill, but now, as she trudged after Matthew with the prospect of a long night of backbreaking work, still aching from the loss of her father and possibly her brother, she had a hard time remembering that excitement. Perhaps Matthew was right. Maybe it was time to leave behind this vagabond life.

She slapped her way through a swarm of biting midges, shoving the rogue notion away as well. Exhaustion sure had a way of dulling her mind. For it had to be fatigue, this nettling idea of wanting to settle. To pack her griefs and troubles into a lockbox and stow the thing under a bed in a solid-framed house. She kicked at a rock, sending it skittering through the grass. Fatigue. She would accept no other reason.

Ahead, Rufus yanked off his hat and slapped his knee, shouting an oath. Apparently he wasn't excited about burying the gold either. As she drew nearer to where he stood talking to Matthew at the side of his wagon, the last of day's light painted his reddening face a deep shade of rage.

"I will have no part of this! I will see you court-martialed for disregarding my father's orders." He stomped off, leaving a trail of obscenities in his wake.

"I hate to say it, but this time I am siding with Rufus." Elias's low tone came out of nowhere.

Startled, she jerked her face aside and stared up at blue eyes pinned on her. How had he caught up to her without rustling the weeds?

"Matthew's doing what he thinks best for us all," she murmured. "I trust him implicitly."

Elias shook his head. "God alone is worthy of that kind of trust."

A grimace crept across her lips. The man sounded far too much like her mother.

Matthew advanced toward them, a shovel in each hand. He threw one to Elias, who caught it without effort.

"The ground is softened where water runs down off that rise." Matthew jutted the tip of his shovel to where the three of them had recently descended. "We dig there. Mercy, hitch those horses and drive the first wagon over, if you please."

They parted ways, Matthew and Elias swooshing off through the grass. She stopped by her wagon to grab a bite of jerky, then braided her loose hair before she crossed to where the horses yanked up tender greens. The munch and crunch was a soothing sound, and for a moment she stood mesmerized, her heart swelling with compassion. The poor beasts had no idea their dinner was about to be ruined. Was that how it was for God, looking down on them?

"Poor fella." She patted the lead horse on the neck and grabbed his rope. "Just when you thought you were done for the day, hmm?"

Night fell with a heavy hand by the time she positioned Matthew's wagon next to the beginnings of a long, shallow ditch. Her task was to take out the heaps of household goods while Elias and Matthew pitched shovelful after shovelful of dirt. Together they unpacked the gold and trade silver, nestling all in the earth, like so many cold bodies into a shallow grave. Once the crate was emptied, she reloaded the goods, pounded the top back on, and moved on to the next.

The night was more than half spent by the time they finished one load and she drove over the wagon she and Elias usually occupied. The ground wasn't nearly as soft as Matthew had expected. Hours later, the cloud cover cleared, brilliant stars dotted the heavens, and the temperature dropped, bringing a chill that, despite her hard work, made her shiver from head to toe.

About halfway through the load, Elias planted his shovel and hefted himself out of the ditch. "Mercy is spent. She needs some rest. I will take on her part of the job."

Despite her exhaustion, her eyes shot wide open. Where had that come from? She'd not lagged, despite her screaming muscles. She'd neither tripped nor bellyached nor gone off into the brush to take care of necessities.

She dropped the bags of trade silver into the hole, freeing her hands to prop them on her hips. The man's command crawled under her skin like a mess of biting ants. He spoke of her as if she were naught but a child. "Thank you for your concern, *Husband*." It was a snippety thing to say, but it wouldn't be stopped. "Yet I will rest when we are all done."

Matthew leaned against his shovel handle and blew out a long breath. "The man's more than right, girl. You need some rest. We all do."

She shook her head. "I'm not sleeping while you two are working."

Elias advanced, his voice warm in the cold air. "You have more than proved yourself. I think I speak for us both in that I or Matthew would not think any less of you."

"*I* would think less of me!"

Matthew straightened. "Then we bury the rest of it whole. We're running out of time as it is. We'll dig deeper and toss in the last of the crates without separating the contents."

Elias shook his head, a disgusted rush of air passing his teeth. But he set back to work, as did Matthew.

By the time they buried the remaining crates and reloaded the wagon with the much lighter contents, Rufus ambled in. Late as usual.

"We ready to leave?"

Two shovels dropped. So did Mercy's jaw. "In this dark?"

Rufus hitched his thumbs in his breeches, the dark silhouette making him more of a scarecrow than ever. "I figure if we near those soldiers soon as they set out at sunrise, we can follow 'em back at a distance, then cut in here and retrieve our load soon as they pass. By day's end, we'll cover a fair amount of miles instead of none."

Matthew's chest rumbled, but whether out of agreement or wanting to throttle the young man, Mercy couldn't tell.

"First we cover this ground with rock and brush, then we will see how close it is to daybreak." Matthew heaved his shovel into the wagon, the scrape of it competing with Rufus's curse.

"Why waste time with that?"

Mercy arched her back. Indeed. Every bone in her body cried out to set herself down on that wagon seat and nod off for a spell. She turned to Matthew. "Do we have to—"

"The faster we cover up this dirt, the faster we get on the road."

They all set to work, and glory be, Rufus did too. By the time they finished and the first hint of gray edged in from the east, a thick layer of rock and briars hid the disturbed ground. Anyone chancing upon it wouldn't be the wiser, especially since they also made sure to beat down the grass in other areas as well, turning the whole glade into a confusing twist of wagon tracks and flattened weeds.

She forced one foot in front of the other, drawn by the call of the wagon seat, longing to sink down. The wood would surely feel like a velvet cushion.

"Mercy, grab your gun and fetch some rope."

Behind her, Matthew's words hit hard between her shoulder blades, and she tripped over her own foot. She knew this was coming. Knew it had to be done. And she wouldn't argue against it.

But as she grabbed the rope from where it hung inside the wagon, she squeezed the hemp as tightly as the squeeze of her heart, wishing Elias wasn't a traitor.

That instead, he was the honorable man she wanted—nay, *needed*—him to be.

Elias smirked as he trudged along the ridgeline. Here he was, marching between two guns again. Mercy in the lead and Matthew behind. This time, though, he strode toward freedom—provided he could work his way out of the bindings that cut into his wrists at his back and retrieve the hidden weapon before they returned.

The coming dawn etched a gray outline on the shaggy tree branches, dissipating the ominous shadows. He'd hoped for thick cloud cover awash with a hard rain, but soon enough, sunshine would poke holes in the dark woods. It would be difficult to cover his tracks, especially from the keen eye of Mercy—and then it hit him. His step faltered. He'd be running *away* from her, putting a forever kind of distance between him and the only woman he'd ever thought twice about.

"Over there, that stand of hemlocks." Behind him, Matthew's voice prompted Mercy to veer westward.

They stopped at a trio of trunks. Nearby, a spruce sapling—tall and thick enough to provide cover—obscured the base of one of the trees.

Matthew tipped his head toward him. "Hunker down between the spruce and that tree." He slid his gaze to Mercy, his gun never lowering from Elias. "Mercy, train your barrel on him while I tie him up. Open hammer."

A scowl ferocious enough to make a grown man back off darkened her face. "You really think—?"

"You know the treachery of man more than anyone."

"No need." Elias crouch-walked his way past the scratchy limbs, working his body into the space between the trees. "I will not fight against you." He dropped to the ground, back against the trunk.

Even so, the click of Mercy's hammer violated the innocence of the morning. Matthew set his gun near her feet and then grabbed the rope.

The whole while the man secured him to the tree, Elias stared up through the breach in the spruce branches to memorize the shape of Mercy. The curve of her pert chin. The hollow at the bottom of her throat. The way her braid swung over her shoulder and rode the swell of her breast, tailing off at the spread of her hips. Even in a torn skirt and with dirt smudged along her jaw, the woman was a dangerous beauty. She belonged here, in these woods, a daughter of earth and light. What would it be like to really be her husband instead of the farce they had been playacting? How passionate? How all consuming? For he had no doubt this woman would give her all to the man she loved.

He lifted his gaze higher, meeting her eye for eye, wanting—*needing*—one last look. She cocked her head. Questions swam in those brown depths, almost as if she knew he was saying goodbye.

Pain dug into his chest as Matthew whaled on the rope, and he grunted.

Mercy scowled. "You're hurting him!"

"Just snugging it tight. Won't be for long. We'll be back before noon. Besides, he is the one who will get a good piece of shuteye while we face the dragon."

Matthew's footsteps circled the tree, then he crouched next to him, smelling of hard work and weariness. "I'm just doing what's got to be done, but I think you know that, aye?"

He nodded. "I would be doing the same, were I in your shoes."

"Good. Then I hope you understand this." In one swift movement, Matthew yanked off his neckcloth and shoved it in his mouth, like a bit in a horse, and tied it tight behind his head.

"Matthew! You're taking this too far." Mercy's voice scraped fierce against the cheerful drone of early morning bird chatter. "He has never once given us a lick of trouble."

Her defense of him was a sweet balm against the way the cloth cut into the corners of his mouth.

The ranger rose and retrieved his gun. "Can't take any chances of him calling out when those French pass. Now, turn around and start walking."

He couldn't see her, not with the way Matthew's hulking figure stood between him and her. But it wasn't hard to imagine the flare of her nostrils as she strained out, "Why?"

"Do it." Matthew's voice was flat, commanding. Deadly.

He bit down hard on the cloth in his mouth. What did the ranger have in mind? For the first time, he wondered if he'd been foolish to allow himself to be bound. Had he misjudged Matthew Prinn's character?

Mercy stamped off. Not her quiet-stepped pace, nor her silent scouting tread. Each thud of her feet shouted her anger.

Matthew turned back to him, gun in hand. "I am mighty grieved about this, Dubois."

He lifted his gun higher.

Elias strained against the ropes, wild to break free—and even wilder to spit out the gag, for a terrible understanding broke as clear as the rising sun. It had been two days since he and Mercy had read the Indian sign carved into the moss on the rock. Whatever that message portended would happen today, and they hadn't covered much ground since then. Danger lurked nearby, and he'd be a fish in a barrel should that portent come to pass. He growled like a cornered bear.

And the butt of Matthew's gun stock cracked against his skull.

Then blackness.

Pure, blessed blackness. One he could lie in wide-armed and float upon for days and days. Maybe he should. So tired. He was so, so tired. Yes, he could live here in this silent dark, nestled in nothingness. . .were it not for the niggling drive to swim out of it. He had somewhere to be, didn't he? Someone to save? An important errand?

Nay, none of that mattered anymore.

Not one thing mattered.

He awoke to a blackfly buzzing on his nose. Pain hammered a beat in his skull, centering just above his left ear. Burning, throbbing, anguishing. So sharp it shot down through his jaws and choked him.

Rays of sun slipped in through the spruce boughs, and he closed his eyes. Too bright. But *how* bright?

He forced his eyes back open, squinting along the length of a beam, judging the angle. Couldn't be much past dawn. If Matthew had meant that wallop to the head to keep him out until their return, he should've taken into account the thickness of his skull and grit in his spirit, for his senses barreled back with surprising clarity. He had to move.

And he had to move now.

Biting down hard on the cloth in his mouth, he wriggled to work the ropes on his wrists against the bark of the tree. Pain bounced around in his head like a shot let loose from a musket, so sharply the world spun. But more than that agony was against him. So was time.

Warmth trickled down onto his fingers as he rubbed away rope fibers and flesh. He worked a steady beat, insanely matching his movements to the throbbing—and then he stopped. Rock still. Listening with his whole body. Had he heard something?

There, between the scampering of squirrel paws and caw of a crow, footsteps rustled the underbrush. Soft. Steady. Stealthy. Moving in from the north. Drawing closer.

Nearer.

The stink of bear grease and man sweat closed in, breaths away. He held his. If a warrior found him here, his throat would be slashed before he could blink.

God, please. Hide me beneath Your wings.

Ten, maybe twelve, warriors slipped past him, stealing toward the ridgeline. Red and black painted their faces. A war party then. Each man's hair was shaved to the scalp on the sides of his head, the rest bristling down his back beneath a stiff roach headdress, the identifying factor for which the French named this tribe Wyandot.

Silently, they fanned out, spanning the rocky cleft above the glade, leastwise near as he could tell from his vantage point. Then stopped. Words passed, quiet as the breeze, too low for him to identify anything other than, "We wait."

Blast! His head pounded. His hands were yet bound. And a war party blocked his way to retrieve the French weapon. What in the world were they waiting for?

The pain in his head shot down to his heart with a sudden, awful awareness. These savages were hunkering down until Matthew, Rufus, and Mercy returned. How they knew the wagons would come back was beyond his reckoning and would have to be pondered at a later time.

For now, his sole focus was to work his way free without alerting any of the killers.

CHAPTER 21

Blue coats surrounded them, muskets at the ready. Mercy sat rigid on the wagon seat while Matthew and the sergeant communicated in a mix of broken French and English. Really, she couldn't blame the enemy squad for such caution—but she did anyway. Were the French not down this far into New York Colony, neither would their native allies have ventured this far south.

And her father might still be alive.

"Put your guns down and take a look." Frustration pinched Matthew's voice, especially when the French soldier stared at him blankly, and he jerked his thumb over his shoulder. *"Regardez!"*

The sergeant narrowed his eyes. Great heavens. . .had Matthew just insulted the man? Maybe they should've brought Elias along to translate. At the thought of him, she ran her thumb over her own wrist. She still hadn't quite squared Matthew's crack to Elias's skull—and had let him know about it all the way here. Had Elias awakened with a monstrous headache, if he yet woke at all? Was the flesh of his wrists rubbed raw from the tight ropes?

With a sharp nod from the sergeant, four soldiers broke rank and marched to the back of the wagon. By the sounds of more feet thudding on the ground behind them, four others had gone around to the back of Rufus's wagon as well. Soon the creak of lids being pried off and the clink-clunking of pots and goods being rummaged through worked their way up to the wagon seat.

Some of the coiled tension in Mercy's nerves unwound, and she was glad now they had worked all night to bury the gold. Those men would find nothing and so have no reason to hold them. They would be on their way in no time.

But when the soldiers returned to their formation with a *"Rien, monsieur,"* the sergeant's glower deepened.

Until Matthew reached into his pocket and pulled out a sovereign.

Mercy's jaw dropped as the gold coin arced in a ray of sunlight and landed in the sergeant's dirty glove.

"*Démissionner!*" the sergeant shouted.

At once, muskets lowered and swung to a resting position on each soldier's shoulder.

"Goodbye, *chiens anglais.*" The sergeant's thick accent dismissed their party, and the entire squad stood aside.

Matthew slapped the reins, and the horses snapped into action.

Once they were out of earshot, Mercy eyed him sideways. "Where'd you get that gold coin? Wait a minute. . .you gave them one of their own, did you not?"

He chuckled.

So did she. Ah, but she'd miss this man.

Her smile faded. In just under a fortnight, they would reach Fort Edward and part ways. What was she to do with her life then? Everything had been so clear before Elias and his load of gold had showed up, but now? She tipped back her head and closed her eyes, giving in to exhaustion with a long sigh.

"You're not going to start harping on me about Elias again, are you?" Matthew's voice rumbled along with the wheels. " 'Cause I'm done jawin' about that."

"No, 'tisn't that." She opened her eyes and faced him. "What is it that made you become a ranger?"

He shoved a finger in his ear and jiggled it. "What kind of question is that?"

She frowned. It was an odd question, to be sure. But maybe—just maybe—if she understood what drove this honorable man to do what he did with his life, it would give her some guidance for what she ought to do. "I want to know."

"Well. . ." He scratched the side of his jaw, whiskers rasping with the movement. "I suppose I wanted to change the world. Right the wrongs, heal the hurts of this land. I aimed to stake my claim of honor by doing big things with my life." A strange smile curled his lips, as if he chewed on a crabapple. "I've come to learn, though, 'tis the small things that really make a change."

"Like what?"

"Like you."

Unease closed in on her. Was he calling her small, or telling her she was in need of change? "What's that mean?"

He slowed the wagon as they neared a space wide enough to turn around, then faced her. "I have come to believe 'tis more important in this life to make one person feel loved than to go around killing and grasping for power."

Such peaceful words were incongruent coming from the war-worn face of a ranger. She searched his gray eyes, yet nothing but sincerity stared back. "You going soft on me, Matthew?"

"Loving someone isn't a show of softness, but of strength, for there is no stronger bond."

She swallowed, shoving down the ember of emotion burning in her throat. How many times had this man thrown himself into harm's way for her? Unbidden, words her mother had planted deep into her heart as a little girl surfaced. "Greater love hath no man than this, that a man lay down his life for his friends," she murmured.

Matthew's jaw dropped. "What's this? Mercy Lytton spouting the Bible?"

A rising smile would not be denied. "Despite raising me in a Mohawk camp, my mother made sure I wasn't raised a heathen."

"Time we get a move on!" Rufus's voice needled them both from his wagon behind.

"Hate to say it, but he is right." Matthew slapped the reins, lurching the wagon into motion. "Close your eyes now while you can. We'll soon have a load of gold to repack."

Leaning her head back against the canvas, she pulled down the brim of her old felt hat, shading her eyes, then nodded off to the quiet jingle of harness and rhythmic vibrations of the wagon seat. She did not awaken until the timbre of the wheels changed from a somewhat graded road to wilder terrain. Tall hemlocks, pines, and oaks closed in on them as Matthew guided the wagon back onto the narrow path leading to the glade.

Blackbirds chattered as they rolled into the clearing. A rabbit bounded off to safety, splitting a trail in the tall grass. The pile of rocks and brush where they'd hidden the gold remained as they had left it. She scanned the ridgeline, glancing from tree to tree. Nothing was different. A man would be hard pressed to find a more peaceful patch of woods.

Even so, the small hairs on the back of her neck prickled.

Something wasn't right.

Matthew stopped the wagon but did not set the brake, nor did he look at her. "You see anything?" His whisper was deadly soft.

"You feel it too," she whispered back, more a statement than a question.

Scanning the area, she began to shut down all other senses—when Matthew angled his body in front of hers.

And she heard the *thwunk* of an arrow piercing him through the neck.

The world blurred, a whirl of green and brown streaked with light. Gasping for air, Elias slowed from his mad sprint to a stop and shored up against a tree trunk, waiting out the dizziness that muddled his vision. The burning of his bloody wrists was nothing compared to the throbbing in his skull. Running full out after a blow to the head was never a good idea, a lesson he knew well. Yet here he was, tearing through the woods like a wolf bent on a fox, wishing for all the world he could put himself between Mercy and the war party instead of skirting the woods behind the killers. His heart branded him a coward, but running off and then doubling back down to the road was the best—the only—way to prevent an attack.

If he could reach the wagon before they swung off the road.

He slowed his breathing. In. Out. Deep. Slow. And the crazy swirl began to sharpen into straight lines. A stand of maples. Squirrels darting. Gnats swarming. All took on shape, and he glanced over his shoulder, hoping, praying he'd not spy a war-painted Indian on his trail. It would grieve him to put an end to a lost one, but better a native than Mercy.

Nothing moved. Apparently the killers had been too intent on the glade in front of them to pay attention to what dangers might've lurked behind—a mistake he'd made only once in his life. And he had the scars to prove it. Time to press on.

He shoved off and broke into a jog. Slow and steady might serve better than breakneck. But with each step, it took everything in him to keep from bursting ahead at full speed. No doubt those wagons were on the move back toward the glade, and if he did not stop them. . . Time slapped him cold, an enemy too ethereal to fight back against.

God, grant that I reach them in time.

Deeming his progress far enough, whether in truth or just because, he swung south, working his way to the road. Hopefully. Hard to tell for certain, when he'd never actually traversed these backwoods before. Yet based on the scant snippets of descriptions Mercy and Rufus had shared, this was the route. It had to be.

Oh God, please make it so.

An eternity later, the woods thinned. He pumped his legs harder, lungs screaming, pain blinding, and nearly overran the road. Staggering to a stop, he doubled over, hands on his thighs, and caught his breath.

Then lost it.

Multiple sets of wagon tracks marred the ground, which meant they had passed this way twice. Heading away from the glade—and heading toward it.

This time he broke into a dead run.

CHAPTER 22

The ridgeline exploded with warriors. Ten. Twelve? No time to count. Heartsick and burning with white-hot rage, Mercy shoved off Matthew's deadweight where he'd toppled sideways against her. She'd have to grieve later—if she lived that long.

As she bent to grab her gun, a rush of air grazed past her cheek. The thwack of an arrow pierced the canvas behind her. Having grabbed her gun, she snatched up Matthew's, his fingers forever frozen in a desperate reach, then dove inside the wagon.

An arrow hissed behind her. Pain seared the top of her right shoulder. The tip ripped through fabric and flesh then stuck deep into a crate behind her. She hunkered down, working her body into a crevice where the cargo had shifted. A poor cover. A deadly one. But all she had for now.

"Rufus?" she hollered. "Rufus!"

No answer. Just the lethal sound of rocks cascading from the rushing tread of moccasins. Men breathing heavy on the hunt.

They were coming.

They were coming for her.

Ignoring the sharp burn in her shoulder, she primed the pan of Matthew's gun and balanced the weapon on the crate next to her. Then she primed hers and clicked the hammer wide. Which way to aim? Front? Back? Clammy sweat dotted her brow. It was futile, this need of hers to fight, but she owed it to Matthew to take out at least a few of his killers.

Oh Matthew. She could yet hear his voice, grumbling with emotion. *"'Tis more important in this life to make one person feel loved than to go around killing."*

Her grip on the gun slackened. He wouldn't want her to kill for him. But she couldn't sit here defenseless either. Perhaps if she could lure the warriors to the front of the wagon, she might have a chance to slip out the puckered hole in the rear and make a run for it. But what to use for a distraction?

Scrambling for an idea, she scanned the wagon's contents. A wool blanket. Some rope. A shovel and a bucket. Maybe she could—too late.

A war hatchet sliced into the back canvas.

She turned and fired. A groaning gurgle followed.

So did the thud of feet climbing up to the front seat.

She threw down her gun and seized Matthew's, hands shaking so much half the gunpowder jiggled out of the pan. *Hold, hold.* It wouldn't do to spend her last shot on nothing but air.

The front canvas rippled. The whites of shiny eyes set deep in a band of black paint peered in and locked onto her.

Mercy pulled the trigger.

A flash. A fizzle. A misfire.

A slow grin slashed across the face of the warrior, and he advanced.

She scrambled back—and an arm snared her from behind, pulling her against a sweaty chest. Her gun fell, and she clawed at the thick arm holding her. A knife flashed, poised to split the flesh of her neck.

"Hunh-ha!" the man in front of her shouted.

The one holding her growled, a low roar that reverberated in her own chest.

But the knife slid away, and she was yanked out the back of the wagon, a captive of a nameless warrior whose face she couldn't see. Another man lay flat on his back, eyes unseeing and a hole in his neck, just like Matthew. Had she done that?

Her stomach spasmed, and unstoppable tremors shook through her. She'd never killed a man before—and never would again. The startling violation of snatching what was only God's to take slammed into her. She jerked her head aside and retched.

The man holding her let go, yanking the hat from her head as he did so. She dropped to her hands and knees and heaved until there was nothing left—then heaved some more.

The black-striped warrior hefted her up by her arm. Sunlight flashed off the ring in his nose and larger silver wheels on his ears as he bound her hands in front of her. She put up no struggle. What was the point? She'd already given her best fight.

And lost.

A thong cut tight into her wrists. Then a wider lash looped over her head and settled around her neck, connecting her to the black-painted man via a short lead. All the while, he studied her with narrowed eyes, some kind of recognition flashing deep within. But what? She'd never seen him before.

Had she?

With a sharp tug on the leather, he indicated she was to follow. He led her past the wagon, around natives hauling out crates and busting them open, and beyond the front seat where Matthew yet lay.

If only she could join him.

Running toward danger was nothing new. It was a way of life. For once, Elias was thankful for his years of rebellion. Any sane man would be putting distance between himself and a band of warriors—especially being unarmed. But he pressed ahead at top speed, straining for a glimpse of two wagons bumping along the road.

He did not slow until he reached the turnoff leading into the glade—and then he didn't just slow. He stopped. So did his heart. Flattened weeds marked ruts through the vegetation. Deep, defined, and sickeningly fresh.

And a gunshot cracked a wicked report.

He was too late.

Or was he? He couldn't credit Rufus with much sense, but Matthew and Mercy? Between the two of them, perhaps they had seen the danger and bailed. Hied themselves off into the woods and taken cover. It was a frail chance, wispy as spider webbing, but he wrapped his hands around it and refused to let go. If only belief alone would make it so.

Drawing upon every shadow-walking skill he'd honed, he backed away from the furrows and eased into the spring growth. Though full bloom was months off, enough greenery lent him concealment. Thank God it wasn't winter.

He darted from tree trunk, to scrub fir, to dogwood shrub, head still throbbing, wrists still raw. A whiff of musk and sweat carried on the air, as did the clank of metal upon metal. Not much farther then.

With one eye on the ground to keep from a misstep, he edged as close as he dared to the clearing and crouched in a patch of toad lilies. Ahead, two wagons sat one in front of the other, barely past the tree line, but no sign of Mercy or Matthew. For the first time since the Indians had arrived, the heavy weight stealing his breath began to lift. Mayhap they had sensed the threat and escaped.

But when a tall native rounded the corner of the last wagon, strutting like a rooster, all air and hope whooshed out of his lungs. Mercy's hat perched atop his shaved head. The old felt that she loved. The one she'd worn when he'd last seen her.

And blood splattered the man's face.

Oh God, please don't let that be Mercy's.

He clenched his jaw to keep from roaring and started counting heads—tallying up just how many he could take down on his own with nothing but fists and rage. Two men threw out crates from inside the last wagon, where four others pried off the tops and emptied the contents. The devil wearing Mercy's hat joined in. That made seven.

He jerked his gaze to the first wagon, where tatters of the canvas flapped in the breeze at the rear. One warrior lay unmoving on the ground, forgotten—for now—amongst a heap of open and abandoned crates. Near the second wagon, a pair of men had unbridled the horses and were leading them toward the rise.

Eight, nine, ten. Blast! Four or five men he might be able to ward off—and that was a huge stretch—but ten? He hadn't felt this helpless since holding François's blue-lipped body in his arms as he'd pulled him from the river. . .yet another time he'd been too late to be of any real use.

Shoving away the memory, he duckwalked closer and huddled behind a wildwood shrub. The leaves blocked his line of sight, but the shortened distance made it easier to distinguish their quiet words.

"White dogs! There is no treasure here."

"English lips cannot help but lie. Their hearts are thick with deceit."

"We are the fools, making a pact with pale-faced devils."

"All is not loss, my brother. Even now Nadowa leads Black-Fox-Running's daughter to camp. Let us return and see his glory walk."

Some of the tension in his jaw slackened. It must be Mercy they spoke of, for he could believe nothing other than she was yet alive—maybe not for long—but breathing at least as long as it would take for the warrior named Nadowa to haul her into camp. For the first time in hours, a ghostly smile haunted his lips. He'd hate to be the man trying to drag her anywhere against her will.

He waited out the pillaging warriors, listening for the clanking of housewares to cease. Eventually, after a final barrage of hateful epithets against the whites, he heard the sound of moccasins padding off. A few rocks clacked down the ridgeline, knocked loose by careless feet. Then the forest returned to nothing but birdsong and squirrels rustling about. Every muscle in him yearned to burst into a sprint and follow their trail, specifically Mercy and Nadowa's. But prudence rooted him until he was certain no one had turned back or laid in wait for God knew what purpose.

Creeping out from behind the shrub, he paused and studied the glade. The wagons stood stripped naked save for the canvas coverings, one of them flapping in the breeze. Up on the ridge, no sign of movement. It was still a risk to expose himself to the clearing, but was not all of life a perilous gamble?

He skulked to the rear wagon, sitting in the late morning sun like a pile of bleached bones and just as devoid of life. No blood. No sign of struggle. He passed it by and moved on to the next.

The slashed canvas rippled. A dark patch of bloody grass cried up from the earth where the fallen warrior had lain. Judging by the flattened trail leading off from it, the war party had hauled their fellow fighter away with them. Weaving through a maze of upturned crates, he worked his way to the front. . .where he nearly dropped to his knees.

Stretched out like a slit-throated buck, the mighty ranger, Matthew Prinn, lay draped over the driver's seat, an arrow pierced through his gullet. Elias staggered. That could've been him. He'd not been happy about Matthew tying his bonds so tight and cracking him in the head, but the man's actions had saved his life.

Stunned, he lifted his face to the impossibly blue sky. "Oh God, bless that man and thank You. Once again You have provided in ways I do not deserve."

His gaze snapped back to Matthew. Blackflies flitted near the wound, his glassy eyes, his gaping mouth. Elias swallowed back a burning ember of sorrow and remorse. As gruff as the ranger had been, he'd be sorely missed. The weeks they'd shared had gone a long way toward healing some of the raw wounds left from his grandfather's death.

"Receive this man into Your arms, Lord," he whispered.

He waved away the flies, wishing he had told Matthew everything, his true mission, and maybe even enlisted Matthew's help. But too late now. Blowing out a long breath and then filling his lungs, he stared at the dead man's chest. Matthew would never have such a pleasure again.

Nor did Elias have the pleasure of loitering.

He broke into a jog, dashed around to the other side of the wagon, and scrambled up to the seat, expecting to see Rufus's corpse inside. An empty wagon bed stared back. Pivoting, he shaded his eyes, careful not to jostle Matthew's repose. He scanned the glade from edge to edge. No more bodies sullied the grass. Apparently they had hauled off Rufus as well.

He lowered his hand, then bent to pull Matthew inside the wagon. Heaving the stiff body proved a challenge, and he regretted the way the ranger landed inside with a thud. It wasn't much of a grave, but it was the best he could do for now. At least the man's body wouldn't be out in the open. He ran his fingers along Matthew's shirt and down his legs, hoping to find a knife. Nothing. The Indians must've thought of that as well.

Sitting back on his haunches, Elias quickly rifled through his options.

Truly, there were only two. Dig up that crate with the French weapon and hightail it out of here for Boston, saving countless lives in the process—or light out after the woman he loved.

He gasped. *Love?* Was that what this burning need firing along every nerve meant?

A groan rumbled in his throat. How could he risk the lives of an entire fort to go chasing after one woman?

How could he not?

Quickly calculating distance, time, and need, he came up with three days. He'd give it three days to find her, then turn around—even if he didn't locate her.

Mind set, he scrambled out through the canvas hole. Though it grieved him to leave Matthew's body, he jumped down to the ground. Time was something he could no longer afford to spend, even on respectful purchases. He trotted off toward the ridgeline and began scouting for telltale signs of passage, one question niggling all the while.

Who were the pale-faced devils who had bargained with the Indians for the treasure?

CHAPTER 23

Two days. One nightmare. An ugly, black, never-ending nightmare. Mercy trudged after the Wyandot brute, the back of her neck raw from the leather thong. If she didn't keep step, the bite of it would gouge a deeper stripe into her flesh—and the skin was already chafed to a pulp from her unrelenting belligerence. Not that it had done her any good. With the big man leading and ten others spread out behind, she did not have a chance. No woman could best eleven warriors. She frowned. The thought should've comforted her in some small measure. *Should've.* But it didn't.

So with each tread, she stored her anger. Her grief. All the frustration of a world turned upside down and shaken into something she didn't recognize anymore. When the time was right, she'd open the door to those foul emotions and run away with them, never to return. But for now, she forced one foot in front of the other. There was nothing else to do.

Yet.

Behind her, footsteps crushed the forest's undergrowth, soft but fast. The man holding her tether stopped and turned. For a blessed moment, the pressure at the base of her neck eased.

Another man sped past her, stopping close to her captor. While they talked, she tried to listen to their tones of voice, hints of emotion, anything that could give her a clue about what they might be discussing, for she didn't know the language. But sweet heavens, it was hard to hear over the rush of rage pumping in her ears—the scoundrel who'd advanced wore her hat atop his head. *Hers!*

She gritted her teeth. She'd have that hat back or die in the trying, for why not? She was a corpse walking anyway. As soon as these men reached their camp, she had no doubt she'd be used in some kind of ritual—the killing kind.

The bigger warrior unwrapped her tether from where he kept it bound to his wrist, then passed it off to the man in her hat. She tensed. This was new. Until now, she'd remained with her original captor. Why would he turn back from the way they had already trekked?

Dark eyes slid to hers from beneath her familiar felt brim, a cold gleam in the man's gaze. Were he not in possession of what belonged to her, she might have given in to fear, but as it was, fury simmered hot in her belly. She'd use this to her advantage. But how?

Slowly, the man pulled the lead taut, then in increments yanked tighter, until the slicing pain at the base of her neck could not be denied. She had no choice but to take a stilted step forward. Again the slow pull, the incremental yanks, the awful buildup of pain until she took another step. Closer and closer, his dark eyes undressing her as he reeled her in, the rope pooling at his feet with each successive tug.

Pooling?

She flicked her gaze to his hands, then away, so he'd not notice her fixation. But one glance was enough. The fool had not wrapped the tether around his wrist like the bigger man, but held it with his fingers, so that the end of it rested on the ground. She flattened her lips lest she smile. This, she could use.

Maintaining the same amount of resistance, she allowed him to draw her nearer, until the rotted-meat stench of his breath filled her nostrils.

She reared back her head, then jerked it down. The front of her skull cracked into the man's nose, breaking it with a sickening crunch. In that split instant of shock and acute pain, she whipped around and tore into the woods.

The world blurred by. She was wind, blowing past trees, gusting over rocks. A mad, desperate race, for the man would give chase. Her gaze shot wild, searching for a hiding place. Anywhere. Anything. A rotted stump or a hidden cleft of a ravine.

Footsteps kicked up a frenzy behind her. If she didn't find something soon, he'd spot her and—

She whumped to the ground, face first, jerked by a misstep on the rope dangling from her wrists. Sticks and gravel bit into her chin. Lungs heaving, she pushed up, frantic to retrieve the knife in her bodice. Fingers met the bone hilt. The blade slid out.

And an iron grip yanked her upward from behind, spinning her around. The knife flew from her grasp.

Blood flowed red from the man's nose to his neck. White teeth flashed in a macabre grin. He swung back his arm and backhanded her full across the mouth.

Her head jerked. She reeled. A coppery taste repulsed her—the warm tang of blood draining from her split lip. She turned aside to spit.

The next strike knocked her flat, turning the world black.

She lived in that darkness for a very long time, but not long enough to make the pain go away. Hours later, when her eyes did open, it wasn't much different. Her head throbbed. The wound on her shoulder still ached deep to the marrow of her bones. So much hurt that she couldn't see straight—could she?

She blinked, trying to focus. Some kind of wall was inches from her face. Deerskin? Birch bark? Did it even matter?

The low drone of voices hummed somewhere overhead. A grating sound, bass and throaty. Her best guess was she'd been hauled into the enemy's camp and deposited in some kind of hut, likely guarded.

Unbidden tears slipped from her eyes. There was no getting out of this. Not this time. No Elias or Matthew to help. Had she ever really thanked them for their care? For the times when Matthew had protected her with a backup shot while scouting? For all his fatherly advice and grudging affection?

Or Elias? The tender touch he'd used in binding up her foot. His thoughtfulness in lending his coat for her warmth—even to his detriment. The way he stood up to Rufus or Logan, defending her honor. She'd never once showed him the kindness of gratitude, had she?

A sob convulsed her, and she curled into a ball. Regret was a living, breathing demon. Not only had she never shown them gratitude, but she'd never had the chance to say goodbye. And now it was too late. She'd lost them. She'd lost everything. Her loved ones, her dignity, her hope. What a failure. She was nothing but a weak woman.

Just like her mother.

Tears flowed freely, choking her, bathing her. Would that she could shove back time, return to her girlhood, and redo how she'd treated the woman who'd birthed her and loved her to her dying day. She reached to clutch the locket.

"I'd be kinder, Mother," she whispered. "Less spiteful. More loving."

"Don't cry, lady."

She froze.

"Your mother must know you love her."

She rolled over—and stared into blue eyes.

Elias thanked God for three things. Nay, four. That he yet breathed. That he tracked a large number of Indians, for trailing any less would have been nigh impossible in this wilderness. And though at first horrified, he was thankful for the small, bone-handled knife lying in the dirt. He knew the blade well, for he'd faced it an eternity ago in the dark of night.

Crouching, he grasped the weapon in a loose-fingered grip, almost reverently. When had it last warmed against Mercy's skin? The flattened growth around him suggested a struggle, but as he narrowed his eyes and studied the length of the blade, the rest of his fear blew away on a waft of late morning breeze. No remnants of blood darkened the steel. Despite the few droplets he'd spied defiling the trillium, he had no reason to believe a slaughter had happened here.

He stood and secured the treasure between belt and waist, most of all thankful he'd not yielded to the strong discouragement urging him to turn around and quit this chase.

With renewed confidence, he strode onward. Having already measured the pace of the warriors, he looked for signs of passage every yard or so. A low-growing branch broken by a careless step. A kicked rock leaving behind a depression not yet eaten up by forest growth. And as he gained on them, now and then he was prized with a slight indentation from the back edge of a moccasin heel.

Smoke, at first a faint whiff, strengthened in scent. So did the pungent odor of man. Calling upon his shadow-walking skills, Elias crept on silent feet, at one point slipping through the outward ring of scouts protecting the camp he neared.

He stopped at the edge of a small clearing, sided on the north by a fast-flowing stream. Squatting behind a leafed-out shrub, he took measure of the site. Two makeshift shelters of skins and bark nestled next to a larger lodge. Off to one side sat a smaller hut, guarded by a folded-armed warrior. Near one of the shelters, two men worked on weapon repair or arrowhead construction. Directly in front of him, three stood in discussion, blocking his view of the front of the larger lodge, but near as he could tell, no women or children lived here. It all indicated that this was a temporary encampment, a staging place for summer forays. He tucked away the information, adding to the intelligence he'd hand over once he reached Boston.

One of the men broke away from the group in front of him—and strode straight for him.

Elias froze, not daring to so much as breathe.

But the man shouldered his bow and passed by, likely off to replace one of the scouts.

Taking care not to snap a twig, Elias eased back, blending with dirt and trees, and waited.

Steps, while quietly chosen, drew nearer. When they passed, he sprang.

Elias grabbed the man from behind, the biting edge of Mercy's knife nicking into the warrior's throat.

"Whose camp is this, my brother?" He whispered the Wyandot words into the man's ear, then lessened his grip just enough to let the man speak.

"Uwętatsih-anue."

Red Bear, here? Immediately Elias released him, smiling wide. "Good. I would speak with Red Bear. Lead on."

For a moment, the man stared at him as if he were mad. And he just might be, so giddy with the blessing of having an ally in this place. If Mercy weren't here, at least his former contact would have plenty of information, especially once a pipe circulated from hand to hand.

Even so, he kept the knife in his grip as he followed the man out of the trees and into the clearing. The warriors working on weapons looked up at his entrance, wary curiosity shining in their dark eyes and murmurs passing between them. The two men who'd earlier blocked his view fell in behind him, no doubt with hands covering the tomahawks strapped to their sides. While the brave he followed led him toward the largest lodge, Elias's gaze lingered on the smallest shelter. If Mercy were here, still alive, that was where she'd be.

They stopped in front of a low-burning fire, more ash than flame, smoldering in front of the council lodge. On the other side of the fire, a man rose, impossibly broad of chest and decorated with three golden gorgets, the ornaments denoting him as the tribe's sachem. A single turkey feather adorned his scalp lock, the black hair streaked with unnatural red glints in the late morning sun. He flicked a glance at Elias, neither acknowledging nor disowning their friendship, then trained his gaze on the native with the bloody nick-line across his neck.

Next to Elias, the man who'd led him here stepped forward. "This man would speak with you, Uwętatsih-anue."

Red Bear grunted. "Where did you find him?"

"He found me."

"Then this day you have been spared by Shadow Walker." Red Bear jerked his head once, dismissing the man.

Without a word, the warrior strode away.

Finally, Red Bear's gaze sought his, and a glimmer of amusement sparked in the dark depths. "I did not think the English would hold you for long, Shadow Walker."

Elias grinned. "As always, great sachem, you speak truth."

Pleasure twitched the man's lips, not quite a reciprocal grin, but a hint of a smile nonetheless. "You come at a good time. We celebrate tonight when the rest of the men return."

It took all his willpower to school his expression into nothing but mild interest. Usually a celebration meant a victory—often one that involved captives. Were both Rufus and Mercy here?

"That is good," he lied. "Yet I am not long for this camp. I seek only information and will be on my way."

"Then come." Red Bear drifted a hand toward the council lodge behind him. "Let us smoke. We will trade what our heads and hearts have gathered."

Red Bear turned and entered the lodge. Elias followed, as did the two men behind him.

Crossing from brilliant light into shadows, he blinked, then sucked in a breath. Red Bear sat next to a warrior already cross-legged on the ground—one who wore Mercy's hat perched at an angle atop his black hair. A sharp-edged anger sliced through him, and his fingers twitched to snatch the hat away and demand to know where Mercy was. But any show of emotion could cause Red Bear to question him, or worse, to demand that he leave.

So he sat adjacent to Red Bear, keeping an angle to view the door. He'd seen one too many men take a tomahawk to the back for want of staying vigilant.

Without looking any man in the eyes, he held out his hands to the small fire. "Tell me of this celebration. Has there been a recent victory?"

"No." The man with the hat huffed. "And yes."

Red Bear lifted the ceremonial pipe from its stand, pausing before he lit it. "It was not the victory we expected," he explained.

"Often those are the most rewarding, Great One."

Nodding, Red Bear lifted the pipe, paying homage to earth and air and fire. Elias waited for the ceremony to begin, not speaking and hardly breathing. Every part of him itched to tear out of here and search the few shelters for sight of a dark-haired, wide-eyed woman, but any impatience on his part would be frowned upon.

Eventually, Red Bear wafted pipe smoke to his nose with one cupped hand, then passed it off to the man in the hat before he spoke. "Long have the Fight-Hard-with-Knives been a burr hooked into our skin. But we have been awarded a vengeance coup. Nadowa believes he has captured the daughter of their dead leader, Black-Fox-Running. I cannot say if she is or not, for my path never crossed with the woman. Only with her father."

The fragrant scent of sweet tobacco began to fill the lodge, far more soothing than Red Bear's words. Could that woman be Mercy? She spoke fluent Mohawk. She bore native features. But was she truly a daughter of a sachem?

"And if she is not?" he asked.

Red Bear shrugged. "We will sacrifice her anyway in exchange for not receiving our promised goods."

The pipe passed to him, and he sucked in a draught of smoke, held it, then blew it out, letting the tobacco work its wiles with his tense nerves. Whoever the woman was, she needed to be removed before nightfall.

Cupping his hand, he wafted smoke to his face, then passed the pipe back to Red Bear. "I may be able to help you identify this woman. Bring her here."

The sachem's brow creased. "You know Black-Fox-Running's daughter?"

"Perhaps."

And if he did, then God help them both.

CHAPTER 24

Wrists yet bound, Mercy shoved her hands onto the ground and pushed up to sit. Pale blue eyes watched her every move. In front of her, a girl—not long before the bloom of maidenhood—sat with her back against a strip-barked wall, knees drawn up in front of her. By Mercy's best calculation, she could be no more than ten or eleven summers, but stillness radiated out from her, like that of a sage old woman. The girl's blond hair tangled past her shoulders, draped over a wrinkled and dirty gown, yet she bore no scrapes or bruises. Apparently their captives were treating her well—which meant the girl would be either adopted or given in trade.

"Who are you?" Mercy asked.

"Deliverance, but call me Livvy, like my mother did." The girl's voice cracked, and she sniffed. Pain creased her brow, and Mercy knew better than to ask. Lord knew what the girl had suffered before landing here.

Livvy's brow dipped lower, concern thickening her young voice. "They did not treat you very nicely, did they, ma'am?"

"No, they did not." The throbbing in her skull and festering ache on her shoulder screamed in agreement. And judging by the way her hands were still bound, she could expect more cruelty to follow.

Even so, she forced a small smile. "I am Mercy, and you are very kind. How long have you been here, Livvy?"

The girl's comely shoulders lifted in a shrug. "Long enough that the days and nights are not so cold anymore." Sunlight slanted through a gap in the wall, illuminating crystalline seas, brilliant and without shores, in Livvy's eyes. "I am certain my papa will arrive soon."

Mercy frowned. That wasn't a likely outcome, especially since the girl had already been here for a month or maybe two. Still, loath to snuff out the girl's hope, Mercy lightened her tone. "How do you know this?"

"Well, besides what God has promised me, there is a man here who speaks some English. He told me I am to be traded."

Mercy shifted on the damp dirt, unsure what disturbed her most—that the girl expected to be traded back to her father, or that she apparently knew God as well as Elias and Matthew had. A fresh wave of sorrow nearly drowned her, and she sucked in a shaky breath. Oh, how she missed those men.

"So," she drawled, desperate to put her mind on something other than loss, "God speaks to you, does He?"

"Of course." Livvy unfolded her legs and angled her head. "Do you not hear Him?"

A bitter laugh begged release. She swallowed it down. Must everyone around her perceive the Almighty's voice while the only whisper in her ears was that of doubt? How could she be so blessed with keen eyesight yet lack so woefully in hearing? What was wrong with her? This turn of conversation was no better than dwelling on the gaping loss of Matthew and Elias.

She hung her head. "No." Misery seeped out with the word. "I do not."

Livvy pushed off from the wall and scooted next to her, wrapping her arm about Mercy's shoulders like an old soul comforting a child. "Don't be sad, Miss Mercy. I can tell you what God says. He says to trust. Always. Trust and believe, for He is your only hope."

The urge to shrug off the girl's hold and scamper to the far end of the hut was so strong she trembled. The words were those of her mother, Matthew, and Elias blended into the unwavering voice of a young girl. Could God have been speaking to her all these years, and she'd just not heard it?

"It can't be that simple," she whispered, more to herself than anyone.

"It is." Livvy squeezed her shoulder.

They both turned when the door flap opened.

A warrior entered, just barely, so small was the space. Crouching, he held a bowl in one hand and a water skin in the other. The savory scent of roasted meat filled the hut like a sweet dream. Mercy's stomach cramped as he handed the food to Livvy. To her, he gave nothing but a dark glower.

"Thank you, Ekentee." Livvy nodded at the man, then held out her bowl to Mercy. "Would you like—"

"No!" The man's voice cut sharp, and the girl flinched. "No food for that one, Liv-ee."

"But she is hurt!"

Dark eyes shot to her, piercing as an arrow. "She is dead."

He reached out and grabbed Mercy's arm, yanking her toward the door. Was this it? Were hot coals even now readied to burn the life from her in front of the men who'd killed Matthew and Rufus? And then what? What waited on the other side of a horrendous death?

She dragged her feet. The man yanked harder. A sour taste filled her mouth. She wasn't ready to die. Not now. Not like this. A hot, ragged sob welled in her throat.

God, please, I will trust You. I will! I am nothing. You are all. Oh, that You would save me.

The ragged prayer, desperate and terrible in intensity, raged inside her as the warrior dragged her out the door.

"Where are you taking her?" Livvy's question was muffled into oblivion by the dropping of the door flap.

Mercy blinked, blinded in the brilliance of daylight. The man jerked her to her feet, and she staggered. No men gathered about. No fire blazed either. But if they weren't going to burn the life from her, then. . . *Oh God.* Did they have something worse planned?

Grabbing hold of the rope at her wrists, the man tugged her toward the largest shelter. The tension cut a fresh stripe into her raw flesh.

She stumbled after him. "If I am to be killed, why do we go to the council lodge?"

The man didn't so much as look over his shoulder. His big strides just kept eating up the ground. But he did answer. "Shadow Walker would see you. His eyes will read your manner of death."

Her shoulders sagged. Whoever this Shadow Walker was, if he recognized her as Black-Fox-Running's daughter, then the torture would be horrendous indeed.

A blue haze hovered just above the circle of the five men seated cross-legged around the council fire. Elias blew out one more mouthful of smoke, adding to the ghostly cloud, then passed the pipe to Red Bear. Did the man notice the slight tremor in his fingers?

He forced his mouth to remain pressed shut, a monumental task when everything in him wished to rage against these killers and then tear out and grab Mercy. But rushing anything—the conversation, the smoking, the vengeance kindling inside—could get both him and Mercy killed.

Red Bear's dark eyes shifted to his. For a while he said nothing, just stared, the etched lines in his weathered face neither lifting nor falling. The man wearing Mercy's hat darted his gaze between them both, a purple swell to his nose, mid-bridge. He'd taken a strike recently, a hard one. The other two warriors merely sat like old women content to perch on a front porch and while away the long day—yet there was nothing frail or feeble about the size of their biceps or the breadth of their chests.

"Know you a General Hunter?" The sachem's question floated as ethereally as the suspended smoke.

Mentally, Elias matched the name from face to face in a collection of British officers he stored in his memory for just such a purpose. None corresponded. "No. Why?"

"We have held his daughter long, hoping to earn Six Fingers back in a trade. Still no word."

Elias hid a frown. If that trade happened, a vicious warrior would once again be on the loose.

The pipe passed into Red Bear's hands. Taking a last draw, the sachem held the smoke in his mouth, then set the pipe on the two rocks in front of him. Straightening, he blew out a white cloud, wafting the smoke back to his nostrils with repeated sweeps of his hands.

Beside the occasional pop and crackle of the fire, quiet enveloped them. It was always like this, the interminable breaches in conversation, the placid pace of information exchange, so unlike the clipped and hurried debriefings of the British.

Red Bear lifted his chin, and Elias leaned closer. "The girl will bring a good price elsewhere, or maybe make peace with Dark Thunder."

Elias tensed. Dark Thunder was as notorious as Six Fingers. A brute of a man. A disease amongst humans. The protective side of Elias would have grabbed a tomahawk and raced out to rescue the girl, no matter who she was. But the prudent side of him held every muscle in check. He counted ten slow breaths in and ten out before he spoke again. "Where did you take this girl?"

Only Red Bear's eyes moved, his gaze slipping as gracefully as the passing of a pipe to the man seated at Elias's right hand.

Next to him, the warrior answered Red Bear's silent command. "The girl was taken en route to Fort Bedford. A small party, two women, the girl, and four soldiers. Hunter is a stupid man to let his women traverse these woods."

Two more women? He chewed on that thought like a gristly piece of meat, not able to spit it out but not wanting to swallow it either. This time he counted twenty breaths. "You hold one girl but not the women?"

"They were of weak blood," the man next to him rumbled, disdain darkening his tone.

Elias's brow twitched as he held his expression in check. The girl must be something special, indeed, to have escaped the blade of the warrior who clearly harbored a sizable abhorrence toward white females.

Outside the lodge, footsteps neared, one set strong and determined, the other with a drag-slide cadence. Drawing in a deep breath of the sweet, left-over tobacco scent, he forced his face to remain blank—which took every bit of his will when Mercy was pulled stoop-shouldered into the shelter like a dog on a leash.

Her captor released his hold of her bound hands, then thrust her forward with a shove between the shoulder blades. Elias bit down hard, tongue caught between his back teeth, and savored the slow leak of blood in his mouth. Any outward show of hostility would be a death warrant—and he'd had his fill of those.

Mercy, God bless her, lifted her nose in the air, refusing to look at any of them. Purple bruised one of her eyes. A cut marred her cheek, and her bottom lip swelled at one end. Her gown was torn, and on her left shoulder, the fabric was matted with dried blood. More blood stained her bodice and sullied her neck, but near as he could tell, not hers. She looked nearly as awful as he had that first day she'd lain eyes on him—but this was entirely different. Not only was she a woman, but the one he'd lay down his life for. . .and just might have to in the end.

For the briefest of moments, her gaze slipped, and she glanced around the circle of men, then froze on him before resetting her proud stance. It hadn't been for long, but in that eternity, the awful questions in her eyes branded him a traitor all over again. But worse was the disappointment haunting those brown pools. Roiling, gut-wrenching disappointment shone deep and dark. The frail bridge of trust they had constructed during the past weeks collapsed to a thousand jagged-edged pieces—and he gasped from the loss, desperate for air.

Red Bear swept his hand toward her. "This is the woman Nadowa believes to be Kahente. You know her?"

A burning ember stuck in his throat. What he said from now on would mean either life or death for Mercy. He swallowed. "Yes."

Red Bear leaned forward, not much, but the movement signaled intense interest. "So this is the daughter of Black-Fox-Running?"

Was Mercy the daughter of a chieftain? He could believe it simply by the way valor straightened her shoulders and courage shone in her eyes.

But thank the sweet Lord she'd never told him her true lineage, for he could honestly say, "I can tell you exactly who she is. . . . she is my wife."

Red Bear leaned back, clearly disappointed.

CHAPTER 25

Shadow Walker has taken a wife?" The question traveled on a ring of whispers, repeated by each man seated at the fire. Disbelief hung heavy in the smoke-thickened air.

Elias slipped a glance toward Mercy, who yet stood willow straight, brown eyes unblinking. Thank God she did not understand the Wyandot language, for if she did, she'd no doubt pounce like a wildcat and scratch his face off for claiming her as his wife. It may not have been the only way to protect her—but it was the best he could think of at the moment. If he'd merely denied her kinship to Black-Fox-Running, at best she'd still have been sold. At worst, they would continue with their plans to burn her come evening.

He turned his face to Red Bear. "We were wed back at Fort Wilderness."

"He is a traitor!" Across from him, the sinewy native wearing Mercy's hat yanked out his tomahawk, until a halting shift of Red Bear's eyes forced the man to lay it on his lap.

Even so, murder darkened the voice of the sachem, lowering it to a growl. "How is it enemy gates open to you?"

Panic spread like a swarm of biting ants over his body. What to say? This whole situation was a tinderbox. The wrong words would spark an explosion.

Give me wisdom, Lord, for I am at a loss. Spare us, leastwise Mercy.

While his mind scrambled to hunt down a plausible answer, he sat motionless, this time thankful for the tradition of unhurried speech. Time stretched like a taut bowstring about to snap. If he remained silent much longer, Red Bear would see him tortured next to Mercy.

God, please. . .

And then it came to him, a gentle sigh of a thought. He tucked his chin, a bull about to charge. He didn't have to answer, not if he parried with another question.

"Tell me, Red Bear, how is it your men knew the wagons' whereabouts?" He narrowed his eyes. "You and I both know that was no chance meeting."

Red Bear's eyes widened to dark caverns. "*You?* You are the one behind this?"

Elias clenched his jaw. Behind what? Was there a spy inside the fort feeding information to the French and their allies?

Once again, he scrambled for an answer. If he said yes, they would pry for more information. And if no, then he was back to being a traitor in their eyes. What to do?

He met the sachem's stare and said nothing.

Each pop of the fire was a gunshot. The breath of every man a dragon's. So much tension filled the lodge that even Mercy shifted her stance.

A quiver wavered on Red Bear's lips, and Elias watched the movement with a wary eye. Would a shout issue forth and a knife slit his throat?

But then the man's lips parted, his teeth bared—and a great laugh ripped out of the sachem, so hearty that the feather decorating his forelock shook and moisture leaked from the corners of his eyes. All joined in, even the villain in Mercy's hat. The warrior next to Elias jabbed him with a playful nudge of his elbow.

In the merriment, Elias once again slipped a covert glance at Mercy. She stared straight ahead, face unreadable, a stubborn set to her jaw. And he didn't blame her. Not one bit. Oh, what torturous thoughts she must be thinking.

He turned back to the sachem. Through it all, he remained stoic. Emotion shown too soon was like a ripple on a pond; he could never know on which banks the gesture may land him.

Finally, Red Bear's laughter faded. "Once again, your mysterious ways serve you well, Shadow Walker. But tell me, my brother"—the sachem's smile vanished, the lines of his face sharpening into a fierce snarl—"if this woman is your wife, why does she not look upon you?"

His chest seized. She truly would be the death of him. She'd shown no sign, not one acknowledgment that she even knew him. A proper wife would've flung herself into his arms by now. He breathed in a measured rhythm, fighting for yet another answer.

"She is overcome," he said at length.

"That one knows no fear!" The man with the hat half-rose from his seat. "Two-Pace's blood cries out from the ground because of her."

Elias's brow twitched from want of raising his eyebrows. She took down one of their warriors? Lord, have mercy indeed.

Ignoring the hotheaded warrior, Elias kept his gaze on Red Bear and tried another trail. "I did not say it was fear that overcomes her. The truth is, great sachem, that the woman is angry with me. We exchanged hot words, and I left her behind. Likely, she thinks I abandoned her."

Elias held his breath. Would the man believe such a tale?

Lifting his face, Red Bear studied Mercy as he might scour a fort's walls for the best place to breach. She stood the assault without a flinch—and the admiration in Elias's heart grew tenfold. What other woman could withstand such a hard-edged stare and not swoon?

A small chuckle rumbled in Red Bear's throat. "Who can know the mind of a woman?"

Elias planted his hands on the fur-lined floor and pushed up before the man could probe any further. "You have given the information I came seeking, great sachem, namely my wife's whereabouts. I will take her and leave in peace. May the sun rise, the rains fall, and the moon shine from a cloudless sky until we meet again."

The sachem lifted his hand, but not in a return blessing. It was a command. A warning. "Take the woman out."

Elias dropped back to the ground, a spectacular feat, since everything in him strained to run after her.

Black gazes darted between the men. Silence crept back in like an unwelcome guest. Everyone, it seemed, held their breath.

"You are free to go, Shadow Walker." Red Bear swept his hand toward the open door. "Yet the woman stays. She is not mine to give."

"But she *is* mine!" Elias pressed his lips flat. Too late.

The warrior in Mercy's hat slid his hand to his tomahawk, his fingers curling like a threat around the handle. Red Bear shook his head at him. The man did not loosen his hold, but neither did he raise it. Would the sachem let such defiance stand?

Red Bear merely angled his head back at Elias. "Nadowa brought the woman in. It is your word against his."

"I tell you true, Red Bear." He swallowed, desperately trying to temper his tone. Making the same mistake twice could send that tomahawk sailing across the fire and into his skull. "The woman belongs to me."

Mercy's hat sank lower on the warrior's brow, shadowing a gaze already black as a new moon night. "You should not have lost her in the first place."

A mighty roar welled in his throat, but he clamped down on it and all the outrage begging to let loose. If he let one word slip, too many would charge out along with it. Though it galled hotter than a branding iron to offer no defense, he couldn't very well admit he'd been bound and knocked out, for that would make him weak in their eyes—and strength was what he needed now.

He threw back his shoulders and faced Red Bear, charging ahead before he changed his mind. "Then I challenge Nadowa."

Audible gasps swept around the lodge like an unholy wind.

Red Bear gave a sharp nod. "So be it."

A smile slashed across the face of the man in the hat. "Shadow Walker is not as wise as the legends say. This day you will die, for Nadowa is unbeaten."

⚜

Mercy tromped after the warrior leading her, heedless of the way each stamp of her feet juddered clear up to her skull. Plenty of slack hung in the lead between her and the man. And why not? She'd rather hole up with Livvy and wait to die than spend one more breath in the presence of Elias Dubois, the scoundrel. The betrayer. Had he planned the whole ambush? Was he the reason Matthew and Rufus were dead?

She kicked a rock, and it skittered into the ankle of the man leading her. The warrior pierced her with a scowl over his shoulder, as black as her raging thoughts. Not only had Elias spoken the enemy language like a native, he'd sat as a tribal member, completely at home with the band of killers. With her own nostrils she'd breathed in the smoky-sweet scent of a passed pipe, a lingering indictment that justified her charge. The man was a traitor. A filthy, lying-tongued conspirator.

But why did that accusation crawl in and unearth such bitter ground in her heart? She'd known all along Elias would be imprisoned as a defector upon reaching Fort Edward. Charges like that wouldn't just disappear, no matter what she desired.

Her step faltered. *Oh no. A hundred times no.* That was exactly what she'd hoped for. His freedom. His loyalty. His love. She scowled. When had she become such a moon-eyed ridiculous woman?

She dug her feet in harder. No more. Not one second more would she yield to base emotions. Ramping up her pace, she drew near the warrior and nudged him in the back. "You. A word."

The man swung around, black eyes smoldering, arm raised to strike.

She flinched but held her ground.

In an astonishing move, the warrior's rock-hard bicep relaxed, and he lowered his hand. "I spare you for the sake of Shadow Walker, but do not push me."

All those times Elias had snuck up on her suddenly made sense as she connected the Indian name to the man. But no matter. Whatever he was called, he clearly wielded some kind of power. What had he possibly said that might stay the hand of the warrior in front of her?

She lifted her chin, a poor attempt at dignity with the blood and bruises on her face, but she'd not cower. "Tell me what is to come."

Hatred glimmered in his eyes, yet his mouth leveled to a straight line. Nothing but the caw of some ravens and sounds of the camp answered her request. If the man had no intention of answering her, why did he not turn away? Yank on her leash? Backhand her as roughly as the brute who'd stolen her hat?

Finally, he sniffed, as if she were the stench of all that rotted in the world. "This night's challenge determines your fate, woman."

"A challenge." She drew out the word, mind awhir. "Who fights?"

"Nadowa." The warrior looked down his nose at her and narrowed his eyes. "And your husband."

"But I have no—" *Husband?* She shut her mouth. What on earth had Elias told them?

A deep voice cut in behind her—Elias's—speaking guttural words she couldn't understand. The warrior holding her tether dropped the lead and retreated to the small shelter holding Livvy. Widening his stance, the Indian stood in front of the door and folded his arms, face entirely unreadable.

"Are you well?"

Elias's question turned her around, and she stared up into blue eyes. Furrows lined his brow as if he were concerned. Hah! Why the show? She barely contained a snort. "Does it matter?"

"Of course it does. Why do you think I came?" He grabbed her by the arms and leaned in close, staring deep. "What has gotten into you?"

"Truth, *Shadow Walker*." She shot the name like the firing of a musket.

He winced. Good. May he feel the pain for such duplicity as sharply as the arrow through Matthew's neck.

"Mercy, I—" His voice was thick and torn at the edges. A small triumph, that. Perhaps he had a seed of humanity left somewhere inside him.

He cleared his throat. "I admit there is much you do not know, but trust me, my silence on matters is necessary."

"Trust you?" She gaped, hating his demand, hating even more the way his smell of smoke and danger tingled along every nerve. "That is a very pretty sentiment coming from your lips."

"There is no time to explain, but I vow that I shall get you out of here. I promise."

For a single, horrifying moment, she believed the passion sparking in his gaze. And more, she wanted him to make everything right. To not be a traitor. To just be a man—one she could love.

Sickened, she jerked up her bound hands and shoved him in the chest. "I don't need your help."

Her voice thundered down on him—and the entire camp. Without turning his head, Elias slipped his gaze side to side, then landed back on her.

"Forgive me, Mercy," he whispered.

"For what? For making me believe you cared—?"

His mouth crushed against hers, stopping her words. Warm. Firm. Neither devouring nor gentle in intensity. It was the kind of kiss that broke her wide open and held her up all in the same embrace, and she leaned into it, her own body a traitor of the worst degree. She was a desert, and he the only water she'd ever wanted to drink.

A low drone of laughter slapped her back to reality. What was she doing? She jerked away, pulse beating out of control, and wiped her mouth on her sleeve.

"What was that for?" she hissed.

"Your life." Once again he grabbed her arms and pulled her close, and before she could wrench from his hold, he bent and spoke for her ears alone. "These people think you are my wife. Play the part well or we both die."

Chapter 26

"You scared, Miss Mercy?"

Was she? She should be. Sitting in the dark of a guarded hut. A harsh language in harsher voices leaching in like a disease from outside the bark walls. And soon she'd belong to either a broad-faced Wyandot or a sweet-talking traitor. But wonder of all wonders, the peace that had crawled into her soul earlier in the day when she'd cried out to God had unpacked and set up house in her soul.

She reached for Livvy's hand with both of hers, still bound, and squeezed the girl's fingers. "No, I am not frightened, leastwise not overmuch."

Livvy squeezed back. "I surely do wish they would have cut that rope from your hands."

"No doubt they soon—"

She jerked her face toward the removal of the framed bark door. Torchlight outside painted a black silhouette of a man. . .and outlined the shape of a floppy felt hat atop his head. She released Livvy's fingers and clenched her hands together so that her knuckles cracked. Surely this thief hadn't been part of the bargain, had he?

She launched toward him. He flinched. And a smile ghosted her lips. Did he yet feel the pain of her earlier head butt?

Grabbing hold of her arm, he dug his fingers into her flesh and yanked her into the night. He hauled her to a ring of men assembled in a loose circle near a large fire. Spectral light flicked over their bodies, painting a nightmarish scene of fiendish ghouls. Two parted, making room for her and her captor. The thrill of a fight brightened the eyes of every man there.

Directly across the flattened patch of ground stood the sachem. Golden gorgets hung from his neck, reflecting flickers of firelight. He stood like a god, arm raised, ready to call into action a battle to the death.

At center, two bare-chested men faced off, ten paces apart, but only one of them commanded her attention. Elias stood with his chin high and shoulders relaxed, at attention but not. A strange mix of nonchalance and wolf about to spring. Though she'd thought on it the better part of the day, she still had no answer as to why he was about to risk his life for her. He could have run free, escaping the locked cell that awaited him at Fort Edward. Why had he bothered coming after her? That question, and a host of others, crowded uninvited and unanswered inside her head, making it ache all the way to her jaws.

Without warning, the sachem dropped his arm.

And the big man charged.

Elias feinted right, then immediately swung back and struck. His first punch glanced off the big man's chin. Mercy did not know much about hand-to-hand battle, but if that was the best Elias could offer, he'd be dead within—

His second fist flew like a musket shot, catching her and the big man off guard. Elias's blow sank deep into the man's stomach, punching him back and doubling him over. Before he regained balance, Elias was on him, knuckles flying, blood splattering, driving him back.

Mercy gasped. She'd always sensed an underlying danger about Elias Dubois. Now she understood why. He struck so hard and fast, he beat the man toward her side of the circle.

Three paces from her, the big man teetered off balance, tipping her way. She retreated, only to be stopped by the chest of the man behind her. But at the last moment, Elias's attacker used his momentum to reach down and swipe up a handful of dirt on his upswing.

"Elias! Duck!"

Too late. The man whipped around and flung the dirt in Elias's eyes. He staggered back, blinded, and furiously rubbed away the grit.

Next to her, a warrior rumbled something low, then held out a hunting knife. Elias's attacker grabbed it and charged.

"No!" she shouted. "Elias, he has a—"

A hand covered her mouth, jamming her head backward against muscle and bone. If Elias's blood was spilled here and now, she'd belong to a killer with no honor.

Elias blinked, the whites of his eyes stark against the dirt on his face. He crouched low, hands out, with nothing to parry but the flesh of his bare arms.

The man advanced, slashing the knife downward. Elias twisted and reached for the man's knife arm with both hands—but the move left his belly open. The big man kneed him in the gut, and as Elias loosed his hold, the man sliced the blade in an arc.

A red line split open on Elias's chest, and she could do nothing but watch as his lifeblood began to ooze out and run down to his breeches in long drips. Elias reeled, and her heart broke. Traitor or not, she did not want him to die.

The men around her howled their approval, and the big man advanced.

Mercy blinked away tears. Elias didn't stand a chance, not against a man a head taller and hornet mad, gripping a deadly stinger.

With each thrust of the knife, Elias backed away, until he crashed into the line of warriors behind him. The men shoved him forward.

A slow smile spread like a stain across the big man's face, the kind of grin only a nightmare such as this could produce. A slow chant began quietly then gained in strength as each warrior in the circle joined in.

Elias's attacker took another swipe, this time kicking his leg forward to tangle with Elias's and knock him off balance.

But on the downswing, Elias spun around to the man's back, seized the arm without a knife, and elbowed the beast at the base of the neck. The big man dropped to one knee—and Elias made a grab for the weapon.

This time the blade came away in his hand. With a mighty roar, Elias slashed a gaping cut across the top of the big man's thigh, then jabbed a kick to his chest.

The man landed on his back, air whumping out of his lungs.

Elias pounced, pinning one of the man's arms with his knee, his free hand pinioning the other arm, and raised the blade high.

The chanting stopped. So did time.

Mercy froze. The muscles of the man holding her tensed. What was Elias waiting for?

Then he struck hard, hitting the warrior in the head with the hilt of the knife. Lightning fast, he raised the blade again and stabbed it into the ground next to the man's ear.

Panting, Elias stood. He flicked blood and sweat from his face and staggered a moment, then faced the sachem. Deadly silence filled the night. Mercy held her breath.

Elias's ragged voice cut the air in words she couldn't understand. The sachem glowered. Warriors to her left and right all grumbled and growled. What on earth had Elias said?

With a wild glance, she looked for the native who spoke English and spied him two men away from her. She wrenched her head free from the brute's hand on her mouth and called out, "What does he say?"

"He tells Red Bear he gives back Nadowa and asks for you in return."

Her blood drained to her feet, and the world started to spin. This was not to be borne, leaving a warrior down but not dead. Surely Elias knew the rules when he'd asked for the challenge. The rules demanded blood.

But if not Nadowa's or Elias's, then whose?

❦

Fire burned a swath across Elias's chest. Thank God the slice wasn't deep, or he'd be the one stretched out on the dirt. Every muscle quivered. Every bone screamed. He wore each of his twenty-seven years like chains too heavy to lift. But if that was what it took to free Mercy, then so be it.

He met and matched Red Bear's stare. How generous was the sachem feeling? For it was no small thing that he'd left the knife blade sunk into the ground next to Nadowa's ear instead of in the warrior's chest.

Firelight glinted in Red Bear's eyes, fearsome as the flames of hell. "There is no honor in this. You shame Nadowa by letting him live. If I let the woman go while there is still breath in his body, it shames us all."

Armed with nothing but an arsenal of words, Elias loaded and shot, praying for a direct hit. "Yet the blood price has been paid, Great One. I wear Nadowa's. He wears mine." He lifted his hands, knuckles split, the splatter of the warrior's blood mingled with his own. "And if you let my wife and me go free, I offer a payment that will benefit all, granting you far more victory and glory than the taking of your finest warrior's life."

A rush of whispers blew behind him, some laced with interest, others scoffing, and a few rumbling with restrained rage.

Red Bear folded his arms, chin held high. "Speak."

"I offer you the very riches your men were looking for when they found my wife."

The sachem's eyes widened. Indians weren't usually greedy for gold, but not so with Red Bear. This shrewd old rascal knew when an opportunity wafted beneath his nose. "How do you know this?"

"Why do you think your men found nothing in those wagons they ransacked? I was the one who hid the cargo out of necessity. I will lead you there come morning."

A slow smile curved the sides of Red Bear's mouth. "Shadow Walker is a man of many surprises. The trade is good. The woman is yours. Come and let us feast."

"Your offer, Great One, is well met." He stepped closer, speaking for only the sachem's ears. "But I have been without my woman for a long time. Grant us shelter alone for the night."

The implication drew a chuckle from the older man.

God, forgive me, Elias prayed silently, for the insinuation and the lie. But had not Abraham done the same when he alluded to his wife as his sister in order to save both their lives? Granted, this was the reverse and he was no Abraham, but even so, far more lives than his or Mercy's depended upon this. *Please, God.*

Red Bear tipped his chin toward the farthest hut. "It is yours."

Elias pivoted and walked tall, hiding a wince with every step. He crossed back to where two men helped Nadowa to stand. The warrior's head lolled, still groggy from the bite of the knife hilt. Some men might gloat over such a triumph, but he found no pleasure in seeing a beaten man. Ah, but he was weary to death of fighting and blood. He crouched and worked the knife free from the dirt.

Mercy stood unattended now, like a lost little girl abandoned at the side of a road. He strode toward her, her luminous eyes watching his approach. Warriors filtered past him, drawn by the fire and the savory tang of roasted venison.

On the way, he stopped and lurched sideways, snatching Mercy's hat off the head of the man who'd stolen it. The man whirled, murder glinting off the silver of his drawn blade.

Again? He'd not yet bandaged the slash on his chest. Even so, he hunkered into a fighting stance, hat in one hand, knife in the other.

Red Bear's voice thundered in the dark. "Shadow Walker reclaims his wife's hat and will pay for it come sunrise. Let it go, Standing Fist."

Working his lips, the man spat at Elias's feet, then stalked off to the fire.

Elias breathed in relief and blew out a prayer. *Thank You, God.* Then he turned and closed the distance between him and Mercy. Reaching out, he placed her hat atop hair so loosened and wild, it spread down to her waist like a mantle. Despite the affront of her capture, the cut on her cheek and the bruise near her eye, the woman was a beauty.

But best of all, and wonder of wonders, the disappointment in her eyes had vanished, replaced by a sheen of awe.

"Hold out your hands," he said gently.

She lifted her wrists. The leather thong cut into her skin, and for a moment he regretted not having killed Nadowa for such a violation.

"I don't know how you managed all that, but"—a gasp cut off her words as he worked the knife between her wrists—"I thank you. . .Shadow Walker."

He flashed a grin as her bindings fell to the ground. "I would say it was my pleasure, but in all honesty, I can think of far more pleasurable things than grappling with an angry Wyandot."

"Seems they are not angry anymore." Mercy rubbed the tender skin at the base of her sleeves. "What did you say to turn away the sachem's wrath?"

"Come, and I will tell you." He led her past the warriors already tearing great bites of venison from two does brought in earlier. Lewd comments followed him all the way to the makeshift longhouse, most about his manliness, some about her curves. All about what they expected would be going on once he was alone with Mercy. Sweet heavens, but he was glad she did not understand the language. It was humiliating enough that he did.

So he forced his mind onto a different trail and glanced at Mercy. "I have not seen Rufus or heard word of him spoken. Was he taken along with you?"

"No." She shook her head. "I assumed he was killed, like Matthew."

He grunted. "There was no evidence. His body was not there. These warriors would have had no reason to haul him off and kill him elsewhere."

"You think he is still alive?"

"Hard to say. But Lord knows the man was ever good at hiding."

He shoved aside the door flap to the shelter and allowed Mercy to pass. Once he stepped inside, his body yearned to stretch out on one of the furs lining the pallets on either side of the wall. Instead, he strode over to where he'd left his few belongings and reached for his shirt—then gasped. Pain seared like a branding iron.

Mercy's light step caught up behind him, her soft voice a soothing balm. "Let me bandage that chest of yours."

Despite the cold sweat dotting his brow, heat ignited a fire in his belly at the thought of her warm fingers tending to his bare skin. "I can manage," he ground out.

"Not easily."

He blew out a breath. It would take him longer to bind up his wound on his own. And time was scarce.

He turned. "Fine. But I will be tending to that wound on your shoulder as soon as you are finished. Ah-ah!" He wagged his finger at the pert angle of her chin. "Do not tell me that injury is not festering something fierce."

Furrows marred her brow as she frowned, yet she snapped into action. Low light from an untended fire at the center of the shelter grew as she lobbed wood onto it from a pile dumped near the door. He sank onto the hardened dirt next to the flames, shivers creeping over the bare skin of his back. He always felt this way after a fight, all jittery and sharp-edged.

Mercy lugged over a skin of water, set it at his side, then said, "Close your eyes."

What the devil did she have in mind? "Why?"

"I believe you asked me to trust you once. I expect the same courtesy."

How was he to argue with that? He closed his eyes.

A bit of rustling ensued, then the distinct sound of ripping fabric. A smile twitched his lips. Of course. She aimed to bandage him up good with the cloth of her petticoat.

"I am finished."

His eyes barely opened when cold water doused him from overhead, shocking and nipping all at once. "Sweet mercy! A little warning would be nice."

"What did you think? That I would bind up a dirty wound?" She clicked her tongue like a mother. "Arms up, please."

He complied, and while she worked to wrap the torn strips of fabric tight against his torn skin, he wondered at her complete ease with the interior of a warrior longhouse and a half-naked man to tend to. But then again, perhaps she truly had grown up in a home such as this.

"Why did you not tell me Black-Fox-Running was your father?" he pondered aloud.

"My past is of no account."

He grabbed her hand as it crossed to the front of his chest and pulled her close. "Everything about you is of account, leastwise to me. Surely you know that by now."

She stared, long and hard, and for some odd reason, tears glistened watery and bright in the firelight. What on earth was she thinking?

She pulled away without a word and went back to wrapping the binding around his chest. The woman was a mystery. A glorious, beautiful mystery.

"And your mother? Let me guess—" He grunted as she yanked the cloth tight at his back. "Was she the daughter of some high-ranking official?"

"Nay, my mother was nothing special save for her claim of her forefathers being the first to settle at Plimouth." Mercy's words kept time to the deft movement of her fingers. "Even so, I am of late coming to view her strength and courage as rivaling that of my father."

She retrieved his shirt and held it out. "As long as you don't go challenging any more warriors, that should hold."

"No more challenging." He grabbed the shirt and eased it over his head, then stood. "But we do have some traveling. We leave as soon as I tend to that shoulder of yours."

"Turn your back, and I will tend it myself."

"But—"

His rebuttal died a fast death from her murderous scowl. Perhaps it was better for her to tend to such a flesh-baring task. He crossed back to where his hunting frock, his belt, his newly acquired knife, and Mercy's blade lay on a fur.

"Why do we leave in the dark of night? It is not safe." The sound of fabric rustled, followed by water trickling off skin—and he nearly turned around when she sucked in an audible breath.

So, he had been right. That wound of hers did hurt something fierce. Blast the man who'd hurt her!

"Elias?"

He jammed his arms into the sleeves of his hunting frock more forcefully than necessary. "We need to make it back to the gold before Red Bear's pack of warriors."

She sucked in another gasp, then blew out a long breath. The sound of her pain twisted his gut.

"Why would they return to naught but empty wagons? They couldn't know. . ." This time the air rushing into her mouth was a threat. "You told them!"

He buckled his belt and snugged the hunting knife at his waist, glad to finally have a weapon, especially with the venom in Mercy's voice. "I promised them the gold. And I am no traitor, if that is what you are thinking. It was the price for your freedom."

"Why did you not simply kill that man?"

At the sound of her next sharp intake, he wondered that very thing. The man should've paid for his rough handling of Mercy. And he would one day, unless God's grace saved him from the same darkness he himself used to wallow in.

His finger traced the hilt of the knife at his side. "It is God's place to take a life, not mine."

More water trickled, followed by a long silence. Finally, she murmured, "You are a complicated man, Elias Dubois. Oh, and you can turn around now."

"You are quite the tangle yourself." He snatched up her knife and strode back to her. A worn piece of petticoat peeked out from the rip on her shoulder, her wound as freshly bound as his. She'd endured it all with but a few gasps. What kind of woman did that?

The kind of woman I want.

He planted his feet wide to keep from staggering. The realization hit him harder than the beating he'd just taken. He wanted this woman so much the yearning ached, warm and pulsing, in his soul.

"Mercy, I—" He what? He pressed his lips shut. This was mad. Heaven help him, now was definitely *not* the time for love. It wouldn't be fair to her for him to spout feelings he couldn't back up with action. Lord knew if they would even make it out of this mess alive.

He shoved down the words he wanted to say and instead held out her knife in an open palm. "I found your knife."

Her gaze shot from the blade to him, admiration shining vividly in her brown eyes—a look he'd never tire of if he lived to be an old, old man.

"You never stop surprising me, Shadow Walker." This time his name was a purr instead of an indictment.

And he liked it.

She reached for the knife, her slim fingers brushing against his skin, leaving a trail of wildfire.

Oh, hang it all. He wrapped his hand around hers and pulled her to him. His heart beat a drum against his chest, eclipsing the pain of battle.

She came willingly and lifted her face to his. "It was no small thing what you did for me, but you have yet to tell me why." Her gaze bored deep into his. "Why did you not just run away to freedom?"

CHAPTER 27

Mercy held her breath, hoping for. . .what? That Elias would speak words of love here in the middle of a Wyandot war camp? Was that what she wanted? Though she did her best to ignore the obvious answer, a charge of warmth shot through her from head to toe.

She did. More than anything. She wanted to belong to the scruff-faced man staring at her with impossibly blue eyes and a mouth she'd tasted sweet and strong.

And that scared her more than a raging war party of warriors.

"Running off was never a choice for me, Mercy. I knew what they would do with you." A storm of anger and restraint clenched his jaw. Then, just like that, the squall passed. The sharp lines on his brow bowed into a grief so great, the weight of it pressed down on her.

He swallowed, his throat bobbing, and his voice came out husky despite the action. "I could not let that happen. Not to you."

The intensity in his gaze reached out, pulling her closer. Without thinking, she rose to her toes and brushed her lips lightly against his bruised cheek, the rasp of his whiskers a powerful reminder of his manliness. A tremor shook through him, through her, through the heavens themselves.

"There is much honor in you, Elias Dubois," she whispered against his skin. "More than I credited."

For a moment, he leaned into her touch, sharing his warmth and strength; then he pulled back, releasing his hold of her. "We need to leave. Find what food you can. I will see to finding some weapons."

He turned and strode to rummage through some Indian's belongings . . .and the loss of his touch was staggering.

But of course he was right. If they were to retrieve the gold with any hope of keeping ahead of a pack of angry warriors, every minute now counted a hundredfold. She joined him in ransacking warriors' belongings for strips of jerky or handfuls of pemmican. Not much was on hand, but she found enough that they would have something to eat along the way.

Wood snapping turned her around. Behind her Elias broke arrows, shaft after shaft. . .which gave her an idea. She reached for a nearby bow and, yanking out her knife, slit the string in two. They fell into a destructive cadence, him snapping, her slicing.

"What is your plan?" she asked while they worked, hoping to somehow ask for Livvy to be incorporated into whatever scheme he had in mind. She couldn't leave the girl behind, especially when the warriors discovered their duplicity. Livvy would bear the brunt of their anger, maybe even suffer a revenge killing. A shiver snaked across her shoulders. She wouldn't wish that death on anyone.

Elias finished the last of the arrows, then faced her. "We get the girl, then the horses—"

"You know of Livvy?" Her brows shot to her hat brim, and it was a fight to keep from gaping. Did the man read minds as well as walk invisible? Her admiration for him grew, blocking out all her reasons as to why she shouldn't trust him.

"Red Bear mentioned another captive besides you." He flashed a smile. "But I'm not promising it will be an easy endeavor. Are you ready for this?"

She slit the last bowstring and dropped the useless bow, then slung a pouch of food over her shoulder. "I am now."

He led her to the back door and nudged the flap aside. Leaning out, he glanced left to right, then turned to her. "Stay low. We will work our way to the girl, and I shall keep watch while you cut a small flap in the back of the hut, taking out any who chance your way. Keep the girl quiet and make for the woods. I will double back for the horses and meet up with you."

Reaching out, he brushed back a rogue coil of hair hanging in her eyes, his fingers lingering against the skin of her brow. Then he disappeared out the door.

She followed, crouching low, trying hard to mimic his moves. It was a risky thing, this escape. Deadly. Her step nearly faltered with the impossibility of what they were about to undertake. . .but had not God kept her safe thus far? A foreign yet welcome surge of faith urged her onward.

Elias moved ahead, stationing himself at the edge of the trees, twenty paces or so from the rear of the hut. The distance was a gaping flatland, making anyone who crossed it a target to be shot. But it gave Elias a wide enough view to spot trouble should any arise.

Dropping to all fours, Mercy crept through weeds and shin-high grasses. She stopped inches away from the bark wall and listened hard. A song chanted on the night air. A few whoops. Some laughter and a holler. It seemed all entertained themselves at the fire—hopefully.

She pulled out her knife and started cutting. Ripping, really. The noise of the blade tearing into dried linden bark scratched a dead giveaway of her location. What Livvy could be thinking was anyone's guess.

Eventually she tore enough off to yank away a big square of bark. "Livvy?" she whispered.

Wide eyes peeked out of the darkness. Livvy opened her mouth, and Mercy shot her fingers to the girl's lips, then beckoned with the same finger for the girl to crawl out.

Livvy's shoulders wedged in the small space—too small for her to fit through. Mercy motioned for the girl to retreat, then stabbed her knife in again, sawing a larger hole. Her blade stuck once, and in that moment of silence, a terrifying sound crept closer from the front of the hut.

Footsteps.

She froze. What to do? She'd never make it to the safety of Elias's side before being seen.

❧

Shallow breaths. Shallow. Anything more and the wound on Elias's chest stabbed sharply. It was difficult to maintain the rhythm though, as he squinted in the dark, concentrating hard on why Mercy might've stopped working.

He scanned the area—and his breath stopped completely. A black man-shape strode away from the fire, ghoulish light outlining his broad shoulders and determined step. And each step brought the beast closer to where Mercy lay low at the back of the holding hut. If she ripped off one more piece of that bark, he'd hear.

For the hundredth time this never-ending night, Elias prayed. *Lord, have mercy.*

Then he slipped the knife from his side and crept forward.

And while You're at it, forgive me, Lord, for what I am about to do.

A hacking cough filled the night air, adding to the ambient noise from warriors who'd swigged too much rotgut. What on earth? The cough issued from inside the hut. . .didn't it?

Elias paused and cocked his head. The coughing barked louder.

The man stopped, his head angling too.

Mercy yanked off another piece of the shelter with the next spate of hacking. The black hole gaped larger, and she dove in.

"Quiet!" The girl couldn't possibly know what the man said, but the threat of his tone was enough.

And as soon as the bark chunks appeared from inside the hut and blocked—mostly—the hole in the back, the coughing stopped.

Elias's lips curved. The girl just might be an asset instead of a hindrance.

But the small smile vanished as the man stalked ahead and rounded the side of the hut. Had he heard something other than the coughing?

The man planted his feet directly in front of the hole. He didn't crouch to study it though, but faced the woods instead of the hut.

Even so, Elias dropped to his belly, fighting a gasp from the pain, and skulked ahead, inch by inch. Would he have enough time to drop the man before he could yell an alarm?

A new sound stopped him once again. Liquid hitting grass, sprinkling in a stream. Elias loosened his fingers from the death grip on his knife hilt, waited until the man finished relieving himself, then tucked the blade away. Apparently far too much drink was flowing this night.

As soon as the man's footsteps faded, Elias crawled back to the safety of the trees, with Mercy and the girl not far behind. When they caught up, he jerked his head for Mercy to follow, her face pale in the darkness. Would that he could gather her in his arms and hold her until her trembling stopped. But no time. Would there ever be enough time?

He glanced at the girl, head even with Mercy's shoulder, blond hair a beacon. Surely he must look as frightening as one of the Wyandot warriors here in the dark, but she made no noise, not even a whimper. Brave girl.

Wheeling about, he led them from shadow to shadow, flinching every time the girl cracked a stick beneath her step. Not often, but enough that should another native venture aside to relieve himself, their movement would be detected. . .unless by now everyone's senses were skewed. One could hope.

And he did.

A quarter mile later, he spied an upturned hemlock, roots and dirt ripped up to form a chest-high wall. With a sweep of his arm, he ushered Mercy and the girl to shelter behind it.

He crouched in front of Mercy, whispering low. "I need one of your petticoats."

The whites of two pairs of eyes shone bright in the dark.

"What?" Mercy breathed.

But now was not the time to explain. "You heard me." He held out his hand.

Turning her back to him, she shimmied a bit and worked loose her under petticoat, then handed over the ragged bit of fabric. The girl shrank back, eyeing them both.

He winked at Mercy. "I owe you one."

Then he ripped the cloth into long strips and set off to locate the horses. It wasn't hard. The smell of horseflesh drew him and any other predator. Hopefully not many men guarded the animals.

He slowed as he came upon a small clearing on the north side of camp. Setting down the pile of bindings, he pulled his knife and melded against the shadows, traveling the perimeter. Only four horses dotted the area. What had happened to the other four? Not that he minded, as it made his task easier, but it made no sense they had left behind the others. Something about this wasn't right—but with Mercy and Livvy waiting on him, he'd have to puzzle over the mystery later.

Near as he could tell, only one brave kept watch—or should have been. The man hunkered down, his back against a heap of bridles and a piece of meat in both hands. His teeth ripped and his lips smacked.

Elias glanced heavenward, grateful once again that a God so big deigned to answer the prayers of a man like him.

He retrieved the bindings, then crept behind the man while he was still busy eating. A quick crack to his head knocked him sideways. As Elias bound and gagged him, he couldn't help but wonder how many more skulls he'd be required to smack this night.

Weary beyond measure, he rose and began loosing horses. He slapped two on the rump, driving them out in different directions into the night. The other two he bridled and led in a circuitous route back to Mercy and the girl. With any luck, the scouts would be confused, especially with the other two horses running who knew where.

Mercy emerged from the cleft of the overturned tree, the girl trailing. He handed her the reins of the larger horse.

She stared into the darkness behind him. "Where are the rest of the horses?"

"We only need two. The girl rides with you. Mount up."

A frown darkened her pale skin. "But we'll never haul the gold with only two horses."

"We are not taking all of it."

"But you said—"

"There is no time. We ride hard. Now." Using the tree as a stepping block, he mounted. Horseflesh warmed his backside. Riding bareback would leave an ache in a few more muscles than he expected.

"Fine," Mercy huffed, then narrowed her eyes up at him. "But you will tell me all when we stop."

He yanked the horse around, leaving space for Mercy and the girl to mount as he had. Would that he could yank an easy answer out for her as well, for the harshness of her whisper screamed determination. How much should he tell her? How much could he? Thankfully he had a hard ride ahead to mull this over, for of only two things was he certain.

Mercy would not be put off.

He couldn't continue keeping the truth from her.

This was exactly why, in all his training, the one thing his commander in Boston had drilled on most frequently was the warning never to drop his guard around a woman.

Now he understood why.

CHAPTER 28

After endless hours of riding, Mercy was spent. In the hollow of a ravine, beneath an overhanging slab of moss-covered rock, she sank onto a patch of ferns barely unfurled. The peppery-sweet scent conjured memories of happier times, of romps through the woods with her brother and of lazy missions scouting for nothing but a place to camp for the night with Matthew. Times when the threat of tomahawks or arrows wasn't just a wild ride behind her.

At her side, Livvy had already curled into a ball on the ground, asleep. It took everything in Mercy's power not to fling herself down and do the same. An all-night ride picking their way through darkness, the morning of speed and distance, and now an afternoon sky draped with clouds like a thick blanket all beckoned her to stretch out. But she pulled up her knees and wrapped her arms about them, refusing to bed down—not until Elias returned from seeing to the horses.

The *tchuk-tchuk* of a blackbird's call drifted down from the treetops, haunting, simple. . .grievous. A sound that tightened her throat and caused her eyes to burn. *Oh Matthew.* She blinked back tears. *Tchuk-tchuk* had been her friend's trademark call, announcing his approach or alerting her to danger. She'd never hear it again from his mouth. The image of Matthew's crumpled body fallen over the wagon seat flashed like a nightmare, and a single fat drip ran hot down her cheek. She'd not even gotten to say goodbye, just like her father. Just like her mother.

She drew in a shaky breath. Was all of life to be like this? Losing those she loved without a farewell? Was Onontio out there somewhere, even now lying cold and stiff?

Footsteps drew near, and she scrubbed away the dampness on her face with the back of her hand.

Opposite Livvy, Elias lowered beside her. "You should sleep. We will not be here long."

His low voice, strong and sure and very much alive, was a balm to her melancholy. Bundling up her sorrow and packing it away into a corner of her heart, she speared him with a sideways glance. "Long enough for me to get an answer."

He snorted. "If nothing else, you are persistent."

Without another word, he eased flat and slung his forearm over his eyes, blocking out the gruel-thin daylight—and her.

She smirked. Did he seriously think she'd be put off so easily? She leaned over and lifted his arm. "Well?"

Only one of his eyes popped open. "Sleep."

"You promised, Elias." She let his arm drop and leaned back on her elbows. "Unless you're the type of man who doesn't keep his word."

She hid a smile at the sigh that ripped out of him. It had been an unfair jab—but it worked, as she'd suspected.

Turning, he crooked his arm and propped his chin on the heel of his hand. "What is it you want to know?"

She narrowed her eyes to keep from rolling them. He knew exactly what she wanted to know. A question for a question was a ploy she'd used herself earlier in the day when Livvy kept asking when they'd stop.

"Tell me what you're really after, Elias Dubois."

"That should be apparent." The blue in his eyes burned brilliant, full of promises and intrigue, altogether dangerous. . .and far too alluring. "I am on the same mission as you."

"Are you?" She flicked away a bug hovering in front of her face and studied him, from the lines of his unshaven jaw to the curve of his cheekbones, landing on the slight lift to one of his brows. How was she ever to know when he spoke truth? "I wonder."

"You know as well as I we can no longer expect to get that load of gold to Fort Edward. Even had we taken four horses and tried to hitch up one wagon, we never would have made it. As it is, we will barely keep abreast of those men, even covering our trail and doubling back. The way I see it, by scattering the horses, we bought us some time as they try to figure out which way we went."

"You don't think they will go straight for the gold like we are?"

"They do not know where the gold is, now do they?"

She pulled her gaze from him and stared straight ahead, the green of the ravine blurring into a smear. He was right of course, and that rankled. Matthew had always been right too, but something was different in the way Elias answered her, always turning things back into a question. Like something tethered the words behind his lips from flying free.

"Then why go back at all?" She spoke as much to herself as to him, trying to work out the logic of why they should bother returning to the cache of gold, especially now that they had Livvy to see to. She swung her gaze back to Elias. "Maybe we should make for Fort Edward and come back with a squad of soldiers."

"If I go to Fort Edward, I will not be coming back."

If? Her eyes widened. "You don't intend to go?"

She drew in a breath, the truth hooking into her like a stickle-burr. She was the only one stopping him from escaping—and after the way she'd seen him fight, she was naught but a gnat to be swatted aside. Not that she blamed him. She might do the same were she faced with years locked in a damp, dark cell. But not paying the debt for a crime he didn't deny wasn't honorable. . .was it? How could she ever reconcile this man's acts of integrity against such a defilement of justice?

He pushed up to sit, a groan rumbling in his throat. That slash on his chest had to hurt something fierce, for the sting on her shoulder from the arrow yet raged when she moved too quickly.

Shifting, he leaned over her. "Regardless of what I intend, know this. . .I will see you and Livvy to safety. I vow it."

Safety? With a pack of angry natives likely even now on their trail? She shook her head. "But we'll never be safe from Red Bear, not after what you did."

"That is a burden not meant for you." He tapped her lightly on the nose. "Sleep now, for we will not rest long."

She frowned. She'd been the cause of that burden, had she not? This man with the purple near his eye and cut on his cheekbone had fought for her to his own detriment.

"I don't understand you," she murmured.

A grin broke white and wide in his dark beard, sinking deep and wrapping around her like a warm embrace. "Would you have it any other way?"

Without waiting for an answer, he eased himself back to the ground, arm once again slung across his eyes. In no time, his breathing evened, chest rising and falling in a deep cadence, sound asleep.

She lay down as well, but her eyes blinked long and hard, his question riding along with the continued *tchuk-tchuk*s of the blackbird. Would she want a man she could predict? One who wasn't full of surprises?

She forced her eyes shut, desperate to escape the answer to that and an even more hideous question that crouched, waiting to pounce at some point in the near future.

What were his intentions?

Elias squatted, studying the base of a tall maple. Morning dew hung like a string of beads along the almost invisible line of a spiderweb. This thick in the woods and with an overcast sky, it was hard to tell exactly where the sun rose, but spiders generally chose the south side of a tree to build their homes because it was the warmest. And a ways back he'd spied a woodpecker hole halfway up a dying hemlock, which was more than likely east. Mind made up, he straightened and grabbed hold of his horse. If they veered just a hair to the left, they ought to hit the ravine by early afternoon.

Using a rock as a mounting block, he swung up onto the animal. Two days and a hard ride without aid of even a blanket as a cushion ached in his backside and legs—but not nearly as nettling as the throbbing of his conscience. The torment of not having told Mercy the full truth yesterday competed with the necessity of his orders to keep silent. Both plagued him every time he looked in her eyes.

He nudged the horse with his heels and trotted back to where he'd left Mercy, refusing to meet her gaze. With a silent jerk of his head, he indicated for her and the girl to follow.

Hours later, the trees thinned somewhat. Ground growth thickened. The heaviness weighting his shoulders lightened a bit as they neared the drop before the glade. Once he retrieved that weapon, he'd see Mercy and Livvy to the shelter of the nearest town—Schoharie, if he calculated correctly—then ride like the wind for Boston. A good plan. A solid one.

As long as Red Bear and his men held off.

He guided his mount down the route at the side of the rock face, and with his first full glance at the clearing, he kicked the horse into a run.

No! God, no!

The broken crates lay in the open air like so many bones. But only one wagon sat at the center of the glade. Weeds lay flattened in two ruts where the wheels of the other one had turned in an arc and headed back out to the road.

And the dirt where they had buried the gold yawned open like an empty grave.

He yanked the horse to a stop and slid to the ground, trying hard to ignore the searing pain of the slice on his chest. How could this be?

Stomping the length of the trench, he scoured the area for clues. Here a shovel cut. There a heel imprint—several, actually. All precisely where they had toiled to hide the gold—and nowhere else.

A skirt rustled close. Mercy's voice followed, pinched and strangled.

"Matthew's body is. . ." She sucked in a shaky breath. "It is still there. What happened here?"

He shook his head, wishing with everything in him his suspicions were dead wrong. "You tell me."

She padded along the roughed-up dirt, her keen eye touching on the same signs he'd detected. Then she whirled, torn skirts swirling about her legs, her slim fingers curling into fists. Red patches of rage darkened her cheeks. "Besides us, only Rufus knew we hid the gold here."

"Are you surprised?"

"Blast!" The word shot from her mouth like a cannonball.

He coughed into his hand to keep from smiling.

"You all right, ma'am?" Livvy asked from behind.

Mercy bit her lip, then hollered to the girl, "I'm fine." Her gaze drifted back to Elias. "I apologize."

He worked his jaw, stifling a chuckle. "No need to apologize. I feel the same. I should have known something was off, seeing as only four horses were taken and Rufus was not held captive along with you."

Mercy shrugged. "Like I said earlier, I assumed he'd been killed along with Matthew."

"Well, there is naught to be done for it now." He pulled off his hat and ran his hand through his hair, a vain attempt to straighten out his thoughts as well. No wonder Rufus not only suggested this clearing, but insisted on their reaching it. . .and put up a fuss at their burying the gold. Likely he'd worked it out with Red Bear to kill off whoever accompanied him, then split the riches with him. A sour taste filled his mouth, and he swallowed. Sweet suffering cats but he'd been wrong about the whelp! He should have known there'd been far more depth to Rufus's deviousness. But where was the man now? And with whom?

He jammed his hat back onto his head and faced Mercy. "Mount up. The trail ought to be easy enough to follow, especially if they turned onto any side trails."

"They?"

"You really think Rufus could do this alone?"

Mercy kicked at the dirt, and though she did not say it, he had no doubt a few more angry words exploded in her head. In the dreary light of a cloudy afternoon and with anger simmering inside, she radiated a fierce beauty.

"Elias." Her brown eyes sought his. "We can't go up against Rufus and who knows how many others with nothing but two knives and a young girl."

A storm was coming. He felt it deep in his bones. One that would blow clear away the secrecy of his mission. He should have run far and fast that first time he'd gripped her hand and the charge had run through him, for he could deny her no more.

"You are right." He spoke slowly, biding time. But for what? The longer they stayed here, the closer Red Bear's men drew. He pierced her with a stare. "And that is why you and Livvy will stay hidden while I get what I came for."

"No."

The word floated somewhere overhead, like a tuft of cottonwood blown by the breeze. *No?* She'd dig in her heels just like that, without nary a by-your-leave?

She folded her arms and tipped her chin, a rock-hard gleam in her eye. "I'm not going one more step with you until you tell me what you're after and why."

And there it was. The fork in the road. The one where he either held tight to his course of silence alone or ran toward her and told all. . .unless he appealed to her sense of fear and avoided the whole thing altogether.

He threw out his hands. It was either that or grab her close and kiss the defiance from her face. "We do not have time for this. I will tell you later—"

"Livvy, get yourself down," she called to the girl and whumped to the ground herself. "We rest here."

"Mercy, please." He gritted his teeth. "You know the longer we stay here, the closer those warriors get."

She peered up at him. "Then you had better talk fast."

Thunder and turf! The woman was as inflexible as a steel-edged tomahawk.

"Stubborn woman." He dropped down beside her and pressed the heel of his hand against his brow, fighting off a killer of a headache. He'd been in tight spaces before, faced death and torture, but never had he felt the need to expose who he was, what he was about, until now.

"What I am about to tell you goes against my orders and endangers your life. You cannot breathe a word of this, not even on pain of death." He measured the words out slowly, methodically, all the while looking for an opportunity to turn the subject on to a side route. "No one would believe you anyway."

How well he knew that. He scrubbed a hand at the base of his neck, right where a rope would bite.

"If you're thinking to scare me, it is not working."

Aye, he should have known better. He lowered his hand, and a smile tugged his lips. "You really will be the death of me, Mercy Lytton."

He sucked in a big breath and let it all leak out. There'd be no turning back now, not unless he jumped up and rode off, leaving the temptation behind. Leaving Mercy behind—and that was not an option.

He turned to her and grabbed one of her hands. A totally irrational move, but needful. A warm reminder she was skin and breath and worth the risk of everything he had to give.

"Elias?" Creases marred her fine brow. . .creases put there by him and his deceit.

He rubbed his thumb along the back of her hand, watching the movement for a while, admiring the way her fine skin yielded to his touch—anything to distract, to keep him from thinking on what he was about to say.

"The truth is," he murmured, "I am not a traitor, leastwise not to the English."

She shook her head. "Then who are you? *What* are you?"

A disappointment. A hellion. A failure.

He shoved back his grandfather's words and looked her straight in the eyes. "I am a spy, sent to infiltrate the French under the guise of a turncoat."

CHAPTER 29

"A spy for the English. Not the French. Not a turncoat. Just a guise." Mercy nattered with an unhinged jaw, knowing all the while it wasn't helping. She could no more understand the words coming from her own mouth than she could from Elias's.

She stared deep into his blue eyes, trying—needing—to sift truth from deception. He didn't blink. He didn't flinch. He stared back, gaze clear and candid as if he looked upon the face of God.

Stunning, truly. All her life she'd prided herself on reading people. Sorting them out like a basket of berries, good in one pile, bad in the other. Had she been wrong about this man just as she had been wrong about her mother all these years? How had she, the one of keen sight, been so blind? And how had he been so cunning as to let her—and everyone else—believe such a thing?

She yanked back her hand from his hold. "You were nearly hanged! Why would you do that? Why did you not tell General Bragg?"

A shadow crossed his face, though not a cloud dotted the sky. He pulled his gaze from her and reached for a pebble, tossing the thing back and forth, palm to palm. "As I said, no one would believe me. The truth of my mission is known only to a major in Boston, and in order to make my role believable, even he would deny me."

Toss. Toss. The stone dropped lazily from one hand to the other, as restless as the information she tried to line up in a neat row. He could be lying, but why invent such a fanciful story?

"Miss Mercy?" Livvy drew close, blond hair as wild and loose as Mercy's own.

She'd have to braid that, as soon as she finished combing through Elias's tale. Mercy smiled at the girl; at least she hoped it came off as a grin instead of a grimace. "I need a moment with Mr. Dubois. Here"—she shrugged off the food pouch strapped over her shoulder— "get yourself something to eat and close your eyes for a few minutes."

The girl reached for the bag, all the while studying Elias. The longer she stared, the more a dimple carved deep into her chin as she pursed her lips. The girl was not dim-witted. She must sense some kind of squabble hanging on the air.

Yet she said no more. She nodded, then retreated back near the horses and sat on the ground with the bag.

Mercy turned to Elias, unsure what to think anymore. Was he a spy? Wasn't he? If he were not a traitor—*if*. . . Her heart beat hard against her ribs as she traced the way the sun wrapped a glowing mantle across his shoulders. If he were a man of honor, then she was in even more danger, for there'd be nothing to douse the affection that had been kindling since the first touch of his hand.

She clenched her teeth, trapping a scream of confliction.

The rock slipped from his fingers, and he snatched it up again. "You do not have to believe me, Mercy. Sometimes. . ." He peered down at her. "Well, sometimes I can barely believe it myself."

She huffed out a sigh, wanting, not wanting. The few crumbs of information he'd served hardly sufficed, and in fact merely whetted her appetite for more. "What are you here for exactly? What is your mission?"

"Originally it was to find out which fort the French next intended to siege, which I did." He tossed the pebble in rhythm with his words. "I was even on my way back to Boston, but as I overnighted at Fort Le Boeuf, the whole thing turned into something more. . .deadly."

The tossing stopped. The rock plummeted. Elias's hands hung still between his knees.

Fear snuck up like a snake, slipping a shiver down her back. She'd seen him face an Indian with a knife, a river bent on pulling him under, not to mention a time or two when she'd swung at him with all her fury. But in all those times, she'd never seen the unvarnished terror now twitching his jaw.

"What did you discover?" she whispered.

He blew out a long breath, and when he spoke, his low voice threatened like an approaching tempest. "I am not sure, which is why I am in such a hurry to get back what I hid in one of those crates. The only thing I know for certain is that I have never seen any weapon quite so deadly."

He shot to his feet, brushing the dirt from his hands along his thighs.

She bit her lip, watching him as he stood there. Could be a ploy. He could be a consummate actor. But the solemn bow of his head, the restless energy rippling out from him, even the way he didn't plead or demand she believe him, all testified to the probable viability of his story.

Still she wasn't satisfied. She stood as well. "If I'm going with you—*if*—I need to know what it is we'll be transporting, especially with Livvy in tow."

He glanced at her from the corners of his eyes. "So. . .you believe me?"

"I did not say that, and stop changing the subject."

His mouth curved up at one side, then just as suddenly the half smile faded. He folded his arms and faced her, planting his feet wide. "All right. There's a battalion of French even now on their way to Fort Stanwix, but it is no regular threat. They intend to deploy a new weapon, one that will kill every man in that fort before a surrender can be arranged."

Every man? Prickles ran along her arms. "What is this weapon?"

"A grenade, of sorts. The likes of which I have never seen. The outside shell is glass, which of course inflicts a nasty spray of skin-piercing shards. But worse are the contents. Small bits of metal, sharpened, jagged, and coated in a substance beyond my understanding. Some kind of poison, I guess. These bits are loaded into the glass grenades, launched over the walls by a new kind of mortar, and when they explode, whoever chances a single scratch by one of those pieces of metal dies shortly thereafter in agony."

"How do you know this?" Her voice sounded strange, even to her own ears. Then again, this whole conversation was morbidly odd. Were the sun not warming her shoulders and a breeze cooling her cheek, she'd question if she were awake.

"I witnessed the test fires"—a fearsome glower etched lines on Elias's face—"as they practiced on English prisoners, mostly men, some women and. . ." His Adam's apple bobbed, and he barely choked out his last word. "Children."

She gulped, suddenly needful of air. This was no playacting. The truth, the horror, the righteous rage emanating from Elias knocked her back a step.

His eyes narrowed to daggers. "If I bring in that weapon and our men can figure out what the poison is, perhaps an antidote can be created. If not, well. . .I know where the poison and the mortars are stored. We take out the supply, and the threat is leveled, leastwise for now."

He'd carried this weight all this time, come for her even when he knew each minute spent chasing after her was one taken from his mission. And he'd not even blinked with the prospect of adding a young girl into his care, despite the strain he already bore. The truth of who Elias Dubois really was punched her square in the belly, and she pressed her hands to her stomach.

"Livvy," she called out, her voice shaky but audible. "Prepare to ride."

Elias cocked his head at her, one brow lifted.

And surprisingly, she managed a small smile. "We've a wagon to catch up to." But then all mirth fled. That wasn't all to be done. Her eyes burned, and she blinked back tears. "But first we have a body to bury."

As much as she understood the urgency of Elias's mission, duty to Matthew came first.

Hours later, after a thorough check for signs of anything that breathed, Elias slid from his horse and emerged from the woods. Ahead, the road forked, one branch bearing south in a sharp turn. He needn't check, really, for Rufus no doubt continued on the northeast trail, toward Fort Edward, but all his training had taught him to be thorough. *Training?* Hah. A smirk twisted his lips. Why follow such minute protocol now when he'd already forsaken the number one tenet?

He followed the road to where it split. None of this would be happening if he'd never hidden the weapon in a crate of gold to begin with. He should've taken the risk of carrying the thing on his body. But hindsight. . . well, hindsight ever had a way of making the present look like a farce.

Slowing his pace, he scanned the ground, looking for signs of wagon wheels. Who helped Rufus was still a mystery, unless the Shaws had turned back and stumbled across him. Of only one thing was Elias certain—that all along Rufus had intended to bring that gold into the fort by himself. He not only would take all the credit for surviving an Indian attack single-handedly, but would receive a fat pay increase and gain another rank for having saved the load. The young scoundrel had been willing to see them all die just for his profit.

Shoving down a rising anger, Elias crouched and studied the dirt where the road divided. What the. . . ? He ran a finger along the weeds flattened in the curve of a rut. No doubt about it then.

"Which way?"

Mercy's quiet voice wrapped around him from behind. He stood and faced her, taking a moment to brand this image of her on his memory. She belonged here, framed by green wilds, one with God's creation. He'd never seen a lioness other than as a child in one of his grandfather's books, but this woman embodied all the traits of the queen of hunters. The way her chin tipped proud, that thick mane of hair riding her shoulders, the confident look in her eye. And now that she knew his secret, the power to crush him with a single swipe.

He scrubbed his face with his hand, wiping away that thought, then hitched a thumb over his shoulder. "Rufus turned off here, going south."

Her floppy old hat dipped low on her brow. "Hmm," she murmured. "A windfall for us."

"How's that?"

"Going south leads us deeper into my people's lands. We can make good time by staying on the road. Red Bear would be a fool to follow."

A bitter taste filled his mouth. "Red Bear is no fool. If he sees our tracks on this road, he will strike hard and fast."

"Yet we don't know for certain he has followed us this far. All our precautions are slowing us, and night will soon close in. I say we gain as much ground as we can by lighting out on the southward fork."

He grunted, then bypassed her as he chewed on her idea. It made sense, but something about it squeezed his chest like an ill-fitting waistcoat. He stalked back to the safety of the tree line, where Livvy sat astride Mercy's mount and his own horse nibbled on some grass shoots.

He peered up at the girl. "Livvy, how about you climb down and ride with me for a while?"

Mercy gained his side. "What have you in mind?"

"You are the one with the falcon eyes, and Matthew always said your scouting skills were second only to his." Grabbing hold of his horse, he swung up onto the animal's back.

Mercy frowned up at him. "Is that flattery, Mr. Dubois?"

"It is the truth. Scout back a mile or so and see if anyone follows." He reached down, offering Livvy a hand up. "We will continue south until you catch back up. If you see no signs, then we shall stick to the road. Agreed?"

Mercy nodded, and the girl wrapped her thin arms around his waist. As he nudged his horse into motion, a sliver of unease poked his conscience for sending a woman—one he cared about very much—into the woods spying for trouble. . .until he reminded himself that that was what lionesses did. She was in her element, and that rankled deep. Would she ever consent to settling down in one place with a man such as him?

"Mr. Dubois?" Livvy's voice chirped from behind. Though the girl was nearly as tall as his shoulder and standing on the edge of womanhood, she was, after all, still a girl.

"You can call me Elias, Livvy."

"Mr. Elias?"

He smiled. Whoever had raised her had done a fine job of instilling manners. How different would his life have been had he listened to his mother and grandfather's lessons at such a young age?

Guiding the horse onto the side of the southward road, he murmured, "Aye?"

"When do you think I shall see my papa again?" Desperation haunted the girl's question.

"Hopefully soon. Miss Mercy and I are doing everything we can to get you to him safely, for he surely must be missing you."

"It must be awful for him managing without me."

Were it not for the compassion riding ragged in her voice, he might almost think her prideful. But over the past two days, seeing her compliance to Mercy, her willingness to please and encourage, he slapped that rogue idea away.

"You are quite the little lady, Miss Livvy." He dipped beneath a low-hanging branch, breathing in horseflesh and leather.

Livvy followed suit, leaning against his back. "I am all Papa has, since Mother. . ."

He tugged at his collar, loosening the knot at his throat. It shouldn't surprise him, the way suffering had a way of grabbing every human by the neck and shaking, ofttimes hard. But it never failed to shock when one so young must endure such tragedies.

Bless this girl, Lord. Hold her in Your hand.

He glanced down to where her hands rode loosely at his sides. How much did her papa ache to have this girl, this flesh-and-blood reminder of a love lost, returned to him? "I imagine your papa must love you something fierce."

"He does."

The conviction in her young voice stabbed him between the shoulder blades. What would it have felt like to have had a father like that? A frown carved deep into his brow. What was this? Self-pity? Had he not laid all that on the altar that stormy night two years ago in a Boston church?

"Just like your papa—oh! Mr. Du—Elias. . .I did not think to ask if your papa is still living?"

Was he? His knuckles whitened on the reins. "Truthfully, Livvy, I would not know."

"That is so sad."

He stifled a snort. Sad? Maybe. But even sadder that both his father and his grandfather had cast him out. "It is a sorry truth, Livvy, but not everyone has a loving father."

Livvy's hands patted his sides, motherly beyond her years. Then again, being held captive in a Wyandot war camp likely had added a score of years she'd never asked for.

"I bet your papa was a strong man, a brave one," she murmured. "Just like you."

"Aye, he was strong. You must be, to be a voyageur." His mind slid back to that first time as a young man, barely older than Livvy, when he'd traveled to Montreal to meet Bernart Dubois. The man was muscle and steel standing there on the banks of the St. Lawrence River. . .reeking of rum and rage.

"My father could haul three packs at a time and once paddled from Montreal to Grand Portage in six weeks flat—a trip that usually takes eight. Indeed, he was a strong man." He spoke as much to Livvy as himself, a good reminder that not all about his earthly father was wicked.

Behind him, Livvy shifted. "And brave?"

He chuckled, low and bitter, and shame stabbed him for the base response. But it couldn't be helped. How brave was it for a man to drink himself into oblivion? To leave behind the woman who loved him more than life, taking her honor, crushing her heart? To lash out at his own son?

Absently, he lifted a hand and rubbed the scar near his ear. "No, Livvy. There was nothing brave about him."

They rode in silence a ways. Just as well, for the girl's questions dredged up ghosts that haunted in ways he hadn't expected.

But a troubling noise behind them jerked him from such painful speculations. Far off, twigs cracked. Weeds swished. Someone was coming.

Fast.

He yanked the horse into the woods, barely clearing the side of the road when he caught sight of Mercy barreling down it.

She reined her snorting horse to a stop in front of them. "We've got to move. Now!"

CHAPTER 30

Death ran headlong somewhere behind them, wielding tomahawks and war clubs—but not many bows and arrows. Mercy couldn't help but smile at Elias's foresight in breaking those weapons before they'd escaped. Without any need to hide her tracks, she urged her horse as fast as possible, weaving through trees, dodging fallen trunks, leading Elias and Livvy southwest.

And by the sounds of it, Elias followed right behind. He hadn't asked one question. He'd just kicked his horse into a run behind hers, giving her the lead. Would she be willing to follow him so blindly? She still wasn't completely convinced all he'd told her was true, though everything in her wanted to. It took time to stop a river of thought and snake it back around the other way.

She cut off onto an old deer trace, taking the turn too sharply, and banged her leg against a tree. The pain barely registered. A bruise was nothing compared to the bloody torment that would be inflicted if those warriors caught up to them. And they weren't far behind. She'd scouted barely a mile back before sighting four braves running point. The horses gave her and Elias a distinct advantage. . .for now. Horses couldn't run forever though. If they could just make it past the Three Sisters, they would be safe—hopefully. One never knew with men driven mad by revenge.

Ducking low, she gave in to the feel of the horse, the heat of it, the speed, praying all the while that Livvy held tight to Elias with the crazed pace. Praying God would spare them as He had at the war camp. Praying this idea of hers wasn't in vain, for it was the only one she had.

A mile later, the trail began a descent. Gradual at first. Somewhat winding. Then sharper, steeper, forcing her to slow her mount. But it wouldn't be long now.

She glanced over her shoulder. Elias's blue gaze met hers, too far back to decipher the questions in his eyes. Livvy's arms squeezed his waist. Good. Mercy faced forward, pressing onward, straining to see the Three Sisters.

Minutes later, at the first hint of a break in the trees, she shut down all her senses save for sight and. . .there they were. A glimpse of gray water, just beyond a massive boulder with a huge tree growing from the base of it. River, rock, and red oak. Hope, threadbare and flimsy, wrapped around her like a worn shawl at the sight.

Once the slope lessened, she dug in her heels and raced down to the banks, then splashed across the river. Water soaked her ragged skirt hem, splashing up as far as her arms, shocking and shivery cold, but a small price to pay. . .if this worked.

At the other side, she urged the horse up the rocky embankment. When the ground leveled, she turned right, following close to the edge of the water. Twenty yards or so more, and she slowed her mount to inspect a patch of barberries growing close to the bank. It would be prickly, the thorns a nettlesome bother, but the branches leafed out enough to provide excellent cover. This *would* work. It had to.

Turning at a sharp angle, she guided the horse into the woods, traveling a safe space—hopefully—to leave Livvy with the animals. She slid to the ground, her backside happy to have ended that wild ride.

Elias trotted up beside her, a grim line to his jaw. "Why are you stopping?"

"We need to know if those men are going to continue to pursue or if they turn around."

"Turn around?" His nostrils flared. "Why the devil would they do that?"

"Come. I will show you." She patted her mount and snagged the lead, holding the end out in one hand. "Livvy, you stay here with the horses. Can you do that?"

"Yes, ma'am."

Livvy loosened her death grip on Elias's waist and made to swing down—but Elias shot out his arm, staying the girl.

He narrowed his eyes at Mercy, a fierce storm churning in those blue waters. "Our lives are on the line here. You are certain about this?"

She tipped her chin. "As certain as I can be."

A slight frown puckered his brow, but he released his hold on Livvy and instead offered his grip to aid her down. Then he swung off and grabbed his own horse's lead, handing it over to the girl.

Mercy spun and retraced her route back to the barberries, Elias's steps close behind. Bracing herself for the tugs, pulls, and scratches of small thorns, she fisted her hands and elbowed her way in, protecting her face.

"No one in their right mind hides in a patch of barberries," Elias huffed behind her.

"Which is why those men won't give this bramble a second glance."

A branch slapped against her neck, stinging pain cutting into the tender place just behind her earlobe. Maybe Elias was right—maybe she was so travel worn that her thinking was skewed.

Eventually, she worked her way in to see the opposite bank, and if she turned just so, the Three Sisters came into view. Elias crashed to a stop beside her, exhaling an "Oomph."

Ignoring his complaint, she lifted a finger and pointed. "See that red oak over there? The one growing out of a rock?"

"I noticed it as we passed. Why?"

"There's a hatchet buried five paces west of it."

He pulled his gaze from the water and turned to her, one brow lifting in question. "Between the Wyandot and the Mohawks?"

She nodded. "Ten winters ago, long before this war broke out, Black-Fox-Running and Red Bear held a peace summit. This river marks the boundary that neither is to cross. They buried the war hatchet at the base of that oak as a reminder. Those warriors would be fools to cross over and bring down the wrath of my people against theirs. . .and you said Red Bear is no fool."

A smile broke, broad and brilliant. "Have I ever told you what an amazing woman you are?"

The warmth in his voice beguiled for a moment, until she remembered what he most often called her. "No, you're usually too busy harping on how stubborn I am."

"Well, I have since come to change my mind." He reached out to pick off a skinny branch barbed into one of her sleeves. "You are going to need a new gown after all this."

She pointed to a tear near his collar. "And you shall need a new shirt."

Quick as a flash of ground lightning, he caught her hand and pressed a kiss to the palm, his gaze never leaving hers.

And God help her, she never wanted it to.

"Mercy. . ." Her name was a whisper, a shiver, a need—one that plucked the same chord somewhere deep inside her chest.

Warmth traveled low in her belly, and suddenly it didn't matter anymore that thorns cut and men killed. That she'd sworn never to hand over her independence to anyone, least of all a blue-eyed soldier with a French name and a mind-boggling story.

She leaned close, drawn by desire, breathing in his scent of lathered horse and heated body. When her lips met his, soft, seeking, a tremor shook through him.

"Mercy." This time her name was a moan.

Heedless of scratches, she reached up and entwined her fingers in his hair, pulling him close.

A groan rumbled in his throat, and his mouth closed in on hers, ablaze with the same hunger that burned inside her. It dazzled, this fire, scorching her in places she'd never known could simmer to such an intensity.

But with the next breath, they broke apart, the moment doused by the splash of men's feet running full into the river.

<hr/>

Heart pounding hard enough for the warriors to hear, Elias froze. If this were his day to die, so be it, but Lord have mercy on the woman warming his side and on Livvy. Short of a miracle, they didn't stand a chance against the ten men tearing into the water. Red painted half their faces, black the other. . .blood and death. And who knew how many more men were still to emerge from the woods?

Fingering the knife at his side, he turned to Mercy and whispered, "Go. Take Livvy and ride."

Her jaw clenched. "Either we stand together or we die together."

She flung the very words he'd told her like a well-aimed tomahawk. Now? She had to choose now to heed what he'd said?

He hardened his voice. "I am not asking. Do it."

"But—"

"Now!" He growled, keeping his tone just below the sound of kicked-up water. "Think of the girl."

A defiant gleam burned in her gaze. Even so, she slowly, carefully parted the lowest branches and crawled out.

Before she disappeared, he turned his attention back to the river.

Two men took the lead, paces now from the embankment, twenty-five yards down from his cover. And only a short sprint away from Mercy and Livvy.

God, please, see to their safety.

He pulled out the hunting knife, gripping it in a moist palm. If he shot up now and sprinted down the river, away from Mercy, they would gain at least some small measure of time to escape. Keeping an eye on the front runners, he crouch-walked backward to clear the hindrance of the briars.

"Cease!"

He stopped. So did the warriors. Red Bear's command halted the very sparrows in the trees from singing.

The old warrior strode from the woods to the water's edge, near the red oak with its roots gnarled around the rock. "We go no farther."

Paces from Elias's side of the river, two warriors stood midstride. One turned, a bristle-haired man wearing a stiff roach headdress, and shouted back, "What of our honor?"

Red Bear folded his arms and stared the man down. "It is for our honor we turn back."

"Nay!" The rebel's voice and fist shook in the air.

Elias shifted for a better view of the uncommon sight. To defy a sachem was asking for more than trouble.

"We will take no life that side of the river." Red Bear didn't budge, in stance or deed. "Especially if the woman is Kahente."

"Your thinking is not clear, Red Bear."

A collective gasp rippled along with the river's flowing waters. No one dared move, let alone breathe. Only the slight breeze ventured to wave the turkey feather hanging from Red Bear's scalp lock and ruffle the hem of his long trade shirt.

Slowly, the sachem's face lifted, an imperial pose. The kind that brooked no argument. "Were your thoughts even a vapor when I, Red Bear, stood on this very bank, seeing with my own eyes the war ax laid into the ground?"

The rebel said nothing. He didn't have to. The baring of his teeth in a wicked snarl said it all.

Red Bear tucked his black-painted chin, the whites of his eyes stark against the scarlet smear of vermillion he wore as a mask. "Are you man enough to dig it up?"

Water churned from the rebel's strong stride as he waded toward the sachem. He stalked past the other men yet standing in the river, all still as a nightmare and likely as incredulous as Elias. Would the fool be brazen enough to raise a fist against the leader of his people?

Elias's brow lowered, weighted with guilt. How many times had he done the same to God? Lifted a clenched hand? Defied the One whom he ought to obey without question?

Oh God, forgive me for such arrogance.

Peace settled over him like a mantle. Would that the warrior now standing in front of Red Bear received such a grace.

The two stared eye-to-eye, ruler and ruled, man versus man. Would Red Bear abide such an atrocity if the hotheaded warrior dug up the war ax? And if he did. . . Sweat dotted Elias's brow. If the sachem stood by and allowed the man to break the peace, the blood spilled would be on Elias's hands for having allowed Mercy to lead them to this place.

A blood-chilling cry raged from the warrior's mouth. Then he retreated past Red Bear and strode into the woods behind him.

The breath Elias had been holding rushed out of his lungs. The other men in the water began striding toward the retreating Red Bear—

Save one.

A bare-chested man broke rank, kicking up water as he raced toward Elias's side of the shore. His feet hit the bank, scrambling on the rocks to make purchase.

The same man who'd stolen Mercy's hat.

Keeping low, Elias clambered out of the barberries. Surprise was his best weapon, for if the man had a chance to cry out a warning, there'd likely be no containing the rebel who'd stood up to the sachem. . .or maybe not even Red Bear.

He ran in a crouch, knife gripped tight and ready to slash. As soon as he gained sight of the man, now several yards in from the riverbank and looking for tracks, Elias pushed air past his teeth in a loud "whist!"

The warrior's head jerked his way. A smile sliced across his face, white teeth sharpened to fangs. The man's eyes narrowed to slits—then he hefted a tomahawk and reared back on the ball of one foot.

CHAPTER 31

Mercy guided the horse through woods she could traverse blind—a blessing and a curse, that. She knew the best hiding places should she and Livvy need to take cover, but she also knew the way so well that it gave her mind free rein to wander off to dark corners. If those Indians snubbed the decade-long peace between her people and theirs, tore right across that river, and discovered Elias, well. . . He'd proven his strength time and again, but not even he could withstand so many men set on killing. Would he end up being just one more person she couldn't say goodbye to?

Behind her, the thud of hooves trotted close, and Livvy drew up along-side her. It was strange to see the girl riding alone, a sharp reminder that Elias had yet to catch up to them. The girl's blond hair frizzled in a tangle. Dirt smudged across her brow, coating everything, really. Her gown hung ripped off one shoulder, her skirts tattered at the hem. The girl had lived a lifetime over the past several months, yet a certain innocence remained in her wide blue eyes.

"Miss Mercy?" she whispered.

Mercy nodded, silent. While it was unlikely anyone would hear should she speak aloud, the scout in her held her tongue on a short leash.

"God's watching over us, ma'am."

The words shivered down her back as if God Himself told her His gaze was upon her. Was this girl flesh and blood? Or was she an angel sent for encouragement? Either way, human or not, Livvy was a godsend. The girl dropped back to follow as before, but Mercy pressed on with a strange peace, and all the while she prayed that God was watching over Elias too.

Veering off on a connecting deer trace, she turned her thoughts as well, trying to forget the danger he was in, forget the passion in his kiss. . .and especially forget that every step of her horse drew her nearer to her village.

The one destroyed weeks ago.

Sorrow pressed down, as weighty as the sullen skies overhead. Part of her wanted to gallop toward home. The other part wanted to wheel about and ride fast and far. There was no escaping the implications of either one. And the more ground her horse ate up, the stronger the urge to slip down and weep hot tears onto the sacred earth of her ancestors.

A little farther on, she pulled on her reins, halting the mare for nothing more than a gut feeling. Birds still sang in the late afternoon air, clouds yet blanketed the sky, muffling light and sound. A squirrel scampered in front of her, and her mount swished her tail. Nothing out of the ordinary.

But even so, she turned her horse about and, with a sweep of her hand, directed Livvy to get behind her.

Elias forced his gaze to remain on the warrior's eyes instead of the tomahawk—one of the few things he'd actually learned from his father. Timing was more than everything now. It was his life. Drop too soon, and the man would rush him, hacking into him before he could rise. Too late, and his skull would be split from the flying ax.

So he waited. Studying. Calculating. Anticipating that one heartbeat when an almost imperceptible narrowing of the warrior's eyes would give away his throw. *God, have mercy.* It was a terrible thing to stare death in the face with nothing to rely upon except a twitch.

And the warrior knew it. His sharp teeth gleamed white against his black-painted face, his lips pulled into a macabre smile. Then his eyes widened.

Widened?

The man's jaw dropped as if the joint came unhinged—and an arrowhead pierced through the middle of his chest, shot from behind.

Elias flattened to the ground, expecting a rain of more deadly projectiles. Had Red Bear changed his mind and even now he and his warriors were breaching the river?

But not one whizz of fletching cut through the air. No thwunks of arrows hit tree trunks or dirt. No splashes or war cries or anything. He lifted his head, listening hard.

The sparrows started singing.

He rose on shaky legs and hunkered back to the barberries. Picking his way inside the prickly shrubs, he went only deep enough to spy the other side of the river.

Not one warrior remained.

He watched for a long time, staring and hoping, afraid to thank God and afraid not to. The last of his battle jitters shook through him in waves, and still he stared, until he was convinced the killers truly had retreated for good.

Indeed, thank You, God.

He emerged from the greenery and blew out a long breath, grateful for life and air and hope. Searching the ground, he spied Mercy's trail, then began to follow it, thanking God all the more. At least there wouldn't be any tomahawks at their backs for the rest of the journey.

But a frown weighted his brow as he trekked along. No tomahawks, indeed, for the danger would be much closer.

He'd be transporting a deadly poisonous weapon on his body.

※

Far off in the distance, a stick cracked, and Mercy held her breath. Her horse shied sideways a step, and she narrowed her eyes, studying the greens and browns and. . .there. A single figure sprinted toward them, hardly more than a smear of a dirtied linen hunting frock and the bobbing of a dark-haired head. Relief sagged her shoulders. Elias. And by the looks of it, no angry warriors trailed him.

Nudging the horse with her heels, she trotted ahead, closing the distance between them.

He stopped as she pulled up in front of him. Dampened hair curled fierce against his temples and sweat dripped in rivulets down his forehead.

While he caught his breath, she slid down from her mount. "They are gone?"

"They are," he huffed out.

She tossed a smile over her shoulder to where Livvy landed on the ground behind her. "You were right. God *is* watching over us."

The girl's grin beamed brilliant in the gray afternoon.

Mercy turned back to Elias, this time searching for any sign of injury. "Are you well?"

"Just winded." He winced, belying his brave words. "I am getting too old for this."

"You sound like Matthew." The bittersweet truth struck her hard. While she yet missed her dear friend, the man in front of her, the one who'd just risked his life once again for her sake, was already filling spaces inside her that Matthew's friendship had never touched.

As if her mount agreed with Elias's words, the horse blew out a snort. Elias reached up and patted the mare's nose. "The horses need a break as well as I. Not much day left anyway. We will camp here."

Her gaze drifted from trunk to trunk, rock to rock. Each one familiar. So many memories. Oh, the dreams she would have tonight should she close her eyes on this patch of land. But in some small way, this might be her best chance to say goodbye to her people, to her father. . .to her mother. To lay to rest all the things she'd never spoken aloud, by chance or by choice.

"I. . ." She swallowed. How to say all that?

Elias cut her a glance.

She straightened her shoulders. The best way to fight an enemy was to run at it headlong. Had her father not taught her that well?

"My village—the one destroyed—is not far. I will take a horse and return. There are some things. . .I must. . .let go of." She stuttered to a halt.

Elias stepped toward her, reaching out as if he'd pull her into his arms, but a whisper away, he stopped. Concern ran deep and blue in his eyes. For a moment, he worked his jaw, seeming to fight his own battle of words. "Are you sure about this?"

"No." She reached to finger the locket at her throat, the smooth stone a reminder of the strength of her mother. "But it is something I must do."

He nodded slowly. "All right. Then we will come along." He turned to the girl. "Livvy, mount—"

"I go alone," Mercy blurted. As much comfort as his presence would bring, this was something personal, something sacrosanct. . .something her very being knew that only God should witness.

He shook his head. "You know that is not safe, even with those men turning back."

She rested her hand on his sleeve, and the muscles beneath tensed at her touch. "Please, Elias," she whispered.

His gaze slid from her hold to her face, softening momentarily. "Fine." And then stern furrows lined his brow. "But if you are not back before dark, I am coming after you."

Elias kneaded a muscle in his neck as he watched Mercy ride off into the maze of trees and continued to stare long after she disappeared. He understood her need to slay whatever demons from her past tormented her. He'd had to slay his own a few years back when he'd first bent a knee toward God. He just didn't like it. Not out here. Not alone. He half-hoped she'd turn around and come back.

Feet shuffled behind him, reminding him Mercy wasn't his only concern. He pivoted, and pale blue eyes blinked up into his.

"Are you all right, Mr. Elias?"

"I am well, Livvy." He smiled down at her. "And you? This has been quite the trek. How are you faring?"

"Well. . ." Her gaze lowered, and she toed the dirt. "I am rather hungry."

"My stomach is pinched a bit tight too." Taking care not to strain the wound still healing on his chest, he slung off the shoulder bag carrying what remained of their provisions. "How about we remedy that?"

He led the girl off the trail to a patch of maidenhair ferns growing amidst random boulders. He sank onto one, she onto another, and he fished out a piece of jerky for each of them.

"Thank you." Livvy bowed her head a moment before taking a bite.

He tore off a chunk of his own meat, marveling. Lord, but this girl was made of strong grace. How many other young ones would not only take such hardships in stride, but remember to thank God for them as well?

After swallowing, she lowered her piece of venison to her lap. A small frown followed the lines of a dirt smudge on her brow. "Mr. Elias?"

"Aye?"

"Are you going to marry Miss Mercy?"

His mouthful of meat went down sideways, lodging as crooked in his throat as the girl's question. He jerked a fist to his mouth and coughed into it. Very funny. Was this God's idea of retribution for all the times as a child he'd flung awkwardly candid queries at his grandfather? Clearing his throat, he lowered his hand. "Well now, that is a big question."

"My papa always says forthright speech is the godliest."

"Your father is a wise man." He dared another bite of jerky. Hopefully he'd dodged the girl's curiosity by getting her to think on her father. Whoever the man was, he surely must be desperate to get her back, for she was unlike any child he'd ever known.

"So are you?" Livvy's blue gaze pinned him in place. "Going to marry Miss Mercy, that is."

He shoved the whole chunk of jerky into his mouth, stalling for time. Despite his hesitation, Livvy's stare did not waver.

The lump of meat traveled down to his stomach like a rock. No. There was no way by heaven or sea he'd give this girl an answer when he did not even want to consider the question. He scrubbed his hand across his mouth. "You think I should?"

"Without a doubt." Gravity sobered her tone.

He hid a smile. Was this what Mercy had been like as a young girl? "What makes you think Miss Mercy would want to marry me?"

Livvy bent forward, leaning close, her long blond hair hanging like a windblown curtain. "I think she needs you."

His brows shot high. "She is a self-reliant woman. What makes you think she has need of anyone?"

"Well, she has not told me, not outright, but. . ." Livvy straightened, craning her neck to look past him toward the path where Mercy had disappeared. Apparently satisfied, she faced him again. "I think she is hiding a whole lot of hurt. Something to do with her mother."

Elias rubbed his hands along his thighs, thinking back on the many conversations he'd had with her. Had she ever mentioned her mother? Try as he might to remember, nothing came to mind. Shoot, he hadn't even known the woman was kin to a mighty Mohawk sachem. He shook his head. "Even if that is true, Livvy, only God can heal hurts down deep."

"Oh, I know, but I think you help her forget. Miss Mercy smiles more when she is with you. My papa says love is that which makes you smile, even when you're tired." She leaned forward again, this time a queer gleam lighting her eyes. "I think she loves you, Mr. Elias."

The girl's words hit him broadside. Not that he hadn't tasted Mercy's need in the kiss they had shared, but love? The thought was too big to wrap his arms around. And even if she did, would she truly give up her life of far-flung freedom to settle down with the likes of him?

Whatever the answer, this was not the time or place to even consider it. He shot to his feet and stalked past Livvy. "I will get some water. After that jerky, you will soon thirst."

"Mr. Elias?"

Ah, no. He'd not be pulled back into that bees' hive of a conversation. He glanced over his shoulder, saying nothing.

She smiled. "Don't worry. I won't breathe a word of this to Miss Mercy. Your secret is safe with me."

"What secret?"

Her pert little nose scrunched up. "That you love her too."

He turned and stalked off. Livvy had far too many years inside her to be stuck inside a little girl's body.

CHAPTER 32

Destruction was the great leveler. It didn't matter what kind of blood ran through one's veins when faced with singed timbers and charred dreams. Wyandot. Mohawk. White. Black. Mercy sank to the dirt, facedown, at the outskirts of what had been her childhood home. She grabbed handfuls of earth, trying to find something to cling to amid such devastation. There was no shame in it. No weakness. Were her worst enemy facing such loss, even he'd drop to the ground and weep.

She closed her eyes—but no good. The macabre skeletons of ruined longhouses had already seared forever into her mind. And though she tried to forget the image, she knew it would never leave. The awful picture of the flattened village was there to stay, like an unwelcome guest who'd slipped in through a half-open door.

Behind her, the horse snorted and pawed the ground. Not that she blamed the beast. Her feet itched to jump up and tear back into Elias's arms.

But instead she sucked in a breath and stood. This was her chance—albeit a late one—to say goodbye to her father. . .and, yes, it was beyond time to bid farewell to Mother.

She padded down what used to be the path between two longhouses. How many times had she skipped here as a child? Followed after her brother in crooked leggings she'd sewn to her mother's dismay, hoping to join him and his friends as they set out on a hunt? Tears burned her eyes. She blinked them away. Tried to, anyway.

She glanced up at a sky as brooding as her heart. *God, why? You protected me. Why did You not protect these people? Why not Matthew? Why not my mother?*

No answers came, but she did not expect any. Her father had required complete obedience from her and her mother even when they did not understand his ways. . .and it was *always* for their good. Though it was impossible to believe anything good could come from the death of those she loved, she must trust that God was sovereign—or that He was not. Yet had He not proven in the past several weeks that He did reign supreme? Not in ways she'd choose, but in ways of His choosing.

Her feet slowed as she neared the blackened ribs of what had been the council lodge. War and peace collided here. The many decisions of when to fight, when to hold off. Had her father sat cross-legged, passing a pipe, when the attack came? Had he been smiling or reverent? Deep in conversation or alone?

She lifted her hand, holding it out as if she might take hold of his and feel the strength of his calloused fingers pressing into hers. She stood still for a long time, listening hard, straining to hear one last time the affection in his voice even as he rebuked her for being so strong-willed.

"Goodbye, Rake'niha," she whispered. *"Skén:nen tsi satonríshen."*

A raven swooped low in a graceful arc, then soared up into the sky and disappeared into the trees. Those more superstitious than she would take it as a sign. She merely lowered her hand. Sign or not, a tentative calm seeped into the thin spaces between flesh and bone. The empty hollow was still there in her chest, right next to the space left behind after Matthew's passing. But just seeing where her father may have spent his last minutes lay to rest a small portion of her grief.

Turning, she picked her way onward to the second longhouse past the council lodge. . .the one she'd shared with her mother.

Countless times she'd walked this way. This time though, when she stopped and imagined the bark-and-frame structure that had housed them, she imagined it with new eyes—and a new heart. Here, in the remnants of violence and death, a quiet appreciation blossomed, replacing her old scorn. Now that she'd tasted of captivity and knew firsthand such terror, she finally understood. How frightened her mother must've been, dragged into this village, not knowing the language or what would become of her. Yet despite the harsh treatment she'd suffered because of her abiding and outspoken faith in Iesos, her mother had survived. . .and never once stopped loving. Not the people. Not her father.

Not her.

She bowed her head with the knowledge. For so long, she'd believed one of the best reasons to be alive was never knowing what would happen next. But maybe an even better reason was to learn from the past to correct a future course.

Kneeling, she reached behind her neck and unclasped the necklace. Tears fell, baptizing the ruby-red heart, puddling in the lines of her open palm.

"I apologize, Mother. Please"—a shaky breath tore through her—"forgive me." Why hadn't she said this when her mother was still alive?

Dampness leaked down her cheeks, chilly in the early evening air, and she shivered. "I did not see your strength because I did not look for it."

She swiped at her nose with her sleeve. "But you'd be happy for me, I think, for I–I've finally learned to trust. Just like you wanted me to."

Her voice broke, and she swallowed, saltiness tangy on her lips. "I believe what you told me, that God will dry each of my tears one day, like He has surely dried all of yours."

The necklace weighed heavy in her hand, and her whole arm shook like an old grandmother's. "I lay to rest my childish contempt. It will ever be dead to me. I only hope that you can forgive me for flaunting it all these years."

She lifted her face to the darkening sky. "Forgive me, oh Father, for leaving undone that which I should have mended."

Setting the locket down, she grabbed a nearby rock and dug with determination. Each gouge reminded her of the grooves she'd surely worn deep into her mother's heart. Regret drove her to a frenzy of flung dirt and ragged cries.

Spent, she pitched the rock aside, then picked up the locket. Pressing the cool stone to her lips, she whispered against it, "I love you, Mother. Let us forever be at peace. Goodbye."

She set the necklace into the ground and covered it up, handful by handful, tear by tear. Pressing the loose dirt into a mound, she laid her hands atop it, finally still. Finally done.

Final.

In the growing darkness, she stood on legs still tingling from her cramped position. Early night air breathed on her like an animal on the prowl, tempting her to return to the same old torment of her darkest memories.

But a newly forged freedom burned like a brilliant light inside her. The memories remained, and always would—but the sharp-edged pain was gone, leaving behind a hard-won tranquility.

Insects began to scratch and whirr. Earthy moistness, pregnant with a damp chill, smelled musty, and the last bit of apathetic daylight melded into shadows. Night would fall hard soon—a darkness so complete, given aid by an overcast sky, that even if Mercy did know this stretch of land, she'd be hard-pressed to find her way back to camp. Elias glanced over to where Livvy curled up near a small fire. He loathed to leave her untended—but he hated even more the fact that Mercy was out there somewhere. Unguarded. Unbidden, his hands curled into fists. What to do? Leave the young girl to go after the woman? Or remain here and leave Mercy in God's hands alone?

Staring harder into the darkness, he ground his teeth, willing Mercy's horse to appear with her atop it. If this was the love Livvy had spoken of, this anguish, this awful burning skittishness to run into the fires of hell if need be just to pull Mercy out, well then. . .he wasn't sure he wanted it. The weighty responsibility of it pushed the air from his lungs.

A shrill cry rent the air, raising gooseflesh on his neck. Just a screech owl. Nothing more. But all the same, he retreated to go grab a horse.

But then turned back around.

Far off, leftover autumn leaves crushed beneath a *thud-thud, thud-thud.* He yanked off his hat and raked his fingers through his hair, relief shaking through him. No doubt about it. This woman would be his death.

Slowly, far too slowly to his liking, a black silhouette approached. Mercy reined in her horse in front of him and slid from her mount, a quirk to one brow. "Why do you stand here? Is all aright?"

"No!" The word flew out like a bat from a cave, but it couldn't be helped. Lord, but he was tired. "Everything is not 'aright.' Not with you traipsing about alone in a dark wood."

Anger shook his voice, and he instantly repented. But it was too late.

Her head dipped, her loose hair falling to the curve of her waist. "I apologize for having caused such worry."

Both his brows shot up. What was this? No defiance? No you-don't-need-to-fret-on-my-account, I-can-take-care-of-myself rebuttal? Alarmed, he studied the woman. There was no change in her broad stance, so unladylike yet strangely alluring. Her same slim shoulders held straight and ready to take on the world. Near as he could tell, not one thing was different in her appearance—but something was. . .what?

He softened his tone. "Well, no harm done, thank God. I made a small fire sheltered from sight, and the smoke is minimal. I did not want to take any chances on those warriors in case they had second thoughts. Go warm yourself. I will see to your horse."

Working quickly, he led the animal to where he'd hobbled his mount, then relieved the horse of its bridle. "Easy, girl," he crooned while he patted her neck. Then he set about looping a rope around one hoof and, with plenty of slack, connecting it to another, keeping the beast from roaming off. After a quick rubdown, he returned to Mercy. By now, naught but coals glowed below her outstretched hands. Next to where she sat, Livvy slept soundly.

Mercy looked up at his approach, her pert chin hiding a smile. "You call this a fire?"

That bit of spunk, little as it was, eased the worry churning the bellyful of dried berries he'd eaten. Maybe she was fine after all. He sank to the ground at her side, opposite Livvy, and handed over the pouch of pemmican. "Did you find the peace you were after?"

A smile split white and broad. "I did."

While she ate, he watched, admiring the soft planes of her face, the curve of her cheeks, the lips that he'd kissed. His gaze sank lower, to her bare neck, the hollow between her collarbone—then stopped. The skin there was naked. No gold chain. No locket.

He jerked his gaze back to hers. "Seems you lost something."

"Hmm?" She chewed a moment more before swallowing. "Oh. . ." Her fingers fluttered to her chest, resting right where the locket should've been. "No, not lost. Given."

He leaned back, eyeing her. "I thought that locket was important to you."

"It. . ." Her lips pressed together, and her hand fell to her lap. "It was time to let it go."

His throat tightened. Ah, that he might remove the unyielding griefs this woman had suffered. "Mercy." Her name came out jagged, and he cleared his throat. "I sorrow for your loss. I know it hurts—"

"No." She snapped her face toward his, eyes burning with the intensity of one of the coals. "Do not pity me. You should know what manner of woman you travel with."

"You owe me no explanations. I am content with who you are—"

"But I am not." She pushed the pouch back into his hands, cutting him off. "Years ago, that necklace was taken in a raid on some whites, led by my father. I was a young girl when the war party returned. My father awarded me with the trinket, for though he could be a harsh man, he was ever soft toward me."

He shook his head. If the thing were that important to her, why had she gotten rid of such a token? "I should think you would want to keep it then, being he is gone."

"You don't understand. This isn't about my father."

Once again her fingers rose, and she absently stroked the side of her neck where the chain had rested since her girlhood. Some kind of memories played across her face as she stared into the glowing coals, twitching her lips, bending her brow.

He waited, giving her the time she needed, wishing he could give her more than that, could comfort, could heal.

Her voice started low and so quiet he leaned in closer to catch her words.

"When my mother saw the stolen locket bouncing against my chest, it was a vivid reminder that she'd been taken in a raid. She asked me to take it off. I refused. She never asked me again, but I persisted in wearing that necklace, drawing a perverse strength from thinking it somehow made me stronger than her."

Her shoulders sagged for a moment; then she straightened them, a new strength rising like an eagle. "But I was wrong, Elias—about so many things. . .and far too quick to judge others when it was my own heart that needed tending."

He grunted. "A lesson for us all, I think."

Her gaze met his—maybe. Hard to tell now, for he could barely distinguish her shape though she sat within reach.

"You're a good man, Elias Dubois."

Mercy's admiration crawled in and made a home deep inside. He'd been called many things by many people, but not good. Not for years. . .not since his own mother had died when he was a lad about Livvy's age. His lips pulled into a smirk. "There are plenty who would say otherwise."

"Well then, they are wrong."

There was no stopping the grin that stretched his mouth—or the chains that dropped from his heart. She could have no idea the healing her admiration brought. He could barely trust himself to speak, so he cleared his throat first. "Bed yourself down. I will take first watch."

He stood, aiming to give her space, but his name on her lips anchored his feet.

"Elias?"

"Aye?"

"Thank you."

He cocked his head. "For what?"

"Not many men besides my brother and Matthew ever look past my independent streak to see me. . .the real me."

He strode to the other side of the coals and sank down, hunkering in for a long watch. "Their loss," he breathed out.

And hopefully his gain—if she'd give up that independence to have him.

CHAPTER 33

Despite stiff joints and a tender bottom, gifts of a long day's ride, Mercy's spirits rose so high, she gripped the reins tight lest she fly away. Last night she'd slept more soundly than a snuggled babe and this morn awakened with a fresh view of the world. She should've made things right with her mother—and God—long ago. And she would have, had she known how sweet that freedom tasted.

Behind her, Livvy shifted. "Miss Mercy, you think we'll be stopping soon? Because, well. . .I need to."

"Aye." The girl was right. She could use a break herself. Not many hours of daylight remained though, so this would have to be a quick reprieve.

She nudged the horse with her heels to catch up to Elias's side, when he suddenly pulled on his reins.

His gaze slid to hers, and he pointed to his ear, then aimed his finger down the road.

She listened. A nearby kingfisher rattled a low call, and a few squirrels played tag off to the side of the woods, scratching their claws against bark. Nothing out of the ordinary. She angled her head. What had Elias heard?

Her lips parted to ask—then as quickly she pressed them together. The distinct jingle of harness and tackle traveled on the late afternoon air.

Elias turned his mount, backtracking a ways. She followed, admiring his scouting sense to move out of range. If they could hear someone else's horses, that someone else could hear theirs as well.

Elias swerved off the road past a stand of birch, then stopped several yards into the greenery.

Mercy waited for Livvy to crawl down before she dismounted. "Here's your chance. Go do what you must, but don't be gone long."

The girl nodded, then darted off.

Giving his horse leave to nibble at the spring shoots, Elias stepped close to her. "Did you hear that?"

"I did. You think. . . ?"

"If it is not Rufus, then we have come a long way for nothing. You stay here, and I will scout it out."

"But I—"

He laid his finger on her lips. "You are better equipped to deal with Livvy than I, should she have needs. I shall be back shortly."

The set of his jaw left no room for argument.

But as soon as Livvy returned, Mercy handed off the care of the horses. "Think you're able to wait here by yourself?"

Blue eyes blinked up into hers. "Yes, Miss Mercy. I'm not afraid."

"You're a brave girl, Livvy." She reached out and squeezed the girl's arm with a light touch. Truly the girl would make a fine scout herself. "Thank you."

Then she turned and followed Elias's trail. Ah, but he was good, even when he wasn't trying. It took all her powers of sight to follow his scant markings of a bent branch or flattened bit of weeds.

The farther she went, the louder the sounds of horses grew. She caught up to Elias on silent feet just behind a screen of elderberries near the side of the road. The scowl on his face as she scooted next to him could make a bear tuck tail and run.

Ahead, on the other side of the shrubs, a male voice tightened into a whine. She and Elias crouched lower and moved in to peer through the branches.

A small clearing opened beside the road. At its center, a wagon—*their* wagon—sat with its back end toward the elderberries, maybe ten yards ahead. They couldn't see Rufus, for he was likely at the front side, but no need. His distinct voice, carping about a need for fresh venison to roast, churned Mercy's empty belly.

A deep voice answered Rufus's complaint. "If young buck wants meat, then he should hunt it himself."

The words twanged with a distinct accent, one that slapped her hard. *Wyandot.* Would they never be free of those villains?

"Yer the blazin' hunter, ain't ya? I oughta see that your pay is docked, you no-good piece of—"

Mercy turned away. She'd heard more than enough.

Elias followed her out, and together they backtracked far enough to confer in whispers. They stopped next to the gnarled roots of an old oak.

"What's the plan?" she asked.

"Nothing."

Her jaw dropped. Had she misplaced her trust? Matthew not only would've concocted their tactical offense but also would've been working out a sharp defense just in case.

Elias smirked. "Nothing until dusk, that is. Semi-darkness is our best asset."

She couldn't argue with that and would have suggested it herself. "Then what?"

"Seems pretty straightforward, unless Rufus and his, er, reluctant friend move the wagon. I will crawl in the rear opening of the canvas, dig out that weapon, then hie myself back to the cover of the elderberries. Assuming I make it that far undetected, I shall head back to you, Livvy, and the horses."

"Oh, no." She folded her arms. "I am not sitting back there waiting to find out what happens."

"Mercy, if I am discovered or that weapon scratches me while I am unloading it—"

"All the more reason for me to be here with you."

A sigh ripped out of him. "All right. But if I do not make it, promise me you will get yourself and Livvy to safety. As near as I can tell, we are not far from Schoharie."

"Agreed. I will go tell Livvy, then return."

He nodded.

But that small task took longer than she expected. A horse had wandered off, for Livvy hadn't properly hobbled the animal. Then the girl had wandered off, her tummy upset from their scant diet. And by the time she grabbed a chunk of jerky for herself and settled the horses for Livvy to await her and Elias's return, the sun lay low on the horizon, ready to dip down for a good night's slumber.

She hurried back to Elias's side in the long line of shrubs. He studied her face a moment, concern etched into the creases at the sides of his eyes. She smiled back assurance. A twinge of sorrow stabbed her. How often had she wordlessly communicated so with Matthew?

They hunkered down, waiting for more shadows to blanket the clearing. She still couldn't see Rufus or his companion, but she could hear Rufus's complaining. The other man's grunts. The crackle of a fire. And the ever-present jingling of bridle and harness. . .wait a minute.

She edged to the far side of the shrubbery, just before it tapered to nothing near the road, and ignored Elias's hand signals for her to return. From this angle, she glimpsed the horses—still attached to the wagon. What in the world? Surely they would not be traveling tonight in the dark. . .would they? But if so, why make a fire? For there, not far in front of the wagon, a fire blazed, outlining Rufus and a large, broad-shouldered man, both sitting in front of the flames.

Frowning, she turned back toward Elias when a new sound stopped her flat. Pounding hooves. Coming down the road, straight for Rufus's camp. She peered past the elderberries. A black horse turned off the rugged track as the last of day's light bled out. The rider was nothing but a shadow—a round, fat blob of a shadow.

"Blast it, boy!" The voice sounded of crushed gravel with a slight slur, giving the speaker away. "What's this?"

Mercy gaped at Elias. Though it was hard to read his face through the maze of dark branches, she could make out the whites of his eyes opened wide. What the devil was Brigadier General Bragg doing here?

The thud of the stout man's feet hit the ground, and she turned back to watch. Rufus sidled up next to him.

"What's what, Pa? I got the gold here, just like you said. Shoot, I got even more than what you expected. So what for do you got your britches all bunched up? Forget to pack an extra bottle, did ya?"

The general's arm shot out. The slap echoed sharply in the early evening air. Rufus staggered from the blow, a string of ugly expletives unraveling from his mouth.

"You're a wastrel and a stain. Were you not my son—and it pains me to call you such—I'd not have included you in on my scheme. By heavens, stand straight when I'm talking to you!"

The first real flicker of understanding and pity for Rufus kindled in Mercy's heart. No wonder he abhorred the world around him, for what a world to have grown up in. Perhaps the real villain here was—and always had been— the general.

Rufus managed to straighten, though he didn't pull his palm from his cheek. And she didn't blame him. It had been a good wallop. Mercy glanced to where the Indian had been sitting, but that side of the fire was now empty. Was he as disgusted by this wrangling as she?

"I'm not talking about the gold." General Bragg swung out his arm. "I can see the wagon's there, you dullard."

Rufus turned aside and spit. "Then what you all riled up about?"

"Tell me, boy, how far will we get when those horses won't pull tomorrow, all because of skin rubbed raw from a night in a harness?"

"Well, I thought—"

Crack! Another mighty slap split the air. This time Rufus dropped to one knee.

Near to her, a crouched shadow slipped out from the shrubbery line, darting toward the back of the wagon.

Elias.

Mercy sucked in a breath, then breathed out a prayer. *And so it begins, eh, Lord? Please, God. Keep him safe.*

Elias ran full-out for the wagon, rage lighting fire to his steps. The general had been the one behind this? That drunken lout of a scoundrel! What a plan. What a horribly devious plan, stealing the stolen gold. . .that the French had purloined from the English. He smirked as he pulled himself up over the backboard. Indeed, the greed of men knew no bounds.

He landed lightly, taking care to move without a sound as he worked his way toward the front of the wagon. Night hadn't fallen hard yet, making the shape of two crates easy to spy. He ran his fingers around the bottom edge of the first one, seeking the notch he'd cut into the box. Outside, the Braggs' voices continued to argue.

"Did you pay off the Indians for their trouble?" the general rasped.

"Yeah, about that. . ."

"Speak up!" The smack of palm against skin once again erupted.

Rufus swore. "If you'd quit hitting me long enough, I'd answer. Dash it!"

"Time's wasting, boy."

The pad of Elias's finger dipped into a notch. Victory. Pulling out his knife, he wedged the blade into the crack between lid and crate. Then slowly applied pressure, bit by bit, so as not to creak the wood. A precaution maybe not necessary what with the quarrel raging outside, but better to be safe.

"I got the wagons to the clearing like you said, Pa." Rufus's voice pinched tighter. "But a blasted band of Frenchies was nearby. The old man and the traitor got it into their heads to bury the gold and ride out past 'em, as if we were nothing but the travelers we were s'posed to be."

A huff rasped from the general. "And?"

Tucking his knife back into his belt, Elias lifted the lid and set it aside atop the rest of the loose cargo. The back of this wagon, filled with pouches of trade silver and bars of gold, surely was an eerie dragon's den. Since the crate in front of him had never been opened, household goods made up the top layer. He reached in and, as quickly as possible, began removing random blankets and other frontier necessities, working his way down to the gold.

"By the time we got back to the glade," Rufus continued, "them redskins were hornet mad for the delay. I lit out of there and waited till Running Wolf returned with the horses. Then we loaded the gold—*all* of it. Worked out better than what you planned. We did not have to pay Red Bear one coin for the use of his braves."

The general grunted. "So the others are dead, yes?"

"The old man and that half-breed woman were killed straight off. The traitor ain't nothing but bones and rope by now, having been tied up in the woods."

Rage shook through Elias. The general had knowingly sent them to their deaths? It took all his restraint to keep from running out and choking the life from both men. What a wicked, filthy scheme!

He shoved his hand into the bottom of the crate, then pulled back just inches from the small leather packet at the bottom. If he grabbed the thing willy-nilly and a sharp point of the metal cut through the casing into his skin, he would be the dead man the Braggs expected him to be. His fingers shook, and he drew a deep breath to steady them, then reached again.

"And where is Running Wolf now?" the general growled. "You were to wait until I arrived to pay him."

"Flit! I can't keep track o' no Indian. They wander like cats."

Elias pinched the edge of the packet and retrieved the deadly thing. It seemed forever ago when he'd first hidden the thin piece of buckskin, wishing beyond anything for a thicker chunk of hide to contain the bits of metal. But just as now, there'd not been a spare minute, with the other French soldiers working so closely to him. He'd been blessed to have slipped the packet from inside his waistcoat without being seen or getting cut.

Ah Lord, would that You might bless me now as well.

With his free hand, he opened the flap on the pouch slung over his shoulder, then eased the packet inside. The deadly bits of metal could weigh no more than ounces, but all the same, the danger pressed down on him. One mistake, one tiny prick, would mean a death like none other.

Trepidation quaked through him, his fingers trembling like a rheumy old man's as he tucked the packet farther into the pouch. The cries of the children, the women's ragged screams, even the pathetic whimperings of the men who'd succumbed to the poison haunted from their graves. He could hear the sounds now—would hear them to his dying day. And Lord willing, that wouldn't be today.

Withdrawing his hand, he closed the flap of the pouch and turned to go.

"As usual, a backwards job by you, boy." The general's voice carried a grudge, and Elias listened carefully to pick up further information as he edged his way to the back of the wagon. "But I suppose you did get the cargo here. The blame will still land hard on those fools I sent with you, should anyone care to look into it. . .but by then, we'll be long gone."

"So I done good, Pa?"

Just before Elias slung his leg over the backboard, he hesitated, then turned back. Bending, he swiped up a pouch of trade silver and tucked that into his bag as well. The money could come in handy for the last stretch of their journey.

"Quit your groveling," Bragg roared. "And for heaven's sake get those horses unhitched!"

Elias straightened.

The horses spooked—and the wagon lurched.

He plummeted backward, out the canvas opening.

Mercy clapped a hand to her mouth to keep from crying out. Elias whumped to the ground, flat on his back, wind no doubt knocked from his lungs. Two heads turned his way from up near the horses. Two guns were immediately primed and cocked.

And two curses rang out in unison.

"Blast it, boy! If you riled up that Indian and he's stealing us blind, you will have the devil to pay."

She pressed her hand tighter against her mouth, smashing her lips, stopping a scream. *Run, Elias. Run!*

He rolled, then stood, staggering.

"We'll see about that." Rufus hacked up a wad and spit, then advanced.

So did the general.

She bit her tongue, trapping the warning scream about to launch from her mouth. Narrowing her eyes, she studied the angles of the dark shapes, from horses, to wagon, to shrubbery, and the position of each man. Elias could still make it to the safety of the elderberries unseen, but only if he sprinted now.

As if reading her mind, he crouched to take off—

Out of the shadows from the other side of the wagon, the tall shape of a broad-shouldered man shot out. The Wyandot.

His musket barrel trained on Elias.

Mercy felt her heart stop, knowing it may never beat again if the lifeblood of Elias drained onto the ground right in front of her eyes. Better that she die here and now.

She dove out of the elderberries toward the road and broke into a dead run. If she could draw their fire, Elias might live—and so would many other men.

If.

CHAPTER 34

Elias had a split-second glimpse of a musket barrel before he snapped his gaze upward and stared into cold black eyes. Violence lived there—but so did intelligence. Slowly, he lifted his hands.

"My brother, do not do this." Elias spoke in Wyandot. "I am unarmed. Come with me." He jerked his head toward the elderberries.

The Indian—Running Wolf?—stared back, impassive.

Rufus and the general's feet pounded the ground, growing closer.

"Why should I?" The man spoke in the people's language as well.

Elias gritted his teeth. Exactly. Why? He'd need a whopper of a reason, for clearly this man sold out to the highest bidder, to have aligned himself with the Braggs. . .and therein might lie the solution. He'd have to up the ante.

"I offer you something more honorable than the tainted trinkets of the English dogs. Hear me out."

Footsteps thudded impossibly loud. Rufus swore. The general wheezed. Any minute now they would be swinging around the back of the wagon.

Running Wolf was a rock-hard shadow, not speaking, not moving.

Sweat trickled between Elias's shoulder blades. Was this where he'd die? Shot down in front of Mercy?

God, please.

The gun barrel lowered—slightly—but it was all the affirmation Elias needed. He sprinted toward the safety of the hedge, the warrior behind. It was a compromising position, running with a loaded weapon at his back, but if the man were going to kill him, he'd have done it by now—and may still if Elias didn't come up with something better to offer him.

Think. Think!

They tore into the cover of shadows just as Rufus's voice rang out, "Ain't nothin' back here, Pa. Blasted Indian musta stumbled to the woods to take a—"

"Spare me the details," the general gruffed out.

Elias turned to Running Wolf and—heedless of his better judgment—offered the only bargain he could think of. "If you bring those two men in to Fort Edward, you will get more than gold. You will get a trade, for they are wanted by the English for murder, thievery, and abandonment. Is not the life of Six Fingers worth more than anything the whites can promise you?"

The duplicity of what he suggested tasted like ashes. Six Fingers was a scoundrel of an Indian, and he'd been glad when he heard the villain had been captured. But if freeing the one gained him his own freedom, the lives of so many more would be spared.

The man narrowed his eyes. "Six Fingers has been captured?"

"Why do you think I am here? I was sent to tell you this." Inwardly, he winced. That was a stretch.

"By who?"

"Red Bear."

And that was an outright lie—one that grieved him to his core. *Oh Lord, forgive me. Again and again and*—

An ululating screech ripped a hole in the quiet, coming from the direction of the road. The cry of a warrior. . .a woman warrior.

Mercy.

His own cry caught in his throat. What the deuce was the woman doing? Why attract attention to herself?

The crack of a musket fired, and then he knew.

She was drawing fire away from him and doing a blasted good job of it.

Another shot split the night.

The sharp report reverberated in the air, shaking Elias to the marrow of his bones. Flay the woman for such courage!

He speared the warrior with a scowl. "Go, now! Before they reload. This is your chance to vanquish those men and free Six Fingers."

The warrior wheeled about.

So did he—but in the opposite direction. He raced to the road and crouch-ran across it, keeping below the line of sight should Running Wolf change his mind and once again join with the Braggs. Speeding along the side farthest from the wagon, he swept the road with a feverish gaze. God help him. If he saw a dark-haired waif spread out on that dirt, there'd be no holding him back.

Across the road, men's voices raged. Another shot rang out. Rufus screamed. Elias used the noise to his advantage, rustling faster along the underbrush. Maybe Running Wolf would have only one man to bring in.

No matter. The only thing of value now was finding Mercy—or not. The thought of seeing her body crumpled and lifeless stabbed him in the chest.

The pouch with the poisoned weapon bounced against his back, but he did not slow until he searched well beyond the makeshift camp. No body slumped in a black shadow on the road. No Mercy. Sucking in a deep breath, he pivoted to retrace his steps back to where they had left Livvy with the horses. If Mercy was there, safe and whole, he just might kill her himself for taking such a harebrained risk. But if she wasn't. . .

His breath stuck in his throat. If she'd been hit and was losing her life's blood, lying cold somewhere in the woods, he'd never forgive himself.

❧

"Livvy? Elias?" Mercy barreled into the brush, feeling her way more than seeing. Good thing they had picked the stand of white birch to hunker down in, so starkly did the trunks contrast with the night shadows.

"Over here, Miss Mercy."

She worked her way toward the girl's voice, barely spying her before she tripped over Livvy's legs. "Is Elias here?"

The useless question flew from her lips before she could stop it. Nor could she keep from peering around the flattened area where Livvy had stamped about—but no dark-haired man graced the small clearing. Of course it would take Elias longer to get here than her. She knew it in her head—but her heart still hoped to find him safe.

"I thought he was with you." There was a shiver in Livvy's voice.

She sank next to the girl, drinking in a lungful of damp air, trying not to tremble herself. "He is not."

Curling up her knees, she wrapped her arms about them and dropped her head. Had Elias gotten away? Or had one of those shots punched the life clear out of his body? And if so, how would she ever breathe again? For that was what he was now. So much a part of her she could hardly distinguish where she ended and he began.

A warm hand patted her arm. "Don't fret, Miss Mercy. I've been praying the whole time. No matter what happens, God is still sovereign."

The girl's faith put her own to shame. If Elias didn't come back, would she even have a faith at all? Her shoulders slumped with the question. It was hard to believe in a God who took as frequently as He gave. Yet not impossible, for the fingers pressing on her sleeve declared such an unyielding trust a reality. Oh, to own such a childlike confidence.

Keep me tethered to You, Lord. . .no matter what.

Her throat closed with the immensity of such a request—but she did not take it back. Not one word.

Livvy pulled her hand away and settled down on the ground. Mercy wished for a blanket she might throw over the girl's small form. But all she could do was scoot closer to her, sharing some of her body heat.

She tuned her ears to listen for the slightest hint of Elias's return. Far off, the eerie howl of coyotes sounded. Nearby, the grass rustled. A field mouse or two, most likely. The skip of a small pebble came from near the road.

And she shot like a musket ball to her feet.

Five steps later, she launched into Elias's open arms and buried her face against his chest.

The scruff of his beard tickled her brow as he bent close and whispered, "Are you hurt?"

Unwilling to pull away, she shook her head, inhaling his scent of smoke and leather and heated flesh.

"And you?" she murmured.

"No."

Then he released her. Just like that. Taking his warmth and strength with him.

She staggered from the sudden loss and peered up into his face. The first pale light of a lethargic moon broke free of a cloud, brushing over the slope of his nose, the shape of his lips, and a glower that would make a grown man retreat.

"What kind of foolish deed was that? Purposely drawing fire." He yanked off his hat and raked his fingers through his hair, then slapped it back on before the growl of his voice had a chance to fade.

Suddenly she was a little girl again, facing her father's wrath for joining the men on a hunt. She swallowed, weak in the knees. Elias was right of course. It had been a dangerous idea.

"You might have been killed!" He grabbed her by the shoulders and shoved his face into hers. "You hear me? Those men were aiming for you. You, Mercy! You could have been shot."

"So could you, and I couldn't bear the thought of it." She still couldn't. A tremor jittered across her shoulders, and she breathed out low, "How am I to live in a world without you?"

Elias deflated, pressing his forehead against hers. "Woman, I swear you are going to be the death of me. Please, do not ever do that again."

She matched her breathing to his. A small thing, but one that linked her to him. "Will there be a need? Are we finished with the Braggs?"

"Aye." He pulled back his head, his teeth bright against his dark beard. "Justice will be served, and by the hand of a Wyandot no less."

Her jaw dropped. By all that was holy, how had he managed that? "What did you do?"

"Let's just say that it is a good thing I speak the language."

She couldn't help but smile back. "You never stop surprising me."

"I should hope not." His hands slid from her shoulders to her back, drawing her next to his body. His mouth came down sweet and slow, lingering on hers so long, a warm ache pulsed through her.

"Promise me one thing?" he whispered against her lips.

"Hmm?" she murmured.

"That you will never stop surprising me."

Elias stood at attention, every muscle squalling to have given in to Mercy's suggestion to board for the night and visit the major's office first thing in the morning. But the sooner this weapon was delivered, the sooner he'd breathe freely. Tonight might be the first time in a year he'd sleep with both eyes closed.

He slid a glance to the mantel clock. If he did not miss his mark, Major Clement would enter before the second hand swept a full circle. A blessing, the man's punctuality, for it would mean less time Mercy and Livvy would remain sequestered in the small foyer with the large private.

Just before the tick of another minute, a door on the other side of the room opened, and in stepped a sprite of a man. The dainty, slim-boned major was the stuff of fairy tales, hardly more than a puff of wind. Elfish ears stuck out from his head. Almond-shaped eyes, brown as a cup of coffee, sat deep above the curve of high cheekbones. His step was light, his complexion even lighter. Most people gave the man nary a second look, so innocuous his appearance. . .and therein lay the irony. There wasn't a more powerful man in all of Boston—not since Elias's grandfather had died several years ago.

The major stretched out a hand, clasping Elias's with a strong shake. "So, the prodigal has returned." Releasing him, the man clapped him on the shoulder. "Good to have you back."

Elias resumed his crisp stance. "It is good to be back, sir."

"By all means, at ease, man! Better yet, sit. You look as if you could use a stout chair and an even stouter drink."

Major Clement strode to a side table and reached for a green bottle.

"Thank you, but none for me, Major." He slung off his pack and set it on Clement's big desk, then sank into one of the leather chairs opposite it. After a month of sitting on naught but a wagon bench, a horse's back, felled trees, or rocks, the cushion beneath him was a cloud. He stifled a sigh. Barely.

"As you wish." The major crossed to his seat behind the desk, a single drink in hand. He tossed back a swallow, then set the glass down—yet did not release it. His finger ran the curve of the rim, round and round, while his gaze studied the sack Elias had placed on his desk. At length, he leaned back in his chair and laced his fingers behind his head. "Seems you have brought me a little gift. Care to tell me about it?"

Elias nodded. "As you know, I infiltrated with the Second Battalion of the Guyenne Regiment. A brutal lot, nearly as rough edged as my father's voyageur ilk."

"Uncivilized beasts, I imagine."

"Worse. Killers, all." His hands curled into fists. For a moment, he saw red—the lacerations of English prisoners hit full in the face by bits of sharpened metal. Then the blood they'd heaved up afterward, bodies convulsing in a torturous death. He drew in a steadying breath. "Brigadier Nicolette's plan is to march on Fort Stanwix, though I am afraid I arrived here too late for you to pull together an ambush. A failure I truly regret."

"Stanwix?" The major grunted, then unlaced his fingers. He pulled open a top drawer, rummaged a bit, then retrieved a slip of paper. "Your apology may be a bit premature. Take a look at this."

Clement held out the scrap, and Elias took it. The edges were ripped and a reddish-brown stain marred one side. Whoever had carried this intelligence had surely paid a price. Charcoal lines scrawled across it, connecting to others. An *X* crossed through one of them. The rendering looked like nothing more than a child's squiggles.

"Turn it the other way," the major suggested.

He did. Still. . .nothing.

"Now imagine that scrap were bigger, with Fort Le Boeuf down in the left corner."

A smile slowly lifted his lips. Those squiggles were a network of rivers—the waterway leading to the fort slated for destruction.

"Let me guess." He handed back the paper. "That *X* indicates the bridge, or shall I say, what *was* the bridge over Mud Creek?"

"Thank God for a cursed damp spring, eh? That ought to keep your Brigadier Nicolette at bay for a while."

Elias grinned. "I never thought to be thankful for a swollen river."

The major shoved the paper back into the drawer, lifting his glass for another drink on the upsweep. "How many are on the march?"

"Three squads, including the Seventy-Second."

Clement choked, setting the glass down with a clatter. "So little?"

"They won't need any more if they deploy this." Leaning forward once again, Elias pushed the pouch with one finger toward the major. "Take care. The contents are deadly."

The major quirked a brow. "Then by all means, I shall give you the honor of presenting them."

Elias rose from his seat and opened the sack's flap. He reached for the major's silver-handled letter opener, then, using the tip, fished out the thin leather packet. A single piece of twine yet remained knotted around the thing, and he carefully worked it loose. Using precise movements, he wedged out a single, pointed bit of jagged metal, not much bigger than a musket ball.

Major Clement bent, his eyes narrowing. "What is it?"

"That is what I am hoping your resources can find out. The metal is coated with some kind of poison. What, exactly, is beyond me. All I know is one scratch will bring down a man within hours."

A muscle stood out like a cord on the major's neck. Lantern light slid along his clenched jaw like a knife blade. And Elias did not blame him. He'd had the same knotted-up reaction when he first discovered the vile thing.

Clement's gaze lifted to his. "How is it deployed?"

"The pieces are loaded into a glass bombshell, and grenadiers shoot them from a mortar."

The major huffed out a breath. "Surely the glass breaks when the mortar goes off."

"No." Elias shook his head. Had he not seen the thing in action, he'd not have believed it either. "It does not, sir. I suspect it is more than simply glass, but I was not able to secret one of those shells away. By faith, I barely got out of there alive with those snippets of metal. Yet if we—if you and your resources—can figure out what the poison is, then perhaps an antidote could be stocked."

"That will take time, Dubois." The major slammed his fist onto the desk, rattling his glass and the metal. "Time we don't have!"

"True, not for the first test load that is even now on the way to Stanwix. May God have mercy." He coaxed the bit of metal back into the leather with the letter opener, adding at least a small measure of safety should the major buffet the desk once again. Then he pushed the whole thing back into the pouch and closed the flap.

"Your words to God's ears, Dubois."

He retraced his steps to his seat and sank into it. "But all is not lost, Major. If we take out the storehouse of both glass and poison, that should buy us the time we need."

Clement's ears twitched as a smile replaced his scowl. "Location?"

"Louisbourg."

A low whistle circled the room. "That will be a hair-raising mission." The major cocked his head. "I don't suppose you are volunteering?"

Years ago he'd have jumped at the offer of adventure and glory. But now? He shifted on the cushion, wincing from scars and aches and too many bad memories. "No, sir. When I said this would be my last operation, I meant it."

"Never hurts to ask, eh?" The major shoved back his chair, then stood and rounded the desk, once again offering his hand. "You have done a fine job, Elias."

He rose, meeting Clement's firm grip. "Thank you, sir."

"Your service has been exemplary." The major's dark eyes twinkled with a hint of hidden knowledge. "You shall have your reward as promised. . .and then some."

"To be honest, sir, I did not do this alone. Would you like to meet my team?"

"Team?" Both the major's brows rose. "By all means."

Elias strode to the door, peeked out at Mercy with a nod, then held the door wide for her and Livvy to enter. He stood at attention as they passed. "Allow me to introduce—"

Before he could finish, the major rushed over to Livvy, grabbing the girl by the shoulders. "Deliverance Hunter? Is that you? I can hardly believe it!"

Mercy shot Elias a glance—one he returned with as much fervor. What on earth?

"It is, sir." Livvy smiled as if they were old friends. "Won't my papa be surprised?"

"He'll be more than that." Major Clement looked past the girl to Elias. "Well, well, Dubois. You shall be greatly rewarded indeed."

Wall sconces shed ample light on the frail-looking man who smiled down at Livvy, but even so Mercy blinked, unsure of what she saw.

Next to her, Elias pulled the door shut, then angled his head toward the man. "Sir?"

The confusion in his tone was a comfort. At least she wasn't the only one to wonder at the odd reunion.

"Ah, yes." The man released his grip of the girl and faced Elias. "You have been out in the field so long, I suppose you missed the arrival of the illustrious General George Hunter, recently in with reinforcements from

Bristol. The man's been quite out of his mind with worry ever since the girl's abduction—and been sparing no expense to find her. How the deuce did you manage to locate her?"

"In all truth, sir, it was providence, for I was not in search of the girl." Elias's eyes sought Mercy's, and he stepped closer to her, the sweep of his fingers resting on the small of her back. A simple gesture, but one that flushed her cheeks. How could this rugged man make her feel so precious by such a mundane act of chivalry?

"Major, allow me to introduce Miss Mercy Lytton. She is the one who found Livvy." Elias turned his face to her—a face she'd never tire of gazing upon, despite the scruff of a beard and layer of travel grime. "Mercy, meet Major Nathaniel Clement."

Leaving Livvy behind, the major settled in front of her and reached for her hand, then bowed over it. "My pleasure, Miss. . ."

Slowly, he released her fingers and straightened. His gaze roamed her face, an inscrutable flicker in his eyes. She stood still as a doe scenting danger. Oh, to own a beaver pelt for each time men measured her so, trying to add up the mixed heritage evident in her features. She'd be a wealthy, wealthy woman.

"Lytton?" The major, slight as he was, stood head to head with her, staring straight into her eyes. "Are you the famed woman scout working with Captain Matthew Prinn?"

Her heart twisted. The slow bleed of sorrow inside her yet continued to drip, and she was more grateful than ever for Elias's warm touch that steadied her.

She lifted her chin. "I am, sir. . .or, I was. I regret to inform you that Captain Prinn is no longer alive."

A groan rumbled in the major's throat. "A shame. The man was the brightest—and I daresay best—of what the rangers have to offer."

A heavy silence fell. The tick of the clock and crackle of the fire in the hearth descended on them all until the major cleared his throat. "But pardon my manners. Please, have a seat, ladies." His brown eyes pierced Elias with a stare. "Unless you have any more surprise guests up your sleeve, Dubois?"

"None, sir."

"Very good." The man pivoted and strode toward an enormous desk. Livvy followed, taking up a chair in front of the thing.

Mercy took the opportunity to lean sideways to whisper to Elias. "How does he know who I am?"

He leaned close, smelling of smoke and horses, a bittersweet reminder they were at their journey's end. "There is none better than the major when it comes to military intelligence."

She took the seat next to Livvy, and Elias remained standing directly behind them.

"I won't keep you long, for the three of you look travel worn and in need of a hearty meal. Now then, Miss Hunter." The major smiled at Livvy. "I shall send a runner straightaway to inform your father of your safe return. I will also arrange for your passage to Virginia as soon as possible, where he has been reassigned. How does that sound?"

The girl beamed. "I would like nothing more, sir."

"Very good." Then he swiveled his face toward her. "Miss Lytton, fortuitous indeed to have you here. You work out of Fort Wilderness, do you not?"

Elias was right—the man was a master of information, especially to have taken notice of a backwoods, slipshod fort. "Yes, sir."

"Excellent." He leaned back in his chair, leather creaking an accompaniment to the movement. "There is a certain matter that has come to my attention recently that perhaps you can clear up."

She pressed her lips flat to keep from frowning. What could she possibly know that would aid a major in Boston, especially since she'd not been on a scout for over a month?

He chuckled. "Oh, don't look so worried, Miss Lytton. I have no doubt you are just the person to ask. Currently there's a load of gold and three men being held at Fort Edward pending investigation. A native, a private, and the missing commander from Fort Wilderness. None of their stories correlate, and in fact all point the finger at each other for all manner of wrongdoing. Do you know anything about this?"

So, Elias's Wyandot had gotten the scoundrels and the cargo all the way to the fort. Not that it would bring Matthew back, but at least the Braggs would pay for their treachery. It was a small consolation—but likely the only one she'd get.

"What I know, sir, is that Brigadier General Bragg and his son are scoundrels of the worst sort. Both deserve a court-martial and time in jail. Or worse."

The major's brows shot high. "That is a strong sentiment."

" 'Tis the truth. The general abandoned his post, conspired with his son to steal that load of gold, and plotted our deaths." She glanced over her shoulder at Elias.

"Miss Lytton speaks true, sir," he confirmed.

The major grunted. "As I said, fortuitous indeed that you are here. Will you write up a document swearing to all you know and have experienced, both of you?"

"We will, sir." Her voice joined with Elias's.

"Then they just might get the court-martial you so desire, Miss Lytton." Major Clement pushed back his chair and stood. "For now, however, the hour grows late. I imagine the three of you might welcome beds to sleep on instead of the ground, am I right?"

Livvy's blond head nodded. Mercy smiled. No doubt even Elias was grinning behind her.

Bypassing the desk, the major strode toward the door. "Dubois, I leave these ladies in your charge until three days hence, when we'll reconvene here."

"Yes, sir."

Livvy shoved her hand into Mercy's, and they both joined Elias's side in crossing the room.

The major held open the door. "I shall see that your expenses for room and board are covered at the Stag's Head Inn. Oh, and Dubois, make it a priority to provision yourselves with new clothing. Pardon my bluntness, ladies"—the major tucked his chin in mock repentance—"but those gowns have seen better days. Good night."

A half smile tugged her lips. The man was judicious in his words. No wonder he held such a position of power.

They had hardly cleared the threshold and the door closed when behind her Elias muttered, "Blast!"

She turned, trying to read the frown on his face and falling far short of what it could mean. "How can you be anything but pleased? The Braggs will get what they deserve, and Livvy shall be returned to her father."

"Aye, all is well save for one thing."

"What's that?"

Elias quirked one eyebrow. "The provisioning. . . .I'd rather run the gauntlet of a Wyandot initiation rite than go shopping."

"Ah, but I believe, Mr. Dubois, that you promised me a new petticoat, did you not?"

A sheepish smile lifted one side of his mouth. "From now on, remind me to be careful what I promise you."

Heat flushed her cheeks, and she turned her face from him. The only thing she really wanted him to promise was to spend the rest of his life at her side.

CHAPTER 36

Mercy worked a pale green ribbon into Livvy's blond hair, smiling with the memory of Elias in the dress shop. His face had matched the ribbon's color that entire day he'd attended them from seamstress to milliner to shoe shop. But he'd had his revenge. The next day he'd escorted them to an afternoon tea, followed by a dinner and then a small spring soiree. She knew enough etiquette to survive the meals—thanks to her mother—but dancing had tangled her feet more thoroughly than a barefoot sprint over moss-covered rocks. If she listened hard, she'd likely still hear remnants of Elias's laughter over her ridiculous attempts. . .until he'd taken her in hand and tutored her until her heart raced.

"Miss Mercy?" Livvy's voice cut into her thoughts.

"Hmm?" She tied off the ribbon, and the girl turned to face her.

"I am surely going to miss you." Livvy wrapped her arms around her waist.

Mercy hugged her back fiercely, certain she would always remember this brave young lady, so like herself and so not. "I shall miss you too, Livvy."

She set the girl from her and bent, eye to eye. "But we shall never forget each other, shall we?"

Huge drops shimmered in Livvy's eyes. "No, ma'am. Never."

Tears threatened to choke her as well, and she swallowed against the tightness in her throat. "There is a word my people use, not a forever kind of goodbye, but one that means farewell for now. Would you like to learn it?"

Biting her lip, the girl nodded.

"Ó:nen ki› wáhi." She drawled out the word.

"Oh-key. . .oh-no-key. . ." Livvy stuttered to a stop.

"Ó:nen ki› wáhi," Mercy tried again.

"Oh. . ." The girl sucked in a big breath. "Oh-nen key wah-he."

Mercy grinned. "Very good. You'd make a fine—"

A rap on the door cut off her praise.

"Are you ladies ready?" Elias's deep voice filtered through the wood.

Mercy held out her hand. Livvy entwined her fingers with hers—and squeezed. They had shared quite an adventure, from backwoods to Boston, and she'd be sad to see the girl leave today. Ó:nen ki› wáhi indeed. May they somehow meet again.

Together they crossed to the door, but when she swung it open, her hand fell limply away from Livvy's, and it was a struggle to keep from gaping.

The man in the corridor was surely not Elias. This was a king, one who weakened her knees by the merit of his stature alone. A deep blue greatcoat rode the crest of his shoulders, with a caramel-colored waistcoat fitted snugly across his chest. An ivory cravat was tied neatly at his throat, set just above a row of pewter buttons. Buff breeches ran the length of his long legs, ending just below the knee at his off-white stockings. Shiny buckles glinted up from his black shoes.

But it wasn't the clothes that stole her breath. Not the planes of his clean-shaven face, the full lips, or the brown hair combed back into a queue and secured by a plain black ribbon. It wasn't even his scent of sandalwood soap with a leftover hint of his trademark smoky smell.

It was his eyes. Only and entirely his stunning blue gaze. The look of unashamed wonder and awe as he studied her ignited a fire that simmered hot and low.

"Elias?"

"Mercy?"

Their whispers mingled in unison, making them one.

Livvy tugged her sleeve. "We'll be late."

Elias cleared his throat, giving his head a little shake. "Of course." Then he held out both his arms. "Ladies, shall we?"

Giggling, Livvy claimed one arm. Mercy rested her fingertips atop the other, memorizing the feel of Elias's strong muscle flexing beneath her touch. He guided them out through the public room and then into a waiting carriage, just as he had the past several days. But today, rather than gawk out the window at the passing buildings and so many people swarming like a kicked-over anthill, Mercy sat silently, staring at the man seated across from her. It was hard—nay, impossible—to reconcile such a powerful-looking gentleman with the scruffy-bearded, hunting-frocked woodsman she'd known for the past month. Neither of them spoke a word the entire ride to the major's office, and even then, he once again cleared his throat to converse with the private on guard.

The major's door swung open, and they entered to not just Major

Clement, but another two soldiers standing at attention.

"Well, well, what a difference three days can make. Ladies, you are absolutely ravishing." The major bowed over her hand and then Livvy's.

"Thank you, Major," she and Livvy both murmured.

The major angled his head toward Elias. "I suppose you are presentable as well, Dubois."

"I try, sir."

Lord, the man did not even need to try, for he'd captured her heart as thoroughly in buckskin breeches and with a smear of dirt on his brow as in a new suit. Mercy forced her hands to remain at her sides to keep from fanning her flushed cheeks.

"Now then, Miss Hunter." The major faced Livvy. "Are you ready to go to your father? You shall have two officers to accompany you. . .and this time, you shall travel by ship. No more Indian adventures for you, hmm?"

"I should like that very much, sir." Livvy bobbed a little curtsy. "Thank you."

"Briggs, Hawthorne." Major Clement turned to the soldiers. "Here is your charge. See that nothing—and I mean *nothing*—happens to the girl until she is safely handed into her father's care."

"Yes, sir!" Both saluted, then broke rank and strode to the door, the taller of the two striding through, the shorter holding it wide for Livvy. "After you, Miss Hunter."

Livvy took one step toward the door, then backtracked and plowed into Elias, surprising them all. "Thank you, Mr. Elias, for keeping me safe. Because of you, I am going to see my papa again."

Elias blinked, then slowly wrapped his arms around the girl and patted her back. "Thank God, Livvy, not me. . .as we all must."

He released her, and she beamed up at him, then stepped over to Mercy. The girl lifted a quivering chin, and Mercy couldn't help but choke up herself. If Livvy started weeping now, there'd be no holding back her own tears.

But Livvy held firm, standing as bravely as one of the soldiers, save for the trembling ribbon in her hair—the only hint of failed courage. "Ó:nen ki› wáhi, Miss Mercy."

Stifling a sob, Mercy tried a smile, a bit wavery, but a smile nonetheless. "Ó:nen ki› wáhi, my friend."

The girl turned and marched out the door, taking a piece of Mercy's heart along with her.

"Miss Hunter is quite the little lady." The major's shoes shushed across the carpet to his desk, where he retrieved an envelope, then held it out to her. "But so are you, Miss Lytton. This is yours."

She exchanged a glance with Elias.

He merely held out his hand. "After you."

Trepidation slowed her gait. The only experience she had with official documents was in the form of translating treaties or passing along intelligence, none of which seemed to bring joy to any of the recipients.

Her lips parted as she grasped the envelope. The thing was thick and heavy. "What is this?"

"Payment for a job well done. You have served king and country without fault."

She looked from the envelope to the major's brown eyes. "But it was my duty, Major. Nothing more." She offered back the envelope. "I require no payment."

He raised his hands and retreated a step, as if she held out a snake. "Yet you shall have it. I insist."

Obstinate man. . .much like Elias. No wonder the two worked together so well. She lowered the packet. "I thank you, Major. You are more than generous."

The major cocked his head. "If I may be so bold, Miss Lytton, may I inquire as to what your plans are now?"

She stiffened. Exactly. What was she to do now with no more Matthew? No more home? No more anything, really. The envelope weighed heavy with possibility in her hand. She could settle, now that she had the means, but did she really belong here in a big city? Could she stand not to run free beneath a big sky and breathe air untainted by man?

She met the major's stare with a confidence she did not feel. "That remains to be seen, Major."

A "hmm" purred in the major's throat. "May I make a suggestion?"

"Of course."

"I happen to know of a certain position opening up." He slipped a glance at Elias, then focused back on her. "A position that might be to your liking. A bit of danger. Lots of intrigue. And you'd report to no one except me."

She snapped her gaze to Elias and searched his face. What did he think of the major offering her his job, right here in front of him?

But Elias—the real Elias—disappeared behind a polished mask of indifference.

"With your background and capabilities, you'd be a valuable asset. So, Miss Lytton"—the major spread his hands—"what do you say?"

Gallows. Musket barrels. Tomahawks and war clubs. Elias had faced them all—yet none were as terrible as the question Major Clement hurled at Mercy. He rooted his feet to the carpet, fighting the urge to throw himself between the two and shield her from such a query. If she said yes, he'd lose her. . .maybe forever. She could have no idea of the dangers involved in becoming a spy. He hadn't when the major first propositioned him, sitting here in this very room, surrounded by the comfort of hearth and the promises of glory—when in reality it was mostly a life of deception, blood, and misery.

He held his breath until his lungs burned, waiting for her answer. The mantel clock ticked years off his life. The scrape of wagon wheels outside shaved off more. And still she did not answer. She just stood there blinking, looking so beautiful his throat ached for want of telling her again and again and again.

Ah, but she'd transformed over the past three days from woodland scamp to a lady of poise and wonder. Her new blue gown clung to her body in all the right places. She'd replaced her ruby heart necklace with a simple ribbon choker. And how easily she moved from one station of life to another was yet one more surprise. The only thing he missed was her long braid, swinging over her shoulder and trailing to her hips, for now she pinned up her dark hair, hiding most of it beneath a beribboned bonnet.

Her lips parted, and he couldn't help but lean toward her. So did the major.

"I am not certain what the future holds." She slipped him a glance, so many questions swimming in her brown eyes it would take him a lifetime to figure them out.

Even so, he breathed in relief. Good girl. She'd not jumped at the offer. He should've known she'd employ her usual shrewdness.

She smiled back at the major. "But I shall consider it."

Blast! If the woman had that much adventure still blazing in her blood, she'd never consent to settling down with him on a farm smack in the middle of a normal life.

Clement pursed his lips. "I suppose that is better than a no."

"It is the best I can give you at present, sir."

"Fair enough." The major turned back to his desk, this time retrieving yet another envelope. Smaller. Thinner. And with *"Mr. Elias Dubois"* penned on the front.

"At long last, Dubois, what you have been working for these past five years." Clement held out the envelope. "The deed to one hundred acres in prime Connecticut farmland, as promised."

He hesitated, palms suddenly moist. This was it. His future. Written on a frail piece of parchment. The thing he'd dreamed of while lying cold, hungry, and, more often than not, surrounded by the enemy.

He inched out his hand, then paused. The prospect of farming tasted like ashes in his mouth, for now that he'd met Mercy, his heart yearned for something more. Her. How could he possibly leave her behind?

The major shoved the envelope into his hand. "And for a job well done..." The man once again turned back to his desk and this time picked up a small leather box. He opened the lid, but his hand hid the contents. "Because of your exemplary work and for the many lives you have saved, on behalf of the crown, I present you with this commendation of honor."

The major pulled out a ribbon with a copper medal dangling at the end.

Without thinking, he shot out his hand, staying the major from handing it over. The land he could accept, work for work. It made sense. But this? A disappointment such as himself did not deserve such a merit. "I apologize, sir, but I cannot accept—"

"Elias." The rebuke in the major's voice pulled him up short, and he snapped his gaze back to the man's face.

"It is time you let go of your past, son. My only regret is that your grandfather is not the one to award this, for I have no doubt the general would have been pleased to see the man you have become."

He froze—but his thoughts took off at a gallop, especially as the major stepped up to him and pinned the award onto his lapel. Major Clement spoke more words of acclamation and Mercy murmured something beside him, but sound suddenly receded. How could he—sinner, wretch, prodigal—even consider wearing such a thing? Him...honorable? Oh, the laugh that surely would have guffawed out of his father's throat. The apoplexy his grandfather would've suffered.

But slowly the incriminations faded, and an intense gratitude toward God ignited—for truly, the award decorating his dress coat was purely by grace and grace alone. Perhaps the major was right and it was time to let go of the past. To stop striving to prove himself to a dead grandfather and instead live to serve a loving God.

The major clapped him on the back, jarring him. "Your grandfather, God rest him, would be proud of you, Elias. As am I." He bowed before them both. "My thanks to the two of you. Miss Lytton, I look forward to hearing from you at your earliest convenience. Elias, Godspeed in your new life."

He drew to attention and snapped a salute while Mercy curtseyed beside him.

"Thank you, Major." His voice wavered, and he swallowed. "Good day."

He held out his arm, and Mercy's light touch rested on his sleeve.

Striding toward the door, he couldn't help but wonder at the sudden freedom filling him at finally, fully feeling that he'd done enough. That he was enough, simply by merit of God's mercy.

Mercy.

He glanced at the woman beside him and silently pleaded that somehow his future would include not only the wonder of God's grace, but Mercy Lytton as well.

CHAPTER 37

The streets outside the major's office writhed with people. Mercy waited while Elias hailed a carriage, unsure if she should stop up her ears or plug her nose, so noisome and smelly was the crush of the crowds. What she wouldn't give for a pair of buckskin breeches and a stretch of land to run clear of this fray. . .but only if Elias were running next to her.

Her gaze lingered on the long lines of his body as he turned and backtracked to her.

"Ready to go?" He held out his hand.

She wrapped her fingers around his, cursing the silly, useless gloves for blocking the feel of his skin against hers. He led her to the coach and steadied her as she ascended. By the time he joined her inside, she longed to be back out on the street. The carriage reeked of fish and sweat and something so cloyingly sweet that the tea she'd taken for breakfast gurgled in her stomach.

Elias settled on the hard leather seat opposite her and rapped his knuckles against the wall. The carriage lurched into motion.

So did her thoughts. The meeting with the major had raised more questions than had been answered. She angled her head, searching Elias's face. "Who are you, Elias Dubois?"

A half smile lifted his lips. "By now you know all my secrets."

"Save one." She leaned forward. "The major mentioned your grandfather. . .a general? Though I suppose 'tis apparent in the way you take charge of things, why did you not tell me?"

His smile twisted into a smirk. "If you recall, you did not inform me your father was a sachem."

She huffed, but of course he was right. Only strutting roosters crowed about their families. She'd come to learn Elias Dubois was many things— obstinate, compassionate, too handsome for his own good—but more than anything, humbleness resided inside that big chest of his. Still, with so powerful a grandfather, how had he managed not to become a man accustomed to privilege and power?

"Your family"—the carriage juddered over a bump, and she grabbed the seat to keep from tumbling—"tell me of them."

"That is quite a tangled story." Shifting, he left his seat and resettled next to her, shoring her up between his body and the wall. "Is that better?"

Much better to keep her from jostling about—but certainly not any safer, judging by the crazed beat of her heart from his nearness. Did he know the effect he had on her?

Ah. . .perhaps he did and was trying to throw her off the trail she'd scented. She speared him with a piercing gaze. "Your family story cannot be more snarled than mine, what with a mother captured by Wyandots and later rescued by a Mohawk leader."

For a moment he met her gaze, then turned his face to look out the window.

She frowned. Apparently she'd pushed him too far. Folding her hands in her lap, she worried a loose thread on the hem of her glove with the pad of her finger—until Elias's low voice murmured against the grind of the wheels.

Instantly, she straightened and leaned toward him, listening hard, for he yet kept his face turned toward the glass.

"I grew up in my grandfather's home. By faith, but he was a strict English patriarch. My mother and I bore the brunt of his wrath for our rebellious ways—her by marrying a rogue voyageur on leave without Grandfather's blessing, I by running wild on the streets. . .the very ones we now travel."

He fell silent, giving her time to wonder on all he'd said. She dared a glimpse out her own window, trying to imagine such a young rebel darting in and out among the crowds. That was easy enough. But Elias had been nothing but kind the whole time she'd known him—unlike anything he said about his grandfather.

She turned back to him. "You are much like your mother, I think. I should like to meet her someday."

He shook his head. "She died when I was ten."

Unbidden, she reached for his hand, and when they touched, he jerked his face back to hers, a question arching one of his dark brows.

She merely smiled.

The carriage listed to one side as they veered around a corner, and she couldn't help but slide up against him. She started to scoot away, but as he looked at the way her hand entwined with his, he whispered, "Stay."

They rode in silence for a stretch, until he finally lifted his face back to hers. "I suppose it must have been hard on Grandfather, losing his daughter and trying to rein in a hellion like me. He sent me packing to my father when I turned thirteen, where I served as a voyageur myself for ten years." A tempest broke in the blue of his eyes, dark and raging—then as suddenly cleared. "He was right to do so, for I learned what kind of man I would become if I continued with my wayward conduct." He shrugged. "The rest you know."

She smiled. "You came back here and became a spy. . .where you still roamed the wilds, looking for trouble. Doesn't seem very different to me."

"No." He grinned back. "I suppose it was not."

"Which is why it suited you so well." She nudged him with her shoulder. "Do you think it will suit me?"

All the playfulness drained from his face, and she shuddered at the stranger staring out at her through Elias's eyes.

"Mercy, I. . ." His words ground to a halt—as did the carriage wheels. Before the coachman opened the door, Elias lurched sideways and flung it open.

Blast! She'd done it again. Pushed him further than she ought have. Foxes and wolves, deer and elk, these animals she knew how and when to approach. But Elias? How could she possibly share all that was in her heart without scaring him away?

She grabbed his hand and stepped out of the coach. With so many petticoats and the weight of her gown, she stumbled as her foot hit the ground, and he tightened his grip, righting her. Thankfully the street in front of the inn was far less crowded with people to witness her inelegant descent.

Dropping her hand, Elias turned to her, a faraway look in his eyes, as if he'd already packed up his gear and moved on.

She froze, terrified. "Elias?"

"I guess this is goodbye." His voice was a husk, an empty shell of what it had been.

Panic welled, and she couldn't contain it even if she tried. "Is it?"

"My service is done. . .but yours? Mercy, if you go back to the major's office, I have no doubt he shall make you an offer you cannot refuse."

"But I'm not interested in what the major might offer."

His brows shot high. "You are going to turn him down?"

Heedless of what the few pedestrians darting back and forth might think, she stepped close to him, as if by sheer nearness alone she could make him know the desire in her soul. "That depends."

"On what?"

"On what you have to offer."

A slow smile split across his face. Life and light and brilliance once again gleamed in his eyes. "I am land rich but cash poor, and the truth is I have nothing to offer you save for hard work and"—he dropped to one knee and gathered her hand—"my heart, if you will have it. Will you, Mercy? Will you give up a life of running free and settle down with the likes of me?"

Behind her, a few whispers swirled like autumn leaves skittering in a whirl, but she did not care. Not one bit. She dropped to her knees as well, right there in front of God and country. "I might, as long as it doesn't involve me giving up my buckskin breeches. But do you suppose 'tis legal for me to marry my husband?"

His shoulders shook with a low chuckle. "You know what I love about you, Mercy Lytton?"

She shook her head.

"Everything." Lifting her hand, he kissed her knuckles.

Blast those gloves! Even so, she couldn't help but grin. "Tsi Nen:we Enkonnoronhkhwake, Elias."

He cupped her cheek with his fingers. "I have no idea what that means, but promise me you shall say it every day for the rest of my life."

"I promise, my love." She beamed. "I promise."

HISTORICAL NOTES

The Lost Gold of Minerva, Ohio
The idea for this story came from a legend that sprang up during the years of the French and Indian War and was first printed in an 1875 Ohio newspaper. Apparently a shipment of French gold was being moved from Fort Duquesne to Fort Detroit. En route, the French soldiers were afraid of an impending attack, either by Indians or by British soldiers—it's unclear which. They decided to bury the gold and then hide until the threat passed. When they went back to retrieve their cargo, it was gone. Where did it go? To this day, no one knows.

Fort Wilderness / Fort Stanwix
There really wasn't a Fort Wilderness, but I did base this fictional outpost on a real location: Fort Stanwix, which I also mention in the story. Fort Stanwix was never under a threat of attack by the French, but it was a key location during the war. It was originally built to guard a portage known as the Oneida Carrying Place, an important thruway for the fur trade.

The Story of Mademoiselle and the Pig
The folktale Elias tells to the Shaw boys in chapter 17 is a story that has been passed down for generations. It can be found in written format in the book *Body, Boots and Britches* by Harold W. Thompson, published in 1940 by J. B. Lippincott Company.

The Klocks
This family truly did homestead in the Mohawk River Valley in upstate New York. Johannes Klock built a fortified house to use as a trading post for nearby natives. The "fort" is still there and open for tours.

Glass Grenades
Grenades bring up images of World War I or II, but really they've been around since the time of the Romans. Grenadiers were originally the soldiers who specialized in throwing grenades. Most grenades of the French and Indian War period were made by filling a hollow iron ball with gunpowder, then sealing it with a wooden plug that contained the fuse. But some

were made of other materials, such as ceramics and even glass. These were not common, but I saw one during a tour of Fort Niagara, and the idea for a deadly weapon took root. No poisonous glass grenades were used during this war—but that doesn't mean they couldn't have been.

Wyandot or Wendat or Huron?
The French sometimes called this tribe of Native Americans the *Huron*, meaning "bristly" or "savage haired" because the men wore their coarse black hair cut in a mane, from forehead to the nape of the neck, and decorated this hairdo with a stiff roach headdress. French sailors thought such a hairstyle resembled the bristles on a wild boar. The people called themselves the *Wendat*, meaning "People of the Peninsula"—which sounded a lot like *Wyandot* to non-native speakers.

BIBLIOGRAPHY

Berleth, Richard. *Bloody Mohawk: The French and Indian War and American Revolution on New York's Frontier*. Delmar, NY: Black Dome Press, 2010.

Drimmer, Frederick. *Captured by the Indians: 15 Firsthand Accounts, 1750–1870*. Mineola, NY: Dover, 1961.

Hamilton, Milton W. *Sir William Johnson and the Indians of New York*. Albany, NY: Univ. of the State of New York, 1975.

Hibernicus. *Letters on the Natural History and Internal Resources of the State of New York*. London: Forgotten Books, 2015.

Huey, Lois M., and Bonnie Pulis. *Molly Brant: A Legacy of Her Own*. Youngstown, NY: Old Fort Niagara Assoc., 1997.

MacNab, David. *Ten Exciting Historic Sites to Visit in Upstate New York*. New York: Page Publishing, 2016.

Thompson, Harold W. *Body, Boots and Britches*. Philadelphia: J. B. Lippincott, 1940.

Todish, Timothy J. *America's First World War: The French and Indian War, 1754–1763*. Fleischmanns, NY: Purple Mountain Press, 2002.

Michelle Griep has been writing since she first discovered blank wall space and Crayolas. She seeks to glorify God in all that she writes—except for that graffiti phase she went through as a teenager. She resides in the frozen tundra of Minnesota, where she teaches history and writing classes for a local high school co-op. An Anglophile at heart, she runs away to England every chance she gets, under the guise of research. Really though, she's eating excessive amounts of scones while rambling around a castle. Keep up with her adventures at michellegriep.com. She loves to hear from readers, so go ahead and rattle her cage.

CONTINUE FOLLOWING THE FAMILY TREE THROUGH HISTORY WITH...

Daughters of the Mayflower: Defenders (August 2021)

3 Early American Adventures Mixed with Intrigue and Romance

The Patriot Bride by Kimberley Woodhouse
Faith Jackson and Matthew Weber are both working covertly to aid the Patriot cause. But will they be willing to sacrifice all for their fledgling country?

The Cumberland Bride by Shannon McNear
Thomas Bledsoe and Kate Gruener are traveling the Wilderness Road when the mounting conflict between natives and settlers will require each of them to tap into a well of courage.

The Liberty Bride by MaryLu Tyndall
Lieutenant Owen Masters and Emeline Baratt meet on a British warship as sworn enemies. Where will Emeline place her loyalties when forced to spy against her country?

Paperback / 978-1-64352-936-3 / $16.99